Critical acclaim for
WINTER HAWK

"Move over Robert Ludlum. Your successor
has arrived."

Toronto Star

"A page turner."

Kitchener-Waterloo Record

"One of the English language's top thriller
writers."

Hamilton Spectator

"A knockout thriller."

Toronto Star

"Thomas weaves a wonderfully complex plot
spiked with an urgency that dares the reader
to set the book aside for so much as five
minutes."

Calgary Herald

"It's riveting stuff."

Vancouver Province

CRAIG THOMAS

WINTER HAWK

COLLINS
TORONTO

First published in hardcover in Canada 1987
This edition published 1988
by Collins Publishers
100 Lesmill Road, Don Mills, Ontario

Canadian Cataloguing in Publication Data
Thomas, Craig, 1942–
  Winter hawk

ISBN 0-00-223285-5

I. Title.

PR6070.H64W56 1988   823'.914   C88-093817-X

Printed and bound in Canada

In Memory Of
MY MOTHER
who died on
4th January, 1985

'The fact is that one side thinks that the profits to be won outweigh the risks to be incurred, and the other side is ready to face danger rather than accept an immediate loss.'

THUCYDIDES: *History of the Peloponnesian War*

PRELUDE

'We come in the age's most uncertain hours,
And sing an American tune.'

PAUL SIMON: *American Tune*

'Two minutes and they're nervous already.'

'How many Russians?'

Anders had seen one fair-skinned face behind the tinted cockpit glass of the nearest helicopter. He continued holding the pocketscope nightsight to one eye, studying the two MiL-24s in the hollow beyond him. The temperature had dropped below freezing as soon as the sun set, and there was a sliver of new moon amid the hard, bright stars. A thin, cold wind pattered fine sand against the shoulders of his sheepskin jacket and insinuated the stuff between collar and hairline. Below the crest of the dune, the thick barrel-like lens of the night observer lay between Colonel Itzhak Jaffe and himself.

Anders could hear the murmur of an occasional voice in the silence, but often the noises might have been the wind calling and chasing around the hollow; and besides, the murmurs were much less clamorous than the remembered voices in his head and the urgency they demanded. His skin prickled on the backs of his hands with nerves rather than the stinging of the blown sand. Jaffe pressed an earpiece to the side of his head. The hollow had been sown with tiny microphones before the MiLs arrived. He could, with difficulty, overhear parts of the conversation between the occupants of the two helicopters – mostly the Farsi from the terrorists in one of the main cabins rather than the Russian from the pilots.

'Two, three,' he finally replied. 'Maybe two or three Iranians, also.' He shrugged expressively. 'What we're using – it isn't the best system.'

'They might have noticed a listening post, don't you think?' Anders murmured. 'Where are your boys?'

'They're coming.' Jaffe looked down the slope of the long dune. A hand waved to him, palm-white, from the darkness below. 'They're coming,' he repeated. He raised the bulky night-sight to his eye, then added when he saw the lieutenant's signal clearly: 'A couple of minutes. From the west.'

Anders felt his body twitch with anticipation as he raised the elevation of the pocketscope. A ghostly cliff opposite slid through the lens.

We have to have those helicopters . . . even now it isn't too late . . .

The Director's voice, even in memory, possessed a quiet desperation. Anders saw that one man had left the helicopters; one of the Iranians, armed with an AKM rifle and tensely alert. Combat jacket, baggy trousers, burnous. But not an Arab, rather an Islamic fanatic. Anders scanned the jumbled landscape beyond the man but could catch no glimpse of Jaffe's *Sayeret* Matkal reconnaissance commando unit moving towards the hollow and the helicopters.

A penetration mission, we have to mount one . . . we have to have two Russian gunships to do it . . .

. . . there isn't any leeway for a mistake – none at all . . .

Anders had asked the Director how much time, *how long do we have?*

The reply echoed in his head, as if an earpiece were clamped to the side of his face and a tinny, broadcast voice penetrated his tension, excitement, fears.

You have to get it right this time – three days. There's only one opportunity . . . that gives Gant maybe two weeks to learn, to get ready . . .

Anders swallowed quietly, drily. Jumped, his whole frame seeming as if electrocuted, as Jaffe's voice announced:

'They're in touch.' The colonel's hand was holding the earpiece once more against his head. Anders thought he could catch the scratching of a radio from the hollow, and trained the pocketscope on one of the tinted cockpits.

Both MiLs, a 24-D gunship and an older 24-A, were in full desert camouflage, but Syrian markings were nowhere in evidence.

'Are their idents holding?' Anders asked, studying both of the helicopters now, as if he expected to see some sudden realization, some sudden activity that would whisk the MiLs up and away from the trap.

Desperation . . . the word came back with the force of a blow. A month earlier, the only serviceable MiL that *Chameleon Squadron* possessed, at least that could pass the closest of inspections, had crashed on a reach-and-recover inside East Germany. The crew had died. For the CIA, the loss of the helicopter was far more critical. It had been one of the pair defected to Pakistan by Afghan army pilots in 1985. One had been cannibalized under examination, the other had been employed ever since on CIA missions. Their only MiL-24.

'They're holding, John . . . don't worry. We found out *everything* from our little group of Shiite friends.' Anders shivered, but not from the chill of the desert night. 'They're being told to hurry now. These Russians pilots don't like hanging around.' Traces in Jaffe's accent of the New York he had emigrated from as a youth, more than twenty years before.

'OK.'

The Iranian on the clifftop was standing more erect. He waved briefly, then turned and waved more vigorously towards the two helicopters. Anders felt the tension tighten like cramp in his calves and buttocks, shiver in his arms as if he were stripped of his clothes. He realized he was still breathing hard from their brief, exhausting struggle to the crest of the dune. Or from tension; he could not tell.

'It's in your hands,' he said with a dry little cough.

'Your people know almost all there is to know about these machines,' Jaffe commented as he nodded in acceptance of responsibility. He gestured down into the hollow where electrics, pumps, machinery whispered. The two MiLs were like nervous, grazing animals, ready for flight at the first hint of danger. 'We even sent you wrecks, bits and pieces before this. You don't want these for evaluation, am I right?'

'Right,' was all Anders offered in reply.

'Forgive me for asking. Something like reach-and-recover, I guess?'

'Don't ever say that again, to anyone.'

'Apologies. Will I get to read it in the newspapers?'

'I hope not.'

Anders raised the pocketscope again. Jaffe rested the weight of the nightsight on the dune's crest. Men had emerged from the darkness and the folds of the landscape. Anders drew in his breath. Seven of them.

'Do they know —?'

'You know the answer . . . yes. We estimate no more than five in the MiL-"A", just the crew of two in the "D" escort. I hope those two babies are just what you want – this bazaar is closing down after tonight.' Jaffe grinned; white teeth in the hard moonlight.

. *it's the only way in. The President has to have the agent and his proof . . . now, we have to have two helicopters . . . any other way and* Cactus Plant *will be discovered missing and they'll start looking for him before he can cross any border anywhere . . . bring in those helicopters . . .*

Anders shook his head as if to loosen the burr-like grip of the words on his memory and awareness. His body was weak with tension, as if he lay in a sexual exhaustion spreadeagled on the sand.

Slowly, the alien, dangerous corner of southern Lebanon became itself again as he watched Jaffe's unit, in Arab disguises and speaking Arabic, their officer with enough Farsi initially to beguile the Iranian waiting for their return; enough to converge without alarm with the waiting terrorist.

Two of the unit appeared to be wounded, leaning heavily against others of the group. Anders had seen some of the final rehearsals but there was no sense of *déjà vu*. Only danger, the possibilities of error multiplying with every step.

Fifteen yards of sand and rock now separated the group from the terrorist who waited impatiently for them. He called and Anders heard a muffled, out-of-breath explanation. Eleven yards, ten, eight –

It all seemed huge and in slow-motion, like the collision of two great prehistoric creatures. He could hear his own quick, shallow breathing and the little expelled grunts of tension from Jaffe. In his memory, the Director's voice possessed a similar tense breathlessness.

. . . Cactus Plant *has given us a possible date, John . . . the launch is rumoured to be on schedule to coincide with the Treaty signing . . . he's not going to be able to confirm that until maybe only a week before it happens . . . one week from launch-time, we'll know for certain . . .*

. . . altogether, maybe we have three weeks maximum – maybe only two, maybe no more than a week before they put this damn' thing in orbit . . . the Israelis have found us the helicopters. Go bring them back . . .

Fear jolted Anders' mind back to the present. The terrorist might sense the strangeness of this approaching group, even behind their scarves and burnouses. Anders flicked his infra-red, one-eyed gaze towards the helicopters. The image of them in the grey mistiness provided by the lens made him twitch with nerves. He felt stretched by the succession of moments. At no point until it was completed, until they had been successful, would he be able to feel they might not fail utterly. There was no relief, no escape.

He could see faces staring up towards the top of the cliff. What would they see –? Might they not see –?

'OK, OK, OK . . .' Jaffe was muttering, the earpiece clamped against his face, his head nodding even as he squinted through the nightsight. 'OK, OK . . .'

Anders switched the pocketscope to the group on the clifftop. Arms now akimbo in welcome, AKM held harmlessly away from the Iranian's body . . . three yards. Three steps . . .

Warm greeting, still relief in the terrorist's tones, even in the moment the group leader embraced him – *now!* –

– small twitch of the whole body as the knife, blade darkened so as not to catch the moonlight, went in. A hand over the Iranian's mouth to prevent a cry, then the unit leader was holding the body upright, turning it . . . Anders watched, unable to breathe. Another embrace and – yes! – the exchange was completed. One of the pretend-wounded had straightened, begun to walk beside the unit leader in place of the Iranian.

Chattering excitedly, his arm around the shoulders of the unit leader in welcome.

The whole group, in single file, began to thread their way down a dry gully into the hollow in the dunes. They were fifty or sixty yards from the two MiLs. Jaffe exhaled noisily, his tension almost as palpable as smoke in the chill air. The two pilots would already have completed their prestart checks. Anders had heard the hum of the auxiliary power units for the past – how long? It did not matter. He knew the MiLs were ready for an immediate engine-start. The moments lengthened, giving no comfort, only prospects of failure.

'Easy now, boys, easy now, easy . . .' Jaffe murmured beside him, almost lovingly.

They were approaching the helicopters from the rear, moving slowly but seeming to Anders to rush towards failure. He could witness the whole scene now through the monocular eyepiece of the pocketscope. Grey, misty light. Rotors unmoving, as yet. The terrorist's dead feet were dragging through the sand, his body supported by a man on either side. Anders noticed guns, now. Kalashnikovs and Uzi sub-machine guns held loosely, slung easily. Forty yards to the MiLs.

Noise. Shattering, unnerving. Engine-start. The rotors moved, began to shimmer in the moonlight. Dust lifted but visibility was not obscured, only shadowed as the pilots held the rpm of the rotors at ground-idling speed. The Israeli unit moved closer as the MiLs appeared to tremble like cold dogs down in the hollow. When they lifted away there would be –

. . . I tell you, John, we have to have those gunships . . . it isn't any exaggeration, God help all of us, to say the future of this country depends on those Russian helicopters . . . you know how true that is, along with maybe a couple of dozen other people . . .

The Israelis would have only seconds before the torque wound up, the rotors were placed in their lift angle of incidence, and the MiLs moved up and away, escaping them. The timing, rehearsed a hundred, two hundred times, was critical.

Twenty-five yards. Another of the Iranians was out of the door of the 24-A now, waving the group to haste. The pilots were

16

becoming impatient now that the MiLs were noisier, audible in the night. It had taken two weeks to bring about this conjunction of a special Israeli commando unit and two Russian gunships. Objective – capture intact, whatever the human cost. Two Israeli helicopter pilots waited in the dunes, a quarter of a mile away, ready and briefed to fly the captured gunships over the border to the waiting Galaxy transport that would hurry them back to the States. Where Gant and his crews would have perhaps two weeks to learn to fly them before they set out for the target of their reach-and-recover mission. Objective – agent *Cactus Plant*, alive, proof intact.

Fifteen yards, waving arms and hooded faces. Exclamations in Farsi. The Islamic Jihad group had been under Israeli surveillance for a long time, operating against Christian and Israeli forces in southern Lebanon and northern Israel; periodic long-stay incursions, piling up the raids, the bombs, the bodies. Always, they were transported to and from their base in eastern Syria by MiL helicopters, flown by Russian pilots.

It had taken days to break just one of them and to obtain the signals, the idents, the codes, timings, landing-grounds, next pick-up point. Days . . .

Anders shuddered. Stepping out of the Galaxy, he had at once become part of it, and driven by his own demons of urgency and desperation; utterly without innocence. Even so, he did not want to consider the Iranian who had been broken and the others destroyed but still silent.

Eleven yards, ten –

He felt his whole frame trembling against the fine sand which had compacted beneath him. Jaffe's hand clamped on his arm, not to steady his nerves but to communicate a similar tense excitement. So many rehearsals –

The Director and the President disappeared from his mind like half-remembered performers in a long-ago play. Fear of failure, desperation, nerves, all became immediate, transmuted into pure adrenalin as he watched the drama's second act begin.

The pilot and gunner were clearly visible, shadowy bulks in the cockpit of the 24-D. They were watching the approach of the

17

unit in their mirrors. Pilot and co-pilot of the 24-A side by side, also watching. *There were so many eyes* –! The slow, broken shimmer of the idling rotors reflected the moonlight like two great, damaged mirrors. Sand scuttled and puffed, but the visibility remained too good. What if –? So many unfamiliarities of detail between remembered comrades and this unit – shape, height, voice, walk, posture. They'd see something any moment now. The noise from the engines and the whip of rotors might not be enough to hide strangeness in expected voices, words –

Anders was aware of the stubby wings of the two MiLs; rocket pods and missiles were slung beneath them, all ironically pointing at the dune which hid Jaffe and himself. Wheels creaked against the restraint of brakes.

Seven yards, six, four –

Recognition and decision in the same appalling instant. The Iranian terrorist half-turned to cry a warning and was beaten down with the butt of the unit leader's rifle. He sprawled on the sand like a dropped blanket.

Movement an instant after decision. The terrorist they had already killed fell slowly sideways as his body was released. Even before his involuntary movement was complete, two Israelis were through the gaping main cabin door of the 24-A and others were running through the swirling sand raised by the downdraught of its rotors. Behind the tinted glass of the MiL's cockpit, Anders saw the flash of a bright torch, inwardly heard the shouted threats to the two pilots, could almost see the stungrenade held in an upthrust hand, thumb on the lever . . . the Uzis pointing. The swift, sudden, chill shock of icy water, the shock of a stun-grenade they could not even use for fear of damaging the cockpit instruments with the shockwave . . .

. . . might have to use grenades on the two separate cockpits of the other gunship, the 24-D. They had always known that. No way to reach gunner and pilot without opening both cockpit doors, both hatches. And the 24-D was further away than its companion, its crew already alerted to danger. The greater prize but the more risky capture. His eye strained at the eyepiece of the pocketscope. Sweat was chill on every part of his body.

Now —

One commando had his hand on the pilot's cockpit latch, a second had climbed to the gunner's cockpit and was heaving at the hinged cover. Flash of gunfire, the noise coming slow seconds later, it seemed. Two rounds at point-blank range from an army-issue Beretta nine-millimetre. Satisfied, the commando dropped back to the ground. The gunner's body was all but below the level of his cockpit sill.

Image of the pilot turning in his seat, arm moving across his body, striking out with something. The commando at his door swung outwards on it, suddenly endangered. A shot from inside the MiL, two more from outside it. The commando fell to the ground and lay still. *The pilot should have been terrorized into surrender, not killed* —

His body slumped heavily in the cockpit. Anders sensed rather than saw his hand leave the control column, sensed his weight transmitted down through the dead body to the rudder —

— the MiL tilted, began to lean drunkenly over, its rotors seeming to stretch out towards the sand. Jaffe's hand gripped Anders' arm and there was a sob of anticipation and shock in his throat. On the 24-A, the rotors had stilled. It was safe. The nearer MiL continued to lean, its fuselage lurching, the tail-boom swinging outwards, the rotor disc tilting slowly, almost with delicacy towards the sand —

— where they would grind, bite, gouge before being ripped off, broken . . .

The pilot had his dead foot jammed heavily on the right rudder pedal. That was obvious. The tail rotor's thrust was increased, the tail had begun to swing. The MiL was leaning drunkenly, sand was billowing as the rotor disc neared the ground. The MiL was trying to climb even as it leaned, shunting about like a wounded bull on the distressed sand.

Jaffe was shouting in Hebrew above the bellow of the rotors and the confusion. Anders understood only the urgency. A shadow ducked into the whirling sand, touched the fuselage, began to climb. Anders watched him, almost paralysed with the imminence of failure. A door swung open. The hollow seemed filled with flying sand. The door shut. Noise, noise –

The rotor disc shimmered, only feet from the sand, the fuselage leaned more drunkenly than ever, the tail-boom seemed to thrash in the sand-cloud like the tail of a pain-maddened creature.

'Christ!' he could not help bellowing at the MiL. Men were scattering from the 24-A. Anders became mesmerized by the rotors of the 24-D, and by the apparent effort of the helicopter to lift off; a wounded bird trying to hop desperately into the air. Hop, hop, the rotors like broken wings, about-to-break wings . . .

. . . men running away – why? Then he saw. The lurching, hopping, leaning MiL was shunting closer and closer to its companion. Both the helicopters would be wrecked, the mission would be –

– *would not be, ever.*

'Christ!' he bellowed again. Four weeks ago, a little more than that, they hadn't even known what the Russians were doing, hadn't any need for MiL helicopters and a reach-and-recover mission behind the Curtain . . . *four weeks* –! The age of innocence. They'd been taken by complete surprise – the NSC, the CIA, DARPA, the DIA, the White House, all of them, totally, completely by surprise . . .

. . . *it was going to fail, going to fail, going to* –

Slowing –?

Slowing –!

The tail no longer twitched, it was steadying. The shimmer of the rotors behind the veil of sand dulled, the noise lessened. The undercarriage righted, came level, thumped back onto the sand. The rotors continued to wind down. Anders realized that the commando had stop-cocked the MiL's engines, starving them of fuel as the quickest way to stop them. Had kicked the dead Russian's foot off the right rudder pedal and stamped hard himself on the left rudder to correct the drift of the tail-boom . . . before he released the rotor clutch.

The rotors slowed to a halt. Anders heard, in the deaf silence, faint, ragged cheering. It might have been Jaffe's voice, even his own. As the tension was released, he felt aged and dazed by it. Jaffe was on his feet, waving to his men, to the lieutenant at the foot of the dune. He was shouting for him to bring up the two helicopter pilots.

Anders stood up and rocked to and fro with exhaustion. It was as if he had run for miles without the least pause. Jaffe gripped his elbow. The colonel was grinning wildly. Below them, as the sand settled, he saw the commando open the door of the 24-D and climb slowly, carefully out, as if bruised or wounded by his own heartbeat and adrenalin.

'I told you we'd do it – told you, man!' Jaffe shouted.

'A – close run thing – too damn' close!' Anders shouted back, beginning to grin. Then he coughed as the cold air filled his lungs. Sand drifted slowly down, making his eyes smart and wink.

'Don't belly-ache! We did it and you've got your helicopters – for whatever reason!'

Anders looked down into the clearing hollow. Bodies were being dragged, arrayed; dealt with casually or tenderly depending on their identity. The two MiLs faced each other like stags about to spar during the annual rut. Two *intact* Russian MiL helicopters. He sighed deeply, still feeling inordinately weak, almost helpless.

Winter Hawk had begun. They had the means to begin it –

PART ONE

All Along
the Watchtower

'You that never done nothin'
But build to destroy
You play with my world
Like it's your little toy . . .'
BOB DYLAN: *Masters of War*

PART ONE

All Along
the Watchtower

distant thunder

A moment of respite, within the storm of tension that he was experiencing, during which he remembered those faded, monochrome snapshots his parents had always kept. It must be because of the camera near his hand and the sequence of photographs he was trying to obtain. They had kept their pictures in a used, threadbare brown envelope. They comprised a sequence, a story, even; of the building of the block of flats in which they had been allocated accommodation soon after their marriage. They must have gone every day, certainly a few times each week, and taken pictures of the slowly rising skeleton, of the piles of bricks, of the dumper trucks and concrete mixers — everything.

The moment of respite was already beginning to pass. His hand jumped on the clipboard, which rested on the rail of the walkway. His parents had, as he was doing, watched something grow, keeping a record of it. His record was not of a block of workers' flats, but of a weapon.

Below Filip Kedrov, the laser battle station's components lay, close to final assembly. The main tube for the laser beam and the large mirror lay like a lance and shield, inert upon two vast benches in the assembly complex's main workshop. Robot arms and lifting gear hung motionless above them; still as items on a building site at the weekend. He knew he must pause for only a moment, there must be no suspicion, no sense of lingering . . . but he could almost savour the extremities of tension because this was the last time, the final day. His spying was almost over.

The past confused and excited him, flying into his thoughts

even as he tried to concentrate on the disguised camera and the shots he was trying to assess. His mother's face when young, hopeful; somehow seeming to reprove herself for the audacity of choosing to be photographed; or cautioning herself against all the hopes represented by the building being constructed behind her. Kedrov felt he must complete his photographic record, just as his father had done when posing his mother next to a silent concrete-mixer and in front of the newly hardened front steps of the completed flats. In that picture, his mother had been frowning at the sun over her husband's shoulder and smiling cautiously with even white teeth. What that final picture in the record had meant to his father, so this last roll of microfilm meant to Filip. In the nature of a triumph, a completion.

The segments of the laser weapon's main mirror, composed of glass coated with vaporized silicone bound by a graphite fibre reinforcement, were all but fitted to the framework. Each segment was capable of being adjusted by the orbiting battle station's computer, using actuators. They enabled the slight distortions caused by the laser beam's heating of the mirror to be smoothed out; necessary if the beam was to be focused and directed accurately at its targets. They'd had trouble with some of the actuators during final testing, but now the mirror worked satisfactorily. He'd told the Americans that a week ago; just as tonight he must tell them that the launch date had been fixed –

– breath small, tight in his chest as he thought of that. Overhearing *that* piece of gossip, of all pieces of gossip in the whole of Baikonur –! The good luck, the *momentousness* of it, made him gasp, even hours later. His nerves jumped and bubbled like an overheating saucepan on the gas – but somehow they did not boil over; completion kept them in check, the idea of finishing, of getting out, of reaching . . .

America.

His breath was again tight as he recognized the little time left, the proximity of safety, of success, of dreams made real.

He had passed everything to the Americans, just as they had asked. All that was left were the rolls of film he had taken, which would travel with him . . . three weeks of films – a record begun as soon as they got the disguised camera to him. Now, he had to hold onto them until they came for him.

And, tonight, tonight he would tell them they must come. He had the proof, they would know the launch date, they would *need* him –

– yes, they would . . . satisfaction hugged him like a warm coat; a fur jacket, a *sheepskin* jacket, because it was never as cold in a centrally-heated country like America. Or a cashmere topcoat, cashmere sweaters . . . slacks and loafers . . .

Because they would reward him – for this, there was no price too high. Perhaps he remembered that block of flats now, with such piercingly clear recollection, because of the life he could envisage for himself, just a few days ahead . . . ? He did not know. All he knew was that dreams made him calmer, suppressed the extremes of tension and fear and danger he had anticipated, driving to work that morning. Half an hour just to start the ancient, unreliable car! Knowing all the time that the last day of his spying had begun.

His eyes cleared. He moved a little along the metal, clattering gantry. Below him, in the rest of the huge workshop, the miniature spacecraft of the laser battle station's outer casing lay open, appearing cracked like the shell of some sea-creature already extracted. Beside it, the huge tanks which would contain the lasing gases waited to be fitted and filled. Nearer, the long, still-innocent tube of the laser with its cylindrical nozzle, and finally the mirror, which would be mounted at the nose end of the miniature spacecraft.

Four days. In exactly four days, on Thursday, the battle station would, fully assembled, be aboard the space shuttle which would carry it into orbit. Within two months, eleven more laser weapons would be placed in orbit around the earth. That was not his concern . . . he had only to signal the Americans that evening, from Orlov's shop, that the launch's exact timing had been fixed, and they would come and collect him. He had been told how, and when . . . *give us the date, Filip*, or *Cactus Plant*, as they persisted in labelling him, *give us the date and bring us convincing photographic proof the weapon exists – and you can come out, come to the West.*

A reach-and-recover mission, they said. A helicopter would come for him – a Russian helicopter. Time and place of his rendezvous was already arranged with them. Before the laser weapon arrived in Baikonur from the scientific research unit of Semipalatinsk, a thousand miles away, he had spied for the money, meagrely-generous though they were with him. He had been an American agent at Baikonur for almost three years.

Now, he knew he was the most important spy the Americans had anywhere in the world. Filip Kedrov understood, with blinding clarity, that his importance could not be overestimated. He had alerted the CIA to the existence of a laser weapon, and the intention to place it in orbit, little more than four weeks earlier, when the pieces of the weapon had arrived from Semipalatinsk by special train. He had heard rumours of its nature and purpose, then overheard scientific gossip, then confirmed it by some casual questions – and told the Americans, who had panicked. Their treaty with the Soviet Union was imperilled, was being flouted, danger, danger, *danger* –

Kedrov cared little. They wanted everything, but they would pay – *no, not money . . . what, then? . . . the West, when I get you the proof you must have . . . very well, we agree . . .*

As soon as he signalled that same evening, they would come for him. He suppressed a sudden yawn of tension or excitement. Tomorrow, the day after, two days' time, they would be here and he would be on his way to the West; he and his priceless rolls of tiny film. They would have to hurry. They needed the films before Thursday.

The clipboard was trembling beneath his hand, as if registering the shock of a very distant earthquake. His left hand, meanwhile, in the pocket of his white coat, touched around, weighed, smoothed the remote control unit which looked no more suspicious than a bulky fibre-tip pen. The camera it operated – the tiny, tiny camera with motor drive – was contained in the large, bright-green, jokey paperclamp which held a sheaf of computer print-outs and graphs to the plastic of the clipboard. The clamp was shaped like a frog; a fat green frog with orange spots. Many of the scientific and technical staff of the cosmodrome at Baikonur used such things – joke clamps, highly coloured clipboards, stickers that poked fun on them, irreverent badges, huge felt pens like the one Walesa used to insult the authorities when he signed Solidarity's agreement with them. It was all part of the thumbed nose to the Army, who ran Baikonur – the two raised fingers. In a small and allowed way, of course. A teenage sub-culture, just like the Western pop tapes, the *samizdats* of satiric novels, the weekend promiscuity, the heavy drinking.

Filip's green frog was as expected and normal as his fornications and his singing-drunk weekends. It had been his own idea, based on a toy he had seen in Detsky Mir on his last Moscow leave. He'd bought one for his sister's little girl. Of course, hers did not possess a lens in its right eye or a silent motor drive, or tiny cassettes of film in its belly and a separate remote control unit.

His thumb once more squeezed the cap of the thick pen in his pocket. He strained to hear, as he always did, but there was indeed no noise whatsoever from the motor as it moved the film on inside the frog. He had practised with it, tested it time and again in complete, breath-held silence, waiting for some tiny, betraying noise –

But never a whisper . . . thank God.

Already this Sunday morning he had filmed, again with this abiding sense of completion, the cracked sea-shell of the battle station's outer casing and the tanks for the lasing gases. And the computer. Now, he was above the last telltale image, the mirror-shield and the lancelike long nozzle. Shown on television – which was obviously what the Americans planned – to the rest of the world, that little cluster of pieces could not fail to represent themselves for what they were. They were not the bits of a telescope or a weather satellite . . . they were the components of an orbiting laser battle station, the first of twelve. Enlargements of the tiny strips of film would tell, reveal, inform, accuse, shock, horrify –

– and make Filip Kedrov the most famous face on television and a hero and a very rich American citizen.

Someone glanced up at the catwalk and saw him. Filip's hand twitched on the clipboard and he stopped pressing the remote control. Smile, smile you silly bugger, he instructed himself.

He smiled. The detached, confident, almost-finished almost-rich part of his mind, controlling what he did and felt, rescued him from his own assault of nerves. He pressed the frog's humped back and it croaked. The technician below him laughed and waved. Someone else looked up, grinning. The guards would only look up if he stayed too long. He pressed the remote control. Fifteen, sixteen, – twenty-one, twenty-two, – moving the clipboard slightly after each shot to draw the frog's gaze across the expanse of the workbenches, from mirror's edge to laser's tail. He moved his hand through a practised, measured, even arc; moving the frog's bulging eye, moving –

– twenty-four, -six, -eight . . . go, go now –

He picked up the clipboard and held it against his chest. Finished, this part of the story, this part of the building work. He remembered once more his father's snapshots, mother posed by the concrete-mixer, her thin cotton dress swollen with Filip's imminent arrival. Now, it was as if he had a record of his new life, the one he had built for himself in America, on those tiny strips of film stored safely in his lock-up garage, in the tins of paint. Everything the Americans had demanded, desired, wanted. They could refuse him nothing now . . . now they would have to come.

Success flushed through him, a wave that excited yet somehow lulled and calmed him. The detached part of his mind remembered to press the frog so that it croaked its farewell. His shoes clicked hollowly along the gantry above the workshop. The clipboard was now under his arm and his other hand was out of his pocket, away from the remote control. Success, a sense of triumph as quick and shallow as the feeling after winning a race at school or scoring in a football match continued to rush through him like a scalding drink. Down inside his chest, warm in his stomach. His whole body seemed to clutch in upon itself like a hand closing around money or some other prize; holding the delight tightly.

He glanced down at the frog, at the ID clipped to his pocket, just above the round yellow badge that instructed everyone to smile. He had every right to be in the main assembly workshop, of course – and that, too, added to the sense of exhilaration, the beauty and self-satisfaction of the completed task. He had been made responsible for the transfer of the lasing gases to their tanks. He had even part-written the computer programme for the operation.

And his luck had not simply been there, and held – it had improved once they had got the camera to him, once he had begun his task. Even the military and their security had hardly impeded him, once he'd got into his stride, so to speak.

He was unwary and unworried about his dreamlike state of euphoria. His job was finished, and well finished. Behind mother, they were completing the plumbing and the wiring for the new flat . . . would they let him live in Manhattan? He grinned. The number of times his parents had made him and his sister look at that series of boring, slowly-changing snapshots –! His shoes clattered down the ladder at the end of the catwalk. He would be able to get into the old town, Tyuratam, and get his last signal off, that evening. Before he did so, he must store the film cassette with its companions, wrapping it in polythene and sinking it out of sight inside an old tin of paint.

Filip Kedrov, *Cactus Plant*, nodded to two technicians who were wheeling an auxiliary power unit through the open doors of one of the main stockrooms. He nodded and smiled to the bored, unsuspicious GRU guard as he passed him, hardly registering the harmless rifle slung across his chest, then stepped through a personnel door into a cold, narrow corridor. A long line of bulky outdoor clothing hung from pegs above a line of boots. He found his own overcoat, scarf, boots, gloves and donned them.

He smiled to himself, hardly concerned with the importance of what he had done, except insofar as it impinged on his personal circumstances.

Impinged? Changed – utterly *changed* his circumstances. It was all that mattered. America. Money and America, money to live in America, to enjoy America . . . The thoughts chased in his head as he wrapped his scarf around his already cold cheeks and made for the exit.

He opened the outer door on the below-zero day and the high, pale sky. Manhattan. It was as if the famous skyline, which he had seen in films the scientific and technical staff were allowed to watch, lay before him now. Yes, Manhattan. He would request an apartment on the east side of Central Park – yes . . .

He blinked and the buildings retreated from the pale Sunday morning, into the near future. A few days away, that was all. He would send that final signal. Tightness gripped his chest and stomach once more. It was so *close* –! Come and fetch me, my American friends. Pay up –!

Lines of high, tinted-glass towers. Fifth Avenue, Sixth. He would at last be leaving that block of workers' flats in front of which his mother had stood so proudly.

He made for the technicians' carpark.

Before he reached his old, third-hand, grey Moskvitch, his mood had changed. The glow vanished, as if the outside temperature had robbed his body of all its heat. He was shivering with fear. Not simply in reaction to what he had done, now that it was over . . .

. . . it was because of the two men in the car parked near the entrance to the carpark. He knew they were the same two men, in the same car, who had followed him to work that morning. He had been so careful of late, so scrupulous in looking for any surveillance, all the time believing himself to be safe. Now, he knew he wasn't. He fumbled his key into the stiff, cold lock. His gloved hand was shaking. He had managed to forget them, forget that he had been followed to work. His quick breathing clouded the car's window. He felt his stomach become watery, then tightly knotted. He wasn't imagining it. He couldn't cling to the fiction that he was mistaken, not now that he was about to summon them to come for him. He had to admit the truth – he *was* being watched.

'He's going on TV tomorrow – Monday!' Calvin announced heavily. 'I've just had the Ambassador here to inform me of the fact – the guy was almost *laughing*!'

The President seemed not to have grasped the significance of *Cactus Plant*'s final signal. The Director of the CIA fumbled emotionally and mentally to catch at Calvin's mood. The transcript of the signal from Baikonur lay on the President's desk like a piece of old and abandoned legislation, as unimportant as someone's grocery list. The Director had hurried from Langley to the White House with it, his mood one of unqualified triumph. An edge of danger, of course, because of the drastic shortening of the time-factor, but a real sense that they could win. But Calvin seemed concerned only with his television encounter with the Soviet President. They had to hurry. Kedrov was spooked, there was no doubt of that. This was the *last* signal. He might already have gone into hiding, and roused a search for him by the GRU. Time squeezed down and narrowed in every direction. Yet to Calvin it seemed less important than –

Four days away. Calvin already knew that, though . . . from the Soviet Ambassador, of all people.

'Monday,' Calvin repeated with a deep sigh that threatened to become both a groan and an accusation.

The Director looked up from the briefcase still balanced on his knees.

'We still have time to get our agent out –' he began.

'The guy's off and running –!' The President accused.

'Mr President, if you study his signal, he's confirmed where to pick him up. He knows how our people will come, what to expect. He can estimate times, that kind of –'

'Thursday! While we're all in Geneva, Bill, they're going to put the first of their laser battle stations into orbit – under the guise of a satellite placement mission and a link-up in orbit with *our* shuttle, *Atlantis*! They're laughing up their sleeves on this one, Bill – laughing at us.' There was evident blame on Calvin's features and in his eyes. He had been let down, left holding the can.

'We *can* get him out, sir –'

'Bill, you're asking me to stake this country's future on a Russian technician on your payroll!'

'He was *always* our only chance,' the Director replied softly, firmly. What had Calvin expected, some miracle? He was unnerved by the time-table, by the proximity of the signing of the Treaty and the launch of the laser weapon. It was tight, yes, dangerous without doubt – but it *could* be done!

'What does he have, Bill? Films, rolls of film. Is that going to be enough to convince the world it's being given the biggest shaft in history?' Calvin's confidence of voice, East Coast with Harvard overtones, had deserted him. It had begun to complain, almost to whine. His hand waved without vigour, dismissing Kedrov and his films and the glimpse of hope they offered. He shook his head. 'It isn't going to be enough, Bill . . .' he murmured vaguely.

The Director brushed the dottle from his cold pipe off the. leather of his briefcase. He pondered for some time, weighing the President's mood and his own words. Then he looked up and said: 'Sir, you approved all of this. You – believed, as I did, as Dick Gunther did, that this was the only way of obtaining proof in the time we had . . . four weeks maximum.' He spread his hands. He reached up and took the *Cactus Plant* signal by its edge, pulling it from the desk onto his lap. He smoothed the paper. Calvin's shoes paced across the eagle and the scroll woven into the centre of the deep green carpet of the Oval Office. The Director cleared his throat. From somewhere outside the thick green glass of the windows, he heard muffled church bells.

'The time-table's more crucial,' the Director continued, 'because we now know it's Thursday for the launch. Before, working on Kedrov's estimates, we assumed another week to ten days –'

'Time we no longer have!'

'I know that, sir . . .'

Calvin continued to pace, dressed in check shirt and jeans, his hands rubbing through his mop of grey hair. His face was cleaned by shock, blank and tired. When his hands were not busy

34

with his hair, they waved uncertainly, as if fending off the circumstances of the morning.

The winter's morning was bright even through the reinforced glass of the windows. He could still hear the bells. Mid-morning services. Kedrov had sent his signal – oh, sometime early Sunday evening, his time. Ten hours ahead of Washington. *Come and fetch me, my friends . . . I am afraid.*

He continued: 'We have to bring *Winter Hawk* to immediate readiness, sir. Today. The mission profile has a forty-eight hour maximum timespan. That's two days and the agent and the evidence can be inside a friendly border. Transmission, editing, anything you require done with the films won't be any problem. Sir, it's nine thousand miles to Peshawar from Nevada, a thousand to the target area, a thousand back. Those are the *only* parameters that really matter. Forty-eight hours maximum, once the mission clock starts running. That's Tuesday or Wednesday – you could blow this up in their faces on the eve of the signing, sir!' The Director's hand was clenched into a fist. Unaware, he had screwed Kedrov's final signal into a damp, grey ball of paper. The sight of it shocked him quite out of proportion to the act. As if he had crushed, abandoned . . .

He shook his head, dismissing the idea. Kedrov was all they had; priceless and unique.

Winter light, aqueous through the tinted glass, fell chill upon Calvin's profile as he continued to pace the room. It gave his features the pointed, marble lifelessness of a corpse. The Washington Monument beyond the glass thrust like a spike at the pale morning sky. Or a launch vehicle, he could not help thinking. Baikonur, Thursday – close, damn' close.

As if to reassure himself as much as Calvin, he reiterated: 'Forty-eight hours maximum. Gant and the other crew can do it, sir. Give me the authority to bring *Winter Hawk* to readiness.'

'Are they ready, Bill? How long have they trained on those gunships? No more than a couple of weeks, less . . . ? *Are* they ready?'

'They have to be, sir.' They have to be. The Director found

himself struggling against Calvin's unmollified expression. He waded upstream against the current Calvin was giving the room. He had hurried here with anxious triumph, to find the party had ended and the guests moved on to another venue. Calvin did not share his sense of success. 'They have to be,' he repeated once more, looking down.

Calvin was obsessed with the political coup the Soviet President had gained. Nikitin would coerce a promise to appear at the signing in Geneva which would give Calvin no room in which to manoeuvre. He would have to promise the world, in advance, that he would honour the Nuclear Arms Reduction Treaty in its present form –

– which excluded all reference to orbiting laser weapons systems, since they did not exist . . . *had* not existed until four weeks ago, so far as the CIA and everyone else thought.

Calvin said urgently: 'Damn your time-table now, Bill – it's fallen down behind the wardrobe. I am going to have to agree to meet him on Thursday – it wasn't supposed to *be* Thursday, Bill, it was to be in two weeks' time! I have to agree to meet him or Congress will crucify me, the American people will help them put in the nails, the press has the hammer, and the whole damned world is going to watch while they do the job!' He rubbed his hands through his hair. 'We just ran out of options. They're calling the tune in Moscow right now. I'm hamstrung, Bill!'

He turned his back on the Director and pressed a buzzer on his desk. Almost immediately, as if he had been hovering at the door, Dick Gunther entered. National Security Adviser to the President. His smile at the Director was brief, gloomy, his eyes studying Calvin like those of a concerned wife.

'Well?' he murmured, moving close to Calvin, behind the huge desk, near the windows.

Calvin shook his head. 'No change,' he muttered. The Director felt himself to be a terminal patient in a hospital room. Calvin and Gunther turned lugubrious looks on him. He felt very young, irresponsible seated in his chair.

'Dick, *you* explain it to the Director,' Calvin said. 'I can't make him see we're fresh out of options!' The President's tone was sharp, almost vindictive.

He walked away, opened a small door which led to a washroom, then closed it behind him on a glimpse of white towels, gold taps, dark wood gleaming like satin. The Director dimly heard running water, then turned reluctantly to Gunther, who merely shrugged.

'Bill, I think he's right . . .' he said eventually. His tone attempted to soothe, but the Director felt lumpy and uncomfortable in his suit, as if his mood had creased and soiled it. He shook his head, staring at the crumpled transcript and the briefcase on his knees. 'We're fresh out of options. There's nowhere to go with this.'

In the Director's briefcase was the entire *Laserwatch* file; a thin and now outdated collection of signals from Baikonur, reports and assessments from DARPA, Presidential demands for action; demands, orders, pleas. When he had received Kedrov's last signal, he had felt the peril of the moment, but also its possibilities. Now, they could act, use the gunships to go in and get Kedrov. But, he had been upstaged, outsmarted. Nikitin wanted the Treaty signed on Thursday. How they must be laughing at his country! Suggesting a rendezvous in orbit, a *party* up there, for Christ's sake, after they'd launched their first laser weapon!

'He's on the hook,' Gunther continued. 'Nikitin isn't fooling around on this. He's going on TV to *dare* the President not to appear in Geneva next Thursday. The man can't not be there and Nikitin knows that.'

The Director sighed, spreading his large hands.

'Dick, I understand all that. There's no answer, nothing but *Winter Hawk*. Dammit, the President has to let us *try*!' He glanced at a group of small, silver-framed photographs ranged near him on the desk. Calvin as college footballer, Calvin as naval officer, Calvin receiving an honorary degree in England, Inauguration Day, waving beside the First Lady. The roles the man had played. 'There's no other way the Agency can help, Dick –'

'You have to, Bill.'

'*How*? You want a *solution* to this mess? Five weeks ago we didn't have the faintest idea the Soviets were within fifteen years of developing a weapon like this and placing it in orbit! We never had an agent at Semipalatinsk . . . all we had was *Cactus Plant*, a low-grade agent-in-place at Baikonur, useful for tipping us off when a launch was about to happen and for telling us what kind of satellite they were putting up. Then, he stumbles on – *this*. We're four days away from the launch date of the first of a dozen satellites and we haven't even gotten our second wind on this thing!' His voice was firm, but tight and small in his throat; angry, guilty, and maybe afraid, too. 'We're four days away from this country becoming a *third-class power* and the President wants a nice neat answer?' Calvin would be listening, of course, but he had to hear it was hopeless unless they relied on *Winter Hawk*.

Gunther's voice was soothing when he replied, but it rubbed like glasspaper; the implacables of the situation scoured.

'All that's history, Bill – already history. He's delayed as much as he possibly can, but no one can work miracles. We can't get the ring of *Nessus* surveillance satellites into operation in time to detect the launching of these weapons. *Nessus* and everything else is going to be at their mercy. That's why Nikitin is hurrying everything forward. The President can't be seen to be dragging his feet now – it's *his* Treaty, dammit! Once the document is signed, there's a two-month ratification period, and by then every ICBM we have left, every satellite, Big Bird, Navstar, Milstar, the whole bag of tricks, will be at the mercy of the laser battle stations. The man is terrified he's going to go down in history as the President who gave his country away on a silver plate! Give him some room to manoeuvre, Bill – a little elbow-room. Work a miracle!'

Gunther had perched himself on the edge of the desk, leaning intently towards the Director as he spoke. Now, he stood up and walked to the window as he continued speaking. The Director felt no slackening of the tension and depression he felt throughout his body.

'He blames everyone, Bill – you, me, our agencies, the chiefs of staff, just about everyone . . . like he's been betrayed.' The chill light of the windows palsied Gunther's cheek. 'This was his

Treaty from the beginning. He blames all of us for not guessing what the Soviets were doing at Semipalatinsk. He blames *us* for advising that he agree to the Soviet suggestion not to bother to include orbiting weapons systems in the Treaty. Neither side had them or could have them inside fifteen years, so what the hell, we all said . . . It was science *fiction* two years ago, Bill!'

'And now it's not. It's a reality.'

Gunther turned from the window.

'Bill, give him *something*,' he pleaded.

Gunther had raised his voice, as to give a theatrical cue, and Calvin re-entered the room. He thrust his hands into the pockets of his jeans and walked to the desk. Gunther moved to one side.

'Have you explained?' he asked Gunther, his voice clipped and hard. The winter daylight was again cold on his face.

'I have, Mr President . . .'

'Well, Bill, well?'

The Director nervously and with great reluctance shook his head. Then he said: 'We have *Winter Hawk*, Mr President, and that's *all* we have. If we initiate *now* —!'

'It won't *work*!'

'It has to . . .'

The silence was stormy, the Director's temples throbbed with the beginnings of a headache. Calvin slapped his hand on his desk, then slumped into his swivel chair. He stared out at the White House lawns, deep in snow, at the pale spike of the Monument. Stared into a close and ugly future.

He announced to the window: 'I have to have irrefutable photographic evidence that these weapons exist. With that much, I can go to Geneva and denounce the Soviets – get their laser weapons included in the Treaty. If I don't have it, world opinion will break me and this country . . .' He turned to face the Director. 'OK, Bill,' he added, raising his palms outwards in what might have been surrender. 'Do it. Initiate *Winter Hawk* today – *now*. Get those guys off their butts in Nevada and into the air before this afternoon. Forty-eight hours maximum, you said. Bill, I'm holding you to that. Tuesday, on my desk – *proof*!'

Sunday nights he was always drunk . . . just like now, but not usually here, in his own flat, because he was afraid to go out, or be seen anywhere. Filip Kedrov looked at his shaking hands, quivering in front of his face. His eyes filled with a leaky self-pity, his body was possessed by an ague of terror. Christ –! He'd tried not to drink any more after he returned to the flat, because of what he knew lay ahead of him, but it had been no good. He'd had to calm himself down, or try to . . . he was so frightened! He'd been back an hour and he was still shaking like a leaf. He had literally fled from the officers' club they allowed people like him to use at weekends, fled because of that telemetry officer opening his big mouth in the toilet while Filip was in one of the cubicles. Christ, why had he had to *listen*! It was terrible, terrible –

His fear was real and deep, in every part of his body like a fever. He clutched the hand he had been inspecting beneath his arm as if he had been caned in school. He folded his arms.

He got up again, knocking over his half-filled glass. Beer foamed on the thin carpet, then soaked into it.

Sick with fear, he wandered towards the window, avoiding the low coffee-table. It wasn't in a sensible position but it disguised a threadbare patch in the carpet. He reached for the curtain, knowing he would not pull it aside – because of the watchers out there.

He walked away. His eyes scanned the room as if he were making an inventory for some insurance claim. Hi-fi, bottles, a cupboard, cheap dining table and chairs. Some pieces that had belonged to his mother, but mostly standard issue furniture appropriate to his status. His eyes flitted, unable to settle, like his body. He'd tried not to drink any more, to keep the remains of a clear head . . .

Not drunk. Just terrified. Tomorrow he would have had to evade the people outside anyway, so he'd gone out to the club because he always did, so as not to show he knew they were watching him . . . *he shouldn't have gone* –! Now, he knew he must go tonight, at once. The big-mouthed officer had seen to that! They'd be looking for him now, and when they discovered who he was, they'd be straight round to shut his mouth – for good. God, they'd kill him for what he'd overheard –!

His stomach cramped agonizingly, and he doubled up, groaning and retching drily. Why couldn't the drunken pig have kept his big mouth shut? Why had he had to overhear what they were saying while they pissed in the urinal? Why, oh, God, *why* –?

Slowly, the pain retreated. Filip's head cleared a little. His brow felt hot.

There were two men in a car at the front of the block of flats at that moment. A third man was in the shadows at the rear, near the lock-up garage. He could place them precisely just by closing his eyes. That's where they'd been when he went out, and to where they'd return after following him back from the club. Closing his eyes made him giddy. There were only three of them, and they still had no orders to close in . . .

But the army would be looking for him now, not just the KGB. It was awful just thinking about it.

He groaned aloud in desperation. He looked at his watch, then at the clock on the tiled mantelpiece. Eleven o'clock, Sunday evening. The small screen of the television set stared back at him, as blank as his own gaze. Eleven o'clock.

He'd gone to the club after sending the final signal to the Americans, his mood almost euphoric despite the car tailing him. Orlov's shop, he'd called innocently . . . God, he would have to go back there, or ring Orlov now, to send *another* message! God, the *look* the captain had given him when he emerged from the cubicle and tried to sneak away!

Kedrov rubbed his cheeks as if scouring them. Why had he had to *hear*? His hands flitted from his cheeks to his ears – unwise monkey. The captain had realized he'd been overheard, almost at once. He had all but moved, almost shouted after him. He had hurried away and out of the club – but they *knew*!

He whirled his body in an ache of fear around the centre of the room, spinning as if to create some spell of invisibility. God, Christ, Hell, *God* – he had to get out *now* –!

They may not have reported him because they were the ones who'd been insecure – but they'd surely come looking once

41

they found out who he was, where he lived . . . Christ, it was *awful* –!

Lightning, he'd called it. Not *Linchpin*, the codename for the launching of the battle station. Lightning . . . it was so awful they would have to kill him to silence him . . . *he shouldn't know what he knew* –!

Lightning.

He stared at the large, bulkily filled haversack on the dining table. As soon as he'd got back, he had feverishly filled it with cans, provisions, spare clothing, aware all the time of the men outside. Especially the one at the back stamping his feet with cold, breathing out clouds of smoky breath, rubbing his gloved hands as he watched the lock-up garages – Filip saw him every time he went into the flat's tiny kitchen.

He'd packed the haversack, ready for flight. And immediately postponed any attempt at escape. He walked stiffly, jerkily towards the dining table, and gripped the shoulder-straps of the canvas haversack. Then dropped them as if they were charged with a current.

He couldn't risk going to the shop again. He must ring Orlov – not on the bugged telephone in the hall, but from a call-box – and tell Orlov to send the message – *hurry, come at once, I am in danger, I have the most – most terrible – important news, I know about* Lightning . . .

Orlov could send the signal then close down the transmitter; disassemble it, hide the bits. If only he could get out of the flats –!

The signal was easy. The rendezvous – he'd decided that long ago, with the Americans. The salt marshes, a pinprick-sized island. They had maps, satellite pictures of the exact location. He had confirmed the pick-up point in his last signal. All he had to say was . . . *hurry, please* –

If only he could move . . .

He gripped the shoulder-straps of the haversack, and did not release them. Hefted the sack, felt the flat's chill and the darkness outside and the three KGB watchers . . . and the captain who had been loose-tongued and was the most dangerous threat of all to his safety, rescue – survival. He swung the sack over his shoulder, his body shivering as it rested like a burden, and glanced around the room. He went into the hall, pursued by the image of the captain's face and the weight of knowledge of *Lightning*. Hurried, opened the door, checked the empty, cabbage-smelling corridor, closed his door behind him with no sense of finality, only with haste. The lock clicked loudly.

He hurried along the corridor, up the concrete, uncarpeted stairs behind the fire door towards the roof. Unlocked the roof door with fumbling hands, opened it, walked through —

— face embraced, arms held —!

He struggled blindly, gasping but not crying out, flailing his arms —

— the washing-line collapsed, the shirts, stiff with frost, the trousers, the underwear and the sheets, draped along the dirty, ice-pooled, gravel-covered roof. He bent double, choking back his coughs, sick with fear and relief. Staring at a shirt lying like a spreadeagled upper torso at his feet, arms akimbo in surrender. He heaved, but nothing came. Slowly he stood upright.

He picked up the haversack, listened but heard nothing, no alarm, and went to the roof's edge. Four storeys down, the lock-up garages. Out of the question. He would have to abandon the car and the rolls of film . . . most of all, the rolls of film in the paint cans. He wouldn't tell the Americans, definitely not —

He crept along the edge of the roof, aware of the man below, at the corner, in shadow. Aware of the car parked at the front. Aware of the drainpipe. Overhang, guttering, drains, pipes. Explored long before with the bravado of imagination rather than the desperation of necessity. Drainpipe at the side of the building furthest from the streetlamps.

He felt weak. Looked back at the fallen washing. The shirt now looked like a murdered man. He gasped at the image. Fumbled his arms into the haversack's straps, balanced its sudden, new heaviness, then cocked his right leg over the edge of the roof. The concrete alleyway below swum darkly, as if he were suffering from vertigo rather than fear. His hands gripped. He straddled the edge of the roof. Then climbed over, hands icily cold but holding on tightly, feet scrabbling for the ledge and the point of

43

emergence of the drainpipe. The gutter was a channel in the gravelly roof, the drain directly opposite his eyes ... his feet found the drainpipe, the tiny ledge, the first clamp. He rested, sweat coldly blinding him for a moment. Then hunched downwards into a squatting position, holding onto the thick metal drainpipe. One foot, then the other. Second clamp. He'd even practised for God's sake —!

Kedrov lowered himself gingerly, fearfully down the drainpipe. His hands were lumps unfeelingly placed at the ends of his aching arms, his feet were numb ... so that they hardly sensed the concrete until he had hunched almost into a sitting position in the alleyway. Then he realized, and leaned his forehead against the pipe, clinging to it still to prevent himself falling and lying — like the shirt ...

He got up slowly, weakly, and pressed into the shadows. Nothing. Silence. A car passing — jump, then relief — and a television blaring in a ground-floor room. Across the alleyway a block of offices rose six storeys. Throwing deep shadow. A ground floor comprising a bookshop, a grocer's, an off-licence. The liquor shop was still open. Just.

Walk now. Quickly.

He stepped out stiffly, as if marching like a bloody soldier —! Lessened his stride, tried to appear to be walking easily, without terror's roboticism. Held the haversack at his side, almost casually. Turned into the lights, poor as they were they were still bright, and hurried to the door of the liquor shop. Turned for one glance only, then walked past the door and the spilled light that tumbled over him, into further shadow. Passing two people, beginning to hurry once in darkness again, listening, listening with all his body, all his senses, but hearing nothing.

They had assumed, even if they'd seen him, that he'd already been inspected and passed by the watcher near the garages. Anyway, he hadn't emerged from the front doors of the block of flats, therefore to them he wasn't a resident. Sweat enveloped him, drying now and chill. He bent forward into his hurrying gait. On his own now, alone. Just the call to Orlov — the cry for help.

Come at once, please – please come at once –!

They had to, they must come – before the army realized he had disappeared and began hunting for him in earnest. Because of *Lightning*, most of all because of *Lightning*. The films did not matter now – they had to know what he had discovered. They must come quickly.

TWO

a flash of *Lightning*

'Sorry, Major – but you're dead – *two times!*'

There was a boyish exhilaration in the voice that remained undistorted or diluted by the radio's rush of static. Gant watched the F-15 curve up and away above the desert, into the pale blue winter morning. Its wings waggled in mocking salute, then speed and altitude transformed it into no more than a straggling, bright, late star. In another moment it was gone, heading back to Nellis, its practice sortie against his helicopter completed – successfully.

Gant was unreasonably, violently angry. Mac began speaking over the headphones like a soothing aunt.

'Shut up, Mac,' he warned. 'I don't need it!'

'Skipper,' his gunner insisted, 'we ain't ready for this – the guy had us on the plate and served for breakfast before –'

'Mac – can it!'

Gant swung the MiL-24-D around a weathered outcrop of brown rock standing like a chimney out of the desert floor. He felt the machine was as heavy and lifeless as a toy airplane at a fairground, whirling around a tower on a steel rope. He had been caught like a rookie pilot fresh out of school by the F-15 attacker which had been sent to hunt them down in this simulation of combat. He'd done it five minutes up from Nellis, and within another minute-and-a-half he'd recorded two kills. Gant had been unable to even begin to manoeuvre the lumbering helicopter evasively, not even with the tumbled, broken desert landscape to aid him. He wasn't ready, not by maybe a couple of weeks.

Below him, on a wide, flat ledge perched above the desert, the

MiL-24-A sat silently, rotors still, the crew of three already relaxed. One of them waved, infuriating him further. Garcia and his crew were even less ready – and now their ship had rotor head trouble and was stranded.

'Garcia – you called home yet?' he snapped, dropping the unwieldy Russian helicopter towards the flat outcrop of rock.

The ether crackled but no one answered him. Garcia could not hear him because he was out of the cockpit. Angry, he eased the MiL in the backwash of its downdraught off the cliff-face until its undercarriage settled. Then he switched off the engines and opened his door. Garcia was ambling across the dust-filled gap between the two helicopters.

'You called them?' Gant shouted.

'Sure thing – right away, skipper. They're sending out a big Tarhe helicopter to lift us off of here . . .' Garcia was grinning, very white and irritatingly. He brushed one hand through his hair now that the movement of Gant's rotors had stopped. 'Say, the guy really zapped you, Major – like that!' His right hand motioned like a gun firing.

'We're not ready, Garcia – I know it, you know it!'

'We ain't going any place, Major, not 'til they can repair what's wrong with my ship . . . one hell of a noise and some really wild –'

'Save it, Garcia – tell the repairman when the tow-truck gets here.'

As he turned away, he saw Mac waggle one hand at Garcia to silence him. Gant's mood darkened further.

'Coffee, Major?'

Coffee –

He did not reply, walking away from the machines and the four men who appeared content to wait for the crane helicopter to reach them, lift the MiL off the ledge and carry it back to Nellis, forty miles north-east. He reached the edge of the flat outcrop. The sun was warm, though the occasional breeze was thin and chilly. The desert below him stretched away on every side, towards mountains to the south, west, and north. Las Vegas lay fifty miles south-east. Nevada. Gant breathed slowly, deeply and evenly to calm himself; squinting into the pale, empty sky . . .

. . . except for the far brown dot, like a speck of dust, which signified an eagle riding thermals up the face of a mountain. He watched the dot float without effort, riding its own element, and felt the sluggish responses and the unfamiliarity of the heavy Russian helicopter through his hands and arms. It was as if he was bound, immobilized both by the machine and the mock dogfight in which he had just engaged.

Unsuccessfully –

Miles away across the desert, a narrow plume of dust followed some invisible vehicle or horseman. Behind Gant, the two Russian helicopters waited like a threat. *Chameleon Squadron* had been halved in size when their only serviceable MiL had crashed in East Germany and killed its crew and the agents they had picked up on a search-and-rescue flight. These machines were new and unfamiliar – they needed *time* –! Time before they could begin *Winter Hawk*. The failure in the rotor head of Garcia's machine cut into the time available. The eagle now floated higher, up towards the peak of the mountain, effortlessly carried by rising currents of warmer air. The wind picked at him coldly.

'Coffee, skipper,' he heard Mac repeat at his side.

He nodded and took the plastic beaker. Swallowed the hot dark drink.

Mac had interrupted the return of peace. The desert had at least given him that. Long journeys, weekends and even whole weeks. He could recuperate. The instructorship at Nellis AFB had given him something more satisfying than companions. Now, he needed to work with these people – Mac, Garcia who would pilot the 24-A, and his crew, Lane and Kopoper. They were young, inexperienced. Valens had died in Germany last month and injured this mission in the same moment he burned to death with his experienced crew. Mac was OK – there was Vietnam to share, and reliability. The others –?

'What about that?' Mac asked conversationally, gesturing behind him.

'The men or the ship?' Gant replied, sipping the coffee.

'You ain't fair on them, Major.'

'Maybe.'

'They're good, Major – my word on –'

'Maybe.'

'You – can't play loner on this one, Major – you know that.'

'Maybe.' Gant continued to sip the coffee, watching the distant trail of dust and the dot of the eagle. Mac confined him on the ledge just as certainly as the damage to the rotor head and the fact that he had been no match for a fighter aircraft, not even with the terrain working in his favour. 'Yeah – maybe, Mac. They're just not ready.' Then, after a pause, he added: 'No one is.'

'Three weeks, minimum,' Mac commented sourly, spitting near his feet. Then, more brightly: 'You'll get used to us being around, Major.'

'I have to, Mac.'

Mac walked away, back towards people he knew and understood. Gant did not turn to watch him, but continued to squint at the eagle in the dazzling morning air. Just warm enough to lift the huge bird, just warm enough. The trail of dust seven or eight miles away was fading, leaving the desert empty once more.

The mission was unlucky; hasty and unprepared. As if the acquisition of the two Russian machines was in itself enough to guarantee success. He'd flown maybe six or seven squadron missions behind the Curtain, using captured or stolen or mocked-up Russian aircraft. But not one like this.

They should never have told them, not even him, the stakes involved. They were too high, they'd *never* be ready. They should not have been told. Garcia and his crew hid from the risks by adopting a casual, callow arrogance. He simply tried to prepare, knowing the time was too short. Eighteen months since he'd brought home the MiG-31, the Firefox, from Russia. *That* mission had had more chance of success!

He finished the last of the coffee, and heard Mac's voice calling him. He realized he had half-understood there was a radio call. He turned. Mac was running towards him.

'– today!' he shouted. 'Nellis on the set – skipper, they've brought the mission forward to today –!'

49

'– crazy,' was all Gant said in reply. It made no sense. He could not believe it, despite Mac's nods, the emphasis of his eyes and his flushed cheeks. 'Those assholes in Washington are crazy – out of their skulls, Mac!' he added as belief gripped, forcing anger. 'What the hell did they say about *that*?' He waved his hand violently towards the crippled helicopter.

'Washington don't know yet, Major –'

'Then why in hell doesn't someone tell them?'

He turned away from Mac. Not because of the message, or because Mac's face was beginning to mirror his own – but because he had seen another dot in the high, clean desert air. Not the eagle – the lumbering crane helicopter from Nellis coming to collect the MiL-24-A. Its symbolism clashed with that of the bird and the trail of dust on the desert floor. Too violently.

'There's no way,' he said breathily. 'Just no way –'

He could no longer see the eagle. The dust from the distant vehicle had finally settled. The desert before him appeared painted, a vast, empty canvas, no longer real.

Colonel Dmitri Priabin of the KGB's Industrial Security Directorate and head of non-military security at the cosmodrome of Baikonur, turned away from the young man lounging with a shallow but arrogant confidence in the office's single easy chair, stifled a yawn and a desire to rub his shadowed cheeks, and clasped his hands behind his back as he stared out into the darkness of the winter night.

Across the expanse of low buildings in front of him lay the main assembly complex and the vast hangar which housed the G-type heavy booster launch vehicle. Its posy of huge rockets was splashed with white light within the open hangar doors; they were end-on to him like the mouths of some enormous multiple gun.

The scene was distant but by no means toylike or unreal. It was all too vast to become miniaturized by mere distance. And it was thrilling, undeniably so. At least, whenever he could forget the purely personal, could step aside from himself for a moment and

50

discover emotions he could share with others – then it was thrilling. He could experience pride, awe, satisfaction, secrecy, even nationalism. A rainbow of clichéd emotions. When he could forget Anna and his past.

His office was warm yet he wore full uniform, including tie and jacket. The pale self that stared back from the dark square of the windowpane was tired, drawn – but neat. The uniform was not to impress the young man who had been brought in for questioning, rather to impress himself. To remind him of who and what he was, and to exclude other, less respectable images. The brown uniform and the colonel's shoulder-boards were a plaster cast inside which he slowly mended.

The rollout of the G-type heavy booster would begin on Tuesday morning. A powerful locomotive waited in a siding near the hangar, to pull the booster on its flatcars the six miles – a short distance by Baikonur's sprawling standards – to the new launch pad. On two parallel sets of railway lines and within a vast erector cage, the booster would make the painfully slow journey. At least, the first three stages . . . the *Raketoplan* shuttle vehicle would follow in its wake as soon as the assembled laser weapon had been installed in its cargo bay.

He stifled another yawn, which might in reality have become a sigh. He felt excluded from the simple emotions aroused by the scene outside. He was excluded by the presence of the general's son behind him, lounging in his chair; excluded, precisely, by his sense of the stupid mistake he had made in arresting the boy at all . . . why the devil had he? Bravado, machismo, reckless-ness – *lack of thought*? Dmitri Priabin profoundly regretted his actions.

It would take nearly twenty-four hours for the first stages to reach the launch pad, and another half a day to move the shuttle and raise it atop the remainder of the rocket. By Thursday noon everything would be ready for that afternoon's launch . . .

He still felt excluded, felt his own concerns press in on him; it could well be a matter of self-preservation . . . and yet, the boy *irritated* him so much –! He whirled on his heels to face the young man, whose eyes were now dull with tiredness rather than

51

drug-brightened, as they had been when Priabin had arrested him. Tired though they might be, the eyes flickered with a pale gleam of contempt, a growing fire of anticipated satisfaction – *wait till Daddy hears about this*, the eyes promised childishly, maliciously. Not only was this little shit a general's son – a Baikonur general's son – but he was GRU, military intelligence. Priabin realized, with a growing nervousness, that he had opened the trapdoor to a snakepit . . . *a can of worms*, didn't the Americans say? It was the boy's expectation, almost his right, to hold the KGB in contempt. GRU really ran security at Baikonur, it was the army that was really in control.

'You still refuse to identify the – source of the drugs, Lieutenant?' he asked with careful authority. 'We really have wasted enough time on this already.'

'Then let me go,' the young man replied, pouting with thin, pale lips. Pale eyebrows, pale hair, faded blue eyes. Almost ghostly. He might have been some aristocrat's jaded, old-young offspring. Perhaps he was, in a Soviet sense . . . certainly the son of a powerful and dangerous man.

Why wouldn't he let the boy go? Spite? Possibly . . . the boy *was* homosexual. Spite might even have been the motive for the anonymous tip-off. One of the boy's circle, offended or jealous, a quarrel, a lack of tenderness? Whatever, he had arrested Valery Rodin, officer of the GRU, on charges of possessing cocaine. Once he had discovered the boy's rank and connections, why had he bothered to bring him in? He could have taken the drugs and kept his mouth shut. But the boy's contempt had stung him, made him angry . . .

Bad dreams of Anna the previous night, contempt for the face he saw in the shaving-mirror just before the call had come – they'd played their part, too.

'You realize how serious an offence you've committed, Lieutenant?'

Rodin shrugged. His tie was loose at his throat, his uniform jacket was unbuttoned. The remains of a plate of sandwiches and an empty beer glass rested on Priabin's desk, near the boy's elbow. It might have been *his* office –

Anger. Useless, harmful anger, doing him definite harm and no damn' good whatsoever . . . but he *couldn't* bring himself to let this arrogant, criminal little shit go free –!

'I know who reported me,' Rodin hissed. 'The *pretty* little queen!' He did not bother to disguise his homosexuality, despite its magnitude as a criminal offence under Soviet law; as if he were immune to KGB charges . . .

. . . which he was.

Neither joke nor crime; just a fact about a young man whose father was a senior officer of the Strategic Rocket Forces, the army's most elite service. A man who was one of the triumvirate of staff officers *running* Baikonur, for God's sake –!

. . . you bloody fool, tangling with that lot.

General Lieutenant Rodin. *His* son could have worn make-up and a frock on duty and little if anything of consequence would have happened to him. And the boy knew that as clearly as he knew who his father was.

And *that's* what enrages you, Priabin told himself – precisely that . . . look at his face now –! Priabin choked on a bile of silent rage. The conversation finished hours ago, as far as he's concerned. Priabin knew he was already on a list of petty revenges to be exacted as soon as the boy was released. In this case, a ruinous revenge if the father took an interest.

'Lovers' tiff, was it?' he asked quietly, unable to prevent himself. The boy set his teeth on edge, infuriated him beyond all measure.

Rodin laughed, not even blushing, not even angry.

'If you like,' he replied, shrugging insolently. Priabin's colonelcy meant nothing, nothing at all.

Somewhere in the building, the damning evidence of the cocaine he had found would have disappeared by now . . . to placate the general's anticipated anger and the son's petty revenge.

'You don't seem to care much, either way?'

'Should I? After all, what can happen?'

There, he'd finally said it. Priabin, angry as he was, still felt chilled, and cursed the shame brought on by his shaving-mirror;

cursed Rodin's initial insolence as his locker was searched; cursed self-consciousness.

It was almost as if he carried within him some urge towards self-destruction. That was the Anna part of him, not the part of him that still worked, slept, ate, shaved, obeyed orders and stared at his uniformed self in mirrors, idled away his posting at Baikonur ... *a cushy number, you're bloody lucky to get it, after everything that's happened*, they had said in Moscow. *Not even demoted* ... yes, he was lucky to have got it after the American's escape and Anna's death ... The part that wanted to convict Rodin, make him sweat, belonged to Anna; the wailing, never-to-be-comforted child she had left behind her, frozen in grief like a corpse trapped in thick ice.

Guilt, of course ... overwhelming guilt for that moment when the border guards had opened fire, when his shouting had panicked them, when Gant —

He snatched his mind away from the images, from the round blue hole in her forehead. The effort to wrench his mind away from that one last image in particular, was as violent as snatching his hand back from a flame. It was that image which, even now, returned more than any other. Often when he tried to remember her smiling, or making love, or concentrating on documents or cooking — her forehead seemed to wear that final badge, the round blue hole. It was clearer and more terrible even than the blood from the back of her head, which had stained his hand and his greatcoat.

He could not remember her *alive*, not for whole days at a time. She was always dead on the icebound road at the Finnish border where Gant had escaped him — and caused her death.

His voice was thin and angry, surprising Rodin out of his slouching posture.

'Listen to me, Lieutenant. Listen carefully. I may be just a policeman to you, but you're guilty of an offence that could land most people with a life sentence — the Gulag ...' Already, Rodin's thin lips had regained their sneering smile. Priabin would have liked, dearly liked, to strike that soft, half-formed face. 'A life sentence,' he repeated. 'I don't want you, I want the supplier. Who supplies the cocaine, the hashish, all the uppers and downers used – people like *you* use? Who supplies? Who fixes?'

'And if I don't tell you?' Rodin asked tauntingly.

'Just tell me,' Priabin sighed, arms folded across his chest. He leaned his head slightly to one side, as if studying Rodin.

'No.'

'Even the general wouldn't – I don't say *couldn't*, remember – but he wouldn't like to keep the lid on this. It might cause him a certain amount of – embarrassment?'

Rodin's features were blank with surprise. Then they looked haughty. The aristocrat's ruined son again.

'You wouldn't tell him! You think he'd *want* you to tell him? You must be mad!'

'If you're charged, he begins to be involved.'

'And you're finished!' The voice was, satisfyingly, a little higher, uncertain; in the upper atmosphere of Rodin's confidence, where it was more difficult to breathe. 'You *know* that, for fuck's sake – you *know* you'd be finished!'

'Lose my cushy billet here, you mean?'

'I heard you were lucky to get it –'

He had been – oh, yes, he had been lucky. They had blamed Anna, the double-agent, not himself. He had lied and concealed and clumsily accounted for his presence at the border, and they had accepted his version of events. It had been the woman who had helped the American pilot to escape, he was still loyal. He had been disloyal, of course – to Anna. Saved himself by exposing her treachery . . . which, naturally, he had only that day stumbled upon, when he realized that his mistress was trying to smuggle the American out of the Soviet Union. Yes, yes, yes, the woman was a traitor, and better dead. Executed, not murdered. Yes, yes, yes . . . he had gone along with it – *all* of it.

His anger became directed at the weak, dissolute, *living* young man in the chair.

'Be careful!' Priabin snapped, his face flushed with anger, tightened into hard lines. Rodin could not muster the satisfied smile that should have followed the jibe.

Why was he doing this? Was he looking for resurrection or oblivion, pursuing this dangerous young man whose father was a general? He *was* desperate, he admitted to himself – he didn't care.

'Rodin – whatever the reason or the consequence, I'll charge you. You believe it. Papa would not be pleased with you, whatever his attitude to me. It's not your first – *escapade*, is it?'

'Don't be stupid, Priabin. Just look the other way – I won't make trouble for you.'

'Uncomfortable?'

'Get lost!'

'Ever thought Papa might grow tired of dragging his queer brat out of the shit, time after time?'

'What are you trying to do, Priabin? *Make* things difficult for yourself?'

'Maybe.'

'Got something against gays?'

'No. Just against drugs. Against you, almost certainly.'

'A Socialist!' Rodin exclaimed with bright sarcasm.

'Aren't we all, comrade?'

'Just walk away, Priabin,' Rodin warned, straightening his tie, preparing to button his jacket. 'Just drop it. Nothing of importance is happening in here – it's all happening out there.' He waved his hand towards the window; pale, long-fingered.

Priabin knew he had been monumentally stupid. The general would be angry at any interruption, four days from the launch. Priabin shook his head. Monumentally stupid.

'Well?' Rodin asked. His jacket was buttoned and smoothed, his cap in his hand.

Priabin rubbed a hand through his dark hair. Nodded.

'You still refuse to tell me?'

'I have nothing to say.' A mere formality of a reply.

'Very well . . .' Priabin sighed, waving a dismissive hand.

Immediately, Rodin stood up. Smiled. Walked across the carpet with what might have been a strut of pleasure, with an authority that made his movements more masculine. He grinned

56

into Priabin's face, his eyes no longer tired, his mouth continuing to sneer.

Dmitri Priabin ignored him, staring out of the window. Beyond the giant assembly building and the glowing hangar, the lights of a dormitory town threw a faint stain on the clouds. The lights of the old town, Tyuratam, illuminated the sky to the south. He could just make out the skeletal gantries of the nearest launch pads against the glow. Across the flat country, towards the eastern horizon, groups of lights appeared like the encampments of units in some vast, invisible army. Missile silos, watchtowers, factories, railway yards, power stations, the airport, towns, villages. The vast settlement of Baikonur; the army's Baikonur.

Now, he wished he had let Rodin go at once – never even arrested him. He was angry with his former mood of bravado. He did want to keep his nose clean, keep his cushy billet until – until he used the tool that had been given him to ensure his return to Moscow Centre with some sort of small triumph . . . now, he might need Kedrov's arrest just to fend off the general's anger . . . *shit* –!

'Just keep looking through your window,' Rodin purred close to his ear. 'You'll have plenty to look at in the next four days. It should keep you occupied.' Priabin glanced at Rodin. He seemed inebriated with release and his sense of superiority over the KGB colonel. His mood seemed excessive, but promised trouble for Priabin. 'You can watch *Lightning* get under way –'

Because the words seemed choked, bitten off, Priabin looked up.

'*Lightning?* What's that?'

'I –' Hesitation? Confusion? Rodin seemed regretful, nervous; emotions pursued a hurried course across his narrow face. Concluding in a tight-mouthed self-assurance and a glance around the office as if to dismiss any authority that might reside within it. 'I meant *Linchpin* – the launch . . . *Linchpin*.'

'*Linchpin*,' Priabin echoed dubiously. 'The launch of the laser battle station?'

'Yes. Just that.' His face was close to Priabin's eyes. Priabin

57

could smell the meat from the sandwiches on his breath, scent the last whiff of the boy's heavy cologne. 'I said nothing else – understand? Nothing –' He moved away, then drawled affectedly and without real conviction: 'I can go now?'

'Yes.'

Rodin nodded, placed his cap on his pale hair, clicked his bootheels ironically, and left the room. Priabin heard him whistling in the outer office. The noise faded in the corridor.

Why had he been threatened? Rodin had forgotten everything else, even his petty revenge, because of that one word, his slip of the tongue . . . it wasn't a mistake, it was an error. *Lightning?* Rodin had quite evidently and deliberately threatened him, told him to forget the slip.

Lightning? What the devil was *Lightning?*

It was important, and it was a secret . . .

He was startled by the opening of the door, having failed to register the polite knock. Viktor Zhikin, his second-in-command, appeared relieved.

'I'm glad you – dropped the matter,' he said at once.

'What? Oh –' Priabin attempted a broad, dismissive smile. '– why try to buck the system, Viktor? Who wants the heartache, mm?'

Zhikin moved his hand almost as if to pat Priabin's shoulder. Priabin grinned unconvincingly. His awareness returned to –

– *Lightning.* Not *Linchpin*, as the first of the laser weapons was codenamed. *Lightning*.

'What?' he mumbled, aware that Zhikin was speaking once more.

'Sorry – are we going to pull Kedrov and the cycle shop owner in for questioning? The surveillance teams want to know. You said tonight –' Zhikin's voice was firm, even parental. It reminded Priabin of his responsibilities. It reminded him, too, that the spy was perhaps the key to his own future, now that he had made an enemy of Rodin, even of the boy's father. It was – yes, it was necessary to have Orlov and Kedrov safe in custody. His bargaining-lever, even his passport back to Moscow. 'They want to know should they go in and try to find the transmitter . . . it doesn't look as if Kedrov is going to go back there since he was spooked by those clods following him —!' Zhikin was angry, self-critical.

'Not your fault, Viktor – they should never have been spotted by an amateur like him . . . idiots.' He rubbed his chin.

'Where's the dog?'

'What? Oh, Grechkova's taken him for his walk – now, what do we do about Kedrov?'

'Where is he now?'

'Still in his flat.'

'And Orlov?'

'In bed above the shop.'

Priabin looked at his watch. Midnight. Rodin had been there since early evening – he wouldn't have liked that, he'd want some revenge for the – the *inconvenience* he'd been put to . . . yes, it would be better to have the agent and his transmitter-man in the bag before the shit hit the fan.

Priabin nodded. 'OK. It is a bit late in the day to let him go on running around – time to chop off that particular chicken's head. We'll go in at dawn . . . warn the teams. You and I will supervise Orlov's arrest. I want that transmitter, and no cock-ups.'

Zhikin smiled. 'Great,' he said. 'Fine – sir.'

'Sure . . .'

Threat, insolence, superiority, arrogance, contempt – he'd seen all those on Rodin's face. And fear, too, together with concern, self-accusation, anxiety – and a clear sense of *danger*.

Lightning. It meant something – something vitally important and concerning the laser weapon. *Lightning –*

What the hell did it mean?

Snow was blowing across the tinted green windows, making their colour colder, almost repellent. The illuminated spike of the Washington Monument looked even more than ever like some spacecraft waiting to be launched. Anders felt uncomfortable in the Oval Office. He wanted to loosen his tie, relax his sitting

59

posture. It wasn't awe, or even tension. It was the weight of events.

New Year, he thought. Just New Year . . . and now this. Anders looked down at the sheet covered with his own handwriting. *Come for me at once, before they find me. I must go into hiding, the agreed rendezvous . . . hurry, come immediately . . .*

Kedrov's panic-button, his cry for help. He was terrified. Of something he referred to as *Lightning* . . . though he didn't explain. *I know about* Lightning, *and they know I know . . . hurry.* The desperation was clearly there. Kedrov had gone into the undergrowth. Gant and his people were stalled at Nellis in Nevada. It was coming unglued, the whole operation —

Kedrov might even have been picked up by now.

Because of the tension, he felt cut off from the outside. Langley, across the Potomac, was separated from him by a vast gulf. He was there to report, at the Director's insistence, as Mission Officer for *Winter Hawk*. But there was nothing to report. The Galaxy transport aircraft was still sitting in its hangar at Nellis AFB in Nevada, two hours after the mission was activated. Three hours now. *Winter Hawk* was stalled.

As if rebuffing the tension, the defeat in the room's air, Calvin was rehearsing old speeches, old hopes.

'We fell for it — we were suckered into this Treaty, Dick! We thought they were so frightened they had to agree . . . they just wanted to *divert* some defence spending! Years ahead of us all the time, and overjoyed when we offered to save them billions of roubles so they could spend it on their own SDI! We threw in *Talon Gold*, our ASAT programme, all in good faith, hoping to encourage them to do the same, went ahead with the surveillance satellite programme instead — and all the time they had their own laser weapon programme going! Dear-Christ-in-Heaven, I won't be forgiven for this — none of us will!' he added darkly, turning to face the others.

Gunther looked down, as did the Director, seated next to Anders. The silence loomed, waiting to be filled. Calvin was staring at him, accusingly it seemed to Anders.

'And now you tell me our last chance is on hold,' he snapped.

Anders glanced at the row of television screens along one wall. The mission room at Langley appeared on four of them in glaring colour, from different angles. The scene appeared slow, undersea, almost inactive.

'Mr President, the repairs they have to effect to one of the two gunships can't be done while they're in the air —'

'How long, Mr Anders — how long?'

'They can't give me a closer estimate than — maybe tonight.'

'*Maybe* tonight?'

'I'm sorry, Mr —'

'That isn't good enough, Anders, and you know it!' He turned his accusing gaze on the Director. 'Bill, you pleaded with me to initiate this operation. Forty-eight hours, maximum, that's what you said. They haven't taken off from Nellis yet and three of your forty-eight have already disappeared!'

The Director shifted awkwardly on his chair like a chastened schoolboy.

Calvin sat at his desk, almost an interloper masquerading as President. His eyes looked lost and afraid.

'There's nothing I can say, Mr President,' the Director offered apologetically. There was only disappointment in his voice, and an overwhelming sense of past events.

'What's the extent of the damage to the ferry helicopter?' Dick Gunther asked.

'It's in the rotor head,' Anders replied. 'And in the hydraulic control jacks below the rotor head . . .' Calvin appeared impatient with detail, as if he suspected lies or excuses. 'They thought they had time to work on it . . . they're flat out now, Mr President,' he said mollifyingly. 'It's a long and difficult job. They can't adapt US parts to fit, not easily —'

'The *hell* with it, Mr Anders!' Calvin snapped. 'Just chalk it up as another Company mistake — in your *catalogue* of error, Bill. You advised me to leave this guy in place in Baikonur until the last moment, you insisted the crews weren't ready to undertake the mission, that more weeks of training were required — and all that it's gotten us is nowhere! We've lost the game, Bill — you've fumbled the pass.'

'I'm sorry, Mr President —'

Anders was angry, but he controlled his features. His brow began to perspire, and his body felt as if wrapped in hot, constricting towels rather than dressed in his grey suit. Calvin was manifestly unfair. He, too, was angry, but angry only that *Winter Hawk* would not have its chance — risky, sure, but their only chance . . .

He glanced at the Oval Office clocks in turn. One of them, a French clock, gilded and ornate, was placed on a low, darkly shining table. It was the First Lady's choice, he assumed. Its blue-numbered face showed a little after three. Sunday afternoon. The snow flew beyond the green glass as wildly as the recriminations in which Calvin had indulged.

'Why the hell did they go ahead?' Calvin was asking. 'Why didn't they trust us?' No one replied.

The Director lit his pipe. Anders was aware of the lighter tapping softly with nerves against the pipe's bowl. Blue smoke rose in the room, drifting across the windows towards the flag. Anders' gaze slid over Calvin's face, and he was shocked afresh by the deep stains beneath the man's eyes. The thick grey hair no longer added distinction to a strong face, it was no more than an old man's good fortune. He entertained an alternative image of Calvin, coming down the steps of Air Force One, returning to Washington from Vienna. Hands raised like a victorious fighter, grin broad, step quick and confident, almost running to the lectern with a genuine excitement, a need to tell. That had been after the first Summit of his term of office, his first meeting with Nikitin. They had agreed the principles of the Arms Reduction Treaty, and the time-table for negotiation.

The voice had been full and resonant as he had stood at the row of microphones. The cameras had continued to click and whir, the lights to flash, as he made his historic announcement.

. . . my fellow Americans . . .

Calvin turned like someone afraid he was being followed, and gazed out of the windows at the flying snow. It was as if he sensed the comparison of images in Anders' mind.

. . . today, President Nikitin and myself have committed ourselves

and our two countries to a resolute search for peace and for genuine, verifiable reductions in our nuclear arsenals . . .

Anders remembered the emotions and the wild excitement the speech had aroused even in himself, a senior career intelligence officer, though he would not have remembered the words . . . except that TV stations had been replaying the damned occasion, over and over, all week now. For four weeks, since they had known about Baikonur, the words had become increasingly hollow. Now, at this crisis, the speech – that first one of all of them – was no more than the naïve utterance of a duped politician. The signing of the Treaty should have crowned Calvin's first term and assured a second. Now, he stared ruin in the face; historic and historical repugnance was his inheritance. No wonder the man looked old and weary.

. . . we have agreed that there will be no special cases, no exclusions. Every weapons system currently deployed or in the development stage is to be on the table, on both sides . . .

The confident Harvard tones had been singing a siren song and the world had listened greedily. Hoping, at last hoping –

A new beginning. Half the Pershings and Cruise missiles and half the Soviet SS-20s had been withdrawn at once, the following day, as a gesture of mutual good faith . . . the world could hardly believe its luck.

But the world still believed in its luck. It didn't know what the men in that room knew. Anders' face twisted in bitterness. He felt betrayed, yes, that was it, betrayed – as anyone would. As they will when they hear . . . if they ever hear.

They will, he concluded. The news would leak out some day – this year, next year, the one after that. The Soviets have us by the short hairs, they've got 'Star Wars' instead of us . . . we're all washed up.

The world had gone on cheering for two whole years, Anders with them. Until *Cactus Plant*'s bombshell out of Baikonur . . . they have transported a laser battle station for launching . . . Christ! Two years had dropped hollow, like counterfeit coins hitting the pavement.

. . . my fellow Americans . . .

63

Now, those raised arms looked like surrender, like newsreel shots of weary and defeated Marines emerging from the hostile Vietnamese jungle. Eventually, Calvin would have to tell the world what had gone wrong, and that he had no answer to the Soviet laser weapons because he'd slowed down the research programmes, cut the funds, believed the Russians . . . they'd crucify him —

Anders realized Calvin was looking at him intently. He felt his cheeks warm under the piercing, accusatory gaze. It was as if Calvin was reading his thoughts.

'You think I've given up, Mr Mission Officer?' the President asked slowly, acidly. His eyes looked inward, with something like distaste.

'No, Mr —'

'Never mind. I want your butt on the co-pilot's seat of a military jet inside of an hour. Get the air force to fly you to Nellis. It should take you three hours, no more . . . and you're responsible for getting those gunships airborne today. Understand me? *Today!*'

Mitchell Gant appeared to sip at the can of beer in his hand with the wary delicacy of a cat. Seated in a crouch on the narrow bed against one wall of his cramped room, he seemed absorbed by the television set, as if he were trying to exclude Anders from his awareness. On the screen, the space shuttle *Atlantis* floated above California while the full text of the NART Treaty, clause after clause of it, rolled as softly as movie credits, superimposed on the shuttle's image.

All three major networks were running the same compilation of images and the Treaty's text. As it ran, the shuttle was shown over every area of the planet covered by its orbit; all recorded daylight shots, countries and oceans immediately recognizable from two hundred miles above the earth. To Anders, each clause that appeared on the screen was one more cruel fiction.

He cleared his throat, but Gant did not turn his head.

'You know most of those guys,' Anders offered.

Gant glared at him, as if disturbed from pleasure.

'Sure, I know some of them . . . Wakeman, the mission commander – yeah, I know them . . .' He seemed to lose interest in the conversation and sipped once more at his beer.

Anders felt oppressed by the narrow, bare room. Bed, table, two upright chairs, two service-issue easy chairs, a strip of carpet. It might have been a waiting-room at some downtown doctor's surgery where all the patients were either black or Mexican. A small refrigerator, metal lockers instead of a wardrobe or chest of drawers. There was a door to a tiny kitchen, another to a bathroom. Yet Gant must have chosen these quarters. His rank entitled him to a bungalow on the base. This was like – like a cupboard for storing machines not in use . . .

He opened the refrigerator, disturbed by his own metaphor, and took out a can of beer. Pulled the ring. Gas plopped softly. Gant had turned down the music accompanying the pro-gramme. The quiet of the room brooded. Gant's presence seemed to charge it with static electricity. Anders shook his head. He did not understand Gant. From his context – this room – he received no clues as to the man's present or past; or future. He looked at the television screen as if through a window onto a larger perspective.

Atlantis had been in orbit for a week. A long scientific mission including the disposition of two new surveillance satellites. The crew was also scheduled to repair other satellites – and, he remembered once more, to rendezvous with their Soviet coun-terparts on Friday, the day after the signing in Geneva. There was even TV talk that the shuttles might land at each other's home bases. Silly talk, but it nevertheless disturbed Anders. The world's present mood was evident in it. The party had begun in earnest and *no one* could call it off now.

On the screen, the Pacific occupying almost half of it now, the earth looked like some huge flower-bowl on which petals of desert, grassland and cloud floated. The shuttle's robot arm hung like a great elbow-joint in one corner of the screen and a Michelin tyre-man, one of the crew on a spacewalk, hovered above the Spacelab in the shuttle's cargo bay. It was a re-showing

65

of the repair job the shuttle had performed five days earlier. The whole programme was a re-run of one long peace slogan.

The lump of the malfunctioning satellite appeared to one side of the screen. Anders sipped his beer, his hand tightening involuntarily on the can. The tyre-man backpacked towards the satellite. The earth below him remained untouchably, impossibly beautiful.

Frustration gripped Anders.

'Christ, Gant – how can you just *sit* there?' he burst out. 'Don't you *care*?'

'Plenty. What good will it do, Anders? I can't repair rotor heads. They're working as fast as they can.'

'We don't have any *time*, Gant –'

Gant ostentatiously looked at his watch. It was seven in the evening, local time, as near as it mattered. Ten o'clock in Washington. Soon, he would have to call the Oval Office – again. He squeezed the can in his hand. Gant was like a pressure forcing itself against him; immobile like a Buddha, silent again now that he was not being spoken to. Then he looked at Anders.

'It could take four hours, it could take all night. You've seen.'

The room oppressed him even more. He felt an imposter in his borrowed flying overalls. His body ached from the unfamiliarity of the co-pilot's seat of the EF-111 in which he had been flown from Andrews to Nellis AFB. Gant's apparent indifference enraged him.

'The man expects you to succeed, Gant,' he said waspishly.

Gant turned his head, his eyes glinting.

'So? The man expects?' He gestured with the beer can. 'When the repairs are through, we go. What the hell else do you want from me?'

'He wants, Gant – *he* wants. You have to give him this agent on a plate, *and* his holiday movies. Can you do that?'

'I'm not his wife, Anders. Just one of the slobs working in the guy's factory, underpaid and underfed.' He grinned quickly, looking suddenly boyish. 'We're not ready, Anders. You know that. Not even me.'

There was a certainty about Gant's pronouncement, negative

though it was; bare like the room around him. A pennant from Vietnam on one of the buff-coloured walls, a few photographs of aircraft, a younger Gant posed in front of a Phantom jet, pilot's helmet under his arm. Little or nothing – yet Anders was impressed by the force with which Gant occupied the room.

'You – have to be ready,' he said.

Gant merely shrugged.

'It doesn't change the facts. We should have had another week, minimum. Those machines are pigs to fly. Tell the man that when you talk with him.' He looked at his watch once more. 'Isn't it time to call home?' His features wore an undisguised cynicism which angered Anders. Gant was contemptuous – of him, of the President – the mission?

'Where in hell are you coming from, Gant?' he snapped. 'What is it with you? I don't need all this crap from you!'

'But you need me, Anders. So does the man. My misfortune, but you do. This idea was crazy from the beginning. Now, it's suicidal.'

'You want out, Gant? Is that what you want?' Anders sneered, the can squeezed almost flat in his fist.

Gant shrugged expressively. 'Out? Why?' He gestured around the bare room. 'You told me, once, Anders, why I work for you. For the rest of the assholes in the Company. Because you let me fly. Uh?' He dismissed Anders with a wave of his hand and turned back to the television as he said: 'I'm in, Anders. I don't have any hankering to face charges that have been tailored to fit me – maybe even a list of charges.' He snorted in derision. 'I'm a big boy, Anders – I tie my own shoelaces and I know the score. I just get parked here 'til you need me. I'm going just as soon as they fix Garcia's ship.'

'OK,' Anders sighed. He leaned heavily against the door. He realized he had never really entered the small room. It and its occupant baffled him. Gant was cocooned, somehow apart. Perhaps he really did despise the very people who needed him, to whom he was valuable. He added in a tone that was intended to mollify:

'If we can have the agent and the material by Thursday, we can still win, Gant – we can bargain.'

Gant studied Anders' angry, tired face. Anders could not change his expression. His muscles were set in defeated lines.

Gant said: 'Maybe. *If* and *maybe.*'

'What the hell else can we do?' Anders cried out. The can in his hand was crushed flat.

Gant shrugged. 'Nothing. But the idea is still crazy –'

'You'll be in Soviet helicopters, you have all the call-signs, the channels and frequencies – you'll be there maybe a half-hour –!'

'They'll shoot a guy on a bicycle on sight, Anders. That place is going to be sewn up tight – and I mean tight.' He looked down at his own can, shook it – it made no sound – then lobbed it into a waste-basket. He closed his hands together as if in prayer. 'And the guy's jumped, Anders. You don't even know if he'll show up when we do.'

'He said. Kedrov knows where to be, he has a transponder only you will be able to pick up. The rendezvous island in the salt marshes is pinpointed. *Winter Hawk* is something they won't be expecting – not in a million years.'

'So you say.'

'So the President says, Gant. To quote him exactly, he said "Tell that guy to get his ass over there – and no foul-ups." His message is clear, Gant.'

'Sure. Otherwise it's a long vacation somewhere where they're always losing the keys. I know.'

'We don't do that –'

'This time *he* will. I have the ball, Anders.' He returned his gaze to the screen. The terms of the Treaty were still rolling softly up the screen, the shuttle still floated invulnerably and apart above the ocean.

'I have to make that call,' Anders said, throwing his can at the waste-basket. It struck the side and clattered on the floor. Gant smiled.

He looked towards Anders as if weighing him. Then he said: 'Give the man my compliments. Tell him Captain Fantastic is just raring to go!' Once again, he snorted in derision.

THREE

gathering storm

'. . . gone, sir. He must have vanished some time during the night, over the roof – we –'

'You were *there*!' Priabin shouted into the car's radio microphone. 'You stupid buggers were on the spot *all night*!'

'Sir, we had all the exits covered –' the voice began once more, its note of apology more calculating and less shocked.

In the Zil's front passenger seat, Viktor Zhikin sighed angrily and banged the dashboard with his gloved fist. His murmur was an echo of Priabin's sentiments.

'Find him!' Priabin barked, his voice unnerved. The silence around him in the car was thundery. The driver had turned off the music from the black-market cassette.

'Sir?' Zhikin asked as Priabin threw him the microphone.

'Don't let's allow Orlov to go the same way, shall we?'

Zhikin snapped into the mike: 'All units – move in at once. Now!' Acknowledgements crackled in the car.

'Come on,' Priabin snapped. 'Orlov will know where his little friend is!' I hope so, he added to himself. I hope so . . .

He opened the rear door and climbed out. The temperature assailed him, biting through his heavy topcoat, his boots. The black car was clothed with heavy frost.

Dear Christ, he thought, the idea striking him cleanly, they've lost Kedrov. Anger welled up at once, almost choking him. He had to find him – his whole career, his return to Moscow depended on it. If it was discovered he had let an American spy escape, he would be well and truly finished. Panic coursed through him like the effects of a drink. He almost lost his footing on the icy pavement. It glinted dully in the red, early light.

He steadied himself against the car, hardly squinting as he looked into the heavy, swollen ball of the sun which had just heaved itself above the flat horizon. Like a heavier-than-air balloon. Its dull red disc was bisected and trellised with launch gantries, the skeletons of radio masts and radar dishes.

Zhikin crossed the narrow, cobbled street just ahead of him. It was veined with grey ice. The windows of Orlov's shop were blind. Paint peeled from the wooden door. The shop's sign was weathered almost to illegibility. A word-of-mouth clientele, Priabin reminded himself humourlessly. Cassettes, expensive stereo items from the West, even the more usual currency of denim. Orlov supplied to the young and to the scientific and technical communities – the army had their own semi-official pipeline which flowed with more regularity, bringing the prized and scarce consumer luxuries. For the army it was a perk, not a crime.

Anger swelled once again in his throat. He banged on the door with his gloved fist, quickly, repeatedly. He realized Zhikin was watching him disapprovingly, head on one side. He went on banging, yelled Orlov's name in the quiet morning of the narrow, old street. Zhikin put his finger to the bell at the side of the door. What if, what if –? Priabin's mind drummed, as if to accompany the beat of his fist.

'Orlov!' he yelled. 'Orlov, open this bloody *door!*' Voice becoming higher.

A helicopter drummed and grumbled overhead. He looked up. A vapour trail crossed the sun. Across the street, he heard the driver's radio. What if Orlov had gone to ground along with Kedrov, slipped away in the night –? If the army found out about Kedrov – they *must do*, now the man had disappeared from his work! – then he'd be bloody ruined.

'Orlov – Orlov, you old bastard, open up!'

He had to get Kedrov back at once, then he might win the game that had suddenly turned deadly.

Zhikin's hand was firm on his arm.

'OK, sir?' he asked, his face concerned and cautioning.

'What –?'

70

'You need . . . to calm down. Orlov will be no help if you . . .' He did not need to finish the sentence. Priabin glared, then swallowed and nodded.

'OK, Viktor, OK – usual style, old techniques . . . sure.' *Come on, come on –*

He craned towards the door, and heard the slow shuffle of something – slippered feet or an old dog's noises – coming through the shop. A bolt slid back. A sigh escaped Priabin's lips, a smoky signal of relief. Zhikin's face settled into satisfied lines.

'He, at least, hasn't buggered off,' he offered as if he read Priabin's thoughts.

'Kedrov knew he was being followed – he panicked. Maybe he came here last night – do you think he's here?' Priabin asked excitedly, the thought striking him for the first time.

'Maybe. Doubt it, sir – first place we'd be likely to look.'

Another bolt, then a security lock. A gnarled hand slid up the blind. Orlov's face appeared, blinking at them like that of a mole becoming threatened and afraid, its tunnel blocked behind it. Orlov wore thick glasses, was thin and elderly, but cunning – already counting them, assessing their mood. His head was bald, liver-spotted like the back of the hand still holding the raised blind. A shrunken but loose stomach sagged like a phantom pregnancy under a stretched grey cardigan.

He opened the door slowly. Priabin wanted to drive through it, rush into the shop bellowing Kedrov's name. Knowing the spy would not be there.

'Yes?' Orlov asked, his voice cautiously deferential, testing their mood like an antenna. His tongue licked his grey lips and his eyes blinked again. 'Yes, comrade Colonel? I'm not open –'

'You are to us,' Zhikin replied wearily, holding up the red ID card in its plastic folder.

'Yes, of course,' Orlov replied. 'Please come in, comrades. How can I help you?' Priabin, enraged by the man's calculated replies, realized he had been forewarned. He had been practising his part all night.

Careful, careful . . . Viktor's right – Priabin could almost *smell* Kedrov upstairs, above the shop . . . he must have come – was he still here? What message had he sent? Steady, steady . . . Orlov's setting the pace just now.

They entered the shop. Bare floorboards, dust; the smells of lubricating oil, heavier greases, welding gas, paint. A litter of parts, a couple of complete bicycles; a new, bright-green man's bike in the shop's bay window that bulged into the narrow street outside. It was ready to be exposed to envying eyes as soon as the blinds and the security meshes were removed when the shop opened. Orlov seemed unwilling to invite them further into the shop's secret bays and reaches. Priabin's excitement was evident in his voice.

'Where is he?' he blurted. Zhikin's face warned.

Orlov stood behind the counter of the shop, as if to serve them. On its surface, yesterday's paper was covered with oil and a bicycle chain. Then he was startled by the noise of locks being smashed at the rear of the building. His head turned wildly. Priabin nodded to Zhikin.

'Search *everywhere*,' he murmured insistently.

Zhikin seemed to weigh his mood, find it acceptable, and nodded. 'I don't think he's here,' he commented, then passed behind the shop counter into the rear of the building. Orlov had begun to whine.

'I – what do you want? I let you in, there was no need to break the door . . .' His voice tailed off as Priabin approached the counter more like an intruder than a customer. He touched the day-old local Tyuratam paper – its reports seeming to indicate a separation of existence between Baikonur and the old town – shunting its edges parallel with those of the counter. The bicycle chain slithered like an almost-dormant snake. Priabin looked up from the newspaper into Orlov's grey features.

A little money on the side, that's all it was . . . he'd call it providing a service, probably. Always reasonably safe, since the KGB bought their new stereo headphones or styluses or pop tapes here, too. Got their Jap hi-fi repaired by Orlov. Priabin himself had done so on one occasion, after the officially approved electrical shop in the town had buggered his cassette player. Orlov was safe –

– until he wanted to start playing in the first division, with the big boys. Being the transmitter-man for Kedrov.

Priabin soothed himself narcotically into the familiar role of interrogator. Softly, softly –

'Where's Kedrov?' he asked almost gently.

'Who?'

'One of your best customers by the number of times he's been here.'

Orlov was distracted by feet thudding overhead, by the destructive noises coming from behind the shop. The ripping of wood, tumbling of contents, the smashing of china, the heavy whispering of moved rugs and carpets; the groans of furniture being manhandled across bare boards.

'I don't understand – you want to know about a customer?'

Priabin swallowed his disappointment. Kedrov was not there. He must have rung Orlov to warn him he was going to ground . . . where the hell was he? Panic mounted; he eased it away with the small rituals of the interrogator's foreplay.

'No. I want to know about the transmitter.'

'Transmitter –?'

A turn of the head, a fearful gleam behind the glasses as the clatter of parts tipped out of some box was clearly audible. There'd be a lot of damage, and some looting, of course. Priabin had no feeling either way; par for the course. New, shiny amplifiers would disappear, and the latest tapes. It didn't matter so long as they found the transmitter. That could be used to open up Orlov like the key to a tin of sardines. The transmitter –

– or its components!

'Viktor! Viktor!' he yelled. Orlov had stayed because he thought he was safe –! He'd *hidden* the bloody transmitter! Zhikin appeared in the doorway to the rear of the building, dust on his greatcoat, his hands grimy. 'Viktor – tell them to look for the *bits* and *pieces* – yes?' Zhikin's face brightened.

'Should I get a couple of technical boys out from the town office?'

'Yes, do that.'

'Phone's in the back – I'll do it now.' Zhikin disappeared,

whistling. Orlov's eyes were narrow with calculation as Priabin grinned at him.

'After all, you could have spent all night taking it to pieces, now couldn't you?' he said lightly. Yes, he could play this role; interrogator-as-seducer. Apart from anything else, it kept his anxiety at a controllable level. He purred: 'Where is it now? Forming the innards of a couple of new hi-fi systems?' He grinned. 'We'll find it, Orlov. You shouldn't have tried to play with the big boys – not the Yankees, anyway. Where's Kedrov?' he snapped suddenly, harshly.

'He's –'

Priabin nodded. 'What did he tell you last night? That he was rumbled, he was getting out? Something spooked him. Did he say what it was?'

'I don't know what you're talking about – comrade Colonel, sir.' His eyes were still narrow with cunning. There was a kind of daring, too, which Priabin was forced to admire. The man wasn't really afraid . . . but then, he didn't know the stakes Priabin had put down on the table. 'I don't understand what you want. You already *know* about this place –! I mean –'

'We know. We know,' Priabin sighed. His gloves tapped on the edge of the counter, flicking back and forth like windscreen wipers. 'But, we just wondered whether you'd got into some other things, say like drugs . . . ?'

'Never!' A prim, virginal refutation – *what do you think I am?* 'I have never touched such things, believe me, comrade Colonel. Never!'

'I don't doubt it, now. That's why we were watching you in the first place, not for the hi-fis. That's how we stumbled on the transmissions, and then onto Kedrov. You see, we've known for a long time. It's why we sent in a burglary squad last week, looking for the damned *transmitter* –!' His voice broke off, his gloves slapped almost playfully, but hard, at Orlov. There was the tiny clatter of spectacles falling behind the counter, and the rustle of the disturbed chain-snake on the oily newspaper.

As Orlov scrabbled for his glasses, Priabin said: 'Where is it? How much information has gone to the Americans, Orlov? How *much*?' The anxiety mounted again, as if he had pressed his tongue against a rotten tooth. It was obvious; the laser weapon. Kedrov had worked on it, part of its huge technical services team. How much had been passed via Orlov's transmitter?

Orlov's face appeared above the counter, spectacles replaced. His mole-features sniffed the danger in the electric silence of the shop.

'Come on, Orlov – I have the power, *all* the power. It doesn't matter if you deny it, if we find nothing, like the burglary squad. You'll never crawl out of the hole I can put you in. You know that, don't you?'

Orlov shuddered; a small, thin, old man's shudder, like the breeze flapping a semi-transparent shower curtain. Priabin could see *through* Orlov, as if he were vanishing before his eyes. He knew Orlov now regretted *everything*.

'And there's always a family, isn't there?' Priabin persisted. 'Son, daughter, grandchildren probably, in your case . . . all flesh and blood, all with jobs, some of them in the Party, expecting to go places . . .' Priabin was smiling an open, almost joyous smile. Orlov was shivering; vulnerable as much as chilly. 'Cars drive too fast on slippery roads, pupils are downgraded and moved out of the Science School to one of the – oh, *agricultural* places –' Orlov appeared aghast. 'You know I can do anything to you, or to them whoever they are. Orlov, tell me about Kedrov. Tell me everything. We might even decide to leave you alone – you never know.'

'May –' After a long silence, his voice seemed rusty, or grappling with a foreign language. 'May I sit down?'

'Where?'

'In – in the kitchen . . . it's warmer.'

'Of course. You can make coffee – then we'll talk.'

Excitement rose in Priabin; anxiety thrust into it like a bout of indigestion. Orlov looked at him with a myopic squint. His nose twitched. The blind mole scenting the air. His cheeks seemed hollow with defeat. Then he said, in a quavering voice:

'I don't understand anything you've said, comrade Colonel. Drugs, transmitters – anything.'

Priabin sighed, pressing close behind the little old man as they went down the narrow, dusty passage towards the kitchen. His head was cocked on one side, as if listening for the noises of the old man's inward collapse. Impatience. He pressed the heel of routine down on it. No one knew, not yet, only his people . . . Kedrov was out there somewhere. Orlov would know, would be able to make an informed guess . . .

When they found the transmitter or its component parts – circuitry, dish aerial, control panel, anything – he would be able to break the old man like a dry stick.

The ice-cold concrete corridor whispered, even after he had stopped walking. His clicking footsteps simply wouldn't stop; they continued, echoing and fading gradually. Yes – silence at last. There was no one behind him except the phantom of his own footsteps, his own fear. He smelt grease, oil, dust. Concrete dust. He touched his hand along the rough wall, seeking the metal conduits that carried the landlines, the firing circuits, the ceiling lights. His ankle ached because he had twisted it – not climbing over the roof, merely slipping in the tunnels leading to this place. He'd stumbled over the rails that had once carried the missiles on their long trolleys along this underground section of the abandoned silo complex.

Kedrov calculated he was seven or eight miles from his flat. It was a frozen, sub-zero morning above ground. It was cold here, too. He was shivering despite his heavy clothing. His hand continued its scrabbling along the icy conduit. He moved his body after his hand, stepping carefully but with the panic that the deep silence had brought. He kept his shoulder, then shoulder and arm, then shoulder, arm and hip in contact with the wall, shrinking to one side of the long tunnel, the air in front of him alive with the danger of becoming solid, a dead-end, at any moment. He had discovered this bolt-hole weeks before, memorized and mapped it – now memory seemed to fail like a weakening bulb. He rubbed his arm and hip along the wall, step after step.

Switch —?

He touched its outlines, the button, hesitated, then threw the heavy switch. It clicked. How could he have simply forgotten the carefully-noted locations? Dusty white light seemed to shower like plaster from the roof. There were pools of light on the concrete all the way down to the steel doors which marked the entrance to the silo. Warning signs, the scribbled graffiti of security and danger, littered the walls. Conduits, rails, the scent of concrete dust and dampness — he shivered. It was *icy* cold down here —

The claustrophobia weakened, fear diminished. He was alone, saw he was alone, sensed he was safe. No one came here, not any longer.

He turned, counting the steel doors that led off the corridor. Four. He wanted the seventh door. He hurried, limping slightly but heedless of the now-innocent rails. Six, seven . . . The room behind it had not even been stripped when the old silo system had been abandoned for more sophisticated warrens elsewhere within Baikonur. The tunnel had not been used since the early '60s.

He touched the door. Icy. His fingers showed momentarily because, even chilled through, his body was warmer than the door, then they vanished. He pushed the door open and switched on the long, narrow room's lights. Bulbs set in the ceiling were protected by wire mesh. He saw the familiar rows of bunks, set four high against the walls. Cupboards he had forced open on a previous visit were filled with unrusted tins of food. There was air and running water. Some last refuge — it possessed an old-fashioned appearance, even while it still had a sense of science-fiction about it.

He unslung his small haversack and dropped it on the nearest bunk. The place struck him afresh, almost as if men still sat or lay on the bunks and there was a murmur of conversation in the room. The drift of cigarette-smoke, the smell of coffee, as they waited to loose their missiles or waited having done so. He rubbed his arms, then laved his hands together to warm them. Cold — it was just the cold. He unbuttoned his overcoat and walked up and down the corridor-like room. There was no need, at the moment, to go into the cramped kitchen, check the water-purifier or the stove. He had done all that on previous visits, there was no need.

A magazine lay beneath one bunk. He glimpsed old monochrome photographs – he thought he recognized the face of Kennedy, once American President, peeping from the shadows. He was part of the geological record of the place.

Food, yes. The water could be trusted, but he was wary. He'd checked the tins – some of them, a surprising number, seemed OK. But he'd brought supplies of his own, enough to last. The tiny bottled-gas stove and heater, he'd brought that, too. Vodka and beer . . . some things he'd stored on previous visits against the necessity – the fear – of having to use this place to hide out.

He opened the haversack, then the greaseproof package he removed from it. Bit into the thick sandwich and its sausage filling. It seemed hard to digest, the bread unyielding at the back of his throat. The empty room seemed to murmur with voices again. In a moment, he must go and turn off the corridor lights – just in case . . . this was a *horrid* place!

Soon, soon they would know he had disappeared. By now, even – the KGB would question Orlov, the army would be told he had not reported for work, that his flat was empty . . . the hunt for him would begin. They'd panic . . . the army would want him, too, because of what he had overheard about *Lightning* . . . they'd think it was why he'd panicked . . . God, it was *mad*–! Those telemetry officers could have killed him on the spot – by now, they'd have found out who he was, reported the incident . . .

. . . *changing the course of history, demonstrating who's really in charge to the Kremlin dodderers* – they'd been half-pissed, loud, stupid – having a pee and not realizing he was in one of the cubicles. God, he'd have had to get away from them, even without the KGB following him!

He opened a bottle of beer. It was gassy, mostly foam as he tilted the neck of the bottle to his lips. But it made the bread easier to swallow, softening it from the half-masticated stone it had become against the roof of his mouth.

Lightning. He giggled with returning confidence, with a growing sense of safety. Nothing to laugh about . . . He bit off another mouthful of sandwich, swigged more beer. Going down easier – he was beginning to enjoy the food.

He was safe, he told himself. The Americans would come. While the army looked for him and the KGB ran around in ever-decreasing circles, he was safe here. He sighed, a windy little noise in the long, narrow room. The Americans would be here in – oh, what? Two days, three . . . he could hang on that long –

– couldn't he?

He shivered again. The bread stuck in his throat.

'Now, Orlov – where is he?'

Priabin's gloves tapped the kitchen table, slapping into patternless grains the little comet's tail of spilt sugar he had created near the opened packet. Some grains had adhered to the fingers of his gloves, some to the circuit-boards and tape-reels that lay on the table like accusations. The technical boys had found it after little more than an hour – it wasn't yet ten o'clock – despite the grumbling reluctance of their search, having been summoned directly from their beds into the winter morning of the old town. Orlov had, indeed, disassembled the transmitter into its component parts. The dish aerial they had found under a pile of old, rusting bicycle parts in the back yard of the shop, the high-speed tape reels in a box of tape-recorder spares; the frequency-agile encoder inside a degutted amplifier case, other pieces in speaker enclosures, inside the hollow frames of bicycles. There was enough on the table – never mind elsewhere in the shop – to represent, undeniably, a satellite-using, American-made transmitter and receiver of coded signals.

For the messages of spies; agents-in-place.

'Where is he?' Priabin repeated.

Orlov shook his head, his face hidden in his gnarled hands. He had crumbled rather than broken; each piece and component of the transmitter had been another wave battering at a worn cliff, eroding it. Orlov had slid quietly and quickly into total defeat.

'I don't know – he didn't tell me. He rang from a call-box last night . . . that's all I know.' He muttered into his dirty-nailed fingers. Priabin sipped his second cup of coffee, and slid his legs out from the table, stretching.

'Don't know or won't say?' he enquired. Zhikin stood, arms folded, at the kitchen door. The others were taking a break at a small, grubby workers' café down the street from the shop; another poor, dirty fragment of this run-down district of Tyuratam. Priabin recited, perhaps for the dozenth time, the litany of threats. 'Sons, daughters, grandchildren, aunts, nieces, nephews . . . schools, Party, prison, unemployment, *hospital* . . . it could all happen,' he sighed, as if the subject bored him. Zhikin nodded approvingly at his tone.

Orlov sobbed, almost retching in fear.

'I don't *know*!' he wailed. 'He instructed me to send a final message, that's all I know . . . that's all . . .'

Priabin snapped: 'What did this message contain?'

'I – can't remember –'

'*Remember!*'

Orlov twitched in his chair. Its legs scraped on the kitchen tiles. His face was white. Priabin nodded at him to speak.

'He – he said he was being followed, that he would go into hiding, until . . . until they came for him –'

'*Came for him?*' Zhikin asked in frank disbelief.

Orlov continued to look at Priabin, afraid of the sudden excitement on the KGB colonel's features.

'They intend to come for him?' Priabin asked.

'He thought so,' Orlov replied.

'How do they intend to – *rescue* him?' he asked, half-mocking.

Orlov shook his head. He shivered continuously now, despite the kitchen's fuggy warmth. The fire in the grate had been banked up by Priabin. It smoked.

'He never said. He believed it, though.' His tone implied that neither he nor the colonel would have believed such a blatant lie.

'What else was in this message? You sent all the messages, I suppose?'

Again, Orlov shook his head. 'Usually, Filip did so himself. To be secure, he said. Last night, he had to tell me the procedure before I could send the message. It took some time before I understood clearly what to do. He had to repeat the codes many times before I understood.'

'The message?'

'He asked them to hurry ... something, he said, called *Lightning*, of the utmost –'

'*Lightning?*' Priabin asked eagerly. 'He said *Lightning?*'

'Yes.'

'What did he mean?'

'He didn't say.'

It was true, Priabin realized with intense, almost childlike disappointment. Kedrov *knew* –! He knew about *Lightning*.

He had to clear his throat before he could speak clearly. He said: 'Then I have to have him. I believe you, Orlov. You must tell me where he is – you must tell me what the Americans know.'

'I can't –!' Orlov protested. 'I would if I knew, I swear to you ... he didn't tell me!' He blamed Kedrov now – it was all Kedrov's fault; dropping him in the shit up to his eyebrows. Orlov would have told him anything he wished to know at that moment – but he knew so *little*!

'Do you know where he might be?'

Orlov shook his head, moaning softly to himself, his face once more hidden in his hands. Old, feeble, weak hands – Priabin despised himself for an instant.

'Did he have anything the Americans might still want?'

'I don't know ... I did it just for the money!' Orlov wailed; the final, complete answer.

'For your favourite charity, of course. Or the family,' Zhikin sneered. Again, Orlov did not turn his head.

Priabin said, in a not-unkindly voice: 'The Americans will not bother with him ... but he may have travel documents, money, an escape-route of his own ... ?'

81

'I don't know, comrade Colonel, believe me, I don't know. I can only tell you that he seemed sure they could come.'

Then he won't be making his own way out, Priabin thought. He's waiting around – to get himself caught, he concluded with a firm, decisive pleasure.

'Viktor,' he said, looking up, 'go and roust out some of those lazy sods down the street – get over to Kedrov's flat and search it. Yes, I know it's been searched – do it again, and thoroughly!'

'Sir.' Zhikin nodded, approving Priabin's conduct of the interrogation, and the order he had issued. Priabin felt a momentary resentment of the older man, his subordinate officer. It passed almost at once.

Zhikin left the kitchen. He heard him barking into his walkie-talkie as he clacked down the linoleumed passageway. Priabin heard the shop door slam, its bell jangling wildly like a warning. He felt hot, despite having removed his greatcoat. Excitements and tensions jumped in his body like sparks; little muscular tics and spasms through his frame. Fear was present, the sense of danger, of a perilous course ahead of him. He was a frail canoe rushed forward by white water towards rapids, towards a narrow gap between high cliffs. He could easily be wrecked, drowned by events. But, if he played quickly, decisively, with nerve, then –

– get Kedrov under lock and key, get *Lightning* out of him, get, get – *out* of *here*, back to Moscow . . . the conquering hero.

He attended to Orlov. His mood was obsequious, fending off the immediate, bleak future with words. He wanted to help, to surrender everything he knew. He was only afraid he did not know enough to satisfy the colonel and avoid his fate. He felt, Priabin sensed, that if he allowed himself to be successfully squeezed dry right there, in his kitchen, then he might not have to leave it.

But he must –

Not too much is going to happen to you, Priabin thought with something close to indifference. You're not important. You can't give me Kedrov . . .

. . . but you know him. You might yield clues. Priabin stood up, picked up his gloves. He dusted the sugar from them.

'OK, Orlov, get your coat.'

'What —?'

'You're coming down to the office. You haven't even started yet!'

He looked at his desk, still flecked with drying spots of paint of various colours; a vile green, white naturally, pink, grey — presumably undercoat — yellow. A dot-puzzle, in colour, which, if the dots were joined up, would reveal the features of Filip Kedrov — spy. Priabin sighed. They'd found the rolls of film in the lock-up garage, waterproofed and hidden in tins of paint. Quite clever. A few scraps of paper, notes of instruction and record, the camera inside the plastic frog, but hardly anything else.

Orlov had confirmed that Kedrov had delivered nothing to the Americans except his radio messages. No courier had been in the area since the transmitter had been delivered, he was certain of that. So, he had expected the Americans to come, he had a photographic record for them. But, would the Americans come? Priabin shook his head. It was impossible to believe. What kind of rescue operation could they mount? And Kedrov had pressed the panic button only hours ago. No. Kedrov was stranded inside Baikonur. But —

— where?

Priabin looked at the first of the hastily developed films. The prints were still sticky, too-glossy. But, everything was there. He had been a good agent — a complete photographic record, punctilious and exhaustive, of the last weeks of the laser weapon project. From the weapon's arrival at Baikonur from Semipalatinsk, almost. The American espionage effort had been motivated by increasing desperation. Everything had depended on Kedrov.

He put down the prints, rubbing his tacky thumbs against his fingers. He might have to destroy at least some of the films — by the time he came to use them, the army would wonder how long he'd known, why he'd not informed them or acted sooner. Peril. The word rather than the sensation appeared in his head. Yes.

Perilous . . . but, he sensed now he could win. Progress convinced him – these films, for one thing. He was getting somewhere, and quickly.

If, if he could win now, Rodin and Rodin's father would be powerless against him. Moscow Centre would have their prodigal son back with open arms and the fatted calf. He might even be able to press a narcotics charge against young Rodin –!

He grinned; swallowed at once as the sense of danger formed a dry lump in his throat. He essayed a laugh. The dog looked up from its position near the radiator, then settled once more, its shaggy red coat looking almost more ruglike than the rug near which it lay. He regarded the dog fondly for a moment, then swung his booted legs onto his desk, unmindful of the still-tacky prints and the spots of drying paint. He lit a cigarette. He'd be back in Moscow, all right, just as soon as he dug up Kedrov. Moscow Centre's gratitude for giving the army the shaft, in Baikonur, would be boundless. He could become the youngest general in the service! He'd get Kedrov straight onto a special flight, as soon as he caught him. Yes, he felt confidence now, a new undented confidence. He'd find the bugger, and soon!

Priabin stared absently at the Party photographs on the opposite wall while he luxuriated in his thoughts and the cigarette. Grim, unsmiling faces they might be, but they no longer disapproved of or suspected him. They were faces he had somehow outwitted, like the cleverest but most disliked boy in his class . . .

. . . so, he thought eventually, stubbing out the remainder of the cigarette, sitting upright at his desk now, why persist with *Lightning*? At least, why draw attention to it by sending Viktor after Rodin's latest boyfriend, a queer actor? Perhaps he had been foolish there – young Rodin would certainly get to hear about it, might blab to Daddy . . . ? Mm. Perhaps it was a mistake; precipitate.

The telephone rang. He snatched it up, as if it might be someone with the authority, the cunning to scotch his dreams.

'Yes?'

'Viktor, sir.'

'Oh, yes, Viktor? What is it? Look, I've changed my mind –'

'I'm at the theatre, sir.' There was an excitement in Zhikin's normally bluff, unmoved voice. 'He knows, all right. Says he doesn't know anything except the word, but there's more to it than that!'

'*Lightning*?'

'Yes, sir – *Lightning*. Put him in a right tizz when I dropped the word out. He's had something whispered in his ear, all right, and by young Rodin.'

'Bring him in, Viktor – bring him in!' Forget your change of mind, Dmitri, he told himself. What a stroke of luck! 'He won't be hard to frighten – he's a civilian *and* a queer!'

'He phoned, sir – caught him ringing someone while he pretended he wanted the bog. I didn't realize they had a phone in there . . .'

'Who did he call? Rodin?'

'He's not saying – but that's my bet.'

'OK, charge him *now* – with sodomy. Get him down here right away. Once he's in here on a criminal charge, Rodin won't be able to get to him . . . we'll have everything he knows in a couple of shakes!'

'Got you sir – with you in, oh, half an hour. I'll come the roundabout route, just to make sure he's not spotted.'

'Good man. When you bring him in, have a real go at him. Play the nice guy. I'll be with our friend Orlov after lunch. I'll join you in your office when I've finished with him.'

Priabin put down the telephone. Stretched his legs and inspected his boots. Tiny spots of paint had adhered to their shiny surfaces. He stood up, stretching luxuriously. Danger tingled, but it was only one element in his excitement. The dog stirred at his approach. He soothed it back to sleep, looking fondly at its grey muzzle. Then he returned to his desk.

He began scribbling questions he would press on Orlov – and questions, too, for the little queer after Viktor had played the nice guy with him. He shook his head, smiling. His was the heavy's part. As easy as opening a can of –

– worms?

'I'm coming with you.'

'All the way?' Gant replied, smiling sarcastically.

'Just as far as Peshawar.'

'Just to make sure we don't turn around at the border?'

'I do what the man says, Gant, just like you,' Anders sighed. 'OK, let's move it.'

Anders looked at his watch. Midnight. The repairs to the MiL-24-A were completed, had been tested. Satisfactory. Forty-eight hours maximum, from now. The mission clock was running. Gant could have Kedrov out and safe by early Wednesday, Washington time. Time —? It had to be enough.

He watched Gant pick up a parka and wrap it around himself, then he followed him from the room. The TV set was showing cartoons. To Anders, there was little appreciable difference between the dashing cat and mouse and the programme which had preceded their antics. Gant had similarly failed to remark the change. Just stared at the screen, hunched within himself, saying little. Anders had left him for long periods alone, hurrying between the hangar and the secure line to the Oval Office. A heavy weight fell on the cat, which shattered slowly like an old vase. It seemed significant, especially as he followed Gant's retreating form along echoing corridors and out into the chill of the night.

Cold moonlight made the snow-covered hills ghostly around the airbase. Light snow flew across the gap of darkness between them and the hangar. The massive bulk of the C-5 Galaxy transport was nose-out from the hangar, its engines still silent.

Anders felt the desert wind cut through his warm clothing. The cartoon image of the shattering cat remained in his mind. *Winter Hawk* was just as fragile. Even though inches taller than Gant, he seemed to be scuttling after the other man's stride.

They walked beneath the huge port wing and its two Pratt & Whitney turbofans. The wind hurled itself into the hangar and around the fuselage. The place was filled with people, and it dwarfed them, as did the aircraft. He nodded to the engineering officer who had reported completion to him. The gunship had already been stowed in the cargo hold of the Galaxy. He took the pocketphone from his parka and began speaking into it even as he climbed the personnel steps aft of the wing, behind Gant.

The door slammed behind them. Only a half-minute before they had been in Gant's cramped room. The shattering cat –

The image vanished. He spoke to the colonel who captained and flew the transport. 'Yes, Colonel,' he acknowledged. 'You can engine-start. We're in your hands.' He switched off the pocketphone and thrust it into his clothing.

Almost at once, he heard the first rising whine of the four huge engines. The wind had disappeared. In its place, the noises of activity, the sounds of routine. Twelve-five. The note of the engines rose and strengthened.

The two helicopters sat on pallets near the tail, rotors folded like the wings of great insects. One mechanic was peeling away a stencil card from the flank of the gunship Gant would fly, the 24-D, to reveal white numerals. Unit, base, designation, something of the kind. The US army drab in which the two ships had been painted during training had disappeared, to be replaced by the olive and yellow camouflage of Soviet Aviation Army units on duty in Afghanistan. Below the camouflage, the bellies of the gunships were painted a sharklike grey. Another stencil was peeled away after white paint had puffed from a spraygun. Cyrillic lettering. Warnings, red stars, instructions were all blossoming on the flanks of the two MiLs. Bolted and tied to their pallets, the two machines appeared strange, unknown. Becoming once more the two helicopters he had seen captured in the Lebanese desert.

The scene oppressed Anders with the sense of its fragility. The machines might be almost ready, it was the crews who were not. Gant himself, Mac his gunner, and the second crew, headed by Garcia. None of them, not even Gant, was ready. There were too many factors in the matrix, like a complicated jigsaw knocked from a table, the pieces all separated and making no sense.

The cockpits of both MiLs were open. Heads and upper torsos bobbed, appearing and disappearing as the flight systems were checked. Anders had a fleeting impression that the machines were still under construction, unfinished. The on-board computers and moving map displays were being updated. The main cabin doors, too, were open. Ferry tanks had been fitted to both helicopters to increase their range. Only by carrying twice his normal fuel and having the 24-A similarly fuelled could Gant make the thousand mile journey from the Pakistan border to Baikonur and retain sufficient resources for the return flight. They would abandon the 24-A once they had transferred its fuel to the other gunship, and make the return crowded into the 24-D, together with Kedrov – the *lost scientist*, he added bitterly.

Weapons, too. Disguised or adapted US weapons to complete the MiLs' armouries. On the short, stubby wings, four rocket pods and four missiles, four-barrelled machine guns mounted in each nose. The weapons were real but their purpose was disguise. It was a charade required for Afghan airspace, a charade played hour after hour . . . weapons, markings, call-signs, idents, Gant's ability to speak Russian . . . thin, so thin as to be almost transparent. Later, hour after hour in Soviet airspace . . . transparent –

Mac and the ferry helicopter's crew moved towards Gant and himself. The Galaxy seemed to shrug at a weight of air pressing on it, against the wind, then began to roll out of the hangar. It was as if the cargo hold was suddenly bathed in a greater light, or some charge of static had built up. Everything seemed clearer, skeletal, stark. A long row of tip-up seats lined the bulkhead. *Fasten your seatbelts, extinguish your cigarettes* – time to go.

Work continued on the two helicopters.

Anders sat down and slipped the belt across his lap. He felt the huge Galaxy turn. Through the window at his side, he saw the maw of the hangar, like a whale's mouth lit from within, retreat into the darkness of the night. Sunday night.

Anders studied the crews like a diagnostician looking at X-ray plates. Mac, Gant's gunner, was the best of them. Garcia, the second pilot was good – but no better than good. His co-pilot was older, wiser, but no better than Garcia. *Chameleon Squadron* had lost a better pilot only weeks ago, when their only MiL had crashed in East Germany. Before the Israelis had been blackmailed into stealing *these* –

Lane, the co-pilot was OK . . . Kooper, Garcia's gunner, was better. Gant – was Gant . . . he'd chosen the 24-D, Anders knew, because there was no co-pilot. Just a gunner. And Gant trusted Mac as much as he trusted anyone.

The Galaxy turned again. Anders glimpsed runway lights and felt the aircraft pause.

'Thank Christ those guys got off their butts!' Garcia exclaimed, sitting down with a nod to Anders, ostentatiously buckling his belt. 'Jesus, are we lucky –?'

Anders watched Gant's face twitch with mistrust. Anders sensed Gant's dislike of Garcia. The second pilot's tension seemed too febrile, wild; like the reaction of a man who had too heavily mixed his cocktails.

Anders studied the others, then the fold-down table near them, the plugged-in computer terminal, the screen, the rolls of charts and sheafs of photographic prints. Too much, there was still too much to do . . . thin, thin, transparent, his thoughts chorused.

The Galaxy surged forward. Anders felt tension grip and hold him. He saw Gant staring at him. The man's eyes were blank and yet fierce; alien, somehow.

Men were sitting down hurriedly now, at the sound of a horn through the hold. The MiLs were left alone, vulnerable. The loadmaster was talking to the flight deck over a telephone link. The show was about to hit the road . . . For a second, he thought of voicing the idea, but Gant's stare disconcerted him. He looked away, at the table. He could distinguish the highest-resolution images of the Baikonur area – one area in particular. A tiny island, kidney-shaped, surrounded by wet salt marshes. Reeds, swirls of shallow water, a white smear in one corner of one picture which might have been water fowl taking off. Could Gant find that at night, with minimal use of the gunship's lamp? That *agreed rendezvous*?

Be there, he thought involuntarily. You Russian son-of-a-bitch, *be there*!

He felt his body moulded to the tip-up seat as the Galaxy lifted away from the runway. Its undercarriage thudded up moments later. He looked at the MiLs.

Banks, glittering shoals, islets, one like an animal curled up, another kidney-shaped. Would they get as far as . . . ? The thought faded.

Be there, he thought firmly. *Be there*.

The tracked army recovery vehicle was nose-down in the river, like a fishing bird. Its powerful crane, mounted over the turret of the converted tank chassis, slowly drew the Zil saloon out of the mud and water. Great broken plates of ice, grey and wallowing like a ship's wreckage, lurched in the space of open water the accident and the recovery operation had created in the frozen river. The water was little more than a soupy dark swirl beneath a clouded sky. The afternoon was already beginning to darken. There was a tiny flurry of sleet in the chill wind, one of Baikonur's very irregular and unexpected snowfalls.

The car's windows and flanks streamed as it was swung over the SKP-5 vehicle towards the shallowly sloping bank, which was churned and printed with caterpillar tracks –

– and the narrower, half-obscured tyreprints from the Zil, Priabin thought, shaken into wakefulness by the sight of the car and the knowledge of its passengers and their condition. The sombre, chilly scene disturbed him.

When he'd finished with Orlov – the old man knew no more than he had already told, he was convinced of it – he'd stopped for tea in the canteen then made his way up to Viktor's office. To find that Viktor and the actor had not returned. Three hours after his telephone call. Immediately, he had begun to worry. He sensed danger, even violence. The actor had called someone – Rodin, it had to be .. . what had happened to Viktor?

Eventually – as if only confirming something he already knew, a police patrol had found signs of – an accident, a car had evidently gone into the river . . . on the route Viktor had said he would take. Yes, yes, I'll come at once . . . what? The army? To get the car out ... very well, you've called in the army ...

Holding the Zil aloft like some cup or trophy contested for and won, the SKP-5 ground and chugged its way back out of the water. The disturbed plates of grey ice slid and grumbled together, as if healing the breach in the river. The streaming car hung nose-down; something tilted and restrained pressed against what remained of the shattered windscreen. Army frogmen, who had attached the crane's cables and hooks to the car after it was located on the riverbed, half-buried in the thick ooze, walked out of the freezing water. Other frogmen, in reserve, hurried towards them with tea or coffee and blankets and warm capes and parkas. Their interest in the Zil was minimal now that it was coming ashore.

Priabin blew sleet from his open mouth and pulled the hood of his parka closer around his head. Like a gesture of mourning. Viktor Zhikin's body threatened to loll out of the broken windscreen and across the car's bonnet; it would then slide like an awry tailor's dummy, fall into the riverbank mud –

He shuddered. The car was carefully set down at the top of the bank; almost a car again, intact for a moment in the poor light. Priabin hurried up the slope, his gumboots slipping on the churned mud, while police and army crowded gingerly around the wreck. The SKP-5 was uncoupled and chugged away, slithering lizardlike towards the tarmac of the road.

A car had crashed, skidding on the icy surface of the road that ran alongside the river. Two people had, unfortunately, drowned. That's all there was to it, Priabin thought. It was simply a coincidence that the car happened to be driven by his KGB second-in-command. *Viktor* –

He pushed the others aside, his emotions supported by his rank. People parted. He touched at, then lifted Viktor's head. Crazy paving; grey, blood-flecked, glass-stabbed crazy paving. Water seeped from Viktor's lips and nostrils. Bruising begun and halted by death. Gashes. He touched the face, feeling the embedded glass pricking and cutting his fingertips, his palm. His eyes watered with the cold wind and with the contact of the dead

91

man's cold, wet skin. He snatched his hand away, sniffing. Moved around the car to the passenger door, tugged it open – no damage to the car, no evidence of a collision to drive it off the road, no violent skid-marks on the tarmac behind it? – and a second body flopped dutifully and dramatically out of the door like dirty water escaping; to loll lifelessly as a doll, wet hair touching the churned mud at the roadside.

The little actor, Rodin's lover. As expected. Priabin felt an unreasoning hatred well up in him at the cause of Viktor's death. No skid marks . . . ? An accident?

Viktor might have died just because this little poof had panicked, tried to grab the wheel, perhaps? Viktor might have died that way, but instinct, damned *instinct*, made him suspect other hands, an arrangement, a plan.

He was aware of the army uniforms that surrounded him, and aware that they outnumbered the KGB uniforms present. Why did he suspect that this was not an accident? Because it had killed Viktor? Was it simply grief getting in the way of reason, like a powerful bully? He stared at the actor's still head. You, he thought, you made a phone call from the theatre, you spoke to someone . . . and then this happened. You'd have been shit-scared, because you were in real trouble and you knew what we wanted to ask you about . . . *Lightning*. The logic of the sequence was as tight and aching as a band of cold steel around his temples. He could not remove it. What had he heard? Loose talk because of the cocaine, mock toasts, murmured in-jokes? Enough to know what was meant, what was intended . . . ?

Viktor, Viktor, he thought. Why did you let him make that call? He must have called *Rodin*, yes . . . Priabin sighed. Coming out from his office, to this spot, driving through the failing afternoon light beneath the low, uncommon cloud-cover, he had become convinced there had been no accident; he had been summoned to witness a design, a purposed thing. Someone had wanted the actor shut up – and they'd shut Viktor up, too.

He felt his chest and throat fill with misery and useless rage. He glanced again at the actor's head near a frozen puddle. The voices of those around him had retreated to desultory murmurs, like those of people attending a funeral. The actor's bald spot was streaked with strands of water-darkened hair. Then he looked across the car at Viktor's greying temples above the scratched, glass-filled cheeks. It would have been so easy – an army patrol to stop the car, quick, decisive blows, a just-as-quick shove to the car, and down the riverbank and into the water . . . slipping out on the ice, breaking through it, vanishing. *It must have been like that –* !

He wiped his eyes and nose. Lit a cigarette, hunching into the folds of his parka to do so. The first exhaled smoke was whisked away by the wind; as insubstantial as any protest, any action he might contemplate. *Lightning* had killed Viktor, he was certain of it. Rodin had threatened him after his slip of the tongue, and he had been frightened, too. Kedrov had used it as a lever, a bribe, to make the Americans sure to rescue him, the little queer actor had panicked as soon as *Lightning* was mentioned, panicked enough to make a desperate phone call.

Every mention of it was like spilling gold; people rushed to retrieve it.

'What?' he snapped, startled back into the cold wind and the enclosing, bare, low hills that hemmed the scene. He glared at Dudin, the senior KGB officer for Tyuratam. The man's face was still shocked, but in a less personal way than Priabin knew must be true of his own features.

'I said – sir . . .' Dudin was careful with the occasion and Priabin's rank. *Captain* Dudin. '. . . can I get the bodies loaded aboard the wagon now? Or do you want forensic to inspect the car with – while they're still in place?' Dudin shuffled his feet, blew on his gloved hands.

'Let – get forensic to examine the car first,' Priabin said carefully, aware of each syllable, weighing its unhurried, neutral tone. Why? Give nothing away, he answered himself. The numbers of army parkas and greatcoats seemed to press towards him like a hostile crowd. Rifles – holsters – guns. Instinct outran logical deduction, but he moved with the certainty of a strong swimmer in calm, familiar waters. 'Yes,' he repeated, 'forensic first.'

The approaching car was moving fast, and its engine noise distracted him. Made him flinch, seeing the crashed, soaking Zil in front of him; as if he heard the accident happening in his head. He turned. Coming from the direction of the main complex, not from Tyuratam. A German car, silver-grey. A small, quick saloon, a BMW. He knew it had to be Rodin's car; the general's wealthy, privileged son's shiny toy. Yes –

Rodin, capless, got out of the car and hurried towards the wreck. His fine, thin hair was immediately disarrayed about his head. He pushed blindly past Dudin, then his eyes met Priabin's with a wild look. He seemed unnerved by the stare of the KGB colonel. Carefully, as if pointing, Priabin lowered his gaze, drawing Rodin's anxious, frightened eyes after it.

To the bald spot, the lank strips of hair like drying leather thonging the stained, soaked, yellow sweater. Rodin sobbed chokingly, just once. He did not look up, though he appeared to wish not to look at the dead actor. Did not wish to touch, kneel beside, stare into the dead eyes of –

– wanted not to be there, Priabin concluded. Yet aware of what he would find even before he saw it. He had not dared to hope for anything better than this. Priabin felt himself embarrassed, as if he had intruded upon a scene of private mourning. Eventually, Rodin looked up, still kneeling.

They understood each other entirely as their eyes met. Priabin's gaze waited for the young man like a statement of arrest. The KGB officer even nodded, half-consciously, confirming what he had learned, what had been confirmed for him. Rodin looked aside, his cheeks blanched, his eyes wet and shameful.

He called *you*, Priabin recited silently. He sensed Rodin gathering his story together like wisps of material to be woven. But you panicked, too, you told others. It was dangerous, but then you had no choice. You knew what you'd done, what you'd find here. He called *you*, and you set the dogs on him and Viktor, my friend –

– because of *Lightning*.

Slowly, now . . .

Rodin's face was bleak as he turned once more to Priabin, his lips primed with their cover story. Seeing the young man's obvious fear chilled Priabin. Ahead of him, something like – he glanced involuntarily at Zhikin's dead face – something like *that*, unless he was careful, so careful. They'd killed now, the barriers had come down, the cage had been left open.

And their *panic* was evident, too –!

Care, care . . . Priabin stared over Rodin's blowing hair, even as the young man began his halting, unconvincing story. The low, surrounding hills were closer in the gathering twilight. Sleet blew spasmodically. He was cold. Tracks down to the river, a mud-stained car. He was alone, even though Dudin's bulky frame was close behind Rodin. He must keep his head down, he told himself; attract no suspicion.

Viktor –

Begin an act, then. Begin to dissemble even while you're listening to this nasty, murderous little creep. *Act a part* – tell them nothing about Kedrov, just find him before they do. He knows about *Lightning*. When *I* know, Viktor, I'll have them.

He couldn't tell anyone, not yet, not until he had Kedrov . . . then, oh, then he could present Moscow Centre with Zhikin's murderers . . . *the fucking army!* He'd screw them into the bloody floor before he'd finished with them, present them on a plate to the Politburo, to the Chairman.

I promise you, Viktor, I promise . . .

So *play-act*!

He sketched on his features a dim attentiveness that was without the least suspicion, as Rodin's story tumbled out. He shivered. Rodin, recovered for the moment, was explaining how he had heard, wondered if the accident had anything to do with . . . Sacha had been arrested, he'd been told . . .

Zhikin's body was being lifted gently upright in the driver's seat, being fed slowly back through the broken windscreen by one of the forensic officers. The man handled the body carefully, almost reverently. But the head flopped grotesquely on its broken neck, filling Priabin's throat with bile.

FOUR

dropping zone

General Lieutenant Pyotr Rodin of the Strategic Rocket Forces, deputy commandant of the Baikonur Cosmodrome, lay awake and stared at the ceiling of his bedroom. The shadows up there, in the corner, were warm and brown, not dark; they mirrored both his satisfaction and his concern. *Lightning* – and his son; the Defence Minister's pleasure and congratulation at progress – and his son's appearance at the scene of the accident which had killed that . . . actor.

The shadows darkened and lightened, as if catching his mood as it varied.

The television broadcast had been amusing – for the most part. The old buffoon Nikitin had appeared against a backcloth of the Kremlin and a frozen river Moskva, Calvin the American President against a snowbound Washington projected behind him. They had danced their mincing, polite dance, the deceived and the deceiver; a farce. Calvin, as predicted, had had to pledge himself to appear in Geneva more than a week earlier than he had expected . . . all that had been satisfactory, most pleasing. Rodin had been able to laugh at both statesmen equally. Nikitin, doing only what the army wished, though he did not know it, thought he was in the driving seat. Calvin would not risk the opprobrium of world opinion by being seen to hesitate now. The final touch to the canvas of the launch of the shuttle on Thursday and its rendezvous with the American craft in orbit was pure comedy. Nikitin thought that a good idea, too, the idiot –!

The broadcast had ended with a flurry of despicable images. Satellites being deployed, SS-20s and Cruise missiles being withdrawn, silos being emptied of ICBMs, barbed wire being rolled up, tanks going into mothballs . . . the music of Beethoven accompanying the lurid betrayals. That last couple of minutes had distressed and angered him. Even Zaitsev's call from Moscow had not sufficed to restore his confidence and good humour. Zaitsev, the Defence Minister and leader of the pro-army faction on the Politburo, had dismissed Rodin's anger as futile. *The withdrawals won't be happening, will they*? he had assured. *Why be angry, then, with the fiction?*

Nevertheless, it was easier for Zaitsev to be dismissive, at *Stavka* headquarters or the ministry, than it was to feel light-hearted at such rubbish here in Baikonur. The images of, of – *surrender* had ruffled his good humour . . . after a few large whiskies he had retreated to his bed. And, slowly, his confident mood had returned.

Only the thought of his son, Valery, disturbed his calm now. He studied the darker shadows on the ceiling. An old cobweb hung there, drifting back and forth in the heat rising from the lamp. Rodin distracted himself from his son by allowing the images of the broadcast to return. And Nikitin's voice and other voices seeped into his mind, to be met with a frozen confident contempt.

We can't afford your toys any longer! That had been one of Nikitin's outbursts at a Politburo meeting, so Zaitsev assured the general staff. *We must have this Treaty with the Americans before we are bankrupted by you and your games! The army must pay the grocery bill!*

My God –

They had laughed, he and his cronies. It had taken almost a year to persuade the Politburo to keep *Linchpin*, the laser weapon project. And to keep it secret and outside the terms of the damned Treaty. A small victory in the middle of the army's defeat by the politicians.

Rodin felt his temperature rising, but did not quell his emotions. They visited him now like the familiar twinges of old age; known and tolerable. And they strengthened his resolve. *Lightning* would change everything. By Friday, the world would be different. The Nikitin faction on the Politburo would be subservient once more. The Treaty would be – worthless to the Americans.

Peasant women bewailing another bad harvest . . . corruption throughout the civil service . . . always the same wailing cries of the inefficient and incompetent – *we can't afford you!* We want to sell you out, sell our country out . . .

The bedside telephone trilled, startling him. His recriminations had been as leisurely as a reverie. He sat up in bed, the shadows in the corner of the ceiling now without meaning. The clock on the bedside table showed it to be almost midnight.

'Rodin. Yes?'

'Comrade General – Serov here. Have I disturbed you –?'

Serov. GRU commandant.

'What is it, Serov?' Why did he always react to Serov's voice or presence with a certain hostility? He shook his head.

'Sir – General – it's a delicate matter . . .'

Serov was being uncharacteristically sensitive and hesitant.

'Is it *Lightning*?' Rodin asked, too quickly. He almost hoped that it did concern *Lightning*. *Lightning* was not a delicate matter, merely crucial. Something prickled in his chest like a warning of illness.

'No, comrade General, it's your son,' Serov announced, his adopted tact no longer present. His habitual sneering calm had reasserted itself. Rodin felt his own hostility rising.

'Valery? Lieutenant Rodin,' he corrected himself. 'What about him?' He wanted to ask – what is wrong, what has happened? And surprised himself with such a wish. Something chilly seemed to wrap itself around his heart like a cold scarf. 'What about my son?' His control of his voice was an effort.

On the ceiling, the shadows were larger. The central heating seemed to have switched itself off.

'I – General, I have considered this matter very carefully . . . I suggest that your son should be sent on leave, perhaps even to Moscow, for the present. Perhaps a two-week furlough?' Serov's manner seemed incapable of retaining deference for much longer. The bully in him was always close to the surface.

'You ring me at midnight to tell me that?' Rodin blurted in

reply. 'To suggest he goes on *leave*?' Genuine irritation had been recovered, he felt more in control of himself.

'I – apologize, comrade General. It's taken me a lot of time to come to this conclusion, but now that I have, I think my advice should be acted on as soon as possible.'

'*Why?*' His voice was too quick, too high.

'Sir, I arranged that accident to – plug a leak. It did not have to involve your son . . .' What was Serov hinting at? What had Valery done? He felt hot once more, his heart stone-heavy in his chest. He was angry with his son; Valery had again caused him trouble, embarrassment, that was more than obvious . . . but, because it was Serov, there was that edge of fear, too. 'Unfortunately, it required the immediate removal of the actor –'

'Well?' Rodin almost shouted, ashamed of his rising fear.

'Unfortunately, after coming to us and cooperating with us, your son has managed to interest the KGB commandant, Priabin, in the matter, and in himself. The accident has become a suspicious circumstance in Priabin's eyes, one in which your son is –'

'My son was not involved!' Rodin shouted. His free hand trembled, plucking at the duvet. His reactions confused him. They were muddied, stirred up like a pool by Serov's words. He tried to analyse his emotions, but was unpractised.

He looked at the photograph on his bedside table, ornately framed in silver. A snowbound Moscow park, a handsome young woman in a tailored suit exposed by her open fur coat, fur boots on her feet, but a fashionable felt hat rather than one of fur on her dark hair. A pram, and a child in it. He had taken that snapshot himself. Had Valery been a disappointment to him since then? No, no . . . only when he had begun to grow, attended school, was too much and too long under his mother's influence . . .

He regained control, and snapped: 'Get to the point, Serov. Are you suggesting my son has been *insecure*?'

'The word I would choose is – indiscreet, comrade General.'

'Then –?'

'Your son has interested the KGB. I would rather they did not talk to him.'

'*You* attracted the KGB's attention by staging that accident –!'

'We *had* to kill the actor, a queer – your son's *friend*! He knew too much and he was being asked about *Lightning* – by the KGB. Does that satisfy you?'

'Serov, you're impertinent – insubordinate.' He began to feel breathless. He pressed his free hand on his chest, hard. And calmed himself. Valery's *actor friend* – the words hurt like a physical pain. Valery blabbing to his circle about *Lightning* – Serov prepared to kill to keep the matter secure . . . kill –

'General, I apologize – it was my professional anxiety . . .' The voice did not soothe, but seemed confidently silky with threat. To Valery –? The man would not *dare* –

'Yes, Serov, yes –!' His voice was high.

'The accident was designed to stop the leak. To warn others . . .'

'Yes.'

'Your son must go on leave.' Rodin felt himself led along a dark path, his guide a creature determined to rob him. 'If he is not here, then all the gaps will be stopped up. There will be no further leaks.'

'But you say my son told – the *actor* . . . ?' He was floundering now, he realized. Serov had assumed control of the conversation. His own authority seemed to have vanished. 'Everything?'

'Oh, nothing of the detail, General, we're sure of that . . . after all, he doesn't know very much, does he?'

'Of course not!' He felt his son's safety, and his *villainy*, working deeper and deeper into him.

'General?'

'I – I will speak to my son in the morning,' he managed to say.

'I recommend –'

'*I will speak to him in the morning!*' Rodin bellowed in an irate voice, thrusting the receiver back onto its rest.

Dmitri Priabin yawned and rubbed his cheeks, then replaced his hands on the steering wheel. He was tired from lack of sleep after the emotions he had endured. He could not fend off those glimpses of the past hours which flickered in his imagination. Zhikin's wife, in particular. He had watched her staring at him as her face crumbled into grief and she began crying in a way that seemed to make her ache. Ugly, mouth open, eyes blind, twisting her apron.

The children had been taken by a neighbour. He'd seen to that before breaking the news of Viktor's death. After a while, she seemed to have forgotten his very presence, as if tied to her chair in a stiff, unmoving posture; staring into a storm that made her eyes stream.

Eventually, he had left her, patting her hand, mumbling justice, revenge, which she heard as little of as she had done his earlier sympathy. He'd told her nothing of his suspicions – *knowledge*, he corrected himself – but he'd wanted her to know something would happen, something would be done to balance things . . . then his flat, and sleeplessness; crowding fears, dim futures. The dangerous path – he knew about Rodin and the little actor. Rodin knew he knew. An ugly, dark stand-off.

But, he had to go on with it.

He opened the car door. Morning leaking into the sky. The wind chilled through him at once. He crossed the yard at the rear of the KGB's Tyuratam building towards the central garage. Rodin's narrow, somehow naked features were vivid in his mind – tempting and threatening – as he bent his face away from the wind and hunched into his greatcoat. Would he have told his father –? What did the GRU know, how much had he told them about his conversation – his slip of the tongue – in Priabin's office?

Rodin *knew* –! He cleared his throat with what might have been a growl. Concentrate on that, not your own skin, he told himself. Remember they killed Viktor . . . whatever else, they did that.

He banged open the judas-door of the garage, startling one of the mechanics.

101

'Well?' he snapped. They'd been working on the Zil all night, presumably. His jaw worked, masticating emotion like hot food. Revenge – no, just making things come out right. 'Well, Gorbalev?' he snapped, more impatiently, catching sight of one of the forensic officers leaning out of the driver's seat of the wrecked car as it rested on an hydraulic ramp in the centre of the untidy, oil-stained floor of the garage. 'Anything? How did they arrange it?'

Gorbalev seemed to study Priabin for a moment, then he climbed slowly out of the car, his long legs seeming to hamper his movements, as if the dimensions of the Zil were those of a child's pedal-car.

'Colonel,' he greeted Priabin, who was still posed in the doorway, the cold flowing in behind him. 'There's nothing on the car,' Gorbalev added. 'Sorry –'

'Nothing?' His voice turned at once from disappointment to temper. 'What the hell –?'

'We've been thorough. Everyone has,' Gorbalev replied evenly, adjusting his glasses, taller by several inches than Priabin. 'There's nothing here. But, come upstairs – Zhikin's body . . .' He appeared almost shamefaced. Priabin looked at the car, glaring at its stained, dented bonnet and empty windscreen. Through *that* –

He shuddered and followed Gorbalev out of the garage, along green-painted corridors, through frosted glass doors into the main building. To the first floor –

– Viktor's body, lying on a table. He winced in anticipation, but there had not yet been a full post-mortem. The scarred, hair-covered upper torso had not been cut, damaged by the pathologist. Zhikin's grimly blank face had been cleaned of glass. The smell of carbolic soap and disinfectant might have been emitted by the grey skin of the corpse.

'Here,' Gorbalev said, pulling the covering green rubber sheet back from the lower part of the body.

Flat stomach, black hair massed around the limp penis, new and old marks on the thighs and shins. Blue stains, like old ink at knee and ankle of the right leg. An arm was damaged, too, the

102

bone breaking through the grey skin just where the faint tide-mark of an old suntan ringed the upper arm. Above the right knee, there was a red weal, indented with what might have been heavy fingermarks. On impact, the steering wheel had impressed itself heavily into the flesh.

'What?' Priabin mumbled, suddenly disorientated, frightened by the body and its distance and lifelessness.

'Ignore the arm. Knee and shin and ankle. All those breaks and wrenches and twists could have been caused by the crash – or . . .' Priabin looked at him but said nothing. Viktor Zhikin was too much like Anna like this, the scene too much like *that* scene, when he had been summoned to formally identify her body. Zhikin's body was too real, too heavy, like hers had been. Solidly dead. Gorbalev continued: 'I think his leg was broken in these places and wrenched out of shape, just to keep the accelerator of the car jammed down hard. The thigh could have been wedged under the steering wheel – explaining the mark above the knee.'

Priabin looked up from the bruises and from his memories. He was puzzled, but anger was beginning even before he understood the reason for it. He looked wildly at Gorbalev, then blurted out:

'Before or after he was dead?' It seemed essential that he know.

Gorbalev took off his glasses and wiped them with a handkerchief; waited for the question to go away, or to make sense.

'I – *before*,' he said eventually, unnerved by Priabin's damp-eyed, bright stare. Priabin sensed himself staring into the same storm that Zhikin's wife had endured. Revenge, now – oh, yes . . .

'It was done deliberately – *they* did it.' He stared at Zhikin's face, which was empty, blank, asked nothing of him; yet weighed him with an intolerable but unavoidable burden. It was easier to feel enraged by the twisted limb than by that dead face.

Zhikin's face, his wife's face, Anna's face . . . all the same; distinct but communal. Fellow victims.

'OK. Keep quiet about this. Your report is to say nothing, except that you're satisfied it was an accident. Understand?'

Evidently, the forensic officer was mystified, but he nodded.

'I understand, Colonel.'

Priabin's fist closed on Gorbalev's lapel. He jutted his face close to that of the other man. 'No, you don't understand. Just do as I tell you. Your report describes those injuries as being entirely consistent with the accident. The car reveals nothing to account for the crash. Zhikin . . .' He looked at the body, as if he were engaged in its betrayal. *Not for long*, he fervently promised. '. . . must have blacked out or swerved to avoid something or simply lost control. He made a fatal mistake. Understand? There are no suspicious circumstances – *none!*'

He glanced, once more, at Viktor Zhikin's body, saw the ink-stained knee and ankle, the twisted shape of the whole leg, and sensed the hands that had done it, breaking the bones with a rifle-butt, or even a sledgehammer. Zhikin had still been alive when –

– hopefully unconscious when they began. With time and care, they could have wedged his foot and ankle without damage. They'd hurried it, taking the violent shortcut . . . and they'd probably wanted to. Twiglike snaps greeted with laughter, the handling of a living human form like a child's rubber doll, bending and breaking the pipe-cleaner skeleton within the flesh and muscle. Priabin felt sick. The damage was as much a warning as the drowning, as the actor's death.

Keep out – restricted area, under military control. Keep out – stay away if you know what's good for you.

Priabin prayed, once more, that Viktor had been unconscious when they began breaking him.

'He was still –?' he faltered, releasing Gorbalev's lapel. He smoothed the jacket's material absently. Gorbalev, polishing his glasses with haste and concentration, nodded.

'Alive? Yes. Water in his lungs. He wasn't dead when he entered the water. Probably unconscious, though. He was hit on the back of the –'

Priabin heard no more, slamming the door of the small, bare, harshly lit room behind him and cutting off the noise of Gorbalev's voice. His chest felt tight, his throat full. He shook with the irrepressible desire to kill someone.

Colonel Gennadi Serov, commandant of military security for the Baikonur area, watched the screen of his television set with a withering contempt. He had not turned up the volume. The puppets appeared more wooden, more meaningless without their words, without commentary. Bobbing, smirking heads posed in front of backdrops of Moscow and Washington. Both of them in darkness . . . the American capital slipping into night, the Moscow backdrop bright, jewelled with lamps. Two heads without authority. Calvin the American puppet and their own dolt, Nikitin. It was another of the endless repeats of the broadcast that Moscow television was transmitting to the entire Soviet Union, the whole of the Warsaw Pact, no doubt, just to make certain. There they were, the fools, grinning their little pact at one another; one of them relieved, the other defeated, he reminded himself. Which only made them all the more contemptible.

That fool Rodin, he thought.

Lightning.

Doubtless the father had talked to the son and then the son had whispered everything into the shell-like ear of the queer little actor . . . the whole matter angered Serov; it was almost an abstract emotion, tinged with his habitual disappointment regarding other people.

He stood with his back to the room, close to the television set. His hands were in the pockets of his uniform trousers, his jacket was unbuttoned; he wore a cigarette in the corner of his mouth, a Russian cigarette with a cardboard tube. The strong, acrid smoke surrounded him. He stood, hunch-shouldered, staring at the two voiceless faces on the screen, as if menacing them. Then, weary of them, he switched off the set. Thursday – it was to be Thursday. Calvin was so sensitive to world opinion at that moment he had been forced to agree to the signing. He was powerless against the wave of events. The launch would take place on Thursday, to coincide exactly with the signing of the miserable Treaty. The real secret would come on Friday, with —

— *Lightning*.

And, because of Rodin's sodomite offspring, and this, this *thing* now sitting on the other side of Serov's desk, quaking in its highly-polished boots because a pal had dropped him in the shit up to his neck —! Because of people like *that*, *Lightning* had been threatened.

Serov glared at the army captain, who visibly blanched. Serov enjoyed the reaction; enjoyed, too, the captain's presence. His own efficiency, his personal stock, would emerge well from dealing with this . . . and from making Rodin toe the line over his son. Yes, if he could manage things with a certain deftness, then he would profit.

The captain's collar was crumpled and his tie was askew. With heavy, malicious humour, Serov thought it looked like the beginnings of an attempt to hang himself. The captain had opened a Pandora's Box — Serov had to find the lid and replace it. He did not doubt that he could.

The captain had been the *direct cause* of the flight of the computer technician, Kedrov. The man had disappeared after overhearing this buffoon's loose talk — in a lavatory, for Christ's sake —!

An evening of boozing, a big mouth, the simple inability to realize he and his pal were not alone . . . the man wasn't just disappointing, he was a disaster! Serov deliberately leaned one fist on his desk, the other rested on his hip. The pose suggested either might strike at any moment. The captain, gratifyingly, shook visibly.

Serov began: 'You're a senior telemetry officer in the main mission control room, your security clearance is high — so high that you were placed in possession of certain *most secret* information in order that your computations would remain valid — you are experienced, you have been in your present post for five years . . . *and you open your mouth in the lavatory, Captain*?' The voice, the long sentence and its subordinate clauses, had been orchestrated to reach a climax accompanied by the banging of his fist on the desk. The captain's tall, slim frame – apparently he was something of a wow with the women – obligingly twitched in response, jumping like Serov's paperweight carved in the form of a tortoise.

'I – I –' the captain tried to protest, his mouth and vocal chords captive in the surroundings of the office, imprisoned by his sense of Serov's boundless authority in police matters.

'*Shut up!*' Serov raged. 'This miserable little computer operator, a *civilian* into the bargain, has disappeared. *He* is the man you saw in the club toilet?' He held up a clear, sharp colour print of Kedrov's head and shoulders, thrusting it at the captain like a weapon. The captain rubbed his arms as if cold. His hands were near the shoulder-flashes that denoted his membership of the Strategic Rocket Forces, the elite. Not for much longer, Serov promised. It would be the Far East, if he wasn't shot. Or perhaps military adviser somewhere in Africa – deep in the bush with the niggers, the fuzzie-wuzzies. 'Is it him?' he bellowed. The captain twitched again. 'Is it?'

'Yes, comrade Colonel, it is him,' the captain blurted out.

It appeared, with this little turd's confession, that Kedrov had panicked, fearing he had heard too much for his own good . . . but he *was* running around somewhere with knowledge of *Lightning*.

'You will no doubt be dumbfounded to learn that this man is not at his work, not in his flat with influenza, with a woman or walking his dog . . . in fact, *he is nowhere to be found!*' Serov raged, amused by the evident terror his words inspired. Mentally, he was ruefully cynical, detached. Guilt was, of course, a hideous weapon. The captain was already, in his imagination, packing for the Siberian Military District and stitching lieutenant's shoulder-boards on his uniform!

Yes, Serov thought, I'll see to everything on your behalf. Afghanistan for you, sonny. There, you'll either be filling your trousers from sheer, unadulterated terror, or your stomach with booze or your head with hashish or your arm with heroin. One of them will see you off and save the price of a bullet in the nape of the neck.

'He's gone, flown, disappeared,' he continued aloud. 'And all because you frightened him off! He overheard you, saw the look on your face when you discovered him, and took off for the hills!' He flicked his intercom switch as violently as if striking the captain, and barked into the machine. 'I want some rubbish cleared out of my office – now!'

The captain's mouth opened silently. Two officers appeared at the door of the office, their smiles masked by urgency. Serov nodded, and the captain was unceremoniously snatched from his chair and bundled out of the office, the door slamming behind him and his escort. Serov gazed at the empty chair, askew but not overturned. The smell of the captain's fear was fading in the warm room. The radiator grumbled.

He suppressed a small sigh which threatened to become a yawn. He had been awake most of the night. Yet he could not regret the interruptions. He'd diminished Rodin, and terrified the captain. Especially that . . . he could not but be pleased – as he always was – when they understood you held their very lives in your hand. He could never resist that.

Hands clasped together behind his back, he crossed to a huge map of Baikonur framed and mounted on one wall. By now, those two young men of his would be kicking the captain – literally kicking him black and blue – downstairs to the cells. It did not matter.

Now, *where* –?

He studied the map, his eyes ranging over it like the passage of a surveillance helicopter. Kedrov, running scared, had twenty-four hours or more start on the search for him. But, he was a civilian, he did not know the place as Serov did, as the GRU did. He must be found. He wouldn't talk unless he was caught, but the KGB – Priabin himself – was interested in him. Black-market goods . . . Serov tossed his head in contemptuous dismissal. Stupid, petty . . . but Priabin had been intrigued by the mention of *Lightning* – stupid little sodomite, Rodin's son! Priabin must not be allowed to learn any more, otherwise he might be just upright enough not to keep his own counsel but inform Moscow Centre.

And all because of *Lightning*. Two people had already had to die. Not that he regretted the acts, only the loose ends they left lying about. Then he had awoken yesterday to find *Lightning* lying about like a whore's telephone number! And that silly little bastard, Rodin, had been there, on the riverbank, staring all his knowledge into Priabin's face!

Would the death of Priabin's man, Zhikin, keep the KGB's heads down? he wondered, rubbing his chin, hearing the stubble rasp. It should do . . . Priabin wasn't a fool, and he'd never looked for trouble. He'd guess what was at stake – his own safety – and that should keep him in order . . .

Never mind Priabin at the moment – Kedrov was the first priority.

His heavy, thick-fingered hand touched across the map's surface, sweeping in vague, narrowing circles at first, then rippling outwards again into the villages, dormitory towns, forest and countryside beyond the main cosmodrome. It was a difficult, perhaps impossible task in the time available. Leninsk, the science city, Tyuratam, the old town . . . buildings, streets, acres of forest and marsh . . .

Where?

– where Kedrov was depended on how frightened he was of being found. Time to begin, then. Get the teams assembled. Start with the man's every known associate, every known contact.

Serov crossed with a swift, assured urgency towards the intercom, his forefinger extended to its switch even before he reached his desk.

The mission had been halted; as certainly as if the Galaxy had struck against some brick wall of air and broken up. Gant's imagination mocked him with images of the simulator tapes he had been watching, as if they represented a prize utterly out of his reach; mocked him, too, with memories of the Saudi Arabian desert over which they had flown, the endless sand stretching away like dusty concrete. Its emptiness, apart from the flares of gas burning off from rigs dotted in the landscape like isolated campfires, was a powerful analogy of his situation.

The Galaxy's tanks were awash with fuel. At Zaragoza Airbase in Spain, they had taken aboard sufficient to make Peshawar in northern Pakistan without landing anywhere, with only one midair refuelling, over the Eastern Mediterranean. Now, they could use only what little remained in the rapidly draining in-board tanks in the wings. The transport's captain was explaining, slowly and clearly as if lecturing trainee MAC pilots.

The Galaxy had looped well to the south of its most direct route, out across the Arabian Sea after crossing the interior of Saudi Arabia and the Omani coast, in order to avoid Iraqi and Iranian aircraft and the unlooked-for hazards of the Gulf conflict. Now, it had already altered course to begin its long northward run to the coast of southern Pakistan, heading for Peshawar and the Afghan border. Langley had obtained permission for a landing only in Peshawar . . . the MiLs were to take-off in darkness that evening – Tuesday evening. He looked at his adjusted watch. Local time, ten-fifteen in the morning. Tuesday morning –

– pointless anger against the sense of time passing; escaping. It had already run out, disappeared as fast as water might have done in that expanse of grey sand that was Saudi Arabia. The green-blue of the Arabian Sea appeared illusory, misted and pearled as it was by the altitude.

Only too real. The Galaxy would have to ditch on that water, and soon. And yet the Galaxy had enough fuel on board to take them another twelve hundred miles –!

Complete failure itched in his muscles, knotted in his stomach. Because of a routine check. Just because of that . . . a handful of caption lights on the main instrument panel and the flight crew had immediately seen the enormity and proximity of the problem they had uncovered. With every passing second, the four huge Pratt & Whitney turbofans were devouring what little fuel remained available to them.

The port side had indicated an imbalance; the fuel was simply not feeding from the outer to the inner tanks en route to the engines. It might be caused by an electrical failure, a closed and jammed valve, a clogging of the suction/relief valves, a fault in the balance controls of the booster pumps. Manual, auto, off – the fuel would not flow, not even with the attempted use of gravity feed. The problem was esoteric; its consequences were all too real. The Galaxy was tiring like a weakened, exhausted bird; it would fall out of the sky just as certainly. The mission was dead.

. . . point of no return in three minutes,' Gant heard the captain drawl in his slow, apparently unruffled Carolina tones. Lecturing to trainees. Gant felt his disorientation swept aside, as if he had snapped to sudden wakefulness. Point of no return –? He had known that, of course, but the words themselves had a douching, cold-water effect. The green-blue beneath seemed nearer now, like a destination. 'We can't make it back to Oman, or Saudi Arabia, and even Karachi is on the wrong side of marginal – *where*, sir . . . ?' Anders was being addressed as mission controller. 'We don't have landing permission for Karachi, anyhow,' the captain added superfluously.

'You're – you are certain of all this?' Anders asked reluctantly, the headset clutched against his cheek like a bandage on a wound.

Gant stood opposite him, body slightly hunched into a tense silence, hands formed into loose fists, as if to ward off the situation. Between them, near the window, a scattering of half-unfolded maps lay on the floor and a moving-map display screen and its linked computer trailed a lead away somewhere across the huge hold to a power source. Various cassette-like cartridges waited to be inserted into the display. Maps of the countries surrounding them, all too distant.

'Sir, it's all been treble-checked. Acting on all our options together to conserve what fuel we have, we can't offer any warranty to any destination, not even to Iran . . . and I guess you wouldn't want to take our cargo there?'

'Is there nothing –?'

'We're going to have to send out a Mayday and ditch in the sea.

111

I'm sorry, Mr Anders, but that's the bottom line. We're fresh out of options.'

Gant watched Anders' face as the man avoided his gaze. His cheeks narrowed and appeared bloodless. His eyes moved rapidly from side to side, as if he were dreaming. Among the maps, the console, the small port windows, he found no solution. Only the waiting, pearly sea below them, still as a pond. Gant took the headset from almost unresisting fingers, and snapped into it: 'There's *no* way, skipper?'

'In-flight – is that you, Gant?'

'Yes.'

'Then you already know the answer – we can't diagnose and repair a fault in the cross-feed system up here!' The careful, almost sensitive politeness the captain had shown towards Anders did not, evidently, apply to Gant, a subordinate officer. His tone was hard, certain, his own numb anger showing through it.

'OK, OK,' Gant replied with controlled vitriol. Condemning the man for possessing no solutions.

'Look, Gant – we're *all* disappointed –'

'*Disappointed?*' he replied scornfully. 'We're not going to a fancy-dress party and you haven't torn a hole in your Robin Hood tights! Another tanker?'

'To fill up the tanks we can use? I've asked, dammit! Nothing could reach us before we fall in the water.'

'Can you land *anywhere*?'

Anders was watching Gant with a kind of stunned admiration; a beaten fighter eyeing his opponent, wondering at the degree of energy, rage and skill that had combined against him.

Gant's mind whirled out ahead of conscious thought, like a rope thrown across a chasm. The water already seemed much nearer. Around him, the hold seemed to enclose him firmly; a trap now, no longer the thin shell which kept them from the numbingly cold air outside. The sea, cleared of its pearly wash, glittered. There was no land in sight, not even the yellowy smudge of a beach, a small atoll, a sandbar. The cargo hold was the clinging interior of a Venus fly-trap –

He shook the image away. Anders' face was pale, his eyes staring through one of the windows, downwards. Mac, Garcia and the others formed a loose, silent group watching him and Anders. They'd heard, but now, after their initial babble of surprise, and nerves, they were silent. Waiting.

His hands clenched more tightly. He waggled the headset's jack plug as if it might be a weapon. His body felt hot with frustration.

'There's nothing . . .' Anders murmured. 'It's fucked, Gant – completely *fucked up!*' His fist banged the bulkhead, which boomed flatly. Then he was quiet once more.

Despite the illusion of the sea nearing, the Galaxy was climbing slowly, conserving its remaining fuel at the highest effective altitude. Pointlessly. It might as well already be falling. They would ditch in the sea, lose the MiLs, and *Winter Hawk* would be kaput, finished; cancelled because some circuits, valves, pumps, even a single switch, had malfunctioned. One *tiny fucking switch* –!

Tension and defeat were palpable around each man in the hold. Jesus – *sweet Jesus* –!

He turned to the window. Far to the north of the Galaxy lay a strip of smudgy yellow-brown. Land, but no landfall. The narrow, hardly inhabited coast of southern Pakistan. No runways, no airfields, no flatness of sufficient area . . . they'd already looked at the maps. Nothing. The coast taunted him with its inaccessibility. The sky was empty and clean, stretching upwards and becoming purple and seemingly infinite . . . all that sky, with the Galaxy hanging on it as on a cliff-edge of air, about to loosen its grip and fall. Two specks of dirt on the perspex, seemed to hang in the sky . . . He rubbed at them. For a moment, they had seemed like other, smaller aircraft, drifting away from the Galaxy –

'A *beach*!' he shouted. He was looking at the MiLs – all neatly palletized for easier loading and storage. Anders seemed startled, and the others turned towards him as if expecting an announcement, or a reprieve. 'A beach . . .'

He stared down the length of the huge hold. The MiLs rested

on large pallets, rotors folded and locked along each fuselage. The railway for the pallets ran the length of the Galaxy, to allow straight-through loading and unloading, to save time. On a third pallet, closest to the tail, there were drums containing their fuel load and reserve. All ready to be off-loaded under cover of evening darkness in Peshawar, a thousand miles away.

'A beach.' He plugged in the headset at the nearest jack point. 'Skipper – skipper, could you make Karachi *empty* – and I *mean* empty?'

'Empty –?'

'Without your *cargo*, man!' Silence. 'Well?'

He heard the pilot consult his flight engineer, but caught only the silence and not the sense of the mumbled reply. The captain was angry when he spoke.

'We can't tell if the engines will flame-out at the end of a landing roll, or maybe the fuel will run out three hundred feet in the air and half a mile from touchdown, or flame-out might happen twenty miles out and five thousand feet in the air – how can I tell you, Major?'

Gant bared his teeth and snapped: 'I take priority, *skipper*.' His tone grated like sandpaper. 'The mission takes priority over everything else . . . the *cargo*. Interrogate the flight management system and find out if, by trading off fifty thousand pounds of cargo against higher fuel consumption at a low altitude, you come out in credit!' He added, with a glint of malice in his eyes: 'What happens after that doesn't concern me. *Do it*, skipper!'

He removed the headset. Anders was watching him; not with anticipation, but as if studying some different species.

'We can't land at Karachi, we don't have clearance . . . the air force and the government would both oppose any landing there. Anyway, we can't even make Karachi.' Anders recited in a tired voice. He had remained unaffected, grasping only dim elements of Gant's objective, scattered pieces of a puzzle he could not interpret. 'Langley would have to get Washington to talk to Islamabad . . .'

'Then make it happen, Anders – now!'

114

'What – are you going to do?' His head was already shaking as he began to perceive the design.

Gant ignored him, staring at the litter of maps and at the console. Then he glared up at Anders.

'I'm going to find a beach on which these guys and their loadmaster can kick those pallets out the back door!' His hand waved towards the MiLs and the fuel drums.

Ridicule and protest formed in Anders' eyes even before he opened his lips.

'I tolerated your bizarre private life – much as it shamed me – just so long as it never involved matters of security!' General Lieutenant Pyotr Rodin growled, angered even further by the feeble, damp-eyed protests of his only son. 'Then, yesterday, I discovered you had been – *insecure!*' It seemed a species of aberration far greater in the general's eyes than sexual deviation. His voice, filled with threat, seemed to loom over the young man on the sofa.

'It wasn't anything – I swear to you it wasn't a *serious* mistake!' Valery Rodin protested, his throat and chest filled with a tight anguish. Fear and the sense of the huge, heavily furnished room surrounded him. The general's apartment was on one of the upper floors of the Cosmonaut Hotel in Leninsk. Outside its windows, the morning sky was clean and remote. To Valery, it offered an illusion of freedom and escape.

'You swear to me . . . and yet, when your little *friend* rings, baying for help because the KGB have become interested in him precisely because you were loose-tongued in front of that Colonel Priabin, you immediately threw the whole sorry mess into Serov's lap. Serious? Not serious? It was *profoundly* serious, Valery!'

The general walked to one of the wide windows and appeared to look out in deep concentration at the square far below his floor of the hotel. Then he turned to look at his son, and said:

'How many of your precious little circle of perverts know as much as the actor apparently did?'

'No one else, I swear it —!'

'No one? Then how did the actor know? Did you whisper it during your sweaty bouts of sodomy?' the general raged. At one time, in the past, he had been unable to use language to confront his son's nature; now, he had found that words could be used as weapons, as a means of distancing the *thing* from himself — even from the son he had watched grow up. 'Did you?'

Valery was appalled. His father knew and hated what he was; but though he had spoken like this before, there had never been such a degree of contempt, such vividness in the insults. He now realized just how much his father hated and despised him. 'No, no, no,' he sensed himself saying, while part of his awareness reflected on his surroundings. The thick carpet, Oriental rugs, paintings, heavy drapes, dark furniture; the apartment of a powerful man. Power that was now directed against him. He quailed. Without his father, he was nothing. A sitting target, without protection. If his father abandoned him now . . .

'No,' he said carefully. 'It was just something that — slipped out. Sacha — just panicked unnecessarily.'

His father sighed, appearing to accept the careful lie. What did it matter now? Sacha was dead . . . he swallowed a hard lump of grief in his throat.

'You little fool.' Rodin was wearing a silk dressing-gown. Normally at that time of the morning he would be at the complex, at his duties. He had waited two hours for this interview with his son.

The breakfast trolley stood in the middle of the room, near an occasional table delicately inlaid with perhaps six different woods. Valery recognized it. It had once adorned his mother's small sitting room. The general had not even offered him as much as a cup of coffee. 'He didn't need to kill him, that mad dog Serov —!' he blurted, immediately regretting the outburst. It was just the way his father swaggered in the big room, and the image of his mother that the table had evoked.

'What else was he to do, in the time available? *You* had interested the KGB in matters they should know nothing about. They were about to squeeze your friend like a lemon. An

116

accident silenced him and warned them. Of course Serov had to use violence!'

'*You* told them to kill Sacha,' Valery said his eyes suddenly damp and weak.

'No, no . . . all that was at Serov's discretion. But, what he did, I would have done . . . he shut the actor up. Closed the door on your insecurity. Even then you could not stay away . . . the KGB colonel was there, and he saw your, your disgraceful behaviour! *Weeping* openly at the roadside for an actor!'

Valery did not look up, merely shuffled his booted feet on the carpet. His movements raised little tufts of loosened pile around him. They had killed Sacha like a dog, a rabid dog –!

He groaned aloud, then heard the general's breath explode like a condemnation.

'*Pull yourself together!*' he bellowed. 'For my sake and for your own, try to behave like a *man!*'

Valery wailed what might have been a single word of protest, but if it was, even he failed to discern its meaning. His father's strong face hardened, his eyes gleamed above his prominent, sharp-cut cheekbones. The face was smooth from a recent shave, the skin still firm though veined and traced with age. Still the hero his mother had married, obeyed, worshipped, feared. The rising star of the Strategic Rocket Forces for more than twenty years, until he stood level with the very pinnacle. He *was* the hidden peak, the *éminence grise* –

– and one of the principal authors of *Lightning*.

'I – I am sorry, father,' he began, calculating and cowed in the same moment. His father's moral and physical presence oppressed him, like the imminence of a storm. The pale clean sky outside seemed a great distance away. 'I am sorry if –'

'No good apologizing!' his father snapped. 'Just try to stay away from actors and drugs for a while!' His hands clenched and unclenched. He moved towards his son as if to strike him. Valery flinched, and the general's face betrayed an appalled and violent surprise. Then bitter distaste. Walking away, he continued: 'Serov has suggested you be shipped out of here for a while – somewhere quiet, until this is all over. I – have not decided what

117

should be done . . .' He cleared his throat. His voice was more impersonal, businesslike. He turned to his son again, and made as if to reach out. But his hand did not move more than a few inches, as if some moral stroke rendered such gestures impossible. 'But, he will undoubtedly warn all your friends to keep away from you. Also, you will confine yourself to your apartment. Do you understand? You will remain entirely incommunicado for the rest of this week. After that, I will decide what is to become of you. I think, perhaps, it is time you attended the academy to – further your military career.'

'No –'

'It will not be your decision, Valery, but mine.' He paused. Through his misery – and relief that his father intended nothing more for the moment – Valery heard his father's stertorous breathing and his own ragged inhalations.

'Do you understand?' his father repeated. 'You see no one, you talk to no one. You stay indoors. You do not answer the telephone. Is that clear?'

'I – understand.'

'Good. You've babbled quite enough already! A week of silence, and then enlistment at the academy, will help all of us . . .' The Frunze Academy, the school for elite career officers. His father's influence could get him a place there . . . dammit! 'Very well.' The voice was unsoftened, and merely pretended to familiarity, to a common humanity between them. 'Now, go. Go – Valery . . .'

He made a grab at the general's hand but his grip closed on air. The hand had been snatched away like that of some Tsar displeased with a menial ambassador.

'Go,' the general breathed from near the windows.

Through the wetness of his tears, the sky appeared almost colourless to Valery Rodin; his father's figure a looming dark shadow against it.

A map was spread near his right boot, pictures unrolled on the screen of the moving-map display like a series of hurried-through slides. He might have been thumbing through some familiar reference book for information he knew it contained.

The three hundred and fifty miles of the coastline between the Iranian border and Karachi flashed by in sections. Narrow coastal strip before the coastal range. Blue of the sea. No islands, no coral atolls, no sandbanks of any size. Just the isolated coastal strip. A few small holiday resorts, a handful of villages. His eyes glanced between the magnified images and the map on the floor, as if seeking reassurance or in growing desperation.

There were people around Gant, silent and expectant . . . and that expectancy was fading, turning cold and sour. He was hardly conscious of them or their changing mood. Aware only of the headset he wore as he sat in front of the display, which was no larger than a portable typewriter.

A box with keys below a small screen — a box without answers . . .

He could not be sure. He had to choose blind, sensing the precise length of a beach, assuming its width between surf and palm, assuming its emptiness — all *before* they overflew it to check it out. If he was wrong, in any of those parameters, they would have no time nor fuel to find a second dropping zone. And all he had in the way of back-up was one of the flight crew acting as an observer, standing between pilot and co-pilot, binoculars ready for the earliest possible visual sighting of the dropping zone he proposed. By the time the beach took on dimension and form in the observer's glasses, it would be too late to make any changes. It would be either go, or no-go.

Anders was in the secure communications room behind the flight deck, talking via satellite with Langley — with the White House by now for all Gant knew. Squeezing permission out of Karachi's military and Islamabad's government. Pressuring the Director and the President to bribe the Pakistanis. *Offer them anything — everyone always wants guns, missiles —*

He muttered to himself, flicking back, flicking forward once more through the sequence of map sections. Holding, weighing, discarding, hurrying on. The stain of yellow-brown was clearer through the small window. It wore a line of green above it now and, more mistily, a jagged line of brown hills. Beach, trees, hills. The dropping zone had to be on the beach, but where, along this length of coast —?

The three pallets would be loosed from the rear doors – fuel, Garcia's MiL, then his own helicopter. Parachutes opening and dragging, the impact of it like landing on the deck of a carrier – and he'd done that, scores of times, though Garcia hadn't and didn't like the idea. With great good luck, the pallets would remain intact and upright and they could release the MiLs, unlock the rotors and rig them, fuel up and take off, to rejoin the Galaxy in Karachi, always praying the transport had made it.

If he could find the beach –

One road along the coast, no more than a wide dirt track. The villages and tiny resorts and occasional isolated bungalows were strung along it like weak and intermittent fairy-lights. He heard the pilot's voice against his cheek.

'It's getting critical, mister.' He no longer used either Gant's name or his rank. Gant was CIA, not air force; an obscure kind of enemy. He was intent upon wrestling the mission to a new shape, and the pilot was no longer in command of the ferry crew. Gant might just kill the crew with his scheme. 'Our best estimate is . . . ETA over the coast in six minutes. That will leave you, at most, another four minutes of flying at zero feet before I have to ditch, or you're out the back door and I can still make Karachi. Got that?'

'I understand,' Gant replied, waving one hand to silence the fierce whispering the pilot's ultimatum had created. 'Where do we cross the coast, on your present heading?'

'Somewhere – Charlie?' Gant heard the navigator muttering, then: 'West of some God-forsaken place called – what? Ras Jaddi – village called Pasni on a low headland . . . got it?'

Gant flicked through the sections of map on the cassette loaded into the display. 'I got it.' Ras Jaddi, a tiny headland, a speck of atoll . . . ? No, nothing except beach, the narrow strip before the trees. That yellow smudge he could see through the window. Ras Jaddi.

'Well, mister?'

Between Ras Jaddi and Ras Shahid, then. Within that fifty mile stretch. He flicked at the buttons, watched the map unroll backwards now, from east to west. Where was there a beach?

He had told Anders to pressure Langley's satellite photography experts into some immediate response. Supply background data, consult photographs, records, files . . . all the while knowing that there would be time only for a blind guess, the one quick overflight and look-down, then the decision of yes or no . . .

Beach —

— sand.

The sea was very shallow for a long way out, just there. The beach should consist of fine white sand up near the trees. An impact on wet sand would be risky — they had to make the DZ above the tide.

'Skipper — alter course to intersect the coast ten miles west of the headland. Somewhere between there and Ras Shahid is the DZ.'

'You have to be more specific, Gant. I got no fuel to spare.'

'OK, OK . . .' He flicked once more through the sections of the map in a feverish hurry. He heard breathing around him, a ragged chorus, like the noise of boxing fans believing their man is going down for the final time. Section after section passed before him, each one covering no more than five miles of coast; detailed, enlarged —

— but only drawings, *sketches!*

There . . .

He made the calculations. The beach stretched for a mile and a half in almost a straight line. High tide reached no more than — it was wide enough. Trees, no villages or settlements, no bungalows. A sand bar almost encircled a small bay.

'OK,' he announced. 'Seventeen miles west of Ras Jaddi — hit that beach and hope to God.'

There was silence for a moment, then the muttering of the Galaxy's navigator, finally. 'OK, mister — it's your funeral.'

'I know it.'

'ETA in five minutes plus. We're at nine thousand feet, cruising at two-forty knots. Twenty miles to run. Beginning my

descent. When we reach the DZ, you have time for *one* look-see.'
He paused, then added: 'Then you say go or no-go.'

Gant envisaged the Galaxy's enormous shadow flickering across the fine white sand, and swallowed the saliva that had gathered at the back of his mouth. The huge wingspan, the weight of the aircraft, its lumbering inability to manoeuvre, everything. He saw it sagging towards the beach, laying its three pallets like eggs – a great prehistoric, reptilian bird. There would be time for the two passes, no more. The beach *had* to be wide enough, long enough, flat enough . . .

He stared at the picture on the display until it began to grow vague and out of focus, then looked up. Mac nodded grimly. Garcia tried to grin, but his lips trembled. Garcia's crew had moved away. He had done what they all wanted, and what they had most not wanted. Garcia was not as good as he was, none of them had his experience; no one had his reputation. Now, he was risking their lives and they resented it.

'Mac,' he said brusquely, 'see the loadmaster. Make sure the guy is up to this – uh?'

Mac was experienced enough for his judgement to be trusted, even in this situation. Mac was the only one for whom Gant did not have to feel *responsible* –! And Mac was in his MiL . . . Mac, perhaps, was lucky.

'Sure, Major.' Even Mac was stiff and remote with anxiety, using Gant's rank as an indicator of doubt.

'The rest of you – you know the theory. Just let it happen to you.' He shrugged. Always, he felt this difficulty, this distaste for risking other people's lives. He resented his responsibility for them. 'Belt in tight and ride down. *You* do nothing. The captain and the loadmaster are the main men. The fuel goes out first, then you, Garcia. Then me on the second pass. I won't drop on your back.'

'Sure,' Garcia replied.

Gant resented the almost-sneer, even as he understood it. Then he saw Anders moving swiftly down the hold towards him, his face no less drawn and pale than when he had departed for the communications room.

'OK,' Gant concluded. 'You got maybe five minutes. I suggest you get on board. Stow everything moveable, make everything secure. OK? Anders —?'

They drifted away from him, completing a departure they had begun the moment his decision was made. Anders glanced at them, looked at the map display — bending to reconcile it with the large-scale map of Pakistan on the floor of the hold — then said:

'Langley says to hold —'

'Tell the skipper. He's talking about five minutes, no more. What kind of holding pattern is that?'

The Galaxy was descending now. Through the window, the strip of sand was still no wider, no more than a margin between blue and green-and-brown. The sea glittered far below, wide and empty.

'I know, Gant — but the government in Islamabad can't be talked to and persuaded all in a couple of minutes!'

'Karachi?'

'Awaiting orders from Islamabad.'

'We have to go, whatever. You know that, *they* know that. Up the ante — a bigger bribe, Anders. Get those guys in Islamabad to see it our way. Isn't it this neck of the woods where bribery's a way of life?'

'It all takes *time*, dammit!'

'Time is the thing we haven't got.'

'You know I can't authorize this, Gant,' Anders said heavily. He leant one crooked arm against the bulkhead, his weight against it. He appeared to be staring down at the sheen of the sea.

'You're just playing politics, man,' Gant snapped, staring at the displayed section of map. *That* beach, *there* —

He was committed. They had to go.

'Whatever, it's been put on hold,' Anders murmured.

'Hold? Those guys in Langley must look like they've run out of a kicked-over antheap! Anders, the computer scenario for the mission is out of date — *tell them*!'

'I did, but —'

123

'We're talking about minutes here! The shit's hit the fan and all those guys are wondering is, who's broken wind!'

'It's still on hold, Gant.'

'It *can't* be.'

He turned to look at the two Russian helicopters. Garcia was already aboard the 24-A, checking that everything was stowed and secure. His co-pilot was alongside him, his gunner in front of them in the forward section of the helicopter cockpit. The MiL, on its pallet and with rotors folded in line along the top of the fuselage, looked helpless, unready. Behind it, the fuel drums were being checked on their pallet. The shadowy bulk of his own helicopter was closest to him. Around all three pallets, the Galaxy's crew moved urgently. Mac stood with the loadmaster. Orders and checks crackled and flew from microphones.

He had already briefed the crew and their loadmaster. Getting Mac to check was only a way of keeping him occupied, and away from himself. The loadmaster was experienced and competent. He had dropped palletized loads at zero feet on previous occasions, but only from the hold of a much smaller Hercules transport. In the end, he would have to do little more than obey orders. The Galaxy's captain would call out the timings on each run, give the green light, and only then would the loadmaster's team, harnessed to the fuselage, release the pallets through the open rear doors.

'It can't be,' Gant repeated softly.

'It has been.'

'Jesus H. *Christ* –! Do they realize? Do they understand? We *lose* these two choppers unless we can dump them on the beach. There is no other way – even they ought to be able to see that, six thousand miles from here!'

'Gant?'

'Yes, skipper,' he snapped into the headset.

'ETA, one minute. When we hit your beach, we have no more than four minutes in the DZ area. *Two* passes only, after the look-see. You got that?' There was an edge of nervousness in the aircraft captain's voice now; something almost apologetic, too. 'I don't have clearance, Gant,' he added.

Gant looked at Anders, then said without hesitation: 'You have it, skipper. I just gave it to you.'

'Let me talk to Mr Anders.'

Anders was glaring at Gant. His body was slumped against the fuselage. The sea was much nearer beyond the curve of his arm. Hills were real, individual mounds and peaks and slopes. The line of palms and other trees, the strip of white sand snaking away westward, losing clarity and finally identity in the faint heat-haze and the sheen of the sea. Gant swallowed.

'OK,' he said, and handed the headset to Anders. 'Tell him,' he said softly. 'Everything's ready.' His fierce whisper contained no element of temptation, merely inevitability. 'We have to go. You can clean up after the horses have left. Do it.'

Anders took the headset as if it might explode in his large hand. His eyes were troubled and vague. For him, the beach ahead of them was not deserted but mined with diplomatic catastrophes. His career, too, was endangered by Gant's simple recklessness.

He glanced at the MiLs, at the voice-filled hold, the hurrying cargo crew, the sea and the nearing strip of sand. Then seemed to look into the distances clouded with heat.

'Can you make Karachi, skipper – *afterwards*?'

'If you're praying real hard, Mr Anders, then maybe.'

'And you, Gant – can you make Karachi?'

Gant nodded. The coast was less than five miles away. The transport was closing on it, beginning to turn onto a new, westward heading. White sand –

Anders urged: 'We can get down just by declaring an emergency – it's *you* they have to let land, after we've reneged on the original deal . . . you're not supposed to be seen.'

'I know it. Look, we have camouflage nets, the works. We'll wait for you to contact us. Send for the rest of the family when you're settled in the new job, uh?'

Anders nodded.

'You have clearance, skipper. *My* authority. Good luck.'

'Thank you, Mr Anders. ETA, thirty seconds. Gant?'

'Yes?'

'We'll set up the visual markers. You'll hear us, but don't give me trouble. It's out of your hands. OK?'

'OK.' Gant sounded reluctant, but took off the headset.

During the first overflight of the beach, the flight crew would select visual markers, make their fixes, define exact distances. Making the strip of sand a grid, a pattern – a dropping zone.

He looked at Anders.

'Thanks.'

'For what?'

'Seeing the inevitable.'

'Shouldn't you –?'

'I want to see that beach.'

They stared through adjacent windows. Perhaps six hundred feet up now, no more. The sea stretched away from them without wrinkling, without waves, like some vast lagoon. The edge of the tide flowed beneath the Galaxy's belly. Its huge shadow, coldly black on the white sand, wingtip over the water's edge. Gant glanced at the frozen frame of the map display, and began to recognize the shallow curve of the beach, the knoll of palms, the cradling arm of the sand bar. The transparent water seemed to run with silver veins, like mercury flowing over a blue-green glass slide. There were no rocks littering the beach, just the sand. He glanced across the hold. Trees flickered in the windows like an old, dark film, beyond the starboard wing.

Straight, flat, wide. The DZ.

'Good luck,' Anders murmured.

'What? Oh, yes. Keep in touch.'

'Wait for my –'

'Sure. It's in the bag. They won't want two Russian choppers sitting on one of their beaches for too long. See you, Anders.'

He left the window. The Galaxy, having completed its check run, was beginning to climb and turn. The flight-deck conversation, relayed to the hold, became more desultory. His stomach felt hollow. Nerves gripped him, shaking his body until he clenched down on them. A flight of sea-birds – cormorants or pelicans – had risen agitatedly into the air from near the sand bar as the Galaxy flew over them. The captain's voice dismissed

126

them as a possible hazard. Pelicans, he decided. Huge beaks and white bodies. Now settling like scraps of blown paper onto the cool, transparent water.

He winked at Mac, who was already strapped into his seat in the gunner's separate cockpit. Mac grinned.

He strapped himself into his seat, fitted his helmet, checked the cabin for anything not stowed or fixed. Fuel tanks empty. There was no way they could have risked a drop with fuel aboard. They'd fuel up from the drums, using the hand pump on the third pallet.

'Mac?'

'OK, skipper,' Mac seemed relieved, fitting once more into his role, their relationship.

'Then just hold on tight. Like the roller-coaster, that's all it is.'

The Galaxy was still turning in its great loop to approach the beach from its original heading. The loadmaster appeared below the pilot's cabin. Gant raised his thumb, the loadmaster responded, then turned to watch the drop signal lamps. He pressed the right earpiece of his headset against his ear and raised his left arm as the red lamp glowed. When the green light replaced it, he would drop his arm and the crewman next to the ramp panel would press the toggle. The drogue 'chute would be ejected into the slipstream of the Galaxy. The main canopy would trail after it, and then jerk open fully, pulling the first pallet out in an instant, a mere twenty feet above the sand.

He could not tune the VHF set to the Galaxy flight-deck's frequency. The intercom system operated by wire, like a telephone. He must sit in ignorance, in silence, until the loadmaster's arm indicated he was on his way. He would know nothing until the drogue 'chute opened, beginning to pull him through the doors. The faces of the Galaxy's cargo crew, harnessed and helmeted, would be the last thing he saw inside the transport; before they began rushing past him, as if seen from a speeding train. Red light, green light, moving arm, the jerk of the parachutes –

'Garcia?' he asked.

'Major?' Formality seemed to assist Garcia, just as it did with

Mac. Or were they still distancing themselves from his decision? Garcia's voice issued from the walkie-talkie secured to the cockpit framework. They would use them for close-proximity communications over Afghanistan and inside Soviet airspace, thus reducing the chances of any radio transmissions being detected.

He flicked to Transmit.

'You OK?'

'Sure, Major!' Garcia's voice was too quick, too hollow.

'Just cool it. Never been backwards out of a Galaxy before?' The mild joke went unappreciated and Gant merely shrugged. 'Just hang in there, Garcia.'

The Galaxy's course was straight and level once more. Its engines rushed distantly, like a wind. The cockpit seemed to close in around Gant. His hands touched the inert controls of the MiL. He glanced in his mirror —

— jaws opening.

The rear cargo doors of the Galaxy were slowly opening, seemingly in preparation to take some huge bite at the whiteness flowing beneath. Gant held his breath, looking down the flank of his own helicopter, past the 24-A and the fuel drums. The doors widened their gape. White sand, the edge of the ripple-less tide, the darkness of trees.

Zero feet. Gant glanced at the loadmaster and the operator over whom he seemed to be leaning.

Three seconds, two —

Green light, glowing to one side of the hold, splashing on the flank of Garcia's MiL. The sand rushed now, a white runway as the Galaxy gave the illusion of landing.

'Sweet-Mother-of-Jesus . . .' someone was muttering. Garcia —?

Edge of the water. Sand. Green light.

Go —

In his mirror, Gant saw the pallet of secured fuel drums lurch towards the mouth of the cargo hold, its drogue 'chute out in the sunlight, the main canopy opening like a daubed mouth.

FIVE

flotsam

Six bottles had contained beer, the larger bottle vodka. They were all empty now. Filip Kedrov studied them, shaking each of the bottles in turn as if tuning a set of musical bells. Then he replaced each with exaggerated care on the bunk opposite his; a rank of brightly-painted toy soldiers. Dead soldiers, he reminded himself, and giggled.

Nothing else to do, he justified his tipsiness to himself. Bloody nothing else to do but sit and wait, just as he had been doing for the past twenty-four hours! Good job he'd brought the bottles, an even better job that he'd stored the vodka and some cans down here on an earlier visit. It had been intended as over-stocking, but . . . the cans were all empty, too. In the bunker's kitchen, in the metal sink. There had been nothing else to do . . .

He flopped onto his bunk, slightly theatrically, hands clasped behind his head, which commenced whirling and spinning disconcertingly. *Keep your eyes open* – He raised his knees gently. The room began to spin.

He sat up quickly. His head lurched and he wanted to hold it but was forced to grip the edge of the bunk with both hands if he was not to become one of those dolls with rounded bases that rocked back and forth for whole minutes after a single touch. His head hung over his knees; he groaned. The sound washed away down the long, empty corridor of the room.

He should have known, should have *known* he would get drunk out of sheer boredom. He released the bunk and held his head softly. After he had cradled it for a time, he looked up slowly. The row of bottles remained still. The opposite bunk did not lurch. He swallowed the sickly saliva in his mouth, and his stomach remained at some distance below his throat. He sighed cautiously.

All the drink had gone now, anyway. He focused slowly on the dial of his watch. Mid-morning. Twenty-four hours had passed down there, two days since he had had Orlov send the last signal . . . well, almost two – a day and a half at least . . . they would be on their way now, coming for him. They *had* to come, didn't they? He felt certain they would, confident of the fact, and kicked his legs over the edge of the bunk like a child on a sea-wall. Soon, he'd have to think about moving from here –

When?

Tomorrow would be early enough. It was difficult to decide, to imagine the distances, the time of their journey. But they wouldn't waste time, not with Thursday only two days away . . . and he had another hiding-place, at the pick-up point, the exact and agreed rendezvous . . . he would go there tomorrow. The helicopters would come in probably disguised as Russian machines . . . from where? Turkey, Afghanistan, more than a thousand miles away –

– stop, stop it! He remembered why he had sought the drink's temporary oblivion. It was the fear of abandonment, the fear of huge distances, of a helicopter attempting that vast, hostile air-space . . . but he was indispensable, wasn't he? indispensable –

Helicopters? One helicopter? *Ridiculous!*

Had they ever said helicopters? Had they – well? Fool, *fool*, can't you remember? He pressed his hands against his temples, but he could not still the debate, could not squeeze certainty back into his head. Isolation, the sense of abandonment, welled up in him. Fool, fool . . . did they ever even mention helicopters? Isn't that what you *supposed*? Tears leaked from his squeezed-shut eyes. He slumped back against the cold wall, his hands loosely lifting and letting fall the stuff of the grey army blanket on which he sat. Then he let his head loll to one side, his cheek and ear and temple against the concrete, his posture magnifying his sobs. He could hear them, great slobbering groans like those of a child sent to bed early. It had only been his dream, the helicopter . . . he had no authority for the idea whatsoever. It was Tuesday morning, and they would not come, not now . . . cars, trucks, trains, would be too slow now . . . the moment was past when they would come.

He wailed loudly. He heard the noise magnified against the wall, almost through the concrete. They would not come . . . how could he ever have believed it?

He heard the noise he was making. Sobbing again now.

Heard —

The corridor on the other side of the wall was like a whispering-gallery.

Heard —

— whispers, shuffles, clicks; movement and conversation of small animals — rats talking and scrabbling . . . he lifted his feet from the floor. He swallowed a sob. What did it matter now?

Whisper, shuffle, click . . . ?

Heard —

— *them*.

The search, the *hunt* . . . Feverishly wiping his wet mouth with his hand, he pressed his ear more firmly against the wall. Shuffle, click, whisper, shuffle-click, whisper, slam, click-click-click, whisper, *whistle* —?

He was shivering with terror, unable to believe that the sounds were as distant as they appeared. He looked wildly around for a glass — remembering something from a detective story — and saw where a tumbler had rolled away from his drunken grasp under the bunk opposite . . . snatched it up, his hands shivering as they clasped it. He put it against the concrete, then rubbed his ear to comfort against it. His blood pounded, magnified, and his breath rushed. He had to hold the hand that held the glass, to still its tremor.

Click, click, click, whisper-whisper-whisper, shuffle, shuffle . . . little rat-noises out there in the dark corridors — where? How far? Slightly louder now, coming closer . . . ? He listened, until it became irrefutable that the noises were gradually becoming louder, moving in his direction. A search — *of every room* —!

His desperation doubled him up with stomach cramp. He wanted to retch. He dropped the glass on the bunk. His mouth hung open, but the nausea from his heart-beat was like repeated soft blows to the back of his head, clubbing him gently down into the rough grey blanket.

He did not understand how he moved to the door, not even that he had done so. He pressed his ear against it, switched off the room lights, then moved the heavy, stiff handle and turned it. He opened the door with exaggerated caution even as the blows continued to bang in his neck and head. His breathing seemed wild, uncontrolled as he looked out. He heard the whisper moving down the corridor but discerned nothing in the gloom. Then he heard and distinguished footsteps clicking, some distance away, funnelled indirectly to him. They were still in another corridor, beyond the T-junction. But *this* corridor was a dead-end. If he moved, it had to be back towards the noises he could hear, towards the crackling exchanges over walkie-talkies, thin tinny voices without recognizable words. The opening and slamming of steel doors. How far down the corridor beyond the T-junction were they?

His head had cleared. The blows of his pulse had receded. He ducked back into the room and, in the darkness which did not seem to delay him, he scrabbled up his haversack – checked that the precious transponder was inside – then scraped and bundled his possessions into it. Half-wrapped sandwiches smeared margarine on the heavy boots he would need in the marshes, he felt its stickiness . . .

He returned to the door.

He could not hide the fact of his presence. They might be at the end of the corridor already . . . no, no, the noises were still too quiet . . . but he would have to head back *towards* the noises! The idea stunned him into immobility in the doorway. The row of lights along the corridor's roof could be switched on at any moment, exposing him. He shuddered, then moved stiffly, like a paraplegic at painful exercise. Walking as softly as he could, moving slowly, limbs unfreezing . . .

Yet, however cautiously he moved, it still seemed as if he was rushing towards the noises that slid and whispered along the concrete walls. Rushing into the narrow neck of a bottle – to become an exhibit, a preserved specimen. There were patches of silence in the search when he, too, stopped, then further crackles, whispers, slams. Occasionally, the calls seemed to be louder, on the edge of comprehension, and those were the most frightening. Closer, closer – he was converging on them. The noises of boot-heels sounded like pebbles dropped down a deep well.

He touched off each door, each yard of wall, hardly breathing. He felt light-headed with panic, but there was a clarity to it. The panic hurried him on, but with caution, with alert senses . . . his ears began to measure the weight and distance of the noises made by the search. Even as his mind whirled with terrors.

Corner. T-junction. Which way were the noises, which way the nearest runged ladder to the surface?

Footsteps, voices – *left* . . . ladder? *Ladder?* Come on, come on, which way, which . . . ? Right, *right*! Thank God . . . relief tumbled into his mind.

He felt the skin across his shoulderblades stretch and become sensitive as he turned down the right-hand tunnel. The furry touch of asbestos against his fingertips. His hand closed convulsively on the pipes, his right foot reached out and tapped against the railway in the middle of the tunnel, and withdrew swiftly, as if its motions were signalling like a telegraph key along the rail. The skin on his back and buttocks was so *thin* –! If they heard or sensed him now, they might just open fire –

He moved, counting each footstep. The tunnel, lower and narrower than the corridor from which he had come, magnified the noises behind him. He could almost hear each time the walkie-talkies were switched from Transmit to Receive. Slamming doors were loud. Boot-steps were distinct.

Hesitantly, he looked back.

– gleam. A flash like a weak, distant glimpse of lightning or the twitching aside of a curtain. Torches. He felt his hand hurrying beside him along the top of the asbestos-lagged pipe. He began to hear his own footsteps as loudly as the first whispers of theirs. Tiptoe, but that was foolish because the drink returned to surge in his head before being kept at bay by fear and the instinct to

escape. They would come for him, no they couldn't possibly –
not at this late stage, but they would come, he was indispensable,
wasn't he . . . ?

He squeezed the thoughts from his head. No, the noises did
that – a shout that might have been the raising of the alarm
stunned him, thrust him in the back to make him go faster – rid
him of all thought except the certainty of capture if he did not
reach the ladder to the surface. There was no time for any other
idea. His heart pattered in his chest like a small, terrified animal.

He looked back three more times. And he saw, on the third
occasion, a torch's beam wash the tunnel wall before turning off,
down the main silo corridor from which he had come. Towards
the room where he had hidden. Where the evidence of his recent
occupation waited to be discovered. Lights flickered on, then the
glow came seeping out of the long corridor, illuminating two
soldiers, little more than silhouettes. His foot splashed in a
puddle; something skittered away from him with a squeak;
nausea filled his throat – *don't be sick now, not here –!* He
blundered on for a few steps, one hand over his mouth, until the
nausea subsided. Ahead of him, a barely discernible light seemed
to drip from the roof of the tunnel.

Perhaps no more – as much as – another hundred metres. He
tried to remember, and did so quite easily, prompted by the new
terrors of imminent discovery. Yes, no more than a hundred
metres now . . . to one of the air-ducts from the surface, closed
only in time of war.

He reached the ladder, touching it almost as he passed, then
clung to it. He saw his own arms, could discern the colour of his
clothing, the whiteness of his hands. A weak circle of light
illuminated him. He looked up. Was it pale blue? He could not
tell –

It was the surface up there . . . He gripped the rungs of the
ladder, released their iciness one by one, reaching his body into a
stretch without moving his feet.

Whistles, then, from the corridor. Summonses over the
walkie-talkies, crackling-squeaky orders. Excitement, discovery.
At once, he moved his left foot, stepped, climbed. Rung over

134

rung towards the broken, twisted-back netting at the top of the narrow chimney, sweating profusely with effort and relief. Up, up –

He climbed with increasing, flooding gratitude. The air in his nostrils was less musty, fresher, fresher all the time with each successive rung.

The Galaxy climbed and began to turn, as if fleeing the scene of an accident. For Gant, even the sound of Garcia's excited, relieved voice from the transceiver could not dispel the image of the huge fan of sand that had been thrown up by the impact of the fuel drums and the palletized MiL. Accident – collision.

'Sweet-Mother-of-God, we made it!'

And behind Garcia's rushing, nervous relief were the noises of his crew, equally stunned. Gant had seen the main canopy of Garcia's pallet open, seen the helicopter snatched like a dandelion-clock through the clam-shell of the open doors, then the sand had obscured everything. The scene had lurched like the image from a joggled camera – sand, lush vegetation, the water, all rushing beneath him, then settling to a steadier image as the transport passed out over the edge of the tide. The white scraps of paper of the pelicans, distressed and alarmed, settled slowly once more on the water.

The Galaxy continued on its turn, lazily and as if time and fuel consumption were of no importance; Gant considered that the sense of detachment belonged only to himself.

No . . . already, the scene below was remote. At an altitude of two hundred feet, it was still impossible to make out details on the beach. The mirror into which he looked quivered because of the mild turbulence outside the Galaxy . . .

. . . sand beneath the open doors once more, not the glittering water. He felt his body tense, then consciously relaxed.

'The fuel drums are all over the fucking place!' he heard in the cockpit. Garcia over the transceiver. His body tensed once more 'No spillage . . . we'll try to move –'

'Gant?' he heard in his headset.

135

'Yes, skipper?'

'We're going to have to let you down nearer the water – to keep you out of the way of those fuel drums.'

'Your decision.' He resented the admission.

'Thanks. Good luck.'

The distances, timings, speed recited by the navigator and the co-pilot became a background, no more. Voices from the flight-deck relayed to Garcia what Gant had been told. In his mirrors, he saw the huge shadow of the Galaxy's tail, dark and cool on the whiteness.

He braced his feet. His hands seemed superfluous in their lack of occupation. He might as well have folded them across his chest, like a child in class told to sit quiet . . . waiting for the schoolbell.

He smiled, in spite of his tension. The edge of the water seemed to glint in his mirrors, then the pilot adjusted the heading of the Galaxy. Height, speed, heading all seemed right to his sixth sense. The sand wasn't really firm enough for a palletized drop, but Garcia had made it . . . nothing to concern him, nothing –

The loadmaster raised his arm. His eyes were fixed on the red light ten paces from the MiL's nose. Gant breathed in deeply, snatching at the breath. Nerves jumped; he was helpless, it wasn't under his control.

The loadmaster's arm snapped down. Then his body seemed to lurch away, as if a blow had knocked the man aside. The beach tilted in Gant's mirrors, and the impressions he received were like reflections in a broken glass. A twitch ran through the huge fuselage, as if the aircraft had attempted some impossibly tight turn; a whale imitating the manoeuvres of a shark. Anders' voice in the transceiver, wishing him good luck – broken by the pilot's expletive. The green light, the lurch and the breaking open of the drogue 'chute –

– beach at the wrong angle, *wrong angle* –! Sky in the corner of the tiny screen formed by one mirror, dark-green trees, the beach – dotted fuel drums, the half-buried pallet of the other MiL, a great stiff wave of sand thrown up on the beach – but all seen wrongly, as if he were drunk and falling –

– scraps of paper, red-white, white, red, red-white, white, scraps of paper *all around him* even as he was thrust against his harness, and the image of a slow-motion film of an accident test returned to his mind. He was the dummy flung slowly and grotesquely through the car windscreen . . . the harness bit into his chest and shoulders, restraining him.

Scraps of paper, red-white, white, whirling and spinning – a pelican's body, headless, thudded against the cockpit, nauseating him; he understood what had happened. The course of the Galaxy had been closer to the water's edge, to the sand bar and the drifting, nervous birds. They had scattered into the air in front of the Galaxy as if thrown up by a giant hand, startling the pilot, making him twitch the stick and jerk the transport off-course for an instant –

– the main canopy opened its colourful mouth behind him, obscuring everything else. The MiL was tilting nose-up, falling. The bird's decapitated body had disappeared from the perspex, leaving a red smear that shadowed the glint of the sun. Other scraps of white flew or twisted above and beyond the MiL.

Split-seconds – the sun blinded – Mac was muttering, but he hadn't reached his third expletive when the pallet struck the sand. The impact rendered him breathless. For an instant, he *was* the life-size dummy in an accident test. He fought for breath. Feeling returned in the gouging of the harness. His eyes opened. He could see nothing. A huge mask of flying sand had been thrown up all round the MiL. Water glinted and sparkled within it, raining down on the perspex like a storm on corrugated tin. Darkness.

'Jesus, Jesus, Jesus . . .' Mac recited his litany.

The straps of the harness bit. Gant realized his body was at the wrong angle. He was sitting tilted forward and to one side in his seat. Hanging there. Splintering noises. Great, aching, tearing noises, and now a steadier though intermittent groaning; the occasional snap.

The sun came back.

'Gant, are you all right? Gant?' It was the pilot.

137

'Alive,' he murmured, unconcerned. The enquiry was irrelevant. 'Mac?' he asked.

'Christ! OK, skipper . . .' Mac's voice was small and shaky, as if lost inside his stunned frame.

'Major, Major —?' Garcia over the transceiver.

'OK, Garcia, OK.'

The great pall of sand and spray fell lazily, half-translucent, half-opaque, into the sea . . . all around him . . . even the pelicans were beginning to fall easily out of the pale sky, to settle gingerly on the water, farther off from the — the sand bar, jutting out from the beach, half-enclosing the little bay of cool water . . .

The sand slid down the perspex like a drawn-back curtain. It stuck to the pelican blood, was plastered in streaks by the water that had been thrown up with the sand. Light flashed through the streaked cockpit from the Galaxy's wing as the aircraft curved gently away in a climbing turn.

The pallet had landed at an angle. Gant realized he was staring into the water; transparent, mercury-veined water, smooth once more after the pall of sand's disturbance.

With a shuddering lurch, the MiL shook off the remaining sand like a dog discarding water from its coat. The horizon was more tilted, the water discernibly nearer. A cold chill gripped his heart. When he looked up, the Galaxy had altered course, heading away behind him, towards its landfall at Karachi. Its diminishing seemed like an act of desertion. The voice of the pilot and the anxious murmurs of Anders filled his headset.

'OK, OK!' he snapped. 'Get out of my head!' His voice was urgent, tinged with panic. The broken pallet beneath the helicopter groaned, then slithered. The cockpit lurched.

'Skipper —!'

'Mac — stay cool. Stay *still*,' he warned. 'Don't *move* —'

'Your angle of impact . . .' the pilot was repeating, his words irrelevant. The cockpit seemed as close and final around him as — as the oxygen tent that had shrouded his father's last days. He shuddered, shaking off the image.

'Skipper — and you, Anders . . . there's nothing you can do, nothing. Get the hell out of here!'

'Gant –'

'Don't bother me now!'

He flicked off the VHF set, then reached up and drew off his helmet. The cries of pelicans like the magnified tearing of paper or cardboard. The almost-still lapping of the tired, cool water. The creaking of the pallet's remnants as they moved uncertainly – downwards . . .

Garcia's voice in the cockpit. Figures along the beach, running as if laboured and laden through the sand. The glinting, retreating dot of the Galaxy. Spars and slivers and torn spears of wood littering the sand bar.

'Just stay cool,' he murmured, releasing his harness gently from his bruised body. Slowly, he levered himself up from his seat, and reached for the pilot's door. Gripped its handle, turned it –

– the MiL lurched, sliding another foot and more towards the water . . .

. . . which, he saw clearly, was not as shallow as it seemed, but was deep enough to submerge the helicopter as far as the main cabin.

He looked up. The locked rotors lay along the fuselage. The MiL could not fly; it was drowning.

There was nothing he could do. As he swung the door gently open over the water, the MiL slid again, with an accompanying groan from the broken pallet. The sea idled, deceptively innocent, less than a foot below the sill of the cockpit. When it moved again, water would begin to slop in. He looked down over the gunner's cabin. Mac's face stared up at him, bemused and afraid. The water lapped against the perspex, level with Mac's arm.

Gant's body felt frozen, immobile, as he waited for the next, inexorable movement of the MiL into the sea.

'He was there and yet you managed to *miss* him? He eluded your search?' General Lieutenant Rodin asked. Serov's admission had distracted him from the ponderous, dinosaur movement of the

139

vast platform on which lay the booster that would carry the laser battle station into orbit aboard the *Raketoplan* shuttle craft.

Serov studied his superior's features before he replied. They were pale and drawn into intent, grim planes by his mood. Rodin was taller than the GRU colonel, and seemed especially aware of the fact at that moment, even though both of them were dwarfed by the booster. The diesel locomotives protested outside the vast hangar as they strained to move the booster's platform from the assembly building along the first yards of the miles of double railway track to the launch pad. The noises of the platform's first movements were hideous, making Serov's teeth ache.

'Yes, he had indeed been there,' he confirmed in a neutral voice. 'My people may – or may not – have alarmed him. Anyway, there was no trace of him in the warren of tunnels and rooms. We were thorough.'

'And what are you doing now?' Rodin asked in an imperious tone. It was as if he drew something of an added authority from the scene around him; as if he had chosen a setting that displayed him to advantage. Serov had not dared keep the information regarding Kedrov secret from Rodin . . . his temerity in suggesting the son was sent away from Baikonur would have earned a greater rebuke if Rodin had found out about Kedrov's disappearance from anyone but himself. He had, of course, minimized the extent of the carelessness the telemetry officer had displayed.

Serov was aware of the scents and noises of the place, aware of the technicians swarming over the platform and the booster, whose great bunch of rocket engines had passed out of the hangar into the pale winter sunlight. The chill of the day stood next to him in the assembly hangar like a heavy body leaning against his frame. His breath clouded around his head.

'Extending the search. Surveillance on all known associates – we'll get him, comrade General,' he added reassuringly, with studied deference. Rodin seemed to smile in a thin-lipped, momentary way, as if sensing the change that had occurred in their relative positions since their telephone conversation. 'I think Kedrov will head for open country now . . . he knows we'll be looking for him.'

'And you're certain he knows little or nothing about *Lightning*?'

'Less than the actor, I imagine,' Serov replied quietly.

Rodin turned away abruptly. Serov enjoyed the general's momentary discomfiture.

A flock of technicians and scientific staff walked funereally in the wake of the platform. Rodin was watching them as if – as if he *owned* them, Serov thought. At the far end of the hangar, where the light appeared dusty and inadequate, the shuttle craft lay on a similar, much smaller platform. Teams of people swarmed over it, bees around honey. He had a minimal interest in both it and the laser weapons as machines. Their power interested him a great deal more. Mere technology wearied him. It was, ultimately, a civilian world.

Chessboard patterning decorated the stages of the booster. Gleaming metal, curving, strong lines, a sense of massiveness; power, too. Serov, with Rodin's back to him, shook his head with cynical ruefulness. A gigantic badge of authority and power.

'I – have confined my son to his apartment for . . . the remainder of this week,' Rodin announced without turning round.

'Very well, General. As long as –'

'He will speak to no one, he will not leave the place. Is that clear? Meanwhile, warn his friends to stay away from him.'

'Yes, comrade General,' Serov murmured. It had to be accepted. Rodin was using the advantage of Kedrov's disappearance to ensure his decision was accepted.

As if pressing home his reasserted authority, Rodin asked: 'What of the KGB's interest in this Kedrov?'

'Pure accident – drugs, we believe.'

'Perhaps. But what *consequences* might follow?'

A group of senior officers was moving towards them. The smallest third stage of the booster passed their position like a slow, submarine creature, out into the sunlight. There was sufficient clear sky for the American spy satellites to observe the moving of the booster. But then, a Soviet shuttle flight had

141

already been announced to the world by Nikitin as a gesture. A rendezvous with the American shuttle in a mission of peace to symbolize the implementation of the Treaty! Rodin merely flicked one hand towards the approaching group, and they halted, still at some distance from him and Serov.

'No consequences, comrade General. Unless they find him first – which they will not.'

'Make sure of that, Serov. You know, I cannot help the suspicion that your – *accident* was precipitate.'

'I beg to disagree, comrade General. It was entirely necessary.'

'Make sure nothing else goes wrong. Understand?'

'Nothing else will go wrong.'

'At this moment, *Stavka*'s backing is absolute. Also, that of our friends in the Politburo.' Rodin essayed a smile, then seemed to reject the expression as something foreign and worthless. 'But, if Moscow were to be, by any means, made suspicious, even alerted . . . then *Stavka* would not go ahead with *Lightning*. There would not be a majority of the High Command in favour of pursuing *Lightning* once the elements of secrecy and surprise are lost to us. That was made clear at the outset – it was made clear to you, among others.' Every utterance, Serov decided, was something *ex cathedra* – Holy Writ, almost. He suppressed a tiny smile. Megalomania – raging megalomania.

'I realize that, comrade General. The High Command will not openly defy the Kremlin – at least, not yet. Not without *Lightning* having been put into effect.'

'Therefore, find this little man who has disappeared and kill him before the KGB or anyone else stumbles across him.'

'Yes, comrade General.'

'We *must* present those old women on the Politburo with a *fait accompli*, with a *result*, Serov. When they see what *Lightning* achieves, the research and development budget for the battle station programme will be unlimited . . .' Rodin's eyes stared, as if he were looking into a vague distance beyond Serov. He appeared to wish to recite old resolutions, cherished dreams as a way of escaping from any thought of failure . . . or his son. This was, Serov realized, a catechism.

'I understand, comrade General,' he murmured, contempt smoothed from his voice. 'We must succeed.' He paused, then added: 'We'll find this Kedrov and dispose of him.'

Rodin nodded vigorously. 'Yes, yes – of course. He has no means of escape or safety . . .' Then his eyes seemed to narrow to a closer attention. 'The army is gambling everything, Serov, in order to regain its rightful power – twenty years of power that has been thrown away or snatched from us by Nikitin and his cronies. So I do not want to step into a dog-turd on my own doorstep, not now . . . find this spy and get rid of him!'

Sunlight spilled whitely into the hangar, seeming to bring a more intense cold to the place, now that the booster's platform had gone. In the distance, the locomotives could still be heard, murmuring in protest at the weight and the effort.

Rodin nodded once, then turned his back and strode arrogantly towards the waiting group of officers.

'If your son hadn't been terrified of you from birth . . .' Serov murmured, then closed his mouth on the remainder of the sentiment. He would do his job, he decided, dropping his salute. He walked out into the sunlight, squinting.

He'd have Kedrov safely dead, long before Thursday. No doubt of that.

The main canopy floated on the surface of the translucent water, becoming sodden. Along the length of the sand bar, back towards the beach, the wreckage of the pallet lay like flotsam. A gouge in the sand, like the careering track of a huge, runaway vehicle, had been scraped out by the impact. Gant's awareness was calm, alert. Garcia and his crew had begun running leadenly out along the bar towards the stranded MiL, which was –

– poised. Still. He was balanced gently, hands and feet taking his weight, half-out of the cockpit door as if about to alight from a bus. The pelicans' cries had stilled, the sea was calm; the Galaxy's engines had retreated beyond audibility. A strangely surreal silence had invested the beach. It was almost dreamlike, except

143

for the spars of wood, the darkly-gouged sand and the floating specks of pelican corpses.

The intake plugs had held fast. Water had not entered the air intakes and thus the engines. All other openings remained sealed. Except for Mac's cabin and his own. He breathed shallowly, his mind racing, as he watched Mac climb from the hinged canopy of his cockpit. The MiL rocked gently, almost subconsciously. Mac was turning his head constantly, like a doll, from the sand to Gant's face. He was treading gingerly as if through a minefield – but he was climbing out against the list of the helicopter. He should not cause it to slide further towards the water. Unlike Gant, who could only exit from the starboard side of the 24-D, into the sea . . .

. . . with the MiL moving after him . . . ?

He concentrated on Mac. One foot and leg over the sill, the slow, ballet-like turn, the right leg, the pause, then the drop. Mac's hands released the sill of the cockpit, and the MiL quivered. But did not move.

Mac looked up at him, grinning through the stained perspex as Gant looked down.

'Easy, skipper.'

'OK, OK, Mac,' he snapped impatiently. He raised his voice, still poised in the doorway of his cabin. 'Garcia – where's my rigging kit?' he yelled.

'All over the fucking beach, Major!'

'Then for Christ's sake get it here!'

'What are you going to –?'

Gant felt as if the force of his anger and urgency would topple the MiL into the sea.

'I'm going to re-rig the rotors – this baby has to be flown off the sand bar!' He looked down. He had no knowledge of tides. It was the imminent danger of the MiL sliding into the water that obsessed him. But, if there was a significant tide, and it was coming in –? He stared into the slight haze and glitter, towards the beach. White sand, all white sand . . . the tide was not retreating, if there was much of a tide . . . he didn't know.

He glanced at the radio, then dismissed the idea of talking to

144

the Galaxy. He studied the rotors folded along the MiL's fuselage. Five rotors, but only four of them needed repositioning . . . it was the only way, and if he didn't get it done, the mission had foundered finally and completely.

'Rigging kit!' he yelled. 'Fuel up your MiL! In that order, Garcia.'

'Couldn't we use his MiL to tow us off . . . ?' Mac began.

'Don't finesse, Mac! For Christ's sake, Garcia, get your ass moving!'

'What do you want me to do, skipper?' Mac asked, wading into the water and edging around the pallet until he was looking up at Gant.

'I'll need you when I start re-rigging. OK?'

'Sure. We got enough –?'

'Don't ask! Clearance? I think so. Another couple of feet and we've had it . . .' He was distracted. Silver fish nipped and glanced near Mac's submerged legs. 'Wade out there, Mac – how deep does it get?' If it was shallow enough . . . ? He watched Mac's waist disappear, then the stain of the water creep to the shoulders of his flight overalls. Shit –

'OK, Mac . . .'

'Too deep, uh?'

'Too deep . . . we have to fly her off . . . she won't float high enough to keep the rotor tips out of the water. The droop on the blades will dip them below the surface.'

The parameters of his situation continued to narrow as they divested themselves of every shred of optimism. There was only one solution, but it appeared impossible. He had to rig the rotors – he needed Kooper or Lane and Mac around this MiL, and he needed, needed –

– fuel, the rigging kit, a rope – rope first –

'Mac . . . get some rope off – get all the rope off the pallet – don't release the chopper yet, she might slide right off . . . we need to lasso each rotor to swing it into position.'

'Sure, skipper!' Mac appeared galvanized by the instruction; as if movement and purpose were reasserted, and offered a satisfactory solution to their situation. Gant glanced across to the beach.

Lane was in the water, pushing something ahead of him. The rigging kit, had to be. Garcia and Kooper were wearily rolling one of the huge fuel drums towards their helicopter, which seemed to sit besieged on the beach, surrounded by the fortifications its impact had dug for it.

'Come on, Lane!' he yelled. Lane nodded. He was skirting the sand bar, where the water was shallow, pushing the rigging kit ahead of him on a section of pallet, its buoyant honeycomb layer intact.

Mac unthreaded a length of rope, measuring its length as he did so. He was as intent as a child engaged in some secret game.

Gant's mind spun out ahead of the moment like a spider's thread. The images did not seem to reach as far as safety. Re-rigging, re-fuelling, rotors having to be clear of the water, the necessity, he now saw, to use the other MiL to ferry the fuel out, the necessity to have that MiL *tow* out the fuel, across the water, without approaching too close to upset his helicopter with its downdraught . . . the tide, too –

He looked down. No edge of stained sand. The tide was coming in – how fast? Would the sand bar be covered? He knew it would be . . . the gouge showed dark, heavy sand, not the fine whiteness of the beach near the trees. They would not even have to wait until the pallet's wreckage slid into the water . . . the sea was coming in to meet the MiL. Already, it was perhaps an inch, two inches further up the flank of the helicopter, lapping gently, deceptively against the perspex of the gunner's cabin. The rotary cannon's barrel was already dipped like a straw into the water. The tip of the airspeed sensor boom toyed at the surface. The MiL was leaning to starboard and tilted nose-down, too. Its weight should be pressing the wreckage of the pallet down into the compacted sand of the bar . . . should be. But it had moved twice, three times, although only by inches. Either it would move as they began to re-rig, or – or . . . the tide –

'Lane! I want you in here – you do the cowhand's job, Mac.'

'Sure.'

'Get the rigging kit onto the sand . . . I need you –'

146

'I release the rotor brake every time you want the rotor head moved, uh, Major?'

'Got it in one. Change places with me – come on!'

Lane dragged the section of pallet and the elements of the rigging kit up the slope of the sand bar, Mac wading into the shallow water to help him, the coiled rope over his shoulder. When they had finished, Mac waved.

'Ready when you are, skipper.'

'OK – Lane, let's change places.' He reached back into the cockpit and tugged the transceiver from its mounting, then clipped it to his pocket. 'Garcia – situation report now.'

'Major – we're making it,' he heard Garcia breathlessly reply, his words accompanied by a soughing like that of the wind. 'We got the wobble pump operational, we're fuelling up now – then we'll re-rig our rotors . . . any more orders?'

'You're going to have to tow out one of the fuel cells to me – just be ready. Out.'

Lane was standing beneath the cockpit. Gant balanced in the doorway, assessed the stability of the tilted helicopter, then jumped into the shallow water. Looked up at once – the MiL had not moved. He exhaled with noisy relief.

'OK, Lane – just take your time, uh?'

Lane reached upwards, grabbing the frame of the open door with one hand, the sill with the other. Like a hunchback, he placed his feet in the niches in the fuselage, hesitated, then scrambled softly into the cockpit, only straightening gingerly after a long hesitation. Something groaned beneath the MiL, but it had not moved. It was simply the tide that shocked – another inch, maybe two . . .

Swiftly, Gant rounded the drunkenly hanging nose and walked up the slope of the sand bar. The water had been warm – he had hardly noticed. The morning was still. The temperature wasn't much over sixty, but it was humid and breezeless. Tension made him sweat –

He squinted into the light, looking up at the locked rotors. Four of the blades clustered over the tail-boom required moving. And first he must re-rig the blade which would hang closest to the water . . . a measurement of the incoming tide. If it dipped below the surface, then when he started the engines it would break – stranding the MiL for good. So –

'You lasso each of the rotors, Mac, and haul them round to the rigged position. I'll lock and secure.'

'Sure, skipper.' Mac had taken the coiled rope from his shoulder. He grinned, wiped sweat from his forehead.

Gant touched gently at the flank of the MiL. Placed his hands firmly on the stubby port wing, above the rocket pod, which stared threateningly into his stomach. He heaved his body onto the wing. The helicopter quivered, rocked gently, settled back. There was a groan of splintered wood, but no sideways or forward movement. Mac's breath exhaled noisily. Gant stood on the wing, then began climbing slowly, using the handholds set in the fuselage. Tension shook his frame; sweat blinded him – just that small effort, and he felt weak, as if the air was that of some Turkish bath. He pressed his body against the fuselage, edging upwards. Lane's features appeared pale and nervous through the cloudy perspex to his left, beyond the plugged air intakes.

He scrambled into a crouched position atop the helicopter, near the opening of the oil cooler intake. He nodded to Mac.

'OK – throw up the tools.'

The wrench glinted in the sun. He caught it easily. Then he grabbed the second tool out of the air, clanging it down against the drum of the exhaust port, which boomed hollowly. He nodded again, paused to look across the water. In a mirror-image of what he was about to attempt, he could make out Garcia atop the 24-A, unlocking his second rotor. Kooper had dragged the first one into position, it was already re-rigged for take-off. It was a race, and he suddenly appeared to be falling behind; and Garcia did not have the urgency of the creeping tide to prompt him.

From his vantage, the sand bar already appeared narrower, a sliver of gouged whiteness reaching out from the shore. No longer like a crooked arm, only as thick as a beckoning finger. The chin radar had disappeared beneath the water, the FLIR, too, was gone. The tip of the sensor boom had dipped below the surface, the rotary cannon was half-drowned. Urgency panicked him, made him feel old and insecure as he straightened up, balancing his weight evenly, one foot to either side of the exhaust. Then he sat gently down.

Minutes, minutes . . .

He unlocked the first rotor.

'OK!' It was necessary and unnecessary to shout, but he did so, releasing the tension that threatened to cramp his arms, his grip on the tool. Mac's lasso floated upwards, Gant grabbed it and crawled along the tail-boom, a four-footed animal disorientated on a high wire, looping it over the tip of the first rotor. 'OK!' He felt the sweat sheening his body inside the flight overalls, and wiped at his forehead and eyes. Raised his body to watch –

Mac walked into the water, tugging the rotor slowly away from its folded position, the rope taut, dropping beads of bright water. The rotor tip moved downwards in an arc. Gant could not breathe.

He scuttled back along the tail-boom, seating himself once more on the warm metal of the exhaust. He began rotating the nut, one eye watching the moving rotor tip as it dipped towards the water. Fish flicked like silver metal fragments. The wrench rotated the large nut, drawing back the triple lugs which allowed their mating lugs to engage in their housings and become locked when the special retracting tool was withdrawn. The rotor stopped moving. Gant almost fearfully studied its tip. Less than a foot from the water. Once any part of it was submerged, the game was lost.

'One!' he yelled. 'OK, Lane – release the rotor brake!'

He moved away from the rotor head. As the brake was released in the cockpit, the rotor head moved, bringing it to a more convenient position. Mac flung the lasso, failed to loop it on the tip of the next rotor – Gant's temperature soared, he clamped his lips shut, watched Mac throw again, catch the tip, tighten the noose. He waved him to begin pulling the rotor into position, retracting the lugs, loosening the nut with the wrench.

A frantic stealth; a tense, almost slow-motion sequence of actions. Lasso, wrench, retracting tool, wrench, the insertion of a wired pin. Hydraulic pressure would complete the locking of

149

each rotor at the moment of engine-start . . . lasso, wrench, retracting tool, wrench, wired pin, rotor brake . . . his back and arms ached, his body was bathed in sweat. The water edged slowly – no, they were labouring slowly, with effort, the sea just slid and rose – towards the rotor tip. Starboard undercarriage beneath the water, the sea lapping high up on the gunner's cockpit, Garcia's MiL in the hazy distance already fully rigged –

'Lash the fuel cell as securely as you can,' he was instructing Garcia, even as he tightened the fourth nut, at the point of removing the retracting tool. 'Make the tow-rope as long as you can – I don't want this baby disturbed by your downwash . . . get that fuel and the wobble pump out here as quick as you can!'

'OK, Major – with you as soon as we can.'

He did not look up at the beach again. He stared instead at the tip of the rotor that leaned out over the water. Inches now – they wouldn't have the time . . . inches . . .

He heard the 24-A's engines start, the rotors wind up. A shattering noise that seemed like laughter mocking the immobility of his own helicopter. He tightened the last nut and removed the retracting tool . . . he reached for the last wired pin, and fitted it . . . the retracting tool slithered from his damp grasp, clanging down the bulkhead, splashing into the water –

– a moment of relief that he had finished with it, that he need not waste time retrieving it, then he realized that Lane, his own task completed and startled by the noise behind him, had lurched across the cockpit to look out, leaning his weight too quickly, too heavily against the frame of the door –

– Mac's mouth opening in surprise, even warning, Gant clinging to the rotor head, still straddling the exhaust as if riding a wild horse, Lane realizing what he had done –

– all in the moment that the MiL seemed to shrug, and tilt and drop its nose and port side. The tip of the rotor disappeared beneath the surface, refraction making it appear like an arm put out of joint. A foot or more of it below the water –!

Water lapped against the gunner's cockpit, almost over it; the sea idled over the lip of the pilot's door sill.

'Jesus –!' Gant wailed. The pallet's wreckage groaned. The

150

movement continued. Two foot, three, almost four feet of rotor disappeared beneath the surface. The next rotor was no more than a foot from the water. He could not take off now. Dare not attempt engine start and let the rotors, one after the other and with quicker and quicker beat, plough through four or five foot of water. Breaking each of them, one by one, flinging the body of the MiL about in an approximation of an animal's dying frenzy —

— couldn't, couldn't.

As if an intrigued spectator, the 24-A glided gently, slowly towards them, towing the fuel cell behind it.

The problem had changed. He couldn't use the fuel now, there was no point, but there was no other way to lift the MiL to safety. Pelicans scattered around the approaching helicopter like gulls around a plough as if mocking the stately progress of the 24-A, which finally stood off in the hover about fifty yards away. The sand bar was now like the thinnest of bony fingers. It was diminishing more rapidly now because of its flattened top.

Mac's face, empty with realization, Lane's features stunned with self-blame, the face of the 24-A staring blindly at him. Faces —

The tow-rope slackened, the fuel cell bobbed on the glittering water. Pelicans wheeled and cried in protest, began to settle . . . slack towrope . . . Garcia would drag the fuel cell closer — *why bother*? Slack tow-rope.

Tow-rope.

Fuel first, or tow-rope — *tow-rope* . . .

'Garcia — drag that fuel cell and the pump onto the sand bar . . . then cast off. I want the rope —'

'I can't —'

'You got to, Garcia . . . tow-rope on the tail bumper, you got to pull this baby out of the water. Then we fuel up and I may have time to lift her off under her own power — now, *do it!*'

Garcia immediately headed his MiL towards the sand bar, to a point thirty yards or so away from the 24-D. The fuel cell bobbed behind it, the pump, on a section of pallet unbolted from the main frame, was bringing up the rear of the tiny, futile-looking convoy. Garcia passed over the bar, throwing up a cloud of fine sand, then the tow-rope tautened as the pallet section drove into the bar, wedged, stuck fast.

'Mac, Lane – get the hell over there and untie that rope –!' Into the transceiver, he snapped: 'Kooper, I want you down here now . . . Garcia, stand by when you've delivered him.'

Gant rose, straightened, then jumped down on the port side. The water was closing over the sand bar ever more quickly, or so it seemed. Garcia's MiL had touched its wheels onto the bar, and Kooper had opened his perspex hatch from the gunner's seat. He climbed out, balanced on the boarding steps, closed his hatch and dropped into the swirl of sand raised by the rotors. Garcia lifted and dodged the MiL away from the sand bar, adopting the hover perhaps twenty yards out over the water. Gant ran, floundering in the churned sand, towards the knot of men around the fuel cell and the wobble pump. His hands waved Garcia in closer. Mac was holding the end of the tow-rope aloft like a prize at some championship.

Garcia's MiL danced slowly, graciously in towards them. Mac began pulling the rope towards Gant, Kooper and Lane picking it up, too, like children rushing to join a tug-of-war challenge. Garcia kept pace with them, standing far enough off not to raise sand. The water, instead, was wrinkled and distressed by his downdraught. It looked darker, colder beneath the MiL's shadow. Gant, too, grabbed the rope and the four of them heaved and rushed it towards the uptilted, drunken tail-boom of the 24-D.

'Make it secure,' he ordered.

He returned to the nose section of the helicopter. The water was shallow enough. He stepped into it, feeling with his feet for purchase, for the resistance of compacted sand, as he leaned against the perspex, and pushed. His feet slipped, then gripped. He was up to his thighs in water. He moved around the nose, then checked the sand along the forward fuselage, below the pilot's cockpit. Enough purchase, maybe –

'OK – Kooper, Lane – get her unlashed from the pallet. She has to roll off when Garcia takes up the strain. Come on –!'

Water was lapping gently against the fuselage. He slammed

152

the pilot's door, preventing it from slopping into the cabin. Sensor boom almost submerged, cannon refracted and bent beneath the surface. Forward undercarriage drowned, starboard undercarriage the same –

Kooper, Lane and he unlashed the MiL from the wreckage of the pallet. His knuckles sprouted blood as he grazed them. Kooper swore. The heat seemed intolerable, as if the air had begun to scorch and burn. His lungs felt dry and raw. Every time he glanced up, the sand bar seemed narrower. The pelicans, settled now despite the hovering MiL, seemed to have gathered to watch; superiorly afloat, able to fly simply by rising from the sea.

He straightened his aching back.

'OK, OK – let's get to it. Garcia – ready?'

'Ready, Major.'

'Begin to take up the slack – gently.'

Gant raised his hand, and Garcia's MiL began to move slowly away, along the diminishing spine of the sandbar. Mac stood by the tow-rope where it was attached to the tail bumper. The rope jerked out, rose from the sand –

'Get ready,' Gant warned Kooper and Lane, waist-deep in the water, shoulders leaning against the perspex of the gunner's cabin and the metal of the fuselage.

The tow-rope snapped taut, scattering wet sand. The knots creaked tight. The rope strained. Hold, *hold, you* –

The sandstorm whirled beneath the 24-A, almost obscuring it. It began flinging hard, stinging particles against Gant's face and hands. He squinted into the murk. The rope seemed thinly stretched; like a thread rather than a rope.

'Mac!' he yelled. 'Come and give a hand!'

He splashed into the water, taking up a position near the forward undercarriage. Straining against the bulk and mass of the fuselage. Mac joined them on the port side, his feet just out of the water.

'Heave – for Christ's sake, *heave* –!'

Downdraught from the straining MiL seeped over them like a slow cloud of heavy gas. He closed his eyes against the stinging sand. He heard the others coughing, groaning with effort. The 24-D resisted, solidly unmoving.

Come on, come on, come on, *come on* —!

He heard Garcia increase the power to his engines. The MiL roared. He seemed in darkness when he slitted open his eyes. His feet began to lose what purchase they had been able to find, he began to slip backwards —

'*Come on — heave!*' he screamed.

He fell forward, plunging his face into the churned, sand-filled water. Beneath the water, he could hear the throb of the MiL and some thin noise like a distorted cheer —

He lifted his face out of the water. Twenty yards away, as the sandstorm subsided, its wheels axle-deep in the sand at the end of three long, deep furrows, his helicopter sat with a kind of elegance; upright, rotors drooping gently.

Water sparkled as it dripped from the rotor which had been half-submerged. Lane was on his knees in the water, Kooper was bent double. Mac had struggled up the slope and was staring at the MiL as it rested near the fuel cell and the pump, as if quizzical about their situation.

'OK, let's fuel her up and get off — we haven't got time to spare.'

Lane groaned, got to his feet. Kooper straightened reluctantly. Mac was already moving towards the MiL. Garcia's helicopter hovered over the water, tow-rope trailing in the sea. By the time Gant reached him, Mac had cut through the rope. Garcia wobbled in the air, as if bowing, then headed back towards the sand bar. Gant waved him away. Garcia gave a thumbs-up.

'OK — be back with you, Major, just as soon as I can.'

The 24-A drifted towards the beach.

Urgency was difficult, as if further effort was grossly unfair and to be resented. They should be safe, after what they had done. Instead, Gant felt his muscles crack and protest as they hauled the fuel cell alongside the helicopter, then dragged the pump beside the fuselage. Gant knocked open the fuel cap positioned just forward of the stubby port wing. Mac attached the hose, Kooper locked it to the fuel cell. Then he and Lane grabbed the handles of the wobble pump, and began pushing and pulling back and forth, pushing and pulling.

'We'll spell you,' Gant said. Water sucked around his boots. The sand was dark and wet beneath the wheels of the MiL. He looked at Mac, then added: 'I want enough to get me to the beach, is all.'

Sweat spread where the water was drying on their overalls. Once more, the air seemed to scorch in Gant's lungs as he relieved Kooper at the pump. A cone of heat and humidity surrounded him. Mac's face, opposite his, was reddened, running with perspiration. Kooper relieved Gant. Water splashed audibly, ankle-deep. Lane took Mac's place . . .

. . . When Garcia arrived, panting for breath after trudging along the narrow spine of the bar, Gant climbed into the cockpit of the MiL. Fuel gauges . . . not quite yet . . .

'Garcia,' he called, leaning out of the cockpit. 'Unplug the intakes.' Garcia splashed through the knee-deep water and climbed onto the fuselage. Gant looked at the rotors drooping to port and starboard. Their tips reached down almost to the level of the stubby wings. The sea had begun to envelop the undercarriage once more. Perhaps two or three feet from the rotors . . . fuel gauges . . . ?

He began pre-start. Auxiliary power unit on.

Fuel gauges?

'OK, guys – disconnect.'

'Jesus –!' someone groaned. Gant heard the hose being disconnected, the fuel cap closed.

Gant reached up, after glancing down at the water rising towards the weapons pylons beneath the wings. He pressed the two start buttons adjacent to the throttle levers. He advanced the levers to ground-idle setting. His arm quivered with weariness and a new sense of urgency. If the water beat him *now* –!

The two Isotov engines growled into life. He checked the main panel, monitoring the small percentage of instruments and functions he required to fly the two hundred yards to the safety of the white sand. The whine of the turbines reached a higher

155

note. Water splashed against the weapons load beneath the wings.

He watched Garcia, Mac and the others retreat in his mirrors, wading back through the water. The sand bar had disappeared. They were thigh-deep in water, walking along its hidden spine. He reached up to the throttles and advanced them to their flight-idle setting. The turbines screamed, the rotors quivered, held by the rotor brake. He stared at the rotor tips to port, then starboard. Six inches, perhaps five –

– released the rotor brake. They began moving, turning as if in amber or thick jelly. Slowly, slowly. Distressing the water over which they passed . . . he held his breath. Quicker, quicker –

The rotor disc shimmered, the tips lifting well above the water. The MiL seemed to shuffle, as if impatient but still restrained by the water. His eyes were blinking away perspiration as his left hand raised the pitch lever, increasing the engine power. His right hand eased the column towards him, lifting the helicopter's nose.

The MiL lifted clear of the water and sand as if climbing out of glutinous treacle. The water rippled outwards from the down-draught, puckered by streams falling from the undercarriage and fuselage. He lifted the MiL over the staring, waving group wading towards the beach, heading for the trees.

He began to breathe more easily. He lowered the pitch lever and gently applied pressure on the rudder pedals. He dropped the helicopter high up on the beach, the fine white sand beyond the tideline whirling up around the cockpit. Then the thought struck him –

– the Galaxy . . . did it make Karachi?

in foreign places

Dmitri Priabin watched the dog's tail wagging lazily just below the television set. He was leaning one elbow on his desk, holding the telephone receiver to his ear. Nodding occasionally, as he listened to the surveillance report on Valery Rodin from one of Dudin's teams attached to the Tyuratam office. They were established in an empty flat opposite the refurbished mansion where Rodin owned — *owned* not rented — a small, expensive apartment.

On the television screen, half a world away and hours earlier, Soviet ice-skaters danced a jigging, doll-like finish to their routine and bowed, then slid towards the camera that would study their faces while they waited for their marks. Another of the endless repeats Soviet television relied upon to fill its programme schedule. The movement of the dog's tail seemed dismissive of their performance. He watched the skaters' shiny, heavily-breathing faces, grinning; and recognized a common identity with them. They were spiritual cousins. Their marks stuttered along the top of the screen. Disappointing. Behind the East Germans. He sensed their anxiety, but without his customary cynicism. They might well be anxious for their new flat with all mod cons . . . would the second-ranked Soviet pair overtake them, take over the flat? He smiled. It was what they were all after — just as he was — a flat on the Kutuzovsky Prospekt. The place had never seemed as inviting to the skaters or to himself as at that moment.

He recognized that his mood had lightened.

'He's been what?' he asked sharply, startled out of his half-attentive mood. A photograph of Rodin lay clipped to the first page of the file opened on his desk. The narrow, sensitive face looked up at him scornfully. The eyes were sharply focused, not as they must be now . . .

The marks for artistic impression were better. The skaters waved with renewed energy. They might yet get to keep their flat on Kutuzovsky Prospekt.

He listened carefully. 'You're certain?' he asked.

'Yes, sir. Silver spoon, sniffing it right up his little red nose, sir,' the KGB man assured him. 'He's practically in a dead faint right now, stretched out on the bed . . . silk sheets, sir,' he added leeringly.

'After drinking, too?'

'Yes, sir. Brandy and coke.'

Priabin laughed. 'Tell me about the telephone calls.'

'Must have made twenty, sir. Do you want the exact log?'

'Not now. Just your impressions.'

Other skaters smoothed onto the ice, bowed and curtsied. Canadians, threatening the Russian medal places.

'Most of them were to members of his little gang, sir. The booze, barbiturate and buggery boys.' Again, Priabin chuckled. 'Tried his father a couple of times, but the general's down at the assembly building – they're rolling out the booster this morning –'

'I know.' He'd watched, from his window. 'Go on.'

'All his friends hung up . . . couldn't wait for him to get off the line. They must have decided he's caught AIDS, mm, sir?'

'Get on with it.'

'We've got everything on tape. The bug's working a treat at the moment. He's been crying and shouting all over the place, pleading and begging . . . right little Bolshoi Theatre star in the making, he is. I almost feel sorry for the poor little sod . . . ?' He offered the remark tentatively, as if testing the water of his colonel's bigotries.

'Daddy's put him out of circulation, then?'

'He did order some groceries, sir – and a lot of booze. That was before he started calling his friends.'

'He's been told to stay in. And not to talk to anyone, no doubt.

158

Now, watch him carefully – I mean *carefully*. I want him soft, pliable, but not useless. When you think he's ready for a visit, call me and I'll come over straight away. When he's lonely enough to *talk* to me.'

With their telephoto lenses and high-powered glasses they were just a few floors above and almost directly opposite. They couldn't miss the signs. Rodin had no need to draw his curtains for hours yet – and before nightfall, he should be ready.

'Sir, we won't miss him picking his nose or scratching his bum, if that's what you want.'

'Anyone else watching him –?' He broke off as the door opened. Katya Grechkova entered, a sheaf of papers and files held against her breasts. He waved her to a seat opposite him. She turned her attention to the skaters, but only momentarily. The second-ranked Soviet pair were on the ice now, gliding into a lift and throw. The girl, in emerald-green and white, flew through the air and landed safely, '– that you can see, that is?' he finished.

'Don't think so, sir.'

'Make as sure as you can. I shan't want to be seen going in there, when the time comes. Stay out of sight. I don't want GRU interested . . . we are *not* interested in Rodin ourselves. Got it?'

'Invisible men, sir, me and Mikhail.' Priabin heard a distant chuckle. Mikhail was at the camera's eyepiece or the surveillance glasses on their tripod.

'Keep it that way,' Priabin replied drily, putting down the receiver. He tapped at his teeth with his thumbnail. A moment of irritation on Katya Grechkova's pale, freckled features, as Priabin looked up at her. 'What's all that?' he asked.

'Kedrov, sir.'

He waved his hand almost dismissively. Grechkova was punctilious in her respect for his rank. It had taken months to persuade her that it was largely unnecessary, entirely unsought. He watched the dog get up, stretch, idle its way as if propelled by the wagging of its tail over to Grechkova; who fondled its shaggy hair, stroked and patted it. The dog licked her hand.

Then she looked up, as if caught out in some dereliction of duty. Priabin saw the vulnerability that normally remained private. She had an estranged husband in the army – this military district, but at army headquarters in Alma-Ata. Had the husband ever seen that small, vulnerable look? She was in the process of obtaining a divorce. Priabin was certain, and relieved, that she carried no torch for her commanding officer. Though he liked her.

'Anything new?' His tone was detached, but not without interest; though he had come more and more to persuade himself that the solution to his problem lay with Valery Rodin. Who knew everything about *Lightning*, without doubt . . . and who helped *kill* Viktor! Though if he found Kedrov, the agent-in-place, of course it would do a great deal of good.

'It's not confirmed, sir – sorry . . . it seems the GRU may have discovered his hiding-place a few hours ago – no, he wasn't there,' she hastened to reassure.

Suddenly, Kedrov was infinitely desirable, captive. The GRU mustn't get hold of him before he did.

'Thank God,' he breathed. 'Where?'

'An abandoned silo complex. He was camped out there, as far as I can discover. But he must have heard them and got away. It's here, sir. Only gossip, but it sounds likely to be true.'

'What else have we got?'

'Not much.'

She tossed her head after frowning over a summary sheet on her lap. She stood up and passed him the documents, tapping at the top sheet, running her unpainted nail down the list it contained. She placed the file on Kedrov over the picture of Rodin.

The second Soviet couple had finished their routine. Good marks for technical merit.

'Hm . . .' He studied the digest of reports on Kedrov – friends, acquaintances, hang-outs, social habits, sexual involvements . . . there really was very little that was new. It was the file of an agent who had disappeared; a spy there seemed little more to learn about. 'Not much, is there?' he commented finally, lifting

160

the file nearer to him so that the picture of Valery Rodin was once more revealed.

'Sorry,' Katya replied, as if being personally blamed.

Rodin's features stared up at Priabin. Just a matter of time now, he thought . . . and felt the impatience vie with the sense of danger. Was he being reckless? Did the danger attract as much as the hope of a solution? I'll get the bastards, Viktor, any way I can, he swore silently, reaffirming a purpose, clouding his self-doubt.

'Can't be helped,' he murmured. He flicked over the pages of the file. Drinker, occasional lecher, cinema-buff, hi-fi enthusiast, bird-watcher . . . his hobbies seemed to offer little or no illumination. 'No, there's nothing here,' he sighed.

Concentrate, he instructed himself sternly. You *have* to find him before the GRU – time's running out, if they're chasing close behind. If they find him first, whatever he knows or doesn't know, you'll be right in the shit! They'll find out you knew all about his activities and never let on.

'Is anything wrong?' Katya asked. He looked up abstractedly. 'What –?'

'Is anything wrong?' she repeated. She pursed her lips as she saw his face become secretive, closed. 'You look worried.'

'I just wish we could find him, Katya. We have to, before those goons in GRU do the job for us. If they even suspect that we were onto him and let him get away – you can imagine the consequences in *this* place!'

'Why are they looking for him?'

'Presumably, just because he's missing from his work . . . let's hope it's nothing more.' He shook his head. 'They can't know anything, not yet.' He stood up and thrust his hands into his pockets. Then he crossed to the window. The booster was almost out of sight now. A snail-like hump in the distance, without real shape or identity, way beyond the assembly building which still contained the shuttle and the laser weapon. Sunlight gleamed on metal; everywhere. 'He could be anywhere out there,' he murmured. 'But *where*?'

'Don't they always run to somewhere they *know*?' Katya prompted.

'Mm?'

'To feel safe?'

'Oh, yes . . . that's the theory, anyway.' His attention had moved from the main assembly complex and the railway leading towards the distant scrawl of gantries which marked the launch site, towards the chimney smoke which was shaded like charcoal scribble along the horizon above the serrated silhouette of Tyuratam. Rodin was there, he thought; he has the key. I know where to find *him* –! 'Yes, they do,' he repeated. But not Rodin – he doesn't feel safe in his flat, just abandoned.

Impatience seized him once again, and he turned abruptly to Katya. She was looking at him, awaiting orders. He wanted to ignore her and leave at once, but her gaze seemed to prevent him. He must attend to the matter of Kedrov. He sighed and threw up his hands.

'Well, my lady – have you any suggestions?' he asked good-humouredly. Katya wrinkled her nose as if she suspected patronage in his familiarity.

'I – well . . .'

'Come on,' he chided, 'just because I've been slow on the uptake and have only just realized you've got an idea. Out with it. Don't be coy.'

'I'd like to look at the abandoned silo, and try to assess how much he'd *prepared* the hiding-place.'

'OK. Unless it's staked out or sealed off by GRU. Now – why?'

'If he'd had it in mind for weeks, then there might be another place somewhere else just like it . . . the GRU will be busy searching every other abandoned silo and underground complex.'

'And get to him first? They've got the troops to do it –'

Katya shook her head. 'He's not stupid. He wouldn't use two hideouts that were exactly the same.'

'So – where and what?'

'Hide – hideout,' she replied mysteriously. Her pale cheeks were slightly flushed; self-congratulation and excitement. She was clever, intuitive, thorough. This was one of her little leaps in the dark. He smiled, encouraging her to explain.

162

'Well, it's flimsy, but –'

'Come on, Katya, forget the false modesty. You don't believe that for a moment!'

'Bird-watching. Something he took up about a month or so ago, that's all. His latest hobby. Soon after he started using the transmitter to talk to the Americans, as far as we can tell.'

'Yes? Go on.' Priabin felt an unfocused excitement. It sounded like nonsense, but –

'He'd never shown an interest before that. There are maybe a dozen or more applications in his name for passes into prohibited areas.'

'To assist his spying?'

She shook her head vigorously. 'Not in the marshes, it wouldn't. Mostly that's where he wanted to go. The reason he gave was ornithology. Time and again – ornithology.'

'Well? You searched his flat. Did you find his books, notes and sketches?'

'Yes.'

'Well?' He had caught her excitement like an infection. Rodin receded in his mind. His gesturing hands hurried her theory, her guesses.

She tugged her halo of tightly-curled red hair back with her long fingers. 'A couple of very ordinary books. I checked them out.'

'He's a beginner, it's a new hobby.'

'I realize that. The binoculars could have been a lot better. His notes are OK – but they don't improve. He's an enthusiast in everything he takes up – spends money on his hi-fi, on cinema history books . . . here, he hasn't. But he went out a lot. I don't think he was *learning* anything.'

'Sketches?'

'A few attempts.'

'A cover, then?'

Katya shook her head. 'Not quite – but not a *real* hobby. Not important enough to him to justify so many trips to the marshes.'

'Then –?'

'Then that's where I think he might be – sir,' she added

163

carefully, looking away from his praising smile. He grabbed her by the upper arms and stood her up. He was laughing.

'Get on with it – and tell *no one*, understand?'

'You mean –?'

'I mean you could be right. Or you might be wrong. Find out!'

'Yes. Now?'

He nodded. 'Now. Take the dog with you, too . . . you know how he likes your company. Misha, come on, boy – walkies with Auntie Katya!'

The dog, which had returned to the rug in front of the television, shook itself upright, its great tail banging from side to side. Katya grinned at it.

'Come on,' she murmured coaxingly. 'Thank you, sir.'

'Find something, that's all I ask. And, go carefully . . .' His own impatient excitement possessed him once more. Tyuratam, the apartment of a privileged young officer, a drugged man sprawled on silk sheets . . . he couldn't wait much longer. He'd talk to Rodin today, hit him hard, get at the truth –

Things were moving. The inertia of events swept him up. He ushered Katya from the office, his hand firmly on her shoulder. The dog waddled ahead of them down the corridor.

'Take a gun,' he warned softly. 'Just in case.'

The sea shimmered in the afternoon sun. It was slightly cooler in the shade of the palms. Netting covered the two MiLs, reducing them to shapeless lumps without purpose or identity. They were parked, like automobiles, as close to the treeline as it was possible to land them. The tide had began to retreat – its depth, as he knew because he had swum out there, would have been enough to submerge the helicopter on the sand bar. The flotsam of his impact had been drawn slowly, garland-like, out to sea. The pelicans were diving for fish or floating like toys on the glaring water. The dead and maimed ones had been taken away by the retreating tide.

Gant wiped perspiration from his forehead. Mac lay near him, smoking, propped on one elbow like a holidaymaker reading a paperback. His posture suggested rest, but the nervous tension induced by waiting – four hours of it now – seemed electric in the heavy air. Kooper and Lane dozed or chatted desultorily, disguising the passage of time. Garcia was in the cockpit of Gant's MiL, taking his turn on radio-watch; waiting for the signal that must arrive, and soon . . .

The Galaxy had made it to Karachi. To be precise, it had put down with the last dregs of its usable fuel at the military airfield west of the city, and only by declaring an inflight emergency. Anders' voice, almost unrecognizable as it emerged from the decoding process of the quick reaction terminal attached to the satellite transceiver, had told them –

– *wait, just wait.*

Four hours of waiting . . . reassurances had come through the communications system Gant would use over Afghanistan and inside Soviet airspace, but no decision; no permission. The mission was still like flotsam on this beach, its clock running away, racing ahead of them. He had to be in Peshawar by the evening, with a thousand miles of enemy airspace to cross to Baikonur. Six hours' flying, minimum. And he had to reach Baikonur that night.

Pakistani airforce jets had made two passes overhead, three hours earlier. Swept down at them, and passed seawards, into the haze, glinting like midday stars. Establishing the fact of a covert mission stranded inside their territorial border. Gant and Anders hoped the mounting nervousness would lead the government in Islamabad, however outraged, to agree to Anders' request – in order to move on the unwelcome visitors, camped like gypsies on the beach.

No sign of people. The coastal strip was virtually uninhabited; barren, infertile, the palms simply a margin between sea and desert. A ship passing along the horizon and making a thin smudge of smoke hang there long after its silhouette had disappeared beyond the nearest headland. Otherwise, nothing. Gant looked at his watch once more; it was a nervous tic.

Three. It would take them almost two hours to reach Karachi, and the Galaxy would take another two hours to reach Peshawar. Seven at night before they crossed into Afghanistan . . . and they had to *wait, just wait* – while time ran out.

Despite his tinted pilot's glasses, he squinted at the sea and the heat haze. His eyes felt tired, strained, and his body somnolent; as if he were within the context of a restless night's sleep, half-waking, always shifting position. The sense of unfairness remained with him . . . they had done enough to *earn* Islamabad's wink and nod, enough to get out of here.

'Major!' Garcia called. 'Anders.'

Gant hurried to his feet, as if startled by danger. Mac looked up, Lane broke off the sentence he had begun. He strode towards the MiLs, lifting the netting and ducking beneath it. Garcia's face was strained with expectation. He handed Gant the lightweight headset, who snatched at it, tugging it on.

'Anders?'

'Gant.' The strangeness of the remote, toneless voice was unsettling as it emerged from the decoding process. Similarly, Gant's voice would be somehow dehumanized aboard the Galaxy as Anders listened. 'Gant – it's OK. Mission continues.'

'Thank God,' Gant murmured. Garcia crossed himself with a fervent detachment. 'Can we leave now?'

'Immediately. To rendezvous at . . .' He gave the map reference, then repeated it. '. . . with Pakistani helicopter units offshore. They'll bring you in – in disguise, sort of. Wolves in sheep's clothing. Fly an offshore routing to avoid visual sighting before the rendezvous point . . . you got that?'

'I copy.' Garcia was holding the relevant map, folded in deep creases, in front of Gant. He saw the rendezvous point clearly. Ten miles offshore . . . they'd go in like a flock of low-flying birds, two MiLs submerging their identities within the flight of Pakistani airforce helicopters. Anders had done well.

'OK. Good luck.'

'How high was the price?'

'You wouldn't believe it, Gant. The President is not pleased. Your debt is climbing.'

'The hell with that. I'll report when we're airborne. See you, Anders.' He threw the headset into Garcia's arms. Grinned. Felt

166

his body shaking with relief. 'OK, Garcia — let's get moving. Close formation, you fly to port of me and a little behind. Constant visual surveillance, and fifty feet off the water. OK?'

'OK, Major —'

He had already turned away from Garcia, lifted the netting, and was shouting towards Mac, Kooper and Lane, all on their feet, like customers waiting for some store to open.

'Let's move it. We're back on the ice!'

Priabin had never before experienced, in quite such a satisfying manner, the *charm* of unsuspected surveillance. Powerful glasses on a tripod, their twin black snouts hardly jutting through the slight gap in the net curtains; the camera's long, long lens beside them. The pleasant ache in his back after stooping for a long time to the eyepieces, the numbness in his buttocks after perching on a hard chair for some time. The aches of a gardener satisfied with his day's work, or a man who has harvested successfully. The beer and sandwiches in the darkened room and the surprising camaraderie among unseen watchers.

It was just after dark now. He straightened up once more, sighing, his hands cradling his back. The glasses were now night-vision binoculars which rendered the world in shades of grey, adding to that inevitable sense of the unreality; the person under surveillance being an object not a human being.

There was special film in the camera. Each of the surveillance instruments had its own pleasure to give. The tape recorder linked to the phone-tap, voice-activated. Rigged to record even their own telephone reports. The laser eavesdropper, which collected the vibrations of a windowpane as it quivered in sympathy with a human voice, had developed a fault, and stood, as if it had transgressed, in one corner of the bare, carpetless room. Priabin shifted his weight from foot to foot. It was easy to let time slow down. He *possessed* Rodin, like this.

Power, that's what it was, in the end. He'd spent what? More than three hours just watching, doing nothing. He made himself move. The other two men in the room, Mikhail and Anatoly, stirred like large, impatient cats. The room smelt of waiting, dust, pungent garlic sausage and beer. And heady, cheap tobacco.

'OK, he's as ready as he'll ever be. I'm going over,' he announced.

'You'll want to be wired, then, sir,' Mikhail observed, moving to one of the suitcases lying on the other side of the room. His companion, Anatoly, dragged a chair to the tripod and at once sat down, adjusting the focus of the night-glasses, humming tunelessly.

'No. Not this time.'

'Sir?'

Anatoly had stopped humming.

'Just take it from me – it could prove safer. He won't tell, *I* won't and you won't . . . whatever I learn. But I don't want any record around of my conversation with the lieutenant the military might get their hands on.'

'OK, sir, if that's how you want to play –'

'Mikhail – believe me. Something big is going on. I can feel it in my water. *He* knows about it, the fairy prince over the way. He'll tell me, if I can persuade him. Now, where does that leave *us*?'

'We've got the message, sir. What we don't hear, we can't let slip,' Anatoly murmured without turning around. 'We'll play dumb.'

'Good. Right, I'll be on my way.'

'Shouldn't one of us –?'

'You think he's *dangerous*?'

'Little bugger could be desperate, sir. Could come to the same in the end.'

'He's up to his eyeballs in coke. I think I can handle him.' He clicked his tongue against his teeth. 'All right,' he added, 'if you see me struggling on the bed with him, don't assume I've fallen for his boyish charm – get over there on the double.'

Mikhail laughed, an explosive noise in the darkness.

'OK, sir.'

Priabin sensed their alertness, all the tiredness of routine and familiarity erased. He picked up his greatcoat and pulled it round his shoulders. Straightened his jacket and tie. First impressions –

168

His boots sounded heavy on the floorboards. He closed the door behind him, walked down the short hallway and opened the flat's front door. The corridor was empty. As he waited for the lift, he felt the place's chill, received its smells of cooking and electricity, heard its murmurs. A number of television and radio sets, laughter. It was a squat, modern block of flats spilling from the science city's boundary and encroaching on the most northerly street of the old town; it loomed over the grander, older house – some Tsarist businessman's idea of a town mansion – where the apartments were allocated to military, top scientific personnel, mistresses. The flats were bought and sold, exchanged for large favours, promotions, used as bribes.

The concierge watched him leave the foyer. He pushed through the revolving doors into the icy chill of the evening. The temperature had plummeted. He stood for a moment looking up at Rodin's windows, two of them lit. He saw again the young man lying on his silk sheets, as if he still watched him through the glasses; or hurrying to the lavatory to be sick; drinking but unable to eat. Afraid. Posed with his sunken head in his hands on the edge of the bed, staring at the carpet and desperate for the telephone to ring. He was ready to crack open like the pod of a plant and spill the seed of his information.

He sighed with satisfaction as he poised himself on the edge of the pavement. Then he crossed the quiet, narrow street, hunching his greatcoat up around his neck. The wind seemed to pass through his clothing with casual, biting ease.

There was carpet in the wide hall. The concierge, summoned by means of the speaker to one side of the door, ushered him in with slight but evident deference. Complicity smoothed his features. He would say nothing, unless directly questioned by someone more imposing than a KGB colonel. Priabin nodded meaningfully at him and took the stairs two at a time. The concierge had no interest in whom he might be visiting.

Outside the door of Rodin's apartment, he was aware of the degree of quiet luxury around him, foreign even to a colonel in his service. Foreign to *him*, anyway.

The carpet was thick beneath his soles, betraying where he had walked. Wool, pure wool. The door was perhaps the original one, whatever alterations had been made to the house. Panelled wood, dark with stain and age. He did not remove his cap as he pressed the doorbell. First impressions –

He felt subdued by his surroundings, and needed to offer Rodin an image of immaculate authority. He must look as if he meant business, would be satisfied with nothing less than the truth, the whole truth, nothing but . . .

He pressed the bell again, held it, heard its shrill summons from beyond the door. Hoped Rodin had not passed out. He'd been sitting on the edge of his bed when Priabin left the other flat, holding his head gently like some delicate, ripened fruit. He had been awake – but in what fashion? Had he left it too late? He became aware of the emptiness of the corridor and the staircase behind him. He was an intruder here, making a secret visit. He thought of Viktor Zhikin, and felt the heat of his body mount to his face; his cheeks burned. He *had* to be awake –!

He kicked the lower panel of the door, savagely. A weak, almost pleading grumble reached him from behind the door. It opened.

He saw a pale-blue carpet, flowers in a tall vase that had begun to droop and fade. Priabin straightened. Immaculate authority He stared into Rodin's sunken eyes and saw them flinch with recognition and anxiety.

'Good evening, Lieutenant,' he said with overflowing confidence. 'I think it's time we had a long chat, don't you?'

He studied Rodin's features. Saw deterioration and experienced satisfaction. He had chosen the right moment. There was tiredness and empty loneliness; dark blue rings under the pale eyes.

'May I come in?' His hand pushed authoritatively at the door.

'I – I, what do you want?' The eyes finally narrowed against a realization of danger. 'Who – what do *you* want?' His drugged awareness picked up disconnected phrases.

'To talk to you, Valery.' His hand pushed the door further open. Large rooms beyond Rodin's narrow shoulder, pale, rich carpeting, ornaments and prints. Just as he had seen through the glasses. It seemed to Priabin, not without irony, like a glimpse into the West from the far end of a long tunnel.

'Why?' Stubborn anger now, gathering slowly like a storm. 'Get out –'

'No.'

He turned Rodin's body with the hand that still held his gloves, propelling him into the apartment's long hallway. Rodin accepted the inertia of his entry and moved ahead, his feet shuffling, his body leaning slightly against the strong hand's certainty, as if grateful.

Prints of hunting scenes and the French Impressionists, red walls set against an almost white carpet. An extravagance of rugs. Priabin could imagine loud rock music and laughter from past parties. He shunted Rodin into the main living room. All the time he had been whispering to him as to a child being shepherded into the dentist's surgery. Rodin seemed to accept the spurious comfort and the imposed situation.

As Priabin had moved through the hallway and past the rooms, he realized that the image through the glasses had not conveyed the wealth here, the possessions, the splashes of carpet, rug, picture, vase, ornament, hi-fi, record collection. It wasn't the taste, simply the income . . . the *influence*, he corrected himself, that could obtain all these things for a mere lieutenant. Cushions, jade, heavy drapes, his thoughts catalogued.

He pushed Rodin gently into a deep beanbag of a chair. The young man adopted a yoga-like posture, arranging his dressing-gown to tidiness. His eyes were blue and blank. He seemed to be staring at his visitor's boots intently. As Priabin lifted his head, he saw the extravagant coving and the plaster frieze of shepherds around the main light fitting. The room suggested the existence of an elite beyond that of his own service. There, the wooden dacha amid the trees was the best that might be hoped for. Obscurely, the room angered him. He was not the simple son of a peasant, his father had been a schoolmaster and Party member, with a medal from the Great Patriotic War . . . he'd seen the red banners rise above the shattered, grandiose buildings of Berlin. Seen the Fascists finished off –

And now this. People in the People's army with all this —!

The ceiling was the last straw. Priabin wanted to smash something. Rodin, preferably. His horizons, despite his loyalty to the Party and his father's loyalty before that, had been founded by ceilings without covings, by walls with new-plaster cracks. Rodin was pre-Revolutionary, belonging to the military aristocracy. Almost a class enemy. Careful, he warned himself. He shrugged off the clichés that had begun to run in his thoughts.

He moved closer to Valery Rodin. And sat on the floor, cross-legged in front of him.

'Tell me,' he said softly, his hand touching the sleeve of Rodin's dressing-gown. 'Tell me about it.' His greatcoat, after he had removed it from his shoulders, lay at his side like a large, untidy dog. He placed his cap and gloves on top of it, making himself look younger, less official. Sympathy, not envy, he cautioned. Pat his arm, but gently . . .

Rodin's features seemed engaged in an effort to regain an attentive pattern around his nose and mouth. The cocaine, as a stimulant to the nervous system and taken, no doubt, to help him climb out of the pit of loneliness his father had condemned him to, had lost its effect. It had been defeated, to some extent, by the brandy. He was now quiescent, but deeply introverted and depressed. Priabin felt himself little different from a bomb-disposal officer approaching a suspicious device.

Rodin's pupils were like shrivelled raisins in his chalky face. Acute paranoia, Priabin recalled from somewhere. Large doses of cocaine and acute paranoia. The bomb might explode – worse, it might be a complete dud and not go off at all. He continued to pat the young man's arm. Rodin did not respond to the contact. Eventually, Priabin said:

'Tell me, Valery – who's locked you up in this expensive cell?' He shook Rodin's arm gently, but the lieutenant dragged it away from his touch. He scowled because his features could not find a sneer of contempt quickly, then the look soured into a drooping snarl.

'Get out,' he whispered, blinking his eyes to make them focus.

Priabin shook his head. 'I know you want company, Valery,'

he asserted. 'You're all alone here. They've seen to that, haven't they?'

Perhaps ten seconds later, Rodin nodded. Once the action had commenced, he continued to nod, like a doll. His breathing was loud and ragged; his lips quivered and his eyes appeared damp.

'Your father . . . ?'

'*Of course my bloody father!*' Rodin hugged his arms around himself, turning into the beanbag, drawing his feet up. His whole body shivered. He began to sob. His voice had seemed to tire after the scream. 'Always my bloody father . . . he made me go into the fucking army when all I wanted to be was a painter . . .' Priabin glanced swiftly around the room. The walls displayed nothing that might have been painted by the boy. 'No good at it, anyway,' Rodin pursued, 'but he couldn't wait to tell me that.' He looked at Priabin then, who arranged his features to express sympathy. Rodin's voice was a transmission from a distant radio station; fading, indistinct. 'In the bloody army for you, my lad,' Rodin mocked, his face twisted, his hand flapping in a caricature of a salute near his temple. 'In the army, make a man of you –' He turned once more to his listener. It seemed that he did not recognize his visitor; did not care who it was. 'Never admitted it, never, never, never . . . all the army gives you is privileges and a chance to bugger the conscripts!'

He laughed raggedly, staring at Priabin. His attention subsided almost immediately, the world around him rushing into a vague distance. His eyes were inwardly focused, and the retreat seemed more profound. Priabin was greedy to interrupt, to begin to interrogate, but restrained his mounting impatience. But it was a race against time.

'Worse for him, really, now I'm in the army and under his nose. He had to – to keep sweeping up after me . . . cleaning up the turds I leave on . . . his doorstep . . . art, culture, acting don't interest him – queers are forbidden, don't talk about them. My mother knows, she understands . . . can't bear it, but understands . . . he can't though, never has . . .'

Priabin absorbed the room once more. The father paid. Every

173

day, General Lieutenant Pyotr Rodin paid. Drugs, affairs, indiscipline; the general had committed a grave error in having his son posted to Baikonur. Custody must have turned into a nightmare.

Away, he suddenly thought. The next logical step, especially now, would be to send his son away somewhere; to avoid any and all consequences of the interest he had aroused — that Sacha's murder had aroused. That was why the boy was in quarantine. He might have no other chance of talking to him, it had to be now. He had to press —

'Why did they kill Sacha?' he asked bluntly, but not without a sympathetic tone.

Rodin's face paled further around his open mouth.

'What —?' He was attempting to concentrate, to realize that it was cold water that had been thrown over him, to wake him.

'Why did they kill Sacha, Valery?'

'*I* killed Sacha! *I* did it!'

'Why, then, Valery? Had you quarrelled? Out of love?'

'What —?'

'Why did you kill him?'

'Sacha? I didn't . . .'

'You said you did. Did you?'

Tears leaked from Rodin's eyes. He began nodding again like a round-based doll, tilting his whole upper body time after time.

'Yes . . .' he breathed at last. Then: 'Yes, yes, yes, yes . . .'

'How? *How* did you do it?'

Would the paranoia hold? Persecution, the sense of isolation, the depth of misery, all conspirators surrounding Rodin, making him spill his little cargo of guilt.

'How?'

'Yes — how? Did you rig the car?'

'What do you mean?'

'You killed Sacha!'

'*I told them about him!*' he cried out, then curled more tightly into the beanbag chair, into himself. He cringed away from further pain.

Priabin stood up, and Rodin shivered at his movement. The

lieutenant was more deeply withdrawn than ever, almost lost to
him. Priabin crossed the room, looking for the bathroom.

Bedroom, bathroom off, he remembered. Bathroom – yes . . .
light on; drawers, cupboards, vanitory unit marble-topped – my
God! Aftershaves, colognes, shaving lotions, hair spray . . . yes,
expensive make-up, French and American. Whose? Sacha's?

He opened the bathroom cabinet. Nothing he wanted there
. . . not the mouth-washes and the creams . . . drawer? No.
Second drawer? Ah, yes.

Silver spoon, packet. He gathered the items and returned to
the living room. Rodin had not moved. Priabin placed powder in
the bowl of the spoon on its thin silver chain – to be worn around
the neck. If he gave Rodin another dose of cocaine now, the
stimulant might make him high enough, temporarily, to talk
about *Lightning*. He had to be snapped out of depression into
a brief nova of clarity and reckless well-being. Rodin was
huddled still into the beanbag, face almost hidden; completely
unaware.

The telephone rang. White powder spilled from the spoon as
Priabin's hand jumped with surprise. He stared at the receiver on
a table near the windows. It continued to ring.

Warning –?

He'd heard nothing outside. The telephone was reaching
Rodin's sunken consciousness. His face turned, wildly hopeful.
He made as if to move.

Priabin picked up the receiver, but said nothing.

'Colonel –?' Anatoly's voice.

'Yes – what is it?'

'Staff car's just drawn up outside the building, sir. Looks like
the general . . . wait a minute –' He heard Mikhail's voice calling
out indistinctly. 'Yes, sir, it's the general.'

'*Damnation*!' he exploded. 'Is he –?'

'Coming in, sir. On the steps now. Do you want –?'

'I'm coming out. Good work!'

He thrust the receiver loudly back onto its rest. Half out of the
beanbag, as if born from its depths, Rodin's face cracked into
desperation as the call ended.

Priabin looked at him for a moment. Perhaps the concierge wouldn't inform the general, without being asked . . . he might just play it safe, anyway. Even the KGB could give him a lot of trouble . . . no time to worry about it. Quickly, leave him –

He felt cheated and was enraged at the fact. He could have made him talk, he was certain of it, with another shot of cocaine to clear his head, loosen his tongue – he was so *close* –!

His hand clenched into a fist.

Leave –

He hurried into the hall and to the door. Listened. Opened the door, heard footsteps below. Closed the door softly and ran up the short flight of stairs to the top floor.

Holding his breath, he watched General Lieutenant Pyotr Rodin use a key to open the door of his son's flat. From the bend in the staircase, he peered down at the top of the general's cap. The door shut behind him.

'Damn – oh, *damnation*!' he breathed, grinding his teeth. He was possessed by the certainty that he would never have another opportunity to talk to Valery Rodin about *Lightning*.

Anders stood in the chill darkness. The wind from the mountains around Peshawar cut at the small exposed areas of his cheeks and forehead and nose. Gritty dust was whirled against his face. Lights were dotted and clumped on the hills around the airfield, and helicopters drifted unseen, their noises muted, across the plain. Light spilled from the open hold of the Galaxy as the first of the two MiLs was pushed down the ramp from the rear doors and onto the tarmac.

The tail-boom of the *Hind*-D, Gant's MiL, dropped like a signalling arm, then the fat body of the helicopter rolled down the ramp. With furious, controlled haste, the Galaxy's load crew unshipped and re-rigged the rotors – as Gant had done on the sand bar. He watched the crewmen descend, move away. Almost immediately, its rotors began to wind up, after the car-backfire of the engine-start. The noise grumbled upwards, towards the final whine. He held the transceiver absently to the side of his face, where his mouth wetted the fur trim on the hood of his parka. Each time the wind dropped or idled, he could vaguely feel the radiated heat from the Galaxy's huge engines. They had landed no more than seven minutes ago from Karachi . . . it was almost seven-thirty, local time. Seven-thirty, too, in Baikonur, a thousand miles to the north of them. Gant had to be in — and out — while the darkness of this single night persisted. He had perhaps twelve hours . . . eleven . . .

He shivered, from the cold and from the accumulated tension of the flight from Karachi . . . from the tensions of the entire day. It was as if they had infected and reinfected one another in the Galaxy's hold with bad nerves, doubts, anticipatory fear; so that the dimensions of that huge space had diminished, pressing in on all of them. He could still see Gant pacing the hold like an animal in a cage, while his MiL was checked and cleaned, Garcia sitting apart, being worn from within by his anxiety, the others quarrelling over hands of poker.

He dismissed the images. It was out of his hands now. He, like an actor whose lines have all been spoken, had to retire from the stage. Whatever their condition, it was up to them. However hard that was to accept.

Gant shunted the MiL further away from the ramp, juggling the stick and the pitch lever to keep the wheels on the tarmac. The second MiL, the 24-A ferry tanker, began to roll down the ramp into the windy night. Anders was a mere spectator. Swiftly, the 24-A's rotors, too, were re-rigged for take-off. The two Isotov engines coughed into life, and the rotors began moving, shimmering in the thin moonlight. Hard stars glinted between banks of white cloud. Involuntarily, he glanced away from the two Soviet helicopters, towards the mountains, into Afghan airspace. He cocked his head, no longer able to hear anything except the noise of the MiLs; the decoy helicopters patrolling up and down the border did not seem convincing.

The MiLs bobbed, their wheels hardly in contact with the tarmac of the runway farthest from the tower and the airfield buildings. He depressed the button of the transceiver. His lips tasted the fur of the parka's hood as he spoke.

'Gant? Are you receiving me?'

'Yes,' came the monosyllabic, detached reply; as if its owner had already departed.

'Good luck and God speed,' was all Anders could find to say after a moment of hesitation.

He shivered. His voice had seemed high and piping amid the turmoil of engine noise and the quiver of his nerves. This is what he had wanted – and now, somehow, he felt guilt approach like a sly messenger, with bad news. It – well, it seemed futile; the MiLs were toys, despite their noise.

'Sure,' Gant replied. His tone might have been mocking, but Anders could not be sure. 'And – yeah, you did OK, Anders. See you.' It hadn't mocked, then.

Gant's *Hind*-D, its camouflage paint palely mottled in the moonlight, rose to the hover and then immediately passed over Anders' head. The downdraught clutched at him, tugged at his clothing, and dust whirled into his face. When he looked again, after furiously rubbing his eyes, he saw through a wet veil the shadows of the two MiLs moving away to the north-west. The Pakistani helicopters waited only a few miles away to shepherd them to the pass that was their chosen crossing point into Afghan airspace. After that, Gant and the others were entirely on their own. He could do nothing; nobody could.

. . . everything has been triple-checked, he caught himself silently reciting like a litany. *All the IDs, the call-signs, the unit, the cover story, everything, everything, over and over . . .*

He felt himself to be an adult attempting, through fear or a crushing sense of inadequacy, to recapture the unquestioning innocence of a child. The litany did not work, it was merely the prayer of an unbeliever.

The noise of the two helicopters, now *Hind*-D and *Hind*-A, gunship and troop transport purporting to belong to the Soviet Frontal Aviation Army and attached to a unit serving in Afghanistan, diminished towards the border. He shivered again and stared at the empty Galaxy. The night surrounded the hard light from the hold and the shadow of the fuselage. The transport aircraft was a remote island in the inhospitable sea of the airfield.

The two vanished MiLs were no more than bottles on water; a cry for help. Unreal, fragile.

Now, he knew it wouldn't work. Too much could go wrong. It was all too *risky*.

PART TWO

Masters of War

'In a world of steel-eyed death
And men fighting to be warm . . .'

BOB DYLAN: *Shelter from the Storm*

bid the players make haste

Gant ran through the moving map display, projected on the main tactical screen, surveying their entire crossing of Afghanistan, a thin, silver snail-trail across the fleeting sequence of maps. Peshawar to Kabul, but keeping well to the east of the capital and its radars and airforce units, and flying through the foothills of the Hindu Kush, which formed a bony radar and infra-red shield. Laghman Province, then Nuristan, Takhar and Kunduz Provinces, before reaching the thick purple line which represented the Soviet border.

Their course stayed as much in the mountains as possible, as far east of the main areas of military activity as satellite surveillance and CIA secret reports from the *mujahideen* fighters could place them. Gant cancelled the runthrough. The main tactical screen went blank. He was flying visually. No infra-red or radar emissions to be picked up. He updated the map display once more, reinstating the current section, matching it to the landscape around him, which undulated now like some great living thing. It was not a mountain range with valleys and hollows and peaks and knife-like passes, but a great, coiling snake; and as dangerous.

The flanks of the mountains gleamed with snow in the bright moon. Garcia's MiL, in his mirrors, was silvered by the light and appeared mottled like a cow because of its camouflage. Mac's helmet, in the gunner's cockpit below him, was like a silver dome. Lights from Mac's screens and displays winked and shone beyond the gunner's shoulders.

He glanced at the fuel gauges. They would not have to set down to refuel until they were far inside Soviet territory, maybe not for two or three hundred miles. The return flight had a critically small margin of fuel. Once they abandoned the second MiL, they would have just enough, *just* enough, to fly the same route home . . .

. . . while *they* waited, alerted and watching for them, all along the thousand miles of desert and mountain.

He dismissed the thought. It interfered with this phase of the mission, to remain undetected in Afghan airspace.

They were seventy miles north-east of Kabul, skirting the mountains that contained the fertile Panjshir Valley. Ahead of them, another hundred and fifty miles to the Soviet border. An hour's flying at their present speed and without deviating from their plotted course, which was already in the onboard computer.

Aircraft activity was heavy, but it was related to a known new push against rebel tribesmen. No one was looking for them, not yet. But it meant that a lot of aircraft and helicopters were in the air . . . his cover, but also his peril. One visual sighting, or straying onto any one of thirty or forty radar screens, and he would be called to identify himself. He wanted to use his radar, instead of relying on eyesight, but it would be like making ripples on a pond, attracting hunting fish. The last time he had briefly employed the radar — counting the seconds it was operating with a mounting breathlessness — he had spotted a high-flying reconnaissance aircraft, slow-moving enough to be an Ilyushin Il-18, moving westward well to the north of them. The flick, too, of a low, fast fighter moving away. They remained undetected. He had switched off the radar gratefully, sweating with relief.

Now, his own radar, and those of Soviet aircraft, were virtually useless in the mountains. The ELINT systems on the lumbering reconnaissance aircraft were incapable of picking them out from the ground-scatter of hills, valleys, snow, rock, rushing water. You're safe, he told himself once more, but the thought struck hollow.

He banked the MiL around the sheer face of a cliff, tilting the rotors away from it. Garcia duplicated his manoeuvre then he, too, levelled his helicopter. Far below, water gleamed in a thin crack. Snow mottled a high peak and lay more thickly in a mountain pass. A black-and-white landscape. At any moment, an aircraft or helicopter could appear, startling him, calling on him for his idents. That danger remained and did not seem to lessen. Minute by minute, it stretched undiminishing into the hours ahead.

He dodged and slunk through the high mountains, the noise of his rotors booming back from rock faces, hollowing down long, narrow valleys.

There were over two hundred assault helicopters stationed in Afghanistan, by Langley's expert reckoning. Two extra could easily be overlooked, especially if their pilots wanted it that way.

On the moving map display, he could pick out the main Soviet airbase at Parwan, the most northerly on their route before they crossed the border. Radar would tell him what kind and degree of activity there was around it . . . but he resisted the clamouring temptation. He flew into an opening where the mountains seemed to part to west and north, and exposed him like curtains being drawn back on a huge, open stage of dark air. He sensed, as well as saw, the moonlight flowing over the MiL, saw its shadow flit and tremble across the valley below. The empty, open sky stretched away on every side –

– hide-and-seek. His eyes quartered the night. Hide-and-seek. He increased his airspeed to one-seventy, and waited – relieved when the noise of the rotors hammered back at him from rock faces as the mountains closed in once more. Cover; the safety of rock.

A stream of Russian, blurting in his headset, alarmed him like the sudden cry of discovery. The radio had been tuned to the principal Soviet Tac-channel as soon as they crossed the Pakistan border. It had been mostly silent until now. The codes Frontal Aviation Army units in Afghanistan used had been broken by Langley; the radio set itself had been reconstructed by DARPA specialists. The voices had been little more than distant, vague whispers.

Until now.

Something was close, perhaps too close.

He turned up the set's volume as the signal frequency locked. It was a . . . helicopter pilot, talking to the AWACS Ilyushin. A quick-fire, sudden, excited burst. What was it? What –? Unidentified radar trace which had disappeared from the Ilyushin's long-range radar screens . . . *your sector*, he heard, chilled.

He had been picked up by the patrolling early-warning aircraft either he or Garcia; it didn't matter which. He listened, knowing that the alerted helicopter would now climb, try to look down, find him again. The interference of the mountains would be like a washing shoal of fish crossing the enemy radar screens. It would obscure any clear blip he might make. At least, he had to hope that would be the case.

Where was it? There was no heading, no positional reference. Where? The Russian continued on the HF set, itself made intermittent by the surrounding mountains. Where? South – *south-east*, he heard, and then the distance. Looking at the moving map display, he knew the MiL was close enough to be dangerous. He must have erupted onto one of the Ilyushin's screens in a clear gap of air where no helicopter flight was logged or expected. He had been visible for long enough to be pin-pointed – but there was no identifying IFF number alongside the blip to explain who he was. To the Ilyushin, he was . . . *unofficial*. If the Ilyushin really started looking –

He wished himself alone, without Garcia trailing behind him and already wound tight as a watchspring. He could not spare the effort, if it really came to hide-and-seek, to watch out for Garcia and his crew when all his energies were needed to stay alive. It was a simple, brute fact.

More voices in the headset; two more call-signs and positions. A routine patrol instructed to alter course, to overfly the *sector in which two unidentified contacts* . . . there was a boyish excitement in the pilots' responses. No one could imagine what kind of unidentified aircraft would be this deep into Afghan airspace – it was probably a false alarm, someone with a damaged radio, u/s

186

IFF transponder . . . but it would be good practice to seek and find, a game, good fun . . .

'Major —?

'Shut up, Garcia!' he snapped into the transceiver near his head. 'Stay close to me.'

He dipped the MiL's blunt nose. Mac raised his hand in the gunner's cockpit. The helicopter's shadow rushed over gleaming snow, down into the cleft of a dark valley. He hugged the ground-clutter like a hedgehog rolling itself in disguising leaves, and pulled the airspeed back to just above one hundred mph. Nap-of-the-earth flying; a feature of all the textbooks. No instruments, no systems — eyesight and reflexes. He felt the exhilarating danger of his plunge. The altimeter unwound with stunning quickness. Garcia, behind him, seemed to fall more slowly than he.

Come on, come on, Garcia —

He levelled the helicopter. Rotor noise boomed back from the pressed-close cliffs on either side. He skimmed down the long funnel of a deep valley-cleft, his eyes and hands aware of each other, his shoulders tense as if the residence of all his reflexes and experience. Stars gleamed at the end of the funnel where the land dropped away. They were cutting across the mountains at the eastern end of the Panjshir, and moving north-east. Off-course, for the moment. Garcia's MiL bobbed in his mirrors like a cork afloat on a rocky sea.

Radio — nothing down here. He had dived into deep water, escaping almost like a submarine by going deep. It was lightless down there, and he had no idea of the whereabouts of the dangerous fish that were hunting him. Safety was a two-edged blade.

Stars, snowfields, a sense of flatness — *are they above?* — a scattering of small lights away to the east of him. The hard stars overhead betrayed no gaps or shadows that might have been the fuselage of a searching aircraft.

Radio — nothing. On the moving map, he pinpointed his position as one hundred miles north-east of Kabul, fifty miles from the airbase at Parwan. Radio —?

Radio.

Russian again. A mobile listening post, for Christ's sake! Here, *here*, close, too damn close!

Langley had logged into the onboard computer and the course coordinates, every major radar installation, every airfield, every helicopter unit of the Frontal Aviation Army serving with the Limited Contingent of Soviet Forces in Afghanistan; every air assault brigade that might have helicopters at its disposal or be flying routine transport missions, every AWACS aircraft and the regular pattern of surveillance flights they undertook ... the satellite diagnosis of their course and its dangers was full, brilliant, almost complete –

– except the mobile radar and listening vehicles. Untrackable, too many to count, scattered over the mountains and valleys. Most of them were deployed further south or west than this.

He had to stall, use the cover story. Invite more danger by averting an immediate threat. He replied immediately, even before his voice had fully unfrozen from shock.

Call signs, idents, radio routine, cover story. It was all there, flashing in his mind like scattered, bright lights. *Give them everything. It will all be so familiar maybe they won't even bother to check.* He knew they would. Someone would. The mission's luck was running that way ... was at the point where he had to begin to think in terms of luck. Kabul contained sufficient of a full army GHQ organization to run down, and disprove, his cover story in a matter of ... in less time than it would take to reach the Soviet border. LCSFA GQH was inside the Soviet Union, at the headquarters of the Turkestan Military District ... but Kabul was good enough and big enough to blow his cover without reference north to GHQ. An unlogged, *private* flight he might call himself, but ...

In his mirrors, Garcia's MiL skimmed over the tiny group of dim lights, over the huddle formed by a bulky, high-sided truck and its screen of a tumbled stone wall, pale in the moonlight. Nothing more than a truck –! The skeletons of antennae and dish aerials threw shadows on the white wall. His passive sensors picked up radar emissions. He *heard* the radio.

'. . . please identify immediately. We do not have you logged. Over.'

Almost polite. His MiL, the *Hind*-D, skimmed on like a flung stone.

'. . . attached to 105th Guards Airborne Division,' his cover story flowed on, 'Kabul. Transfer of top classification documentation from army HQ, Kabul, to Central Asia Military District HQ, Alma-Ata. That's all you're allowed to know, Mobile Unit 476. Over.' Despite his tension, he grinned. The last elegance of the bluff, *not* letting everything spill out with the haste of denial of a child caught with the jam still round its mouth.

Gant's eyes scanned the black, star-pricked sky. Scanned his engine instruments and flying displays out of habit, wishing he could use other sensors and radar but knowing he must now preserve his cover story . . . in such a mission he would be flying visually. Even on the mission he would eventually admit to . . .

They were out there, like sharks waiting to smell blood or feel movement through the water – and the mobile listening post could guide them to him the moment he failed to satisfy it. He could outrun none of the aircraft. He couldn't even outrun another *Hind*.

Peaks loomed ahead. Cover. He scanned the sky, the gaps between the mountains to the west of him, then the north-west – *there*! He swallowed. Red and blue dots that were not stars, but tiny navigation lights winking on two fuselages catching the moonlight.

Cockpit lights, fuselage lights, the silver of metal. Less than two miles away.

'Major –!'

'I see them!' he snapped into the transceiver. 'Leave it to me, Garcia. *Out.*'

Speed of the lights and the flash of metal against the background stars –? MiLs. Gunships, like his own. Drawing his gaze away from them, he quartered the sky . . . no fighters, nothing but the two helicopters. Two against two . . . *come on, come on, swallow the story*! There was no alarm, not yet, no request to the helicopter patrol to investigate.

189

He eased his speed to one-twenty, one twenty-five, checking in his mirrors to see that Garcia was scuttling to keep up with him. Yes.

The mountains of the Khwaja Muhammad range neared, promising obscurity, loss of detection. But they knew he was here, now. Unless they accepted his story and allowed him to continue unmolested and uninvestigated, they would want to find him again. Everyone would want to find him. On how many screens was he pinpointed by now? The two MiLs had him, the AWACS Ilyushin would have seen him, how many fighters . . . ? They *had* to believe his story!

The aircraft, including the Ilyushin, would all be from Parwan; thus his cover story originated his flight in Kabul. The capital's squadrons of MiGs, Sukhois and MiLs operated mainly to the south and west of Kabul, those at Parwan against the rebels in the Panjshir. They would accept his story, *should accept it*. He felt the tension tighten in the wrist and hand that held the stick. Sweat prickled his forehead, spreading like some oily measurement of time as the seconds passed. The ether roared emptily in his ears like the noise of his own blood.

'Helicopter 2704, please confirm your point of departure. Over.'

Digging. Not deeply, but digging. Garcia's image in his mirrors was like a wasp on his windscreen, something dangerously distracting. The 24-A dogged him faithfully, but he was *responsible* for it. The lights of the two MiLs to port seemed to have neared; the two gunships flashed more brightly in the moonlight –

– the mountains crowded ahead like an encouraged illusion. He flicked his *Hind*-D to one side, jumping a ridge of rock like a flea. He lost sight of the two approaching helicopters. He drove into a narrow, high pass where snow gleamed and his own shadow pursued him across its whiteness. Perfect for a visual sighting, a difficult place in which to manoeuvre.

He did not climb or alter course. His first – only – priority was to answer the mobile unit, to answer the single voice before other voices took up the questioning, began to bully for answers.

190

'Origin of flight, Frontal Aviation central airfield, Kabul. Over.'

'Thank you, 2704. Please hold this frequency.'

'Mobile Unit 476 – I am under orders to maintain strict radio silence. Can we get this over with? Over.'

'I'm sorry, 2704. We have no record of your flight-plan logged with Parwan. We have to check with Kabul. Over.'

Gant believed he could see the rigidity of tension in Mac's hunched shoulders just below him in the forward cockpit. The narrow pass opened out ahead. He squeezed the *Hind* over and around a naked outcrop, bobbed over a huge flying buttress of rock, then dropped into a wide valley. He glanced at the moving map. Assured himself of his position, his course.

Checking with Kabul –

Gant hesitated, then gambled; felt an exhilarated fear. *Give them everything . . .*

'Unit 476 – go easy, will you?' the mountains were beginning to break up the signal on the HF radio. But he had to satisfy the unit before he lost contact with it, had to dissipate any idea of pursuit.

He climbed. He bobbed out of cover like a startled bird, hanging in the clear dark sky with the mountains below him. Garcia followed like a cork rising to the surface of the thin air to starboard. Gant slowed his airspeed to less than one hundred, as if someone idling in a conversation, not quite walking away from a companion. Bluff. Whoever was watching would have him pinpointed now. For the moment, he had thrown away all secrecy. *They mustn't check with Kabul . . .*

He wondered whether to employ his own radar, know how many there were out there, and exactly where, then decided against it. If the cover story didn't work, then would be the time to know the odds. The Soviet border was now less than a hundred miles to the north-west of his position at its nearest point.

Now, he told himself.

'Mobile Unit 476 – whoever else is out there – I repeat, go

easy . . .' He scanned the sky. Yes, distant winking stars and the mirrorlike fuselages of the two MiLs. Not hurrying to close the gap of dark air between themselves and him, not yet. *Now* – 'I – look, it's not documentation. We're empty at the moment. Got that? *Empty*. Understand? Over.'

Sweat dampened his shirt beneath his arms. His free hand, having released the collective pitch lever, quivered with tension. Not too much, he hadn't said too much, not yet. Let the revised cover story drip like water onto a stone.

'Helicopter 2704 – please explain. Over.' It was still the voice of the operator from the mobile unit, at the prompting of his officer, who couldn't be more than a lieutenant at most. The MiLs were hanging back, waiting.

'I – it's a private flight. I'll be in trouble with *very* senior people if you check with Kabul. I'm – not supposed to be here. Be discreet, uh? Over.' He grinned quiveringly.

The *Hind*-D was swimming slowly through the thin air, operating close to its service ceiling. Perhaps still a mile away, he could see the two Russian helicopters, their shadows moving beneath them across rock and snow; across the peaks and the high glaciers and icefields. The world seemed shrunken. He could almost believe himself to be in a jet. The Hindu Kush climbed away to the south-east as far as eyesight could reach. A huge army of mountain peaks marching on China through Kashmir. High above him, against the star-filled blackness, he saw the silhouette of something swift – MiG or Sukhoi – crossing his course at perhaps forty thousand feet. He was swimming slowly forward and the hunting fish had caught his scent, his movement.

Come on, tumble it, you bastard. Don't be dumb, his thoughts insisted, their urgency mounting. He willed realization on them. Reach out and grab the answer that's in front of your face. Come on, *come on* –

A minute of silence.

'2704 –' He was startled by an unfamiliar voice. 'Are you on a shopping expedition? Over.'

One of the two approaching gunships was now less than five

hundred yards away, well within rocket or cannon range. It waggled its stubby little wings. A pleased, waddling dog recognizing another dog. He moved his own column, flicking the MiL slightly from side to side.

'Sure,' he replied with evident relief; that would fit the cover story, it didn't matter if they thought he was scared. 'Glad someone understands, at last. Thanks. Over.'

The closest of the two Russian helicopters passed across his nose, slightly above him. The pilot and the gunner, who would have been listening, both waved. The gunner raised one fist, his other hand at the elbow of his bent arm, signifying sex. Gant raised his thumb in acknowledgement.

They understood now; he was explained. It was one of the smuggling runs for senior officers. Runs which were frowned upon then ignored, even encouraged, but were always carried on under a cloak of fictitious secrecy. He might have been on his way to collect sex videos from army HQ, pop records, drink by the case, cigars from Cuba, women . . . oh, yes, most importantly women. Flown in for parties or changed whenever the local girls, the mistresses, or the last imported batch of whores – top-class, indubitably clean and expert – became tired or over-familiar . . . the gunner in the Russian MiL probably imagined he had six or more girls aboard he was on his way to Alma-Ata to part-exchange. He grinned.

The second of the two Russian helicopters slid nearer, as if to contradict hope. Gant swallowed. The pilot of the second one waved, too, then both of them dropped away towards the mountains. He heard the patrol leader inform the mobile unit and the AWACS aircraft and the MiG that had passed overhead of the purpose of his mission. Fantastic detail flew and gossiped over the air. Coarse laughter, envy –

It was working. They were satisfied.

'Christ, Major – you did it – they're going!'

'Can it, Garcia!' he snapped back, hearing the relieved chatter of Garcia and his crew over the transceiver; sensing Mac's relief, his own, too.

'Sorry to have troubled you, 2704,' he heard the original voice murmur, amusement in the operator's tones. 'Good hunting. Over and out.'

'OK,' Gant said into the transceiver. 'Let's ride with the luck while we can. Forty minutes' flying time to the border. But don't count on a free ride all the way.'

'What's wrong?' Garcia asked warily.

'Maybe those pilots have flown sex-missions before – they swallowed it. It only needs some suspicious little Party shit on the AWACS aircraft to call Kabul – just to make sure – and we're blown wide open. So – stay keen.'

'Uh-huh.'

He watched the two Russian MiLs diminishing below and to port. Heading west, back to Parwan. Even if not at once, or in half an hour, someone was eventually going to suspect – *know*. Long before he got to Baikonur and back out again, someone would have checked . . . and they'd be waiting. Looking and waiting. He ground his teeth audibly, then lunged the MiL towards the mountains that stretched away towards the river Oxus where the border lay.

The wind raced almost horizontally across the frozen marshes. Filip Kedrov teetered against its force as he crossed the long, dipping plank of wood from the rotting mooring to the hulk of the houseboat. Thankfully, shivering, he stepped onto its deck, rubbing his gloved hands together with cold and genuine relief. He bent his head into the wind as it sliced down the flank of the houseboat, blowing sleet into and through the gaps in the deck's planking and the panels of the main cabin.

He flicked on his torch, spraying its feeble light around him until he located the steps. He clattered down them, afraid each time one creaked, afraid of falling, of breaking his neck. He shut the doors behind him and wedged them with a thick chunk of wood. Then leaned a decrepit old chair against them, too. The doors rattled on their hinges with the force of the wind. The houseboat groaned and sighed and seemed made of rotting cardboard in the howling wind.

It was small and low and no one had used it for years. Kedrov could not imagine who might ever have done so. Perhaps some officer's sexual hideaway, perhaps it had belonged to someone before the army came . . . one of the entrepreneurs the old town used to boast? It did not matter. It suited him. Long, low, bargelike. Just holding together enough to keep most of the weather out. He saw in the pool of yellow light from his torch that the blankets on his bed were damp; sleet had been blown through cracks in the peeling woodwork and soaked them. His breath smoked in the light-and-dark of the room. He washed the torch over the cabin. He was alone.

He unslung his haversack, laying his torch alongside it on a deal table in the centre of the boat's single cabin. The windows were wet, blank squares of darkness. Swiftly, he drew the thin curtains and pinned them together at each of the windows; it was a practised, almost effortless task. His breathing sounded loudly above the muted noise of the wind. At each window, his breath formed a target-like circle of fogged glass. When he had finished, he returned to the table, then lit an oil lamp which sat in its centre. It smoked and glowed and smelt in the narrow, confined cabin. He coughed.

He needed coffee, some of the tinned food he had stored here a week ago, and a check on the transponder which was his lifeline to the rescue . . . *don't think about it*, he warned himself. Don't *start all that again* . . .

But he knew the thought would return. He had rushed upwards, as if on a child's swing of hope, after his escape from the silo complex . . . he would swing down again, just as certainly.

He drew the transponder from the haversack. It looked like a transistor radio. Cheap, Russian-made, unreliable – thereby attracting even less attention than a Japanese portable would have done. Its cheap look depressed him; as if it foretold the malfunctioning of the thing, indicated that the Americans held him in no great esteem, had spent no money or effort on his rescue . . . *stop it!* Oh, stop it . . .

He was an explorer in a strange new country. All the nervousness, the exhilarating fear and tension of the past weeks of his spying paled into insignificance now, beside these – terrors, which leapt out at him. This was territory he had not visited before, and its landscape enclosed him, wore him down.

Tonight was the earliest they could possibly come . . . but tonight was Tuesday. If they intended rescuing him, if they meant to come, it would be tonight. Had to be, otherwise they would be too late. He understood their schedule, by instinct rather than information. They expected to be able to use the photographs – those he had had to abandon in the paint tins in the lock-up garage – on television, in the newspapers, to expose what was intended at Baikonur; to prevent the launch. They had to get him to the West before Thursday – they knew that . . . thus, tonight was the earliest and the latest they could come . . .

. . . and would not come – oh, stop it, *stop it please –*!

The cheap cabinet of the transponder made it impossible to envisage the complicated microcircuitry inside. If he used it, even then, he would not know whether it worked – a light was supposed to come on, but what would that mean? – and he would hear nothing. It was simply a homing device, sending out a carrier wave which only his rescuers could receive . . . science fiction! His own expertise, his own technical background availed him nothing. He simply stared at a toy he was certain would not work. It had been given to him just to keep him quiet, keep him working . . .

He tried to sigh, but the noise became a sob in his throat. His mouth was filled with saliva, which he found difficult to swallow. He was shaking. He distracted himself by looking at the lamp, trimming it, then at the walls and fixtures of the boat. He had repaired some of the worst gaps in the planking and panelling, he had hidden food here, the lamp, beer . . . He shuddered as he remembered the closeness of his brush with the GRU, hugging his hands beneath his armpits. Hour after hour in the freezing cold, all day and most of the evening, until he had worked his way on foot to this last safe-house. He was intensely weary –

– which was why he was so uptight, so frightened! The explanation paled, overcome by the noise of the wind, the groans of old, rotting wood. Ice – the soupy slush around the hull – grumbled beneath his feet. Sleet puffed like thin cigarette-smoke through gaps in the wooden walls of the cabin.

He slumped onto the bunk, all his anticipation and returning warmth seeming to evaporate. It was impossible to sustain the fiction of rescue here, with the occasional cries of a night-bird and the disturbed honking and barking of wildfowl in the darkness outside. The Americans would not come.

Please let it be tonight, please let it be, he kept repeating. *Please –*

He was worn almost transparent with fear. His doubt had increased, gnawed its way to full growth. He had nothing left, no reserves with which to fight it.

Please let it be tonight, please –

He huddled into himself on the bunk, the transistor radio unnoticed in his lap. Knees drawn up, cradling it. Presently, he began to sob with self-pity.

It was eight-thirty in the evening. He cried, oblivious to the passage of time.

Katya Grechkova took off her spectacles and rubbed her eyes. Looked at her watch. Eight-forty. She yawned, tiredness and satisfaction mingled in the stretching of her arms and back. She stood up, lit a cigarette and walked to the other side of her small office – the office she had shared with Viktor Zhikin. Her head was aching, but its dull throbbing failed to blunt the edge of her pleasure.

She stood near the window, looking back at her desk, at the pool of white light from the anglepoise lamp falling on papers, then stared at its shadows thrown on the Venetian blind. Then back to the desk, posing the scene as if for a forensic photograph; exactly capturing the source of her satisfaction. She puffed on the cigarette with a conscious hint of melodrama. Zhikin had always – not unkindly – teased and joked at her for her fastidi-ous, intense manner of working, the degree of her absorption in any task to hand. As if she were hiding from life in her work, he had once said – her own life, perhaps? Then he had broken off at once, seeing the naked, pained look she could not keep from her face.

She puffed quickly at the cigarette. The room was smoky, the ashtray littered with stubs. She did not want to think about all that, not now. Work was no longer a solace or an escape . . . and Zhikin would never have understood that she was escaping from an insight into herself, not from her husband's character or their failed marriage. Captain Yuri Grechkov had been someone she had suddenly discovered and, in that moment of discovery, contempt had entered and occupied the place of all other emotions. He had failed to attend his mother's funeral; simply not bothered to apply for leave from army manoeuvres. Katya had gone, wearing a black armband on her uniform sleeve. And she hadn't even liked his mother. He'd known she was dying and hadn't returned from wherever he was, hadn't come even after she telephoned to say *it won't be long, can you come at once . . . ?*

Not even for the sake of avoiding the guilt to come, would he break off from his silly army games somewhere in East Germany. It wasn't much, but the revelation was, for her, like a collison with an express train. She seemed to understand him, see his shallowness and indifference, and despised him for his failings.

Her view of him now was more fixed than a photograph; an oil painting, framed and hung. She would never see him in any other pose. What she avoided, what Zhikin would never have understood, was her inability to forgive or make allowances. She had sentenced him, finding him guilty, and there was no appeal.

So, after the weeks of quarrels and silences and shadowy, separate living, she'd left Alma-Ata and got herself posted to Baikonur. Got a flat, a few sticks of furniture from central stores, some prints to replace photographs, which he was fond of taking, developing and framing – mostly of her . . . and begun a new and partial existence on her own. It had taken a long time to accommodate the new knowledge she had of herself. To have made such demands, to have had such standards for him, to have such *ideals* —! She had had to descend from some dreamy, cloud-cuckoo place to a life of daily contempt because of one single failure on his part. He'd shattered her image of him. She had thought herself quite, quite *evil* for a long time, in a little-girl, final way. She could not live with him, could not bear him to touch her —

But all that had faded —

Cold satisfactions, those to be gained from being successful in her work, being adept at it, had sustained her. Those, and the transmutation of Yuri into poor straw — the minute catalogue of his faults and weaknesses — from which bricks could not be made, had pardoned her self-knowledge. Her work was her independence, it made her eager, active, clever, a more flattering mirror than her marriage had ever been. Now, the satisfaction was intense, almost unmarred by memory or insight.

She believed she had discovered where Kedrov the spy was hiding.

She returned to her desk. The dog's tail thumped against her legs as he joined her from his corner of the room. She patted his head, stroked his neck, felt the wet muzzle and nose against her palm. Looked at the map she had been working from.

Her forefinger and index finger, still clamping the remainder of the English cigarette, stroked a slow, diminishing circle around a small area of the salt marshes. The dog wandered away from her other hand. Yuri would not let her have a dog, didn't want the trouble and the loose hairs in their bright, well-furnished apartment in Alma-Ata . . .

She shook her head and replaced her spectacles, which glinted in the lamplight as she raised them from the desk. She bent forward, as if to check something. Yes, just there —

Katya knew the marshes. She'd hiked there often enough to have been able to make her clever guesses. With ease, she could recollect sites on the map in three dimensions. Trees, islets, swampier areas, ornithological hides, hunting lodges — a few of them from before the Revolution, now used by senior officers who imitated the pleasures of an older aristocracy — old, ruined boats and huts, even villages long abandoned, game wardens' cabins.

Kedrov's books and maps lay on the floor. Now beneath the dog, who was looking up at her, eyes wide, tongue lolling pinkly. His eyes were moist with the illusion of devotion. Using the maps and notes, she had narrowed and narrowed her search, until –

– this place. She tapped it on the map. There was a rudimentary sketch in one of his notebooks, a chart warning himself of deep water in one place, of the existence of a hide in another. A hide that had once been a houseboat. Almost in ruins now . . .

So, she felt she had him. Other references, other places in his notes and on his maps were possible, but she had put the old boat at the top of her shortlist. Tomorrow – impatience surged even as she reaffirmed the need to wait until daylight, the need to report to Priabin.

Fortunately, she had not needed to see inside the old silo complex. The DANGER signs, mint-new, that had sprouted everywhere, the fact that her KGB ID card had not got her inside, the soldiers' gossip and the precautions of guards and the barbed wire that had uncoiled like a plague of snakes all over the scrubby, undulating ground – everything told her that Kedrov had been there and had gone.

She snapped awake as the dog stirred on the maps and notebooks, rustling them. Her fingers moved on the map as if she were beginning some incantation. He *was* there – daylight would prove it with his discovery and capture.

She must tell Priabin.

She looked at the dog. If she were careful, very careful . . . She'd drawn a gun, she could use it. She had waders, a torch, a dog from some hunting breed that couldn't have forgotten everything its ancestors had once known, a car, a map –

She grinned, tense with excitement. Shivering with nerves.

Tonight, tonight, *tonight* . . .

She cleared her throat. 'Come on, Misha – *walkies*!' she called out. The dog lumbered to its feet, wagging its broadsword of a tail in delight.

The *Hind*-D's shadow glanced like a blow off the long, hanging beard of a frozen waterfall which pointed like a gesture to flat snowfields, a clump of stone huts, tethered camels and ponies in the moonlight. A shuffling figure glanced upwards out of the folds of a cloak and a long, old rifle swung ready for use. The figure was, in an instant, miniaturized in the mirrors. A white plain broken by a frozen river stretched before the helicopter and its shadow, which raced across the snow, the MiL moving above it like a dark insect.

Gant skimmed the ground at no more than thirty feet. His whereabouts were secret once more. He had picked up no information over the Tac-channel to indicate anyone still remained interested in him. He was, for the moment, safe.

Garcia's helicopter was tight behind him, zig-zagging, skimming, flicking and dancing through the terrain. Garcia had become infected by the exhilaration of danger; now he was alert, confident, flying on instinct and even passion. Yet he nagged at Gant's awareness; a liability, someone to have to be careful for, someone whose mistakes could be fatal.

On the moving map display, the dot that represented his position was well to the north of the Panjshir valley and the airbase at Parwan. He was little more than fifty miles from the Soviet border. Ahead, directly north, lay the main highway from Faizabad to Mazar-i-Sharif, running east to west like the huge river valley of the Oxus which lay beyond it and which marked the border itself. It was flatter land there, less easy to hide in, more populated; roads, railway lines, villages, irrigation canals, airbases and military camps. The golden road to Samarkand.

He glanced at his watch, at the map once more, then around him. Mountains were retreating in the mirrors, the land opening out ahead. Patches of brown rock jutted through the snow, naked outcrops – and a tented encampment was suddenly beneath and alongside them; still lumps that were camels, the flicker of a cooking fire. Dark tents bulging like the backs of huge creatures trying to bury themselves in the snow and sand. The river gleamed. The country had altered. He wanted to use the radar, now that it would begin to be effective, out of the mountains, but he dare not allow any electronic emission to be picked up and pinpointed. Not now, not this close. He was seven hundred and fifty miles from Baikonur. It was almost nine in the evening. He had to make it before daylight – get back out before daylight . . . He crushed all thought of the hours of the return flight, skulking through Afghanistan in broad daylight. He had perhaps nine hours in which to be on his way back – well on his way . . . Haste, haste, his thoughts cried, and his hand twitched on the stick, his eyes glanced at the throttle levers over his head.

Russian from the HF radio, startling in his headset.

. . . positional report, one MiG, he guessed. It was about twenty miles away from him. The AWACS Ilyushin would be there somewhere, too, and the helicopters. There had been no alarm raised, he reminded himself. No one is interested in you. They think they have you pigeonholed. No one is interested. He withdrew his hand from the main panel where his fingers had twitched near the switches that would activate the radar. *No* –

The huge, sandy desert of the river valley was beginning to spread out before him now, beyond a line of low hills. He could now be seen by look-down radar; the ground-clutter was less effective in concealing him in these lowlands. The moonlight gleamed on the fuselage.

If the MiG was alerted, if the Ilyushin picked him up again, would it dismiss him? Would its crew simply chuckle, remember his cover story, make lewd jokes and go back to their routines?

More Russian from the radio. The helicopters. Less than ten miles away, *less*, as they reported in. Why? He'd heard nothing, only routine messages and few of those . . . but he'd been hiding in the mountains and the radio had squirted with static for whole seconds at a time. He'd lost contact with them on numerous occasions, so how could he know what they'd said to each other?

He must stop.

He studied the terrain. As yet, there was no need to refuel. He felt urgency prick at his skin, invest his stomach. The land was bare and inhospitable. Should he go to ground in it? Until he could assess the situation – without giving them the opportunity to fix his position and course – should he?

The *Hind* flipped over a ridge and the land rose once more as he approached the line of snow-capped hills. The Oxus and the border lay just beyond those hills, at the end of the valley of the Kokcha river which would be empty of water until the spring thaw in the mountains to the south of him. He dabbed at buttons and the computer bled into the moving map the disposition of watchtowers, camps, radar installations, listening posts, patrols. The border sprang to life, gleamed on the map's colours and contours.

In the dry river valley of the Kokcha, then. Somewhere. Shunting the two MiLs beneath some overhang, some tuck in the terrain, to wait until the situation could be assessed, analysed. They were too close and not accidentally close, he believed. They were still interested, though for the moment they could not find him.

He gained altitude because there was no defile that he could see. He was climbing to cross the hills but climbing into radar sight, too. His shadow chased him across the sheets of snow and the bare ridges of rock.

Tension prickled his hairline, made his shoulders ache. He shifted to greater comfort in his seat, feeling the harness cut into his body. The silvering moonlight pried over the cockpit. He increased speed to one-seventy, one seventy-five, and Garcia and their two shadows raced across the bare hills with him. He felt exposed, naked. The MiG and the MiLs might not pick him up, but the Ilyushin was capable of spotting him . . . and he was increasing the chances of that by the speed of his flight. Slow down —

He eased off the power, dropping the MiL's speed to little more than half. Garcia almost overshot him to port before he re-adjusted his own speed. The hills slipped beneath. The MiG, out there somewhere, preyed on Gant's nerves. It was less than twenty miles away, only a minute away, allowing for a change of course and a cautious approach. Cat-and-mouse . . . he sensed the cat, the heat from its fur, its breath . . .

Then, it came. Without introduction, without call-sign, he heard his position, as if he himself were reciting it from the moving map in front of him. The AWACS Ilyushin had retained its interest in him. Unlike the professional pilots of the MiG and the helicopters who had buzzed him and retired laughing and gesturing, the AWACS aircraft, because of its sensitive role, would carry a GRU officer or a GLAVPUR political officer – the aircraft's real rather than titular commander.

His position, heading, speed were repeated and acknowledged by the MiG.

'It's blown wide open,' Gant said over the transceiver with a grim calm that surprised him. His hands, unlike his voice, quivered. 'Let's hide – first, I want to take a look . . .'

He switched on the radar. Wiped the moving map from the tactical screen. Which greened. Immediately, on the north-west edge of the screen the AWACS aircraft appeared. The two MiLs were to the south of him, and westward. They were more than five minutes away. They could be outrun. The border ahead remained unalerted, for the moment. Nothing was in the air to prevent his crossing. He counted the passing seconds, as if making a call that was being traced through the telephone exchange . . . how long before his emissions removed all doubt about his position and heading? He was electronically waving at them. The MiG, the MiG –

He summoned the head-up display. Along the cockpit sill, figures stuttered. Course, speed, altitude, distance. Twenty-five miles away, speed four hundred, altitude dropping quickly. Time to convergence, one minute forty seconds. He snapped off the radar, and the image of the MiG moving purposefully towards the centre of the screen remained as a retinal after-image.

He flipped over the back of a hill; Garcia's helicopter flea-jumped behind him. The long, riverless valley stretched ahead, a mile wide and sloping down to the border and the Oxus. It was wide enough for the MiG to be able to manoeuvre within it. Gant cursed his luck, his eyes scanning the valley walls, its dry riverbed. Rocks, overhangs, outcrops, ledges. As soon as he had disappeared from the radar screen of the MiG, it would have increased speed. The AWACS Ilyushin would be guiding it. It would be unlikely to have lost its fix on them. The convergence was – inevitable.

He reinstated the moving map, searching it frantically for a narrower side valley, something to draw tightly round the two helicopters and prevent the MiG from turning or manoeuvring. Nothing. He ploughed on, the border no more than thirty miles away now.

'Garcia – find somewhere we can put down – and fast!' he snapped into the transceiver. 'Split up – take the eastern wall of the valley, I'll fly the western wall – make two targets . . .' He hesitated after the word had been spoken, but the situation could no longer be disguised. 'Do it,' he added.

'Gant – he knows where we are, right?'

'He knows.'

'OK, let's play hide-and-seek!'

Garcia was edgy, but brightly nervous; confidence fizzed out rather than dripped or leaked. He wasn't believing in the situation. It was still a game, training. Gant didn't know if his mood would change the moment the MiG appeared.

Garcia's *Hind* drifted out of the mirrors and across the wide valley; beginning to lose shape and identity against the coloured rock, snowdrifts, bare outcrops. The camouflage concealed it almost perfectly. Gant squinted to make it out. Garcia, like himself, had dropped his speed dramatically, further losing himself against the background. Good. Gant watched the valley wall to port, a grey-white curtain. Waited.

Like a shark, sudden and fast, the MiG – a *Flogger* air-combat fighter – flashed above the valley, its belly lit to ghostliness by the moon. It vanished almost at once to the east. A new star climbed and turned in the black sky a second or two later.

'Anything, Garcia?'

'Only for sitting ducks.'

Gant watched the distance in front of him. The star dropped towards the valley, winking palely. Gant felt a strange envy, which became anxiety in a moment. He sensed the MiG pilot's superiority, his eager, unworried confidence. The *Hind* was no match for the *Flogger*. It entered the valley perhaps five or six miles ahead of them. The two MiLs behind them would now be working with the MiG, via the commands and sightings of the AWACS aircraft, and hurrying to overtake them. He estimated they would enter the valley in no more than three minutes. At maximum speed, just over two minutes from the position they had held when he had briefly used the radar. Then he and Garcia would be in a box, with the lid screwed down.

The MiG-23 howled up the valley towards them. Another sighting pass, he thought. One more look, one attempt to communicate after that. Too late to hide now; the bluff had to be continued and it had to work.

'Arm all the firing circuits, just in case,' he said almost casually over the transceiver. Garcia would hear him, so would Mac –

– whose helmet turned. Mac looked up at him, then raised his thumb. Wide eyes, white teeth in a pale blob of face. That was all Mac was.

The MiG was level with them for an instant. A glimpse of dark cockpit, as if the aircraft was pilotless. Then it roared away, into an immediate climb and turn. On its infra-red screen two spots would glow hotter than the surrounding icy rocks. Two spots, one each side of the valley. The pilot would be pleased, would retain his confidence, even though he knew the *Hinds* were armed and were more manoeuvrable in the box of the valley. He had fixed the targets, and he had assistance. Gant turned his head. Once more, a new star climbed and winked in the night.

'All weapons systems to my control,' he announced, then added: 'Garcia – do nothing 'til you hear from me. OK?'

Over the transceiver, Garcia's voice was tightened by tension; yet almost elated, too. It was still only training, only practice. They'd never done it for real. They did not know what *real* was. Could not understand it . . . Gant understood it too well. But real hadn't killed him yet . . .

'Gant, what the hell *is* there to do?'

Beneath the elation, Garcia was peeling open. Soon, the proximity of the rocks, the speed and armament of the MiG – AA missiles, a gun pack, look-down, shoot-down radar – all would

206

begin to weigh more heavily. He was unnerved now, but even Garcia probably thought it was excitement, not fear. But, his confidence was being stripped away.

'Forget it, Garcia. Set down as soon as you can, where you can. On your own. Just don't get in my way.' Because that was the only message he had for Garcia, the only one that possessed value; *don't kill me along with yourself.*

The new star was falling back towards the valley once more. Gant ignored the distant speck of Garcia's MiL and its wavering shadow. The radio tuned to the Soviet Tac-channel blurted in his ear. The star fell with frightening swiftness. Gant experienced it with Garcia's taut nerves, sensed he and his co-pilot, Lane, craning to follow its course. He was suddenly aware of how much fuel the other *Hind* was carrying. They were riding in a giant petrol tank. Now, Garcia and the others would have begun to smell the fuel by a trick of fear on their senses. Its volume and proximity would be scraping at nerve and will.

The *Flogger* dropped back perhaps as much as three miles behind them, its pilot's voice in his headset broken by the terrain and the slow bend in the valley which made it invisible for the moment. Gant sensed confidence and suspicion through the static.

'Unidentified helicopters – you are in restricted airspace without permission. Please identify yourselves. Over.'

The MiG appeared in Gant's mirrors, rounding the bend and rapidly overhauling them. He glanced across at Garcia. He was maintaining speed and heading, hugging the rock face, the MiL's shadow breaking up and re-forming like dark water.

Gant replied at once, knowing that the cover story had been checked and found wanting. Someone in the AWACS aircraft. Just routine, but just in case.

The pilot of the MiG pounced upon the fiction.

'Unidentified helicopter – try again. Kunduz requests your positive ID for Parwan. Kabul central army aviation field has no record of your flight. Please explain your purpose and authorization. Over.'

The MiG, moving at low speed, gradually enlarged in the

mirrors. The pilot was cruising along the valley at their altitude. Herding them while he waited for their answers.

'My mission has the highest security clearance from Kabul army HQ,' Gant persisted, knowing he would not be believed. Anders was talking in his head now and the noise angered him. It reminded him of the priorities of the mission, of the price of failure, when all that interested him was the span of a single minute and his own survival. 'Why the hell are you taking so much interest, comrade? Over,' he added. And then waited. Anders nagged again. Garcia's *Hind* remained steady. He could hear, where his right ear was free of the headset, the man's ragged breathing from the transceiver.

The MiG was level with them.

'Kabul won't vouch for you, *comrade* – no one at central airfield even remembers two MiL-24s taking off tonight. Please identify. Over.' A brash, amused, contemptuous irony in the pilot's voice; it reassured – but why?

What was in the MiG pilot's mind? It was something to do with the degree of suspicion, or the kind of suspicion . . . what? What did he think . . . ?

The MiG, unable to match their speed without stalling, had slowly moved ahead of them. Then it lifted sharply – just in case, aware of the armament of both helicopters. It rolled, flashing like a shark in the moonlight, then turned tightly to drop back into the valley behind them; levelling off, pursuing once more.

. . . deserters or unsanctioned black-marketeers! One or the other, maybe both. That's what he thought! Illegality, not penetration. Profit, not espionage. He studied his mirrors. Moonlight glinted on the MiG's sleekness, and on two more distant spots. The Soviet helicopters. There would be others gathering now – or maybe not? The degree of confidence, even of amusement in the pilot's voice? There might be no general alert, not at the moment –

– what to do with the *Flogger*?

His mind was cold; body hot, but alert rather than jumpy. He had passed through nerves to tension. He replied to the pilot, easing the right amount of nervousness into his voice. *Almost* pleading.

'Look, comrade, you check with the top brass at Kabul. And I mean the *top* brass . . . and apologize from me for dragging them into it. Over.'

'Sorry, comrade – you'll have to do better than that. Kabul doesn't know you. Parwan wants to know why you were using the roundabout route, and Kunduz wants you to divert. Climb immediately to four thousand metres and take up a heading directly for Kunduz military airbase. Confirm when you have a revised ETA. And remember I'll be watching you. Over.'

The MiG was level with him once more. Between himself and Garcia. Gant's mind was suddenly cold with doubt. The sleek air combat fighter was only a couple of hundred yards to starboard. The pilot would be wary, but he evidently didn't expect trouble from them. Deserters or black-marketeers, people to be despised, even discounted.

He could see the outline of a flying helmet in the MiG's cockpit, and the AA missiles beneath the wings – and the gun and the laser rangefinder beneath the forward fuselage.

'I copy. Acknowledge diversion to Kunduz airbase and climb to four thousand. ETA – sixteen minutes.'

'You will be accompanied by the two helicopters astern of you. Take up close formation with them on rendezvous. Do you copy? Over.'

'I copy.'

Gant glanced at the moving map. The MiG was lifting away once more, burning fuel prodigally in its manoeuvres. Its mission range –? Would it have to return to Parwan or Kunduz to refuel in another minute or so? If so, another MiG or a Sukhoi would already be on its way to take up station. He watched it, willing it to return rather than depart. Images flashed in his head, but seemed like reflections from distorting mirrors. The Soviet border was less than ten miles away. Kunduz was fifty miles to the south-west.

'Shit –' he breathed. It was impossible to shake the MiG, and if it needed to refuel, it wouldn't abandon them until a replacement arrived. The two Russian MiLs were clearly visible in his mirrors.

He heard the incoming surf of Garcia's breathing; faster, more ragged. Shit –

He clenched the control column more tightly, altered the collective pitch lever, climbing out of the valley into the dark sky. His head was turned, to watch Garcia follow him.

Mac said: 'Skipper, shouldn't you call Langley –?'

'The hell I will!' he snapped back. He was listening to the tenor of Garcia's breathing as if with a stethoscope.

Break –

Garcia's voice yelped in his headset and t! e tanker helicopter lifted sharply, nose-up, out of the valley. The falling star of the MiG dropped more quickly, as if alerted. It banked fiercely round behind them, levelling off. When the pilot spoke, his voice was tightened by G-forces.

'Maintain your former heading – climb to four thousand metres and wait for your escort. Repeat, climb to four thousand on your former heading. Do you copy? Over.'

Garcia flipped out of sight – Gant climbed more rapidly until he could look down on the scene. He saw the two pursuing MiLs also climb and begin to divert. Saw the MiG-23 racing from behind and below. Had he picked up Garcia after his turn?

'Garcia – for Christ's sake get back here!' Gant yelled into the transceiver. Ether replied, and hoarse but more relieved breathing. Excited murmurs he could not make out. The MiG swept up towards Gant, past him, and locked onto the tail of Garcia's MiL. Garcia had increased his speed to perhaps one-fifty; not nearly enough. The MiG pilot was flashy, but good. Good enough. Gant felt his stomach lurch. Mac's voice protested.

'Return to your former heading and maintain. Abandon your present heading. Reduce your speed. Wait for your escort. Do you copy? Over.'

The two aircraft raced away from Gant, diminishing in size. Garcia was already another half-mile away from Gant in the split-seconds that had passed since he broke – cover, formation and nerve. The MiG coursed behind him. The two MiLs were hurrying, panicked into movement, towards the point of disobedience. They could smell blood. Ahead of Garcia were hills which might hide him. He might have taken the decision based on surprise and the nearness of that covering terrain. No. He had panicked himself into risk, into confidence.

And was wrong.

Gant increased his own speed, rushing across the mile-wide valley, his head moving from side to side like that of an animal at bay, seeking cover. He knew what would happen, with a sick certainty, and he was already on the other side of the experience, considering only his own survival and escape.

'Skipper –!' Mac protested.

'No,' he replied without emotion.

All three Soviet aircraft were distracted by Garcia, forgetting him for the moment.

Where?

A solid wall of snow-streaked rock on either side of the valley. No avenue of escape, no narrow cleft which would keep out the MiG. Its pilot's voice pursued Garcia; commanded, ordered, threatened –

– threat. Only a matter of seconds now.

'Garcia – for Christ's sake slow down!' he yelled, knowing it would be useless, but somehow satisfying Mac, and some small part of himself.

In a moment, all their screens would be blind. He had time –

– hung in the air in the middle of the valley, watching the helicopters and the MiG and the tiny speck that was Garcia's *Hind*. Could not help but watch.

He scanned blank cliffs.

'Find somewhere, for Christ's sake,' he murmured to Mac.

Threat. Challenge.

He could hardly think ahead now. There was only survival. He had been caught and he had to survive this situation in any way he could. Look, *look* –

Final warning.

211

A spurt of flame, from an igniting rocket motor, no bigger than that of a flaring match. An AA-8 missile, infra-red homing, had been launched by the *Flogger*. Even though he anticipated it, was sure it would happen, he felt stunned.

I am authorized to open fire if you do not obey my instructions, lingered in his head. *You are in restricted airspace . . . I will open fire unless you –*

One of the few Russian phrases Garcia had ever bothered to learn hung on the ether and in his mind for a moment – the moment of the missile's spurting, glowing flight. *Go fuck yourself –* Garcia's voice was high-pitched.

Look, look for an escape, don't be distracted, look –

The MiL spun in the hover in the deserted, blank valley. There was no hiding-place. He *had* to watch Garcia's *Hind* as the AA missile hurried after it like a burning arrow. It hunted just for a moment for a warm, electrically-alive object above cold, unmoving rock – then it struck.

The whole sky seemed to become orange and white at the moment of impact. Burning fuel washed like a waterfall the few hundred feet towards the flank of a hill. Garcia groaned through the transceiver and began a scream he did not complete or even understand. The *Hind*, shattered, spilling burning fuel, tumbled against the hillside, split further, opened and crumpled. Gant had snatched up the night-glasses from their pocket in the cockpit door. The scene was enlarged, clear, horrific. Rotors flew like separate metal sycamore leaves, great half-molten pieces of fuselage bounced and tumbled. Fuel ran like lava down the hillside.

His fuel, *his* fuel –

He could think of nothing else, having ignored the fact until the moment of the explosion. Not Garcia's death, not the deaths of Lane and Kooper, not even his own immediate danger . . . he thought of nothing except the fact that his reserve of fuel had burned up. Now, he could not reach Baikonur, despite his own ferry tank . . . he could never get back.

Even as he heard Mac whisper 'Oh-sweet-Jesus-Christ' in the transceiver, he knew that the MiG pilot had aborted *Winter*

212

Hawk. He was surrounded, unable to escape – there was no point in even trying to evade capture.

He hovered, stunned.

EIGHT

oasis

A hole in the cliff.

Gant flicked switches, knowing that it did not matter now, knowing that he was below the shield-edge of the valley walls, knowing that their screens would be blinded by the nova of the explosion and burning of Garcia's MiL – knowing that unless he explored, analysed, *found* the hole in the rocks in the next few moments, it was finished anyway. He felt relief as the helicopter's main panel and principal screens sprang to life – stuttering to green and red, lights and LEDs winking, systems coming on-line.

The infra-red display glowed like a sunrise. The green of the radar screen was still awash with flying metal and fuel and confused images – Garcia's helicopter continued to explode on his screens.

Hole in the rocks –

Blackness and moonwashed cliff. Less than half a mile away, the readouts proclaimed. Was it a retinal image from staring into the explosion?

He dropped the *Hind* like a huge stone towards the floor of the valley; as familiar as if lowering into Nevada or New Mexico, because it represented safety – at least, for the next few minutes. His attention was mesmerized by the sense of the two Soviet MiLs and the *Flogger* grouping like dogs around a quarry already torn.

He saw and sensed Mac in the gunner's cockpit but he hardly registered. Gant was saving himself and the machine. Nothing mattered beside the reality of the gaping black hole that now

214

enlarged – not a retinal image, then . . . A cave, a cavern, a cleft. Safety.

Qualification. Dead end. He was running like a sheep into a pen.

Imperative. Get out of sight.

The entrance to the cavern had to be big enough . . .

He could see crumbled sections of rock face, openings, the gouge of the river bed waiting for the spring; boulders littered the floor.

He edged the *Hind* towards the eastern wall of the valley. He glanced continually in his mirrors, quartered the sky through the cockpit perspex. Nothing, yet –

The imperative overcame the qualification. He needed time to think, to plan, to revise, a time when he wasn't flying. He turned the helicopter slowly nose-on to the cavern, and shunted the machine gently towards it.

'Horizontal clearance – nineteen metres . . . vertical, six metres thirty, skipper,' Mac's voice murmured from the transceiver. The mouth of the cave *was* wide enough, tall enough – though it was close.

'OK, Mac.'

He whirled the *Hind* on its axis like a matador's cape, scanning the clifftop above him, the valley around them, the empty sky, pinpricked with stars, lighter where the wash of moonlight spread from the full, pale disc. No shadows, no silhouettes, nothing. He poised the helicopter opposite the mouth of the cavern.

'IR lamp on,' he announced, tugging the infra-red goggles over his helmet and adjusting them. A grey world, the light from the lamp splashing like dull paint into the blackness. The sense of the cavern's size impinged upon him; the place, opened out behind the entrance, retreated in every direction beyond the reach of the lamp.

He shunted the *Hind* forward, its undercarriage hanging just above littered boulders. Most of all, he was aware of the rotors whirling above his head. The dimensions of the cavern's mouth were as clear in his mind as if he were reading them on white

215

paper. Mac's voice murmured directions to slip to right or left. The main panel glowed; he scanned it continuously with the rapidity and repetition of a child avoiding cracks in the pavement to fend off bad luck.

Ice glittered. The cavern mouth loomed as if about to swallow them.

Now.

He suppressed a shiver. The rotor tips caught the infra-red lighting thrown back from dark, cold walls. The rotors formed a disc – not touching the walls of rock. *Not touching . . .* Mac was inside the cavern, then so was he. Rotor-noise boomed in the enclosing, retreating dark. The pale, ghostly light from the IR lamp made the interior open up into dusky, shadowy heights like the nave of an ill-lit cathedral. The goggles revealed hanging ice, drifted snow, rock, undulations like those of the seabed, and a roof stretching upwards beyond the light. His breath eased out, controlled. Mac exhaled noisily.

'Cold in here,' was his only comment.

Gant turned the *Hind* slowly in the hover. He flicked off the IR lamp and pulled off his goggles. The mouth of the cavern was pale with moonlight.

'Mac?'

'I can't hear anything, skipper. I'll go take a look.'

Gant lowered the undercarriage until it bounced and the *Hind* settled. He switched off the two Isotov engines and the rotors grumbled down to stillness. Silence seemed audible after the last echoing noises died away. He opened the cockpit door. Icy cold assailed him like a bully. Mac opened the hinged canopy of the gunner's cockpit and dropped to the floor. Gant removed his helmet. The cavern was huge around him. He felt the darkness as if it were moving. He jumped from the door, a lamp flicking on in his hand. Mac's lamp wobbled its light towards the mouth of the cavern. Gant flicked the powerful, inadequate beam around him as if to locate a dangerous animal. A dry gouge in the floor stretched away towards the back of the cavern; the course of the former river or tributary that had excavated this hole in the rocks. He saw the lamp's beam glance off a waterfall of ice. There were no stars or moonlight above him, only at the entrance.

His head still rung with the noise of the rotors, as if he had been flying the *Hind* for days without pause. He had, in fact, been in the air for two-and-a-half hours. He leaned for a moment against the fuselage, his hand and arm remaining numb from his fierce grip on the control column.

'Mac? OK?' he whispered into the transceiver he had detached from its fitting in the cockpit.

'Skipper —' Mac's hoarse whisper replied; it seemed loud in the silence. 'I can hear the MiG — turning, I guess. Coming this way, for sure. Jesus, I'm *cold* —!' His tone was expressive. He hardly needed to add: 'What in hell's name was Garcia playing at?' for Gant to understand the force of his reaction. He focused his night-vision — having flicked off the lamp — and could pick out Mac's body at the entrance, hunched as if in illness.

'OK, Mac — OK,' he replied, realizing there was a shiver of reaction in his own voice. 'OK . . .'

He heard the approaching noise of the MiG wash into the darkness.

'She's coming,' Mac announced, his teeth chattering. 'Skipper — Christ, did you *see* it?'

'I saw.'

The *Flogger* howled down the valley, its engine noise booming against the cliffs and into the cavern. Almost at once, the noise began to retreat. It was maybe five or six minutes since he had picked up the MiG. It had already flown perhaps as much as three hundred miles of its combat radius. In another five minutes, it would be forced to return to Kunduz to refuel . . . but a replacement would be in the air before then and on-station when the *Flogger* turned for home. They would still be trapped in the cavern . . . but he couldn't regret his decision, not even in the moment when the darkness was beaten like a gong by the noise of the MiG's engine. He could never have outrun the fighter; never have avoided its missiles — Garcia hadn't been able to —

'He just broke up,' he murmured into the transceiver.

'Where does that leave *us*?' Mac almost wailed from the entrance. 'Skipper – this situation is *shit*!'

'Maybe. What about the gunships?'

'I can hear one, maybe both . . . no, just one.'

'I'm coming to take a look.'

After he had walked a few paces, he looked back at the *Hind*. There was the faintest glow from the main instrument panel in the cockpit, but the bulk of the helicopter was in total darkness. It would not be seen from outside except, maybe, by means of an infra-red lamp. The mouth of the cavern was a pale expression of surprise. Stars glinted. Mac's bulk, to one side of the entrance, was pressed back against the rock. He was holding the bulky Noctron night-viewer to his face. Its range was more than five hundred metres, maybe better than that with bright moonlight. Gant could hear the approaching MiL.

'The second one's moved off to the south,' Mac whispered as Gant reached him. 'This guy's gonna get swallowed by this cave-mouth if he don't slow down!' He ducked further into the shadow.

Gant looked around. A lamp might just reach the *Hind* – just.

'Here, let me take a look.'

'Sure.' Mac handed him the night-viewer. His voice seemed fierce now, angry. He appeared able to suppress his realization about the loss of their reserve fuel, hide it inside his rage at Garcia's death. The thought of the fuel made Gant shiver; the darkness spread around him like the inhospitable country in which he was stranded.

He leaned gently out of the shadow.

The gunship hovered in the valley, moonlight splashing on its camouflage paint. It was a twin of the helicopter behind them, a 24-D. No troops, then – just the crew . . . no, if it didn't have a ferry tank aboard it could still be holding up to eight soldiers. He watched it. The main door remained closed. Its blunt head turned towards them. The Isotov engine-intakes were like insect eyes above the squat, gleaming cockpit. Its noise masked the engine of the coursing MiG, away out of sight.

Only minutes, Gant thought. Because of the rock that

surrounded them, he could no longer monitor the Soviet Tac-channel. If only they would give him a gap, a sliver of time between the departure of the *Flogger* and the arrival of its replacement. He could not even listen to the MiL talking to its base. If only they sent more helicopters, not more fighters . . . fighters were virtually useless for the kind of work the Soviets needed to do in the search for him. They had to, he decided. It was too obvious a tactic to ignore. Helicopters – this gunship and the *Flogger* had, doubtless, already requested back-up. Excitedly reporting the one kill, the temporary loss of the second target – yes, they'd send out more gunships.

Ferry tanks? The *Flogger* had been carrying one under its belly, but no wingtip tanks. It had been flying a lo-lo-lo mission, with no high-altitude work. Its combat range would have been severely reduced. It should be leaving –

He saw the MiG, winking like an intruding star, high above the valley. Then it banked to the south-west and was gone almost at once.

And now, perhaps only *now*, calling for more helicopters . . . there would have been a delay-time induced by success, by the frightening exhilaration of a *real kill*, maybe the pilot's first, before he reacted by the book and decided on reinforcements.

'Fifteen minutes maximum, if every guess of mine is right,' he murmured, almost to himself. Yes, fifteen at the outside.

The gunship faced them, hovering thirty feet above the rocky floor of the valley. Alone. Four hundred yards away from where they stood. There were too many guesses, too many factors he had placed on his side not on theirs. But he could do nothing else – defeat was banging behind him like a door being closed.

'You think they'll send choppers,' Mac divined.

'Wouldn't you?'

'Sure.'

'They got troops aboard, Mac?'

'I sure as hell hope not.'

The night was icy through the thinness of his flying overalls. A deeper chill of isolation and abandonment was spreading through him. He had to keep that off, stop it numbing him.

219

'Cabin door,' Gant snapped.

'What do we do?'

They watched. Mac seemed to want the night-viewer, but Gant kept the eyepiece against his face. He refined the focus of the single 135mm lens. The face of the Russian crewchief appeared, his head leaning out of the cabin door. Gant saw the sloping pencil-mark of the rifle he was holding against his body. He switched his attention back to the shadowy cockpit. Gunner in front, pilot behind him. Immobile, almost idle in their lack of movement. He switched back to the cabin door. The crewchief lowered himself slowly down a trailing rope –

– followed by one, two – *two* flat-helmeted soldiers. The MiL remained at its easy-to-manoeuvre height. The three men became lumbering shadows in the dust raised by the downdraught, then they emerged, moving away to the left of the cavern, spreading out, all of them armed with Kalashnikovs, heading towards another, smaller cave.

Gant looked at his watch. Had the three armed men left the MiL because assistance was only seconds away? Were they being too eager or did they know for sure help was almost with them? It couldn't be more than fourteen minutes before other gunships arrived – it could be less than one.

'Go get the guns, Mac,' he whispered.

'What – ?'

'The Apaches are here, Mac – go get the guns.'

Mac hurried off into the darkness. Gant heard him misplace his footing and curse softly, cutting the words off as he remembered the proximity of the three Russians. Gant watched the space opening up between the three men and the MiL. He studied the cockpit. Infra-red trace, seeking engine heat. They'd be bound to be using that . . . laser rangefinder, too. If he so much as stepped into the mouth of the cavern now, out into the open, they would see him. Just a shadow to eyesight, but a wavering, warm shape on infra-red.

The MiLs would be in the air by now, heading towards the position of the gunship that blocked their escape-route. He shuddered. Escape-route? To where?

Hold on, dammit, *hold on*, he told himself, clenching his teeth together to prevent them chattering uncontrollably. Halfway between here and Baikonur he would run out of fuel, over the desert. He would exactly repeat the situation he was now in. They were cut off to the south, west, and maybe the east. Only the north would be open . . . maybe. To the east, the Hindu Kush rose above the service ceiling of the *Hind*. He could not cross the mountains and, anyway, only China lay beyond them. To the north lay the border. He *could* cross that. To run out of fuel somewhere between the Oxus and Baikonur . . .

Hold on –!

Both hands gripped the night-viewer. The impossibilities chimed like harsh, untuned bells.

The three armed men had moved out of sight into gullies or the shadows of boulders. Effectively, they were now cut off from the MiL – which, seen through the Noctron, became less than a threat, more of a target. It was the only way in which Gant could overcome the shuddering chill induced by the hours stretching ahead of him. An immediate, violent solution. Target.

Mac was hurrying back but already the handguns and the two Kalashnikovs were as outmoded as arrows. Garcia's helicopter exploded once more in his mind. Now that he had removed the night-viewer from his eye, he could see a thin trail of dark smoke crossing the full moon like an old scar. The explosion repeated itself, a series of starbursts from some huge firework display, and he saw the MiL directly in front of him vanish into an identical orange fireball. There was no other way; he could not simply wait for defeat to arrive, he had to strive to outrun it.

Minutes – even one or two minutes – of confusion might be enough for him to be swallowed by the landscape; cross the border and drain into the desert like water. MiL for MiL; this Russian pilot and crew for Garcia and the others. An eye for an eye – and a way out.

'I know what the gooks felt like, now I'm staring into that face,' Mac observed through clenched teeth.

Vietnam trembled like a thick cover of leaves about to be parted. Gant snapped: 'Shut up, Mac – I don't need it.' Mac

221

grunted, handing one of the rifles to Gant, who simply stared at the target.

His awareness narrowed. He breathed steadily but quickly. The noise of the MiL's rotors insisted. The three men on foot had not reappeared.

'There's a way out,' he murmured. 'Kill the target.'

'What then, skipper?' Mac replied, lifting to his eye the Noctron that Gant had returned to him. The rifle was folded in the crook of his right arm. 'What do we do when we've burnt her?'

'Cross the border.'

'And run out of fuel, skipper?' Mac's voice was outraged. 'I never took you for a gung-ho bastard with a need to get killed. Why now?'

Gant glanced at Mac. 'There's nothing else – unless you want to surrender?' His voice snapped like a thin whip because of his own desperation.

'No, but –'

'We might as well surrender, Mac. If they'll allow it. Maybe they just want to fry us, too, like Garcia?' Mac's breathing was rapid and frightened. 'You want to wait for an order or are you volunteering?'

'OK, skipper,' Mac replied after a long silence; reluctant and almost surly.

'Let's go – and let's see how good you really are, Mac.'

They stumbled into the darkness of the cavern, not daring to use their lamps. The perspex, given the faintest gleam by the instrument panel, loomed mistily out of the blackness. Mac, after missing his footing once, clambered into the gunner's cockpit. Gant closed his door softly. The noise of the MiL, washing through the entrance where the moonlight made a pale carpet, was still audible until he put on his helmet and stowed the transceiver in its fitting. His hands were clammy, shaking, and his body was alert with nerves.

Target, he reminded himself.

Lights flickered on in orderly rows in Mac's cockpit.

'Mac?'

'Sure.'

'After you launch the missile, make for the entrance. I don't want anyone outside . . . one Kalashnikov could bring this baby down.'

'Got you.'

His palms dried. He flicked the low-light TV picture to the main tactical screen. Ghostly. The MiL was a dervish whirling in a small dust storm. The edges of the cavern's mouth were like dark curtains revealing a tiny stage. On that stage, he could see the gunship.

And a warm body registering . . .

Posed in front of the MiL, merely a shadow on the TV image, but a shimmering glow on the superimposed infra-red display. One of the soldiers! It unnerved him. Flesh, not just a machine. For a moment, he could not disregard the information of the infra-red. His hand sweated. Then his mind restored the imperatives of ruthlessness.

He said: 'It doesn't exist. Concentrate on the gunship, Mac.'

'Skipper.'

The quality of the flickering, warm image changed as it entered the cavern. It shone out more brightly. And was clearer, more recognizably human.

– get out of the way . . .

As if aware that it was silhouetting itself against the pale entrance, the warm shimmer moved to one side, into what it thought was invisibility in the darkness.

'Mac?'

'Ready, skipper.'

In a moment, if it moved any closer, it would see the reflection of panel lights on the perspex of the two cockpits. Gant held his breath.

Through the mouth of the cavern. A straight line. The MiL continued to hover in its own little storm of dust. It was neither lifting nor falling, but soon it would climb out of their sight because the dust was beginning to rise around the cockpit, reducing visibility.

The warm image continued to swim towards them on the

infra-red. The MiL turned in the air like a sycamore leaf, the lights were in rows of readiness along Mac's panel.

'When ready,' he whispered at last.

The MiL began to lift. Mac's breathing quickened as he watched the warm body moving towards the centre of the screen.

Launch.

He heard the ignition even as he heard the horn sound in his helmet, signalling that Mac's rangefinder and IR had locked on to the target. He could almost hear the switches and the buttons and the circuits. The cavern dazzled with rocket flame; exhaust smoke billowed. He saw, garishly lit, ice tendrils hanging high above them, the huge roof of the cavern –

– and the man, in uniform, lit by fire and stunned into immobility. The AA missile tore free of the *Hind*'s stubby port winglet, rocking the helicopter. Its flame lanced towards the entrance, and something too-illuminated to see clearly fell away from it. Even through the perspex there was a thin, high-pitched cry. Smoke rolled in the dying glare as what was now a small lance of flame vanished through the entrance. Distantly, he heard the noises of Mac's departure from the gunner's cockpit, and saw his dim shadow move away.

Gant stabbed buttons – ignition of another kind. His stomach churned. The rotors above his head began to turn slowly. Something was still screaming. Mac was running towards it, his lamp wobbling like a weakly held white stick alongside him. The rotors accelerated, their noise booming in the cavern.

On the main tactical screen, displaying the low-light TV image, the little bright tail of flame drove towards the bulk of the Russian helicopter. Microseconds passed.

The MiL, rotors turning, eyelike air-intakes staring into the cavern, swallowed the missile. Light spread on the screen and spilled into the cavern so that he could see Mac bending over the scorched soldier. On the screen, the MiL opened almost like a mouth about to scream, staggered in the air, split, flew to pieces. Metal bounced into the cavern like pebbles. In the glaring light, Mac was pressed against the wall, his face averted. The place was

224

alien, as if the rocks themselves were burning. He moved his shocked hands slowly, with extreme effort. In his mind, substitution whirled – he must contact Kunduz, inform them that the runaway had been destroyed like its companion . . . *intruder destroyed, mission accomplished* – slacken the pace of the pursuit, buy time. Then on their radars he would be Russian, he was explainable. It might gain him as much as minutes.

Above his head, the rotors were dishing, bathed in lurid orange light. The *Hind* struggled against the restraint of the brakes. His hands gripped the column and the collective pitch lever. On the main screen there was a glow from outside, but the low-light television picture revealed nothing solid, no object out there.

A shadow appeared in the entrance, outlined by the fire behind it. It startled Mac – dim exclamations reached Gant through the helmet and the perspex – and flame spat before the shadow fell to one side and vanished from the entrance. Then Mac was waving him urgently forward.

The *Hind* struggled; he released the brakes. It rolled forward down a shallow slope, hopped over the gouge of the dry watercourse and eased towards the mouth of the cavern. The glow from what remained of the Russian helicopter increased, making a bright lance of the airspeed sensor boom. Flame and smoke roiled about Gant, as if he were thrusting the whole machine into some furnace. Mac ducked his way to the side of the helicopter. Gant heard him slide open the main cabin door. There were – how many soldiers out there somewhere? Gant heard Mac's boots thudding on the metal floor behind him. The door was left open.

His breathing was stertorous, but his body still felt calm, even cold. The *Hind* eased more swiftly towards the exit from the cavern.

The Russian MiL was rubble, its fire already diminishing. He lifted the *Hind* over it, rising softly through the pall of smoke into the moonlit night. He flicked on the radio and prepared his signal. A moment of illusory calm –

– so that he hardly heard the gunfire, even though he saw the squat figure of a man on the ground. Saw flame, only vaguely heard the shots cry and bang on the fuselage. Kalashnikov on automatic. Moonlight splashed on the cockpit. Someone cried out from the transceiver . . . cried out −?

Mac fell as Gant held the *Hind* in the hover. It was almost as if he had jumped, his shape seeming right for an attack upon the Russian, who was lying spreadeagled. Dust rose slowly around Mac from the impact of his body. Mac's own Kalashnikov buried itself upright near his body, like a marker.

'Mac −!' he heard himself shouting, over and over. 'Mac! Mac!'

Mac had killed the one surviving Russian, the only one who could contradict the lies he intended. But, the Russian had killed Mac . . .

His hand had closed the Soviet channel almost as soon as he had begun yelling. It would be just another cry in the night as the intruders died . . . he had not given himself away. The moon silvered the perspex. Survival became a panic in him, obscuring everything else; even Mac's death. For which he was responsible − he should have been more aware, should have taken the *Hind* up quicker . . .

Panic obscured his recriminations; obscured everything. *Survive.*

He opened the Tac-channel, and immediately his voice was an acted enthusiasm, a cry of delight mingled with shock.

'Got the bastard!' he yelled in his mother's Russian over the Tac-channel. 'Got the deserting bastard!'

'You lucky bastard, Ilya!' he heard immediately, as if his pretended excitement was infectious. 'You lucky sod!' Then: 'What's your position, man?'

Without hesitation, Gant supplied the coordinates. Mac's shrunken form lay still on the valley floor, near the Russian soldier. There was nothing on Mac's body to betray the mission or his origins . . . not for hours yet would they learn Mac came from nowhere, had no record. The pretence made Gant tired. His desire to flee, to survive through speed, had to be restrained at a cost.

The Russian pilot replied: With you in four minutes – lucky sod!'

'Roger. Out.'

He flicked off the radio. Felt nausea rise to the back of his throat. Made himself not look down again, except to inspect the rubbish that was all that was left of the MiL. Even there, if he were lucky, there would not be enough to betray him . . . only the dog-tags, and even they might have been damaged enough to be unreadable except under laboratory conditions . . . at least, *at the very least*, he had four minutes!

He summoned the moving map to the main screen and bled in the disposition of radar defences, watchtowers, camps and barracks, villages and farms and towns, the listening posts and the missile units. In the vast valley of the Oxus and the mountains that rose beyond it, inside the Soviet Union, the defences were mainly long-range – especially since 1979. Crossing in a low-flying helicopter would be easy –

Fuel.

He glanced at the gauges. He had perhaps as much as four hundred miles of flying at his most economical cruising speed before the ferry tank dried up. It would leave him three hundred short of Baikonur. Three hundred miles short – somewhere in the deserts of Soviet Central Asia; Uzbekistan. He felt cold, his body slipping into a mild paralysis. He could not go back. He would never make it to Peshawar, all the way south back across Afghan airspace, not once they identified even one of the bodies below or some part of the ruined airframe . . . he was utterly trapped by the situation.

Panic surged in him. *Go now, go before Kunduz begins demanding a full report* – expecting one . . .

He felt his body flood with anger.

Mac –

No, it wasn't because of Mac; it was because *he* was trapped. It was like the Firefox, its fuel running out, before he reached the ice-floe and the submarine that was *Mother One* . . . but there was no submarine out there in Uzbekistan, there was no fuel out there . . . run, run –

Mac —

Survive.

His hands moved almost automatically, and the *Hind*'s nose whisked up. Still low and within the radar-shield of the valley, he increased speed. Bowed to the pressure of the panic to survive. In six minutes, he could be across the border, inside the Soviet Union. His mind shut out the hours ahead, thought only of the next few minutes. He wasn't defeated, he hadn't lost — not yet. And he would survive.

One hundred, one-twenty, one twenty-five . . . the *Hind* skimmed along the wide, dry valley, raising, as it passed, a small trail of dust no bigger than that of a single horseman. Going forward represented the prospect of opportunity. And there was something in the back of his head, *something* —

He could not focus, not yet . . . but it allowed him to expand his vision of the minutes ahead.

Nine-fourteen, local time.

Even the thought that he would never reach Baikonur could not halt or slow his northward momentum. To go back was to return to the certainty of death now rather than capture — he had killed three of theirs, five including the pilot and the gunner he had incinerated. All of them friends, acquaintances, comrades of other people . . .

The north promised more than that. Most of all — time; time in which circumstances might change, or might be altered to his wish . . . time which might focus the vague something at the back of his mind.

He looked at the gauges. Maybe as much as four-twenty miles before his fuel ran out.

Not enough —

President Calvin's hand swept in an angry gesture towards the screens against the wall of the Oval Office. Winter sunlight through the tinted windows paled and made more insubstantial the television images. Though the Director of the CIA still found them as easy to recognize as if they were personal memories or hopes.

'Why the hell are we paying them to even bother to learn how to do that?' Calvin shouted. His voice seemed to contain as much anguish as anger, as his finger pointed accusingly at an image of the shuttle *Atlantis*. The transmission from the orbiter was from the camera's viewpoint along the spine of the shuttle, revealing the bulk of the Spacelab in the cargo hold, and beyond it two tyre-men with back packs floating like huge white bees around the satellite they were repairing. The remote manipulator arm hung at the edge of the screen like a weak, broken limb. The earth appeared to be almost entirely ocean; virtually cloudless. The vast Pacific, impossibly blue. It was as if it unnerved Calvin for a moment, for he remained silent. Then he burst out again: 'Answer me – you, Bill, or you, Dick – why should the country pay out the billions of dollars to teach those guys how to repair spy satellites?' He glared at his two companions. Filtered sunlight glanced across his shock of grey hair, and his stubborn profile, gilding his features. He raised his hands, then slapped them against his thighs. 'Those guys up there would be better employed learning how to repair Russian automobiles! A skill they could come to need – *that* up there is just about as advanced as a tow-truck and nowhere near as useful any more!'

On companion screens, beside the image of the *Atlantis*, Baikonur. Russian broadcasts to the rest of the world, demonstrating their *peaceful mission in space . . . just like that of the American shuttle*, a forerunner of *future cooperative ventures, the* Soviet Raketoplan *shuttle will be launched on Thursday, to coincide with the signing of the Treaty, the two shuttle craft will rendezvous in orbit in a symbolic gesture of peace, on Friday . . .* The subtitled commentary seemed to mock the men in the room; enrage Calvin further. On other screens, images from around a frightened world. Frightening, frightened, beginning-to-be-relieved . . . *hope is alive in the world again . . .* Calvin shook his head almost in shame. He had said that only a few weeks ago, in his State of the Union message to Congress. *Hope is alive*, dear God in Heaven –!

He studied one screen after another like a list of indictments against him. Barbed wire being rolled back on one screen, the symbolic demolition of concrete emplacements on another. Fences, silos, missiles on others . . . being moved, opened, shut for ever, torn down. A montage of withdrawal as potent as a magnified sigh of relief. On yet another screen, an English-language documentary on the city of Geneva and the location of the signing session – the Palais des Nations. A wide-angled view showed the snowbound city, the gunmetal-coloured expanse of Lac Léman, the tiny, distant, frozen tail-feathers of the Geneva Fountain.

Calvin turned away from the screens. His desk was littered with dozens of newspapers. Some of them had slipped and lay scattered on the dark-green carpet with its scroll and seal. Headlines glared and lay abandoned, like the decorations for a Christmas past. Celebration, optimism, unqualified approval and praise. Calvin began to imagine that he had surrounded himself with the newspapers and the screens in order to torment himself. Mirrors to reflect his scars.

Failure inhabited the Oval Office, though his desk and the floor were strewn with success. He knew his anger was only a bluff, a device to hold failure at arm's length. Dick Gunther knew the game was up, so did the CIA Director. Their faces told him that quite clearly. Gant, that last fond hope, that last desperate stake, had disappeared. He had run into the desert sand like a trickle of water.

Calvin raised his glance as he heard the Director clear his throat.

'I'm sorry, Mr President,' he heard the Director say. It was no more than a repetition of the first words he had uttered on entering the room little more than ten minutes earlier. Even before he had explained, he had begun to apologize. As soon as Calvin looked at him, the Director looked down.

'OK, Bill,' Gunther soothed. 'That's the end of it. There's nothing any of us can do now.'

'Nothing? Nothing, Dick?' Calvin stormed. 'They're going to put a laser battle station into low earth orbit the day after tomorrow and you say there's *nothing* we can do? Find something, dammit! That battle station will be capable of taking out spy satellites, ICBMs, even *Atlantis* and the other shuttles. That's the hole we have to get out of!'

Gunther shook his head. He was perched on the corner of the desk. Calvin saw the gleam of calculation in his eyes; but he was only weighing the Presidential mood, looking for soothing, meaningless words.

Calvin looked back at the row of screens. The blue earth shifted, as if knocked from its orbit, as the camera shot changed to a close-up of the two astronauts at their repairs to the surveillance satellite. A KH-11 type which watched the borders of Israel. Its manoeuvring rocket was failing to respond to transmitted instructions. And Spacelab. Weeks of experiments to find purer pharmaceuticals, high-strength alloys, high-purity crystals for electronic components. Not an aggressive element aboard the *Atlantis*.

Gant was missing, presumed dead. The long-range AWACS aircraft above the Pakistan border had lost touch with the helicopters. Gant had vanished into a whirlpool of Soviet aerial and radio activity. They must have discovered, exposed and now finished him. It was that news the Director had brought with him. It was noon in Washington, the end of Tuesday morning. On Thursday he would have to sign in Geneva – or earn the world's embittered, enraged scorn. Something no President could afford.

The telephone rang. Calvin's hand jumped, then he reached out to take the reply to the call he had made on hearing the news of Gant's loss. He concentrated on keeping his extended hand steady. Gunther handed him the receiver.

At least one explosion, the Director had announced. *A lot of radio traffic, radar emissions, all the trappings of a search-and-kill mission . . .*

. . . the Soviets had indeed had a quarry. Gant.

Calvin snapped on the amplifier and placed the receiver in its cradle. The others, too, could listen to this –! He spoke to the US chief negotiator in Geneva.

'Yes, Frank. Yes, we all feel that, Frank. I want to know what's

231

happening at your end.' Giordello's sympathy and the appalled, lost tone in his voice irritated Calvin.

'But, Mr President, in view of –'

'Listen to me, Frank – what is my *time-table in Geneva*?' He did not look at either Gunther or the Director.

There was a short silence, then Giordello began reciting the litany of protocol and procedure and procession. Midday, Thursday. The bald fact emerged and grew, looming in the Oval Office like a shadow. Cloud had removed the pale gleam of sunlight. The Presidential seal on the carpet was dulled, and the images on the screen blazed out. A fool's errand, a fool's journey on which he must set out before midnight, so that he could sign away America before the weekend.

He sighed. And he could no longer keep the pain and distress from his features as he listened to Giordello's voice. He was beaten and he knew it.

Nevertheless, he would sign away America. He was politician enough to do that rather than earn the world's immediate wrath.

Katya remembered her father, almost like childhood prayers. It is my litany because I am afraid, she told herself. Nothing more than that. She remembered the factory worker's face in the local Party newspaper, on a huge hoarding that gazed across the cobbled square of the town. Her father's eyes had been apologetic, asking almost *why am I here, what have I done to deserve this?* As if he were a criminal, photographically displayed to a shocked public.

In the darkness, the ice-bound marsh possessed a sheen from the moon. Frozen sedge scraped against her waders. She moved forward gently, her slow pace seeming to lend an extra cold to the frozen night. A thin wind cried across the marsh. Some bird honked in the dark. Ahead of her, she could discern a thin vertical line of dim light. And another, horizontal line which joined it. Like heated, magnetized iron filings, glimpses of light shone through gaps in the rotting planking of the houseboat.

This is my litany, she recited once more. The first *new*

232

Moskvitch, for which they had waited another three years after her father's output at the heavy industrial boot factory qualified him for one – output and Party loyalty, of course. An example to his fellow workers. *What am I doing here?* Her father's bemused, even fearful features looking out from the hoarding had rendered him less than a hero; once and for all.

Bare, utilitarian, unreliable; blue. The Moskvitch. Hard to start from the autumn to late spring. Impossible to use from November to March. Its wipers stolen two days after it was delivered. The spare tyre a week later. Her father's pride and joy. *What have I done to deserve this? Why me?* As always, overwhelmed by the generosity of the Party.

She glanced at her watch, the memories not interfering with her alertness. Eleven. The leaking light from the houseboat drew her on. Sedge scraped and snapped and brittlely rustled. The dog, too, distressed it, panting and shivering alongside her. The boat was less than fifty yards away now. Again, a bird honked. The dog growled and she soothed it to quiet. She descended the knoll of reeds she had climbed, one of the many tiny islets dotting the marshes. To the east, the sky had a pale, chilly glow; the thousand arc-lights around the cosmodrome and the occupied launch pad. There were further, dimmer gleams from the science city, from villages, from watchtowers and silos. Yet here, above the thin mourning of the wind, she could hear the mutter of nocturnal animals disturbing the sleep of water-fowl.

Katya shuddered in her coat, her face chilled inside its upturned fur collar, her beret seeming to do little to keep the aching cold from her head.

On her way to school, she had passed her father's bemused glance from the hoarding every day for a month. Schoolfriends sometimes mocked, or were silent out of envy or contempt. He was, and remained, only a factory worker and had no right up there alongside teachers, scientists, engineers, officials of the ministries. The cold wind of March had rattled the portraits, making their heads turn this way and that, ever vigilant. Her father had seemed cold and uncomfortable up there, as if he, too, knew his place. Memory invaded her, radiating warmth, calm.

She slapped her arms across her chest, pausing so that one foot could test the ice, then move her weight onto it, followed by the other foot. The dog slithered, then regained his balance. His great tail banged against her waders. She must get even closer, to make sure . . . though she *knew* that Kedrov was in there . . . Kedrov the spy.

She glanced the torch's beam across the thick ice. Moved gingerly. As if to demonstrate its safety, the dog skittered ahead of her. Nothing to fear . . .

The ice seemed to strike coldly through the soles of the waders, through both pairs of thick socks. The iron-filing pattern of the leaking light beckoned her. She stepped more confidently towards the houseboat, its outline low and huddled against the faint-glowing night. Ice groaned, but quietly, as if disturbed in its sleep. The wind insinuated and moaned, her noises were indecipherable. Kedrov would not be alerted.

She reached the mooring and wiped the torch-beam over its rotting wood above her head, over the plank crossing from jetty to deck. The boat's movements in the wind and the water had reduced the ice around the hull to a soupy, treacherous slush which groaned and slopped. How deep was it? Could she wade in it?

The wooden jetty would be noisier, but in the wind, with the noises of the boat's rotten wood . . . ? Gingerly, she reached out and touched each step of the jetty. Then she climbed, moving slowly, very slowly. Creaks, the night-glasses banging once before she pressed them against her breasts. Her breathing was ragged in a sudden hush of wind. Then, once more, the wind struck through her gloves and clothing, urging her on. The dog's big feet scampered beside her, increasing their noise. His breathing was louder than hers. She knelt at the top of the steps, half-way along the jetty, the boat directly ahead of her, and shushed the dog, made him lie down. Then she straightened. The dog's tail slid back and forth in the torchlight, but he did not attempt to rise.

'Good boy,' she murmured. His tail increased its speed. Then she began creeping towards the houseboat. Her gun was in her gloved hand, her gloves almost too thick for her forefinger to fit into the trigger guard of the Makarov. The pattern of light from the gaps in the boat's planking was clearer, more inviting.

This is my litany because I am afraid, her mind whispered. The memories were random now, flying like sparks.

A plank creaked. The past vanished. She shifted her weight gently and released the wood; it groaned with relief. The dog still lay where she had left him. She moved forward on tiptoe. She was no more than a dozen yards from the boat. Some of the gaps in the planking were wide enough for her to discern a shadow moving inside. Her heart banged.

When she reached the boat, her heart slowed. She knelt down on the jetty to bring her eyes level with a wide, jagged crack of light where the shadow had moved, then settled. She squinted into the crack, half-poised like a runner on blocks. Her waders squeaked against one another. Her gun rested on the rotting wood, clutched unregarded in her left hand.

Kedrov.

Her heart began to thump once more. He was holding a mug. Beyond his shoulder, a haversack. A transistor radio lay on the small, bare section of table she could see.

She *had* found him!

Self-satisfaction warmed her like scalding coffee. She seemed to touch his features with her intent, squinting look. Nose, mouth, profile, thinning hair. The features matched those of the photograph clearly in her mind.

She was very aware of her quick, light breathing and of the gun in her gloved hand.

And of Priabin.

She sighed, but the warmth of pleasure remained; pride was like a blanket into which she snuggled. She checked once more – radio, mug, Kedrov, radio, coffee-mug, *Kedrov* –

– then straightened up, feeling light-headed with success. She tiptoed back towards the dog. Her body urged her to hurry the first yards of the mile or so back to the car and the radio mike.

Kedrov —

She ruffled the dog's fur and laughed softly, luxuriously at her own success.

The bare, scoured landscape flowed slowly beneath the belly of the *Hind*. Gant was vividly aware of the fragility of the machine that enclosed him, that kept out the freezing night temperature and the cut and noise of the wind; aware of its power to kill him. Perhaps within minutes now. Just like his father's life-support machine; tubes, a tent, a mask covering the resented face. The doctor, his sister, her husband the trucker, all approaching the moment in different ways. He in his uniform, cap beneath his arm, body stiffly to attention. He'd decided for all of them and switched off the life-support. The opaqueness of the tent pitched over his father's shrunken form had slowly cleared. A small, old body without the capacity to evoke feeling of any kind had gradually been revealed.

He squeezed the thought from his mind. Now, over this bleak, cold desert, this machine was keeping him alive — and it would switch itself off and kill him when the last drops of fuel drained from the reserve tank. Like the MiG-31 over the North Sea, the *Hind* would make an attempt on his life.

Icy perspiration. The dunes slid beneath the *Hind*'s black shadow. Sand flew off their crests at the helicopter's passage. Distance to Baikonur, a little less than four hundred miles; location, Soviet Central Asia, following the course of the River Oxus towards the Aral Sea. Below him, the emptiness of the Kara Kum; the huge, decayed, toothless jaws of the valley carved by the Oxus opened on either side of him. Dunes and the diamond-sparkling sky stretched away in every direction. Far to the north, too far to concern him, thin cloud hung like the grey smoke from a cigarette.

However precisely and carefully he described the landscape to himself — with whatever assumed detachment — he knew he was unravelling like wool in a cat's claws. Panic had approached and he was conscious of forcing a mental door shut against its increasing pressure. Soon – perhaps even before the fuel ran out – he would not be able to control it.

The MiL had drifted closer to the single main road running parallel with the river, between it and the railway line. Occasional headlights and once the smoke and blaring light of a locomotive glanced across his vision. On the moving map display, the desert appeared to stretch infinitely away beyond the river, road and railway tracks. He had deluded himself, pretending that a solution lurked unformed at the back of his mind. He had run because there was nothing else he could do. He had, he admitted, run in the wrong direction. Mac's shape spread on the ground came back to him vividly, as did the sense of having abandoned the body.

Lumped, broken country stretched away to the north. To the south lay a plateau of ugly grey rock and sand. The *Hind*, with Gant imprisoned within it, hugged the ground on the last of its fuel. He had disappeared successfully into the landscape after crossing the border. His whereabouts were unknown. They would remain that way.

Fuel gauges on Empty. All of them. Wool in a cat's eager claws; unravelling.

The road was less than a mile away now. Unconsciously, he was drifting towards it, as if it were a solution. It wasn't. Straggling closer than the road was the gleam of the river.

Think, *think* –

His mind was empty, except for the seeping of panic, and the urge to survive like the noise of a rat scrabbling at a cage; frantic and desperate. His arms quivered with the effort of holding the *Hind*'s course and height. Its shadow drifted over the broad, straggling, grey river. Was there something at the edge of his mind? He couldn't think, he was too hot, his mind too jumpy and unfocused. He needed to be clearheaded. The *Hind* glided now, as if grace was to be its last skill. The water seemed shallow and muddy, more like a creek than the force which had formed the landscape around him. The dim glow from some encampment stained the night farther to the south, beyond the road and railway – his whole body leapt in anticipation, even as he

237

dismissed it. They would have no fuel and they would kill him for his clothes before they stripped the helicopter naked. Ignore it, *ignore* –

The campfire glowed like a promise. Deliberately, he slowed the helicopter to a crawling speed above its shadow. His arms ached with tension, and fear. His brow and the back of his overalls were wet with perspiration. Not here, not in this lost place, he heard his thoughts repeating. Another mile, another ten, fifty . . . please.

He was at the hover, sand drifting off the side of a nearby dune, hanging like some vague curtain. The *Hind* was in a hollow, surrounded by low dunes. Not in this place – keep going, keep going, *not in this God-forsaken place* –

His resolve snapped in his head like an old dry stick. His body quivered. He could hear his teeth chattering. He could not clear his head.

The undercarriage bumped, then settled. He released the controls. Dust whirled around the cockpit. He switched off the engines and the rotors whined down through the scale and slowed with a sense of finality. He cursed the weakness that had made him land even as he opened the pilot's door and jumped to the ground, coughing immediately because of the sand and dust.

He groaned aloud. As soon as he had walked away from the settling dust, he breathed deeply, again and again. He looked behind him. The *Hind* was already cold and lifeless, and the suggestion of its immobility was like a great, icy wave breaking against him. He was shivering, though he hardly noticed the small, biting wind. His hands clenched and unclenched in futility.

His father returned, then. Machines . . . his father's only use to people, and only then when he was sober. The memory was a supreme mockery now. His father could repair any machine; irons, fridges, lawnmowers, sprinklers, cars – anything you wanted fixed . . . until he had been beaten by a machine in the end, when Gant had switched off the life-support. His father seemed to be watching him now – not gloating for once, just detached and judging.

Painfully, slowly, he climbed the shivering, rattling sand of the dune. Immediately, the glow of the campfire – *no*! The flash of a vehicle's headlights miles away along the road. No suffused glow of a town or village or barracks . . . He rubbed his hands through his hair, the presence of the silent helicopter pressing against the back of his head like a migraine.

Machine, machine . . . His father watched. Think, t-h-i-n-k . . . *think* . . .

He stared at the empty road. Heard the thin wind and shivered in it. Heard the oily sliding of the river and the silence of the helicopter. Empty country, empty road. He was breathing rapidly and deeply, despite the ache of the icy air in his lungs. The beginnings of a terminal attack. Empty road, empty . . . something, something, *Christ* –! Empty road . . . its very emptiness was the clue, the answer, empty . . . stretching away like, like –

Roads home. Roads at home. Slow rise and fall of seemingly-endless roads, empty most of the day . . .

– a gravel road in Iowa, and . . . an old biplane sagging down out of an empty morning sky onto the road and taxi-ing towards . . . the gas station. An airplane . . . His Saturday job, to serve at the gas station where hardly anyone called, and where he spent his time reading magazines about air aces and dogfights. The biplane might have jumped from the pages of one of the magazines . . . that first airplane, the *first* one he'd ever sat in . . . it had just rolled slowly up to the gas-pumps and the pilot had looked down, grinned and said, *Get the windshield, check the tyres* . . .

. . . and filled the airplane's tank from the pump!

Gant whirled around, and stared in utter shock at the *Hind* resting in the hollow. Turned back to the empty road. Looked again at the helicopter, his panic becoming urgent again, but eager now, not final.

There *had* been something in his memory, he hadn't merely panicked . . . a single-engined, prop-driven biplane, flown by an ex-Air Force pilot disgruntled with postwar America. An itinerant crop-sprayer, taxi-ing with complete arrogance on a road in Iowa to fill his fuel tank at a gas station.

Gant ran stumblingly down the dune, sand flying and slithering. Urgency possessed him, as if the engines of the *Hind* were still running and he was using fuel by his very movements. He clambered into the cockpit and flicked on the moving map display. He summoned the largest scale maps, hearing his breathing hoarse and loud in the confined space, hearing the humming excitement in his ears, his heart pounding. He searched the map feverishly for signs of human habitation. Road, railway, river, all heading towards the Aral Sea . . . along the road, follow the road . . .

North, east and west the land opened up, becoming ever more empty. Damn the emptiness of this place –

Desert shading into green on the maps as he ran them again. Temperate. Soil not desert sand. Trees, crops – people. Northwest, where the river turned like an enormous python up towards the Aral Sea, its vast, eroded valley like a huge skin it had already shed. Green – people . . .

Engine-start.

The *Hind* jumped like a flea into the night, out of the hollow. The cockpit was solidly around him, no longer a fragile eggshell. He saw the road, the river as if for the first time.

Along that road. Main road. Gas.

He tried to grin. The gauges had registered Empty for miles already. How much –?

He did grin. The machine wasn't going to beat him. He would survive.

'We're gonna make it – I promise, Mac –' And then he remembered that the gunner's cockpit was empty and Mac was dead and already hundreds of miles behind him. His voice failed.

In its greed, which now reflected his own, the *Hind* hurried through the empty landscape. As he flicked over the crest of a dune, the river gleamed to starboard, and the road was a pale trail to port.

Suddenly, he began to fear once more that the machine would win.

The urgent bleeping of the radio woke Priabin. Ridiculous, he realized in the moment of waking . . . He'd fallen asleep in his car while it was parked outside his office building. The lights, he saw fuzzily, were still on in his office. He scrabbled at the dashboard, reaching for the radio mike, half-expecting the dog to bang its paws on the back of his seat and lick his ear and neck. But the dog was with Katya. He clenched the mike, flicked the switch, and said:

'Priabin. Yes?'

Her voice was breathy, excited. Priabin was sharply disappointed. He wanted the call to be about Rodin, but knew that Katya must be calling about Kedrov.

'– found him!' the girl almost shouted. 'I've found Kedrov in the marshes! Colonel – he's here!'

He glanced up at the lights in his office. Security pressed down on him like a constricting weight; survival, too.

'Katya – hang on, I'm in the carpark. Wait until I can listen on the office scrambler –'

'Sir!' The girl's frustration amounted to outrage.

'*Katya!*' he snapped in reply. 'The car isn't *secure.*' Kedrov, Rodin, the GRU, the military . . . Viktor dead – anything to do with Kedrov was important, might be dangerous. 'Just give me a minute, Katya, then we can use the secure channel.'

'Yes,' Katya replied automatically.

Priabin dropped the mike and flung open the door of the car. Now Rodin was distanced in importance. Katya had found Kedrov. The pieces of the broken ornament that was his future were miraculously coming back together. He hurried across the frosty concrete. The wind flung itself into his face. He ran up the steps and thrust open the twin glass doors into the building, surprising the foyer guard – who instantly relaxed and saluted as he recognized Priabin.

He fumed at the doors of the lift until they opened. Fumed as it ground its slow way upwards. Ran along the thinly carpeted corridor, and unlocked his door –

– locked it once more behind him.

'Katya?' he said breathlessly into the radio, switching on the scrambler unit as he did so. 'Katya – tell me everything!'

Kedrov – Viktor . . . They were linked, too. Like Viktor was

241

bound to Rodin and *Lightning*. It was all of a piece; his future was restored. Dear *God*, the girl had done well –!

He flicked on the anglepoise lamp. In its pool of light, he saw the map of the salt marshes. As he dragged a notepad and pencil towards him, she said: 'I *knew* he'd be here!'

'Well done, well done, you *clever* girl!' he replied lightly. It was infectious. The drowsiness induced by lack of sleep and the car's heater had – well, simply vanished. He felt re-invigorated. He was denied access to Rodin, but now he had Kedrov, who knew something about *Lightning!* He had the answer in the palm of his hand.

Katya's story spilled out excitedly. He listened, enthralled; asked her to repeat details merely in order to savour them; scribbled on his pad, marked the position of the houseboat on the map that lay like an untidy tablecloth across his desk. When she had finished, he said, chuckling:

'Well done – oh, *sweet* girl, well done!' He heard her moment of hesitation almost as if she audibly demurred from his praise, sensing patronage. Then he heard her laughing, and added, more soberly: 'Do nothing – no, don't argue, don't do *anything*! This is too important – no, it's too dangerous, too. You wait there. I'll call Dudin at once – I'll come out with him and his men and we'll all take him together . . . no, no bullshit, no heroics. We'll make *certain* we take him.'

His free hand was clenching and unclenching near the pencil and the notepad. He was racked with impatience like a child.

'Yes, sir,' Katya replied, reconciled to good, sensible precautions. 'But, please *hurry* –!'

'Look, don't worry. Just sit in your car and play that Paul Simon tape I *know* you bought last week from one of the backstreet dealers in town – and we'll be right with you. OK?'

'Yes, Colonel,' she replied in a sobered, careful voice.

'You know Paul Simon's not only an American, but also a Jew – and *very* subversive,' Priabin added. He joined her laughter, then said: 'Well done, Katya – really well done. Hang on – we'll be right with you!'

He switched off the radio. He would make certain that Katya's part in this was recognized by the ponderous, dinosaur committees – just as he would use the capture of Kedrov as his return ticket to Moscow Centre. He had begun to dial Dudin's number but his hand, as if understanding his mood, had replaced the receiver. He found himself staring at the dark square of the window as if at some screen upon which long-anticipated images would shortly be projected. It was only gradually that the haze of light from the distant launch complex made itself apparent against the glass. He rubbed his chin, then watched his fingers drumming with growing impatience on his desk . . . . but the moment was good, and he deliberately held onto it for as long as he could. His fingers were pale in the lamp's pool of white light. Slowly, almost luxuriously, he made those impatient fingers reach towards the dial – Dudin, and the capture of Kedrov –

– the telephone began to ring.

Katya's danger was almost the first reaction that began to surge in him, until he realized it was not the same telephone. It was the one he had been going to use to call Tyuratam's KGB chief.

His mood vanished, he grabbed up the receiver and almost shouted into it: 'Priabin. *Yes?*'

'Sir –?' It was Mikhail.

'Mikhail – look, I'm busy, urgently busy. Clear the line, will you? I'll take any report later on –'

'Sir, this is important,' Mikhail announced heavily. Priabin could clearly hear restrained anger in his breathing.

'Oh, very well, Mikhail,' he sighed. 'What is it?'

'Two things, sir . . . we've been trying to get hold of you –'

'Yes, yes,' he snapped. 'What two things?'

His body twitched with impatience. Katya was out there in the icy night, close to Kedrov. In an hour, they could have him –! He closed his free hand into a tight fist, clutching his image of Kedrov.

'His father rang him almost an hour ago – to confirm the poof's leaving first thing in the morning. The early flight out.'

'Why?'

'When the old man was here, sir, he – he *beat his son up*. Raging anger. Knocked him about . . . we couldn't hear, but we saw a lot of it. Old Rodin was shouting his head off. Now we know what he was saying. It's tomorrow –'

'Damn,' Priabin said softly, but the news was strangely without impact; a small pity for the son, an abstract dislike of the father and his behaviour . . . but the disappointment, the sense of being cheated that Mikhail implied he should feel – were both absent. 'That's it, then,' he added with a sigh.

'Sir – the other piece of news!' Mikhail's exasperation was insubordinate.

'What?'

'He – he's asked to talk to you, sir – the poof, not the father . . .'

'Asked –?'

'He must have checked, found the 'phone was bugged . . . little sod just picked up the receiver and spoke to us! Demanded to speak to you – said he had something to tell you!'

'Something to tell . . . ?' Priabin began. It was as if a drug injected minutes before only now began its stimulating effect. His mind seemed to become urgently intent. He leaned forward in his chair, his hand scrabbled for his pencil; Kedrov and Katya and the marshes retreated. He was tempted and greedy. 'What *exactly* did he say?'

Mikhail's tone changed, became enthusiastically relieved. 'Said he had to talk to you, sir . . . you want to hear the tape of what he said?'

'No, just tell me.'

'He said he had something important to tell you – something you'd be interested to hear. He said he had to talk to you tonight because, as we no doubt knew already, he was leaving for Moscow on the morning flight. Cheeky little bugger –'

Lightning – had to be . . . *Lightning*.

He could have it all. He felt dry-mouthed with anticipation.

'When was this?'

'Fifty-two minutes ago, sir.'

244

'He hasn't rung back?'

'He's been packing. Quite calm, by the look of it. No drugs, just one brandy. He seems to be waiting for you, sir – as if he's sure you'll come.'

Priabin shook his head. If he was that certain, then it was *Lightning*.

'I'll come. Straight away.'

'One other thing, sir. He says he won't let you in – you'll have to talk to him from here – stand where he can see you. Talk over the 'phone.'

'Why?'

'Who knows, sir?'

Priabin was puzzled, but that was unimportant. Dudin could go to Katya's assistance with a team . . . they could hold off until he could get there himself. First, he had to hear what Rodin had to say. Katya's maps and notes lay on the desk, scattered like archaeological evidence of some lost civilization. He could hardly think of Kedrov now – Rodin was the prize. Rodin had had Viktor killed and Rodin wanted to talk to him about *Lightning* . . . and he would know so much more than Kedrov! Anticipations raced in his mind, clear and quick as glimpses into a certain future.

'No one's with him?'

'He's alone, sir. No one's rung, either. He hasn't called anyone else . . . he's just waiting, sir.'

'The waiting's over,' he announced excitedly. 'I'll be there as soon as I can. Is he up or down?'

'Neither. Suspended, sir.'

'Good. I'm on my way!'

He clicked the rest then dialled Dudin's number immediately. He would make sure Katya was safe and didn't go in single-handed – as she just might if no one turned up soon – and ensure, too, that Kedrov couldn't slip away . . . his heart bumped and his forehead felt hot. His cheeks burned as if with embarrassment.

'I promised, Viktor,' he murmured as he waited for the telephone in Dudin's office to be picked up. 'I promised . . .'

Midnight.

Gant touched the rudder pedal with his left foot to maintain his heading, eased the column, maintained his height with the collective pitch lever in his left hand, and listened to the fluctuating, reluctant rpm of the two Isotov engines. He was aware of each of his tiny movements, most aware of the engine noise as the *Hind* moved at thirty feet above –

– that. On the main road between Urgench and Tashauz. Closed, apparently deserted. Lifeless. A gas station, kiosk windows boarded, weeds moving in the downdraught all over the forecourt. He had seen nothing else except a few parked lorries, lights extinguished and drivers presumably asleep in their cabs, a couple of cars streaming white light along the ribbon of the road. The lights of Urgench were the palest smear in the mirrors.

He was beginning not to believe. He was beginning to sweat, to panic. The gas station should have been open – its remains were there, sliding into ruin! – it was shown on the moving map, but who in hell would have thought to update the positions or financial viability of gas stations?

It was closed. Thirty feet below the *Hind*'s belly, with boarded windows. It had been deserted years ago. Petrol pumps, hoses bent hand-on-hip, a corrugated plastic roof that was dirt-covered, clumped with mosses, a wooden garage with drunkenly-leaning doors, the single-storey wooden house which was lightless, where –

– lights flicked grubbily on behind a thin curtain! His heart lurched with relief. Not lightless, not abandoned . . . immediately, he dropped the *Hind* carefully towards the forecourt. The engine noise was fragile, uncertain, like the beat of an ancient, weakened heart. He felt the wheels touch, the helicopter bounce as if pleased, then he throttled back to ground-idle.

The low house – shack, no more – needed painting . . . it had looked so dilapidated he thought it must have been empty. Its door opened. A man in a thick coat and dark, baggy trousers stood in the light of Gant's main lamp, hand shielding his eyes. Gant adjusted the lamp so that it shone directly on the man –

garage manager or whoever he was . . . it didn't matter; there was fuel beneath this weed-strewn, dusty concrete.

Stay smart, he told himself. Stay smart. Tension coursed through him, indistinguishable from relief.

The man walked into the light, waving at the beam as if fending off insects or repeated blows.

He moved the throttle levers to flight-idle, and the rotors growled into a disc reluctantly. He eased the column forward and gently raised the lever until the helicopter shunted forward — waddling and uncertain in its progress. He watched the edge of the shining rotor disc as the *Hind* moved gently towards the corrugated roof.

He watched the pumps intently, watched the roof's lip, watched the rotors, whirling —

— satisfied he was as close as possible, he lowered the lever, eased back the column, applied the brakes. The helicopter sank, bounced, stopped. He altered the throttles — noise boomed around the cockpit from the roof and the pumps — and stop-cocked the engines and applied the rotor brake.

Check the tyres, get the windshield . . . He grinned. The *Hind* was drawn up like a huge, grotesque car. Dust settled on the cockpit and shimmered downwards around him. He could do nothing for the moment except stare at the gauges, then glance at the petrol pumps. *Premium Grade*, they announced in Cyrillic and some other script he did not recognize. He could use petrol instead of paraffin or aviation fuel without short-term damage to the engines. He *had to*.

The garage manager — in Soviet Central Asia he might even be the owner — ducked beneath the drooping, still rotor blades with inordinate care and suspicion. They rested more than ten feet above his head.

As he approached the cockpit, Gant swung his door open and called out, beginning to control the situation, damp down suspicion: 'Gauges must be out — ran out of fuel! Sorry, comrade, to disturb your well-earned rest or whatever else you were doing back there . . .' He was grinning broadly, but his features adopted command, the expectation of quick and questionless

247

assistance. 'Your stuff will have to do until I get home – fill her up!'

The engine noise had died out of his head now. Around him, the night seemed to spread outwards like a black pool stained with moonlight. He sensed distances, and isolation beneath his relief. The man looking up into his features was an Uzbek with a narrow, dark, unshaven face. His eyes glinted reflections of the cockpit lights. Tiny rows of green, red, amber, blue from the still-alive panels made his pupils those of an automaton.

'Who pays me?' the man asked, seemingly unaware of the cold or the wind. His accent coated the Russian words thickly like a rough varnish. His thin, hook-nosed face stared impassively up at Gant, as if it were indeed a car that had drawn alongside the pumps. He was simply waiting to see money.

Gant glanced at his watch. Midnight plus five. Three hundred and forty miles to Baikonur. Two hours, maximum, with full tanks; and a full ferry tank. He could still make it – just – if Kedrov was waiting for him . . . ingress and egress before daylight. Hopes, estimates, tension tumbled together in his mind and invaded his frame, even as he maintained his disarming, superior, expecting-to-be-accommodated smile towards the surly Uzbek. He gripped the door-handle with his right hand, his thigh with his left, and calmed himself.

'You'll get paid – what's your worry, comrade?' He leant over the Uzbek, his rank and uniform overalls evident. So, too, the holster on his hip containing the Makarov pistol. 'I'll write you a receipt – OK? You'll manage to read it?' he added with a small sneer. The Uzbek was unimpressed, more reluctant than before. Evidently, he owned the garage. It would be *his* loss. Gant snapped: 'The army pays, comrade.'

Then he jumped down from the cockpit, landing close to the man, and was immediately taller than the Uzbek; who understood the change in their relationship. He flinched. Gant was still smiling, but his hand was lightly on the holster now. The flap was unopened as yet, just as his lips were unopened in the smile.

The night chilled through the thin flying overalls after the hothouse of the cockpit. His sweat dried like forming ice. The moon-sheened darkness oppressed, unrelieved except where headlights rose and fell over a dip of the road, perhaps a half-mile away; a vehicle heading for the garage. He looked up, picking out the distant navigation lights of a slow-moving aircraft. A commercial flight out of Tashkent, he guessed. He shivered, desiring movement, assertion; the headlights flicking into view once more at the periphery of his sight. Bouncing nearer like a ball.

He bent over the *Hind*'s flank as if it were that of a car, and flicked open the fuel cap.

'There you are, comrade – fill her up. Then fill the ferry tank in the main cabin.' One hand still on the holster flap, the other on his hip in challenge. 'Your hose won't reach from the pump,' he observed with continuing casualness. 'Find an extension hose and a funnel – get on with it, comrade!'

The Uzbek seemed to subside slowly into his coat, shrinking. Then he shrugged and turned to the nearest pump, dragging the hose from its rest. He unlooped a length of hose from a hook on the side of the kiosk, and picked up a tin funnel from the shelf inside. The door banged in the wind. The Uzbek cursed softly as he thrust the nozzle of the hose into the extension, then dragged it towards the *Hind*. The headlights of the approaching vehicle bounced against the cockpit. The funnel clattered into the fuel tank; the man returned to the nozzle of the pump and squeezed its lever. Fuel flowed after the click. Gant felt as if he had drunk cold, fresh water. Oasis. The fuel's transfer was sweet. The headlights were flat beams now, colliding with the wood and metal of the garage. Ice sparkled on the corrugated roof above him and on the weedy forecourt. Stiff grass rattled in the wind.

Gant remembered needle-like outcrops rising over the hills through which the *Hind* had flitted. Minarets and mosques sparkling with ice in the hard moonlight. Perhaps Bokhara, perhaps some other town. His flight over Soviet Central Asia had been like rushing down some narrowing tunnel; hills, stretches of sand that seemed red even by moonlight, dry rivers, oases, encampments where camels lumped together like full sacks on the ground, as still as the tents near them. Fires dying down, scuttling and alarmed figures moving. Herds of goats, trading caravans. Still irrigation water and reservoirs. It was as if the oncoming headlights illuminated the past hours. They were now clear, confined by the emerging dark shape around them which had become a truck. The Uzbek looked up from the nozzle of the pump without real interest. Gant's hands tensed, bunched into fists, and his face twisted to the beginnings of some cry of protest. Army —?

Civilian . . .

He sighed audibly with relief. The hours of avoiding radar, other aircraft and helicopters, towns and villages had worn at him like waves at an old cliff. He stood more erect, as if to deny his weariness. The truck drew onto the forecourt. The Uzbek made a noise in his throat that might have signalled recognition. The truck pulled to a halt. Gant heard the handbrake scratching on.

The young man who got down almost at once from the passenger side of the canvas-hooded truck was wearing army uniform. Gant's heart banged in his chest. He was grinning as he stared, hands on his hips, at the *Hind* drawn up at the pumps.

Uniform? *How* —?

The canvas covering the back of the truck rattled in the icy breeze. The driver, who wore a sleeveless sheepskin jacket and a cloth cap, got down from the cab. Only the passenger was in uniform.

And was approaching —

— Russian, not Uzbek. White skin in the moonlight, white teeth, a white hand raised in greeting. A captain, but young. A yawn, one hand stretching away cramp. The driver hung back, as if out of respect. The young man grinned again. Gant felt his attention mesmerized by the uniform, the shoulder-flashes.

At seven yards, Gant saw that the captain was GRU, military intelligence —

— and went towards the younger man, disarming him with a smile, an extended hand.

The captain took his hand, shook it. Despite the icy wind, the GRU man's hand was still warm from the heated cab. His features registered a slight shock at the coldness of Gant's grip. There was a sharp smell of vegetables – cabbages? – on the air; presumably the truck's cargo.

Why was a GRU captain stepping out of *that* vehicle?

Cabbages, onions, the earthiness of potatoes. Gant's sense of smell was heightened by nerves. The driver's firm's name was in Uzbek, not Cyrillic. He wrenched his mind away from the irrelevant. The captain's scrutiny was inexperienced, but nevertheless there. No hint of suspicion, but questions were forming in his eyes . . . a military helicopter, *there*?

Gant's own rank matched that of the captain, but the younger man would assume the precedence of GRU over Aviation Army rank. Gant's attention concentrated, narrowing every perspective, on the shoulder-flashes, the arm badges – the tiny, untwinkling jewels of the man's significance.

'You're a long way from home, comrade!' he announced heartily.

'– words out of my mouth!' the captain replied. Laughed. Finally released Gant's grip. 'A bloody helicopter at a filling station? You must be the squadron joker!'

'Ran out of fuel,' Gant complained.

'Long way from home? Not as far as you, man! I'm just hitching a ride to Bokhara, then on to Samarkand.' His accent was Moscow, perhaps Ukrainian – Kiev? European Russia. The master race. Gant's own accent – his mother's accent – was distinctive. 'You're Georgian, by your accent?' the young captain added.

'Yes,' Gant replied. 'From Surami – you know it, the thermal resort.' His shoulders shrugged.

'Away from the Black Sea?' Gant merely nodded. 'Don't know it,' the captain continued. 'One-horse town, is it?'

'Just about.' His voice was easier, lighter. He spun the web of conversation, rank and comradeship. Then the captain asked:

'Afghanistan, if I'm not mistaken?' His eyes were sharper as he studied Gant. They were alert, as if studying some mental list of explanations. The night and the distances leapt at Gant, reminding him that the *Hind* was misplaced by hundreds of miles, was suspicious here.

251

He was suddenly aware of his own cover story. *Where was he going? From where?* Alma-Ata, army headquarters, was eight hundred miles to the east. His cover was now outdated, an obvious fake.

Beneath their conversation, their camaraderie and humour, the fear continued to flow like a river. Gant shivered. The wind seemed to be strengthening. Yet the two Uzbeks seemed oblivious to it; they were smoking near the pumps. Gant heard his teeth chattering and saw the captain grin.

'Adamov,' the captain announced.

What is my name? His identity lay in his breast pocket, with his papers.

What is my name?

He had forgotten his cover name.

The captain's eyes glazed with suspicion.

heart of the matter

'Let's find ourselves some coffee. This Uzbek moron can fill the helicopter on his own – my driver can keep him company.'

Gant realized that the captain's words, as he gestured towards the low wooden bungalow, were meant to extend the moment of suspicion. Just how long would this pilot take to introduce himself – explain himself? The moment was an elastic band being stretched to breaking.

'What in hell are you doing getting down from a cabbage truck, comrade?' Gant exclaimed, forcing laughter. 'A captain in GRU – not quite the right sort of transport, uh?' His hands came out, palms up. Friend, harmless, they suggested, while his voice asked *who are* you, *man*?

The captain was disconcerted, but it might have been no more than his resentment of the familiarity of Gant's tone. It was the captain who should patronize if either of them did.

'Just finished a job upcountry,' he replied, his hand still patting at Gant's shoulder and turning him towards the wooden building, where a grubby light filtered through thin, unlined curtains. The wind moaned, rattling the corrugated plastic above his head, making the drooping rotor blades of the *Hind* quiver. There was a mutual sense of cursing in the conversation between the truck driver and the garage owner; racial suspicion and hatred. 'Some of these fucking Moslems are giving trouble – don't want to fight their Islamic brothers in Afghanistan . . . you know what they're like. Pigs!' He spat obviously and loudly, turning towards the two Uzbeks as he did so. The wind carried the gobbet of spittle and splashed it against the side of the petrol pump, near the bending garage owner's head; which did not turn or look up. The truck driver's eyes flickered, but the expression died as easily as a match-flame in the wind. 'Pigs,' the GRU captain repeated, evidently convinced of the manifest truth of his generalization. 'We shot a few – *a number of the conspirators and mutineers were tried and executed according to military law,*' he corrected himself solemnly. His eyes were smiling and flinty with satisfaction. Then he belched and Gant smelt the drink on his breath for the first time. 'All done by the book, according to the book, for the book.' Captain Adamov grinned. 'Bang!' He strutted a few steps, hand curled at the end of his outstretched arm. His trigger-finger squeezed perhaps half a dozen times as he paused behind remembered necks, watched remembered corpses –

Gant, controlling the shiver that the mime had induced, watched Adamov as he returned to his side, nudging him. 'The rest of them have been shipped off now,' he remarked. 'A few more GRU and GLAVPUR people among their officers, of course . . .'

'Where –' Gant cleared his throat, glancing at the dial of the petrol pump still spinning as his tanks filled. After the underbelly tanks, the ferry tank in the cabin. It would be minutes yet . . . 'Where was this, comrade?' The driver and the garage owner were gabbling rapidly in Uzbek, their words still carrying the strong accent of hatred.

– *pig, pig, Russian pig . . .*

The words became a remembered litany in his head. He had heard them often, through the thin, cracked-plaster wall as he lay next to his sister's cot. Only understanding years later what it must have been that his mother was refusing his drunken, demanding father. He shook his head. Adamov seemed confused.

'Where was this little problem?' Gant asked.

'Oh, barracks outside Khiva. Low-grade conscripts. They had some of their officers tied up – full of hashish and threats the whole lot of them –' He grinned. 'Making demands – you know *them*! Cut the balls off one poor sod and shoved them down his throat . . .' He sighed theatrically. 'Not a lot of resistance, once we'd explained the position to them and the hashish wore off.'

254

'How come you're here now? Must have been a big op?' Gant shrugged as convincingly as the cold would allow.

'What do you mean?' Adamov protested, as if he suspected the presence of another policeman.

Gant understood. Adamov had been due some leave, had perhaps wangled or forged the papers granting him a few days off in Samarkand before he reported back to headquarters. His presence there was a weakness, but the man was still dangerous.

Degree of cover, training prompted him. *Imagine you're standing there naked, reddening with embarrassment until you can put on some clothes . . . what can you add to your cover? Remember background, experience, training, anecdote, expertise, rank – convince them you are who you say you are.*

Afghanistan . . . you're just back from there, and finding that Adamov is fighting the good fight right here . . . *Uzbek pigs!*

'OK, coffee it is,' he said, quite easily. 'Borzov, by the way,' he added, remembering his cover name easily now. Adamov nodded, relaxed by the identity he felt was emerging.

'Good, *good*!' Adamov's hand came back to Gant's shoulder. They moved together towards the low house, bending slightly into the increasing wind . . . which nagged at Gant's awareness. His mind estimated the windspeed, considered take-off, flying.

Twelve-twenty, he saw, glancing surreptitiously at his watch. Time wasting. *Cover story!*

'Cleared your desk early, mm?' he asked with assumed heartiness.

Adamov glanced at him with renewed suspicion, then relaxed. 'Just so, man. Cleared my desk early!' He pointed an index finger, then curled it shut in a squeezing gesture. Hero of the slaughter. He laughed. 'I *like* it! Cleared my desk early.' His laughter was snatched away by the wind after it had buffeted Gant.

Adamov had enjoyed the killing – perhaps he had even been given his early leave for services rendered? Gant shivered. Adamov said abruptly: 'I recognize the flashes on the MiL, the idents. Alma-Ata's your home base, then?' He hardly paused before he added: 'Then you must know old Georgi Karpov? He must have been posted to Kabul the same time as you were – same flight, or squadron or whatever you call it in the FAAs . . . How is he, old Georgi – mm?'

Adamov had paused on the step up to the wooden porch of the bungalow. Dust flew around them. The captain's eyes were bright, as bright as the full moon. Only one thought took precedence in Gant's mind –

Who was Georgi Karpov?

The laser battle station, ostensibly the first component of *Linchpin*, in reality the very heart of *Lightning*, had been transferred to the main assembly building, still in its component parts. The main mirror, the laser tube, the power source – each provided General Lieutenant Pyotr Rodin with a hard, diamond-like satisfaction. Each component was as evocative as memories of the ranks he had held, the promotions he had received during his years of service.

That very evening, shaving for a second time in order to appear at his most groomed here and now, he had watched his worried face in the mirror – and wondered how people viewed his only son. Did they see, as vividly as he did, the weak chin, the full, loose lips, the pale, delicate skin . . . ? Did they see his wife, as he did . . . ?

No, of course not, he had reasoned – reasoned again now. They could not because they had never seen his wife. Not out here, not in Baikonur. Very few of the High Command had met that quiet, mousy woman who hardly left fingerprints never mind made an impression on anyone's memory . . .

. . . and who had ruined his only son.

Dismiss –

Staring at the components of the laser weapon, he watched his son's image whirl away into the darkness in his head.

The following night the laser weapon would be lowered into the gaping cargo bay of the shuttle craft, the doors would close on it, the shuttle craft would be drawn out of the building on its short journey to join the booster stages at the launch site . . . there was nothing else. His son did not concern him – did not *deserve* his attention at this time.

Even the presence of Serov could not dim the moment, tarnish the hard glint of his pleasure. The GRU commandant was to his right, while to his left an army technician stood beside a television set mounted on a wheeled trolley. Its power lead trailed away through the small knot of aides and scientific staff and out of sight. On the television's screen, the earth glowed blue and white and green, hanging in the blackness of space. Africa lay green and brown beneath his glance.

Then the picture switched to another camera's view. The hold of the American shuttle craft, *Atlantis*. The picture seemed almost in monochrome. In the centre, two astronauts in pressure-suits were working on a satellite they had rescued. They were attached to the hold by twining, snakelike cords. Rodin's fingers plucked at his lower lip. His gaze was intent, as if he were deciphering some complex puzzle. It was, however, anticipatory pleasure he experienced, not doubt or confusion.

In less than thirty-six hours' time, the Soviet shuttle would be launched into low earth orbit. Nothing could go wrong here, not with their schedule. Nothing must go wrong –

– and the express hoist at the launch pad needed repair. It would be used to place the shuttle craft atop the G-type booster, and now it had developed an hydraulic failure. It must be repaired. At once. Thus he had spoken, and they had assured. He understood enough of the jargon – besides which he trusted his aides – to know that it was not crucial, that the repairs could be effected in time to move the shuttle during the early hours of Thursday morning. Which would put it into orbit to coincide with the Treaty signing . . .

. . . and bring *Lightning* into effect on Friday.

But, better to say it once more than to leave any doubt, any doubt whatsoever.

'Thirty-*five* hours, comrades,' he announced to their immediate attention. He disliked the word, *comrades* – a Party word, not a military one. *Gentlemen* would have fitted more easily. His eyes scanned them like some surveillance camera as his head turned once more to take in the details of the shuttle which lay open like a gutted fish, beached on its massive transporter. The railway lines ran the length of the huge building and out into the arc-lit night. 'Thirty-five hours.' Power flowed like adrenalin. 'The hoist is to be repaired before this craft moves from here – you have assured me it will be done.'

White-coated civilians nodded, murmured again. Military aides confirmed with nodding heads, with shoulder-boards and uniforms and medal ribbons. Rodin was satisfied, even though his gloved fingertips prickled with impatience. He nodded by way of reply.

'Good.'

He turned to Serov. His son whirled back out of the darkness in his head. Why did he feel any necessity to explain to Serov? Why, why was he *afraid* of the man?

Because Serov had the kind of mind, stark and untroubled in its ruthless clarity, which might reach towards the final cleanness of an accident to Valery similar to that prescribed for his actor friend . . . and Rodin could not contemplate that thought. Guilt sprang unfamiliarly, and he hated the weakness and fear it aroused in him. He would carry out his plan and get the boy away from Baikonur – away from Serov – back to Moscow and the Academy . . . where he could begin to call upon favours and discretion. The boy could even stay with his mother.

He cleared his throat and said to Serov in a hard, quiet tone: '*Stavka* requires assurances, Serov, concerning your missing technician. They've been in touch with me and specifically mentioned the matter of security. You understand?'

Serov's face darkened at Rodin's challenging tone, but he merely said: 'In two hours, comrade General, I shall be able to brief you on every aspect of security surrounding the – project. My people are updating everything at this moment.'

'Good.' Rodin smiled slightly at Serov's tight-lipped acquiescence.

Then the colonel hit back softly, sharply.

'We shall expect no further embarrassments from your son,

258

comrade General . . . ? I approve your scheme to remove him to Moscow in a few hours' time.'

'You *approve* –?'

Serov continued as if Rodin had not spoken: 'The KGB are keeping the boy under discreet surveillance, but they have made no move – and they're not likely to.'

'You people *seem* to have acted wisely, after all,' Rodin replied, unable to eradicate a slight quiver from his words.

'Thank you, comrade General,' Serov replied with evident irony.

Rodin turned his glance away from the GRU commandant, once more to the *Raketoplan* shuttle and the laser weapon's components. Light gleamed from the great shield of the main mirror. His body seemed filled with reposeful confidence. He saw the mirror, the tube, the shuttle, as extensions of his own authority, as if they were as vital to him, as much a part of him, as his limbs.

The others might, even now, change their minds. They could scrap *Lightning* even after it was launched. The shuttle's launch had to be on schedule, it must appear technically *perfect*, and it must coincide with the signing of that filthy, weak Treaty in Geneva . . . then they'd show their real power to the dodderers in the Kremlin. What was it Peter the Great had said, at the launching of a man-of-war in St. Petersburg . . . ? *It is now our turn . . . you may happen even in our lifetime to put other civilized nations to the blush, and to carry the glory of the Russian name to the highest pitch* . . . yes, that was it. Pyotr Alexeivich, Peter the Great. With that Treaty on the point of ratification, it was not easy to believe in sentiments as broad and certain as that – except for *Lightning*. Now, he was poised on the edge of the great chasm of the next day and a half. After that, the Defence Minister, *Stavka* – the General Staff – and their supporters in the Politburo, would have all the leverage they required to treble, even quadruple the budget for orbital weapon development. They would have the leverage to do *anything* – and he would have given it to them.

Lightning was their private tearing up of the Treaty. After it, they could move forward, become the power both real and hidden. *Lightning* promised a reincarnation of the army's waning power. No self-satisfaction could do justice to that thought. It was the arm twisted up behind the Politburo's back until it broke like a dry, old stick.

Images of violence and power coursed through Rodin like rough, heady wine.

'Let me come over,' Priabin whispered, staring out of the window down towards the window of Valery Rodin's flat. Even without the aid of the glasses, he could see the livid bruising on the young man's face. 'Let's talk face to face – this is ridiculous.'

'I've locked and bolted the door.'

Hashish and drink. He'd started again perhaps half an hour before Priabin had arrived. Rodin had come to the window at once, as soon as Priabin lifted the receiver. Through the glasses, his face had been that of a whipped and frightened animal. Alone in the dark, he had been suddenly, unstably grateful for the contact of Priabin's voice and his shadowy image in the window opposite. He had even raised one hand in what may have been a wave of recognition.

But, he wouldn't open the door, wouldn't allow Priabin into the flat. It was like a wall of silence, a huge gap of night between them that depressed and offered no promise. Rodin seemed as if he had tricked him into coming; there were no revelations, no confidences . . . just this idle chatter, this need for company on the young man's part. A salve for the bruises his father's hands had inflicted.

The boy was desperate. Quietly, certainly desperate. But still unbroken. And Priabin could not operate with surgical precision down a telephone line on a figure glimpsed only at a distance. Frustration made him jumpy. Mikhail and Anatoly had retreated into a tense silence away behind him in the room's shadows. Katya was out in the marshes and Dudin was on his way to join her. Kedrov the spy was in the bag . . . this boy was wasting his time.

'You're wasting my time!' he snapped. Mikhail murmured

260

something he did not catch. 'You hear me, Rodin?' he persisted.

'Am I?' Rodin replied breathily, with contempt.

'Why did you call me? What did you want?'

Priabin studied Rodin's figure. A joint between his fingers, a balloon of cognac in his hand. His body swaying slightly. There was music on in the room, Priabin could hear it mutedly. It seemed familiar and evocative, but he could not catch either tune or words.

'To talk.'

'Last time we spoke you had nothing to say. What's changed – *sweetheart?*' There was a qualm of sympathy in his chest and stomach, but he ignored it, even though he could clearly see Rodin flinch at the insulting word. It was like a slap, turning his head quickly to one side. His body stopped swaying. He even raised his hand to his bruises. Priabin sensed instinct guide him, but it was all but obscured by his frustrated anger. 'What is it you want? You want to lodge a complaint against your *assailant* – is that it? Well? Who did it to you, then? *Who was it?*'

'You know who did it – your bastards were even watching! Don't be *smart!*' Rodin suddenly yelled into the telephone. It was a child's playground yell, half pain, half threat; self-pity, too. Priabin saw him swig violently at his glass, then wipe his mouth with the back of his hand. He puffed nervously at the crumpled cigarette. Priabin felt himself close to the young man, as if suspended on some window cleaner's hoist just outside the window where Rodin stood in his silk dressing-gown.

'Let's talk about *Lightning*, then, shall we?'

He could see fear ingrained like dirt on Rodin's face. As livid as the bruises. Rodin shook his head.

'No! Let's talk about Sacha –!' His narrow neck seemed stretched. Priabin bent for a moment to the glasses – dammit, he was attempting to break a man at long-distance! It was all but impossible – he had to get into the room with Rodin!

'Why him?' he snapped back quickly, unsure as to whether or not professional instinct guided his response. 'The queer's dead, after all . . .'

'*You sound just like my father!*'

The two men in the room with him stirred at the tinny scream that even they could hear. Priabin winced with pain, knowing he had made an error.

'So, I'm just like your old man,' he responded, his voice mocking. Anna dragged at his sleeve like an importunate child. He had not even noticed her memory entering the room. He felt hot, and guilty. Shaking his head – still bent to the glasses on their tripod, the receiver against his cheek – he continued brutally: 'We've been through that, Rodin. You and your father. What's your father doing right now? What is he doing *now*?'

Have to watch his face, watch his face . . . Anna, leave me alone, he whispered into the darkness at the back of his mind. Not now, not now . . . she was there, of course, to tell him not to break Rodin, to understand him; to remind him of how alone Valery Rodin was, how desperate. Not now, Anna, *not now* –

Rodin's mouth was agape, then it closed to a cunning expression as if biting on something edible. Anna, Viktor . . . Viktor supplied his urgency, his unfeeling grip on the boy across the street. He couldn't let go, couldn't let Viktor down. It was why he was here . . . Anna and Viktor.

Revenge for Viktor was achievable. He could never avenge Anna's death upon the American pilot, Gant – Viktor would have to do.

'Just remember, Valery,' he whispered into the receiver, 'I'm more dangerous than you. I have a dead second-in-command on *my* conscience, not just a not-very-good actor who was your lover.'

And he knew he had been right, that it was instinct guiding him, when Rodin screamed back: 'He could have been a great actor!'

'Because he flattered *you*?' The riposte was automatic, pure technique. At once, his next line was there, as if in a script. 'Because he made you feel good in *bed*? My God, he must have been good if he could do that for *you*!' The contempt was acted, yet absolute. In his head, Anna stared reprovingly. And he saw her face the moment after she had died, when he had held her body. He winced, almost protested aloud, then controlled his reactions, and listened.

Rodin seemed to have drawn calm from the silence. He said in a quiet voice: 'Just like my father.'

'If I'm like your father, Valery, then what did you want from me?' Priabin's voice was softer, almost soothing. Anna's face retreated.

He glanced at his watch. Twelve-thirty. He stamped almost viciously on his impatience. He had to stay with Rodin. The boy wanted to talk, must be made to talk usefully, to the point.

'Just to talk,' Rodin murmured. The hashish had calmed him thoroughly. His voice was slow, easy, detached.

'Why did you want me to come, Valery? Why now? Why at the moment when you're being sent away?'

'Because I knew *you* would come,' Rodin replied dreamily. He even raised his balloon and swallowed off in a mock-toast what remained of his cognac. Priabin straightened from the glasses. The boy's eyes were unfocused, wide-pupilled from the drug and from staring into the night. 'I knew you'd come,' Rodin repeated.

Time was diminishing quickly now. The boy wasn't frightened any longer. He had to be slapped into wakefulness; Priabin had only his voice and his experience to do it. Anna, go away . . .

'What did Daddy say, Valery?' he probed, his voice insinuating like a needle. 'Why did he beat you up? Just for being queer . . . or was he giving you a taste of what's in store for you?' Priabin sensed the others in the room leaning forward, attentive and appreciative. Anna's dead face flashed like a warning. Go *away*!

'What —?' Rodin breathed, shaken.

'Has he abandoned you, Valery? Told you he'll never drag you out of the shit, ever again? Is that what he was telling you with his fists . . . you're on your own now?' Rodin's quickening breathing, like some indistinct climax, accompanied his words, raced ahead of them. 'It was, wasn't it? You'll be at the mercy of everyone at the Academy . . . they don't like sodomites there, do they? He's going to *cure* you, Valery, isn't that it? He thinks enough beatings and you'll settle down with a nice young wife, eh? *Eh?*' Priabin laughed mockingly.

'. . . shut up, shut up, shut up . . .' Rodin was collapsing in his pain and distress and fear for the future. Future? At the Frunze Academy without his father's protection he had no future! He'd be the butt of jokes and casual violence from fellow-students and instructors alike. '. . . shut up, *shut up, damn you*!' Like the scream of someone being beaten into confession in a distant room. Priabin shuddered.

Rodin's voice had degenerated from words to sobbing; self-pity controlled and enveloped him. Priabin let the noise continue until it faded into a breathy, swallowing quiet. Rodin had walked away from the lighted square of his window and sat heavily on the edge of his bed. Next door, the subdued lighting of the living room showed the place like something in a brochure, for sale or rent; already abandoned.

Eventually, Rodin said in a tiny, empty voice: 'You're right, policeman — you're right. He's finished with me. Daddy's finished with his naughty little boy . . .' Priabin bent to the glasses. Rodin sat unmoving, head bent into his hands. The remainder of the joint was burning a hole in the thick pile of the grey carpet. He might have been posing as a model for some bronze statue meant to symbolize defeat.

'Then talk to me,' Priabin replied after a moment. No, he corrected himself. Not softly softly — not yet. 'I haven't got time to waste, Valery.' Commonsense approach, brisk and shallow. A man with a lot on his plate, things to do. 'Do you hear me? Unless you have something for me, I'll have to abandon this interview. Be on my way.'

Silence, stretching so much that Priabin winced against its breaking. Then: 'No. Don't do that.'

'Why not?'

'I want to talk to you — I have something to tell you.' He would not look up, like a child pleading in its misery, cowering in a corner. Afraid to look at the adults in the room. 'I — you can come over. I'll unlock the door.'

'I — don't have much time to waste —' Priabin said with difficulty, the pretence of indifference now almost impossible.

'I won't waste your time,' Rodin replied, looking up and

out into the night. 'I know what you want to know – you come over . . . who knows? I might even tell you!'

The step onto the wooden porch felt greasy, treacherous beneath Gant's boot. Adamov's eyes, although peering into the dusty wind, nonetheless gleamed. Before Gant glanced away from the man's face, he noted the tightness of expectancy around Adamov's jaw, the slightly flared nostrils. Gant looked at the helicopter as if seeking some quick, complete escape. He felt dangerously inadequate, his feet on the step, the lee of the dwelling offering little protection from the wind. The two Uzbeks remained near the *Hind*, as if detailed to guard it. Gant felt himself without resources. He could not simply run, simply *kill* –

He unclenched his hands and looked directly into Adamov's face, and sneered.

'Georgi *who*? Who's he, comrade, when he's in the house?' He felt his chest tightening as he held his breath. Adamov's features narrowed, as if only now responding to the cold wind. His eyes squinted – then he rubbed at them, clearing flying dust.

'Georgi Karpov? You know *him*, surely?' he laughed.

Gant shook his head, watching Adamov's hand, the holster at his hip, the hand, the holster, the hand . . . which came unclosed slowly, purposefully, then passed the holster, moving up to the peak of his cap. His shoulders shrugged.

'I've never heard of him, comrade Captain – and neither have you,' Gant said slowly, evenly. Then, more quickly, he added: 'What's the matter with you, *policeman*?'

The hand left the cap, hitting Gant's shoulder like a statement of arrest. Then Adamov laughed.

'I thought he was posted to Kabul . . . haven't heard from him for a couple of years, though. Could have moved on . . .' He shivered. 'Come on, man, let's get out of this *bloody* wind!' Then he added as easily as taking his next breath: 'Bloody *country*!'

Gant glanced quickly towards the *Hind*, then said: 'Sure.' He allowed himself to be pushed ahead of Adamov, the skin crawling hotly on his back almost immediately, despite the chill of his body. The wind knifed along the porch, the dust curled like brown waves across the concrete of the forecourt.

'You can give me a lift, maybe?' Adamov said behind him as his hand gripped the handle of the door. Then he slipped on a loose board and giggled.

Gant seized on the advantage, gripping it fiercely. Adamov was half-crocked with drink. When he turned, Adamov was holding a leather-bound silver flask in his hand, waving it encouragingly.

'Something to go in the coffee – kill the bugs!' He grinned. 'Had to start on the flask. Rum –' He sniffed it. 'Not bad, either. Couldn't drink the vodka – got no smell. Wouldn't have drowned the stink of that Uzbek pig!' He gestured towards the truck and its driver. 'Come on, get the bloody door open – I'm freezing!'

Gant stepped into the narrow, shallow passage behind the door. Wooden floor and walls; uncarpeted, undecorated.

'How the hell can I give you a lift?' he asked.

'Why not?' Adamov replied, then bellowed: 'Come out, come out, whoever you are!'

His fist banged against the thin wooden wall, which groaned as if in protest.

A door ahead of them opened. A woman in black. Moslem dress. Face hidden below the gleaming eyes. A wisp of greying hair. Olive skin. She stood aside, without reluctance and without welcome, simply attempting not to exist. Gant strode past her as Adamov would have expected Captain Borzov of the Frontal Aviation Army to do. *Lift, passenger,* his mind repeated endlessly, creating waves of heat. He could not, *must* not kill Adamov. Too dangerous. People might know where he was, might be expecting him. The Uzbeks knew he was here. Yet there seemed no other solution. Time was elongating, being wasted. There was no other solution . . .

. . . and soon . . .

Adamov bellowed something in Uzbek at the woman, as if spitting out something which made him gag. There were evident crudities, an oath, a command.

'Told her to make some coffee and be quick about it,' he explained.

The woman backed away, black robe sweeping the floor of the low room. Single rug, log-fire – no, cakes of something that might have been dried dung – a bare table and chairs, one battered armchair near the fire. It was like a weekend cabin, suggesting no one lived there on any permanent basis. The woman closed the door of what must have been the kitchen behind her. Adamov slumped heavily into the armchair, which puffed dust and creaked with age.

'God,' he murmured. Inspected the flask, and adjusted his holster so that it no longer dug into his hip in the narrow chair. Offered the rum. 'Not while on duty?' he asked ironically. 'Bad for your night-vision, uh?'

Oil-stains on the arms of the old chair, on the bare, scrubbed wood of the table. Gant's eyes cast about as if trying to avoid the question. He did not want to drink, should not, but knew that he had to – he had to do more than keep Adamov tipsy, he had to make him drunk. Malleable. He smelt the coffee from beyond the closed door; the smells of cooking, spicy and strange, remained in the dead air of the room. There were loose threads, bare patches, in the one old rug on the floor.

'Drink?' Adamov asked again.

'Sure – why not?' Gant replied, taking the proffered flask and tilting it to his lips, sipping at the apparent generous swallow through clenched teeth. He wiped his lips and handed back the flask, coughing and shaking his head ruefully at the quantity he had pretended to consume.

You can't kill him, there's no easy way, you can't get rid of the body . . . so watch *him.* The killing of a half-drunk man slumped in an armchair would be easy. Almost any part of him could be broken before he could even move. The situation in which Gant found himself, the watch on his wrist, the *Hind* outside, beyond where the wind rattled the window, all made him jumpy with the tension of wanting to kill and not daring to.

He crossed to the window and tugged back the thin curtain. He watched the garage owner straighten, check the reading, then say something to the truck driver. He removed the extension and the funnel, then clipped the nozzle of the hose to the pump. Finished. Full tanks. It was difficult not to sigh with relief.

The woman returned and put down two tin mugs. The liquid in them was thick and black. She glanced at neither man. Gant realized she was not pretending she didn't exist – it was they who did not exist for her; simply scraps of something blown in by the wind. Adamov cursed her for not handing him his coffee by the fire. She continued to stare at the floorboards as she turned back towards the kitchen. Adamov grimaced at her bodily odour, or perhaps merely at her existence. He rose unsteadily from his chair and lurched towards the table.

The Uzbek who owned the garage was coming towards the house, slouching against the wall of the wind. Adamov joined Gant. The two of them were framed in the square of window.

Rum-breath, a hand on his shoulder, a grin near his face, eyes unfocused. The whingeing, familiar voice.

'Come on, comrade, you can spare the time to give me a lift to Samarkand . . . nice knocking-shops in Samarkand, good clubs. For the tourists. Clean girls, dirty nights –!' He roared with laughter, slapping Gant across the shoulder-blades four, five, six, seven times . . .

'Anyway,' he continued, leaning heavily against Gant, slopping a few drops of the thick black coffee down the breast of Gant's overalls. 'I reckon you can't refuse me, can you? Can't refuse me, mm? More than your future's worth for HQ to get to know you were all the way up here – skiving? What you up to, comrade? What's the fiddle? What's your *game*?'

His stubby, thick forefinger, the trigger finger, was prodding against Gant's breastbone, six, seven, eight, nine times, to emphasize the force of his suspicions . . . twelve, thirteen, fourteen –

Gant caught and twisted the wrist to which the prodding finger was attached. Adamov yelled in pain.

'Don't do that, *comrade*!' Gant hissed. 'And don't even *ask*!' He released Adamov's wrist. Immediately, the hand made as if to strike, then dropped to the man's side, obeying the gleam in Gant's eyes.

'All right —!' Adamov snapped. 'Fuck your business, anyway!' He turned away —

— out of the window's well-lit frame, which showed him and Gant like objects in a camera lens to the two Uzbeks. The garage owner was near the window, turning to the steps of the porch. Adamov was pouring more rum into his coffee, his face twisted against the pain in his wrist.

'OK, a lift is what you want — you can have it!' He announced, his voice full of mock comradeship and loud enough to be heard —

— movement, quick and sudden, his hand coming down across the back of Adamov's neck, rabbit-punching him even as he turned. Coffee flew at the chair and fireplace, sizzled on the burning dung, splashed on the dirty floorboards. Adamov's eyes glazed as Gant hugged the body against him.

The Uzbek entered the room sullenly, staring. Adamov leaned against Gant, his unconscious breathing loud and drunken. Gant glared at the garage owner. He hefted Adamov's weight against his side and growled at the Uzbek: 'He's drunk. Understand? You speak Russian — pig?' He winced inwardly as he added the obligatory insult. The Uzbek nodded, rubbing his unshaven chin. Then shrugged.

'Pay me,' he announced in a thick, almost indecipherable accent. And held out his hand to underline his demand.

'The army pays,' Gant replied. The man was in the doorway. Adamov's weight bore against him. He wanted to flee.

The *Hind* was outside with full tanks. Reaction to the blow he had struck at Adamov coursed in him. Two minutes before wind-up, all systems on-line, take-off. The empty, clean sky was two-and-a-half minutes away from him.

He flung Adamov into the narrow chair, which squeaked on the bare boards but did not overturn. The GRU captain lay like an abandoned ventriloquist's dummy. The Uzbek's eyes narrowed, and his hands twitched about his belt as if he were searching for a weapon he had mislaid.

Gant reached into the zip pocket on the breast of his overalls. The Uzbek flinched. Perspiration hovered along Gant's hairline. He withdrew a notepad, a pencil held against it with a rubber band. He removed the band and flipped open the pad.

'Come here,' he snapped, and moved to the table. He began writing. Each sheet of the pad was headed with the insignia of the Frontal Aviation Army and the details of his regiment. He made out a receipt, snapping only once at the Uzbek to check the amount of petrol he had supplied. Then he tore off the sheet and handed it to the Uzbek. 'There – an official receipt. Any complaints?' His hand rested lightly on his hip, just above the holster.

The garage owner shook his head, reluctantly. He folded the receipt with an air of resignation and slipped it into the pocket of his baggy trousers. Then he wiped his hands on his coat, as if they had become contaminated.

'Good,' Gant remarked. 'I'm taking this one – tell your pal, the driver.' He plucked Adamov's frame from the chair with ease, and moved with him to the door. 'Open it!' The Uzbek scuttled to do so. Action revived Gant. He lumbered the unconscious captain into the corridor, the man's boot-toes dragging like fingernails down glass. The Uzbek pressed back against the wall as Gant flung open the outer door and leaned into the wind, clutching Adamov like a shield.

Steps – yes. He counted them, careful of his balance. Dirt, and no noise from Adamov's boots until they reached the concrete and the toes of his boots began to scrape once again. 'Fucking passengers!' Gant yelled to the wind, for the driver's benefit. 'Bastard's pissed as a fart and fallen down!' The driver, leaning out of his cab, smoking, tossed his head and grinned, as much at Gant's struggle with Adamov as with relief that the GRU man had found other company.

Gant turned to the driver. 'You shouldn't have let the officer drink so much!' he barked. The driver was indifferent.

Gant leaned the unconscious Adamov against the fuselage of the *Hind*, and slammed back the door of the main cabin. Then he bundled the body aboard. He glanced at his watch. Twelve thirty-five. He climbed into the main cabin, squeezing close to the ferry tank which occupied most of it, and dragged Adamov to one of the fold-down seats troops used when being transported. He fumbled the straps – excitement now outstripped him, making him clumsy in his furious haste – and strapped Adamov into the seat. He reached for some webbing and used it to bind the captain's hands. Finally, he gagged Adamov with . . . Mac's scarf, lying on the floor. He removed Adamov's pistol from its holster, dismissed Mac's memory, and turned away. He jumped down and slammed the cabin door shut. If Adamov woke, it wouldn't matter. He was no longer a problem. Dumb, secure and unarmed.

He climbed into the cockpit. Shivered. The driver watched him from his cab, the garage owner from the porch. He touched at the controls, the panel, other instruments, then began.

His hands reached, gripped or touched, flicked or depressed, bringing the MiL to life. The auxiliary power unit he had left on. He pressed the start button of the first of the Isotov engines, moved the throttle lever above his head from Stop to the ground-idle position. The engine began to wind up from a hum to a grumbling murmur. He pressed the second start button, moved the second throttle lever. The turboshaft hurried in pursuit of the noises from its companion. Slowly, the rotors began to turn, drooping at first then gradually smoothing into a disc. Gleaming in the wind and moonlight. The *Hind* began to buck, as if restrained by a trap.

The woman was standing on the porch behind her husband. The night pressed around their shadows. Gant reached up and moved the throttles to flight-idle, released the rotor brake, engaged the clutch. His eyes scanned the instruments as they came on-line, especially the fuel gauges; and the temperature, and pressure and output power, he reminded himself. This is petrol, not kerosene. For the length of his journey, the ordinary automobile petrol would do no harm to the engines, but its performance had to be watched – closely.

He flicked on the moving map. The rotors flurried dust around the cockpit and the scene was dimming. Two minutes . . . the *Hind* rolled forward as he released the brakes, away from the canopy over the pumps. The place was suddenly very small, a needle in the haystack of the landscape around him. But he had found it and that was all that mattered. Relief was now far too late and unimportant.

He glanced to either side, then over his head. Clear. He was well clear of the corrugated roof and the power lines. The *Hind* continued to waddle, ready to lift. He eased the column laterally, in the direction of the wind.

He raised the collective pitch lever, applied rudder to remain headed into the wind, and felt the *Hind*'s undercarriage lift from the ground and the wind buffet the helicopter. Then he increased his airspeed, and entered a climb of more than two thousand feet per minute, rushing up like an elevator on the side of some tall building. The ground diminished beneath him, bathed in moonlight. Gant checked the moving map, his distance and course. Two hours' flying. He moved the column to starboard and the helicopter banked. He eased back on the stick. On the moving map, he watched the white dot that was the *Hind* resume its original course. Baikonur lay almost due north. He glanced at his watch once more. Twelve-forty. He was late; darkness seemed already to be slipping away like water into a drain. The moon was old and lower in the sky. His head spun with the flickering, separate illuminations of times and distances. He had just enough time – *just enough!* – to get out again, with Kedrov, before daylight. His pulse slowed and his temperature seemed to fall back towards comfort. Just enough time . . .

Be there, you bastard – *be there!*

Priabin wanted to bruise Rodin's face just as the boy's father had done. Urgency should be obeyed, not put aside like a book being loaned between friends. Kedrov was out there in the marshes, for the taking. Valery Rodin, having admitted him, seemed only to want to prolong the conversation. He was greedy for company.

'Let's talk about *Lightning*, shall we?' he snapped at Rodin. Technique, often a steel rope, frayed and parted; as likely now to

272

injure him as Rodin. He knew he could blunder in this situation, go astray and cause Rodin to clam up. Then, he would have nothing.

He swallowed the whisky Rodin had poured for him and attempted to calm himself. The room incensed him as much as it had done on his visit earlier that evening. The coving and frieze and the smell of hashish and cognac – the scent of his own expensive Scotch whisky. Priabin felt the anger mount. This boy must not be allowed to waste his time!

'Let's talk about *Lightning*,' he repeated. His tone was threatening.

Valery Rodin's head snapped up. His eyes were wakeful, clearing from their drugged, drunken glassiness. Then the young man shrugged. Priabin sighed inwardly and controlled his own anger as Valery Rodin continued talking as though Priabin were some kind of confessor figure, not KGB. He was not afraid of Priabin, or of his rank or organization. Priabin was, in Rodin's eyes, the only visitor who was *not* dangerous. Ludicrous –

Priabin felt the battery and the tiny microphone against his ribs. It was recording the maudlin details of Rodin's past, nothing of importance.

'. . . I'm to train for the *Sukhoputnye Vojska*, the Ground Forces, would you believe – specifically, the Tank Troops. I am to become a career soldier, hence the Academy . . .' His lips pouted with anger, helplessness. 'A career officer!' he barked thinly, the noise of a beaten animal protesting.

'But why?' Priabin asked.

'To make a proper man of me, of course!' he sneered. 'I'm to follow in his footsteps!' His voice was a venomous hiss. 'And it gets me out of the way very neatly,' he added.

'Why?' Priabin asked, too eagerly.

Rodin winked at him slowly, exaggeratedly. 'We'll come to that, all in good time.'

'I meant, why *now*? Why change branches of the service? Why are you in the GRU if your old man wants you to be a tank officer?'

Rodin swallowed cognac. He was very drunk, but somehow in

273

command of the situation. Priabin could not bully effectively; and could not leave, despite images of Katya and Kedrov, Dudin and his men going to the girl's assistance . . . he had to know, had to open the oyster that was Valery Rodin. However long it took.

'Most of his closest pals in *Stavka* are in the intelligence directorate – it just worked out that way. And he could really trust those pals to keep an eye on me – keep me under control.' He giggled, but the noise was cynical, contemptuous. 'And in this God-forsaken place, he can keep a personal eye on me. He can surround me with *watchers*!'

'And now you think he's had enough?' Technique. Patience coming like a memory of training, calming Priabin's anxiety.

'Right. That's right. He's bloody had enough.' Rodin tossed his head. His eyes glazed once more. He stared down into his lap as he sat on the bean bag like a Buddha; a thin, blond idol. 'I told you, didn't I, that all I wanted was to paint?' He looked up and Priabin nodded as if interested. 'I've told *everyone*,' Rodin added ironically. 'But you, I didn't fill in all the details. My mother plucked up the courage to put the idea to him, when he was home on leave. She made sure he had the best food the house-keeper could cook and she could buy . . . French wine, good cognac, a cigar . . . he was expansive, know what I mean?' Again, Priabin stifled his impatience and nodded. 'When Mother put it to him, he just looked straight at me, sardonically, and nodded like a judge. He even smiled, but that was cold, too . . .' Rodin waved his free hand, shooing the oppressive elements of the memory further off from him. 'He went to the best experts, to Academicians, touting some of my water-colours, my sketch-books and canvases like a penniless student . . . and showed all of them. It took him a *week* altogether! Then he came back, with a *typed report*, summarizing everything they'd said. Top copy for me, carbon for Mother. He made us sit there, in front of him, on dining chairs and read the report!'

'And – they said you were no good?' Priabin said softly into the silence. The words echoed like the splashing of pebbles in a deep well. He saw Rodin once more without barriers, and could not avoid pity for him.

Rodin nodded furiously. 'Yes, yes, that's what they said. They confirmed all his suspicions, answered all his prayers. I'd never make it as an artist. He had me in an army training school inside a month. Mother never raised the subject, ever again. All the theatre visits stopped, the allowance was strictly controlled, no parties, and above all, *no friends of a certain kind* — I'm quoting him . . . I couldn't be unsuccessful, not as his son. So, he put me in the army, where if your father's a general you can't *possibly* fail!' Rodin wiped his pale lips, rubbed a hand through his fair hair.

'I'm sorry,' Priabin said eventually. Rodin swallowed cognac by way of reply.

Priabin glanced at his watch. One in the morning. Kedrov was out there —

— *Lightning* was here!

He twitched with indecision and impatience. How *vulnerable* was Rodin, would he break soon?

Rodin said cynically: 'I have it all to look forward to, don't I? Once he abandons me, I'm lost.' He swallowed fearfully. 'God, I'm *lost* —'

'Why does he want to do that to his own son?'

'What —?'

'Why does he want you to suffer? You won't have a prayer in the Frunze, once they realize your old man isn't protecting you any more . . .' He winced, anticipating Anna's sudden return to his thoughts. 'They'll make a bloody punch-bag out of a queer without connections . . . they're all shits in the Frunze, you know that. *He* knows that! Why? Why do it to you?'

'Because I *know*, and I *told*!' Rodin shouted at him. His eyes were wild, large and moist like those of a hunted deer or rabbit.

'Why did he have Sacha killed?'

'Because Sacha's the one I told! Don't you understand? If you know, you don't talk, not to anyone!'

'Nothing's that important. Nothing could make him punish you like this, surely?' Priabin soothed and pressed. He was leaning slightly forward in his armchair, his eyes watching Rodin intently. It was a huge effort to let technique take its course. 'Tell me — what's that important?'

He got up, and crossed to the bean bag. Rodin seemed to cower into it as Priabin leaned over him.

'Tell me,' he murmured. Had Rodin broken? Was he snapping like a stick now? He placed his hand on Rodin's shoulder and the shoulder shuddered into his grip.

'You really want to know? Something so dangerous?' Rodin asked with a strange, wild cunning. 'Really? Aren't you afraid?'

'Tell me about it.'

Rodin put his bare feet onto the carpet. Priabin stood aside as the young man crossed the room in his creased dressing-gown, to the racks of LPs, cassettes and videotapes. He looked back once at Priabin, then began pulling tape boxes from the shelving. Priabin's body was taut with anticipation. Anna was still absent, Kedrov was much further than ten miles away, one in the morning was an early hour.

Rodin was breaking open like a watermelon dropped from a tall building.

Rodin brandished a videotape box, neatly labelled, in his hand. His face was shining, eyes gleaming. 'You want to *know*? You really want to know *why*? *Look!*'

Vanity, secret knowledge, cleverness all conspired to rescue Rodin from his self-pity and isolation at that moment. They all delivered him to Priabin. Soon, he would know.

Rodin pressed the video cassette into the recorder beneath the television set. He flicked on the set, then began to run the recording on the tape. Priabin did not understand, but his tension was extreme, excitement was making his head spin.

The first images emerged. He was sharply, deeply disappointed. He did not understand. A swirling whirlpool slowly cleared into an image of the earth seen from space. Rodin stood beside the television like an eager, insistent teacher, watching him, one hand resting on the set. Then the Americans' latest space shuttle floated into view, gradually filling the screen. It floated like a white bird above tresses of cloud that partly masked a vivid, utterly beautiful blue expanse. The Pacific Ocean. He still did not understand. This was nothing, a cheat – these pictures

had been on television, world-wide, for the past week or more
. . . there was nothing here for him!

It was a test, he told himself. But he was failing the examination miserably. He glanced at Rodin's face.

The shuttle drifted, hanging like some great albatross over the
ocean.

'What is it?' he asked eventually, almost mesmerized by the
images on the screen, angry with himself; afraid that there was
nothing to know – that was his deepest worry – that Rodin knew
nothing!

'That's *Lightning*, you bloody stupid *policeman*!' Rodin mocked.
'Can't you even hazard a *guess*?'

'Find him, Serov – find him tonight!'

Gennadi Serov's features indicated nothing more than the
recognition of General Lieutenant Rodin's seniority and the
order he had issued. There was no evident response, however
momentary, to the insulting ten minutes of cross-questioning,
the almost manic reawakened concern with the escaped Kedrov.
He was no more than a computer technician, he just *might* know
a *little* about *Lightning* . . .

. . . yet Rodin had kept him standing in this icy wind, which
blew into his face so that he had to squint into it, while he
pummelled him with questions. The general seemed impervious
to the temperature as they stood together at the top of the short
flight of steps outside the principal senior officers' mess. Rodin's
breath smelt of cognac. When they encountered each other –
Serov coming to report on overall security, as ordered – Rodin
had not asked him inside. He had been made to report just there,
like an errand-boy.

'Yes, comrade General Lieutenant,' Serov replied in a neutral
tone. 'Everything possible will be done.' Of course, Rodin and
the others were paranoid about the security surrounding *Lightning*, were unnerved by the idea of Kedrov running around loose
. . . and the job of tidying-up had been delegated to him. Serov
seethed beneath his adopted calm.

277

'I don't think that Kedrov represents a danger to our – enter-prise,' he added deferentially. Your son does, he thought, but not Kedrov!

'That isn't for you to decide, Serov,' Rodin snapped back, tugging his gloves smooth on his hands, as if before a mirror. 'You maintain he isn't a danger – *anyone* who knows and who can't be relied upon, accounted for, *trusted* . . . is a danger. Shut him up before the KGB find him!'

'I don't think they have any idea –'

'I don't want to hear that they have! But, they're looking for him – *you* find him first. Tonight!'

'Yes, comrade General.' And your son – isn't he a danger? his anger added silently. You don't realize how much of a danger . . . shall I do something about him, too? There was a fierce, dark satisfaction in the mocking defiance of his thoughts. The superi-ority of secret power; not as grandiose as that which Rodin enjoyed, but – ah, welcome in the icy wind and in the humiliat-ing position he found himself, one step down from the general's tall, forbidding figure.

'Good, good,' Rodin murmured. 'We are too close to the time, our time . . .' he sighed. The portentousness of the words were ridiculous to Serov; it was the old man's way, making a mission, some kind of holy war, out of whatever he was doing. Then his words became precise once more. 'Use extra helicopter patrols, put more men on the task.'

'Yes, General.'

Rodin leaned over him. His face appeared to age quickly. It was narrow and pale from the wind, but it seemed drained and weary, too. Serov enjoyed the old man's moment of weakness. The light above the door of the mess hollowed Rodin's cheeks and created large stains beneath his eyes.

'Listen to me, Serov,' he commanded, and his gloved hand gripped Serov's arm roughly, squeezing. 'My son –' Serov con-trolled a sudden intake of breath. It was as if the old man had read his mind. '– my son *is* to return to Moscow today. He will there enrol at the Frunze Academy. Today. You understand me?' The hand shook his arm. It was a gesture of strength, yet it seemed at the same moment like a plea. 'He will travel under surveillance, of course. He will talk to no one —' He broke off for a moment, as if the tone he was using was some strange flavour on his tongue which must be carefully tested. Then he blurted out: 'He is not to be *harmed*, Serov!' His hand dropped Serov's arm.

Serov saluted formally, crisply.

'Comrade General, there was never any danger —'

'Good. I believe you . . . but, the boy — will be better placed in Moscow . . .' Then the moment of weakness, of something approaching ordinary humanity, passed from Rodin as quickly as the wind plucked away his smoky breath. 'Meanwhile, concentrate on this man Kedrov!' he added sharply.

'General, I assure you that everything —'

Rodin merely turned his back on Serov and walked through the door of the mess. Serov's face clenched into rage. His mind was filled with images of Valery Rodin rather than the general. Something had to be done about Rodin. Priabin was back there, talking to him. He had had the boy under surveillance since the actor was killed . . . Priabin was no fool . . .

Serov descended the steps. He rubbed his numb cheeks to life as he walked to his car. Valery Rodin certainly knew about *Lightning*. What were he and Priabin talking about? Rodin had not left his flat, there had been no opportunity to place bugs — Priabin had the advantage there . . . but, if Priabin learned of *Lightning*, what would he do?

His driver opened the door of the Zil, but Serov remained deep in thought, one hand resting on the roof of the car, the coldness of the metal seeping through his glove. His other hand rubbed his chin repeatedly, as if to conjure something from it.

What would Priabin do? Talk to Moscow Centre —? Yes, he would. He'd enough brains to grasp the enormity of the whole thing, and realize he couldn't handle it without the Centre's help — without the backing of Nikitin and his gang in the Politburo, come to that! So — Priabin might try to call, or radio — even fly out . . .

Serov was appalled. Priabin could have everything out of that weak, queer little bitch, if he was any good at all! And that, *that* must be prevented – at any cost.

'Get them on the radio!' he snapped.

'Who, sir?' the driver asked, bemused, startled by the sudden emergence of the colonel from his abstraction.

'That damned team watching the general's son – who else, you idiot!' he roared. 'And quickly!'

'What does it mean?' Priabin asked slowly, hesitantly. 'I – don't understand what you mean by it.'

Rodin's young, vulnerable face was angry. He was important, his secret was important – but only if Priabin understood! Knowing his father's most profound secret – *Lightning* – had helped fill some of the hollows he had found in himself since they rendered him incommunicado. He wanted to boast again now, as he must have done to Sacha and to others.

'*What does it mean?*' Rodin mocked him in a squeaking, school-girl's voice. His hand banged the television set in frustration, but the American shuttle craft remained unaffected by the blow. It continued to float above the peaceful blue ocean. 'It means that *Linchpin* is only the weapon – *Lightning* is the codename for the *use* of the weapon! That's why I'm to be punished for the rest of my life, Priabin, and why they killed Sacha – because I let the cat out of the bag! The beautiful, expensive, marvellous American space shuttle *Atlantis* is nothing more than a *target* –!' Rodin's mouth was wet with excitement, his body was hunched over the set. 'They are going to use the laser weapon to *destroy* the American shuttle in orbit . . . *a test of its efficiency*, that's their joke!' He wiped at his forehead and leant more heavily on the television, as if his words had caused him acute physical exertion. 'Now you understand what's at stake. Why Papa can't love his little boy any more? Do you understand?'

Priabin stared at the floating, silent shuttle.

'They can't . . .' was all he could find to say in a weak, breathy whisper. He had no idea of the length of the silence that had preceded his words.

Valery Rodin laughed.

'Don't be a *moron*, Priabin!' he mocked. 'Of course they can do it. It will be seen as an unfortunate, tragic accident. The Americans will never suspect how it was done . . . or, even if they suspect, they could never prove it. The shuttle will disintegrate, become *dust*!'

'But *why*?' Priabin's hands floundered in front of him, as if a great, drowning wave had broken over him. His thoughts seemed loose, like unsecured ballast or a freed cargo. The shuttle floated serenely; invulnerable.

Vulnerable, he realized now. So very vulnerable . . .

'Why – why again?' Rodin taunted. 'You're being very slow tonight, Priabin – or are you always that thick?' He left the television, as if no longer needing its support, and slumped with what might have been confidence into the bean bag. He lit a cigarette, and Priabin could see his hands were shaking. Then he said: 'To show the old dodderers in the Kremlin – and the ones who are only old in their ideas – to show them once and for all who it is in charge of things. Who really gives the orders – who knows? Who cares? They're going to do it. The *why* of it only a policeman would want to know!' He shrugged. 'Maybe they want to make sure things go on just as before when that Treaty is signed.' He was talking quietly now, intelligently, as if revealing another part of himself, one that would further win Priabin's admiration. He did seem calm, in control of himself – unlike Priabin, whose head beat with the knowledge, with its terrors and implications. Rodin continued: 'Nothing will change, will it? Whatever the old women in Moscow want to do about agriculture, schools, medical research, consumer goods, cars for every family, *food* for every family! – it just won't happen . . . the army will have the icing on the cake, just as always. They'll have the laser weapon, they'll have shown they can use it. The project will never be scrapped or signed away. The greedy men of the Politburo will want a slice of *that* cake!'

He studied Priabin's wild expression, seemed to find it satisfactory, then plucked a grain of tobacco from the tip of his tongue. Unfiltered American cigarettes, not hashish, Priabin noticed. His eyes catalogued the furnishings of the room, his mind unable to cope with Rodin's words. Terrible, terrible . . . but his thoughts could get no further. Green carpet, the frieze of shepherdesses and their rustic swains, vases, a couple of pieces of jade, the hi-fi, the racks upon racks of LPs and cassettes . . . even one of the new compact disc players. Terrible, terrible . . .

'They'll agree to all the money they need for research, they'll build them all the laser weapons they want . . . just like the American President would do, no doubt, if his army had *Linchpin*! Killing the shuttle will give them backbone – it will be the starch in the Politburo collars . . . no one will ever limit or abandon the laser weapon project if its *power* is demonstrated, will they? All they have to do is kill *that!*' His fingers, and the smoking cigarette, pointed at the screen like a gun. 'Bang. See?' he added in a quieter voice. 'See now?'

Priabin shook his head. 'Why?' was all he could utter.

Rodin's mouth made a simpering gesture of sympathy. Then he grinned. The boy had found a small, precious superiority and was clinging to it. Priabin could not cope with Rodin's information, his opinions.

'*Why?*' Priabin asked again, finding technique held out like an assisting hand. The boy had to go on talking now, had to be used, had to –

Priabin remembered the microphone, imagined Mikhail and Anatoly in the darkened room across the street, imagined their shock, their sense of possessing dangerous knowledge. It was all on tape, but it would make no sense without Rodin. He had to use the boy as his proof. However he did it, and he had no solution at the moment, he needed Rodin, in person – in Moscow.

Technique stilled the swirling of his own fears and imaginings. So, when he asked *why* yet again, he tried to sound uncomprehending, dim.

Rodin grinned comfortably.

'What is it *ever* about, policeman? *Power* . . .' He raised his hands to acknowledge the room, the flat, the benefits that extended beyond the windows, beyond Baikonur. '*This* – this is

282

privilege . . . bought by power. The power to divert contracts, twist the arms of suppliers, find out and blackmail the local Party officials and the local black-market . . . but you already know all about that. Even *you* can tap in to that much of the system. But it isn't power, is it? It's just playing at things. My father never plays. He likes real power, not the gimmick of privilege. You *know* people who like privilege – beavering away in every city of the Union, finding the lever, assessing the fulcrum, tipping the scales in their own favour. But that's just kids' stuff.'

Priabin clung to the analysis, to the cool mind that supplied it, the almost bored tone of Rodin's voice. He clung to it because he dare not think of the other thing. Now that he had been informed, he knew he must act . . . and could not even begin to contemplate action.

'And that's what the general wants – real power?'

Rodin shook his head.

'It's what the army already has – it's a question of preserving the power they have. For them, the issue's *simple* . . . the laser weapon is not an offensive system, it's to protect the army! Don't you see that?' He shook his head once more in reproof of dullness. 'Papa –' he announced with deep, bitter irony '– Papa told me a lot. He had to have an *audience*. My mother is in Moscow and he would not have told her in any case. I served as his audience. It's all about moving the wheel when you put your shoulder to it, not being defeated by the wheel's size and weight. Moving events.' He stubbed out his cigarette, murmuring, like a taunt or even a temptation: 'Haven't you ever wanted to be sure you could do that, if it came to it – control and change events?'

Priabin's features had come to reflect stupidity, incredulity. His mind swirled like the clouds interposed between the planet and the image of the shuttle on the screen. He realized *Lightning* would work. Yet he clung to the concrete-like set of his facial muscles, drawing Rodin out, making him the superior, making him want to go on talking. Even now, as he spilled the whole of the story, he was implying that he was still his father's confidant, that they were really close. His father could relax only in his company.

283

'No,' he admitted as an answer to Rodin's challenging question; it was like an admission of abnormality.

'Then you haven't been on the mountain-top!' Rodin giggled. 'They *all* feel like that, *always*!'

'And they killed Sacha, just like that.'

Rodin's head jerked back as if avoiding a blow. His thin face became enveloped in shadow. What might have been an involuntary tear gleamed. Rodin snapped, wiping at his eye: 'Let's have some music on. I'm bored with all this talk —'

Priabin watched him cross to the hi-fi. There was no urgency in the KGB colonel; as if his knowledge restrained him in the armchair to which he had returned. He felt empty, as if at the end of a passion, or some great defeat of his most cherished hopes. Tired —

'I wonder what you like, policeman?' Rodin murmured to himself. His long fingers flicked along a shelf of LPs. 'Ah – what about this? About your era, I would have thought.'

He stood up, unsheathed the record, placed it on the turntable. A few moments later, the words struck against Priabin's thoughts as if Rodin had seen into some secret part of him and was using interrogation techniques in his own right. Softening Priabin up.

Anna. The song was Dylan, of course. The American CBS album, no cheap copy. Not political Dylan, which Anna had always preferred, but the Dylan Priabin himself would always choose – *had always chosen* . . .

He was intent on the words, his face paled by the shocks of memory . . . and the likeness of his own history to the present. Anna and that damned wheelchair that had become part of the weapons systems of the Firefox. A wheelchair for the totally disabled, governed by brain impulses, corrupted into a thought-guided weapons system . . . its inventor, Baranovich, corrupted too. He shook his head, hating the clarity of the past. Rodin studied him, his own face abstracted, filled with memories.

. . . if I could only hear her heart a-softly pounding . . .

He glanced at his watch. One-fifteen. Time was racing ahead of him – Kedrov in the marshes . . . Rodin here, the weight of what

284

he had been told . . . it seemed impossible to act, to lift that weight. A growing dread seemed to have invaded his frame, making him weak.

. . . and if only she was lying by me . . .

The song pained.

'But we need this Treaty,' he heard himself saying, sensing that he wished to avoid the song and prolong the talk. Talk meant inaction.

Rodin shrugged. 'They don't . . . puts them out of a job, drops them from the top of the First Division, wouldn't you say?' He returned his attention to the music.

. . . I'd lie in my bed once again . . .

. . . yes, and only if my own true love was waiting . . .

'You *do* understand, Priabin?' Rodin asked him after a time. The song had almost reached its conclusion, its final statement of loss. Anna —

'What?'

'All this, man!' Rodin's arm gestured towards the soundless pictures on the television. Then he got up, crossed the room and switched off the record. He stood, hands on hips, as if in challenge. 'You *do* understand?' he repeated.

The shuttle floated. Priabin concentrated upon it. It was over South America. Cloud draped the planet like a wedding veil. The image was unbelievably beautiful. He could not make himself care what happened to the shuttle, or to its crew . . . not for a long time. When he finally spoke, he saw that Rodin had sat down once more, and was half-way through another cigarette. He did not look at his watch but simply said:

'They can't do it. They can't be allowed to . . . we can't *afford* it!' He shuddered, felt cold. The nasal, almost-whining song was gone, and Anna, too, had faded below the level of consciousness; as if she could safely leave him to his own devices. He lit a cigarette, blew smoke at the frozen shepherdesses, at the floating shuttle *Atlantis*. 'No one can afford this project, you know that,' he said. 'The Union's bankrupt. Are they mad they can't see that? Why else would we be signing the bloody Treaty?'

'I'm not arguing with you.'

285

'We all need the bloody rest, dammit! The whole of the economy's fucked – people are fed up with having nothing in the shops and no money to spend anyway . . . it's as simple as that in the end. The army can't be allowed to screw them again!'

'Oh?' Rodin replied archly. 'They can't, can't they?'

'We have to stop it!' Priabin blurted. His thoughts buffeted him like a wind. Maybe he could send a coded message, but they wouldn't necessarily believe him . . . and to whom would he send the message, the bloody Chairman himself? They'd ask the Defence Minister to confirm or deny, always supposing they didn't dismiss it out of hand as the ravings of a lunatic . . . and then he'd be screwed like Sacha and Viktor! God – what could he *do*?

He studied Rodin.

Relief surged through him . . . *Rodin was being flown to Moscow today*. All he had to do was book a ticket on the same flight – once they were in Moscow, he could begin to do something, talk to people, persuade them . . .with Rodin as his prize piece of evidence, *proof –*

'Not me,' Rodin replied, his face dark with suspicion and self-concern; no longer confident.

'You *must –*'

'And put my head in the gas-oven? Piss off, policeman!'

'You have to help me.'

'What? You must be joking.'

'It's your only way out . . .' He left the sentence evocatively unfinished. His features wore an implacable look.

'Joke over, Priabin!' Rodin got to his feet and flicked off the television with a sharp, punching movement. Then he turned to Priabin. 'Forget it, brother! Forget I ever told you – or you and I will end up where Sacha is now!'

'I can't – not now. It mustn't happen.'

'It will happen. Nothing's more certain. It's early on Wednesday morning . . . tomorrow isn't such a long time. Go home and go to bed and get up on Friday!' He moved closer, appeared threatening though slight and dressed only in a robe. 'Nothing – say nothing, Priabin. For your own sake –'

'No. We both know now – and we have to do something about it.'

'You're crazy! You want to die? Like Sacha . . . they killed him like *that*!' He clicked his fingers. 'I'm staying alive. Whatever my father has in mind for me, I'm staying around for it.'

'You *can't*!'

'Just watch me!'

'You have to help me –'

'You can't beat them.'

'Listen to me – just listen . . .' He had grabbed Rodin's slim arms, holding them fiercely. 'You're on your way to Moscow – you just have to do what is already arranged for you. I'll get a seat on the plane . . . we can both be in Moscow in time to stop this thing.' Rodin was shaking his head, but in a shamed sort of way, eyes cast down at the carpet. 'It's an act of *war*! And if the Americans ever suspect we had anything to do with the loss of their shuttle, there'll be a holocaust! Do you want that?' Kedrov's told them we have the weapon, he thought. They'll *know* we destroyed their shuttle!

'You're talking rubbish –'

'No! No, I'm not. It's your only hope of safety, and it's the only thing we can do. Your Papa and his pals are mad. They have to be stopped.' He was shaking Rodin's arms roughly. Then he released them. Rodin began to rub them at once, walking away towards the window. The tape would have to be wiped – or taken with him to Moscow . . . yes, taken to Moscow. Just in case –

Mikhail and Anatoly must be told to clean up thoroughly, and keep their heads down.

Katya and Kedrov in the marshes . . . Dudin was involved now. Kedrov should be kept under wraps until he got back from Moscow. Would he be safe out there? Anyway, he'd have to arrange all that tonight – in what remained of the night. One-thirty. He'd have to hurry. The air ticket wouldn't be any problem, and he could be incommunicado as far as any callers at his office were concerned . . . he could do it.

'Well?' he asked Rodin's narrow back.

'No.'

He made as if to move towards the young man, but then remained standing near his armchair.

'You have to,' he said.

'They'll kill me.'

'Not if we *win*!'

'And the rest of my life – and yours?'

'You'll be protected – for God's sake, we have to do it!'

Would Rodin help him?

Ticket. Get on the flight, even if he won't agree. You can have him arrested in Moscow and taken to the Centre . . . you'll have the tape to open him up with – a pre-recorded corkscrew. Get the ticket, get on the plane, get Kedrov stowed safely . . .

One-thirty, thirty-two . . . come on, get moving . . . Heat and energy seemed to mount in him. He steadied himself against the chair, and felt his strength return. Then he said:

'Think about it. It's your only hope – *our* only hope!'

'My father will have me killed if he ever finds out I betrayed him. You realize that, don't you?'

Rodin would not turn to look into the room but continued to stare out into the windy night. Priabin could clearly hear the wind howling at the building's corners, crying down the narrow street.

'He won't be able to harm you – not any more.'

'So you say.'

Priabin was possessed by impatience; technique was deserting him. If he stayed he would say the wrong things, close the oyster again and alienate Rodin. He had other things to do, arrangements to make –

– leave him, then? He did not want to . . . felt he could not risk . . . but he had arrangements that must be made. Leave –

'Look, I'm leaving now –'

Rodin turned.

'Who are you going to tell?' he shouted, his face white, the cords in his neck standing proud.

'No one, no one . . . not *here* – you think *I'm* mad? It's my life, too. No, I have things that need doing.'

'You're going to be on that plane?'

'Yes.'

'*Damn you, then!*' Rodin screamed.

'You told me knowing I was a policeman – you told me because you were afraid of it.' Priabin soothed. 'Think about it. I can save your life!'

'The hell you can – get out, damn you – *get out!*'

Rodin's fists were formed into claws, and raised in front of his chest. He looked dangerous, and unbalanced. As if he might fling himself in an attack upon Priabin, or throw himself from the window.

'Think about it!' Priabin shouted back. 'Lock the door, don't answer the telephone, and *think about it!*'

Priabin turned away, picked up his greatcoat in the hall, opened the door and let himself out of the flat. He sighed with fear and weakness, leaning back against the door for a moment, head raised. He was sweating profusely.

Rodin, he knew, should not be left alone. But, he couldn't involve Anatoly and Mikhail. If they were suspected, they were dead. They had the tape and they must keep their heads down until the storm had blown over. Kedrov he had to hide somewhere, in Katya's custody . . . Dudin had to be bought off with some cock-and-bull story about security . . . he had to get a seat on that morning flight! His head spun.

He crossed to the staircase, and began to run down the first flight. Every moment he was away from Rodin would be filled with anxiety. Hurry, then – be as little time as you can – *hurry!*

Dear God, he thought as he reached the foyer of the building. Dear God, they're going to start the next war –!

TEN

collision course

There was still no glow from the tiny light on the receiver. Kedrov had not activated the transponder hidden in the cheap radio. It was not receiving Gant's signal and sending its precoded reply which only his receiver was able to pick up. Gant knew where Kedrov should be – less than twenty miles away. Either he wasn't there, or . . .

Gant dismissed the thought as it bullied against his resolve. Kedrov *had* to be there. Alive.

The white dot that represented the *Hind* remained motionless on the moving map display, hovering to the north-west of the marshes, outside the farthest security perimeter of the Baikonur complex; just outside. Fifty miles behind him, the shore of the Aral Sea, twenty miles ahead the salt marshes. The *Hind* shivered like a restrained and impatient horse as he held the machine twenty feet above the distressed, dull surface of a man-made lake. Trees quivered or leant in the wind, encircling the lake like a stockade's wooden wall. The helicopter was hidden from sight by the trees, yet Gant could not bring himself to land and switch off the engines and await Kedrov's response to his signal.

Beyond the trees, the desert was etched with the fine engraved lines of irrigation channels. In a later season, crops would grow there. In summer, people would swim in this artificial lake. He remembered the satellite pictures of the area used in his briefings. He had been able to pick out the heads and lying torsos of swimmers and sunbathers in the vastly magnified, grainy monochrome pictures. Now, in winter, the tiny resort was closed; changing huts, the café, the boathouses all deserted and lightless. They'd made certain the place was unoccupied in winter before suggesting it as a target point for his arrival.

His hands, feet, whole body it seemed, made the constant tiny movements and adjustments that kept the *Hind* steady above the lake. He glanced at his watch. Time of arrival, two-ten, Wednesday morning. He had perhaps five hours' darkness left . . .

. . . and there was no transponder response. Kedrov wasn't there, twenty miles east of him in the marshes. Waggling into the sky perhaps a couple of miles to starboard of him, he saw the headlights of a vehicle as it bounced over the undulations of the main road from Aralsk. He had crossed the road only three minutes earlier, on course for the pleasure-lake. To reach it and hover here, near the strange pagoda that had been erected in the middle of the lake, hanging like a zeppelin near its mooring tower.

He had flown most of his route over the Aral Sea itself, low and fast. Fishing boats, the lights of an occasional village on the straggling shoreline. The shallow sea was virtually empty of commercial traffic, as was its shore of habitation. It was little more than a vast, moonlit puddle across which he dashed, disturbing the calm, icy water with his passage. The barren, flat landscape was relieved only by the mounds and peaks of frozen waves reaching out from the shore.

And now hurry had drained away; destination had been achieved, but purpose had been foiled. There was no light on his receiver to show the reception of his signal —! And he was a thousand miles from the nearest friendly border.

They had selected the north-west of the Baikonur complex as his point of ingress because it was the boundary closest to the salt marshes and the least protected by radar patrols. The surveillance defences of Baikonur seemed to straggle away into the desert just like the vegetation; or perhaps they considered that the Aral Sea supplied some natural obstacle to intrusion.

Gant studied the tactical screen, which was alight with flitting dots whose pattern of movement he had already discerned.

Helicopters patrols. An outer circle of them, around the perimeter of the complex – expected and easy to avoid, or to use as a cover for his own movement. They would not come as far as this deserted place. Others moved with what seemed a greater urgency, criss-crossing the map on which they were superimposed. CIA intelligence had indicated that there was no more than a single *zveno* – flight – of MiL-24 gunships based at Baikonur. There were extra, unexpected patrols –

– purpose; to discover Kedrov, the missing agent-in-place. Minutes before, as he was still skimming the Aral Sea, the first radio transmissions he had picked up on the HF set had worried him. Was he expected? Were they waiting for him, too? Now, he did not think so. And the urgency of the dots on his screen was belied by the routine responses and acknowledgements over the headset. They were looking because they had discovered Kedrov was missing, not because they knew he had a rendezvous with a helicopter.

Their search had included the marshes. *Was* including it, now. Dormitory towns, villages, isolated settlements, farms, factories, radar installations – everywhere. The search was being coordinated, and involved foot patrols, cars and helicopters. Needle in a haystack . . . Gant had little worry they would find Kedrov. They might, however, find him.

Gently, he lowered the *Hind*, the decision taken before he became clearly aware of it. The helicopter skimmed the artificial lake, raising its water into tiny waves, then Gant shunted it beneath the young fir trees, watching the rotors intently. Branches waved and lashed above the cockpit. The undercarriage bounced on sand, and he closed the throttles. The rotors wound down into silence, out of which the wind's noise leapt, banging against the perspex. The trees above his head continued to sway and lean. He sighed, eased his frame in the restraint of his straps, and watched the tactical screen. Fireflies –

The stream of orders and reports filled his hearing, but he did not remove his headset or helmet. *Not here, not here, not here . . . couple of kids, looks like we might have found a black-market drop here . . . not here, no, nothing here, nothing nothing . . .* The reports poured into his mind. They hadn't located Kedrov, and they evidently had no idea where he might be. It was a blanket search which was turning into the boredom of routine.

Gant watched the perimeter patrols. They were calling in, too, but maintained their conventional role. Because of the proximity of the launch, the security system of Baikonur was operational. It was its own justification. The closest helicopter to the bathing area was five miles away. It would pass perhaps three miles to the east of him as it swung onto the southward leg of its patrol. The next helicopter would pass perhaps twenty minutes later. On the ground, only listening posts and mobile units interested him. Those he could bleed into the display at any time from the satellite's model of security patrols. Tonight, there were more of them, however.

He had to thread a path between them, avoiding everything — aural and visual detection most of all. Keeping low —

— changing idents. He opened the cockpit door and the wind buffeted him. He gritted his teeth and squinted against the flying sand that pattered on his overalls, slapped his cheeks. He removed a shallow box from the rear of the cockpit, releasing the straps that held it. He climbed down onto the sand, cursing his luck with the wind. Against the sky, he saw distant towers and gantries and radio masts, and their proximity unnerved him. Distances extended without limit and took on the complexion of something animate and hostile. He sensed the silence of the machine by which he knelt, remembered Mac — then, muttering inarticulately, he opened the box to search for what he required.

Strips of adhesive plastic, too flimsy . . . but he couldn't use the spray-cans and the stencils, not in this wind. Beneath his hands lay the means of changing the *Hind*'s identity to that of a GRU or KGB patrol. The insignia, the numerals, the ident flashes were all accurate —

— useless. He stood up, closing the box savagely, then thrust it back into the cockpit. His fist banged against the fuselage. He ground his teeth. There was no transmission from Kedrov. He could avoid visual sighting, in this darkness with the moon ageing and dimming, and could avoid the listening posts and the car patrols – or be mistaken for one of their own – if only he could go now, move at once, just the twenty miles to the marshes –!

Distantly, he heard the helicopter patrol away to the east . . . as predicated and expected. He banged the fuselage again with his fist. Where in hell was Kedrov? Where was the signal . . . ? Away behind his hunched back, the miles unrolled towards Afghanistan and Pakistan. A thousand of them. To the west, beyond the Aral Sea and the Caspian, Turkey lay a thousand miles away. He shivered.

Eventually, he climbed back into the cockpit. He huddled into himself in his seat. On the tactical screen, the fireflies moved with darting, seemingly-purposeful activity. As he reached for the headset, his hand quivered. Then he jammed the earphones against his head. The transmissions flew back and forth; response, acknowledgement, report, description, response, order, position, reference, report . . . *nothing here, cleared this area now, nothing here, nothing, nothing, nothing* . . . They hadn't found Kedrov, they had no idea where he was. Gant's hands had clenched into fists in his lap. He realized he had been sustained for the last hours – since Garcia's MiL had been destroyed – by the single, simple idea that Kedrov was not the problem. Getting to him was the task, the mission, not *finding him* –!

Nothing, nothing, nothing . . . Where in hell was he?

He felt the first tremor of panic. Unease was sliding towards anxiety like an unbalanced cargo inside him. He looked at his watch. Two-thirty. They'd be looking for him, on both sides of the Afghan border. Which escape-route could he use – back that way or west towards Turkey? The thought of escape made his mouth dry. The priority route was Afghanistan, but that had been before they'd stumbled across the mission and shot down the ferry helicopter. They'd killed Garcia and his crew, and by now they'd long known he had escaped, leaving Mac's body behind. They'd be waiting for him. It had to be Turkey . . .

Where was Kedrov?

Two thirty-one. Twenty minutes since his arrival. Time was operating like a thermometer, recording an inexorable rise in his temperature, and his tension. *Twenty minutes already gone!* He had perhaps no more than five hours of darkness left ꜱd a thousand miles meant a minimum of five hours' flyinꜱ ꜱe. In another minute, slow daylight would begin to encroach on the other end of his journey, exposing his last moments in Soviet airspace. How long could he afford to wait for Kedrov?

He could not ask the question clearly. His head spun with a storm of anticipations and shied from any answer. How long? Where was Kedrov? Two thirty-two.

He remembered Adamov, presumably conscious by now, tied to the jump-seat in the main cabin. And now, with a narrow, cold certainty, he knew why the GRU captain was still alive. Not because his body might have been found, not because there might be a search for him . . .

. . . because he might need the uniform. The papers. Even the man.

When he tried to get out. He might have enough fuel, he might not . . . superstitiously, he was afraid to risk another gas station. He might need a uniform, ID, information. So, Adamov was alive.

He was growing numb with cold or something else. He blew on his hands, shuffled his feet. He turned in his seat, staring westward. No longer towards the marshes and Kedrov. He looked at the instruments.

Still no glow of light from the transponder. Kedrov's set was not responding to the signal, he couldn't be at the agreed rendezvous.

He was hunched into himself, his hands like frozen claws in his lap, his head bowed, chin on his chest. On the unregarded tactical screen, the defences of Baikonur sparkled like cold stars — radar, missile launchers, gun emplacements, listening posts. Gant felt nothing but emptiness around him.

Where was Kedrov?

Where . . . ?

'What's he doing?' Priabin whispered.

'He's just woken up — he fell asleep,' Katya added, as if

surprised by Kedrov's behaviour. 'Curled up like a frightened child, head under the blankets – look.' She tapped the TV monitor. A cable snaked away from it across the frozen stretch of marsh, along the rotting jetty to the borescope which had been inserted into a narrow gap in the houseboat's planking.

Priabin studied the image. A low-light television camera with a needle-like probe was attached to the hull of the boat. One of Dudin's team had approached Kedrov's hideout and checked that the camera and its borescope could be installed without Kedrov being aware of the fact. More than a hour ago. Now, the monochrome image of the houseboat's cabin could be observed from a quarter of a mile away.

Priabin rubbed his gloved hands to warm them – perhaps almost to express a kind of gloating pleasure. On the screen, in the centre of the circular image, Kedrov stirred on his narrow bunk, and looked at his watch. Priabin involuntarily did the same. Almost three o'clock. The effect of the time on Kedrov was alarming. He sat bolt upright on the bunk, stiffly flinging aside the blankets that had covered him. His face was clearly appalled – as if he had not-quite-woken from a nightmare. Priabin exhaled wincingly, so real and close was the man's fear. Kedrov was a terrified man – had he sensed the camera, the men surrounding his hiding-place?

A helicopter passed distantly. GRU patrols. There were more of them than Priabin expected. Looking for *him*, the man on the TV screen? Extra security because of the launch? Priabin was sensitive to the pace of events. He could still lose this race . . .

. . . Rodin. He must get back to Rodin, soon. The boy was dangerously isolated and afraid. The ticket for the morning flight was waiting at the Aeroflot desk. Kedrov had to be taken now, and hidden elsewhere. Katya must look after him . . . once he'd mollified Dudin.

Kedrov stood up. His frame had enlarged as he moved across the narrow room towards the hidden needle-like lens. His face was white, distorted by the fish-eye vision of the tiny lens. He was leaning heavily on the table in the middle of the room, staring down at the – what was it? Priabin leaned closer to the screen. Yes — a transistor radio, unremarkable in every way. Kedrov was staring at it with the same mesmerized attention a rabbit would give to a snake. His whole frame could be seen quivering, as if an earthquake had struck the boat. What was wrong with him?

Kedrov tore off the back of the radio, exposing its circuit boards and wiring. Touched at it, studied it as if it contained his whole future, looked at his watch, studied the radio, looked at his watch . . .

Katya, beside Priabin, next to Dudin, was puzzled but silent.

'Colonel —' Dudin began.

'Not *now*, Dudin!' Priabin snapped. His breath was smokily whipped away by the wind crying across the marshes. The canvas windbreak erected around the screen rattled as loudly as the frozen reeds and sedge. He concentrated on Kedrov's puzzling behaviour.

Watch, radio . . . something glowed in the centre of the radio's innards, though Priabin had not seen Kedrov switch on the set. Had he missed it?

'Did he switch it on?' he whispered.

'What —?'

'Did you see him switch on the radio?' He raised his voice as another helicopter passed overhead; closer than the previous one. There were no lights around him, no radios or walkie-talkies being used — and not just so as not to alarm Kedrov. Priabin could not risk attracting GRU attention to their stake-out.

Katya shook her head. 'No, I didn't,' she confirmed.

'Pity we haven't got a mike rigged up . . . why has he taken the back off the set?'

Kedrov shook the set as if he, too, wondered whether it was working. Evidently, there was no sound from it. One of its batteries fell from the case, then another detached itself. Kedrov appeared momentarily alarmed, then grinned. He replaced the radio on the table. He seemed calmer, though his face was etched with creases of anxiety. He looked at his watch again, then the radio, then his watch . . .

. . . radio. The windbreak rattled. Priabin hunched forward on the small, folding chair placed in front of the screen. The noises of the stiff spikes of sedge were ghostly. The helicopter's drone diminished in the distance. Radio . . .

A point at the centre of the radio's exposed circuitry still glowed. Without batteries? Kedrov had retreated, and had sat down once more, his eyes still on the table and the radio. His shadow no longer fell across the transistor set. Where was the power coming from, without its batteries? It should not be working . . .

– but it was. It wasn't an ordinary radio.

His hand gripped Katya's arm. She winced with pain, exhaled. He shook her arm excitedly.

'It's not a radio,' he whispered fiercely.

'Sir –?'

'It can't be. It's working without batteries – there's no lead . . . it's a dummy set. What the hell is it? It must have some other power-source, something that doesn't look like an ordinary battery.' He was murmuring quickly, to himself as much as to Katya; chasing ideas that ran ahead of him. 'What's going on, Katya? What?' It's working, but not as a radio, he thought. Why? For what reason? 'It's still working,' he said aloud, 'but not as a radio set . . . it can't receive without its batteries . . .'

And then he knew.

Transmission. It was some kind of transmitter, the glowing light only to inform Kedrov it was operating . . . the signal was inaudible – dear *God!*

'It –' He had to clear his throat. 'He – he's signalling to someone . . .'

Dear God, Kedrov expected to be rescued. *He was waiting to be rescued!*

'How?' was all Katya could say. Dudin had overheard and was crouching beside them now.

'I don't know!'

'Colonel, let's move in now,' Dudin offered.

'Not yet – let me think!' Rescue, rescue . . . someone was coming for Kedrov – at least, Kedrov believed it. But who, and how? Should they make sure of Kedrov, now? Or – but how the hell could anyone get this deep into Baikonur? The idea was impossible.

'Sir?'

'Colonel –!'

'No, no – just let me think!' He stood up. The wind leapt on him over the top of the canvas. The navigation lights of a helicopter glowed, moving against the background of stars. He could just make out its engine noise above the wind. How –?

Everything, his imagination tempted. Everything – there for the taking . . . just wait. Kedrov has run out of time, he's terrified he's too late already – it must be soon. A half-hour, an hour at most . . . sooner than that. Just wait –

Rodin was forgotten.

'Someone's coming for Kedrov,' he said, looking down at his companions, whose faces lifted from the screen, and were palely lit by its monochrome glow. Between their features, Kedrov stared out unseeingly, desperately hoping he was on the point of rescue. 'We're going to have him, or them, too!' Priabin added, his voice eager.

Serov stood opposite the window of Valery Rodin's flat. The empty room around him was the very one used by Priabin's KGB surveillance team until only a couple of hours earlier. He was alone. Overcoated, hands clasped behind his back, standing. Near his toe, scratched into the floor-boards, were the marks left by a tripod. He had seen them in the light of his torch. Otherwise, there was little trace – beyond remaining scents and the feeling of recent occupation – of the surveillance team.

Priabin. It rested on the answer to the question, *was Priabin dangerous*? What did he already know? Serov had consulted the file on the KGB's head of industrial security at Baikonur. The man's history was intriguing – the dead woman, the Firefox fiasco, his survival of an incident which should have ended his career, perhaps even his life . . . Priabin was a survivor. But there

299

was something about the man . . . he was difficult to comprehend, to thoroughly know. Priabin was a mystery to Serov and therefore dangerous.

Something might have to be done about him – and soon. Just as decisive a something as the act soon to unfold at the uncurtained window opposite.

'Door's open,' a voice whispered in the shadows of the room, disembodied – unnerving except that Serov knew it came from the small transceiver clipped to his greatcoat.

'Go ahead,' he murmured in reply. The room seemed charged with the static from the open channel. He raised to his eyes a small pair of binoculars, suitable for low-light conditions. And studied Rodin's form stretched on the bed.

The team was in the flat. Breathing, quick and tense, filled the room. Lockpicker, two heavies and a doctor to administer the overdose of drugs . . . whichever drug was decided upon in the next few minutes. They were in the hallway. Rodin lay on the bed, robe in disarray, deeply unconscious; drink and hashish. He was a drugged, incompetent, dangerous *mess* –

– rubbish to be thrown out. Serov listened to the team's cumulative breathing, felt his muscles tauten and contract with their tension. For himself, he was prepared to assume the calm of the detached observer, certain of the outcome of the drama he witnessed.

The door opened behind him, startling him. He turned angrily. A young radio operator, carrying his set, apologized awkwardly.

'You said, sir –' he began.

The older sergeant, accompanying him, merely snapped: 'The comms unit you requested, comrade Colonel.'

'Yes – very well, get it installed and working – over *that* side of the room.'

He turned away abruptly, in time to see the door of Rodin's bedroom opening. He stared. The team were in black civilian trousers and sweaters; ski-masks. He felt excited by the menace they so thoroughly portrayed on the screen of the window. Two, three of them, and the doctor . . .

. . . Rodin sitting up, startled awake, one of the team moving to

300

him, another to the curtains at the window, dragging them closed –

– sharp disappointment, Rodin's distant, tinny voice protesting, breathing from one of the team as if engaged in strenuous exercise, the heartbeat of another, all filled the room. Serov's frustration at being cut off from the unfolding drama was as audible to him as the sounds from the transceiver, and the noises of the two men behind him.

'OK, sir,' the sergeant murmured.

'Not now!' he stormed, hand moving as if to clutch at his heart. Then he added more softly: 'In a *moment*, sergeant.'

'Sir.' The sergeant clumped away.

He uncovered the transceiver on his breast like a treasured pet. Breathing, Rodin's repeated, frightened questions, the laughter of one of the team – Grigori, possibly. The comms set at the back of the room crackled and hummed, awaiting his attention. Serov stared at the closed curtains, as if anticipating some vivid shadow-play to be thrown upon them by the lights of Rodin's bedroom.

He could trust the team – just as he could trust the two men behind him. There was no risk in using them to dispose of a general's son. They were his creatures.

General Rodin would be an implacable enemy, should he ever discover the truth of his son's death . . . . however, there was no danger of that. But, he would ask. A sacrificial goat might divert any suspicion from himself. He recalled the general's cold, stiff features looking down at him. The glittering eyes had seen Serov's capacity to destroy his queer son. When he heard of Valery's death, Serov might be the first person he thought of in connection with the event. Might indeed –

Suicide, then . . . Serov rubbed his chin. There was the smell of cigarette smoke in the room now, the scrape of matches as the sergeant and the radio operator lit acrid Russian tobacco. Serov wrinkled his nose fastidiously. Watched the curtains opposite, then looked at his watch. Three in the morning. Rodin hadn't been gagged – no bruising must appear around his mouth.

'Why, why, why . . . ?' came repeatedly from the transceiver, not *Who? Who are you, what do you want?*

Serov could not resist saying: 'You know why.'

'Who —?' Rodin blurted. Someone laughed once more — yes, Grigori, whose stereotyping even included the slightly manic giggle; it was surprising how often members of his special teams fulfilled their cinematic stereotypes. Then: 'Serov? Is that you, Serov? For Christ's sake, where are you? What do you want, man?' It was both question and bribe.

'Yes — I'm across the street, Rodin. Where your friend Priabin had his men installed.' The sergeant cut off a guffaw of laughter in the shadows behind him. 'You remember your friend Priabin? What you spoke about together . . . ?'

'You've been watching me?' Rodin's voice was terrified, certain of its future.

'Everyone's been watching *you*, dear boy.'

'For God's sake —! I told him nothing!' Rodin bellowed; but the small noise from the transceiver was contained, even swallowed, by the room. 'My father — he can't want you to do this, he can't —!'

'He doesn't even know.'

'Then you can't *do it!*' Hysterical relief, the voice at the point of breaking. 'You need his *order* —!'

'Security is my concern.'

'I told him nothing!'

'I don't believe you . . .' Serov stared at his gloved hands, flexing the fingers, spreading them in front of him. He smoothed the gloves as he had seen the general do only hours earlier, on the steps of the officers' mess. Businesslike, fastidious rather than sinister.

'I told him nothing!'

'Now you're protecting him, too,' Serov observed calmly. 'Security is my responsibility — it's security I'm interested in here. I'm ensuring things remain — secure . . .' He listened for a moment to Rodin's ragged breathing, then he said: 'Very well — do it.' And above Rodin's scream of protest and terror, he added loudly: 'Make it suicide. *Suicide!*'

302

He stared at the curtains. A delicate blow to the head or neck, or a gripped nerve to render Rodin unconscious . . . silence the noise he was making.

'Don't bruise him!' he snapped as if he could see the struggle taking place on the bed rather than simply overhearing it.

A narrow tube down the throat, and whisky or cognac – the choice was unimportant – and then the valium or whatever tranquillizer or sleeping-pill the doctor discovered in Rodin's bathroom cabinet or bedroom drawer. No overdose of heroin or cocaine, but a signposted suicide; sleeping tablets washed down with drink. The boy would be unable to avoid swallowing the mixture. The tube would leave nothing but a little rawness at the back of his throat which would not interest the coroner. Murder would not be a possibility.

The initial spluttering, the exerted breathing of the team, the murmured instructions, went on for some time, but slowly, inevitably subsided. There was a cadence about it, a diminuendo, which Serov quite liked; and a decency in the violence taking place off-stage, as it were – behind closed curtains. Something domestic and suburban and inescapably ordinary . . . so fitting. So belying. Rodin's father would believe in the suicide, and if he wondered why, then –

– Serov turned abruptly from the window. The room could be redressed with KGB surveillance paraphernalia, easily. Now, he had given himself the option of incriminating Priabin, should it prove necessary. Over the transceiver he could hear calm breathing noises, movement, whispers, routines; as if they were arranging the body for viewing – which, in a sense, they were. Yes, it might be best to implicate Priabin, arrest him . . . tonight? Certainly today. He postponed decision. If he didn't use the suicide to involve Priabin, then it would simply bring the pain of guilt to the general. And that was satisfactory, too.

He turned to the window, briefly. Still curtained. They'd draw them back before they left, switching off the room lights. Someone would see the body from this block of flats when daylight came. Yes, all very satisfactory, neat.

'All done here, sir,' the transceiver said over his heart.

'Very well. Stage-dressing completed?'

'Almost.'

'Hurry it along – but miss nothing. Well done. Out.' He turned to the sergeant and the radio operator, who came swiftly to attention; impressed, perhaps even abashed by what had occurred across the street. 'Very well. Put me in touch with headquarters – Captain Perchik.'

'Sir . . .' Call sign, fine-tuning, then he heard Perchik's voice. He took the proffered microphone, snapped down its Transmit button, and said: 'Give me a full report, Perchik. Quickly! One of your one-minute digests I enjoy so much for their brevity!'

'A good night, sir?' Perchik asked, his voice responding to the eager lightness of that of his superior; a momentary camaraderie. Perchik knew what he had been doing.

'A good night. Now, hurry. I want this Kedrov – what have you got as the chef's recommendation on the menu?'

'Chef's recommendation, sir . . . stay away from the social contacts, the sexual contacts are a bit off tonight, we haven't any of the close-friend hiding-place – it's off . . .' Serov smiled, even chuckled. Perchik was clever as a cat at obsequiousness. 'But the chef does recommend recent pastimes and hobbies as something you should try.'

'And –?'

'Going through the man's whole behaviour pattern, his every move, for the last month, we've come up with a bicycle repair shop – really black-market – in Tyuratam, but Kedrov isn't there and the KGB hauled in the owner of the shop two days ago.'

'So, he's offered no leads or they'd have Kedrov by now. What else?' There was a clipped, military manner about Serov now, something lighter and less intent than the observer of Rodin's murder. This efficient portrait was another part he enjoyed playing.

'Bird-watching – the feathered kind, sir,' Perchik added without creating any sense of time-wasting. 'Out in the salt marshes. Where we go duck shooting, in season.'

'I know, Perchik. Disgusting sport, if you can call it that –

bird-watching, mm? He's applied for permits from the KGB? Or from us?'

'KGB handle that sort of minor stuff, sir.'

'Many times?'

'We've counted almost a dozen, sir – those marshes are full of rotting hulks, old hides, hunting cabins, you name it –'

'That will do for a start. Priority air search of the area of the marshes . . .' He looked at his watch, holding up his wrist so that the dial caught the light of the streetlamp. Three-fifteen. 'Order that at once. It's a long shot, but he must be somewhere – why not there? He must know the area . . . get it done, Perchik.'

'Sir.'

'Out.'

Serov dropped the microphone into the sergeant's waiting hand, and walked to the window. The curtains had been drawn back once more, but the room was in darkness. Light crept in from the street like an orange fog. It touched Rodin's stretched-out legs, his disordered robe. One arm hung over the side of the bed – yes, he could make that out with the glasses – the other lay folded on his chest. A sweet, dreamless sleep; a nice touch of fiction. Sooner or later, someone would wonder why the boy didn't move, he'd be found eventually . . . maybe even his father might call –

– a pleasant anticipation.

'Outside, sir,' the transceiver announced.

'Good,' he said at once. 'I'll join you.'

Serov turned away from the window without hesitation; as if he had seen the movie that window-screen had to offer, many times before; the re-running of a popular success, without suspense because the ending is known.

'Tidy up, sergeant,' he snapped as he opened the door. 'This set may have to be re-dressed today or tomorrow.'

'Sir.'

Serov closed the door behind him.

Gant looked up from the insistent, unnerving image of his curled, stiff hands. His watch, showing three-twenty, had ceased to evoke further anxieties. It merely recorded the passage of wasted time. He now had almost an hour of first light to negotiate in Soviet airspace. Even at the MiL's maximum speed, that might be as much as two hundred miles of flying before he reached either the Pakistan or Turkish border. The situation had become hopeless; he had slid wearily into acknowledgement of that, his fears deadened by familiarity.

He stared across the harshly lit main cabin – the primitive heating failed to resist the chill of the night outside, which was intensified by the banging of the wind against the fuselage and the creaking of the rotors. Opposite him, trussed into the jump-seat, was the cause of his sullen, muddy depression. Adamov. Soon, he would have to kill the man . . . after gaining as much information as the man could supply. Throttle or suffocate him, so that the uniform remained unmarked. Adamov's uniform would fit, just. His collar-size determined the fact that he would have to be murdered.

Helicopters droned distantly to the south and east, but the *Hind* remained undiscovered. It seemed no longer like something parked near the picnic area, but rather a dumped vehicle, long abandoned and left to rust. And still he could not kill Adamov and leave this place.

The man's eyes seemed to ask, again and again, *Who are you?* He did not seem afraid, nor to anticipate a violent demise. His eyes were vivid with curiosity and anger. Had they not been, he would have been easier to kill. There was a hollow in Gant's chest and stomach that was watery, queasy with danger and the dread of violence still to be inflicted. The watch measured the slow, reluctant steps he was making towards hurting Adamov. Soon – it would have to be soon . . .

. . . the incident at the gas station, the flight across the Aral Sea, the waiting here, all seemed to have finally drained him. He seemed to have nothing left. He had lost control of the mission. He could not even bring himself to return to the cockpit, to look for the signal light on the transponder. He knew the light would be dead. Kedrov would not be making the rendezvous . . .

. . . then *go*!

306

The lethargy was huge and frightening, like a great weight of water above him. He'd let go. Already beaten.

Gant was weary of Adamov's dumb yet too-vivid presence and the intermittent drumming of his bootheels on the cabin's metal floor. He stood up awkwardly and quickly, like a drunk getting to his feet. His head whirled emptily. Adamov flinched, even attempted to cower, securely pinioned as he was. Gant ignored the momentary fear. Avoided it, rather. He dragged open the cabin door and leant gratefully into the freezing wind, which did not even begin to clear his head. He jumped down.

Bitter cold immediately, chilling through him, so that he believed that he must have been warm in the cabin. He tugged the fleece-lined flying jacket closer around him, with a sudden loathing of the huddled figure he made. The wind seemed to cry from a great distance, thin and fitful though it was. He felt each of the thousand miles to safety, each of the twenty to where Kedrov had not arrived, and the great emptiness around him.

And Kedrov slowly faded in his mind and the reluctance he had felt at hurting Adamov also lessened. Soon, he would be able to go through with it, make him talk, use the uniform. He rubbed cold hands hard against numb cheeks, leaning his back against the fuselage. He sighed with deep, tired, empty anger. The sighs became an expression of failure and isolation. He should have turned back when he'd filled the tanks . . . should never have believed he could make it.

He shivered continually with cold. To warm himself, he began to walk, patrolling the margin of the man-made lake, beginning to think of his own safety. He could abandon the helicopter inside Baikonur, steal a car or truck, make it out that way . . . he could take the *Hind* as far as its fuel allowed and then find a vehicle . . . he could fly to the nearest American consulate or embassy or diplomatic mission and walk in and ask them to get him home . . . just as soon as he disposed of Adamov, put on his identity and his uniform. And that would be soon now, *soon* —

The startling calls of ducks, other wildfowl. The dull, fretted lapping of the water, the stiff, dry rattling of sedge and reeds, the thin, searching cry of the wind. He walked on, deliberately oblivious to the passage of time. Occasionally, the drone of distant, hunting helicopters sounded above the wind, but he sensed no threat. He was safe until he chose to move —

— a startled goose flung itself into the wind from the reeds at his feet. Gant flung up his hands to protect his face and stumbled backwards as if pushed. He almost fell. Involuntarily, he cried out in a stranger's high-pitched voice, a near-scream of shock and terror. The wild goose skittered across the ruffled metal of the lake's gleam, then gained height and grace and curved behind the pagoda, carried by wind and fright and wings. He stood, idiotlike, staring open-mouthed at its passage and the widening circles of its flight.

Then he turned and ran, shaken out of every feeling except panic, back towards the *Hind*. He felt as if his limbs had been untied, his mind cleared. Get out, get out, *get out*, his thoughts insisted.

He blundered against the helicopter, dragged open the cockpit door and heaved himself into his seat, newly afraid. No —! No light from the transponder . . . He had been terrified that he would find the light illuminated, Kedrov's summons peremptory and unignorable. The APU was still on, the main panel glowed with other lights. Two minutes warm-up, two minutes to take-off. Even as he completed the pre-flight checks and decisions, his eyes continued to stare at the transponder and its unlit signal. Not yet, not yet — he's dead, dammit, forget Kedrov, he isn't there. In two minutes he would be airborne . . . and he knew where he was going, knew it for certain. Kedrov's contact has been from the diplomatic mission in Tashkent. He had easily enough fuel to get him to Tashkent . . . he would walk in to the mission, and ask for the Company's man . . . easy. They weren't looking for him, not yet, they wouldn't have the place guarded, blocked off. He had the time —

Engine-start. He switched on Baikonur's Tac-channel. Throttles open. The rotors moved with an initial reluctance, then began turning more swiftly. He would not need to kill Adamov — at least not until later. He began to listen to the reports from the patrols, a feverish excitement mounting in him, all thought of Kedrov and the mission banished.

He released the brake. On the tactical screen, the fireflies were more numerous, more concentrated – but nowhere near him, nor between him and the Aral Sea . . . he would have to loop well to the south before taking up a heading for Tashkent. As long as they had no idea he was there, they would not close the mission in Tashkent against him –

– glanced up through the perspex, searching the night for the bird that had startled him. It must have settled or flown off. Like a talisman, he couldn't risk harming it.

Twenty feet, thirty, forty . . . fireflies, the search that must have found Kedrov hours before and was now just waiting for *him* to show . . . fifty feet. Gant swung the *Hind* around on its axis, pointing it westward. Fifty miles to the Aral Sea.

Then he saw the light on the transponder. And groaned. A steady light – *now!* Kedrov had switched on. The fireflies of the search were concentrated in the area where he should be –

No, the bastard was dead, no . . .

The *Hind* was moving westwards, increasing speed, the trees distressed by its passage, the lake shrinking in his mirrors. Seventy miles an hour, eighty, the airspeed indicator hovering around one hundred – he was out, safe –

Over the Tac-channel, he could hear cars involved in the search, troop units being moved by helicopter and truck, MiLs congregating – just where Kedrov should be. They were searching the marshes now. Someone had ordered it, it wasn't an accident. Reports and positions flew.

He was five miles from the lake. Then he heard the name *Kedrov*. The poor bastard was alive, free, and they were looking for him. Six miles away, seven now. He was almost thirty miles from Kedrov and leaving him behind fast.

The *Hind* slowed. He cursed the light on the transponder and he cursed Kedrov. Raged at the swarming helicopters that filled the tactical screen. Damn it, damn you, you stupid sonofabitch – why now, *damn you*? The *Hind* took up, as if of its own volition, a new heading. To pinpoint Kedrov in the marshes, he would have to fly a north-south patrol until he obtained a triangular fix on the source of the response.

He listened to the tangle of orders and responses, he watched the tactical screen as closely as he might some poisonous creature about to strike.

The area of the agreed rendezvous was being patrolled at that moment. If Kedrov was exactly where he should be, and not somewhere else, then he was right in the middle of the search. He exploded the scale of the moving map until it showed only the islet which was the agreed rendezvous. There were still two helicopters registering even on that tiny pocket of earth and frozen water. One of them was dropping troops into the marshes.

He had to try to get Kedrov out as soon as he pinpointed his position.

Not there, not right there – please . . .

'Everyone's ready?' Priabin asked breathlessly. Dudin nodded, clearing his throat.

'As instructed, Colonel,' he confirmed. The windbreak rattled like a high flag at his back. Katya stamped her feet for warmth, arms clutched around her, hands beneath her armpits. Her face was pale.

'Well concealed? This could be a helicopter, someone could come on foot –'

'I was clear about that,' Dudin remarked with evident offence. His own impatience seemed not to exist, his excitement dim and contained by careful routine.

'Good man, good man.' Priabin looked up from the screen. Kedrov was sitting or pacing in the cabin of the houseboat, his tension like a silent scream. Above Priabin and the others, a GRU helicopter passed slowly across the night, its navigation lights winking. They had intensified their search of the marshes. Somehow, they'd made the same kind of deduction Katya had made, probably from the same evidence. Kedrov was here somewhere.

Priabin felt success about to be snatched from him; Serov's

310

GRU people, with their vaster resources of men and machines, might have pinpointed the agent-in-place and be simply waiting for a signal to close in . . . just as his men were waiting for a signal.

Go in now, then. Claim the bloody prize! Get your hands on Kedrov before they do – wait for the collector to arrive! If he comes, another part of his thoughts answered more pessimistically. If he bothers, seeing the opposition in the area . . . go in *now*! Serov's people might well get their hands on whoever was coming to Kedrov's aid – and GRU troops would be here soon, he'd heard enough of their radio chatter to know how thoroughly they were searching – so get *your* hands on Kedrov!

'OK, OK,' he murmured, teeth chattering, gloved hands rubbing furiously together as if to ignite a fire. 'We're set. Make no moves, Dudin – just let whoever the rescuers are come on – close in behind them.'

'Colonel.'

'Katya – you found him, you can come in with me. Dudin, when you spot them, *only* then contact me by transceiver.'

'Colonel. You think they'll come in force, then?'

'I don't *know* –' He glanced down at the screen. Kedrov had begun pacing once more – good. Creaking planks and the noise of his footsteps would cover their approach. 'Once I report we're in, and have Kedrov, get your men to remove the borescope and the cable. I don't want whoever's coming to spot *them*!'

'Shall I get the dog from the car, sir?' Katya asked.

'No. Kedrov doesn't appear to be armed . . . I think he's pretty much beaten already . . . let's go in now.'

He turned as if to issue another order to Dudin, or to check previous instructions, then waved his hand apologetically; even grinned. He stepped out of the windbreak, out of the shadow of the clump of bushes and stunted trees, down the slope onto the ice. Treading warily. The wind hurled itself against him so that he staggered. The ice creaked unnervingly. As Katya caught up with him, he looked at his watch. Three twenty-four. He walked, leaning slightly backwards, square-footed like a fatter man, feeling his greatcoat plucked and whirled like a cape around his legs. Katya hurried at his side, gun already drawn, body hunched forward. The ice betrayed their passage as if muttering to Kedrov.

The jetty, then. He climbed the rotting steps carefully, easing his weight onto each one, then to the one above. He kept his hand away from the rail. Eventually, he crouched at the top of the steps and Katya, moving with much less noise, joined him. Her breathing was rapid, excited.

A helicopter passed above them, perhaps no more than a couple of hundred feet. Still scouting. The moon was old and low in the sky, they were just two shadows amid shadows. But Kedrov must be getting panicky at the insistent over-flights . . . Priabin wanted to hurry, scuttle on all fours like a dog along the jetty, bang open the cabin door, gun in hand, make *certain* of his quarry.

'Come on,' he whispered. 'Follow me.'

The helicopter's noise diminished towards the south. Priabin, bending low, hurried forward, caution no longer expedient or even desired. It was not a stalking game now, but a kill. Kedrov was *his* now.

He scurried beside the limp snake of the borescope cable, still carrying the images of the houseboat's interior. He was thirty yards, twenty-five –

– stopped. Because of Rodin.

He was playing for ridiculously high stakes. Kedrov, his would-be rescuers . . . Rodin and *Lightning*. Katya reached him, leant into his body for shelter, looked up at him urgently.

'What is it?'

'What –?' It was all too risky, too dangerous. He had been blinded by the dazzle of complete success. He had wanted it all. 'I –' He shook his head. 'Nothing – come on,' he urged. The wind was at his back, blowing him towards the rotting houseboat like a scrap of paper. If he was quick, sudden –

He had whole minutes yet and a great desire to see shock subside into fear and defeat on Kedrov's face before he returned to Rodin.

'Come on –'

He was running without caution. Clattering along the jetty, his

312

noises masked by the wind and the protests of the old boat. He jumped onto the deck, drawing the Makarov pistol from his holster. His opened greatcoat flew aside. He raised his right boot at the doorway, two steps down from the deck, and kicked savagely at it, as if already cheated and circumvented by events. The doors flew open, crying and splintering. He stumbled down the steps. The wind caused Kedrov's shadow to flicker and enlarge then shrink as the oil-lamp's flame wavered and smoked.

'Kedrov – you're *done*!' Priabin shouted, almost laughing, pleasure welling up in him.

Kedrov was stunned, then further startled to see Katya's small frame emerge from behind Priabin's coat, her gun, too, trained on him. His mouth plopped open and shut, open and shut, like that of a goldfish. Priabin clasped Katya's shoulder, and said:

'You can arrest him, Katya – you found him!'

She moved carefully towards the bunk. Kedrov's shadow, their own shadows, danced and mingled and loomed at one another all around the room. A beer can rolled to Priabin's feet. He kicked it with the kind of pleasure he might have felt kicking back a boy's football in a park. Katya motioned to Kedrov to extend his hands. She handcuffed him. The man's mouth continued to open and close. He could find nothing to say. Katya stood back, her narrow face flushed with excitement, her gun steady.

Priabin moved to the table. Tapped the transistor radio with the barrel of his pistol.

'Works without its batteries, I see,' he murmured knowingly. Further shock was impossible on the stretched, blanched mask of Kedrov's face. He spoke, however.

'How –?' Like an actor forgetting his lines, he dried after the single word.

'We know someone's coming,' Priabin said, offering no explanation of his knowledge, not even referring to the borescope. 'We'll all just sit and wait for him, shall we?' His voice was still musical with success. Katya, too, was smiling.

313

'When's he due to arrive? Soon, I should think, the way you keep looking at the door . . . soon? Good – *excellent*!'

Priabin looked at his watch. Three twenty-eight. He'd give it until four. Then the worries returned. Rodin – I should have told Mikhail to watch Rodin, stay with him.

Would he somehow be made to pay for *this* success . . . ? He felt himself almost superstitious, needing signs and portents. The ticket to Moscow on the morning flight was waiting at the Aeroflot desk. He'd simply checked the Aeroflot computer from the KGB offices – the airline, thank God, was still KGB rather than army, even out here. Mikhail had the tape of his conversation with Rodin. Yes, that was safe. The little incantations of his successes that night calmed his breathing, cooled his body. He looked at Kedrov's face, crumbling like waxy, old cheese . . . the portrait was almost complete. Kedrov's rescuers next, then Rodin . . . the thought of Rodin was like the hollow tooth to which the tongue inevitably returns. He winced. But, if he had not left the boy, he would have just continued to refuse, even threatened Priabin with his father, denied everything. He had had to be left alone with his growing fears. Through them, he might come to help.

His anxiety would not go away. To allay it, he snapped at Kedrov: 'What do you know about *Lightning*, my friend?'

As if he had been practising his response to just that question, Kedrov flung back at him: 'Nothing – nothing at all. What are you talking about?'

'You know something, Kedrov – you know,' Priabin murmured. 'It's in your eyes.' Priabin felt calm once more, albeit temporarily, he suspected. The cabin seemed less shadowy and cramped. Katya and Kedrov and he formed a still, restful painting as they waited.

Until four o'clock . . .

. . . then Rodin would have to become his *absolute* priority.

His speed was no more than ninety mph. The *Hind* wove its way along the channels and roads and railway tracks of a derelict silo

314

complex. Canal-like gouges in the flat land. The complex had been abandoned in the early seventies, when all passages and missile railways had been tunnelled underground. Satellite photography had shown this place unchanged for more than fifteen years. Dust flew up behind the helicopter. Kedrov's transponder was less than five minutes away now.

He jerked the *Hind* aside violently, avoiding a fallen power cable which suddenly draped itself in front of the cockpit as if hanging from the dark sky. The helicopter rolled, then he righted it.

He studied the map display. He was working to the largest scale now, and the details were more sketchy, adapted from countless satellite pictures. The thin dark trail of a shallow stream, barely running on the surface at all, lay ahead of the white dot that represented the helicopter. He lifted out of a gully. In his mirrors, skeletal gantries and towers leaned or remained upright without purpose. Beyond them, the bathing-place was lost to sight. On the map, fireflies moved now that he was in open sky. Russian crackled and flew in his headset.

His conflicting emotions had receded, lost in routines, in flying the helicopter. There was an abiding sense of moving closer to the centre of a web, of deliberately putting his foot on a branch-covered pit. Otherwise, the fear had diminished, the sense of panic that had made him turn west and begin to run was under control. He was wound tight as a spring, but there was an unreality about the danger and an excitement that welled in him. He believed he could get to Kedrov, believed he could get him out . . . despite the odds against him. He had recovered his ego. There was a cold, machine-like exhilaration about his attempt which swept even self-preservation aside, for the moment. But the whole thing was narrowing like a blind alley. It was going to be close, *very* close.

He noticed sedge waved and bowed like corn beneath the *Hind*'s belly, as he was approaching the salt marshes. The troop transport, a heavy MiL-8 *Hip*, had collected the GRU search party, and was moving on a course almost parallel to his own. If he glanced to port, he could just make out the distant white legs of twin searchlights walking across the landscape, shining down from the MiL-8's belly. Collision course between himself and as many as two dozen armed GRU soldiers. He dropped over a low bank into the winding course of the stream which led into the heart of the salt marshes. Ice gleamed like fragments of a broken mirror.

He lost sight of the two walking legs of light and of the forest of abandoned gantries behind him. Airspeed, eighty-five. Time – he glanced at the clock on the main panel – three forty-two. He looked up as the *Hind*'s shadow skimmed a stretch of frozen water. No navigation lights, only the cold stars. He was sweating freely now. Distance to target, four miles. A clump of dwarf bushes leaned from the bank of the stream. Icy sedge stood out from both banks like the spikes of an insect-devouring plant, ready to close over the helicopter.

Call-signs, reports, instructions rang in his ears. Though he knew they were not aware of his presence, not yet . . .

KGB helicopter, routine flight, would be his story. By the time they checked him out – despite the absence of a flight number on their radars, which would make them curious – he would have completed ingress, be on his way out again . . . *be there Kedrov, be there, you bastard.*

The padding of his helmet above his eyebrows was damp, and rubbed as he moved his head from side to side. He was too hot in the leather jacket.

As the marshes spread out more flatly, he glanced to port. Yes, the lights walked on in the distance. The MiL-8 was now slightly ahead of him, or so it seemed. Stunted trees in a clump – the *Hind* rose –

– flicked aside. Violently, as the rotors of another helicopter caught the moonlight, and cockpit lights enlarged in his vision. He swung to one side of the MiL-2 and slightly higher. Altitude, six hundred feet, rising like a bobbing cork onto every radar screen monitoring the area.

Russian bursting from the headset, a stream of oaths and curses and a challenge that was without suspicion; just simple fear and relief flooding the ether.

316

'. . . calm down, comrade,' he heard himself saying through clenched teeth. The other MiL was turning in his mirrors, to face after him. Reeds and frozen water flowed beneath the *Hind.* '. . . no damage done,' he continued to soothe. 'KGB flight Alpha-Three, what more do you want? Fucking about the sky like a swarm of fucking locusts . . .' He listened, then.

'. . . purpose of flight?'

'None of your fucking business . . . we have choppers, too, comrade.' He flew on, watching the MiL recede in his mirrors, watching its blind face turn slowly away as if to resume its inspection of a plotted route. He heard its pilot or co-pilot reporting the almost-collision, reporting his cover story. He was logged in. Now, the questions would begin. He dropped down to fifty feet, disappearing from radar.

Islets, stretches of reed-filled ice, stunted trees. The marshes. Navigation lights to port and starboard, but patrolling not converging. The MiL-8's searchlights a dull glow away to port, but closer now. Collision course – he felt weak. Dear-Christ-in-Heaven! He forced himself to study the map display, to draw his gaze away from the clock on the panel, to ignore the fireflies superimposed on the sketchy landscape.

Something flicked at the edge of eyesight as disturbed water birds rose in the night. The white dot on the map converged on the islet curled like a sleeping cat and the other that was kidney-shaped . . . the agreed rendezvous!

He adjusted the contrast to improve the low-light TV picture on the main screen. Grey shapes glowed unreally. He bobbed over a rise – airspeed seventy – drew the *Hind's* shadow like a black cape across a stretch of ice, glanced to starboard . . . yes?

Then rose onto radar screens once more, but he had to be sure . . . a hundred, two hundred feet, then the shape of the islet revealed itself. Catlike – kidney-dish islet lying across a stretch of frozen water from it, the skeletal shadow of a rotting jetty.

He dropped the *Hind*, as if determined to break through the gleaming ice. Navigation lights around him were lost in the background of stars. The wind seemed no longer to hurl itself against the helicopter. The agreed rendezvous. He was there; target. The white dot that represented the *Hind* was as still as the Bethlehem star.

He flicked away, keeping low, making the reeds bend into the wind with his passage. Stunted trees in the foreground, jutting out of the land's slight undulations. He slowed his speed, judging distances, watching the screens, the radar altimeter, port and starboard of him, the ground . . . where were the lights from the MiL-8? He could not see them. He put the helicopter into the hover. Dropped the undercarriage onto a slight incline, bounced the *Hind*, rolled it forward, wheels hardly in contact with the frozen ground, until the dwarf firs seemed to surround it. Switched off the engines.

Silence.

The wind, then —

— and nothing else. Reeds grew as high as the miniature trees, as if springing up that moment around the helicopter. He felt like a prey-animal amid veldt grass; there were lions out there he could not see. Still, cooling, the *Hind* was overlookable from above. The world consisted of only two dimensions. The reeds were almost as tall as the fuselage. Good enough.

He opened the cockpit door. He did not concern himself with Adamov, who was securely tied and gagged. He drew a sketch map from his overalls, checked the compass display on his watch, orientated himself. Islets to the south-east of him. He could see the clump of trees standing up like frightened hair from the knoll's scalp. Half a mile.

Searchlights —

— leaping onto the ice in front of him, cutting off his glimpse of both knoll and trees. As the belly of the MiL-8 lumbered into view, he pressed against the fuselage of the *Hind*.

Two hundred yards away, the transport helicopter moved across his sight, walking on its searchlight legs, something like an umbilical cord dragging from its belly and tossed by the wind . . . a ladder, a rope ladder. He heard a dog bark, more than one dog, and glanced wildly around him, the noise of the rotors beating in his head. The noise had come from within the MiL . . . the dogs were still aboard but the cabin door was wide now, light spilled from it outlining a human form. Dogs, men, guns.

The transport moved away, oblivious of him. He saw a bulky shadow starting to descend the rope ladder a quarter of a mile away. They were beginning to drop men and dogs in their prescribed places . . . they were looking for Kedrov –

Go –

He could not move, not for a long moment, not until the MiL-8 had moved further off and its noises were less insistent. Then – compass, sketch, night-glasses, visual sighting of the knoll and islet where the jetty was, then –

Gant clambered down the slight incline, onto the first stretch of ice, sedge and reeds scraping like steel against his legs. His hand on the pistol –

– Kalashnikov. He turned, scrambled back up the slope, breathing already harsh, and opened the cabin door. Adamov's white face resented him. He climbed in, took down one of the rifles from its clips, checked its magazine, its weight in his hands, looking only once at Adamov, forcing himself to wink, tossing his head to emphasize a gesture he did not feel. He shut the cabin door behind him. Jogged more easily, familiarly down the incline onto the ice. Continued to jog, leaning into the wind, head down, rifle clutched across his chest. Half a mile. Three-fifty.

Be there!

Gennadi Serov's imagination prickled with points of information just as the night sky, seen through the window of the speeding car, seemed alive with the cold, separate lights of stars. There was a comfort in the analogy, just as there was exhilaration about the details of the report rendered by the team leader and the doctor. They were now seated in silence in the rear of the car, Serov preferring to ride next to his driver. He felt light-headed – yes, that was apt – with the risk he had taken and was still running. It had been a dangerous, even a challenging, move to have young Rodin killed . . . but therein lay its greatest satisfaction. When the body was discovered, the general would be deeply wounded.

And, if he became suspicious, asked for causes, occasions, reasons, he would plant evidence of KGB surveillance in the empty flat across the street from Rodin's apartment. After all, they had been there.

Routine reports, issuing from the radio, washed over him like the sensation of a warm bath. The helicopter search, the cars and the troops on foot, had not yet located Kedrov. They would do so . . . and, if they did not, General Lieutenant Pyotr Rodin would have enough to distract him when the body of his son was discovered.

Apparently, Valery Rodin had subsided quite easily, even strangely. Given up, as if his heart or will had surrendered. The tranquillizers had been administered via the tube, it had all been over in a few minutes — they had left Rodin so deeply unconscious he would never recover.

The car coursed through the trafficless streets of Leninsk, the science city of Baikonur, heading south-east from Tyuratam towards GRU headquarters, a complex of white buildings close to the Cosmonaut Hotel. Out of Baikonur itself, there was something commercial about it, business rather than army or science. Serov enjoyed the separation of the GRU from army headquarters . . . detachment implied independence. To the north of them, the complex was bathed in light from a hundred sources, the sky softened by its glow. To the south, over the darkened city, the stars burned. The car was passing an ornamental fountain at the entrance to a leisure park. The wind had shaped the spray into a peacock's tail before the temperature had frozen it, despite the anti-freeze they mixed with the water.

Radio reports, radio noise. He sighed. Kedrov was unimportant, only the general's anxiety made him otherwise. A dozen helicopters, a hundred men or more, all looking for this one pathetic little shit —! Even out as far as the marshes. Perchik might have a good idea there, might not . . .

He closed his eyes. Details of the reports sparkled like jewels in the darkness behind his lids . . .

Snapped open. He sat upright. His driver was looking at him expecting to receive a change of orders.

'What —?' he asked.

His driver handed him the radio mike. Serov depressed the Transmit button and demanded: 'Repeat that last information, Unit —?' He turned to his driver, clicking his fingers impatiently. 'Unit Air-7,' he added when given the designation. The driver steered the car to the kerb and they slowed to a halt. The handbrake rasped on. 'Unit Air-7, what was your report?' Serov barked. 'This is Serov, understand? Your *report*!'

His fingers drummed on the fascia board. Through the window, misting a little with his sudden tension, he could see a war memorial looming at the end of the wide thoroughfare. They were no more than two minutes from the office. Yet the driver had been correct to stop until this matter had been dealt with — had he misheard?

'. . . helicopter we can't account for, just sitting under some trees — engines stopped, no sign of the pilot . . .' The report continued. When the pilot of Air-7 had finished Serov was silent for a few moments . . . why had it woken him? It was strange, but not sinister or threatening. In the silence, the pilot added: 'A gunship, sir. And it's not a member of our *zveno*. Stranger . . .'

'What markings is it carrying?' he asked. 'Can you see?' He forgot to add 'Over', but the pilot of Air-7 seemed to divine that he had finished; or was, perhaps, simply frightened into efficiency. An unidentified gunship? From *outside* Baikonur?

'. . . picked up the engine heat on IR,' the pilot explained, his voice distant and unreal, but somehow enlarging the significance of the abandoned MiL-24. '. . . see it now on low-light TV . . . army, sir, not ours or KGB — joy-rider, comrade Colonel?'

'Don't be stupid!' It *was* possible, however, in a place like Baikonur — student-like stunts and stupid acts of indiscipline; boredom. Most of the GRU's work had to do with things like that. But, in a gunship? Nevertheless, he added: 'If you can't see his white arse going up and down in the reeds, then it may not be a joy-ride! Get down there and check it out — now, sonny!'

He threw the radio mike towards his driver, and rubbed his chin. Intuition was pressing at the back of his thoughts, attempting to bully its way in. Why? How much significance should he attach to this . . . ?

'Very well, Vassily – drive on!' He banged the fascia as if to startle a horse into motion. The driver started the engine, put the car into gear, and pulled away. The war memorial, sword up-lifted in threat rather than reconciliation or sorrow, loomed closer. It was a huge shadow against the lights of the square behind it. Should he order the MiL surrounded, as intuition seemed to wish? No, wait –

The car rounded the dark memorial, crossed the square. The empty ether hissed from the radio. What was it? Why did he still feel it important?

'Sir – Colonel, sir!' A different voice, perhaps the co-pilot.

'What?' This time, he remembered. 'Over.'

'Sir, an officer – one of ours, GRU, tied up in the cabin – sir, he's claiming he was kidnapped –!'

Serov wanted to laugh, especially as the car skidded rounding a corner as Vassily's surprise transmitted itself to the steering.

'What kind of joke –?' Instinct pressed: he added urgently: 'Get his story – better still, get him to the radio! And get help to stake out that helicopter. Do it *now*! Get that idiot, whoever he is, to the microphone!'

Vassily whistled through his teeth. Serov could feel the mys-tified excitement of the two in the back prickle the hair on his neck. What in hell was going on –? His fingers drummed on the fascia with an increased urgency as the car drew into the fore-court, then beneath the archway of GRU headquarters. Serov did not even spare a glance towards the hotel or the windows of General Rodin's suite. The square was nakedly empty, as was the inner courtyard of the building.

'*Where is that idiot?*' Serov bellowed into the mike.

The trunk of the dwarf fir seemed to move to collide with his back, so violently did he lean against it to conceal himself. A helicopter's shadowy belly slid above the ice between him and the rotting jetty. He forced himself to observe it through the night-glasses. The fleecy lining of his jacket, near the collar, was icily damp from his exerted breathing. It numbed his cheek as he leaned back, lowering the tiny pair of binoculars. The helicopter passed northwards. He tried to listen, but nothing other than the retreating MiL and the cry of the wind came to him. The landscape might just be deserted.

Gant clutched the Kalashnikov against his chest, made himself study the open space of ice across which his path lay. Empty, gleaming palely as if lit from far below its surface. Deserted. He raised the glasses once more. Starlight and moonlight were intensified. He scanned the stretch of frozen water. Carefully, repeatedly.

He saw nothing, but could not trust the evidence of his eyes. There could be men out there, hidden and waiting or simply approaching in a search-pattern laid down for them. He would not know. He understood his limitations. This was not his element; here, he was ordinary, dangerous to himself. He looked at his watch. Three fifty-eight. His approach had been careful and slow, but it had been textbook, not instinctual. What had he missed? He studied the jetty and the houseboat through the glasses. Thin bars of light stood out, indicating a source of light inside the boat. It had to be Kedrov. This was the agreed rendezvous. He scanned the ice again, then the sedge and the reed-beds, then the clumps and tufts of trees and low bushes. They were impenetrable, could hide an army. He shivered, hating the thought of the *Hind* half a mile behind him. It seemed like a home he had abandoned.

He moved slowly through the reeds and out onto the ice. Time urged him, and he moved quickly across the frozen marsh towards the jetty, until he pressed against groaning wood, into the shadows cast by the jetty. He listened. Heard the wind. Saw distant navigation lights. No dogs . . . *listen for the dogs!* The MiL-8 had dropped men and dogs at their appointed places in the pattern of the search. Could he hear dogs? He held his breath, listening into the wind. Distant rotor noise, nothing more.

He climbed the steps, crouching at the top, sensing the skin on his back and buttocks and neck become fragile. He felt colder, as if naked. The rifle seemed unreal, held in numb hands that gripped like claws. The boat was only yards away. He could see the bars and strips of light clearly. He scanned the open ground once more with the glasses. Nothing. Then he ran in an awkward crouch, the wood of the jetty announcing each quick footfall, the wind seeming encouraged to unbalance him by the cramped and difficult posture he adopted. He stepped carefully onto the boat's deck. Eased along the side of the cabin, bent down . . . sensing some kind of expertise emerging now, as if he had undergone a whole course of training in the last few moments. Looked through cracked wood, saw nothing, then through a gap where two thin curtains did not quite meet. Saw him –

– Kedrov. Had to be. A radio, back open, exposing the source of the signal, lay on the table in front of him. The man was down, that was obvious. Head hanging, face in shadow, staring; hands still, but weakly clenched in a child's grip. Not believing someone would come for him. Gant felt relief, felt the urgency of the minutes that had passed since he left the MiL; felt the possibility of success. Rose and eased himself further along the narrow deck until, down two steps, he reached the cabin doors. Touched their wood, felt the grain and the peeling paint because his hand was suddenly warmer. They creaked as he pushed them open.

He stepped into the narrow, shadowy room. Was startled as he heard a helicopter's rotors close, saw Kedrov's face lift to his, was warned, but not quickly enough because there was a prod of something metallic, hard, in his back. A hand reached for the barrel of the rifle and held it tightly before he could begin to turn. And a girl, gun held stiff-armed ahead of her, emerged from the shadows at the far end of the cabin. He felt a moment of rage which he might have used, but shock drained it away. The girl was afraid, surprised, pleased. Kedrov was appalled. Gant realized the face should have warned him, wearing defeat like a badge. He let the rifle go and it was snatched away somewhere behind him. A helicopter seemed to be in the hover outside. He heard the first dog cry distantly but eagerly. He shivered.

The place seemed to rush in on him. *Winter Hawk* was finished; blown. Finished just as he was.

'American?' a voice asked behind him. The metallic rod jabbed in his back. It would be foolish to move, it said. Your hands would not be quick enough. 'Well?' The man spoke English with competence as he said: 'We have been waiting for you – all of us, but perhaps for different reasons. Turn to face me, please – very slowly.'

Outside, the helicopter had landed, the engines were running down. Human orders were being shouted. The girl seemed surprised at the activity. His hands relaxed. He turned.

KGB. Colonel's shoulder-boards on his greatcoat. Gant's own age –

– familiar.

The colonel's face dissolved as if under a great pressure, then it re-formed into a wild, unstable mask. The eyes burned, and Gant recognized –

– Priabin. The girl, Anna, who had died at the border . . . last image of her body cradled by, by this man, beside the car they had been using to escape . . . this man, Priabin. Her lover.

'Gant,' he said. Then again: 'Gant.' The tone of the voice suggested he had already killed an enemy. Priabin sighed. The hatred was there, but the features were composed around the eyes, strangely at peace. There was even a smile –

– as the Makarov pistol was raised between them after Priabin had stepped back two paces. As it was levelled at Gant's face. Priabin was smiling, his features were calm and satisfied. He seemed to have travelled quickly through shock as if it were an unimportant way-station; passed through hate, too. Passed almost beyond the shot he intended firing.

'Gant,' he sighed once more. His finger squeezed the trigger of the pistol.

PART THREE

Shelter
from the Storm

'You and I, we've been through that,
And this is not our fate;
So, let us not talk falsely now –
The hour is getting late.'

BOB DYLAN: *All along the Watchtower*

PART THREE

Shelter
from the Storm

ELEVEN

a fortress deep and mighty

Katya could not understand. Her mind whirled with speculations and anticipation, but she could make no sense of the fact that the two men recognized each other. Impossibly, they knew each other, from some occasion in the past —?

And then the name surfaced. It was fixed in place by the banging of the houseboat's doors as she watched the tip of her own pistol move upwards and begin to cancel Priabin's strange, fulfilled pleasure. *Gant. That* American . . . the one who had stolen the — the one who had caused the death of . . . impossible —

The wind howled, entering the narrow, low cabin. The planks and boards of the boat creaked and groaned like an audience. The room seemed to quiver, reflecting the tension between the two men. She sensed that Priabin was as quick and ready to die as he was to kill the American, whose gaunt, weary face stared at Priabin's pistol. She felt her throat tickle with the smoke blown from the flickering oil-lamp, shadows enlarged and seemed to struggle with each other on the planking above her. The pistol wobbled, but had its target. The American's stomach, chest, then forehead.

The doors banged once more, startling her from her trance. Priabin was posed with his arm stretched out, his pistol aimed at the American's head. He leaned into the contemplated shot, his finger closing on the trigger —

— the American spy . . . *their* prisoner.

'*No!*' she screamed, her voice thinner and higher than the wind.

Priabin's hand shook. The American turned his face to her, as if only now acknowledging her presence. Her eyes concentrated on Priabin as he, too, turned to her.

'No! No! *No!*' she shouted as loudly as she could. Her words rang and echoed, unrecognizable as her own, in the low, narrow cabin. Her own pistol was raised, her body was crouched; she was half-ready to scream, half to shoot, and she knew her face was distorted with a sense of panic. '*No —!*'

And Priabin turned fully . . .

. . . the American was still . . .

. . . their eyes on something other than herself. They were both looking at Kedrov, huddled on the bunk, hands wrapped across his chest, knees up to his chin. Their – *object* in the room, *both* of them.

'No!'

Had the American been on the point of action? Yes, he was now letting his hands return to his thighs, letting his face sag out of its tight folds of expectation. His pale eyes gleamed at her, cold and baffled. She thrust her gun three, four inches further forward. A sigh emerged from his whole frame. Priabin's face, alerted by her cry, was thin and sour with the knowledge of being cheated.

'Please . . .' she breathed, feeling a wave of tiredness lap at her, not knowing what to do next.

Radio – crackling voice, commanding and urgent.

– walkie-talkie, lying on the scarred, stained wood of the table, bursting into chatter.

Faces moved and shifted expression and purpose. The shadows beat about her head like birds' wings, growing and diminishing as the flame of the lamp was driven by the wind. She shook her head, kept her pistol moving between them. Kedrov's features formed the only still point of the scene as he cowered on the bunk, unable to take advantage, defeated long ago by a forgotten war with himself. Shadows, the doors banging, walkie-talkie.

'No –' she said once more. Both men were still, the voice from the walkie-talkie invaded. The American's face finally subsided into the narrow, bitter fury of capture.

'Answer that!' Priabin snapped, his pistol reasserting itself, less menacingly, towards the American. Gant – *that* American, she reminded herself. Priabin added: 'It's Serov's voice.'

Her hand moved towards the table, she touched the walkie-talkie with her fingertips. It snapped orders at her.

She glanced back at Priabin, afraid.

'Colonel, you were going to –' she blurted.

'Kill him? Easily,' Priabin announced in a strange, quiet voice which seemed filled with disappointment. 'Don't worry,' he said.

Katya paused, then turned away and picked up the walkie-talkie. It was over. Like a nightmare. She had woken Priabin from it. She shivered, sensing reaction begin. *That* American . . . the one who had caused Priabin's mistress to die . . . Priabin's lover.

'Colonel?' she asked. 'What shall I say?'

'He is *our* prisoner, you will do *nothing*!' Serov's voice insisted amid the crackle of the ether and the noise of the wind outside. 'This is a GRU matter, *not* KGB!'

Shadows flickered, the thin trail of smoke from the distressed flame of the lamp rolled and split. Kedrov's hands gently covered his head, as if Serov's words rained down like blows. His body quivered. It seemed he had exhausted himself with waiting.

Dogs barked. The American flinched. He was no longer dangerous. Slowly, foggily, he wiped the sleeve of his flying jacket across his forehead, then his eyes. Almost gently, Priabin took the walkie-talkie from her hand. His grey eyes were vague and troubled. They made her feel cold.

'This is Priabin,' he snapped, pressing the Transmit button. He kept glancing at the American, then at Kedrov, as if trying to identify them.

She subsided into holding her pistol routinely on Gant; her shiver becoming more pronounced.

Gant stared at Kedrov, and felt he was looking into a mirror. The agent's defeat was total, had happened even before he arrived. Gant shivered. Vietnam. The water-filled pit was coming back, crawling around the edge of the barrier his mind had learned to erect against it . . . the pit, the bamboo stretched like a grid over it, just close enough to touch with his fingertips . . . the icy water, the howling of other people already dying, the murmur of voices in the chilly darkness, the glint of fires . . . the water, the water . . . he began shivering uncontrollably –

– the dog's warm body bullied him aside, he heard someone cry out in Russian as he fell against the planking and turned his head to see the open jaws, the lolling tongue, the long white teeth of the huge dog. He saw the uniformed man's rifle slung across his chest, heard the dog howling, eager to tear – saw light glinting from its choke-chain, and the soldier's grimace of effort to control the animal.

Dmitri Priabin backed away from the dog with as much calm as he could muster, the walkie-talkie in his hand, about to address the impatient, angry Serov. The dog strained on its leash towards Gant.

'Quiet that damn' thing!' he roared, keeping his thumb down on the Transmit button. 'Get it *out* of here, damn you!'

Another GRU man, another dog, almost tumbling down the steps into the cabin. Serov's hard laughter. He waved his hand at them.

'Get out!'

Priabin remembered Rodin, the airline ticket, the flight to Moscow, and saw them all retreating. He was enmeshed in this situation – and, when he looked at Gant, watchful and defeated with his arm across his body as if expecting an assault from one or both of the dogs, his rage surged in him again. Anna's face was omnipresent in the room's shadows. He still wanted to kill Gant. Oh, yes, how much he wanted to kill the American who had caused . . .

The dogs' noises quietened. Their handlers were rebuked by Priabin's uniform and rank; nothing else. The shoulder-boards held them on more fragile leashes than the dogs' choke-chains. Pink tongues lolled, teeth glinted, saliva specked the planks of the floor.

'Everything's under control here, Serov,' he snapped. 'And the American is *my* prisoner.' He grinned shakily, but only so long as he looked at Katya, standing hunched next to him, her gun ready for the dogs. When Priabin's gaze fell on Gant, his expression twisted. He shook his head. 'Where are you, Serov?'

There was a silence, ether and breathing coming from the walkie-talkie. Then 'Do *nothing*, Priabin. I'm taking command here.'

'Naturally.' Priabin forced himself to drawl in an easy, confident manner. 'We're waiting. Out.'

'Get those damn' dogs out of here, both of you!' he snapped. 'Your boss is on his way —' He grinned again, waspishly. 'He doesn't *like* dogs!'

The dogs were dragged out, protesting and reluctant. The wind's noise replaced theirs. There was the occasional sound of a whistle outside.

'You're not —?' Katya began.

He had raised his gun once more towards Gant.

'What?' He looked at his hand, at the Makarov. 'Dammit, *no* —!' he yelled, protesting against his inability to act more than to reassure the girl that he would not do so. His voice and look evidently frightened her. 'All right, all right,' he soothed. He shook his head; it seemed with regret. 'Serov can have him alive — much good that will do *you*, Gant.'

Gant made no reply, simply shook his head.

Serov came through the banging doors theatrically, urgently. He seemed surprised by the expression on Priabin's face; pleased at the obvious sense of capture the scene displayed. Two armed guards remained in the doorway — until Serov placed one of them at Gant's side. Serov pushed the table to one side and stood in the centre of the cabin.

'Kedrov, the missing technician,' he announced rather than asked, pointing with the glove he had removed. His cheeks were blanched by the night's temperature.

'Kedrov,' Priabin agreed formally. 'Lieutenant Grechkova here is responsible for his capture.'

Serov looked at Katya briefly, nodded as to someone who had brought him a routine report, then turned his gaze from her to

Kedrov, then to Gant. Priabin saw that Serov's face was mobile with anticipations.

'How did you —?' Priabin could not help asking.

'We found his helicopter,' Serov murmured, pointing at Gant. 'A cavalier approach — not really clever.' He seemed pleased with Gant's silence, with the drawn expression on his features. 'Mm — who is he, Priabin?'

'He's — American.'

'Of course! You've established nothing *more*?'

'I know who my prisoner is, if that's what you mean,' Priabin replied. 'I know all about him.'

Serov turned on him, his eyes dark and angry. He was perhaps two or three inches shorter than Priabin, but broader. His face was set in hard, angular lines and blunt planes. His expression warned. Priabin sensed his own weariness, and a new caution at the back of his mind. Rodin — *Lightning*, this man knew everything about *Lightning* and must not so much as suspect that Priabin knew. His thoughts rushed in his head like vertigo. He kept his face expressionless, except for the slightest indication of self-satisfaction, as Serov snapped:

'Then who is he, Priabin — who is he?'

Serov turned away to look at the prisoner, and Priabin said softly: 'His name's Mitchell Gant — formerly Major Gant, United States Air Force . . . doesn't the name ring a bell, Serov? Not one small bell?'

Serov turned, stung by the insolence of Priabin's voice, his face sharp with anger, his removed glove raised as if to slap at the speaker. Then shock caused his mouth to open soundlessly. Priabin smiled.

'You know him, then?'

'*That* one?' He whirled around once more. 'Him? He's *that* American?'

'He is, Serov — oh, *yes*, he is . . . they sent him for Kedrov, obviously. They need Kedrov before the Treaty is signed.'

Serov turned to face Priabin. 'How long have you known about him?' he demanded. His voice accused like his eyes.

'It was —' *Care!* '— accidental,' Priabin explained. The heat and

334

tension in the cabin of the houseboat affected him. He sensed Serov's disbelief. 'We were looking for drugs . . . that's how we stumbled across Kedrov.'

'Just like that? An American spy you just *stumbled* across! How much do they *know*?'

'I'm – not sure. Enough, certainly, to send Gant to collect him.'

Serov considered his next words for some moments, then said: 'We must get them back – we must know everything the Americans know! You – you're to be congratulated, Priabin . . . and you, Lieutenant. Both of you, yes . . . congratulated. You've saved – the secrecy . . . the Americans evidently have nothing, otherwise they wouldn't want this bundle of rubbish in the corner! Yes –!' He turned to Gant and his guard. 'Get him outside – shoot to wound if he doesn't go quietly . . . *quickly*, man! You – take this spy with the American – get moving!'

Priabin studied Gant's face. Complete failure was clearly branded on it. All anger and fear had died. Priabin attempted to feel satisfaction that Gant, though living, was a prisoner with only a brief and violent future before him. The satisfaction would not come.

Rodin. Valery Rodin. *Lightning*. That was what he had to do now. He had to accompany Serov, make his report, try to leave as quickly as possible . . . this complicated matters. Damn Serov's stumbling across Gant now! He had to make that Moscow flight in the morning. His head whirled with anxieties. Serov was dangerous, though distracted for the moment by his two prisoners. The weight, the enormity of *Lightning* lurched against Priabin's frame as physically as an assault. He had to be calm, and careful, and get to Rodin as soon as he could.

He followed Serov and Katya out of the cabin, ducking his head as he went through the doors. The wind hurled itself at him. The dogs accompanied the prisoners, growling and yapping. Tail-less Dobermans. Gant and Kedrov were surrounded by armed GRU troops as they were ushered along the rotting jetty. A MiL-8 transport helicopter stood on the ice fifty yards away. Gant had lost, Kedrov had lost –

– *he* had to win. *Had to* –

– could not, not *now* –

Priabin gagged, feeling his throat hot with nausea. He pressed his gloved hand over his mouth, tried to swallow; felt his stomach surge again and again with shock, and growing, virulent fear for himself. The lockpicks dangled from his other hand, ignored. He tasted sickness, and saliva, then swallowed, and tried to calm his body, his sense of his own danger.

When there had been no answer to the bell, to his knocking, he had anticipated something bad, but not this.

Rodin's skin was cold, white-blue. The empty pill bottle lay betrayingly beside the rumpled bed. Priabin did not believe its statement – it was too obvious. So they *knew* . . .

He backed away from the bed, withdrew unsteadily from the bedroom – flicking off the lights and turning in one movement, ready to fly the scene. The lounge was grey with the morning's first slow, leaking light. The furniture assumed vague contours, a half-life. He went to the window from which he had watched Rodin. Scanned the block of flats, the curtained windows, the stained concrete – a light here and there, most of the flats still in darkness. It was six in the morning. Two hours before the Moscow flight left. He had come to collect Rodin and found him dead.

No bruising, but the throat was slightly raw. He knew what had been done and by whom. Serov, Serov – who had seemed willing to credit the KGB with the capture of Gant and Kedrov, seemed careless to detain him, even ordered him home for a well-earned sleep . . . a bluff heartiness . . . false, just an act. Katya he'd kept behind like a schoolmaster while she wrote out her report on Kedrov. Himself he'd allowed –

– to come and witness what had been done. Rodin killed easily, quickly, faked to look like suicide.

He was alone with the secret of *Lightning*. Gant was insignificant, Anna's memory was not apparent anywhere in the cavern of his thoughts. It was only himself, his life – or death – he admitted slowly. He was his only concern. Serov held him in his hand, he already knew everything . . .

– then get out. Get that flight to Moscow. Get out – *now*!

Proof . . . ?

They would *have to listen*!

Six-five. Call the airport, check the flight isn't delayed, then get out. *Trap*. The thought loomed. Serov's people could already be outside, already on the stairs. He looked out of the window – no, nothing yet – call the *airport*!

He picked up the receiver with a gloved hand. After touching Rodin's cold face, his stiff jaw, his neck where there was no pulse, he had replaced his gloves . . . then the gagging nausea had risen to his throat, minutes after he had entered the apartment –

– selfishly, he acknowledged as he feverishly dialled the airport. Selfishly, as the suspicion had emerged and blossomed that Rodin had been murdered, had not taken his own life . . . *come on*, come on, *answer the bloody telephone*!

He was sweating inside his greatcoat. The central heating had come on, the flat was warming up . . . the curtains in the bedroom were open, people would see Rodin lying there and disapprove . . . eventually, someone would report his not having moved for hours or days – *draw the curtains across . . . no, leave everything just as it was, you were never here*.

'The Moscow flight!' he blurted as soon as the woman at the check-in desk identified herself. Aeroflot. 'Is it scheduled to leave at the usual –?'

'No flights will be leaving today.'

'Listen!' he snapped, knowing the circumstance even before it was explained. 'This is Colonel Priabin, KGB. I have a seat reserved on the Moscow flight – what time does it leave?'

'I – I'm sorry, comrade Colonel. All flights have been cancelled –'

'*What?*' He looked at his watch. Six-fifteen. Dawn sliding across the carpet like a slow grey tide, lapping near his boots. The room constrained him. Already? Already? It shouldn't happen yet –

'– the usual emergency, sir . . . just been brought forward twenty-four hours. Routine, comrade Colonel – I'm sorry if you –'

337

'I have the most urgent meeting in Moscow today!' he bellowed.

Frosty tone, then. 'I'm sorry, comrade Colonel – we have our orders here.'

'Yes, yes –' Let me speak to someone in authority, he began to say in his mind, but the order slipped away. It was pointless. 'I understand,' he said. 'Code Green has been initiated a day early. I understand – thank you.' He put down the receiver thoughtfully, his hand moving in a slower, simpler world than his thoughts.

He had to get out. Code Green, the usual security measures surrounding any launch at Baikonur. The whole of the complex became isolated from the rest of the country; no flights in or out, no trains, no radio or telephone contact. But, this was twenty-four hours early – this was Serov.

Effectively, he was already bottled up inside the Baikonur complex, cut off from Moscow. There was no other reason than *Lightning* for imposing normal launch security a whole day early, there could be no other reason. He tried to think, to consider rationally, but the effort of it made him more fearful. His body seemed to fill with it; mercury mounting in a thermometer.

He found himself at the bedroom door. His hand flicked on the lights. Soft pink warmth from the bedside lampshades, Rodin's face still and aristocratic in profile, his limbs easy on the rumpled bed. There was no *proof* – that had been eradicated . . .

. . . remember. It was difficult. He concentrated on the corpse. Remember *what*? Kedrov and Gant were a huge, blank wall between himself and the recent past. What was there, on the other side, when he had talked to – to this here, on the bed, when it had still lived? What –?

. . . proof, proof, proof . . .

The tape! He had been wired for sound, it was all on tape! Mikhail had the tape, he had intended taking it to Moscow, they could identify Rodin's voice, surely? It was some kind of proof, it would force them to begin to act.

Mikhail. Priabin glanced at his watch. He'd be at home now, keeping his head down as ordered. Tape —

— flight cancelled. No trains, no radio, no telephone. Roads — perhaps the roads . . . he had only to get as far as the nearest KGB office outside the complex, in — in *Aralsk* — two hours, a little more, by car. Six-eighteen, hurry.

The fear would not go away, not even diminish amid the exhilaration of imminent action. He left the bedroom door ajar as he had found it, switching off the lights. Rodin's body retreated into shadow, but the corpse was not so distant now, not so removed — he had the boy's voice on tape, he still had *Lightning*. He hurried into the hallway, carefully opening the front door. The corridor outside was empty.

He took the stairs quickly, but not in panic. He did not wish to be remembered, timed and logged by the janitor who might be working for Serov.

Outside, the leaking daylight was bleak, and a wind flew into his face. Hurry —

Gennadi Serov regretted leaving Kedrov and the American, even for this journey, this call. They had become the centre of the game; the essence of success. Proof that the Americans had no proof, that the whole business was still secure, intact. And Kedrov, with his hanging, victim's face pleased Serov and tempted him. He would gut Kedrov the technician, the spy, like a fish; fillet him with drugs or violence — the method did not matter, only the execution of the thing.

He stepped out of his staff car. The wind tugged a few isolated clouds across the lightening sky. The block of flats appeared shabby, crouched at the side of the highway. Behind him, the road narrowed across the flat country towards the distant gantries and launch towers and radio masts scribbled on the horizon. Smoke hung over Tyuratam to the south-east, other factory complexes smeared the sky with fumes as separate and identifiable as fingerprints left on glass. He studied the flats. A car started up and pulled away from the lock-up garages at the rear. It headed west along the highway, its exhaust signalling in the chilly morning air. It passed the low restaurant, the shops, the other blocks of flats.

One of the members of Priabin's surveillance team, who had watched the little bitch Rodin, lived in this block. Serov rubbed his hands together, as if in anticipation of a welcome. He walked rapidly away from the car, motioning his driver and his team in the second car to remain where they were. He waved the walkie-talkie at them to signify his confidence. He pushed open the glass doors of the block, entered its carpeted foyer. Thin nylon carpet, but carpet – security people, some technicians, factory managers lived there. They qualified for foyer carpet, for two bedrooms each, in some cases, and for proximity to a *beriozhka* shop and a restaurant. And cars – quite a number of them parked in front of the flats, more in the garages behind. There was also a janitor, who indicated Serov's presence by tactfully ignoring it, having identified the uniform and the rank.

The lift door opened. Graffiti on the walls like a challenge to him, harmless though it was. Some drivelling, misspelt protestation of love, another of sex; some comment on a football team, on the army . . . He ascended to the third floor.

A woman in the corridor, coming out of the door he wanted, saying goodbye to her friend. A drab, frightened, worn woman, as if recently bereaved, two children with lost faces, the small boy still eating a round of toast. Jam on his cheek. He let the woman and her children pass, studied the door the woman opened, read the name of the occupants – *Zhikin* . . . smiled.

He realized the other woman was watching him. Hardly alarmed, more curious. He touched the peak of his cap with the glove he held in his hand.

'Your husband – Officer Mikhail Shubin – is he at home?' he asked with brisk authority.

'Comrade Colonel, I –' the woman began. His tone had not been intended to disarm, and it had not done so. Her eyes were alert, shadowed with the expectation of concern.

'You must know,' Serov insisted. 'My name is Serov – GRU

commandant here,' he added carelessly. 'I wish to speak with your husband.'

He had already moved close to her. He could smell bedclothes still, and cooking. Cigarette-smoke, too. He was allowed to all but pass her before she squeezed against him and they walked almost comically down the linoleumed corridor towards the flat's kitchen, close together, as if he held her in the crook of one arm. Serov was amused as she seemed to wish to scamper ahead, warn –

– Shubin, it had to be him, was sitting tousle-headed at the foldaway table erected against one wall of the cramped kitchen. Coffee steamed in front of him, the stove steamed with something on the boil – eggs, perhaps? Serov recorded the details with the eye of a painter. Cracked and discoloured lino on the floor, a child seated on Shubin's lap, rolling a small toy car across the morning's copy of *Pravda* open on the tablecloth. Cloth – clean, too, and not oilcloth or newspaper. Precisely, Serov noted the fine gradations that would have told him, had he not already known, the rank, income, privileges of the man at the table. Condensation from the boiling water covered the window. The woman moved to the saucepan – yes, Serov could hear eggs bumping softly against its metal – and turned down the gas.

'Mikhail –' she began in a remonstrative tone, then continued: 'Colonel Serov –'

Shubin placed the child on the table. One of his large hands held the toy car, the other rubbed at his head. His eyes, however, were furtive and quick. Serov felt pleasure rise as tangibly as the steam in the kitchen.

'Comrade Colonel,' Mikhail acknowledged, nodding his head almost in what might have been a bow. 'What can I –?'

Serov held up his hand, sitting immediately at the table. Shubin collected his child in his arms and he, too, sat down. The eggs stopped tapping against each other and the sides of the saucepan. The woman tended them with concentration; placed slices of bread on the grill pan, slid it noisily under the gas, which she lit with a plop –

– which made Shubin's hand jump. Serov thought of Viktor

341

Zhikin's widow two doors away, and her children, and considered the eventual, inevitable absence of this man from this scene.

'Shubin, I won't beat about the bush, I'll come straight to the point,' he announced, clearing his throat, laying his gloves on the table, near the now-ignored toy car.

'Coffee, Colonel?' the woman asked from her position at the stove.

'Thank you. Black.'

Shubin lit a cigarette. Puffed at it nervously. Serov felt Priabin must have confided in the man – or there was a record of what was said . . . and there'd been a warning, too. The strain of appearing calm was creasing Mikhail's face into hard, tight lines. He smoothed again at his hair where the boy's hands had disturbed it; as if waiting for an interview. He needed to feel tidy. Serov glanced very obviously at the man's felt slippers, at the bottoms of his pyjama-trousers, at the dressing-gown. All weaknesses, disadvantages. Serov all but sighed aloud, anticipating the ease with which he would obtain what he wanted.

A kettle boiled, further clouding the window. The woman brought his coffee, in a cup, unpatterned but china, not in a mug like her husband was using.

'Sugar?'

He raised one hand to refuse. Shubin swallowed coffee quickly. Then Serov said: 'You and one of your fellow officers maintained surveillance on a certain apartment in the old town until the early hours of this morning – that is correct?'

Shubin swallowed. He had a prominent Adam's-apple which bobbed as he swallowed his renewed fear. He attempted to shake his head. The little boy had picked up his toy, and one of Serov's gloves. Serov reached out and held the child's hand; removed the glove and squeezed the hand as he held it. The child uttered a cry, perhaps of surprise. He dropped the toy in his father's lap. It fell onto the floor. Shubin held the child wonderingly, staring at him as if at some unexpected piece of information. Then his wife snatched the boy up, and soothed him. Kissing the squeezed hand.

342

'Answer, why don't you?' Serov prompted, sipping his coffee. The woman retreated to the window with the child; they became less important than silhouettes, except that the woman would hear and understand every word. Her presence made the filleting process easier, in this case. It was always easier when you could hint at futures that might darken. 'Well?'

'I – comrade Colonel, you should speak to Colonel Priabin, my commanding officer –'

Serov's hand banged the table. Coffee splashed and the cloth and the newspaper were stained. At the instant he began to shout, Serov heard Shubin's feet moving the discarded toy on the linoleum.

'Your commanding officer may possibly turn out to be a traitor! I am talking to *you*, Shubin – do you understand me? To you!'

The boy wailed in the ensuing silence. He heard the woman calming him, and raised his hand to warn her as she tried to take the child from the kitchen. Shubin's face was ashen.

'I, sir, I –'

'You were following orders, Shubin. I realize that. Now, you simply follow my orders. What happened between them?'

'I don't know, sir – really I don't!'

'A tape, man! Don't tell me comrade Colonel Priabin talked to Lieutenant Rodin without being wired? Are you that sloppy in the KGB out here?' Serov shook his head in mock reproof. 'Of course not. Now – what did they say to each other?'

Again, the woman tried to leave the kitchen, the boy in her arms. Serov raised his hand once more; and saw Shubin shake his head vigorously, warning her to remain where she was.

'Well?' Serov whispered, sipping the last of the coffee, careful that the sleeve of his greatcoat did not touch the wet tablecloth.

'My family, sir –'

'Quite.'

'If I –'

'Not if, *when*. And when is now. At once. You have no alternative. Oh, get *on* with it, Shubin!'

'Sir, there was a tape . . .'

'Yes?'

'We – I mean, we weren't monitoring . . .' Shubin seemed to retreat from Serov's enquiring, exploratory gaze. It was true, Serov decided. The man had a tape, but hadn't listened in, knew little or nothing. Not that it mattered. He would be destroyed, along with Priabin and the others, as soon as *Lightning* was under way. Perhaps he could even be allowed to live . . . His knowledge would be irrelevant, once *Lightning* had happened. Priabin, of course, would have to go. 'We know *nothing*, comrade Colonel Serov!'

'Why was Lieutenant Rodin placed under surveillance? No, sit down, you can get me the tape in a moment. It is *here*, I take it?' Shubin nodded. Serov stretched his feet under the table; encountered the toy car and placed his foot on it. He gently applied pressure, and felt the cheap tin begin to give under his heel. 'Tell me,' he encouraged. Shubin picked up his disregarded cigarette and puffed at it. 'I want to know what's been going on here, for the past couple of weeks . . . a general's son under surveillance? A GRU *officer* under surveillance by the KGB? Very irregular. Yes – out with it, then. Everything.'

Everything offended him deeply, with a separate, sharp shock for each recognition of his son's – *sybaritic* lifestyle. Quickly, as if for the purposes of healing, anger erupted and grew to replace the constriction in his throat that he understood to be grief. Yet this, *this* –

– these *garments*, behind the louvred doors of the fitted wardrobe. Garish colours, silk, narrow leather trousers, the shirts more like women's blouses, the shoes, even the slippers that whiffed of decadence, the bathrobes and the dressing-gowns – each item offended him even as he continued his helpless inventory of his son's wardrobe. He felt anger becoming nausea. He kept his back to the room, to the bed. This, this was no *man's* wardrobe, no *soldier's* wardrobe . . . and he could not escape that judgement, that condemnation, not even when his eyes dimmed. He sniffed loudly. The insistent clichés did not seem irrelevant or superannuated by his discovery. He clung to them, even as his hands, veins standing proud, gripped the edges of the louvred doors.

He uttered a strangled growl that he did not himself understand, and slammed the doors together so that they almost keeled from their runners. He could not look into that – mirror into his son's private life any longer. He turned to the bed. He had thrown a bedspread over Valery's limbs, but could not bear to cover his face . . . but the anger coursed, even now, even as he looked at the body. His son . . . his *son*! To live and die like *this* –!

On the dressing-table – no, on the carpet now, some of the bottles broken, the stench of the perfumes heady in the dry, silent room – the aftershaves, the colognes, even the make-up – General Lieutenant Rodin gagged at the image, at the smears of eye-shadow and lipstick that his angry, violent bootsteps had produced on the carpet. As if he had wanted to grind each item out of sight, crush the images each evoked.

He turned his head from his son's cold features, almost regretting that he had shut the sliding doors of the wardrobe; needing visual stimuli to sustain the anger he knew had arisen to conceal feelings he wished not to recognize. He strode from the bedroom without looking over his shoulder, and entered the bathroom. Flung open the wall cupboards. Creams, make-up, powders, and – the drugs. The silver spoon on its thin silver chain, like, like a *medal*, for Heaven's sake –! Worn like a medal –

He snatched up a handful of small packets. White powder. He ripped and tugged at the plastic of the packets, covering his hands with the powder like an untidy cook flinging flour . . . ran the tap, washed his hands, washed the drugs away.

Fear had driven him here. Fear for – for Valery, yes, but fear *of* Serov. Fear on behalf of Valery . . . only to find, to find –

He grunted like a very old man, asthmatically. His head hung on his chest, as if he were on the point of vomiting. His arms were shaking as he leaned on his knuckles over the washbasin. He felt hatred surging in his body, shaking it like an ague. Hatred of Valery, of these creams and powders and colours and drugs that filled his thoughts; the perfumes that seeped from the bedroom and were released from these cupboards. He had not been able to sleep, but it had not been the launch that had filled his restless mind, not even *Lightning* . . . his son, instead. Robbing him of needed sleep, robbing him of all anticipation of success. And now, now he had seen into his son's − soul. He'd opened cupboards, drawers, wardrobes, and seen his son's private world mock him.

Why had Valery done it? Why? What fear had it been, what ache or despair? The concealed striplighting hummed softly. He could not look at his face in the mirror; lit from above, it would have been too naked, too old. Why? What had he been afraid of?

Love . . . ? He sobbed aloud, as if at sacrilege. The idea appalled him, but he could not resist it; it was as if someone was whispering insistently in his ear. Love? He groaned, staring at the water still running into the basin. The mirror was steaming up. He inhaled the heat as if trying to cure himself of a cold. Love −? Impossible . . . for that *actor*? For *him*, for *that kind of love*?

There was no sense of self-blame, no tint of self-condemnation in his thoughts. The KGB colonel, Serov, that pathetic little homosexual actor − as if different in persuasion from Valery − all of them had played their parts in this, in what Valery had done to himself. All of them . . .

Eventually, his body calmed, the bathroom filled with steam from the wasted hot water, he re-entered the lounge and picked up the telephone.

An ambulance. Without explanation. The boy's mother would have to be told. It would break her heart, the heart secreted from him, spent extravagantly like a windfall inheritance on her son − yes, it would break her heart. But, that was duty, and easy. He would inform her as soon as . . .

He dialled, staring out of the wide lounge window at the cold sunlight seeping down the stained concrete of the building opposite.

Dmitri Priabin shivered, as if in a fever's spasm, and clutched his arms, wrapping them around him. He leaned his weight

against the side of the car. He could not stop shaking —!
Couldn't —

She was watching him from a window of the flat. Wouldn't let
him in, pretended that Mikhail wasn't there, had gone out,
didn't know when he'd be back . . . then, reality breaking
through the hesitant lies, she'd cried out from behind the thin
front door — *go away, get away from us, leave us alone, for God's sake
leave us alone, can't you?*

Apart from the crying child, Priabin had sensed Mikhail close
behind the door. The woman's sobbing became muffled as if she
were crying into someone's chest. He had banged on the door,
even though he had already accepted her plea. The banging had
brought Viktor's wife — *widow* — to her door, along the corridor.
She had looked at him with what he could only perceive as
accusation. She had not spoken, simply stared, then retreated
behind her door, where there was a muffled hushing of curious
children.

. . . *go away, we can't help you, go away — sir —*

He had not even challenged Mikhail's words, simply accepted
the fear with which they were uttered.

. . . *has the tape — sir — please go away* . . .

He had nothing. The cold sunlight glanced from the car's
chrome. He could not stop shaking. Only Serov could have
frightened Mikhail and his wife that much . . . they hadn't even
used his name, as if in fear of its invocatory powers. Don't name
the Devil and he won't come . . . but it had to be Serov, who now
had the tape and knew the whole game, knew that Priabin knew
about *Lightning*.

. . . and Dmitri Priabin *knew*, with absolute certainty, that
Serov *had* had Valery Rodin put to death like a farm animal taken
to an abattoir. He had always known it, of course — this was the
confirmation. Serov would have Mikhail removed, just like
Viktor — and he would remove . . . yes, his head nodding
violently in agreement with the sharp, brutally clear picture in
his mind, yes . . . Serov would have him killed too.

His fear narrowed. Serov was his enemy; it was Serov he had
to evade — and frustrate. He had already attempted to radio, and

to use the telephone, both without success. Code Green was fully operational and Baikonur was severed from the rest of the Soviet Union. He could contact neither Moscow Centre nor the nearest KGB offices in the town of Aralsk, less than a hundred miles to the north-west. He could only –

– go there, go to Aralsk; break out of the security net spread over Baikonur, and use the high-speed transmission equipment, even the telephone link, from Aralsk to the Centre. Without proof, without a shred of tangible evidence? Go, go now, he tried to tell himself; and heard a part of him reply, *just a moment, in another minute, not just yet.*

– get in the car –

In another moment, when I feel stronger . . . get in the car, they may be watching Mikhail's place, waiting for you to collect the tape!

The thought had not occurred to him, not even dimly, until then. He tried to make himself not stare wildly around at parked cars, at windows. Got into the Volga, gripped the wheel with both hands to still them in their renewed tremor. Saw the windscreen fog with the heat of his tension. Looked through its cloudiness, looked through the rear window, checked the side windows after switching on the engine and engaging first gear – so that he appeared only to be checking for traffic before pulling out – checked again, then once more –

– saw . . .

Checked carefully. Two shadows in a small, anonymous car, fawn-coloured, a Polish-built Fiat or something like it. A car easily ignored. Exhaust puffed like hasty breathing from its rear. Just now, it had not had its engine running. They had known he would come, they had waited.

One chance now, he realized, his knuckles white from his grip on the wheel, his stomach churning again. One chance to get out – bluff . . . or maybe there weren't roadblocks and barriers yet . . . maybe –

He accelerated, but not too violently, pulling away from the flats and out onto the almost-deserted highway which ran between the river and the railway line west and then north-west. At its end, beyond Aralsk and Orenburg and Kuybyshev and Ryazan was Moscow . . . fifteen hundred miles away. His heart, still beating wildly, seemed to lurch in his body. He swallowed drily, and tried to concentrate on Aralsk. He need only reach Aralsk . . . you don't have to go further, just as far as Aralsk.

Where would the checkpoints be? Telegraph wires scalloped between poles accompanied him, paralleling the empty railway track. Below him, to his left, now that the buildings were set down like randomly scattered lumps and blocks, he could see the frozen river in its shallow valley; grey and imprisoned.

Where would they stop him? Because stop him they would . . . the fawn car followed with an almost leisurely certainty. Priabin's mind, though his eyes darted and flitted across the topography, was without its own familiar landscape. His position was unique in his adult experience; it was that of – of a criminal. The hunted. His thoughts were shapeless and gloomy. He did not know what to do in this situation. He simply had no experience of being anything other than a man of rank and authority. He'd worn his officialdom like clothes, like his own skin, for years – and now it was gone, stripped away like old paint from wood. *What did he do now, for God's sake –?*

The highway ahead of him narrowed to a point at the vague, uncertain horizon, almost invisible because of the flatness of the country. He passed a restaurant – where he had once eaten with Viktor and his wife – a garage, a dirty, weed-filled place, the grass stiffly upright and icebound, where the building plots had never received their designated houses or factories – then there was openness that was oppressive, stretched ahead, surrounded him . . . nothing but –

– *Novokazalinsk*, he told himself suddenly, with an audible grunt. That's where Code Green's maximum security perimeter was always set to the west, on this highway. Dear God, why hadn't he even been able to remember that until now? It was as if his mind was frozen solid, like the river down there. Ducks waddled across the ice, but otherwise his surroundings were lifeless. A hut amid scattered trees, smoke straggling from an iron chimney . . . beyond the railway track, the marsh country was beginning, clumps and islets of trees, tall grass and sedge. The fawn car was still in his mirror. Above the road, the pale sky was empty; so featureless it might have been rushing away behind him, and always fleeing ahead of him, making him appear unmoving . . . no, some geese provided a false horizon, straggled across the sky like a hurried autograph as they flew towards the marshes. If only he could *fly* −!

He kept his speed to fifty, even though his nerves jangled and bullied him to flee. He had to pretend, had to go on with the illusion that he was in no hurry, that this was routine − he had to − for the sake of hope, and his nerves.

A helicopter enlarged beyond the geese, moving along the highway, perhaps two hundred feet above it. Routine patrol. The geese diminished in the distance to his right, still indecipherable. Passing over abandoned launch towers, power cables, the tiny tilted cups of radar dishes. Far to the north, beyond the geese, the sticklike antennae and gantries of the principal military launch complex suggested an horizon. Ahead of him, there was nothing. He looked at his tripmeter. He'd done five miles − Christ, only *five*? − and there were another forty-five to Novokazalinsk.

He felt worn. The black helicopter had become grey-bellied, green-mottled, somehow less sinister as it floated above him and passed eastwards towards Tyuratam. Yet there was no relief in its lack of special interest in him. Glancing at the map that he had half-opened on the passenger seat had been a mistake. There were roads everywhere around Leninsk and Tyuratam and the other towns and villages. But where he was heading − in fact towards the perimeter in any direction − roads narrowed, straggled, disappeared, merged . . . they needed perhaps no more than a dozen barriers to seal off the whole of the vast Baikonur complex from the rest of the Soviet Union; just so long as they stopped the trains and the planes, as they had done −

− plane, light aircraft. He felt sick as he remembered. During a Code Green the previous year, a light aircraft had strayed into maximum security airspace and been shot down without challenge or apology or warning. Baikonur was a place of logic, of

350

inescapable necessity. Things were not weighed, simply laid down in orders and regulations and systems. One huge steel box whose lid could be slammed shut at a moment's notice. Had been.

Fifty-five. Priabin eased his foot on the accelerator. The Volga's heater seemed more inefficient than usual; he was chilly, even within his greatcoat. His forehead was cold with drying perspiration. The fawn car could be seen in the mirror. The helicopter had disappeared. He glanced at the car's clock. Nine-seventeen . . . three hours since he had been in Valery Rodin's bedroom, since he had found the boy's body – *three wasted hours!* Telephone, radio, trying to contact the Centre – he'd known almost at once he wouldn't get through, but he'd gone on trying, arguing, hoping.

Just to find himself on this road, tailed by the GRU, knowing that the security of Code Green had bottled him up. He would get only as far as Novokazalinsk and no further. It was like a brick wall with which he was destined to collide.

He thought of the main hangar and the shuttle craft and the laser battle station as pieces of a huge jigsaw on the point of completion, missing only the last few segments of the pattern that was *Lightning* in all its enormity. He ground his teeth. He could do nothing, *nothing!*

Fifty-eight . . . he slowed the car without thinking. Nine-nineteen. Ten miles from the flats now, perhaps forty more to go – why bother? *Forty more.*

He hardly thought about Gant. Strangely, the American was reduced to insignificance now. Serov had Gant. Gant was as good as dead. Perhaps he hadn't ever wanted revenge, then? No, he had – just never expected the opportunity – and now, now he had himself to think of.

False horizon, very close. Against the narrowing road, a group of black silhouettes against the pale sky. The cars were carelessly disposed across the road, there were converging lines of red and white cones, even a barrier. One truck, men in yellow overblouses laying the cones out, military cars – four of those . . . and the coffee-stall parked at the side of the highway, a shabby grey caravan with a side-window and a ledge. Men near that, too. Men in the road, cones, barrier, truck, cars, greatcoats, uniforms, guns . . .

Brick wall. Collision. His body felt jolted, shocked by something as real as physical impact. Not Novokazalinsk, then. *Here* — they were waiting just for him . . . Serov's GRU people.

The fawn car slowed, maintaining its distance behind him. One of the officers ahead was waving his arms to emphasize the paraphernalia and authority of the temporary arrangements on the highway. Priabin knew his journey was over. He stopped the Volga, fifteen hundred miles away from Moscow Centre.

TWELVE

solitary confinement

Kedrov's form, strapped into the chair, seemed tense and resentful, struggling to defy the questions that buzzed and murmured around his head. Veins stood out on his arms and the backs of his hands where they gripped the padded arms of the black chair. Veins on his temples, too. Fierce concentration, the effort of denial, furrowed his brow. He was as taut as an overwound spring and yet utterly helpless. The contradiction amused Serov, satisfied him in a way he did not analyse; *never* analysed. Only Kedrov's lips and tongue seemed involuntary agents. The willpower being suggested by his whole frame was absent from his mouth. He could not help himself answering the questions of the interrogation team.

Of course, the pupils of Kedrov's eyes were unnaturally open, considering he was facing the window. His eyes were too bright, with a stare that reminded Serov of utter disbelief – *how can this be happening?* – as it always did during such drug-assisted interrogations – *why am I talking? I don't want to talk . . .* Such involuntariness, such childlike, babyish inability and weakness was always – what? Satisfying to watch? Yes. He possessed Kedrov and the American, he had robbed them of everything, even will. In Kedrov's case, he controlled the man's mind.

Serov rubbed his chin. It was smooth from a recent shave. The landscape of his thoughts was open, rolling, sunny; he could see a great distance from the promontory of his successes that night. Rodin, Kedrov, the American pilot – whose story he had learned from that clown Adamov, discovered tied up in the *Hind*'s main cabin. The pieces had fallen like lucky cards. Serov was confident, even eager. Priabin, too, would soon come entirely within his orbit. Then, it would be finished with.

There was a trace of excitement in him, like a strange liquor tracing its way to his stomach. But it was a sober sensation. When there was time, the American would be – *gutted*, emptied of everything he knew, and he would know a great deal, while Priabin would – disappear. Kedrov, of course, would meet the fate of a spy and traitor once he had confessed.

'. . . long have you been spying for the Americans, Kedrov?'
'What did you tell them?'
'How much do they know?'
'. . . send your signals?'
'Orlov . . . ?'

Serov watched Kedrov's face attempt control around the mouth that no longer belonged to him. His voice stuttered like a cold engine, then the spy began helplessly to condemn himself, spilling his answers like water from a leaky bucket.

'. . . bicycle shop . . . don't understand –? American equip – 'quipment . . .'

One of his people, standing behind the straining Kedrov, shrugged with the ease of the interrogation. Serov nodded slightly, condescending to share the man's amusement. Sunlight fell coldly on the sweating, straining man in the chair, his whole body thrust forward against the restraint of the straps.

'. . . every, every week – *don't*, can't – *remember* . . . told them, told them – no, told, *no!* – told them when, when . . . arrived from Semipal, pal, pala – tin . . . sk –' The sweat was soaking his shirt, running on his face as if he had just plunged his head under a pump. '. . . know – know no . . . *nothing*, everything –!'

'Tell us what they know, in every detail.'
'Do they know dates, times?'

And so it would go on. Not long now. He looked at his watch. Nine-forty. Kedrov was like a tooth where all the enamel and even the soft inner had been drilled through; they were down to the nerve. He'd told them almost everything, it was all on tape.

'*Lightning?*' he snapped, impatience disturbing him, spoiling

354

his sense of satisfaction. 'Kedrov, what do you know about *Lightning*? What have you told the KGB about *Lightning*?'

Kedrov did not even look in his direction, but continued to stare as if he could see nothing ahead of him. But he spoke almost immediately, answering Serov.

'. . . noth – not asked, nothing, told him – don't know noth – know, *know*! Heard – in the *shithouse*! – heard, heard, told noth, nothing . . .' His voice babbled on, his will a tiny, shrunken ball kicked about between the questioners. He could not help himself.

Priabin knew from Rodin, then, only from Rodin. Another tiny jigsaw piece that fitted satisfactorily. He rubbed his chin once more, after indicating that he had no further questions. Besides, it was becoming too routine, he was losing interest . . .

. . . nine-fifty. He looked up – not really looking at Kedrov any more or even listening to the questions and answers, but half-sunk in a vague reverie – and one of his lieutenants beckoned to him. He mouthed urgency, even as his eyes surveyed the room, and his nose wrinkled at its scents and odours.

Serov indicated that the interrogation should continue, and moved to the door.

'What is it?' he snapped, closing the door on Kedrov's babble.

'Comrade General Rodin – he's *here* –!' For a moment, Serov could not understand the cause of the lieutenant's concern, even surprise. Then he remembered.

'Calm down. You know nothing – if you can't keep your face straight, stay out of his sight. Understand?' Rubbish – he always had rubbish to deal with. This one – part of the team that had removed Rodin, and worried as soon as the little shit's father shows up! For Jesus' sake –! 'Where is the general?'

'In your office, sir.'

'Very well – oh, go and get yourself a cup of coffee, man! And stop filling your trousers. It's over and done with. Go on –'

Serov waved him away and turned to the stairs. One flight up, why wait for the lift? Serov composed his features to a mask of enthusiasm and success as he climbed the stairs. A window showed him the square, and the Cosmonaut Hotel on its other side. Traffic, normality, sunlight, cobbles and statuary. When he entered his office, he must appear to greet Rodin with the news of Kedrov's successful interrogation. Rodin's news would – must – be like a douche of cold water thrown over that enthusiasm. Yes.

He mounted the half-flight of steps, leaving the view of the square. A patrolling helicopter had buzzed above it like a fat bee. He paused for a moment outside his office door, then went in. His male secretary nodded towards the inner office. Serov entered the room, his face bright.

'General, Kedrov is spilling everything he knows –' he began, crossing the thick carpet. Rodin was standing near the window, looking out across the square. 'The Americans obviously know, but they have no *proof*, none at –' He paused, measuring his reaction as carefully as some dangerous chemical, then said: 'General, what is the matter? You – don't look well . . . please –' He indicated a chair. Rodin's face was ashen, as if he, too, had newly adopted a mask, one of pain and grief. He'd seen his son's body. 'What is it, General? What is it?'

Rodin held his wrist tightly, perhaps for more than mere support.

'Valery –' was all he said.

'Your son, General. Yes, what is the matter –?'

'My son is dead.'

Rodin would not let go of Serov's arm, thus he could not move that dramatic half-step away from the old man. His features were in close-up; Rodin was inspecting them searchingly. Yet there was something blank about his eyes, like those of the drugged Kedrov.

'Dead –? I don't understand . . .'

Rodin's eyes studied him as carefully as the fingers of a blind person identifying braille. Serov produced shock, concern, sympathy. Then Rodin let go of his wrist and turned back to the window.

'Suicide,' he whispered. Serov's frame relaxed. He was surprised at his own tension.

'Suicide? How can you –?'

356

'I *saw* him!' Rodin wailed. 'I found him, earlier.' He turned back to Serov. 'Who? *Why*?' Careful, *careful*, Serov thought – this is the moment . . . 'What made him do it? Who is responsible?' There had been nothing, no trace of honest expression for Rodin to witness. He turned away once more. Sunlight haloed his form. 'Was it you, Serov?'

'I –?'

'Hounding that actor, getting rid of him . . . ? Or that KGB colonel? Who *was* it?'

'Your son was being questioned, perhaps pressured –'

'This man *Priabin*!' Rodin growled. 'What does he want? Why is he – was he interested in Valery? This – *drugs* business?'

'Perhaps. Perhaps something else.'

Rodin turned quickly. '*Lightning*? I can't believe –'

'Who knows what he suspects, General?'

'Then find out!'

'Arrest him?'

'If necessary. If he, *if* he . . .' His voice cracked and he turned to the window. There was no colour, not even anger, in his features. 'Find out, Serov. Find out if he was responsible.'

'Of course, General.'

'I want – my son will be flown back to Moscow, and he will receive a full military funeral. Is that understood? You will make the necessary arrangements. There will be no breath of any – irregularities. He died – in the course of duty. Duty. Do you understand?'

'Completely, General.'

'I want to know, Serov, whether that man was responsible for my son's suicide.'

'You will, General.'

There was silence, then, for a long time. Serov quietly moved to his desk. Rodin continued to stare out of the window. There was a new kind of frailty about the slope of his shoulders, about the way in which his head seemed cocked to one side. Serov glanced through the reports on his desk.

Afghanistan? He read the sheet quickly. That's how . . . he couldn't have made it. They'd shot down his tanker helicopter, evidently . . . which fitted with Adamov's ridiculous story of filling the tanks of the *Hind* at a petrol station near the Amu-Darya . . . Serov smiled. The American had come on, hadn't given up. How desperate the Americans must be for proof, how desperate –

He looked up. Rodin was staring at him.

'Now,' he said. 'I want to see this American – *the* American.' His voice was younger now, his face reaffirmed in habitual lines and planes.

'Of course.'

'What condition is he in?'

'Tired and beaten – defeated, General, not assaulted.'

'Psychological assessment?'

'Tough. He will take – time.'

'And he was entirely alone?'

'Their last, desperate throw of the dice, General. I'm certain of it. They know, but they are impotent without proof. That's why they had to have Kedrov instead of just leaving him to stew.'

'Your search for other Americans has not been abandoned?'

'No, it's continuing. But I'm sure –'

'Very well.' Rodin sighed, but choked off the sound, as if it threatened to remind him of unrelated things. 'Then *Lightning* is safe . . . but this man, this KGB colonel – he might talk?'

'To whom, General? Code Green is initiated. He's cut off – inside the fortress, so to speak. He can't communicate with anyone outside.'

'Arrest him anyway!' Rodin snapped. 'Arrest Priabin at once!'

President John Calvin paused at the top of the passenger steps of Air Force One, and waved once more to the television cameras and the rows and clumps of dazzling flashbulbs. He quashed all sense of masquerade such as had assailed him during the drive from the White House to Andrews AFB. Even as he had prepared himself for this interrogation – this challenge – by camera, he had been as unfamiliar with his role as an actor bereft of his script. But, adrenalin was flowing now, he could play the part

358

expected of him. He could smile, and wave, and brush at his grey hair as it was lifted and distressed by the breeze. His pale cheeks would be the result of the chill, nothing more. His tired eyes would, on TV and in the newspapers, seem concerned, filled with the gravity of the occasion rather than its awful emptiness.

He waved, suitably serious. The sharp tip of his raincoat collar tapped stingingly against his cheek as the wind blew it. As if trying to wake him from the dreamlike role-playing. Flashbulbs burst out afresh, and he wanted to shout that they had enough pictures to last a lifetime and . . . He smiled at the cameras. The First Lady was already aboard. Remsberg, the Secretary of State, was aboard, Dick Gunther, too; his advisers, his Press Secretary. Everyone . . . the whole pack of liars and actors.

He had made his speech without a stumble or uncalculated pause; but it had wearied him. *My fellow Americans . . . on Thursday, we shall make history* . . . Mockery. Calvin nodded towards the bottom of the passenger steps, at Miles Coltrane, his Vice-President, who grinned and suddenly raised his hands, clasped together, in a signal of triumph such as a champion boxer might have given. Like shaking dice, Calvin thought. Miles — you're maybe a better actor than I am . . . then Coltrane saluted him and backed away as the ground crew approached the ladder. Calvin looked out over the cameras towards the roped-back crowd, already being shunted farther from the runway. A sea of featureless blobs — black and brown and white faces . . . *My fellow Americans*, I leave you to engage upon the greatest betrayal of my country any American citizen has ever contemplated or achieved . . . He waved once more and stepped back off the passenger steps, ducking his tall frame to pass into the interior of Air Force One.

Uniforms, civilian clothes, salutes and acknowledgements. His wife's pale, relieved features. He patted her shoulder, then passed her seat, towards Remsberg and Dick Gunther.

He understood their expressions, as clearly as if they were miming for his benefit.

'Nothing — nothing at all?' he snapped, waving his hand at the huge map-table in the centre of the aircraft's main section.

He did not even look down at its surface. Both men seemed surprised at the persistence of optimism.

'It's twelve hours now, Mr President –' Dick Gunther began. The CIA's Director joined them like a man uncertain of his reception. His face was drawn, his eyelids heavy with lack of sleep. Calvin looked at him with the distaste he suspected he might show towards a mirror at that moment.

'*Twelve* hours! And you know nothing more than you did then? What the hell is happening over there?'

The operators and technicians manning the command centre studiously avoided the small group around the map-table. Senior officers hovered, as if out of their natural element. Calvin saw Danielle, his wife, watching him as if for signs of exertion or illness. Rings flashed on the pale, long fingers of the hand that rested on the seat. The aircraft's captain hovered, too, another futile uniform.

'There's been no signal – no nothing, sir,' the Director offered. Remsberg's heavy jowls quivered as he shook his head in solemn negation. Gunther merely shrugged.

'Then I don't have anything?'

'You could try to challenge Nikitin – when you meet before the signing . . . bargain with the guy,' Gunther murmured. 'Stall for time – pretend we know what's happening – maybe even go on TV and call his bluff?'

'They'd fry me, Dick – and you damn' well know that!' He looked over their heads, then snapped at the captain: 'For Chrissake, let's get this show on the road, Colonel!' The aircraft's captain flinched, then saluted. Calvin shuddered. Already, they would be beginning to despise him . . . he couldn't stall for time, not even that. No one, no one in the whole damn' world would stand for it. 'OK, OK – let's take our seats.'

As he sat down next to Danielle and patted her hand – which reached for his but which he would not take and hold – he glanced through the window. The crowd was at an anonymous distance now, hardly distinguishable in the flashing darkness, yet he felt their pressure on him just as surely as if they had surged against the fuselage. He looked into his wife's face. It was drawn, the fine lines around her eyes and mouth were emphasized – he wanted to flee into a contemplation only of her.

Without proof, he could not delay. Without proof – The engine note changed, and he felt the restraint of the brakes. He swallowed, as if fearing air-sickness or an accident during take-off. Danielle grabbed his hand. He felt the impression of one of her rings – it had turned on her narrow finger and dug into his flesh.

He looked out of the window. Miles Coltrane could still be picked out – he'd been called Uncle Tom by some militant blacks when he agreed to become part of the Calvin ticket. What would they call him now, a party to *this* deal –? He turned back to his wife and attempted to grin. The Inauguration Ball came back suddenly, ambushing him with triumph. Her smile, her pleasure for him that night, amid the whirl of people and the endless handshaking and backslapping and the glittering chandeliers and the brisk waiters and the deals beginning to be struck and the lobbyists to meet – but the *success* of it, the winning! Now, its fragmented scenes merely made him dizzy . . .

. . . like his Inauguration speech, recollected in its most strident and hollow fragments, which now made him want to retch. *A time of hope . . . . I pledge this administration to work unceasingly, with every nerve and sinew, in the cause of peace . . . a planet fouled and desecrated with nuclear weapons . . . a time of opportunity . . . on the edge of the abyss we might also be at the border of a Promised Land . . . our children . . . a time of hope, time of –*

He shook his head savagely, as if to countermand the aircraft's first movements. He must meet Nikitin tomorrow – he glanced at his watch . . . *today*, Wednesday. It was twelve-ten on Wednesday morning. Today. In Geneva. Twenty-four hours before the signing ceremony . . . and he could not stall or bluff or call Nikitin to show his cards, because if he did then the Russian President would act up his outrage and go directly on TV to challenge him to explain to a desperate world why he wouldn't sign the treaty the billions of inhabitants of the planet were waiting for . . .

. . . all day, on TV screens around the world, they'd have seen the wire being cut and rolled away, that obscenity of a Berlin

361

Wall being dismantled, the bombers going into mothballs and the aircraft carriers in drydock – the missiles being loaded aboard flatcars and being taken home under joint military supervision – Calvin remembered his own particular desire to see the sleek, black-backed dolphin-like submarines coming home, rendez-vousing off the east coast, from Maine to Florida, emerging like a forgotten and terrible army from beneath the sea. So *many* of them . . . the Trident force, the deterrent – rising out of distressed white water . .

. . . intended as a final symbol and gesture of peace. Every US submarine on the surface, identifiable and heading home.

And he had failed – utterly. Air Force One trundled slowly along the taxiway. He patted his wife's hand with increasing urgency and obliviousness. He did not want to look at her concerned expression. Her ring dug into his palm. He had failed.

Twelve noon. Twenty-four hours before the shuttle was to be launched . . . no, twenty-eight, Priabin corrected himself fever-ishly, with inordinate self-criticism for his error. It was to co-incide with the signing in Geneva, and Baikonur was . . . it was *twenty-nine* hours! Baikonur was four hours ahead of Geneva – the launch was to take place tomorrow afternoon. He rubbed his hand through his already dishevelled hair, in reaction to the strange, distracting panic of his concern over time. Time, after all, was irrelevant.

Katya, he saw, was watching his every movement; like a faithful dog or an animal ready to spring, he did not know. The dog itself was oblivious, untidily heaped near the radiator. Katya had returned him – when? Half an hour ago . . . before she was aware of *Lightning*. A time of innocence.

'I'm sorry,' he blurted out. 'Sorry I told you – I shouldn't have. I've endangered you.'

Katya shook her head. 'It doesn't matter,' she murmured; evidently, it did. She did blame him for imparting his secret to her. Sunlight fell across his desk, across her pale hands as she twisted them together on the edge of the desk; across her denims

362

where she had crossed her legs at the knee; across the carpet to the toes of his boots as he stood staring into the blank square of the window, fuzzy in his vision. 'It doesn't matter now . . .'

He moved to her and gripped her shoulder. She flinched. 'It does matter,' he muttered through clenched teeth. 'That's the bloody trouble – it does matter, more than anything else.'

She looked up at him almost wildly. 'Then what the *hell* are you going to do about it, Colonel?' He released her shoulder, as if he had received an electric shock from her, and she turned more fully to face him. 'Dudin's got a cold, so he says, the radio room is sealed and guarded, you can't make anything but a local call by telephone, the roads are guarded – *I* can't do anything, what are *you* going to do?'

Having crossed the office, he turned to face her. The dog appeared curious, even alarmed by their raised voices. Its tail banged against the radiator like a soft drumbeat.

'*I'm sorry* I told you – it, it just spilled out, as if it was too heavy for me to carry . . . Christ, Katya, I don't want *you* involved!' Again, he rubbed at his hair and began pacing the floor. 'I just don't know what to do! There's nothing *to* do.'

At the roadblock, they had politely, firmly turned him around and pointed him once more in the direction of Baikonur and his own office. GRU troops, supervised by an experienced captain . . . not that it mattered. The guns were in evidence, the implacability of their obedience to orders like the sharp smell of woodsmoke permeating the scene. Even the helicopter had reappeared and accompanied him most of the way back to town . . . it had been simple. Almost an anticlimax. Turn around, please, Colonel, there's a good boy.

And he had done. And sat here, scribbling on a pad like a psychiatrist recording nightmares – schemes and plans that were impossible to put into practice – or pacing the carpet or drinking coffee or smoking. The air of the office was blue with cigarette-smoke, thick like that of a drinking den. And all to no avail. There was no solution. He could not get out of the Baikonur area, could not get to Aralsk or contact Moscow . . . and Serov, who knew how much he knew, would make his move soon.

He crossed to the window. Any of the cars down there, any of the many he didn't recognize, could have his office under surveillance. Serov needn't hurry, he wasn't going anywhere! He flung aside the corner of curtain he had moved, groaning aloud, then turned and saw the surprise mingled with contempt on Katya's face.

'What the devil do you expect me to do?' he challenged guiltily. 'What *can* I do, dammit?' His fist banged the desk in muffled, limp emphasis. What was the point of taking it out on the girl. He shouldn't even have told her, used her as a sympathetic ear for *this*, of all things! He could have sentenced her to the same fate as himself, if Serov ever suspected that she . . . 'Sorry,' he murmured, waving his hand indecisively. 'Sorry.' He walked quickly away from her. 'Dear-Christ-in-Heaven, I almost wish Gant had got away with it!' He turned to face her. 'And you understand what *that* thought is costing me!'

'Can't we do *anything*?' Her hands might have been held up in sign of surrender.

'What?' he shouted. '*Me*, not us – can't *I* do anything? It's not your problem, you keep your head down.'

'But I *know* –!'

'Then forget!' He rubbed his head and began once more to pace the room, motioning the old dog back to its position near the radiator. After a few moments, when Katya thought he would never stop and that her head would burst, he turned to her, then to the map on the wall. Posed himself in front of it, hand cupping his chin, head slightly on one side; a furious effort of concentration, or no more than an actor's posture – she could not tell.

'What are you looking for?' she asked finally, hearing her fingernails drumming on the desk and unaware for how long the noise had been going on. He did not answer and she stood up and moved across the room, to stand beside him.

'Aralsk is a hundred miles away,' he murmured, as if thinking aloud. 'There's a little more than a day left . . . say, half a day if I'm to use the night to hide in.'

'How?' she asked.

'I'll have to walk it.' He turned to her. 'I can't just sit around and wait for what's bound to happen.' His eyes were wide, looking beyond her.

'You can't walk it, not in a night, not in twenty-four hours.'

'Then I'll drive as far as I can, to the security perimeter.'

'Which way?'

His hand indicated the map. 'The way poor bloody Kedrov went – out to the deserted silos, then across country here . . .' His fingers stroked circles rather than a course of escape, yet his voice appeared convinced by his scheme. 'Back through the marshes might be best.'

'That's less than half the distance – it can't be done.'

'I can't wait here!' he snapped. 'I don't want to end up like that poor sod Rodin! Pills stuffed down my throat or falling out of a high window! Serov *knows* I know – don't you understand, Katya?' He had gripped her upper arms and they hurt with the pressure of his fingers. He was shaking her like a disobedient child with whom he had lost patience. 'I'm frightened out of my skin, Katya, and I know I have to do something. I'm afraid for myself, I'm afraid for you, even for Kedrov – I'm afraid for the whole bloody world if these madmen have their way!' He was utterly unaware of the pain he was causing her, the degree to which she was being shaken. 'The whole bloody world – the poor, tired, sick-to-death bloody world!'

'Dmitri –!' she shouted at him, and his eyes focused, saw her, felt her arms, and released her, shaking his head as if to clear it.

She rubbed her arms gingerly, regained her balance.

'I'm sorry –'

'It's all right.' She forced herself to stop rubbing her arms. 'You won't make it,' she asserted. 'It's too far.'

'Then I'll have to steal or commandeer a car or a truck or a fucking *tractor* once I'm outside the perimeter!'

She walked away from him, considering his desperation and his scheme. She was afraid for him.

'I'll need food, walking boots – my gun . . . you'll look after the dog?' She nodded absently. She realized he had to make the attempt, some attempt, but she could only visualize failure; and his death. *Lightning* or whatever he called it was still unreal to her; less real than the enmity of Serov. Her horizons were narrower than his; her practicality did not allow her madcap schemes or desperate remedies, but enclosed her in a narrow steel box of facts that could not be breached. She could not *think* – especially while he talked.

'. . . a backpack, a good map, this way, across the marshes – they'll be empty now . . . making what? Five, six miles an hour. If I drive out as far as here . . .'

A truck pulled into the carpark below the window. A military truck.

'. . . what's the time at this point? Say – eight, eight-thirty, outside the perimeter – I need to know more about the terrain up there, the security . . .'

Soldiers, GRU troopers, descended from the canvas-flapped back of the truck, whose exhaust plumed greyly in the icy air. Six soldiers and an officer –

'Dmitri –'

'. . . farming . . . that would take me further west if I wanted to find a car – maybe this road here.'

'Sir –'

The soldiers moved towards the building; looking up at the windows, spreading out to cover the exits. The officer strode to the main doors. Katya turned.

'. . . one farm – yes? Yes, another there – what's the distance?'

'*Colonel!*' she shouted.

He looked round at her, plainly startled. 'What is it?'

'It's too late – they're here.'

'What?' Priabin's voice suggested complete surprise. She looked at him. His face registered a slow coming to terms with what she had said. Then the colour drained from it and the realization gave him a stunned expression. He moved jerkily to her side at the window, in time to see the officer and two of the armed soldiers enter the main doors. Priabin whirled round, as if itemizing his office furniture, his possessions – a man about to be robbed. He ran his hands stiffly down his cheeks.

'What do we –?'

366

'Get out! Katya – get out of here! You're not involved – just go back to your office – look as if you've been working there all the time – go *on*!'

He had grabbed her by the arm and was pushing her roughly across the room.

'What about you?'

He shook his head. 'Depends what they want – look, whatever happens, you know *nothing*!'

'But, if you're arrested, taken away, what do I –?'

'Nothing – there's *nothing* you can do. Just keep your head down.' Misha stood up and shook himself, tongue lolling. 'Take the dog with you,' Priabin added. 'Quickly! Come on, Misha – quick, boy!' He opened his door, pushing Katya and the dog into the outer office, snapping at his secretary: 'Lieutenant Grechkova hasn't been here – I've been alone all morning! Understand?'

His secretary, red mouth still wide, merely nodded.

'I have to –' Katya began.

'Nothing – understand me, Katya – nothing! Now – *go*.'

Dmitri Priabin closed the outer door behind them, and felt the perspiration stand out on his forehead. His secretary, the widow of a KGB officer, appeared concerned.

'We're in for a visit – GRU. They may want to talk to me, I might have to go with them . . . just a routine panic!' He grinned shakily at her. Soothed her by patting the air in front of him with his hands. 'Nothing to worry about. Just remember, no one's been here, I haven't even spoken to you. I'll explain when it's all blown over.' He had walked to his own door, paused holding it open, looking back at her. She was nodding her understanding; her eyes were bright with anxieties, her hands fluttered above her typewriter, as if he were dictating to her. 'OK, Marfa – just play dumb. It's me they want to talk to. When they get here, show them straight in.' He nodded, smiled palely, and closed the door behind him.

He looked at the map on the wall with a deep, sharp regret. He sat down at his desk, lit a cigarette quickly, puffed at it hungrily then slowed his exhalation, trying to find a pose of relaxation, so

367

that he should be surprised. Fear, regret, a looming sense of disaster regarding *Lightning*. He felt the jangling of his nervous system in his chest and arms. Try to relax –

– secretary's face, then the GRU officer's features and bulk behind her, beside her, in the room ahead of her. He assumed surprise, moulding the shock he could not prevent. Two soldiers were in the room immediately behind their officer. His secretary mumbled an apology, but he waved to her to calm herself even as he addressed the GRU major. A major . . . arrest, then.

'What is it, Major? What prevents you from waiting to be announced?' he asked with studied lightness; a sting in the tone, too, because that helped dissipate his fear.

'Colonel Priabin?' the major asked stolidly; aware of his authority, confident, but tied to a defined script. A minion.

'Naturally. What is it you want, Major? I'm rather busy, as you can see.' He lazily waved a hand over his desk, then drew on his cigarette. Puffed smoke at the ceiling. 'Do you need those two men just to speak to me?'

'Colonel Priabin, I must ask you to accompany me to GRU headquarters . . .' Priabin was on the point of interrupting him, but the major ignored his hand, his poised lips. 'Colonel Serov wishes to interview you.'

'Oh. Concerning what?'

'I am not able to divulge that, Colonel,' the major announced stiffly, staring past Priabin's shoulder; but there was no sense of awe, of being daunted. Just the indifference of a machine. 'Should you decline to accompany –'

'It's an arrest, Major – I understand!' Priabin shouted, standing up quickly, surprising the two armed soldiers, whose guns moved then stilled in their hands. He sensed the confidence with which he had begun ebb from his face. 'An arrest,' he repeated firmly. 'Ludicrous!'

This minion was not his enemy, and he had tired of the fencing-match. It did no good, it merely wasted breath and energy. He would need all his wits, all his cunning and strength for his meeting with Serov, who *was* his enemy. If he was to save his life –

He could not complete the thought. Instead, Rodin's somehow decadently splayed limbs spread on the rumpled bedclothes, filled his imagination. The same fate, the same fate, he heard the soft drumbeat announce, pulsing in his temple. He plucked his cap from the coat-stand, glancing at the map on the wall as he did so. It seemed such a huge place, suddenly; so many miles, so many hectares in which he might have hidden . . .

Regret, failure – his stomach churned with fear. Rodin's limbs, the blue hole in Anna's forehead. He swallowed sickness, kept his features an inexpressive mask, tight and false though his skin felt. Anna dead, Rodin dead, himself –

'Let's go, Major!' he growled. 'Well? I don't have all day – let's go!'

They were already engaged in the process of breaking him down. It was natural to them, and inevitable. There might be beatings, there might not; humiliations, drugs, starvation, half-drowning . . . it might take weeks or hours. They would choose. He could choose either to endure for as long as he could, or to crumble like an old, honeycombed wall. It would not matter, just as it did not matter to that poor bastard Kedrov he'd failed to rescue. At the end of the breaking, there would be the disposal of what remained. Very little; husks of corn or empty peanut shells littering the floor.

Gant watched his clenched hands shivering. His wrists rested on his thighs, his hands faced each other like armoured and frightened crabs, weighing each other. The shiver was not simply muscular. It was fear; *the admission of fear is not of assistance*, he remembered . . . some psychologist, some expert: *keep fear at arms' length or you may not be able to control it – it might end up controlling you . . . forget perspective –*

. . . if you don't have a future, don't think about it . . .

What was that crap? Why was it here now, like laughter in the dark? He was cold, he was hungry – par for the course – and the walls of the cell had started to contract in his imagination. He was waiting for the first interrogation, the first pain or the first enema of the mind, of the *personality* that the drugs would bring. That was almost more difficult to bear – never mind to resist – than the beatings and the starving and the electrodes. The sense of being utterly without will . . . Gant shivered more violently. He knew he had begun to think too much . . . He had enlivened his imagination instead of drugging and sedating it with numbers or distractions of other kinds. Worst of all, he'd admitted to himself that there was no way out; no way back.

Because he was Gant, they would gut him like a catfish . . . catfish? *Catfish* . . . He squeezed his memory like an orange, but nothing flowed. He could not get back to his youth, to the valium of the past. They would want everything he knew. He would be in no condition – *no* condition – to be returned by the time they had finished with him.

He was cold. The shiver was in his arms now, in his body, too. Cold –

– door. He could not stifle his gasp of relief – fear seeped whole seconds later – as the cell door opened. He had not even seen the preliminary eye at the peephole. The pit in Vietnam, in the 'Cong village, which had been approaching him again, retreated in his mind. He looked up with an almost pathetic eagerness.

Smell of spicy food. One of them had a rifle and kept his distance, the other moved closer with the food. Thin stuff, he saw, slopping in the mess tin – then it splashed on his flying overalls, down the sleeve of his leather jacket, soaked the thighs and crotch of his trousers . . . He snarled and almost rose.

The rifle moved, drawing a bead on him, the first round clicking into the chamber of the AK-74. Gant dropped back against the icily cold wall, hands pressed against his thighs, his body posed as if ready to absorb a blow. The corridor outside taunted him with its inaccessibility. The guard close to him was grinning, the armed one anticipated pleasure. Gant, involuntarily, flinched. The nearer guard unzipped his trouser flies, chuckled, then began to urinate on Gant's one grey blanket. Gant sat immobile, staring down at the food stains on his overalls. The guard whistled, as if using some public convenience. The urine spread in a pool. Both guards watched Gant greedily.

370

The guard finished.

'Should have drunk more beer,' he called over his shoulder, zipping his flies.

'You can't piss worth a kopeck, anyway.'

Gant felt the shiver in his body and attempted to quell it. The casualness of the humiliation was worse than a beating. A clear statement – you are ceasing to exist.

'You want a turn?'

'Piss *on* him, you mean? Who cares – there'll be plenty of time.'

Gant stared at the rectangle of tiled corridor he could see through the open door. They had left the door open to undermine him further. The fact that he understood what they were doing did not help. The urine stank, but he did not move. He heard a squeaking noise in the corridor, a voice murmuring. Boots.

The surgical trolley stopped directly opposite the door of the cell. He recognized Kedrov's profile, saw the blank, wild eyes staring at the ceiling, saw the furiously working mouth . . . and heard the insane, disconnected, drugged babble of sound coming from Kedrov. He was still deeply drugged. Here he is, they were saying. Your role-model; your future. He hunched further into himself, wanted to fold his arms across his heaving stomach, wanted to concentrate on something, anything other than the darkness that loomed in his mind. Two attendants in white coats peered into the cell. Kedrov babbled, screamed, denied, confessed, complied, rejected . . .

. . . they had overdone it. Kedrov might be lost for good in his own head, amid the ceaseless, whirling jumble that filled his mind. He should be sedated now, quiet; spent. Instead, he raved like a lunatic. They'd most probably done it deliberately, just to make an impact on himself.

He growled, but the noise seemed to whimper in the cell. Kedrov raved. The guards watched and weighed, the attendants looked round the cell like prospective house-buyers. Gant's lips were wet. He continued to growl but could not make the noise assertive or defiant.

Kedrov's voice vanished. The cell was darker. The urine's stink predominated. They were gone. Gant groaned softly, cradling his chest and stomach with his arms, head forward.

And slowly but insistently, the stench of the guard's urine became transmuted into the smell of stagnant, muddy water. The bamboo cage was opened, he was thrust into the pit, the bamboo grille was closed over his head. The walls were wet, the water reached his chest. The strange, small Eastern faces looked down at him then left him alone; utterly alone.

After a while, when he covered his face with his quivering hands, his father's face seemed to look down through the slatted bamboo, and be satisfied. Gant knew he would die. Once he had been emptied of everything he knew, every tiny chipping of information.

Kedrov —

He groaned. Rage was pointless. He had no future, not as himself. No future —

— Kedrov . . .

Standing on the metal catwalk outside the long glass windows, it was as if he were able, at last, to look down not only on the main assembly building and its contents, but on recent events. That appalled and appalling silence at the other end of the telephone connection with Moscow, the silence that had gone on and on until he thought his head would be crushed by it. It had been as if his wife had died, too, at the moment he gave her the news concerning their son.

The silence had had the effect of allowing a slow, betraying light to leak into his mind, illuminating dark corners he did not wish to inspect; his failings, his treatment of Valery, his lack of affection for his wife . . . eventually, he had tried to soothe her, gain some response. The line went on humming, and he could not make her reply. Possibly, she was no longer even in the same room as the telephone — somewhere else in the flat — staring at photographs, at Valery's room, at —? Rodin could not guess and was reluctant to pursue his questions. He had, after a further time, put down the receiver. And yes, he *had* wanted to tell her it was suicide, and his suspicions as to Valery's motives – but could not . . . not quite . . .

He tried to clear his thoughts, use the scene below him to erase his memories. Uniforms, white coats, the *Raketoplan* shuttle, the laser weapon, now assembled and undergoing its final scrutiny . . . uniforms, uniforms . . . army, army. The repetitions, the sights that filled his eyes and thoughts, began to clean his mind. He could begin to think of Valery as – as a soldier. The detritus of his recent life was being cleaned from him, like pigeon-droppings from the statue of someone honoured and eminent. Yes, a cleaned statue . . . yes, he could begin to think along those lines now. His breathing became easier, his chest seemed to expand, as if he were exercising his lungs before a window on a cool, fresh morning. His head felt cleared, sharply attentive.

He looked about him and beckoned a senior technical officer, who hurried to his side.

The greatcoated colonel had clattered along the echoing cat-walk only moments earlier. His heavy features were still sharp and blanched by the outside temperature. Despite his anxiety, Rodin smiled at the man; greeting someone who shared his secrets, his outlook, his background, as if smiling at the portrait of an ancestor, or a son.

'Well, Suslov – Yuri . . . well? The express hoist at the pad – you have news? Well, man, well?' It was as if his eager, breathy questions were releasing something more than anxiety.

Suslov was nodding, regaining his breath, unable to prevent a smile of relief and satisfaction from spreading.

'Yes, yes – sir, it's working again. Fully operational!'

The small group of technical officers attendant on Rodin moved to surround Suslov, congratulating him. Rodin turned away, hands gripping the rail in front of him, staring down at the shuttle craft, back opened like some crustacean with its shell surgically removed. The laser battle station had come together now. Lasing gas tanks ready to be filled, the mirror complete, the long, lancelike nozzle positioned. The nuclear generator, which was only to be activated once the shuttle reached its orbit just before the launch of the battle station, was housed in the main section of the weapon's oildrum of a fuselage. Rodin itemized the battle station like a clerk; each constituent, seen as if with an X-ray machine, adding to the satisfaction he received from Suslov's report.

'Fully operational . . .' he murmured. Suslov was at his side, gloved hands on the rail, eyes looking down. The kingdom –

'Yes, General,' he affirmed, his voice sounding abstracted; as if he were on some high place and looking across the border to a homeland long missed. 'We're back on schedule.'

Rodin turned to him. 'We must obey the Politburo's time-table,' he instructed, as if passing on information he disliked. 'We must launch when the Treaty is signed. For the *television* transmission. Twelve in Geneva – the crew will reach orbit at that time. The opening of the cargo bay will coincide . . . so Nikitin and the other old women have ordered.' He smiled at Suslov, easily, mockingly. 'Don't worry, Yuri – careless talk will not cost, lives, not here, at least!' He turned back to the group that hovered behind them on the catwalk. Glanced through the glass into the assembly building offices and control room. Television sets, including on some of their screens the American shuttle craft in its orbit . . . the launch pad, with the booster stages upright in their gantry, the mission control room of Baikonur.

The battle station would be detached from the cargo bay of the Soviet shuttle and its boosters fired to place it in its thousand-mile-high orbit. Then its infra-red sensors would align the mirror and the nozzle, the laser radar would scan the target, the fire control system would trigger the main beam, and . . . and the American shuttle would vaporize; a tragic accident. A perfect, undetectable crime. What debris there was would remain in low earth orbit or burn up in the atmosphere as it fell earthwards – towards the Amazon forest or the remote Sahara. It was irrelevant – there would be nothing left.

'Pictures,' Rodin announced. He snapped his fingers, as if the word had struck him with the force of an original idea. 'I want a photographic record, from this moment, Yuri.' He turned to his hovering staff. 'Organize it. There will be Politburo and *Stavka*

374

members who will not understand without pictures!' His voice was light, his mood almost jolly. 'The older ones, the tank people, the *infantry* commanders.' His staff smiled conspiratorially. 'Yes – and others will want to savour what we have witnessed.' He looked down once more. 'Especially the moment we first move the shuttle . . . but everything else, too. Loading the weapon, the cargo bay, the crew boarding – out at the gantry . . . everything.' Excited by his own orders, he glanced at his watch. 'It is now one-thirty. The shuttle begins its journey to the launch pad in *ten* hours' time! Back on schedule, as you so rightly say . . . gentlemen, *lunch!*' He clapped his hands together, as if at the sudden thought of food. They parted for him, a closely-knit group of satisfactions; smiles, confidence – just what he wished to see . . . Valery. A soldier, like these men, he forcibly instructed himself. Already uniformed, lying in an open coffin in the mortuary. Waiting to be flown home, as if fallen in a war.

Lunch.

He opened the door of the control room. Television images erased the presence of his son, as did the anger they evoked. Pictures from Germany – Strategic Rocket Forces officers and men, supervising the loading of SS-20s onto trains – *trains!* – to bring them home.

It will stop, he promised, whether to the men he saw on the screen or those around him, or even himself, he was not certain. But it was like the taking of an oath. It will stop – the trains will halt and be turned around. The army will *not* be broken by the politicians!

'Lunch!' he made himself announce with hearty pleasure. 'Later, there'll be little time for eating!'

'Yes, yes!' he snapped impatiently, his eyes glowering at Marshal Zaitsev, the Defence Minister. 'This is not the time or the place to press these matters, comrade Marshal.' Nikitin's voice warned. His hand waved around him to indicate the private departure lounge, the gathered small groups of uniformed or overcoated men – the press and the cameras and the photographers herded into one far corner. 'What I have agreed to approve the Politburo *will* approve —'

'But, comrade President, the revised budget is no more than a fraction of what is required —'

'Zaitsev — *drop* this matter. There are — other factors. Do you expect us to divert rivers, make deserts bloom, *feed* our people with *lasers*? You will have enough money for research, then for development — when we are convinced you *require* it!' His hand made a firmer gesture, dismissive of protest. He deliberately turned his gaze from Zaitsev and looked out of the huge windows of the lounge and across the snowbound tarmac of Domodedovo airport. A snow-clearing plough plumed a thick, darkened fountain of snow in an arc. His aircraft waited below the windows. To the north, hardly discernible in the heavy midday cloud and threat of further snow, the hills and towers and domes of Moscow were insubstantial. Crowds had gathered, or been gathered; black-coated, headscarved or hatted, they waited in the icy temperature for the departure of this flight — perhaps for this flight above all? Nikitin was — no, not *moved* by the sense of occasion, but affected, certainly affected by it. And by his own sense of himself as an historical figure, he observed with a semblance of humour. He would bring back hope, he supposed. The Americans would look at things in that light — perhaps much of the world. For himself, it was a question of necessity; historical inevitability.

Well, whatever he called it, it was necessary. Zaitsev, of course, would protect the army — the *bloody* army! — to his last breath, realist though he often appeared. So, he'd offered the army something of a reprieve. This laser weapon business would distract them from the cuts in the budget, the other reductions, the diversion of funds to agriculture, consumer production. They could play with their new toy, make it bigger and better — while people ate and watched television. Yes, it was a good bargain to strike with *Stavka* and their allies in the Politburo — and it was the dagger in the sock, the gun up the sleeve as far as the Americans were concerned. It couldn't, it really could not, be better . . .

. . . except when Zaitsev and his cronies started to be greedy again – and now, of all times!

'It's time to go,' he announced to the window, to the grey, lowering scene beyond it. He turned to Zaitsev. 'Yes, yes,' he soothed with almost elephantine humour in his voice. 'Don't *sulk*, comrade Marshal! I'm right – you'll see. And I *won't* emasculate the army, either.' He slapped the Defence Minister's shoulder with hearty violence, then stared across the room at the waiting press cameras, the television crews. 'Come – stand beside me, for the photographs.' Then: 'Come, *come!*' he bellowed to negotiators, generals, Politburo members, waving them to him. 'Time to have our pictures taken, for posterity!' He laughed in a great roar. Then he looked at Zaitsev. 'And remember to smile, comrade Marshal. This is a wedding, not a funeral!'

The press contingent, garnered and selected from the foreign press corps in Moscow, moved forward. The pick of the crop, he observed, recognizing faces he had seen across tables in the past weeks as he gave his carefully prepared and monitored interviews. As cameras rose to eyes or bobbed on shoulders, he barked with mock severity at the Defence Minister, 'Smile!'

THIRTEEN

the key to the prison

Serov smoked as if he were the one undergoing interrogation. Priabin was not certain how much of a pretence it was, like the pacing up and down, the staring from the window, the lengthy silences. Or perhaps Serov's adrenalin surged in situations like this one, as he worked towards the revelation of their true identities, prisoner and gaoler. Dmitri Priabin kept his hands still in his lap, his features calm; Priabin, colonel in the KGB, with a waft of Serov's magic wand becomes —

— nothing; lost; irrecoverable.

Serov made another display of lighting a cigarette. His square, blunt face bullied by its very lines and angles. His eyes glared. Priabin saw a change in Serov's mood. They had been there for more than an hour. Priabin had been neutrally uncooperative.

'I'm just about pissed off with you, Priabin,' Serov announced heavily, leaning forward. The leather of his chair creaked, his face was angled so that the sun behind it shadowed and strengthened his expression. Anger, frustration, the losing of patience. Priabin concentrated upon his own role; innocent suspect, man of authority.

'What is it, Serov?' he all but sneered. 'I've told you I don't know how many times already — I don't know what you're talking about. Yes, I saw Rodin, no, I did not harass him, yes, I'm sorry he's dead, yes, it was about drugs.' He threw his hands in the air. 'What the hell else do you expect me to say?' He leaned forward, hardly pausing, summoning a pretence of anger on his own part. 'And, while we're at it, when do I get the credit for catching our friend Gant — *and* Kedrov?' His index finger tapped the edge of Serov's desk peremptorily. Then he leaned back, acting a mood of self-righteous superiority, and lit a cigarette of his own . . .

. . . careful not to draw in the smoke too greedily. It was his first cigarette since leaving his own office. Careful.

Serov's face was full of anger, his eyes were brimming with contempt.

'You stupid little prick,' he murmured, and it sounded like a threat rather than an insult.

'Have you finished with your questions, Serov? I'm busy in my own little way, just as you are. Can I go?'

'No you can't go!' Serov bellowed.

Priabin made as if to stand. 'I don't see the point of any —'

'*Sit down!*' Serov screamed. Priabin could not prevent his whole frame from flinching from the voice's assault. 'Sit down, you pretentious little turd and I'll tell you just what's going to happen from this moment on!'

Priabin made a huge effort to shrug with a modicum of nonchalance. Serov was physically intimidating. Their fencing was at an end. The man's real interrogation technique was simple and brutal; old-fashioned and direct — the inspiration of fear. Priabin sat down slowly, smoothing the creases in his trousers, crossing his legs. He flicked ash into the china ashtray on the desk and looked up at Serov.

'For Heaven's sake, get on with it, Serov. What's troubling you — a clash of authority? Territorial imperatives?'

Serov remained standing. 'There's no clash of authority. You don't *have* any authority, except by my say-so.'

'I see. Then — what the devil is the matter with you? Not sleeping well? Is that it?'

'Smart little bugger, aren't you?'

'I'm not trying to be.'

'You're not being.' Serov sat down with a sigh. He waved his hands over open files strewn on the desk. Brushed ash from one sheet. 'Let me tell you what's happened to one of — *your* prisoners, shall I?' He smiled without humour. Priabin braced himself. Serov cleared his throat. 'Unfortunately, Kedrov couldn't take it. He's told us everything.' He drew on his cigarette and coughed. 'I don't know what scrambled state his brains will be in when he comes out of it. Still —' He shrugged. 'We found out how long he'd been working for the Americans, what he told them — everything . . . even what he overheard concerning *Lightning*.'

'What's that?'

'Too pat, Priabin — too pat. I *know* you and Rodin talked about it — I've got the tape, sonny. From your friend Mikhail. I *know*!'

'Bully for you, Serov.' He could not eradicate the quaver from his voice, and Serov bellowed with hard laughter, his hand slapping the desk violently.

'Shall I tell you why we've been fencing for an hour or more?'

'Probably because you enjoy it.' Priabin carefully stubbed out his cigarette.

Serov nodded. 'That, too,' he admitted. 'When I've got time for it. But, in this case, I wanted to know how far you'd go to hide the fact that you knew as much as you did. Quite a long way, apparently.' He plucked at his full lower lip, extending it into a deformity. Then he said: 'Now I know for certain you'll try as hard as you can to spread the news — don't I?'

'Sorry —?'

'You want to tell someone, don't you? About the naughty secret you've discovered? Moscow Centre, the Politburo, oh — Lenin's stuffed and mounted corpse for all I know! It's why you were at the roadblock, why you tried to use the radio. You should have come in here and told me everything, tried to convince me you were on our side, believed in our point of view. I wonder why you didn't?'

Priabin cleared his throat. Why hadn't he? 'It didn't occur to me,' he replied quietly.

Serov laughed, like a dog barking. Banged the desk with his palm once more. 'You're all the same, you Party pretty-boys!' he mocked. 'Give you a nice new uniform and you can't help believing you're immortal, can you? You came in here unable to conceive that anything nasty could possibly happen to you! Deep down, you couldn't *believe* —! That uniform's as much good to you as a cardboard gun, sonny!' His palm banged again and again, punctuating his words. 'You'll get years for this — you might never be seen again – like Wallenberg . . . Oh, heard of him, have you? It happens to colonels in the KGB, too, not just to intellectuals and scribblers like Solzhenitsyn – *you*, too, can *disappear*, is our motto!' His laughter made him cough; it did not weaken the fear he had created in Priabin. 'It's up to you,' Serov continued, 'which way we proceed from this point. You want the drugs? You want Rodin to believe that his son was harassed to death by your interrogations? Or do you want to – tell me . . . ?'

The silence was immediate. Priabin's temperature had jumped, his body itched and strung with uncontrollable nerves. He stared at Serov, but sensed the paleness of his face, the weak, small movements of his lips. His mouth was dry. Serov meant to have him finished with. The brute fact of his situation was unavoidable. How could he have lied to the man? He could never have persuaded him of his harmlessness. Perspiration prickled on his brow. His collar chafed. No, he could not have taken him in, not for a moment . . . but Serov was right, too. Whatever his fear when he was brought here, he had not believed, not with every part of himself, that this would be the outcome. The damned *uniform*, the *authority* – they'd deceived him, *lulled* him!

'Tell you what, exactly?' he asked, his voice almost casual.

Serov glowered, but his eyes sparkled, as if his enjoyment had achieved a new level of satisfaction.

'Oh, I couldn't trust you, could I? Not for a minute,' he said. 'Even afterwards, when all this had been resolved, you'd still be trying to cause trouble. No, I think I'd better wash my hands of you now.' He chuckled. Shook his head as if in reproof of a friend's poor joke. He clasped his hands behind his head and leaned back in his creaking swivel chair. 'You're too much of a survivor for me, Priabin. I don't like you – never have, come to that.' His voice was almost meditative. 'How you bloody well survived that cock-up over the MiG-31, I'll never know! Let your dead girl-friend take all the crap, I don't doubt.' He did not look at Priabin's face; Dmitri felt himself flush. 'Even got this cushy posting out of the deal – talk about falling in the manure and coming up smelling of flowers! You should have kept your head down, nose clean – walked away from trouble, sat out your tour . . .' He sat upright, looking keenly at Priabin, leaning his arms on his desk. 'You see, that's the trouble with you – you don't know when to leave well alone. Do you, eh?'

'Can I get up?' Priabin asked after a while.

Serov shrugged dismissively. 'Why not? I think we're about finished, don't you? *You* are, at least.'

Priabin stood, almost to attention, testing the strength in his body before moving. He walked to the window, standing beside Serov, looking out. Serov turned to watch him, heavily amused. There was nothing he could do.

'Going to throw yourself out?' Serov asked confidently. 'Could do worse, old man.' He saw Priabin's body shiver. 'Could do a lot worse. We've got *our* Serbsky Institutes, and our Gulag, too. I don't think we'll be hearing from *you* again – if you get that far!' He did not raise his voice. His tone was that of a judge passing sentence. Priabin thrust his shaking hands into his pockets, staring blindly into the afternoon outside. Gantries, cables, pylons, masts, radar dishes, low buildings – away beyond the square and its cobbles. An endless vista of – army authority.

He turned to Serov, as if to speak, then returned his gaze to the world outside the room. The square. The heavy military statuary, the modern Cosmonaut Hotel, the cars and the people. He saw nothing except his brief and violent future. Fear, real fear quivered through him. Serov was indeed going to kill him.

'There's no way out for you,' Serov was murmuring. 'No way out.'

His words were like a quiet but demented refrain; Priabin's mind caught them up, set them spinning together with his thoughts of Anna, Gant, Rodin and now Kedrov. No way out, no way, *no way out* . . .

He wanted to press his hands to his ears, as if the words were still being spoken and he could shut them out. But Serov was silent, standing back like a painter to observe the effect of his last brush-strokes. No way out, *no* way out . . .

. . . Anna, Gant, Rodin, Kedrov, Anna, Gant . . .

No way out –

– there must be *some* way . . .

. . . *some way* —

— *there must be some way out of here . . .* said the joker to the thief —

God, why Dylan *now*? The song ran in his head together with Serov's taunt. No way, *some way*, no way out, *some way out*, no way out of here, *some way out of here* . . . It was like contemplating the onset of madness, his mind was so helpless in its desperate attempts to avoid realization. No way, some way . . .

— thief, thief, *thief* —!

Gant!

He whirled around. Serov was smiling. Priabin's hand slapped against his empty holster. Serov laughed, raising his arms in a mocking gesture of surrender. His whole face was violent with laughter. Priabin had no scheme, no inkling, no —

— *thief!*

He snatched up the heavy, long paperknife from Serov's desk and before the man could move had thrust it against his neck, pricking the skin just above the collar, near the jugular. He grabbed the pistol from Serov's holster and stepped away from him as his boots lashed out to try to cripple him. Priabin moved round the desk holding the pistol on his opponent, fighting to close his mind against the emptiness that suddenly loomed after his desperate movements.

Serov dabbed his neck with a handkerchief, swivelled in his chair. His eyes shone and his features were flinty with contempt.

All Priabin could hear was the beating of his heart and their mutually ragged, tense breathing. He sat gingerly on his chair, both hands holding Serov's pistol, gripping it tightly, almost inexpertly, to still the quiver his hands were transmitting to the barrel of the gun. He steadied its aim on Serov's body with a huge effort. Gantries, pylons, power cables, radar dishes, stretched away behind Serov, to the indistinct, distant horizon, which offered no sense of escape. Army territory out there, all of it, for mile after mile.

'You bloody fool! That has got you precisely *nowhere!* There's no way out. Don't you realize that? No way — you're as good as dead.'

The office she had shared with Zhikin was pressing in on her. His desk stood near the window, its surface slatted and barred with shadow and pale gold like an animal's hide as the afternoon seeped through the Venetian blinds. His death was in the room with her, as was her awareness of his murderers' identities. A prologue to Priabin's tragedy. She tried to rid her consciousness of the desk by reducing it to veneer, leather, papers, a swivel chair. But it was in those freer moments that her husband's image proved most strong. Uniformed, smiling sardonically, he seemed to stand at her side like a pedagogue. He was there to represent the army. The memory of him, her knowledge of him, convinced her more than anything else of the truth of Priabin's wild allegations and fears. Her husband would have been breathless with excitement and ambition at something as fantastic as *Lightning*. His image seemed to voice a thousand words of contempt for politicians, for the civilian population . . . for anyone not in the army.

Priabin was convinced that they were enacting their most dangerous fantasy – and she could not help but believe him.

She got up from her desk, her hands twisted together. She remained well away from the animal-striped desk that threatened near the window, and began pacing the room, not for the first or even the tenth time. The dog watched her, his tail flapping idly, aware of her tension, aware that he was ignored.

'Why did you have to *tell* me?' she almost wailed. Her conscious thoughts were filled with blame for Priabin. What was she doing, trying to justify the fact that she wanted to help? Or disguising her fears for Priabin's safety? 'Leave me alone!' she shouted. The dog looked up. She growled at him not to move. It was even *his* dog! Its eyes became hurt, even wounded. 'Oh, God –!' Her mind was like a boiling mud-pool; bubbles of escaping ideas and imaginings and emotion kept breaking the surface. Her hands knotted into fists as if she was about to beat the air about her head. She had never felt so, so *trapped*.

Priabin had enlisted her, that's what he had done. He had known she would help him if she could, had relied on the fact. She should be keeping out of sight, but instead she was frantic with concern for his safety, even in the midst of her self-concern. It couldn't possibly come to a war, it just couldn't –

– he believed it. She could not refute it, just as she could not waive her husband from her mind. *You don't understand* – he always prefaced his remarks with some such phrase. *You don't begin to understand* –

Katya's rage expended itself on the image of her husband. She held her head in her clenched hands as in a vice, to squeeze Yuri out of her imagination. She wanted to escape him and she wanted to rid herself of loyalty, affection, duty, terror, even self-preservation and leave her mind clean and empty. She growled in her anger. The dog's tail signalled the animal's anthropomorphic sympathy. After all, what could she do – what could she possibly *do*? It was already too late to help Priabin – Serov had him, and she could not get out of Baikonur, just as he had been unable to do.

She sat down quickly behind her desk, and lit a cigarette with trembling fingers. The hiss of gas from the cheap lighter was audible and somehow frightening for an instant before the flame spurted. Her head was tight almost to bursting. Her hands would not stop shaking; it was the same earth tremor that Priabin must have experienced when Rodin first told him about *Lightning*. Must be –

What could she *possibly* do?

She drew at the cigarette as at oxygen, as the boiling mud-pool seemed to threaten to choke her. One hand clutched the other while her whole body trembled at the thought of what she must attempt. She tapped ash feverishly into the full ashtray. She was unable to move from her chair, hunched slightly forward in it. Yuri had vanished, gone somewhere to his habitual place at the far back of her mind; but he was like an accident that leaves shock behind. She felt, perhaps for the first time in her life, real terror. Quaking terror –

– telephone. Her heart jumped in her body. Her stomach was water. The telephone continued to ring; demanding she answer its summons.

Her arrest . . . ? Priabin's implicating her . . . ? Serov . . . ?

She snatched up the receiver. 'Grechkova!' she cried in a high voice, holding the receiver with both hands against her cheek as if expecting news of a death.

'Katya – is that you? What's –?' His voice was strained. But it was *him* –! How . . . ?

'Colonel!'

'Yes – are you alone, Katya?'

'Yes – why? How are you able –?'

'*Listen!*' His desperation was clear. Had he told them about her? 'Listen to me, Katya! No, don't say *anything!*' She thought she caught the noise of soft laughter, further from the mouthpiece into which he was speaking.

'*What is it?*' she pleaded.

'I need your help – I have to have your help, Katya. Now!' He paused, but she could say nothing. Eventually, he said: 'Katya – are you still there?' Again, she heard the distant noise. Who was it, laughing like that? Then she knew – Serov was *there!*

Trap, trick, deceit –

'Yes,' she answered. 'I'm here.' She felt very cold, yet still. Serov's image ushered the chill. He would be listening on an extension, enjoying every word, watching his prisoner reel in his accomplice; prove that she knew about *Lightning!*

'Listen, Katya – you're the only one who can help me!' he cried excitedly, fearfully. 'You've got to.'

'I can't help you, Colonel,' she announced with a dull empty calm.

'You *must!*' he almost wailed. Again, the indistinct sound of Serov's laughter. 'You're my only hope, Katya!'

'I can't help you, Colonel,' she repeated. 'I know nothing, I can do nothing.'

The noise was louder. She shivered at the sound of Serov's voice, though she could not make out the words.

'Katya – *please!*'

'I can't –' she began, then she heard Serov's roar of triumphant laughter, heard him yelling.

'. . . scared shitless . . . knew it would happen, should have asked me . . . rats deserting . . .' Laughter again, almost choking

386

off the triumph. She lost the words and clung to the tone in which Serov went on.

Deceit —?

He hadn't, hadn't . . . Serov was laughing *at* him, at her failure to help him . . . it wasn't a trick.

'Colonel, *Colonel!* What is it? What do you want?' Then, more carefully: 'What can I do to help?'

The silence crackled like a bad connection between them. She could hear his breathing, filled with phlegm and tension as he attempted to calm himself. She no longer heard the laughter from further into the room. What had he done, managed to do?

'Thanks,' he said eventually.

'Can you talk?' she asked, becoming the eager partner.

'What? Oh, yes — Serov's here, of course . . . I have his pistol.'

'*What?*'

'True.' There was almost a chuckle in his voice. 'He's a bit annoyed about it, as you'd expect . . . I'm wasting time. I can't get out of here without your help. Will you —?'

'Yes. I promise. Whatever —'

'I want our surveillance helicopter ready for take-off. As soon as maybe. Go there yourself and check it out. Don't take any bullshit, just get them to do the full pre-flight check, fuel up, everything — *my* orders!'

'Yes, yes —'

'And then bring a uniform here — to Serov's office. Don't worry, Serov will tell them to let you in — won't you?' he added with a kind of malevolent amusement, talking into the room, to be answered by silence. 'He will, anyway. Now, do you under-stand all that?'

'I don't understand why —'

'Dammit, you don't have to understand why, woman — just *do* it!' he bellowed. Then, almost immediately, he soothed: 'No, no, I'm sorry, Katya — but please do as I ask. The helicopter first. It has to be ready to fly immediately, tell them . . . then the uniform. Got it?'

Strangely, through the thicket of questions that confronted her, one emerged; the silliest, least vital — or so it seemed to her.

'What – what size should the uniform –?'

'Size?' he bellowed as if at a dim and truculent pupil. 'The American pilot's size, of course!'

'What a brilliant scheme,' Serov observed. He scratched the side of his broad nose with a fingertip, his body leaning back in his chair, which creaked as he shifted his weight in a pose of leisureliness. Priabin returned to his own chair, the pistol held in both hands with the same suggestion of inner conflict and desperate urgency. Serov's face mocked him. 'Brilliant,' he sighed. Then he leaned forward in his chair. Sunlight fell across one side of his face, removing any trace of expression. Dust-motes whirled as his hands waved dismissively. 'You aren't going to make it, Priabin. That I can confidently predict. You're falling apart too quickly, too much. You aren't going to make it.'

'Shut up, Serov. Pick up the telephone.'

Serov waved his hands across his desk, as if wiping crumbs quickly from a tablecloth. 'Not yet – perhaps not at all,' he murmured. 'Listen to me, schoolteacher's son.'

'You think I'm soft because my father wasn't a horny-handed son of the soil like yours –? If you even *know* who he is!'

Serov's eyes glinted, but he roared with laughter. 'You're just a little boy in a grown-up world! Little Mitya, his Mummy's pretty, darling son. You won't make it. Still, I'll make sure you merit a disused mineshaft as your final resting-place – I promise you that. Somewhere quite quiet, and lonely.'

'Pick up the telephone!' Priabin yelled.

Serov shook his head. 'I've told you no . . . not yet, anyway. It's two-thirty already, Priabin. Time is on my side. You can't walk out of here without me – they'd stop you, or check with me at the very least before they let you pass. So – you can do nothing to me, not even make me pick up the telephone. Is that clear, Priabin? You ceased to exist the moment you entered this room.'

Priabin stood up, snatching up the receiver. 'Get the American brought up here – *now!*'

Again, Serov shook his head. 'Impatient boy,' he sighed,

enjoying his situation. Even with the pistol in his hand, Priabin appeared impotent, Serov possessed that degree of power that rendered bullets harmless. Priabin's body jumped and twitched with possibilities, as if his muscles responded to the rapidity of his thoughts. 'Sit down, Priabin – you look foolish.'

Priabin replaced the receiver, sat down obediently. He placed the pistol harmlessly across his lap.

'What have you got?' Serov asked. 'One girl who may or may not be in love with you – not much to rely on, love, in this situation, I'd say . . . getting your helicopter ready. Where will it take you? I'd say Aralsk, wouldn't you?' He grinned as Priabin felt his face redden with confession. 'I thought so. Where you were making for by road. But, you need a pilot, and you need a witness. All right, I'll pick up the receiver for you, but to make a call of my own . . . no, you can listen on the extension.'

He dialled swiftly. Priabin felt the situation beyond his grasp, beyond recovery. Something in him had surrendered to the room's trap; to the central heating, the sunlight dazzling through the window, to Serov's authority. It hadn't been a scheme, something rationally developed, just a madcap insight, a momentary instinct of survival.

Serov nodded at him to pick up the extension. He did so and could hardly feel the bakelite in his grip.

'Ah – Ponomarov? Good. What's the condition of the patient now – no, the *spy*! Yes, that's right, I want a report.'

Priabin listened fearfully.

'Twenty-four hours before he comes round, at least that long. We consider he will be able to be questioned again by Friday, but *gently*, Colonel, without the use of more drugs. Really, some of your people . . . mind might have been irreparably . . .'

Eventually, Serov snapped: 'Thank you, Ponomarov. I don't have time for morality. Just keep him safe. Is he under guard?'

'Your people are here, yes.'

'Good. *Thank* you, Ponomarov!' He slapped the receiver onto its rest, and grinned, spreading his hands as if in innocence. 'There, that's your witness for you. To have him brought here would be peculiar enough to arouse suspicion, to collect him from the infirmary suicide. That's your one witness taken care of – see how it shakes you, Priabin? See how much of a blow that is? You're falling apart!'

'Send for the American – *do it!*'

Serov rubbed his chin, then his nose, then plucked his lower lip, elongating the silence until it drummed against Priabin's ears. He ran his hands over his cropped hair, even pulled at his ear-lobes. A whole language of relaxation, confidence, contempt. Priabin raised the pistol and carefully aimed it at Serov's broad, creased forehead, above the gleaming eyes. Serov's smile remained.

'Send for Gant,' Priabin said quietly, aware of the inadequacy of his voice, its lack of command. 'Do it now – because, as you might now begin to guess, you have turned over the stone and found the scorpion under it.'

'Poetry?'

'Even the son of a peasant should be able to take my meaning,' Priabin attempted to drawl. Using contempt steadied his hand, his bluff. 'You *know* what I mean. You've made my situation hopeless – where does that leave *you*?' He smiled shakily, but its effect on Serov was minutely visible. The man's eyes narrowed in calculation. 'I'm not going to let you live so that you can kick seven kinds of shit out of me for making a fool of you here – am I? Without *you* supervising what happens to me, I might even qualify for a neat, military execution at Rodin's orders – mightn't I?'

'Don't be stupid –' Serov began. Priabin's hand waved him to silence, and he stopped in mid-sentence. Another signal of uncertainty.

'Think about it. I shoot you in – oh, in a struggle for the gun, then I ring Rodin and get him to come over. Surrender myself to military discipline. I could ensure your death and something slightly more civilized for myself than if I give you back your gun. Mm? What about it?'

'Rodin's already beginning to think you harassed his son to suicide.'

'Then I'll tell him the truth – I saw you kill him. *Your* people . . .

do you think he'll expect proof? I wouldn't be surprised if he doesn't have an awful suspicion already that something like that —' He broke off. 'It doesn't matter. You now know that *you* won't come out of it smelling of roses.'

Serov's face was vivid with hate and bafflement. His hands moved more quickly over his face and head now; without pretence. There was no fear, because he knew how to keep himself alive and unharmed. But, he could be beaten!

'You — little *shit*,' he snarled.

Priabin's fears and possibilities bubbled inside him again, now that the iciness he had required had been exhausted. Katya, Gant —

— having to use Gant, Gant! Dear-Christ-in-Heaven, he would kill Gant when he'd used him! He *had* to kill him. He looked quickly at his watch. Two-forty. It would be dark in a couple of hours . . . Wednesday. Twenty-four hours before —

'Pick up the telephone,' he ordered. 'Have Gant sent up here for — interrogation by you. Do it, Serov. You know now I could easily use this gun on you. Pick up the telephone!'

Vividly, he heard the strange, chirruping voices of Charley in the darkness. The water up to his chest was icy, his body already numb and maggot-white from immersion. Occasionally, a narrow-eyed, child-sized face would peer down at him; occasionally, a torch-beam flashed over him. Chuckles. Charley laughing, talking in the distance; the noises of women and the cleaning of weapons.

They did not feed him, nor did he receive any water. Eventually, he cupped in his hands some of the filthy, stagnant liquid in which he stood, his stomach heaving at the idea and the reality; he had urinated, evacuated his bowels in that same water. After the first night, the Viet Cong villagers paid him not the least attention. For them, he had ceased to exist; had begun to cease to exist even for himself, as if the soupy, filthy water were dissolving him. The occasional distant noise of aircraft tormented him.

Gant sat in his cell in GRU headquarters, arms folded tightly into his chest, body hunched in a sickly, ill posture. He was breathing shallowly and quickly, as if staving off nausea or memory. Vietnam had strengthened its hold on his imagination. He had escaped then – been rescued, rather – but here it was different. No one would come; he was trapped just as certainly and for as long – if they didn't kill him – as Clarkville and Iowa had held him.

Church, flag, the flat, uninterrupted land, school; his father. They all seemed to him now like pieces of a complex plot to bring him to this last place – to his disappearance. Gant understood the creeping, strengthening hopelessness welling up in him, but he was too weary to fend it off; he could only disguise it by memories of other imprisonments – earlier escapes. He had escaped Iowa, even Vietnam; but not Baikonur, because he had never escaped flying. Not from that first aircraft, billowing the road's dust about, heading for the gas station. A crop-duster who'd flown in the war. Church, flag, flying; all a trap.

At some moments, he looked quite rationally at his watch – they'd left him that – and smelt the dried urine on the grey blanket he had flung into the corner; he could even smell the spiced gruel that had stained his overalls and hands. The afternoon was halfway to darkness, almost three o'clock; local time. The last time-zone . . .

It had been like a fever, that first flight. Each loop and spin and dive and climb – the engine popping only a little more loudly than his mother's sewing-machine – was a rise in temperature, the fever taking firm hold of him. Clarkville as he looked down on it was nothing; dotted buildings, a few narrow streets, scattered farms, the corn everywhere, the gently rolling landscape that, from the air, seemed endlessly flat . . . his father shrank to insignificance. He knew, with a fierce delight, that he had broken out, escaped; loop, turn, dive, climb, spin, upside-down, roll; free movements. The fever had never left him.

Almost three o'clock. His mind returned to Vietnam, towards the third dawn and the terrible numbness throughout his body, the collapse of will and the awful loneliness amid the bustle of the village; his past was better than his future. In memory, he was close to being rescued —

— door, startling as it was meant to do by being flung open. He looked up, frightened. Now, it began —

'Get up!' an officer barked at him, posed with his hands on his hips in the doorway. One armed guard behind him was as much as Gant could see. 'Get up!' the officer almost screamed. Yes, now it would begin, the drugs or the beating.

He rose slowly, shakily to his feet, unable to ignore the weakness that seemed to have drained everything from his frame, even the blood.

Loop, roll, turn, dive, climb . . .

'Quickly — this way!' the officer bellowed. Everything he said was shouted, had exactly the same volume and tone. The guard outside, carrying his rifle across his chest, stepped back to allow Gant into the corridor, keeping a precise distance between them. 'Upstairs, you! To the lift — quickly, the lift!' It was the voice of a machine. The officer had drawn his pistol. Gant moved at a shamble that he could not improve or disguise; like the numbness that had made him stumble and fall when they had hoisted him out of the pit. Marines, the rattle of gunfire, the noise of helicopter rotors . . . loop, turn, dive, roll, climb, spin . . .

The officer's gun was thrust into his back. The guard's rifle had its stock folded. An AKMS, something in him identified. The guard was jammed into the corner of the lift behind him, next to the officer. Gant faced the lift's closed doors. He took no notice of the numbers illuminating and flicking off as they ascended. Then the doors opened onto a carpeted corridor. He was pushed along it. The guard was allowed to swing the barrel of the rifle against him in encouragement, but he hardly felt the blows; numbness was something he required now. He encouraged it.

'Halt!' the officer cried in a parody of authority. He knocked at the door at the end of the corridor, listened, opened it. 'In here — wait!'

There was no one, no secretary, in the outer office. The officer seemed surprised, but knocked at the inner door. Gant heard a voice he might have recognized had he not been sinking into himself, then the officer opened the door.

'The prisoner, Colonel, as you ordered!' he snapped out robotically. Then he turned to wave Gant forward. The guard buffeted him almost casually in the back with the AKMS. Gant stumbled towards the voice that announced:

'Thank you, Lieutenant — that will be all. Return to your duties.'

'Should your outer office be manned —?' the officer began.

'It's not *your* concern, Lieutenant. That will be all.'

Gant had passed the officer, shambling into the office where he saw Serov outlined against the light from the window. He was still squinting after the darkness of the cell. The light hurt his eyes as much as the blue sky had done over the Vietcong village. There was a second officer in the room, he noticed as the door was closed behind him.

Closed — change of atmosphere, of tension; excitement here, even rage. But not directed at him, he sensed like an animal exploring some outbuilding at night. Alert, led on by hopeful scents, aware of danger, confused by contradictory sensations. What was it about this room, these two —? Who was —?

'Gant!'

Priabin, he realized . . . and the KGB colonel had a pistol drawn. Priabin, who wanted to kill him. He stared at the man, unable to move or speak, as if exactly repeating their previous encounter.

'Thank God,' he heard then. Serov —? No, Priabin.

Serov slumped noisily into his chair, hands raised. His voice betrayed nervousness, suppressed or burned-out rage.

'So, you've got your pilot, what now? It's three already. I've been closeted alone with you for a long time. We've refused two urgent calls and other, more routine ones must be piling up at the switchboard . . .' He sighed theatrically, lowering his hands slowly onto the desk, fingers spread. Gant was baffled; kept turning his gaze to Priabin, to Serov, to Priabin . . . Serov added, with greater mockery: 'I even sent my secretary on a pointless errand — but he will be back soon. Anyone could walk in here, at

394

any moment. What are you going to do?' He was all but gloating – even though he appeared to be Priabin's prisoner, Gant realized with slow, painful thought. 'Where's your girl-friend, mm? It's not happening *quickly* enough, Priabin!'

'Serov, be quiet – you're boring me.' Priabin replied, moving towards Gant. His nose wrinkled at the foodstains, at the dirt on Gant's hands – his eyes were concerned at the features he studied, at the defeat and weariness Gant knew his own eyes proclaimed. He shook his head, not knowing what he intended by the gesture. 'Are you OK?' Priabin asked in heavily-accented English.

'Maybe,' Gant replied in Russian. Priabin nodded at the word, as if remembering Gant more clearly. 'What – gives here?' he added, gesturing at Serov, who watched them both.

'You are now my prisoner once more,' Priabin replied.

An exchange of prisons . . . ? The room's atmosphere was wrong, there was something else here – as if Serov were the prisoner, though he couldn't be.

He watched the emotions on Priabin's face; hate, yes, but purpose, too – fear, desperation, the wild excitement of overcoming something . . . what had happened in this room?

'You said pilot,' Gant observed, turning to Serov. 'Why are you handing me over to this guy? He wants to kill me.'

'We all want to kill you, my dear fellow – in our own good time and our own way, but Colonel Priabin –' He lit and drew on a cigarette. Blue smoke rolled above his head. '– Colonel Priabin has a use for you before he kills you . . . and make no mistake, he still wants to do that. You are able to see that quite clearly for yourself, I imagine?'

Gant had turned back to Priabin. Yes, he still wanted it. Gant felt his body coming back to life, prickling with cramps and heightened nerves. There was a prison here, but he was no longer sure on which side of the bars he stood. He slowly, innocuously flexed his hands, shifted his feet.

'So?' he asked Priabin.

'Not if you help me, Gant – not then.'

'No, I don't believe you,' Gant replied. He might even want to

395

mean it, but the woman's death would make him do it in the end.

'I'm your only way out, Gant!' Priabin snapped, with an anger that seemed it had been suppressed for a long time. 'You'll do as I say.'

'What?'

'Fly me out of here – with the good Colonel here, of course, for company. Wonderful conversationalist!'

'Why? Why do you need me?'

'Tell him, Priabin – why don't you?' Serov scoffed quietly.

Priabin's face expressed urgency. He glanced at his watch, as he had done repeatedly ever since Gant had been brought there.

'All right – I can't get out because of the security surrounding the launch . . . yes, the laser weapon. Your people were right to be worried – they've done it, we've done it, we have one and it will be loaded aboard the shuttle tonight. I have to get out of Baikonur, to another KGB office a hundred miles away – do you see?'

Gant shook his head. 'Who's stopping you?'

'I am,' Serov announced quite calmly.

'Why?'

'Because I have to try to stop the launch, that's why!' Priabin yelled, looking once more at his watch. Three-one. The sunlight was pale now, sliding down the far wall of the room like splashed paint. 'Don't you understand?'

'Of course he doesn't, Priabin. You could hardly expect him to, now could you?'

Priabin seemed at a loss, then his face brightened. '*Lightning* – of course, you don't know. Our precious army here intends to *use* the weapon!'

'How?' Gant asked after a long silence.

'Against your shuttle craft now in orbit. *Atlantis* will be vaporized on Friday – unless you get me out of here. I have to talk to Moscow – is that enough explanation for you?'

Gant felt his jaw slacken, his mouth open. Confirmation lay exposed in Serov's smile, his glittering, watchful eyes. Dear-Christ-in-Heaven! Wakeman and the others, just – gone.

'I don't have time for your shock and recovery, Gant!' Priabin snapped. 'You'll obey my orders and fly our surveillance helicopter from here to Aralsk – as secretly as the way you got in. Understand?'

Gant nodded. The man was giving him the pilot's seat in a MiL – a hand reaching down, two, three, four hands, into the vile water, and pulling at his numb hands and arms until they lifted him from the pit and he lay weak and exhausted and crying on the earth beside it. Fires burned all around, rotor noise howling about him, rifles on automatic . . . this Russian was going to give him control of a MiL helicopter; help him escape. He fought to prevent his relief appearing in his eyes, around his mouth. Clenched his hands behind his back.

'He's already thinking furiously how to turn all this to *his* advantage, Priabin,' Serov remarked.

'That makes two of you,' Priabin snapped back, looking again at his watch. Three-three. 'We'll make it, Serov – won't that annoy you!'

Ideas whirled in Gant's head. The laser weapon itself, the weapon being used, the shuttle and Wakeman its commander, whom he knew, the Treaty, distances, the promise of the MiL. Priabin must be used, for his safety; Priabin *had* to succeed – an aftershock ran through him like an icy chill. Using the battle station! Wakeman, *Atlantis*, the Soviet shuttle, that night, orbit, the Treaty, the army, the distance to the nearest border . . .

. . . climb, turn, loop, roll, spin, dive . . . the key to the prison was in his hand, that was his most immediate and recurrent image – *escape*.

There was a knock on the door. Priabin, startled, turned the aim of his pistol towards the noise. Serov sat immediately more upright, as if about to spring.

'Watch *him*!' Priabin demanded.

Gant moved towards the desk, hearing a voice from beyond the door. A woman's voice.

'Colonel?' Then: 'Dmitri!'

Priabin hurried to open the door, almost pulled the girl into the room, slammed the door behind her. In her arms was a uniform. Serov's breath hissed between his clenched teeth. Gant caught the paperknife Priabin threw in his direction. The Russian was elated by the girl's arrival. Her wide eyes were taking in the room, its tensions and reliefs, its promised dangers for her, for all of them except perhaps Serov. Her hand touched Priabin's arm proprietorially, concerned. He seemed to be ignorant of the contact as he turned to Gant.

'Get into this KGB uniform, Gant. It should be about your size – quickly!' He turned to the girl. 'Katya – the helicopter?'

She nodded. 'They grumbled a lot, said you couldn't get permission to take off, they didn't want to be shot down . . . but it's ready for your arrival. I told them it was urgent, you'd come with the right papers.'

'Good girl. I'll have the right authority, all right – *him!*' He pointed at Serov with the pistol; he was euphoric, almost drunk with the jigsaw he had successfully put together. Gant distrusted his mood. 'What's happening outside this room?' he asked, still animated. 'Did you have trouble getting in?'

'Back stairs – poor security from the clodhoppers. I didn't see a soul. We could use –'

'Front stairs – the lift for us down to his car in the basement garage. A nice little party on urgent business. Come on, Gant, hurry, man!'

'What about the guy I came for – don't we need him?'

'He's heavily sedated. Too hard to move him. They'll just have to take my word for it, won't they?' His face seemed struck by light. 'No, they bloody well *won't*, will they, Serov?' He crossed to Serov's desk, tugged open a drawer, rummaged in it, tried a lower drawer, rummaged, then held up three cassette tapes. 'The ones *we* used – even neatly labelled by Mikhail!' His gaiety was dangerous, consuming all caution; in his own mind, Priabin had already won the game. He threw the cassettes to Katya. 'Look after these with your life!' he quipped. 'Gant, are you ready?'

'Yes.' He stood to attention in the corporal's uniform to be inspected. Priabin studied him for a moment, then nodded.

'You'll do. OK, let's go. Serov, you'll walk beside me in our little party, with Gant and Katya behind us. *Both* armed. One false step – but you know how the dialogue goes. Don't worry about Gant, Katya – he has a vested interest in helping us. We're giving him a chance to go on living . . . just in case, take the pistol from him as soon as we reach the helicopter – OK?'

'Yes, Colonel.'

'I think this farce has run for long enough, don't you?' Serov drawled, smiling.

'Get up!' Priabin snapped at him.

Gant saw no movement of Serov's hand, only his rising from his chair, then an alarm howled outside the window, answered by the baying of other alarms in the retreating distance of the corridors beyond Serov's office; all over GRU headquarters. Priabin was stunned by the noise. Gant thrust Serov aside and felt for the alarm button which had to be in one of the desk drawers Priabin had opened – found it, but was unable to stop the noise.

Serov shut the drawer on Gant's left hand. He yelled in pain and struck Serov across the temple with the gun Priabin had handed him.

'No –!' Priabin wailed. His look of triumph had vanished.

Gant winced at the pain in his hand and continued to fumble it clumsily around the drawer's interior. His mind was filled with the prospect of broken skin, broken bones, the uselessness of the hand . . . it touched another button. Silence.

Then he examined his hand, cuddling it, testing it. Broken skin . . . the fingers bent slowly, in turn. No broken bones. Just bruising. The silence in the room, in the whole building, thudded against his ears like noise. His hand would have to be good enough to fly the MiL. Serov was satisfyingly slumped in his chair, blood seeping down his cheek from the cut on his temple.

'No . . .' Priabin breathed. This time it was a plea.

Furniture of the room. A hurried impression as Gant's eyes roved like a quick, unfocused camera. Drinks tray, glasses, chairs, waste basket, papers, *papers* –!

Cigarette-smoke, lighter . . .

'*Help me!*' he yelled at Priabin.

'What?' came the dazed reply.

Gant flicked the desk lighter, crumpled paper into the waste basket. The girl, eyes concentrated and squinting, watched him, then snatched vodka bottles from the drinks tray. Handed one to Priabin, unscrewed the tight cork from her bottle, twisting and tugging at it with almost comic desperation. Priabin, realizing, tugged the cork of the other bottle with his teeth.

'Drunken bastard – spilt the stuff, lit a cigarette, we sounded the alarm, but put out . . .' He did not concern himself with other explanation. They doused the waste basket, then the surface of the desk. Gant flicked the lighter. Priabin soaked the front of Serov's uniform. The man's eyes cringed at the sight of the stain and the flickering lighter flame.

'*Now!*' Gant shouted, almost throwing the lighter at the vodka. Flames licked over the desk, dribbled to the carpet, flared in the waste basket. 'Get him on his feet!'

He bundled Serov's frame out of his chair. 'Move it!' he bellowed. 'Use the extinguisher, for Christ's sake!'

Katya snatched it from the wall, inverted it, banged it on the arm of a chair, and foam sprayed wildly. Gant glared at Priabin.

'Help me get this guy to the door!' Priabin was watching the gouts of foam as if mesmerized. 'Damn you, Priabin, move your *ass!*'

He threw Priabin the pistol and bundled the half-conscious Serov across the room. The man seemed unwilling to protest or resist. Gant watched the door, then opened it –

– two guards spilling into the outer office, rifles awry, curiosity as much as threat in their expressions, their eyes already glimpsing the flames and smoke beyond their colonel and the uniformed man who held him. Gant's hand ached. His was a KGB uniform, so was Priabin's and that of the girl . . . three of them and the semi-conscious Serov.

'Drunk!' he yelled. 'Started a fucking fire in his own office – cigarette –!' The men were nodding. Gant turned. The girl had doused the flames. Acrid smoke filled his nostrils. 'All right, get out of our way, the Colonel needs medical attention – quick, move it!'

They began to back away from Gant and the muttering bundle

in his arms, from Priabin as he pressed behind Gant, from the woman completing the group. Moved out of the outer doorway into the corridor. Gant thrust Serov forward, his feet dragging. Smoke seeped after them, stinking and choking.

The lieutenant was in the corridor beyond them, emerging from the staircase, running –

– saw the group they made, his retreating men, his slumped superior officer. Suspected. He'd questioned Serov about the manning of the outer office, he'd come expecting something to be wrong, but not a fire.

'Wait!' he shouted, still running. 'What's going on here? Wait! What is the matter with –?' He stopped, mouth opening at the sight of Priabin's face – that of a prisoner – and Priabin's gun, impossible in an arrested man's hand . . . recognitions flickered. He raised his gun.

'Do it and this bastard's *a dead man!*' Gant yelled at him. The two guards were slowly beginning to understand. Gant saw the narrowness of the corridor, the lift doors at the end of it, the lieutenant and the two guards. It was never going to work.

He coughed in the rolling smoke and pushed Serov towards them like a shield. Priabin thrust the muzzle of his pistol against Serov's forehead. Gant felt the man in his arms become rigid with his sense of danger.

'We mean it!' Priabin shouted. 'Get back, get out of our way!'

Gant moved Serov like some overlarge toy being manhandled by a child. His feet dragged, but otherwise the GRU colonel did not resist his bundled passage down the first yards of the corridor. Gant felt the vulnerability of his own frame behind that of Serov. Priabin's shoulder rubbed against his as they moved together, Priabin still pressing the gun against Serov's head. Come on, come on, *move* –!

The two guards retreated into the lieutenant and, as if goods trucks colliding softly, set up a reaction, moving him, too. They shuffled backwards reluctantly, staring at Serov's head and the gun. Gant was sweating furiously; he felt his volition draining away. To counter the threat, he offered Serov's form like a

401

challenging flag at the three retreating men. It seemed to hurry them.

He knew they'd be in the underground garage, they'd be everywhere in the building . . . no one had done anything but cut off the alarm. It hadn't been cancelled by some telephone call, by an all-clear. Serov's boots dragged like brakes on the carpet.

He glanced at Priabin's face. It contained a desperation as clear as his own.

'We mean it, we'll kill him!' Priabin shouted at the guards and the lieutenant, waving the pistol then replacing it so hard against the man's temple that Serov groaned. 'Come on, get back!'

'Get away from those doors!' Gant bellowed hoarsely, his arms aching with Serov's weight, his own unwashed scent rank in his nostrils, his heart pumping wildly. '*Hurry* it!'

'Drop the rifles – your pistol, Lieutenant.'

To Gant, the lift suddenly seemed nothing more than a steel box into which they were stepping voluntarily; incarcerating themselves.

Priabin had summoned it. The rifles lay like sticks of black wood on the carpet. The three GRU men were beside the lift doors. The lieutenant was looking down an empty staircase, hoping for assistance. Katya trained her pistol on them.

Gant slumped against the wall, Serov's weight hugged to him, Priabin stood opposite the doors of the lift, pistol held out towards the frozen trio near the stairs. A moment of suspension, as if they all floated with some deep, slow current undersea. Then the click, the opening of the doors with a sigh.

Gant's head turned wildly –

– empty . . .

Empty!

Luck, incredible luck, which meant they would be down there . . . Priabin kicked the rifles and the pistol into the lift, then helped Gant throw Serov after them. The colonel had begun to move, desperately but too slowly, trying to writhe out of Gant's relieved grasp. Gant flung himself against him and they clashed dully onto the far wall of the lift. Gant locked his arm across

402

Serov's throat, snarling. Serov's body slumped into defeat once more.

The girl backed into the lift, her gun still held level at the three men outside. Priabin covered her, then he pressed the basement button and held it down. Gant heard banging – already fading – on the outer doors. His own smell was suddenly more apparent in the confined, slowly-moving box. His breathing and that of the others was magnified. Sweat ran into his eyes. Priabin's face was mobile with conflicting anticipations, eyes flickering again and again to the floor indicator above the doors. The lights winked on, winked off, but the lift did not stop –

– don't let it stop, don't let it, don't –

'They'll be waiting,' he warned. Priabin nodded.

Gant gripped Serov's body more strongly, keeping one arm across the man's throat, feeling the bobbing Adam's-apple against his sleeve; hearing the gurgling swallows of Serov's breathing, as if the man were drowning. Priabin placed the pistol muzzle almost ceremoniously against the blood-seeping temple.

Something in Gant's head had counted the passing seconds. Two and a half minutes since the alarm had been switched off. He shifted Serov's weight against him.

Ground floor. The lift did not stop. He felt the luck of it in another surge of adrenalin, but it seemed thin and ineffectual.

The lift jerked to a stop, the doors opened. The icy temperature of the basement garage struck into the compartment; jolting Gant. He shivered. In his arms, Serov growled. Priabin jerked his head up. Serov's eyes were narrow with hatred.

'Gant?'

'I go first, sure –'

The basement was silent, apparently empty.

'Dmitri what if –?' Katya began.

'Don't *think*!' Gant growled at her. 'It has to work!' He adjusted Serov's weight so that he could push him ahead. 'Rifle,' he added, nodding at the floor of the lift. Their noises seemed lost in the echoing cold and concrete reaches of the basement. Gant listened. He could hear no footsteps, no running men.

Rasp of metal on metal. Glimpse of a rifle trained, resting on the bonnet of a car ten yards from him. Other men, perhaps five or six. Two officers, too. Men with uniforms undone but already dragooned into order and purpose.

He crushed Serov's body against him like a shield, feeling his own vulnerability; aware of every vital organ beneath the thin, stretched envelope of skin.

The noise of the first shot seemed swallowed by the low-roofed cavern of the basement, echoing harmlessly into the distance. The bullet chipped concrete flakes and dust from the wall near Gant's cheek. Dust filled his eyes, he felt his cheek sting.

'Stop firing, stop firing!' an officer bellowed through a loudhailer, his voice distorted and booming. 'You idiot, you'll *kill* the Colonel!' he added unnecessarily. Then he said, directing the open mouth of the loudhailer towards Gant: 'Stay where you are! Drop your weapons – you're outnumbered. You can't get out of here.'

Gant coughed as he attempted to reply.

'There's no *time* to talk!' he heard Priabin shout. 'We have nothing to lose – get out of our way. Don't attempt to stop us or Serov will be killed! You'll answer for that death, Captain. Think about it!'

He stood alongside Gant, now thrusting the barrel of an AKMS rifle against Serov's head.

'Dmitri, the keys are in this car!' Gant heard Katya call out.

'Start moving towards the car,' Priabin whispered fiercely. Gant nodded, dragging Serov so violently off-balance that his legs stuck out in front of him and he became a drunk being towed rather than a shield. His heels scraped on the concrete floor. Oil-stains, the smell of petrol as Katya started the engine of the car Gant had not dared turn to see. The captain and his men made as if to move forward, their poses tense, threatening danger through reckless instinctive action. 'Serov's head will *disappear* if I squeeze this trigger!' Priabin roared. 'Stay where you are. Don't move a *step!*'

Serov's bulk shifted against Gant, the dragging legs attempted to push the body upright. Serov cried out:

'Let them go! Don't interfere!'

Gant felt the body of the car against his back, felt the open rear door scrape against his sleeve, jab into his upper arm.

'Get in, get in!' he said urgently, dragging Serov backwards with him onto the bench seat. Serov struggled out of Gant's hold, but Priabin pushed him across the seat with the rifle and almost tumbled into the car. Gant felt exhausted beneath their combined weight. Priabin slammed the door, and the car immediately jerked forward, engine racing, tyres squealing on the concrete.

The soldiers moved aside, losing their purpose and pattern as the car rushed at them. The captain jerked away from the bonnet at the last moment.

'Keep down,' Priabin urged. Katya's form was bent over the steering wheel. 'It's three kilometres, no more.'

The car bucked onto the bottom of the exit ramp. Roared up into fading daylight, bouncing and skewing onto the cobbles of the square, beneath the archway and towards the dark statue surmounting the war memorial. The whole car smelt of petrol; the engine howled. The traffic was light, the girl weaved through it out of the square onto a broad dual carriageway. Serov's eyes gleamed in his face, in contrast with the delicate, infirm manner in which his fingertips touched at the drying blood and the bruise on his temple.

Priabin's face was excited, elated. He laughed, the rifle across his stomach and jabbed against Serov's ribs. He studied his prisoner with a wild satisfaction. Then looked at Gant, his features clouding. He shook his head as if to rid it of memory.

'You'll —?'

Gant was cradling his hand. It was already lividly bruised. He flexed his fingers in demonstration.

'I can fly,' was all he said in reply. Then he turned to look back through the rear window.

'Two cars and a truck,' Katya said through clenched teeth.

'We're immortal as long as we have this bastard with us,'

Priabin replied. 'Katya – turn on the radio. Let's find out what they're up to.'

After the click of the switch, orders and counter-orders, ideas and schemes and warnings flew like escaped birds in the car, adding to the strain of tension between its four occupants. They guessed the KGB helicopter at one point, others discounted it, they queried the use of roadblocks, voices demanded action, authority leapt and changed and was questioned and recognized. They agreed on the priority of Serov's life; agreed, too, that the helicopter was a possibility. Behind them, Gant saw the cars and the truck maintaining but not decreasing the gap between them and their quarry. In the distance, away above and beyond office blocks, the first helicopter could be discerned against a pale sky gradually being stained dark.

The modern buildings thinned, leaving gaps of sky and flatness between them, until the town opened out into low buildings, fenced perimeters, the sense of a military place. The girl turned the car off the highway onto an approach road. The first car followed, only hundreds of yards behind. Gant heard the orders, transmitted ahead, that the car was not to be stopped, the barrier was to be raised. High wire, parked aircraft. The pole of the guardhouse barrier lifted like an arm beckoning. Armed soldiers stood back, almost at attention as if for a visiting dignitary. The car swept past them, slid as it turned violently, then straightened again. Hangars, repair shops, control tower, vehicles and aircraft.

An army truck was parked outside the hanger for which the girl was heading, soldiers already debouched from it, but loosely grouped as if given a break from some training exercise. An officer with a walkie-talkie. The cars and the truck surging closer behind them as the car slowed. White faces peering to check on them, on Serov.

Katya drove the car into the hangar, then slowed to a halt. A cramped, low building, gaps of sky visible through holes in the corrugated roof. A single helicopter, a MiL-2, unarmed and designed for aerial surveillance. Small, light, vulnerable, its top speed seventy miles an hour slower than a MiL-24 gunship. Gant felt his hands quiver with disappointment.

406

He opened the car door, entering the tension of the hangar, his awareness narrowing to a matter of seconds ahead.

'Can you?'

'Yes, damn you!' he yelled back at Priabin. 'Get that bastard in the cabin – watch *them*!'

They were all on the far side of the car from the entrance to the hangar, shielded by its bulk from the soldiers outlined against the poor daylight; they still had a loose-limbed, uncertain air about them.

'It won't be long,' Gant murmured, reluctant to move from the shelter afforded by the car, 'before someone gives them an order they can't question – kill them all.' More troops in the doorway as they climbed out of the truck which had pursued them. A droning of rotors, closing. There was no evidence of any ground crew, no KGB uniforms. The helicopter required two minutes to bring its instruments and systems on line. If they'd fuelled up, if no one had had the foresight to disconnect, damage –

He had to know, yet he could not force his body into motion. Serov seemed to sense his indecision, but could take no satisfaction from it. What Gant had said had struck him forcibly. He might, at any moment, become a victim himself, as much a target as his captors.

'Got to go,' Gant said softly, as if to himself. 'In the cabin. I need another two minutes – you have to watch and listen for me, understand?'

Priabin nodded. 'Two minutes.' He was pale. The girl was shivering with cold, perhaps with reaction now that she was no longer driving.

Facing the entrance, they moved slowly away from the car, towards the fuselage of the silent MiL-2. Its metal was cold against Gant's backward-stretched hand. He fumbled for the handle to the hinged door of the main cabin, his legs against the undercarriage wheel.

'Get in!'

Then he moved quickly, forgetting them, aware only of his own unarmed vulnerability. He slid back the pilot's door and clambered in – knowing his back was turned to a dozen or more

Kalashnikovs for two, three seconds – then he slid the door savegly shut; as if it rendered him immune.

Polish-made, at Swidnica, under exclusive licence. A cramped single cockpit, instrumentation and systems – familiar enough. A sophisticated helicopter. Two minutes. Electrics, hydraulics – on, on, on, on –

He glanced to his left, towards the hangar door. If they blocked them –? Trucks could be used, they had two trucks out there . . . the instrument panel glowed, the hydraulic systems sighed as the pressure increased to operating level. They'd be bound to think of it.

Non-retractable tricycle undercarriage – height of the aircraft perhaps thirteen feet, height of a truck maybe ten, twelve feet, height of the doors, no more than twenty-eight, thirty feet . . . just –

– unless they closed the doors, *closed the doors!*

Ignition.

He could not avoid watching the doors. They would think of it, had to – just as soon as the rotors began to turn, proved he was a pilot, could fly the machine. Had to.

Ignition of the second Isotov turboshaft. Throttles. The tail rotor had begun to turn, and above his head the three-bladed main rotor moved heavily, slowly, as if through a great pressure of deep water. Then quicker.

Soldiers revived to purpose, hurrying. No trucks, just the sliding shut of the heavy doors. Unarmed helicopter. The rotors whirled, roared. The MiL bucked against its brakes. Holding his breath, he gripped the control column with his left hand, closing it gently. It ached, was stiff, but would suffice. Satisfied, he moved the throttles above his head, nudged the column, touched at the pitch lever. Released the brakes. The MiL bobbed above the concrete floor of the hangar. The doors began to slide ponderously towards each other, like hands closing on a butterfly. He looked up through the perspex at the disc of the rotors and was intensely aware of their fragility.

'Gant! They're closing the doors!' he heard in his headset. Priabin's voice, rising in panic.

The gap of fading daylight narrowed measurably. The air beyond the doors was as unknown and dangerous as the lightless cave into which he had shuffled the *Hind*. The rotor diameter of the MiL-2 was close to fifty feet, fifty —

He thrust the column forward with a burning hand and raised the pitch lever. The helicopter leapt towards the daylight like a startled animal. Fifty feet, fifty . . . fifty . . . *fifty* —!

The wheels skimmed the concrete, the gap of daylight narrowed, the doors shuddered closer together, grabbing at his anticipated path. His awareness was totally concentrated on the doors, on his measurement of the shrinking air. Priabin's voice was a wordless, continuous cry of protest and warning, which he ignored.

Slowly moving soldiers, slowly gesticulating officers, the now hardly altering gap of darkening air, the blur of things to either side of him . . .

. . . so that he hardly heard the noise of shots in his headset, the shocked cry of protest, the banging of the cabin's hinged door — all of them loud, but hardly impinging, hardly real.

Not even Priabin's terrible, sobbing cry was real.

As he corrected the MiL with the gentlest touch, he saw in his mirror, a figure rolling on the hangar floor, but could not identify him. The rotors, the gap, fifty feet, fifty, fifty, fifty, fifty . . . the scene was frozen now, the MiL its only moving part. The corrugated ribbing of the doors, their heavy bolts, the patches of rust, the rotors, the rotors, fifty feet, fifty, fifty —

— left hand, right, left, right, fifty — his breath suspended, everything about his body tensed and still in anticipation of the first wild lurch and the tearing noise of a rotor blade — fifty, *fifty*, *fifty* —

Air.

Fading daylight, level flight for a moment and the rushing blur beside him cold and empty. *The doors in the mirror* —

He banked the MiL savagely, then climbed as rapidly as he could as they began shooting. His body was bathed in sweat, as it returned from shock. His hand began to burn with pain. His mind, no longer icy with judgements, knew they could not escape, not in this small, unarmed helicopter . . . he was merely alive, but not safe.

He heard —

'That bastard's shot her — *shot* her.'

last ditch

Time would not elongate beyond two minutes. A clock had begun to register in his head, second after second. He could see no further than the two minutes advantage he had over any organized helicopter pursuit. Eight seconds had already passed. He was becoming accustomed to the lightness, the individuality of this MiL, which type he had never flown before.

He eased the column forward, ignoring the wail of protest and horror which gathered in the tiny cockpit. Yet he could not isolate Priabin and the moans that must be the girl by switching off his headset. The ground beneath him diminished in the last of the daylight. He flicked on the radar, studying it at once, his mind closed to the sounds in his ears.

At six hundred feet – where they can see you, he told himself angrily – he slowed the climb until the MiL entered the hover; then, using the controls with new deftness and certainty, he made a three hundred and sixty degree turn. Eyes flickering from the radar to the scene darkening outside the perspex, to the radar, to –

– the blip of a patrolling gunship already changing course, summoned back towards him. There was nothing else in the air, as yet. He lowered the pitch lever and the MiL began to drop back towards the ground. He heard in his ears Priabin's plaintive cry.

'Gant – you must land the helicopter. I can't staunch the bleeding . . .' Then something about *stomach, huge loss of blood, looks pale, barely conscious – pain* . . . 'You must land, we must get Katya to hospital!'

'Serov got away!' Gant growled. He had intended a question

411

but it became an accusation. 'You let him get away – we have *nothing*!'

'Shut up!'

'Listen to me! There's no way out of here, Priabin. This airplane has no *weapons*! It can't outfly a crow, damn you!'

The MiL moved steadily away from the airfield, crossing boundary lights strung below like a warning. Gant flicked on the moving map display, which glowed to life on the photo-reconnaissance main screen. The section of the PR map surprised him with its detail – getting lost would be easier with this much information.

For how long? For what purpose? Pessimism insisted, elbowing hope aside. Priabin still protested and demanded in his ears – almost inside his head now. He continued to head the MiL south, towards the old town, the Moscow road, the shelter of the river. Anywhere he could find ground-clutter to confuse their radars, low cover, even a place of concealment. Because he had no alternative. It was simply a matter of time – thirty-eight seconds of the two minutes' freedom had passed. In the gunships, APUs were already warming-up, rotors waited to turn, hands were poised near throttle-levers, final flight-checks were made, orders poured into headsets. He dismissed the crowding thoughts and switched off his radar. The solitary patrolling gunship was not in pursuit; it was waiting for new orders, for the pack. The tiny MiL drifted no more than forty feet above scrubby, frozen fields, scattered wooden buildings.

Gant studied the helicopter's main instrument panel. A PR adaptation, familiar enough; cameras, low-light TV, infra-red, neither defensive nor offensive systems, just recording instruments. The moving map slid with him, repeatedly throwing up details that suggested safety, soon dismissed and ignored. Tyuratam's lights glowed against the darkness to port and to the south-east. In his mirrors, the Baikonur complex was a haze of white light.

They had nothing now, only Priabin's wild story. What they needed – what they had had with Serov as their prisoner – was proof, corroboration. This – *Lightning* . . . He shied away from the

412

thought. They intended it; they would achieve it. Their mad wild card on the table, changing the basis of the game, declaring the eventual winner. *Lightning*. He could not think of it rationally, thus refused to think of it at all, except to understand that there was nothing he could do to prevent it.

Survival dictated other priorities. He watched the moving map record his increasing distance from the hangar and the airfield. Sixty-two seconds of the two minutes had vanished, slipped from him. He felt weary, hungry, still numb in parts of his body and mind from the shock of escape. Hope had drained him of adrenalin.

'Gant? Gant, are you there?' he heard.

'Yes,' he snapped.

'She's unconscious – I, I think she's dying . . . for God's sake, turn back and land. I'll show you the hospital complex – turn back before it's too late.' Priabin's voice was strange, as if a recording of a long-past crisis. Gant remembered the Finnish border, the woman's body cradled in Priabin's arms beside the car. The girl in there, evidently dying, was Anna, not the junior KGB officer with whom he worked – maybe even slept.

'No,' he said carefully, firmly.

'Yes, *damn you!*' Priabin almost screamed in his head.

Gant flicked on the radar. Nothing ahead of him. Against the town's haze, he could see power lines, radio masts. He threaded a course dictated by the details of the map, designed specifically to assist low altitude, even night flying. He flicked off the set again.

'No. She's dying – you said it. You can't save her – or yourself, that way. She's on your conscience, Priabin,' he added without pity in his voice. 'You messed up back there – the girl got shot. It happens.' Better to finish it quickly, encourage the rage, burn it off like gas from a well. He needed Priabin's brain, not his feverish, guilty imagination.

And Priabin raged; cursing, blaming, pleading. The MiL drifted south slowly, hidden by folds and dips, masked by ground-clutter. Gant poised his hand over the radio, waiting to tune to the principal military frequency. He would need to know when they began the hunt, how they began it. Priabin's anger slid into incoherence, into harsh breathing, sobs, then a soothing murmuring to the unconscious girl.

Gant exhaled carefully, deeply. The haze of the town was closer, the road and railway and river no more than a few miles ahead. Lights from a scattering of homes, headlights on a minor road to the west of him, bouncing and imitating searchlights; the image made him shiver with anticipations. Yet, with only the haze ahead and in his mirrors, the scattered lights, the last strip of orange-gold marking the always indistinct desert horizon to the west, the murmuring voice of Priabin – it was all unreal; deadening like a sedative. The MiL was comfortable now, like a familiar car. He flicked on the radio, tuning it.

A roar of voices after the swish of static. Like a great anger. Command, commands, commanding – eventually a voice emerged, and it did not seem to be that of Serov, even distorted by rage and distance. An older voice. Snapping out orders, giving advice, directions. The hunt was up.

Literally. Airborne, the first two gunships, heading south at close to maximum speed. They wouldn't care if, at first, they overran him. *Kill on sight, destroy on contact, end, finish, make certain, no survivors, destroy on contact . . .* the litany unnerved him. He returned the set to its neutral, safe swish of ether. He would not be able to evade them. Fuel gauges registering full . . . he'd get no more than – what? One-fifty, carrying only two other people in the main cabin? One-fifty. The western shore of the Aral Sea? Not even that far. Gant groaned.

Priabin's voice was silent. Just an occasional movement, the scraping of a boot on metal, the whispers of a shivering body in his ears. A small, weak, unconscious groan. He listened instead to the retuned radio.

Positions, speed, altitude, pattern, all immediately supplied, as if they were reporting to him. Once the pattern was established, they might go to another channel or into code – but it was all too diffuse as yet for the controller to resign the authority and success of the search to his units. He wouldn't be able to see most of them on radar because they were keeping low now, rushing through the early night, eager and assured. Positions, visual scan, IR traces, ground-clutter –

'Priabin.'

'What?' A man startled from sleep or reverie. His voice was dull with misery.

'We, we need proof! Proof they can't mistake or misunderstand. *Real* proof – not like those tapes. Real . . .' The idea was still formless. 'Right. Like – pictures . . .' He clenched on the thought, grinding his teeth, forcing its birth. 'TV, infra-red – *cameras*, right? Transmission, video recording – range?'

'What?'

'What's the *range* of this damn' transmitter?' he bellowed.

'I – I'm not sure – a hundred miles, fifty, I don't know.'

'Then you'd better hope.'

'Why?'

'You use it, to transmit PR pictures direct?'

'Sometimes –'

He lifted the MiL over power cables. The road was ahead, cars moving along it, lights rising and falling, spraying out into the dark countryside. Scattered houses, the early moon, stars. The darkness appeared unsafe.

Nothing in his mirrors. The two minutes had come and gone. Two minutes thirty. At high speed, they wouldn't be more than a minute behind. Maybe a minute and a half – then *use* the time!

'Aralsk – the nearest KGB office . . . receive the pictures?' He was incoherent in his struggle to shape the idea. 'Uuuhn,' he groaned, as if the notion resisted and he were grappling with it. '*Damn* it!'

'I don't know . . .'

'Talk to them!' he yelled. '*You* talk to them. Is there a radio back there?'

'Yes – what pictures? Gant, what –?'

'Maybe some . . .' His voice was soft now, his breathing stertorous but relieved. IR, TV – low-light TV, transmitter, recorder, cameras of different kinds in the main cabin, Priabin would have to describe them . . . Christ, Priabin was going to have to *use* them!

His voice gabbled. The idea was loose, slippery. He held onto it only by bellowing the fragments.

He had slowed the MiL almost to a hover, twenty feet above a darkened and dilapidated wooden building. Barn or warehouse. Its bulk – he dropped alongside it, but kept his undercarriage perhaps six feet above the ground – disguised his radar image. Lights streamed along the road. Headlight beams washed over sand, over the ditch alongside the road, caught the gleam of icy railway track, all as if seeing him rather than simply moving across his sight. His head rang and whirled, his voice was breathy, threatening to crack.

No more than a minute now, the clock in his head insisted.

'Assembly building ... shuttle vehicle – laser weapon aboard?' He did not pause for a reply. 'Pictures – *pictures*! From the doors ... roof – shuttle and weapon, all we need ... transmit to KGB receiver – proof, other people know, Moscow – *everyone* ... otherwise we don't survive, this could keep us alive ... once their secret's blown, we might be safe – assembly building –'

His voice failed.

'Gant? *Gant*?'

'What –?'

'It's madness – you realize that? I *can't* do it!'

'Forget her!' he roared back. 'Forget the woman – she's *dead*, Priabin – we're all dead unless we get some leverage – now. Understand me? I can't get us out of here, I'm not Captain Marvel. Can Aralsk KGB pick up a transmission?'

Priabin was silent for a moment, then he said: 'I'll ask them.' Then, as if uttering a betrayal, he repeated vehemently: 'I'll *ask* them!'

'Do it now,' Gant said with a sigh he could not prevent. He almost added something more sympathetic about the dying girl, but refrained. Priabin's conscience, his grief, was inconvenient, possibly dangerous.

Gant held the MiL in the hover, seven or eight feet from the ground. Beyond the road, the river caught the first pale moonlight like a winding slug-trail. He felt a breeze elbowing against

416

the fuselage, heard Priabin's breathing, his movements in his ears. Let his own body subside.

Not the doors . . . the booster stages had been moved to the launch pad, the doors would not be open. The roof, then. Skylights.

Holding the MiL occupied his instincts and his limbs. His mind cooled. TV camera and even infra-red . . . Priabin would have to get out of the MiL, use an IR lens on a still camera, unless –

'You got a portable TV or film camera back there?'

'Um – yes, I think so.' Priabin searched. He heard the man pause, then sniff audibly. 'Yes. Videotape recording, not TV.'

'OK – use that. I'll take TV –'

'Can you operate the equipment?'

'Pray I can.'

He had been assessing the control panel. Lights, camera, action – yes.

'Gant –' Priabin protested.

'Not *now*!'

He summoned the sections of moving map he would require. The main assembly building which now housed the shuttle craft and the laser weapon was more than twelve miles to the north-east. He assessed the distance, the obstacles with a strange detachment. A ring of silos, an intricate web of roads and railway branch lines, test facilities, factories, support areas . . . danger symbols, restricted areas strung like the constituents of a minefield. His hands were aching and his legs cramped from holding the helicopter still in the now turbulent breeze. He looked up, seeing navigation lights amid the stars. Nothing yet.

'Is the girl secured?' he asked, as if of a piece of cargo.

'I –'

'You want to save her pain, Priabin, make sure she can't move,' he instructed through clenched teeth.

'Gant!'

'Just do it. You talked to Aralsk yet?'

'They're standing by for a transmission – it's all right, I explained that our office's receiver was out of commission. They don't know – *yet* – what it is they're going to see.'

'When they get the pictures, tell them to transmit them direct to Moscow – they can do that?'

'They'll have to use a relay to Gur'yev or on to Astrakhan, even Baku . . . to the nearest satellite facility.'

'Warn them to be ready on that. There isn't going to be much time. OK?' He attempted to trust Priabin; but images of the dead woman on the border road, defeated him. Priabin would work with him – possibly. Priabin had his own life to save – possibly. But the dead woman and the dying girl – what had they done to him? 'OK?' he insisted. 'You ready?'

'No,' Priabin replied immediately. 'But we're on the same side, Gant. For the moment, and by the strangest accident – but we are. I have to stop them, too. There's nothing standing in my way,' he added as if he divined the source of Gant's doubt. His breathing was harsh, contradicting his statement. Gant let it go.

'OK. Talk to Aralsk, then get ready to use that video camera.'

Begin.

The MiL rose gently from the shelter of the wooden barn. The wind cuffed the fuselage as it moved out of the shadows, into the betraying moonlight. Bright moon, strong wind – Gant loathed the night.

He scanned the night sky, his gaze sliding from the starry darkness towards the wash of the moonlight. Nothing. No lights, no insect silhouettes. The wind struck the fuselage. He glanced down at the moving map display. Twenty feet above the ground, the MiL began to move north-east, away from the Moscow road, towards the main assembly building of the Baikonur complex.

'I should not have had to come here, Serov – I should *not* have had to *come!*'

Serov's broken arm was held in a sling made from someone's uniform belt. His face was ashen with pain, his whole bulky form somehow diminished by his injury. To Rodin, he appeared – for once – subordinate. Rodin's voice echoed in the empty hangar. GRU officers and men had retired to a respectful, even nervous distance, anticipating some kind of detonation. Rodin slapped one removed glove in his palm, as if weighing a selected target. Serov had become the object of his rage, but more than that; the general felt a desire, almost a need, to vent some deep, anguished wrath on the man who stood in front of him. There were pools of light-rainbowed petrol around them where the stolen KGB helicopter had stood.

'I – comrade General, I am sorry that –'

'Be quiet, Serov – be quiet before you say something that further displays your incompetence.' Rodin's glove slapped into his palm like an anticipation. His staff, too, stood away from the two of them; near the open doors of the hangar – through which the American had flown the MiL and *escaped* –! It hardly bore consideration, it made his body overheat, his collar seem tight. It evoked intense contempt, even hatred, for this, this *creature* in front of him.

Rodin cleared his throat of angry phlegm. 'They *will* be found, Serov, within the hour. At liberty, they are an element of the most critical importance. This American – Gant – you seem to have underestimated him just as you did the KGB officer. You *let* them take you!' The anger was back, and he did little to suppress it. His hand moved, without restraint, slapping the glove hard across Serov's face. The colonel's features winced as he jerked his head aside. Colour appeared on his grey skin, below his left eye.

'You –' he snarled.

Rodin knew. Some deep instinct convinced him that Serov was involved in Valery's death. He could not analyse or even continue the idea. His wife was broken, and he could feel pity for her; just as he could feel his hatred of Serov. He knew that Serov, too, understood. His eyes gave that away.

'I will make it my duty to inform *Stavka* of this day's business, Serov,' he promised. Had Serov killed his son? Impossible . . . but he had had something to do with it – had he hounded the boy? Showing him his future, in a cracked and distorting mirror? Had he destroyed Valery? 'They will be recaptured,' he continued, as if some rehearsed and uninvolved part of him continued with the business of security, and *Lightning*. 'The measures taken must not fail . . . it is now out of your hands, Serov. Rather, it is being

419

put back into your hands. You'll come with us to mission control and run the search from there. Understand? You *will* succeed.'

'Comrade General, my arm —'

Rodin waved a dismissive glove, airily. 'There is no time to have that set and plastered. You will come *now*. You have control of four gunships and another eight helicopters, as well as GRU and army units. You will use them to find these runaways — *come!*'

Rodin turned away from the ashen, carefully neutral features. His stride did not falter. Inside himself, he felt a dark tide moving his heart and stomach. Now, now he could blame others, entirely, for Valery's death . . . others would pay. Valery would be — avenged. The record put straight.

He reached the tight, expectant knot of staff officers. He waved them ahead of him out into the evening and the icy wind. He looked up at the stars. Somewhere out there, one small helicopter posed a danger. Critical — but it was difficult to believe that the American could evade the hunt for more than an hour or two . . . before midnight, before the shuttle and the laser weapon began their journey to the launch pad, he and Priabin would again be in custody — or dead. He felt the wind snatch at his breath. It flew away like smoke. He bent his head to climb into the staff car's rear seat.

Dangerous, but not mortal. He looked out of his window. Serov was cradling his broken arm as he came out of the hangar. A gunship droned overhead. More distantly, lights flashed from other MiLs. Searchlights flooded down from the bellies of two other insect shapes in the distance.

'Mission control!' he snapped. 'Quickly.' Then, as he made to settle back into his seat, his glance turned once more to Serov, waiting in the cold for his own car. He tapped his driver on the shoulder as he heard the gears bite and the engine note strengthen. 'Wait!' he snapped, and wound down his window. 'Serov!' he called. 'Come here.'

Serov walked the few yards in evident discomfort. He leaned slowly, like an old man, to the open window.

'Comrade General?'

'Where will they make for, Serov? What will they attempt?'

'Telephone – radio?' Serov replied dully. 'Priabin will want to talk to Moscow Centre.'

'Exactly. Where, then?'

'Aralsk is the closest office with the necessary comm –'

'Then do something about Aralsk! I don't care what it is – close the office, commandeer the equipment, destroy the place if you have to – just make it impossible for them to use Aralsk KGB. Understand?'

'Yes, comrade General – at once.'

'Driver – you can go.'

The lamp set beneath the MiL's belly was on. The monochrome television picture, four inches square and set above the control panel, showed the uneven ground over which the MiL passed with grainy inexactitude. Gant flicked off the camera. The surveillance equipment was effective in searching for moving figures, and vehicles – it would have to be good enough from the roof of the main assembly building. Distance to target, seven miles. Groundspeed, less than forty miles an hour.

Ten minutes now. Occasionally, in his headset, their voices barked and called. Areas clear, coordination with ground troops, consultations with the command post – Serov's voice was back, strangely weak and old, but decisive with what Gant sensed was desperation. The other voice had disappeared. They were concentrating the search to the south of him, to the west, too. Looking for a fleeing animal. He was within the net but they were still casting it and not pulling it tight. He huddled close to the terrain, slipped beneath power cables, nosing like a dog rather than flying – but he had reached the curving rampart of silos, tracking radars and the power grid at the perimeter of the military launch complex to the north of Tyuratam.

Noises in his ears. *Nothing, clear, sweep of area completed* – and always Serov's angry dissatisfaction whipping them on. Silos like craters surrounded him, passed below his sight and the cockpit coaming. Priabin had been silent for a long time. Occasionally, he heard the girl coughing or moaning. He deliberately dissociated the noises from any human experience. They were only the distant night-sounds he had heard in Vietnam; monkeys calling or men burning. Eventually they merged and lost identity.

The network of power cables straddled the road he was following. He slid gently beneath them, crossed another road, two parallel railway lines. The craters of the silos slipped behind him; radar dishes stared like blind eyes, ahead and around the MiL.

With the lamp on, at his speed and lack of height, they were no longer looking for him; he belonged with them, as familiar as a uniform or a waving hand. The wind, however, waited to ambush him. Rocked and jolted the MiL, rendered it egglike and fragile.

Six miles, five and a half. Lights along the flank of a low building, presumably a factory. He lifted a little and passed over it, splashing the light like a declaration of intent over the roof and the shadows that clung about the eaves. Dropped the MiL behind the building, moved on north-east. A truck stationary on a minor road – the glimpse of searchlights playing amid fuel storage tanks – a soldier looked up, his face white in the light for an instant, his eyes blind, his hand –

– waving.

Gant exhaled noisily.

'Priabin?' he said softly. 'Priabin? Is the girl . . . how is she?' Asking after the girl, assuming sympathy, was like touching wood, or crossing his fingers.

'Unconscious again.' Priabin's voice was dragged by pity and sadness. 'Gant –'

'Don't say it,' he warned.

'But, *afterwards* –!' Something continued to protest within Priabin, like a qualm of conscience he could not be rid of.

'Afterwards, we hide until the cavalry comes for us,' Gant confirmed. 'Serov would kill us – *you* – as soon as he could. I might be valuable – you wouldn't be. You took him – he'll kill you even if everything's blown up in his face. Understand?'

'Yes, yes, dammit, Gant, I understand,' Priabin breathed, as if not wishing to be overheard.

Four miles now –

A haze of lights, like a stadium's glow after dark. The assembly buildings for Soyuz, G-type boosters, satellite final assembly, Salyut construction and training, shuttle craft assembly . . . laser battle station assembly . . . target. Three and a half miles and five minutes away. He felt himself tense.

A net of moonlit roads, the trails of purposeful snails. Cars and trucks moving, swaying and bouncing their lights. The navigation lights, the downward-thrust searchlight, of one of the hunting gunships away to the north, another walking white limb of light to the south-west. He felt the tension constrict like drying bandages wound much too tightly. It was a moment of drowning extended for minute after minute, mile after mile; holding his breath for longer and longer.

The haze of lights was nearer and individual stars of light had begun to appear. A row of lamps along a road, clusters of lights over loading bays and railway tracks. Two miles, a little over three minutes –

– dogs barking. *Area clear*, directions and orders, new headings, callsigns . . . he had begun to understand their movements, recognize and determine the position of each helicopter that reported. They had reached the point of farthest travel and were turning to trawl back in; they were on the point of pulling the net tight around him.

A mile and a half.

There was no escape afterwards. Merely hiding, if they survived.

'Aralsk,' he said gruffly through his nerves. 'They still standing by?'

'Yes.'

It had suddenly seemed important to ask, as if Aralsk hung by a slender thread, another spider dangling as dangerously as the MiL he was flying. His helmet chafed where sweat had sprung on his forehead and neck, then dried, then appeared again; tide-marks of his successive fears.

'OK – you understand what you have to do?'

'Yes.' A boy's small voice, reluctant but obedient.

'The battle station – don't finesse, Priabin. Just use the zoom to close in on it, and hold the shot. Let them see the shuttle, then what's in the hold.'

'We won't need –'

'Damn you, just do as you're told! You don't know *shit* about the ten *seconds* that follow what you're asked to do. You don't know *anything!* We need all the ammunition we can lay hands on.' Stop it. Wasted energy, he told himself. 'You're the back-up,' he continued in a calmer, more official tone. 'Just get the shots – OK?'

'OK.' Silence, then the sliding back of the cabin's main window on the port side, directly behind him. The main observation window. Priabin must be leaning out, watching the assembly complex slide closer like a great fungus of light. Then he heard Priabin say: 'Gant?' His voice seemed to hold a threat, but was without excitement.

'What?'

'I've just remembered how much I want to kill you.'

Gant's wrists jumped with reaction, his body shivered.

'I don't need it, Priabin. Not here and now. Just do the job.'

Then he attended to the callsigns trickling through the ether. Headings, groundspeeds, reports, requests. Headings . . . they were moving back, closing on mission control, he presumed, from where the hunt was being coordinated. A point only two miles or so behind him. He was the fly in the centre of the web. The closest helicopter, by his guess, was little more than five minutes from him, coming in from the north-west.

Half a mile. Less than a minute. He could see the main assembly building quite distinctly, ahead of him. Scattered trucks, the locomotive that would tow the shuttle out to the pad, soldiers gathered like ants around their parked vehicles. It all seemed enlarged, as if viewed through a telescope of exposed nerves. One quarter of a mile. He flicked off the lamp in the MiL's belly because now it drew attention, conspicuous in so much light. He banked the small helicopter lazily and hung tilted sideways in the hard-lit evening, approaching the vast building which rose like a line of cliffs. He ascended gradually, innocently into the air until he could see beyond its vast corrugated roof to where Baikonur vanished into the dark.

He glanced soldiers staring up at him disinterestedly; a glimpse of the yellow locomotives, the grouped trucks, a sense of the renewed wind, as it banged at the fuselage. Then, as he levelled, he could see only the huge, sloping roof beneath and around him. Target. He drifted the MiL slowly, very slowly, along the gully that ran between the two sloping cliff-faces of corrugated sheets. Looking for the skylight he needed.

The channel between the two slopes of corrugated iron seemed endless, so slowly was the MiL moving forward. Noise beat back like blinding sunlight from the roof, deafening him, making it almost impossible to hear Priabin's shouts in the headset. His eyes scanned the length of the roof on either side, studied the mirrors, looked ahead, again and again. As if he expected the helicopters to jump into sight like giant fleas.

Tension beat like quick, successive waves of a storm; his ears throbbed. Too slow, *too slow* –

Yet he spoke calmly to Priabin, enunciating clearly; the volume a yell, the tone one of encouragement. 'You can *see* it?' *Twelve*, he counted. Twelve of the skylights on either side already passed. How many? 'Where will it be? Remember it . . .'

Priabin was counting, too, as he leaned out of the cabin window. But he had to lean back inside each time he spoke, and shout above the rotor noise, holding his microphone against his lips.

'Shuttle – moved to middle – building . . . laser weapon – cargo hold. Middle, *middle* of the building – eighteen, eighteen windows!'

Gant strained to hear, and to believe. It had to be like an X-ray, and as accurate. He had to be above the right skylight, he had to be able to *see* the shuttle and its cargo hold on the tiny TV screen in front of him. To point the camera lenses downwards, hold steady, let the videotape soak up the images below like litmus paper – all the while juggling the MiL in the wind that howled down the channel between the two slopes of iron.

'OK, OK,' he replied. '*One-eight*, eighteen.'

Fourteen, fifteen – close now. The clock ticked in his head as precisely as ever. The closest gunship was less than three minutes away.

He couldn't use the IR sensors on board. Too much icy metal directly around and beneath, too vast a space within. It had to be guesswork, relying on what Priabin had already described of his last visit to the assembly building – rubber-necking like a tourist – and his estimation of the present position of the shuttle and its by now adjacent or even loaded cargo. He *had* to be able to *see*!

. . . seventeen, the helicopter seemed to hang like a model in a wind-tunnel; undulating, disturbed, but not flying. Seventeen . . . eighteen – *eighteen*.

He held the MiL-2 at an angle that was difficult to maintain, its whole fuselage tilted away from the roof's slope. The skylight was blacked out, as he had expected.

'Eighteen!' he yelled.

'Eighteen!' Priabin cried back at him, his voice almost lost in the noise and the wind.

'Are you ready?' Gant estimated the skylight was directly beneath one of the wheels of the tricycle undercarriage. Priabin had to check.

'*Yes!*'

'*Camera?*'

'*Check!*'

'*Go!*'

He strained his hearing but caught no sense of Priabin's boots clatter onto the corrugated iron when he dropped. Then he saw a bent, hunched, almost-lying figure just ahead of the MiL's nose; waving. Greatcoat flying, boots losing purchase, camera straining at its straps, face white with fear and tension. He was frantically directing the nose of the helicopter away. Gant shunted delicately in the wind, with a vast expense of energy and adrenalin. He waited, arms and shoulders crying out, until

426

Priabin stopped waving; raised his thumbs. He was so close Gant would have seen the gesture clearly without the aid of the lamp's splash of light, which he'd switched on once more. *Now –*

He dropped the MiL's starboard wheel. He heard the noise, felt the damage, the restraint of the skylight's remains as he tugged the undercarriage clear and righted the helicopter; returning it to its abseiling posture against the slope of the roof.

TV screen. Priabin was waving wildly like an excited child. TV screen. He studied the viewfinder's image. The crater of twisted metal, broken wood, splinters of glass, shards of wooden black-out –

Focus.

There –

– what he had come for. *There –*

He caught his breath. On the tiny television screen the viewfinder's monochrome image wobbled, blurred and then re-focused. The maw of the shuttle's cargo bay gaped, the long-nosed metal anteater of the laser weapon hung over it, suspended from a crane. Caught in the act.

Gant could see Priabin at the farther edge of the skylight he had broken with the undercarriage, his hands waving and pointing, the video camera clutched against his chest – then operating. The light from the MiL's lamp splashed into the skylight. Wait, wait –

He switched on the videotape, holding the image firmly, with vast effort, his muscles aching with the strain of holding the MiL against the buffeting wind. The tape began running; evidence, proof . . . he'd done it, he had it all . . .

Then the alarm, even as he cautioned himself once more. Wait –

– the first shooting, from inside the assembly building. Antlike figures staring, running, posed to attack or panic. Glass still showering down, shards of wood and buckled metal rattling and bouncing on the flanks of the shuttle – smaller than its target, *Atlantis*. Gant's thoughts raced, uncontrolled. The alarm would be reaching the closing gunships – shock, response, orders, further concerted response. Full speed, heading certain – kill,

kill, *kill* . . . now, the closest MiL was half a minute away from the corrugated roof. The knifelike channel was like a cul-de-sac, trapping him. The videotape slid softly, with aching slowness, gathering the images that were required. Bullets struck the belly of the MiL, whining away, their high noise audible in the roar of the rotors. In their panic they risked the MiL being damaged and crashing through the roof, onto the shuttle.

Priabin had drawn back, stunned by noise and the bullets. Gant yelled into his microphone.

'*Get back inside* – that's enough – *enough!*' Priabin looked towards the cockpit with the sudden movement of a startled deer. His headphones and their lead had been forgotten; Gant's voice had boomed in his head. He raised his arms in acknowledgement and scuttled back beneath the MiL's shadow. Television screen. The helicopter bucked in the wind's violence and the videotape recorded the corrugations of the roof for six seconds until he juggled the image of the shuttle and the laser weapon back onto the screen. Soldiers, too, and gesticulating ants. He could not prevent the surge of success catching at his breathing again, making his whole frame weak –

– a flea jumped; a giant flea . . . up over the lip of the roof and down the slope towards him; seconds to weigh, decide, obey the voice that was crying in Gant's headset – kill them, *kill them.*

It happened in the slowest of motion. He glanced at the scene through the skylight, the frozen arm of the crane, the dangling anteater of the battle station, the shuttle's gaping maw – and the movement of the gunship seemed just as frozen and recorded. Sense of the tilted MiL, the noise of the cabin door banging shut – the movements of his hands like those of an old man – then his MiL jumping away as if to continue some rapid abseil. The gunship bore down and over him, and he sensed the machine he flew falling backwards, then dodging like a small, agile opponent as the cannon beneath the gunship's nose opened fire. Tracer rounds hurt Gant's eyes by their proximity.

'Gant –!' Priabin yelled, then cut off his voice, realizing his helplessness.

The MiL-2 rose up the opposite corrugated cliff, as if backing away from the bully of the gunship. He hopped the helicopter over the peak of the roof, flinging it like a stone away from the assembly building, and up into the darkness. The gunship turned like an angry adult towards a disobedient child, the cannon still firing in short, awful bursts of tracer.

He turned on the radar. There was no point, no purpose in concealment; he needed to see them, even as his peripheral vision glimpsed winking navigation lights less than a quarter of a mile off to starboard.

Never this close, never this close before — obsolete fighter aircraft tactics and manoeuvres gleamed like false lights in his mind. Useless to him.

'Transmission!' he yelled. 'Do they acknowledge in Aralsk?'

'Yes — yes!' Priabin shouted in his ears after a silence which was filled with the noise of the MiL and the girl's moaning. 'They want to know what it is!' Priabin seemed almost amused, a feverish excitement making his voice high and boyish.

'Tell them to re-transmit!' Gant yelled, his eyes flicking from the scene beyond the perspex to the radar screen. Three of them now, including the gunship still firing its gleaming bursts of tracer, unstitching the darkness. Gant was caught in a wash of light for a moment as he drove downwards and beneath a great sagging loop of cable. Unnerve, *unnerve*, he told himself, his hands twitchy with anticipation, his body bathed in sweat. 'Tell them to re-transmit *now*!' It was as if he projected his own immediate fear as far as the Aralsk KGB office. '*Now!*'

In his mirrors, the heavy *Hind*-D, like the one he had flown into Baikonur, hopped over the power lines and came on. Gant estimated distances. The rocket pod beneath one of the *Hind*'s stubby wings bloomed orange. Voices yelled and countered in his headset.

He was half a mile from the main assembly building, heading east. He banked savagely, the whole area of his mirrors seeming to be blinded by the orange glow from the *Hind*'s port wing. Capable of penetrating eight inches of armour, thirty-two rockets to each pod, four pods on this gunship. One hundred and twenty-eight chances to kill. The first burst passed alongside his flank as the helicopter lay on its side in the air for an instant. Range, twelve hundred metres . . . he was almost out of range. The smaller MiL could, just, outmanoeuvre the *Hind* at low speed. He flung the helicopter towards a long, low warehouse. *Shut up*, he yelled silently as the girl cried out in pain and terror from the cabin behind him. The *Hind* possessed poor low-speed handling qualities. But there were four of them now, the second closest perhaps less than a mile away, the others converging as orders were screamed and reiterated over the radio. Gant hurled and twisted the MiL through the low canyons of the warehouse complex.

'. . . lost them,' he heard in his headset.

'What?' he shouted back. The engines of the helicopter whined and screamed as he turned violently. He felt the whole airframe shudder. The MiL's shadow loomed like a hunchback on the wall of a building, light spilled from an open door. The mouth of a furnace glowed. Industrial support unit. He was still heading east, his undercarriage skimming the concrete, his twists and turns as tight and violent as he could make them. The girl must be in agony at the assault of G-forces.

'Lost them. Gone *dead!*' Priabin shouted. The mirrors were clear for an instant, as if he were alone.

'Dead?'

'Just cut off – middle of conversation. About to transmit on to Baku, for the satellite.'

'Forget them. They won't be able to help.'

'– happened?' was all he heard in reply.

'They're *dead* – you said it yourself!'

The single videotape was all the evidence that existed. A *Hind* turned into view at the far end of a long corridor formed by the walls of two buildings. Smoke, sparks flaring from beside the cockpit, another welding job or a small electrical furnace – sparks, flash from the eager *Hind* astern. Rockets.

He jumped the MiL-2 into the air like a startled cat. It jerked rather than flowed upwards, and the rockets passed like a firework shower beneath the helicopter's belly. Explosion as they diverged, one striking the wall of the building, penetrating the corrugated iron, another exploding on impact. The remaining rockets raced on, their flame suddenly dying out.

He rolled the helicopter in a banked turn over the roof of the building and slipped into the darkness beyond it. He increased speed.

The four gunships were controlled, but they had lost formation, purpose had become almost hysterical. They would leave gaps, blind-spots – Serov insisted on retaining command of the helicopters. It was a weakness, it had to be exploited. Serov was relying on radar, visual sightings, positional reports all reaching him in a constant stream, but there were whole seconds which passed between information, decision, response. Chinks, tiny gaps of time – he had to slip through one of them.

The *Hind* was back in his mirrors, lumbering until it reached open darkness and then bearing down with frightening speed. If he had only been armed, he could have taken the *Hind* easily. Outmanoeuvred it, got behind it or above or beneath and ripped it open with rocket and cannon fire.

The *Hind* seemed to have discovered patience. It was now merely stalking him. Gant increased his airspeed and the pilot in the *Hind* matched it but made no move to overhaul him. Gant rose to a couple of hundred feet, as if declaring a surrender. He was visible now – he saw the other gunships on his radar, all close, too close, and dropped the MiL savagely down in the steepest descent possible. Somehow, now that they had re-assumed a pattern and a definite purpose, he had to rid himself of one of them. Create a gap of time and air through which to escape.

'. . . she's dead!' he heard Priabin cry out. It did not matter. Priabin's grief or lack of hope did not matter, just as the girl's death was irrelevant; no more than the distant announcement of an aircraft's departure. His sole interest lay in his own survival.

He could not shake off the *Hind* astern of him. A stream of positional fixes flowed from the co-pilot/gunner back to Serov, pinning him down, like a moth to card. Darkness was unusable, hugging the ground no longer a weapon. They had him, they were closing at almost maximum speed.

Radar dishes, gantries, pylons, radio masts. He was approaching the vast power and tracking network to the east of the main control and assembly area and south of the principal launch facility. Scattered lights, a network of roads strung with pale globes, lights shining from huts, from portacabins and even caravans. A strange suburb of Baikonur. It was a minefield designed to assault helicopter rotors, but it was cover, too. It was too precious to be damaged in a wild attack. They would be cautious, almost as if unarmed. They wouldn't be able to use –

As if sensing Gant's intent, the *Hind* trailing him launched from one of its underwing rocket pods. A flare, then the quick leap of the unguided rockets towards him, enlarging in his mirrors, rushing out of the night.

He jerked at column and pitch lever.

Too close, too close –

The amphitheatre of tiered seats and rows of screens and monitors that was Baikonur's mission control was only an audience to what was happening down on the room's vast floor, fifty yards or more away from the nearest spectator behind his telemetry screen and console. A strange, vivid frenzy of voices, movement, panic and imminent success, like a dramatic, surprising play.

Military personnel mingled on the stage, at the centre of which there was a huge, upright map rising from a wheeled dolly. Cables snaked away from the map across the concrete floor. A small jumble of screens and consoles had accreted like mussels on a rock around the map. VDUs and terminals, radio and radar screens were like fragments broken from the orderly rows of equipment of the security section of mission control.

Voices called and bellowed, squeaked or rang metallically. The air was filled with sharp ozone. And tension and excitement and the sense of imminent death. Rodin looked up at the map's surface as a new area of Baikonur was displayed, keyed in from the console that controlled the fibre-optic projection. At once, a single red light jerked across the map and settled. An operator pointed a long rod towards the red light, his face intent upon the information flooding into his earphones. He acknowledged, and wiped the pointer like a wand across the grid-referenced projection. The red light remained where it was, but a snail-trail of light drawn by the pointer showed its heading, speed, its changed position on the map. Amid the telemetry and tracking complex. Two other operators traced in the paths of the two closest gunships with similar snail-trails, one blue, one green. Gant's track was red, like his light.

Serov stood beside Rodin, his headset awry from his right ear so that he could hear the general. His arm was clutched in a makeshift sling, his face was drawn and dusty grey in colour. Rodin had once more assumed control of the hunt, superseding Serov, using the facilities of the main control room rather than the security room that was Serov's headquarters.

'This American is clever – dangerously clever,' Rodin murmured, looking down at Serov.

'We have him, comrade General,' Serov asserted without the energy to perform any but a subordinate role. Weak hatred swilled in him like something slowly draining from a leaking water-butt, but he simply could not assert any strength. His arm hurt vilely. 'He's moving very slowly.'

'We can't achieve a kill, not while he's in there,' was Rodin's clipped, scornful reply. 'We can't risk any damage before tomorrow – obviously,' he added with an extra sting of contempt. He rubbed his chin while voices and acknowledgements flew about them. 'Move two mobile patrols out to the area. Their rifle fire should drive him out – up and out. Then he's naked.' Rodin pronounced the word with a curious, even salacious relish.

The operators wiped their trails of light across the map. Their earlier markings were visibly decaying. Gant and the two gunships were treading slowly, like men in a minefield, through the tracking and power grid network. The remaining two *Hinds*, the other members of the gunship helicopter flight, stayed outside the network, awaiting orders and a clear field of fire. The American could not remain there indefinitely. As long as they tracked him closely, carefully, they would have him. More gunships would have helped, but Baikonur had had no need of them. Security at Baikonur had been, until now, an internal matter, and had been effective. Should he call up units from airbases to the west and north-east? MiGs would be unusable here, more gunships –? Flying time? Too long. He would destroy the American with what he already had in the air and on the ground.

The coloured trails glowed and diminished in brightness on the screen. A slow, balletic dance, like the streamers used in a Cossack wedding dance, whirling, curling, twisting in the air . . . he was clever, the American.

Serov attended to a voice in his headset, nodding occasionally, his face greyly satisfied within the pain it registered. Then he announced to Rodin:

'Aralsk KGB office is – out of commission. Permanently. No doubt the work of terrorists,' he added with a flash of his former vivid competence.

'What did our people discover?'

'A recording of the transmission we monitored from the surveillance camera on the MiL.'

'It had not –?'

'No. No onward transmission. The recording was destroyed. There is no shred of evidence – outside Baikonur itself.'

Rodin nodded, his cheeks flushing slightly at the ease of success. His hand closed into a fist, squeezing air or an image in his mind.

'Good. Then it is contained.'

Something on the screen struck his attention, then riveted it, as if the trails of light were whirling hypnotically. Rodin became fascinated, absorbed; and there was an edge of excitement, too. Gant's MiL had increased speed, weaving and dodging like a cornered rat; the two gunships lumbered more slowly, picking their way through or over the obstacles in their paths.

The voice of the *Hind*'s pilot was breathless and excited. He pressed the headset close against his head with both hands, as if to keep the words secret. He smelt the ozone from the electrical equipment festooning the floor, growing around him like a small, rank garden, felt his heart pause, his breath fade.

'He had to lift over the cables – a moment . . . there's a patch of empty ground beyond . . . bring him down there –?' the voice yelled. 'He's lifting now – a hundred feet up, a clear shot –'

'No!' Rodin shouted into his microphone. 'Wait. He must be over clear ground!'

'. . . turning now, high-G turn . . . he's over the open area, *now* – waiting . . . ? He's banking and turning as tight as he can, spinning like a top – why? Clear shot, General – clear!'

'Make *absolutely* certain,' Rodin said. 'Damage *must* be avoided at all costs. Kill only the American – *not* our project.' Then he waited. He stared at the map, listened to the voice, his hands gripped on the earphones of his headset like claws. His chest ached with tension.

'. . . climbing, twisting to get away, I'm following him. Yes – no, almost, yes . . . climbing and turning, descending again now, climbing again, turning, turning, tight high-G turn again, yes, gone . . .' The pilot was waiting to use one of the missiles slung beneath the wings, radio-guided. At that range, it could not miss, but the pilot was waiting for the optimum moment while Gant squirmed and wriggled like a fish on a hook.

Rodin sighed loudly.

'. . . tighter turn, in a descent . . . now he's climbing again, we've got him now – tight turn, follow, then –' There was the noise of a thud. It was quite distinct, as distinct as the alarm in the pilot's voice that became a cry that was all but a scream of terror. Then his voice disappeared, there was a grinding, rending assault upon the metal of the gunship, then the hissing ether.

'What happened?' Rodin roared.

'. . . crash,' he heard dimly a few moments later. The pilot of the second, observing gunship had begun to report, his voice distant with shock.

'High-G manoeuvres . . . like the early days in Afghanistan,' he murmured. 'The American made him follow a high-G turn the MiL-24 just can't make, the rotor struck the tail-boom – seen it happen before in the mountains – *he forgot it!* He cut off his own arse, shredded the rotors, comrade General.'

'Is, is –?'

435

'Burst into flames when it crashed, comrade General. The American fried them, sir!' It was an outraged wail.

Rodin tugged off his headset and threw it aside. He raged at Serov, as if in pain: 'Kill the American! I don't care how, just do it now! Understand – do it *now!*'

Flames gouted and died quickly fifty feet below and a hundred yards away. The gunship was incinerated, out of the game. His body was racked with the pitch of tension the manoeuvres had effected.

Now, carefully . . . Their low-light TVs and thermal imaging and infra-red were all blind; flaring into indistinctness because of the fire on the crashed gunship. That had been a bonus. He could not have planned the lurch of the stricken *Hind* into a radio mast, then a radar dish, its tail broken but still flailing like that of a maddened insect, its rotors churning the icy ground – its fuel tanks erupting into a volcano.

Quick, then. He had drawn in the other three, they had converged like an audience acquired by a juggler, wondering what sleight-of-hand was in progress. He had twisted and turned and lifted and dropped the agile little MiL more and more puzzlingly, more and more hypnotically. And always over that bare, dark space of sloping ground where the *Hind* would think it safe to kill. Until it had begun to attempt to match his movements, to get behind or above or alongside for long enough to ensure the kill. Following him, turning tighter and tighter. He'd seen it happen on guerilla film smuggled out of Afghanistan by the CIA. Finally, the pressure on the rotors from the created G-forces was sufficient to slap the rotor tip down onto the tail boom like a knife of dramatic sharpness slicing through flesh. A stagger in the air, a maddened, dervish whirling, then the crash and the explosion . . .

. . . seconds ago already. He edged the MiL-2 through and beyond a sprouting clump of subsidiary radar dishes. Firelight flickered and washed over them, threw his shadow.

Tracer roared and flashed past the cockpit, the fuselage of the

436

MiL jumped and bucked, struck by cannon fire. He lowered the helicopter even closer to the slightly undulating ground, his airspeed minimal, his body twitching and shifting in his seat as if he were trying to manoeuvre only his physical form through the jungle of cables and pylons and dishes that confronted him. He attempted to steady the MiL, tense against a renewed burst of firing. Changed course once, again, again, as he waited for the damage to the MiL to become apparent, even deadly. Instinct compelled him to dodge and evade even as his mind explored his body, the cockpit, his sense of the main cabin. Something was wrong with the MiL . . . his shadow had been spotted, one of the gunships had loosed off cannon rounds more in desperation than certainty . . . but something was wrong with the MiL; the sensation of tight bonds becoming looser, the sense of a car's brakes becoming spongy, its steering soft, unresponsive. He could feel it in his hands, in – in his *feet!*

The rudders were slow in responding, the helicopter had acquired a determination, growing every second, to drift to port. He touched at the rudders with his feet . . . the MiL was drunk, hard to keep on its heading or to manoeuvre.

He emerged from the tracking network's forest almost at once. The passive radar warning had been improved on this helicopter, none of the gunships behind him had radar locked on. For the moment, they'd lost him, just as he had hoped.

The MiL yawed, almost zig-zagging as he struggled to bring it back onto its heading, south-east towards the road and the river which marked the boundary of Baikonur. Darkness, space, lack of habitation, he'd seen it on the moving map and decided to lose himself and the pursuit there, then –

But the lack of plan no longer mattered. He wrestled with the increasingly drunken helicopter, his injured hand on fire, the veins standing out on his wrists, his muscles in arms and now legs aching like overstretched . . .

. . . no radar pick-up anywhere. They were still blind. Tyura-tam glowed away to starboard, but darkness pressed on him. Undulating ground, gritty sand flying in the downwash of the rotors. Stars overhead – he could see them now. He groaned aloud as it took whole seconds to swing the blunt nose of the helicopter back to face the heading he demanded of it. Southeast. He was flying much too slowly, much too drunkenly. If the remaining three gunships in the Baikonur *zveno* acted in concert, if Serov directed them coldly rather than in rage, they'd find him before he got ten more miles.

Radio noise . . . silence, apart from the hiss of ether escaping like a gas. They'd switched to a secure frequency. He had lost them, just as they had lost him.

The radio silence intensified in his head, as he struggled to maintain his heading against another lurch of the MiL to starboard. The lights of Tyuratam stayed directly ahead for whole seconds before they slid back to starboard. 'We can't get another ten miles in this machine,' he finally announced. 'It's shot, Priabin. Understand? It's over – finished!'

FIFTEEN

the limits of the cage

It seemed the icy wind blew the fleeting sunlight like frozen scraps across the tarmac of Geneva's Cointrin Airport towards the rostrum and the band and the guard of honour and the dignitaries and Air Force One. It glanced from the airport buildings in splinters of brightness that hurt Calvin's tired, stinging eyes. The cards on which his address was printed in large, black handwriting appeared about to be plucked away by the wind. His hands were already almost numb with cold.

The anthem completed, he heard the silence that seemed to stretch away on every side until the wind filled it. He glanced down once more at his speech, then his eyes roamed almost without focus or purpose across the scene; an undirected camera. Cameras –

He alerted himself, adjusting his features, to the battery of long-lensed cameras and the bobbing, shoulder-resting TV and film cameras. The scene closed in as the clouds once more masked the sun and the surrounding mountains seemed to retreat; even the snow on their flanks appeared grey.

He began speaking. Below and to one side, Remsberg, Danielle, and Giordello the chief negotiator, were arranged like figures in a tableau. In front of him, the guard of honour, the military band, the cameras; the rest of the world. He coaxed depth, vigour, honesty into his voice, adding the ingredients like a careful but dishonest chef, while fragments of his situation spun like slow coins in his memory and imagination. The slowing down of the US laser programme, *Talon Gold* and the other projects, because of cost and by his orders . . . the frantic race they would now be in to recover the lost years . . . his country's

439

inability to match the Soviets for at least five years, so DARPA claimed . . . the contumely that would haunt him to the end of his life once the existence of the Soviet weapon became known, as it must . . . the terrible, helpless clarity with which he saw the whole awful race to destruction beginning once more. During the last strains of the anthem, his heart had been beating sullenly under his hand as he saluted.

'. . . to the people of the whole world, I say this – we are here to make an end of the beginning. This is a time of hope – as an illustrious predecessor of mine once said, *we have nothing to fear but fear itself*. I ask all of you to remember that. Fear is an old coat we can, thankfully and by the blessing of God – *throw away!*' The wind seemed to catch the emphasis in those words and fling it away, so that he hardly caught the sound of his own voice. Nervously, he glanced down at his wife; who smiled. Remsberg, the Secretary of State, was watching him keenly, Giordello's dark features displayed only rigid formality as he stared ahead. Then Danielle, sensing that his thoughts were wavering, urged him on with the address with a quick, decisive nod of her head.

The Soviet army at Baikonur had gone to their Code Green customary security status a day early, but there was nothing in that . . . they wouldn't launch earlier than scheduled because they were safe, in no hurry, no sweat . . . Gant was lost.

'All of you have seen the nuclear arsenals of our two nations being declared, withdrawn, dismantled. This is no game, no quick popularity stunt – *we mean business!*' At the hustings, at a rally, that would have brought an explosion of shouting and applause. Here, in the wind and the briefly returned sunlight, only a ripple of diplomatic applause.

'You have heard, many times over the past weeks and months, of the importance of this place and this time. I can only repeat that to you now, and to echo the words of the great writer, Charles Dickens – we must begin the world. Let us begin the world together. Thank you and God bless you.'

A moment's pause, then he raised his right hand and waved. A drowning man, he saw himself to be. A man of destiny, so his features proclaimed and the occasion suggested. He stepped down from the rostrum into the company of the Swiss President and the members of the Federal Council, the members of his own party, the Soviet ambassador and his retinue. A shoal of black Mercedes saloons drew slowly towards them like the constituents of a funeral procession. He shook hands with warm automatism, smiled and offered a suitable *gravitas* to everyone who looked in his direction.

On the bonnets of the cars, stiff and rattling little flags. The flag of his country, the hammer and sickle, the United Nations blue, the Swiss white cross and the flag of the city of Geneva, the eagle and the key. The same symbols cracked and writhed outside the main terminal building. The eagle and the key – the American eagle and the key to the prison. He could not avoid the idea.

John Calvin climbed into the rear of the appointed Mercedes and felt himself slump like an invalid into the soft upholstery. Danielle clutched his hand as if to comfort and congratulate in a single gesture. He gripped her hand, patting it up and down on his thigh, as if measuring solemnly the passage of some short, remaining period of time.

The plantation of firs surprised him, coming out of the evening darkness with the sudden leap of something animate and mobile. He lifted the MiL, restrained its swing to port, and leapt the trees as if they were part of a racecourse. Then slowed the helicopter even further, so that it hung lazily above the ground. The nose yawed to port, the rudder pedals were spongy and unresponsive. Whatever the damage sustained it was intermittent, but each time it returned it was like the nearing crisis of a fever, shaking the helicopter more violently, making its control all but impossible. His hands and feet and body and awareness all knew that the MiL-2 was becoming unflyable. Ten miles or ten minutes – no more. There were no additional factors in the equation . . . the MiL was finished.

– lurch, yaw, the trembling sense of fragility as the whole airframe shuddered with his effort to re-establish control. The tail-rotor bit, swinging the tail back into alignment. Sweat dampened his forehead and armpits. Gant looked down at the small plantation of firs, curved like a windbreak. Moonlight revealed light, bare soil stretching away southwards, a cluster of small, warm lights beyond. Farming country, reclaimed desert. Irrigation channels and ditches scarred the flatness. Dykes and canals.

The passive radar receiver was silent. They'd lost him. Maybe they considered him still inside Baikonur, couldn't yet believe he'd slipped through the net. The radio was silent, too. He could not find the Tac-channel they had switched to, hadn't the freedom of his right hand to reach forward to do so. He had to grip the controls fiercely every moment, despite the throbbing ache in his bruised hand, fighting the sensation of lack of control, of the emptiness that lay under his feet. They'd find him soon . . . a car or cart on a road, a farmer's ear, a soldier, a disturbance of ducks or cattle . . . something would give him away.

He held the MiL in the hover, in a small space of relief when the rudder pedals responded. What to do –? He felt empty at any thought of abandoning the MiL, however fragile and damaged, yet he knew he would find no secure cover which would enable him to examine the aircraft and possibly repair it. He would become the honey-pot as soon as he put down for any length of time.

To abandon the MiL . . . on *foot*? Find a car, any vehicle, drive – the thousand miles *to Turkey or Pakistan?* Or just to – the nearest *surviving* KGB office . . . and what happened to him, then? After the success, when Priabin turned around with the look from the houseboat on his face . . . ? Gant shivered; the airframe was obedient like a grazing horse around and beneath him.

What should he do?

Go – rudder pedals responding . . . he turned the MiL gingerly like a child balancing on one leg and turning through a complete circle . . . gently, gently. The wind had lessened, as if satisfied the damage provided a sufficient complication of the situation, but he was still wary of it. He held his breath as the nose swung slowly like the lens of a surveillance camera, remote and obedient. He was through eighty, ninety degrees, the tail stabilized, the MiL steady on the spot and at a constant height – fifty or sixty feet. One hundred and ten degrees –

– buffet of wind, then, as if displeased at his skill. The tail swung, the nose yawed violently. Rudder pedals more necessary because he had passed the downwind position of the turn and the rate of turn had speeded up. The extra force of the wind demanded more rudder – too much, too quickly. The MiL turned on its side like someone about to die, and as he righted the machine the thin, rippling darkness of the fir plantation was instantly closer. The MiL was shivering throughout its fuselage. The nose was swinging out of control, the helicopter was becoming a wild sycamore leaf at the mercy of the windy air . . . north, west, south, east . . . the helicopter began to turn like a dancer in some mad balletic spin, faster and faster . . . north, west, south, east, north, west . . . it would fall in a moment, undirected and on open ground near the firs. Terrified at the thought of fire, he stop-cocked the engines and then pushed the main electrics switch to OFF. All he had left was rotor inertia between himself and the trees – he had to *control* the crash . . . He drove the MiL downwards the last few feet, felt the undercarriage touch, then dig and skid and snap . . . saw the rotors eating at the trees like flailing saws, saw the tail as he looked over his shoulder lurch against young firs and gouge and snap them . . . then crack open Rotors grinding with a sick and hideous noise, then one snapped, and the MiL lurched into a slide, a fall, a stillness.

Still.

He heard silence ascend through the scale and become as real as noise. It had taken only moments. He had thought nothing, imagined nothing, simply waited for the crash to be over. He had known it would not kill or injure him; it had just been the end of the MiL.

Then he breathed, raggedly and loud and often. And heard Priabin in his headset. Shaky-voiced, almost afraid to do anything but whisper.

'Gant? Gant – are you all right?'

Gant stared through the perspex, through fir-branches and smeared resin. A small gap of starlight and moon-sheened sky.

No huge tear in the fabric of the plantation . . . good. The MiL was tilted, but there was no surviving tail to thrust out of the trees.

'OK,' he murmured absently before the minutes ahead invaded his thoughts. 'OK. You?'

'OK, I think . . .'

There was a quiet horror in his voice, from the other side of shock, on behalf of the dead woman. Now, Priabin would blame him more than ever. Become dangerous. That was the future and he dismissed it, sliding back the door of the cockpit. He heard a thin branch snap, felt the chill of the evening invest the cockpit. Released his straps, climbed awkwardly up and out – dropped to the ground. Branches cracked under his feet. He smelt seeping fuel on the cold air.

He looked up – cover? Almost. He had driven into the firs sideways-on, at a downward angle. Some of the trees had bent and slipped back like dark curtains while others had snapped or leaned drunkenly. Night – all night, perhaps. Unless they came very close, they'd see little until daylight.

The main cabin was intact. The tail-boom had snapped off behind the aerial lead-in, a third of the way along its length. It stood like a ruined statue less than thirty yards away, masked by trees.

The door of the cabin swung open. He turned quickly to face Priabin, then took off his helmet and threw it aside. Immediately he listened to the night, his ears still ringing from the headset's confinement. First, the disturbed cries of birds, then the soughing of the wind in the firs. Nothing else. Baikonur's single gunship – *zveno* had lost his scent.

Priabin's face was a white, pleading mask in the cabin door. Gant realized that Priabin's shock would delay him. He felt a resistance mounting within him, but he accepted Priabin's priorities for a few moments longer. He did not want to look at the girl, as if he had contributed to her –

– he had, he admitted.

Clambering up and into the MiL-2's dark main cabin, he heard his own breathing, heard Priabin's too . . .

The girl became reduced in importance. He did not enjoy his

renewed sense of his own priorities, but accepted the necessity of disregarding the girl's death. Priabin had covered the girl's body. She was — Gant made himself believe — no more than a heap of coats on the cabin floor. He stood very still for some moments, staring at the fuselage. Guilt lessened, faded. A heap of coats.

Slowly he realized Priabin was murmuring her name, over and over. The sound contained grief, guilt, affection. He could not tell Priabin it was time they departed.

Maps, torch, the gun, flares, even the radio . . . ? At least, if he couldn't remove one of the sets, he had to listen. He had wasted time here, he thought ashamedly, yet he was convinced he was right. The girl was dead — he had to survive. He had to know where they were, what they were doing. He jumped down to the litter of fir needles and broken branches on the plantation floor. He listened again. They were still safe. He looked at his watch, holding its dial close to his face. Six-fifteen.

He clambered back into the cockpit. Snatched out the folded, heavily-creased maps from the pocket beside his seat. Found the torch, snapped the rifle out of its clips behind his head, high up on the cockpit bulkhead. Cradled these things like precious possessions. He needed to use the radio. Reserve battery power only — if the aerials had not snapped off, if the set had not been damaged . . . He checked the code cards in the slot beside the set. The helicopter's usual KGB pilot had scribbled the military channel frequencies below his own codes . . . Wednesday. He hesitated, then switched on. Voices leapt into the cockpit's silence.

Almost at once, he realized their error. Some unidentified aircraft? No, a vehicle moving on the north-south road beyond Dzhuzaly. As much as fourteen or fifteen miles away to the north-east. What was it? *Patrol tried to stop a truck, no camouflage or insignia — broke through the barrier, patrol vehicle damaged, unable to pursue . . . All helicopter units to proceed immediately . . .*

Black-marketeers, drunken soldiers, thieves, it did not matter which. Time had opened like a carelessly-left window, and they could climb through it like burglars. They had to take advantage of it.

Gant continued to listen. Different crises signalled like lamps in a storm. The three remaining gunships of the Baikonur *zveno* had already acknowledged, and detailed their changes of course to rendezvous to the north-east, where the truck had broken through the barrier. They each reported no contacts in their current sectors. Serov – he recognized his voice easily – was too eager, too ready to believe; deceived by his need to recover the situation. Rodin, the general, was riding on his back. Gant savoured Serov's error. He listened to the man divert a troop-carrying MiL-8, a couple of road patrols in light vehicles. He heard him direct units to erect roadblocks, order UAZ light vehicle patrols to cordon off areas. He listened for a moment longer, then turned off the radio.

As he climbed down from the cockpit, he carefully cradled the rifle, torch, maps, bars of chocolate. He paused for a moment, then climbed reluctantly into the MiL's main cabin.

Even the exercise of power in desperation was a source of satisfaction, Rodin realized. His voice raged with insistence, unreasonableness, even threat, his features were highly coloured, but none of them dared sustain their objections in the face of his determination; his power.

'The launch will take place in nine and a half hours from now,' he repeated like the closing of a door on some argument in a distant room. 'Not tomorrow afternoon, gentlemen, but before dawn. The weapon will be placed in its orbit one hour later. It will be used as soon as possible thereafter. Do you understand me clearly? You all have your tasks –' He had not paused for an answer to his question but plunged on. 'Your responsibilities. See that you carry them out. It is now –' He glanced at his watch. 'Six-thirty. Launch time is set at 4 a.m. tomorrow. Very well. Dismissed, gentlemen, dismissed!'

They moved away from him, their boots echoing on the catwalk where he had gathered them. He did not concern himself with their faces, the expressions they might now allow themselves. He had issued his orders. It was simply a matter of telescoping the launch schedule from twenty-four hours to nine and a half. The task could be accomplished –

– must be. The American was still loose and his sense of Serov's ability to stop him had diminished. His sense of other and larger failures had increased. He felt the distance to Moscow as tangibly as the black thread of a telephone cable, and *Stavka* at the other end of the connection. He would have to tell them, but not yet. His goal was clear. He must achieve the object of *Lightning* before there was any possibility that the American could reach a friendly border – reach *anyone* at all. Priabin might have persuaded him that it was best to try for a KGB office within the flight radius of the stolen helicopter.

Their – their *freedom* maddened him like a goad. He was diminished by their being at large, hampered and confined by it. While they were at liberty, he had only the illusion of action, the illusion of choice. They had evidence for the old men of the Politburo, including Nikitin the *social reformer, the open hand of our society* as *Pravda* called him again and again! Rodin's hands whitened in their intense grip on the guardrail of the catwalk. He was blind to the scene below, as if undergoing some strange fit or blackout. Nikitin and the others would raise their hands in horror and back away – disown the army and the laser weapon and the research and development programme and continue with their emasculation of Russia's defences. They would not stop until they had butchered the army, just as the pig Stalin had done – for other reasons – in the Thirties. The motive did not matter; the country would be weak, ineffectual, unable to defend itself. *The open hand of our society* . . . baubles, television sets, cars, packaged food, was what Nikitin offered them, and, and they seemed to *want* it . . .

Rodin shook his head. His vision cleared. The weapon was directly beneath him, loaded and locked into the shuttle craft's cargo bay. In minutes, the cargo doors would be closed, the signal would be given and the shuttle would begin its journey on the transporter. It should take thirteen hours for the transporter to reach the launch gantry – twelve at best, and another three hours to hoist it on top of the booster stages. He had ordered the

447

whole operation to be completed in seven hours maximum. Beyond that, fuelling would take another two hours, and final checks a further half-hour. Then – launch. Nine and a half hours. Impossible, they claimed. Do it, he had insisted.

Power, emanating from the scene below, the renewed urgency he saw and sensed, the speed of movement, the first noises of the closing of the cargo doors of the gleaming shuttle. Power –

The logic of what he intended was inescapable, yet it seemed elusive. It was his responsibility. He *had* to demonstrate the weapon's capabilities, like a crude sideshow trick to capture the attention of peasants. Othewise, the Politburo would retreat, renounce –

He nodded his head. The transporter's locomotives roared and howled below. Still-life for a long moment, everyone watching. Then, with a tremor like anticipatory nerves, the shuttle moved inches, then a foot, then more . . . A cheer, echoing in the vast spaces. He looked up rather than down, at the splinters of wood and the crazed metal that hung from the shadows of the roof. The American had broken in like a vandal, stealing evidence. The glimpse of the broken skylight, the vague future it sketched, confirmed his decision. Serov had to recapture them. Meanwhile, he would put the weapon into orbit . . . then think, consider the consequences of his decision. The shuttle was moving slowly, inexorably now towards the gaping main doors. He smelt diesel, ozone, metal, heard the cry of mechanical effort.

If the American lived, if Priabin proved . . . ? A howl of protest around the world like the noise of Krakatoa, its cloud of contumely following. Russia would be vilified, the situation thrown back in their faces – and the army, *he*, would be responsible . . .

. . . desperation, he admitted. He would have caused – what? War? No, not with the Americans, not war . . . what, then? He shook his head, not knowing, knowing only that if he did nothing, if *Lightning* were to be foiled and defeated, there would *be* nothing – a weak army, a weak Russia. Surely they would understand, as he did. He nodded his head this time. The locomotives were half-way through the doors into the night.

Stavka would agree with him and, in time, so would Nikitin and the others.

Bleakly, he qualified his optimism. Even if they didn't understand, he was not prepared to leave his country and his service defenceless as the Americans seemed ready to do. He could find a calming sense of purpose in that.

'I want to know which way out they plan to take – now!'

Drugs – no. Beatings – no. Electrodes – no. Sense-deprivation – too long, and *no*. He wanted to employ the instruments of his craft. With Priabin, he had underestimated, miscalculated. Not taken the man seriously because he looked little more than a boy and had messed up badly in the past. Here, with Kedrov, it was different. He wanted to use the *skills* . . .

But it was a matter of power, the power of his presence, his will. Like recovering a lost faculty. He knew that this was part of a programme of recuperation, like a special diet for an invalid, and however much Serov wished to ignore insight, he could not avoid that debilitating image of himself. Priabin had *held a knife at his throat* and he could all but feel its vile tickle now as his throat constricted with remembered fear and present hate. His broken arm throbbed, but he could easily have clenched his fist and beaten it time and again into Kedrov's face, lying there on the pillows and looking helplessly up at him. He had to gut Kedrov by will and presence alone, without the other aids.

Kedrov's eyes blinked a number of times. Serov could see his soft, exposed throat swallowing, again and again. Antiseptic and the other disliked hospital smells filled the small, narrow room in which Kedrov had been restored to something like his former self, drained of the drugs.

Eventually, Kedrov said in a hoarse whisper, his throat evidently sore from tubes: 'I don't know . . . I don't know anything.' He shook his head slowly from side to side like an uneasy sleeper to emphasize his denial.

'You *must* know!' Serov snapped, then controlling his voice. 'The American was coming for *you*. You must know the *route*!'

'I – don't . . .' Kedrov sighed. Fear trembled on the point of overcoming lassitude, but failed. His eyes appeared weary and damp, his skin almost translucent.

Serov felt an itch of anxiety that he had to prevent from becoming a shudder. The truck that had crashed through the roadblock had been a false alarm – *drunks!* They'd crashed into a ditch – he'd see they got years for what they'd done. Afghanistan was too good for them. His hand clenched behind his back, his nails biting into his palm. When he heard they were drunks, he had felt deeply unnerved, almost too weak to stand upright. He hadn't yet reported to Rodin – Kedrov and the idea that he knew the answer had come like a desperate last gleam of daylight. And the man didn't *know*!

Must know . . .

'You must,' he murmured in a voice he would normally have disclaimed as his own. 'You know, Kedrov, you know.'

Again, Kedrov shook his head slowly, sleepily, like a child not wanting to hear any more of a story, wishing to sleep. Christ, had he had himself driven like a madman from mission control just for *this*? It was ten minutes since they'd found the drunks, since the gunship *zveno* and the other patrols had been scattered once more to resume the search . . . ten minutes wasted. He wanted to shake, beat, terrorize, but knew he needed the self-respect that only Kedrov's breaking at the sound of his voice, would give him. And Kedrov hardly heard, hardly cared that he was in the room with him.

Priabin and the American had made a fool of him. He knew the story of his humiliation had become common gossip, common property in GRU headquarters. People sniggered behind his back, out of earshot. Serov wanted to beat –

'I don't,' Kedrov confirmed.

'Who was your American contact? How did he get in and out?'

'Train . . . car? I don't know. He brought the transmitter to Orlov's, then we never saw him again . . .' Kedrov was willing to talk freely now, without drugs or fists. It confirmed that he was telling the truth when he claimed to know nothing. Of course he knew nothing!

'What about the others?' he cried. 'How were you recruited in the first place? Not by the old man, surely?'

Serov felt the edge of the bed press against his thighs. He stared down into Kedrov's open, amiably uninvolved features. The man might have been smoking hashish, or lying back smugly after coitus.

'No. Years ago . . . I was recruited in Moscow when I visited my sister. I wanted money – oh, a lot of money, I offered –' He smiled, then continued: 'I offered my wares, the Americans wanted to buy . . . the laser weapon was a real bonus.' Immediately he paused, his eyes began to leak tears which ran into his ears, then wet the pillow at either side of his head. Kedrov appeared to pay no attention to them and continued to murmur his story. 'It was my way out, to America. I would have money, a flat overlooking Central Park, a new identity, women, good clothes, anything I wanted . . .' There was no emphasis, no timbre in his voice. 'I would have had everything I ever dreamed about.' His eyes were still leaking, and Kedrov seemed to be staring at something through his tears. 'I didn't know who was coming, how they would come, which way we would leave – I only knew they had to come for the photographs and everything I could tell them . . . I think it was all a last-minute thing, too hurried to work properly.' His tears neither increased nor diminished, his voice simply stopped speaking. He did not look at Serov.

Serov looked down at Kedrov's features, then turned quickly away. Their blankness, their introspective tears, their unawareness of him, their pale resignation, all defeated him. For Kedrov, he hardly existed.

He slammed the door of the small room behind him. The GRU guard snapped to attention, his rifle vertical, barrel in front of his face. Serov hardly looked at him as he snapped:

'There's some rubbish that needs clearing out of that room. See that it's done tomorrow morning – dispose of it!'

He walked down the corridor towards the lift which would take him down to his car in the basement garage . . . where Priabin and the American –! He stared at the carpet beneath his feet, acknowledging no one. Gant and Priabin had – had undermined him. They had made his future a simple matter of a single success or failure. The knowledge burned inside him like a poison, spreading through every organ, every artery. It increased the sapping pain of his broken arm. He had to have them, *had to*.

Gant glanced at his watch. Fifteen minutes . . . he knew they'd have discovered their mistake by now. The search would have spread out again; soon, they'd be combing this sector. Their chance to escape had gone. And he still could not persuade Priabin to move, or persuade himself to abandon the Russian. Nor did he understand his indecision; it was a huge, creeping lethargy.

Priabin sat opposite him in the darkness, the other side of Katya Grechkova's body. He had covered her pale face at last with one of the uniform parkas hanging in the cabin. Gant was slumped on a fold-down seat, Priabin sat loose-limbed on the metal floor.

'I've had it, Gant. I've resigned from the human race as of now.'

'For Christ's sake, Priabin, I *need* you!' he repeated for the tenth or twelfth time. 'You have to help me get this film out of here.' He could dimly see, with the aid of filtered moonlight, that Priabin was shaking his head. A mask of wisdom seemed palely gilded on his features.

'No. I don't have to help you. There's no point, anyway.' Then his voice became bitter, accusing. 'Why do people have to keep *dying* around you, Gant?'

'You'll die if you stay here. Listen, Priabin, get this film to a KGB office, send the pictures to Moscow. That's all you have to do, man!'

Priabin stirred his legs, as if he might get up, but he did not rise. Shook his head once more. 'I can't, Gant. I feel too tired to make the effort . . . .' He sighed, but Gant heard a choked-off moaning sound behind the attempt at listlessness. Sixteen minutes. Outside, the plantation and the air above it were dark, silent. But it was only a matter of time. 'Serov killed her like an animal – to stay alive. Isn't that your remedy, staying alive? Well, I'm not joining in, Gant . . . we can't beat them. People are too *disposable* around here, I feel cold and empty and my skin feels too thin. Do you understand? I'm *not* going with you.'

'Christ, I *need* you!'

Did he? Something like a faint and momentary spark seemed to glow in his thoughts. Did he?

'You don't, Gant. You don't need anyone.'

'Were you and she –?'

'I was *fond* of her, Gant, that's all. Now she's dead.' He paused, and then said: 'I used to be good, Gant. Like a hawk in the hover above a landscape, waiting for something interesting to move. I was good at what I did. But I stopped caring very much when they killed Anna, and I'm finished with it now they've killed Katya. I don't believe we can stop it and I don't even want to try.'

'They'll kill you, for sure.'

'Perhaps. They've killed everyone else, including that poor queer . . . or perhaps I did that.' His voice became quieter. 'Yes, I think I did that. But, it was just another moment in my skating routine. Skating across the thin ice and never falling in . . . oh, Gant, why don't you *get on* with it?' He suddenly snapped, dismissing an irritating visitor. 'Get on with staying alive. Who knows? You might even make it!' He laughed, short and soft.

'Get with it, Priabin, you can't stay here.'

'Gant – just *go*, will you? I'm tired of it. I've been through idealism, optimism, daring, excitement, all those things, in the last few hours. It doesn't amount to anything. I can't beat them, neither can you.' His voice was stronger now, with the determination of clear insight. He waved his hands. 'I didn't expect this, you know. I assumed we'd go on – until they caught up with us or even until we made it to some safe place, but, there it is. I'm finished. I don't believe anyone but the Americans could stop it now. Even if *Nikitin* knew, I don't think he'd stop it . . . perhaps he wouldn't even have the power.'

Gant stood up. The spark at the back of his mind had lit some kind of fire, which glowed dimly. His body felt ready to move.

'Then to *hell* with you, Priabin!' he growled. He quickly slung the rifle across his shoulder, slipped the torch into one pocket of the parka, the emergency rations into another, the maps, the first aid, the spare clips for the Kalashnikov – and the cassette of videotape, then the smaller cassette from the camera Priabin had used . . . all as if putting on armour. His body felt chilly, but alert. 'To hell with you,' he repeated, though he might have been expressing some good wish or merely a farewell.

'Stay well, Gant,' Priabin murmured. 'God speed.'

Gant stood in the doorway for a moment, then said: 'You wanted to kill me.'

'Not now. I can't do any more of that. It's become too real here. I think that's it. It was something of a game until I stumbled across *Lightning*. It's too real . . .'

'Stay alive, Priabin . . .' Gant's voice faded, and he said nothing more. Dropped to the ground and was gone. He was instantly absent, distant. Priabin could hear nothing of his progress.

He stared obsessively at the heap of coats that covered Katya's body, but he saw the snowbound road, the border crossing and the dead, pale face he crushed against his uniform. Anna. He'd caused her death, caused Katya's death, too, by involving her. Caused Valery Rodin's murder because Priabin had made him talk about *Lightning* . . .

His stomach felt queasy with guilt. Gant would not have understood, hadn't understood a word of the little he had said. The night was cold and silent. He looked at his watch. It might be hours yet before they found him. He patted his pockets, looking for his cigarettes.

Found the cassettes Serov had obtained from Mikhail and which he had given to Katya. Gant had forgotten them. He should have taken them . . . didn't matter. Gant wasn't going anywhere, either – not in the long term. His attempt was only an illusion of freedom.

Again, he stared at the heap of greatcoats and parkas. Katya was under there. His queasiness affected his head, made him dizzy even though he was sitting. He drew up his legs, pressing his knees against his stomach gently but firmly. His throat was sweet with nausea. He was robbed of all volition, purpose, optimism. The carefully dressed imitation he had become was exposed as a fake. He was, suddenly and completely, riddled with guilt, like a cancer. The only vague surprise lay in the knowledge that it was Katya's death – someone of whom he was merely fond – rather than anything else that had so completely robbed him of his illusions.

He was overcome by an accumulation of guilt, he told himself with a kind of desperate detachment, like the gradual, inexorable pressure inside a volcano.

He found his cigarettes and lit one quickly, clumsily. And choked on the acrid smoke, coughing violently and bringing tears to his eyes. He wiped them viciously. Then inhaled gently, coughed, exhaled and leant back against the cold metal of the cabin fuselage. Queasy and weak. But, he thought, as long as he remained still and did not move either physically or psychologically, staying with the wrecked MiL and his own decision, he could contain the nausea. What was it he had said to Gant in accusation –? *People die around you*. It wasn't true. It was around himself that they died. It was he who was guilty. Now, he had to be found, taken back – he had to give himself up. Meanwhile, until they came, he could still imitate calm, just so long as he remained still, and quiet like this . . .

The UAZ light vehicle was parked almost innocently, posed and silhouetted against the haze of lights from Tyuratam to the west. Its two uniformed occupants were engaging in a desultory search along the raised embankment which carried the dirt track across that stretch of the irrigated landscape. Their lamps swung and passed and waved like hands accompanying a rambling, purposeless conversation.

Gant crouched in a ditch, his eyes level with its rim, his body pressed against its slope, fifty yards from the Russian vehicle's silhouette. The noise of the approaching UAZ had growled suddenly out of the darkness, taking him by surprise as he jogged along the track, himself a clear silhouette in that deserted place.

He had dropped into a ditch, panting, shaking with shock, gripping the packed dirt with gloved fingers and shifting toes which sprinkled tiny pebbles and earth onto the ice at the bottom of the ditch.

It was almost eight. The temperature was well below freezing. He was perhaps six miles from the plantation where he had abandoned the MiL –

– and Priabin. Gant refused to acknowledge the sketchy but insistent insights, the understanding he had of Priabin. It would weaken his own resolve. Shock had drained him already and he could spare no more of his flagging energy. He watched the vehicle, watched the lamps wobbling over sand, dirt, ice, and waited. His hooked fingers were numb with the cold, their grip feeble. Voices called, the lamps turned to each other as if for company or reconciliation, then began to wobble back along the raised track. Calls, casual obscenities, exclamations against superior officers and the chill of the night. Gant felt the skirts of his parka rustled and fingered by the bitter wind that kept the sky clean.

Once, one of the remaining three gunships had passed low overhead, but had not caught him in the glare of its downward-probing searchlight. It had droned away towards the south-east. He had jogged, crept, dodged, weaved his six miles – the first six of the thousand – in good time, but this enforced halt was fatal to confidence . . . movement was its own justification.

He bit his lip, not simply to prevent his teeth from chattering. His body pressed against the chill ground, his feet shuffled in tiny movements to retain purchase. Ten or twelve feet below him, the ice was cloudy with the pale moonlight. He had passed a couple of low dwellings – a cart beside a barn at one of them, a parked tractor at another. He could not even find a car.

U-A-Z. The three letters appeared separate, distinct in his mind. Two men. For the first time, he felt the rifle between his stomach and the side of the ditch. UAZ. An army vehicle, an army radio. He wouldn't be out of touch, he'd know where they were. He listened to their voices – they were drinking something. They were fifty yards away. If he climbed out of the ditch, he would have to cross fifty yards of moonlit open ground – or be certain of killing them at this distance with a rifle not fitted with a nightsight. U-A-Z. It tempted like luxury. He ground his teeth in indecision. Eased the rifle from beneath his body, hanging on with one hand, his feet scrabbling audibly to keep him where he was. Then wriggled upwards until his elbows held him on the rim of the ditch. The rifle was in his hands. He heard the crackling chatter of a radio. Darkness faded as the moon emerged from behind a cloud. The UAZ, the intervening ground – the fire zone – was silvered, the men more solid, tinged with colour and dimension. He picked out paintwork, camouflage patching, the stretched folds of the canvas hood, the gleam of glass and metal. One of the two was partially masked by it, but clearly visible, the other was silhouetted against the haze from Tyuratam and glisteningly illuminated by the moon. Two good targets. He could even see the thin stream of urine glittering in the moonlight as the man farthest from the vehicle relieved himself. Slowly, carefully, Gant took aim with the Kalashnikov, the pressure on his elbows making his forearms quiver.

Should he? Wouldn't it be like waving a flag, pointing to himself, calling out to them? But it was a vehicle, it was movement. Fifty miles an hour, sixty, seventy, the main highway, the camouflage of driving an army vehicle and he was in uniform already, spoke Russian. He felt his temperature rise, felt the tremor still in his forearms, noticed that the man had finished relieving himself, heard the other's coarse comment on his performance . . . heard the radio crackle again, a tinny, angry little voice flying like an insect across the fifty yards that separated him from the UAZ – his finger closed on –

– they were in the cab almost immediately. The engine fired noisily in the silence. A face looking out, a white, momentary spot, then the UAZ moved and he could have squeezed the trigger and damaged the vehicle as well as killing the men, but did not, cursing silently. The UAZ roared noisily away, raising a slight flurry of icy dirt as it trundled along the embankment. He had waited too long –! The radio had summoned them peremptorily elsewhere, they had moved with the speed of guilty dawdlers and were gone. Awkwardly, he scrabbled out of the ditch, sliding over its lip on his stomach.

He stood upright. The UAZ was already out of sight, hidden by the height of the embankment. Not even the glow of its tail-lights. He cocked his head, listening, despite the intensity of his disappointment. There was a silence in the air except for the whistling of the wind. The gunships and the troop-carrying MiL-8s were elsewhere. This empty farmland to the south of the river was still, being beyond the security perimeter, the periphery of their hunt. Perhaps that very embankment represented the outer ring, the edge . . . ?

Wearily, he climbed the slope, his body hunched into the parka, the Kalashnikov clutched across his chest. He hoisted his heavy body onto the track and straightened. Two dim red eyes in the distance, obscured by dust. The UAZ was gone, and he felt he had been abandoned. Turning through a full circle, he scanned the empty sky, the empty country, flat and featureless; lightless, too.

He bent on one knee and took the small torch from a pocket of the parka. Unfolded one of the much-creased maps, flicked the beam across the map's surface, then drew its light back more slowly. Dotted buildings, scattered like specks of dirt. He found the embankment, found the direction he sought – west, after the UAZ – found the closest speck to the embankment . . . no, two, three, six specks. The name of a collective. A car –? His breath seemed to come shallowly at even the thought of a car. This – none of it – could be rationally pursued. A thousand miles lay out there in the darkness . . . he turned to the north-west, where light ran along the whole of the horizon like a false dawn. Where, he knew, Rodin the general would be not just hunting him, but making damn' sure that *Lightning* went ahead. Precisely because he was still running around loose they'd want to make sure he didn't mess up the party. The time-table would be moved up – what difference could they make to the launch schedule? Halve it . . . no, down to two-thirds, with God's good grace, two-thirds. He had until dawn, until the early morning light. A thousand miles . . .

He stood up groggily, swaying in the wind as it buffeted him. He held the rifle like a comforter. The collective was maybe two miles west, a dotted collection of buildings in the middle of nowhere. Farm headquarters, barns, and maybe a car or a truck.

He forced his legs into motion, forced his frame into a quick jog, despite the huge inertia of disappointment and futility that weighed on him. A car or truck would mean quicker movement away, would be a means of staying alive that he did not possess while on foot. It wouldn't take him a thousand miles, maybe not a hundred, but it was better than this, better, better, better. His heavily pounding boots drummed and reiterated the word, as did his pounding ears. He would stay alive, stay free for twice as long, three times as long as on foot . . . better, better . . .

His elbow seemed to pain him more in Rodin's presence, like an old wound reacting to imminent changes in the weather. He did not cradle it with his good hand, however, not before Rodin's grey, almost fanatic stare. There *was* a madness about the damned old man, he decided, even though he felt, along with the others in the room, that Rodin was right to pursue *Lightning* with all possible speed.

Eight-fifty, Wednesday evening. Digital clocks and calendars littered the walls like urgent graffiti, adding to the tensions and pressures of that vast humming room. Serov smelt the ozone of a hundred screens and keyboards and fibre-optic maps. Banks of mission controllers retreated like an audience into the shadows behind and almost above the lights. On the huge upright map nearest to him and Rodin, the American shuttle, *Atlantis*, weaved the slow path of a weary fly; a poisoned fly about to die. Serov's vitriol was sluggish without the antifreeze of his best health. The elbow drained him like a disease rather than a fracture. It was an effort to hold his features clear of pain, even during those short periods when Rodin, turning occasionally from his senior officers and technical staff, looked directly at him. His courtiers were sycophantic and filled with enthusiasm, fired with the old man's purpose. Serov knew that if they lost this one chance . . .

bows and arrows and menial tasks, cleaning shithouses like Afghanistan, training the fucking Cubans and Palestinians and Shiites in half a dozen countries. It was as plain as the nose on Rodin's face – the army's last chance to keep its grip on the Politburo's collective balls.

Rehearsing the old war-cries kept the pain at a tolerable level.

'Where is he now, Serov?' Rodin hissed at him, his head snapping round to fix his grey gaze on the shorter man. 'Where is your American and his little KGB friend? You haven't come to tell me you've caught them, by any chance?' Almost languid, almost joking – almost.

Serov shook his head, his features grave. 'Not yet, comrade General,' he said with regretful confidence. 'It is, of course, only a matter of time.'

'It had better be.' And yet Rodin was detached from the fate of Gant and that stupid little prick Priabin. The screens that curved in a crescent to their left showed the shuttle moving towards the distant launch pad, showed the waiting booster, showed the crew in their quarters – intruding on their sleep like spy-cameras. The murmurs, if one concentrated, were a chorus of instructions, orders, reports, checks. *Atlantis* moved on the map, the weaving line that traced its course slipping across Africa. 'It will be,' Rodin murmured, and turned back to one of his people, launching into an immediate discussion on the shaving of minutes from the boarding and pre-flight checks by the crew. Serov waited to be dismissed.

He gazed at the screens, the huge map, other maps, a chart of the pattern of radar and telemetry stations across the Soviet Union that would follow the shuttle in orbit, the banks of controllers at their screens and keyboards, rendered identical by the shadows and by their each wearing a headset and microphone. Cigarette-smoke rolled and billowed amid the suspended lights. He looked up towards the tinted windows of the GRU's security room. Squinting, he realized that one of his people was waving to him, urgently pleased. The immediate leap of tension and the beat of his heart enforced his fear of the condition of his nerves. Could it –?

He nodded to the unseeing Rodin, who was insisting that another ten minutes be trimmed from the handover-ingress routines, when the crew boarded. Then Serov hurried across the cable-littered floor towards the door. Along the cold, concrete corridor. He clattered up an iron spiral staircase, careful not to knock his broken arm in his haste. He could clutch it now, protect it. He hurried down the narrow corridor to a single door. He thrust it open, entering the security room surprising its half-dozen occupants. Ozone again, VDUs, radios, fibre-optic maps. The hunt for Gant was once more *their* business, returned to their charge by Rodin.

'Is –?' he began.

The lieutenant was nodding. 'Yes, Colonel, they've found it, on the ground, too . . . here!' His finger dabbed at a screen which displayed a map – where? South of the river? Yes.

'Thank Christ!' he could not help but exclaiming. Then: 'Are they still with the machine?'

'Priabin, the KGB colonel, sir – he's there.'

'But Gant is not?'

The man shook his head. Serov did not even bother to recall his name; no requirement to be congratulated or commended officially. He was just the bearer of a report. Yet a small, secret pleasure welled from his stomach to his chest. He felt the knife tickle at his collar again, the pain in his elbow surged through him as he remembered – then cleared as he anticipated. Priabin would pay, he'd beat the little shit to a pulp, with one hand tied behind . . . he grimaced. With his one good fist, then.

'What does Priabin have to say?'

'Do you want to talk to –?'

'Just give me the *gist* of it, man!' he roared.

'Sorry, Colonel . . .' the man lowered his eyes and rushed on: 'He said he was waiting for – our people to turn up. Sir, that's exactly what he said! The woman you wounded is dead, sir. The MiL suffered damage during its encounter with the *zveno*, just as they suspected – rudder controls inoperable, the report says. The American was forced to crash-land, about two and a half hours ago. Gant has a videotape of the – assembly building with him, a

461

rifle, food. He's on foot. Priabin has no idea where he's gone, and says he couldn't care less . . .'

Serov realized how muddy, how defeated his thoughts had been. The impact of what he heard struck him only after the lieutenant had finished his summary. Then he hit his head as if to jolt his mind to activity.

'Then he's on *foot!*'

'Yes, sir.'

'Thank Christ for that! You realize what it means? He's as good as in the bag. He can't possibly get anywhere on foot! My God, we've won, we've stopped it . . . tell them, the gunships, the ground patrols, *everyone* – two hours to find the American. Two hours!'

He turned away, walking across the room towards the windows. Immediately, he located Rodin. Right, you old bastard, he thought carefully, precisely. I'm no longer here on sufferance. I have a *right*.

Quenching a sneer of triumph, he turned quickly towards the door. He'd tell Rodin *now*.

Resolve and will had turned against him, robbing him of strength as they, too, ebbed. His imagination was using energy at a suicidal rate. His legs had become leaden, hard to move, and his head felt light, as if he were greatly hungry. The sense that it was hopeless, that he could go on for only a little longer, waited at the door of his conscious mind, pushing it slowly open.

Moonlight, gleaming on snaking ice, sheened on the early frost glittering across the stretches of sand and dirt. Clouds moved across the sky like great dark shoulders heaving at something that resisted their solid force. The rifle banged against his ribs as he jogged, with repeated, sapping blows. The others – the dead girl and the KGB man he hardly knew who had wanted so much to kill him, even Serov and the pursuit – were increasingly behind him, distant and unreal. His head was becoming fuzzy with exertion and defeat. There was nothing in front of the next few heavy thumps of his boots, nothing behind other than the slow distance he had come.

How many miles? Three, four since the last glimpse of the map? Gant gritted his teeth, hearing his breath roar in his ears, his blood pound. His head was dipping, his eyes joggled like a camera pointing downwards, held by some running man. Nothing had come near him, no other vehicle, no helicopter. They had no idea where he was —

— find him before daylight, nevertheless.

The certainty grew that he was merely expending energy to no purpose. His body ran with sweat, the rifle banged, even the videotape cassettes weighed heavy in one pocket of the parka. The ground beneath his boots seemed to shift, become uncertain and sandy. Trees filtered the moonlight darkly, as if hoarding it.

Trees.

He staggered to a halt, his head reeling like a drunk's, his body quivering. He looked around him wildly, as if he had been ordered to halt. He dropped to one knee, flicking on the torch, waggling the map's creased folds beneath its thin beam. The map shivered in his hand, but not from the wind which distressed his hair and was chilly on his damp neck and throat. His eyes traced the way he had come — flatness, flatness, a small plantation, yes, he remembered it, a narrow, clattering bridge across a main irrigation channel, two other planklike crossings, yes . . . this small fir plantation? His mind jogged back along the track. He did not remember, and shook his head in puzzlement and fear. Like a driver on a long straight highway, startled to realize that the last miles were a blank in his memory. At any moment, they might have surprised and taken him, at any moment. He shivered. The wind was increasingly cold, his body small and vulnerable. The track was a pale, moonlit strip running between the two dark, high banks of trees. Stars glinted coldly. Warmer light insinuated between the narrow boles of the farthest trees of the plantations . . . warmer light, represented a danger now to his exhausted mind, not a destination. He stood up slowly, like an old, arthritic man.

Breathed deeply to calm himself, but felt only colder because he was not moving. Gripped the rifle with gloved hands, but thought it to be little more than a harmless stick he had gathered somewhere. He looked up, his gaze swinging across the strip of sky he could see. It was empty, but the fact brought no reassurance.

A cloud hid the moon.

Startling him. He studied his watch, holding the dial close to his eye. It was already eight-fifty in the evening. Again he shivered in reaction at his inability to account for the past half an hour. How long since the UAZ had driven away?

The landscape refused to become less than alien, however much it resembled Nevada in its sandy barrenness. He had struggled to make it familiar but it had resisted him, remaining a place a thousand miles inside hostile borders, a place where he had no resources and no future.

He doubled over with stomach cramps, thrusting the rifle against his abdomen to resist the pain. It was psychological or it was hunger, it was not fear, it was not isolation, it was not fear – he repeated the formula of words, breathing stertorously, groaning softly. He would not kneel, would not rest against a tree, but stood in an invalid crouch as if retching silently, the gun hurting his stomach and pelvis. Eventually, the griping waves of pain receded and gingerly he was able to stand erect. His mouth was wet, his hands shaking, his body cold with drying sweat. He did feel more awake; shaken or startled into wakefulness. He squinted, studying the pale but warmer lights sparkling between the boles of the separate firs. It had to be the farm buildings of the collective. He listened, but heard only the wind, the stir of the young trees, the tiny noise of gritty dust against his parka and across the boots he wore – he looked down as if surprised to find himself still wearing the KGB uniform the dead woman had brought. His mind pursued the recent past, concluding that Priabin was no danger because he had no idea in which direction Gant had gone. Even when they found the wreck of the MiL, the wreck of Priabin, they would learn nothing except that he was on foot.

He moved cautiously, with new alertness, keeping in the

464

shadows of the trees, just off the dirt track, painted once more by the returning moon. The trees gradually opened like dark curtains . . . buildings, low and functional, with an abandoned air despite the lights that shone from them. Two, three, five, half a dozen, scattered like the counters of some abandoned game. Seven buildings, all one-storeyed, some large, the largest of all in darkness. The quiet noise of a radio creeping towards him. No other human sound, nothing moving. There were numerous windows aglow, many of them in the same building. Barns, tractor and cultivator stores, grain silos most distant of all, other huts that had all the frontier appearance of bunkhouses from an American past. He could not see a single vehicle as he crouched in the shadows of the outlying firs. As his eyes registered more and more of the scene, he saw the dim glow from even more windows, curtained. The gusts of chill wind brought the murmur of voices, the rattle of utensils, the noises from other radios and television sets. The place took on life and peril.

He stood up, leaned against a fir, studied terrain, distances, the shapes and angles of the buildings. Listened intently, then began running, crouching low, rifle across his chest, safety-catch off. His shadow, a deformed and dwarfish thing, scuttled beside him like a mocking effigy. Then he sprinted, his whole body tensed against the first cry of curiosity that would become alarm and challenge. The UAZ had undoubtedly preceded him, warned them to keep a look-out . . .

His back and shoulders banged concussively against the wooden planking of the barn. The eaves threw down darkness like a cloak. His breathing was loud, too loud, and he stifled it as well as he could, dragging in slow, hard breaths, through his teeth. He pressed his cheek against the rough, cold planking, but there seemed no sound from inside the building. Ten yards from him, an ugly breeze-block shed or storeroom. The huts with lighted windows were further away than the shed. They formed an incomplete, untidy crescent, as if a builder had begun a town and failed to complete even a single street of it. A bankrupt, isolated place. Beyond the huts, the desert country undulated

465

just perceptibly, raised banks and ditches and canals criss-crossing it; firs growing in clumps. He edged along the wall, pressing back into shadow, face averted.

He reached a blacked-out window, tried it, but it would not move. Continued. Half-way along the side wall, another window. He raised his arms, rifle now slung across his back by its strap, and pushed. The window-frame cried out, as if to alarm the workers in their huts. Gant paused, his cheek distorted against the wood. He stifled his breath and listened more intently. Rough shouting that was louder – greetings, he recognized, a casual obscenity, then the banging shut of a door. He continued to hold his breath after that for a long time, fearing the noise of a dog or another door opening, a quizzical human voice registering alarm as it discovered his shadow crouched against the wall.

Eventually, he straightened in a continuing silence filled only by the loutish wind lurching against the collective's buildings. He gently, slowly-so-slowly raised the creaking, protesting window. He felt through the opening, his fingers touching some sacking material which blacked out the glass. He smelt petrol like a heady, reviving drink. Vehicles. Oil, too, on the icy air before the wind snatched the scents away. He raised himself level with the sill, then levered his body across it, resting on his stomach as if stranded through exhaustion. He tore at the sacking, then let it fall. The darkness of the barn seemed impenetrable. None of the barn's windows let in the moon. Blinded or boarded? It did not matter. He grasped the torch and heaved his arm out in front of him, flicking on the thin beam. He played it waterily over the ground immediately below and in front of him.

Cans, empty tins, rubbish, bundled rags, a pitchfork, a workbench, concrete flooring. An inspection pit gaped like a grave. Vehicles. Oil-stains. He flicked the beam of the torch further into the room like a lifeline desperately flung. The beam wavered and darted like a small, feeble animal. He heard disturbed chickens somewhere outside. Someone coming . . . ? His body was weak, shivering. The chickens quietened, disturbed only momentarily. He grunted with relief.

A tractor's huge, ridged tyre and red flank . . . ploughshare, the superstructure of a combine . . . no good. A covered truck . . . an open-backed pick-up . . . yes. He held the beam steady, then played it like a voyeur's gaze slowly, caressingly over the small grey truck. He inhaled the scent of petrol. A pick-up – flick of the torch, a crazy, wobbling search until . . . petrol cans. Vehicle, fuel.

Gant was aware of his body straddled like a side of meat across the window's sill. He raised himself on his arms, began to swing one leg up to the sill, heard his boot scrape on the flaky wood. Wind snapped along the side of the barn. The dog's bark was on it, as if the animal itself were already rushing towards him. A human growl, questioning the dog or ordering it –

– frozen. Hands, elbows, wrists locked like a tumbler supporting the huge weight of the rest of his troupe. The quiver through his arms like a nearing earthquake. The dog again – where? *Where* –? Wildly, he swung his head from side to side. Away to his left, back towards the half-circle of huts and other buildings . . . the human voice was there, too – a door opened, someone yelled, the dog barked, an answer came on the wind – *sodding patrol, fuck the cold, ballocks to you, Sergei, coffee . . . ? Why not – heel, heel, damn you, heel . . . don't make a fuss of the bloody thing – supposed to be a guard dog – up yours, too . . .*

He unfroze and dropped to the ground, still listening intently to the voices coming on the wind. He cowered in the shadows as he heard the conversation of the two men and the low, continual growling of the dog. His head was reeling with the sense of the truck in the barn behind him. He knew the dog would come, the man would probably be armed – even if only with a voice to cry out or give the dog the order to attack. Knew he must go, must –

– dog distressing the chickens, growling with movement, the man thanking Sergei, exchanging friendly obscenities, calling the dog which therefore could not be leashed – *this way, damn you* – the voice coming closer, the man's whistling becoming louder. Go, get out now! Growling of the dog. Gant stared down at his boots. He had already left his scent, he must get as far away as possible before the dog picked it up.

He staggered out of the shadows of the barn and ran hunched across moonlight which lay like a pale carpet. His blood rushed in his ears so that he could hear nothing else. He dared not pause to try to pick up the first noises of the pursuit – as if the distance behind him threatened like a jagged crack in thin ice pursuing him as he ran. He reached the darkness of the trees but even so did not pause, his thoughts filled with the dog and its freedom, its strength and speed. Panic filled him. He could not stop running.

Trees, the narrow track, moonlight, cloud, moonlight again, a long, slow rise in the track, then a steeper dip, then the false horizon of more trees, their shadow –

He staggered, the breath knocked out of him. He leant heavily against a tree, and looked around him. A thin belt of trees beside the straight track. A windbreak for more buildings, another collective? Dogs?

He knelt down, squinting into the darkness. He could see no lights. Rising to his feet, he began to jog cautiously, as if testing either his body or his resolve; or both. Evidently, the dog's discovery of his scent had been dismissed, the opened window investigated and considered an accident. Or perhaps the man who had exchanged ribaldries with Sergei had no interest in anything beyond the limits of his reluctant patrol. Whatever, there was no pursuit ... they might have called the army; probably not. It did not matter. For the moment, he was still safe. Reassured, he jogged on.

The building had a lean-to on one side of it. It was barnlike but lower than the collective's barn. It was lightless and silent. Locked, too, he saw in the moonlight. Cautiously, avoiding any delay, he crept towards the lean-to. A row of smeared windows. Open, flat landscape beyond, itself deserted. What was the place? There was only the single building. It might be an implement shed, some kind of store ... a vehicle? Unlikely. Not this far from the collective. He moved on, regarding only his own footsteps and their exact, soft placement.

He rested in the shadow of the lean-to. His boot had kicked a tin hidden by the longer grass around the building. An oil-tin; empty. He heard, then saw, a length of corrugated iron sheeting

468

tremble in the wind. It was rusty and hung away from the lean-to. He listened, then got down on his stomach and crawled through the gap. Smelt, tasted rust. Smelt – smelt *petrol* . . . no! Paraffin –? Oil, too. Rubber, dust, concrete. His eyes became accustomed to the faint light through the dirt on the windows. Tins on shelves, tools, oil-drums, fat-tyred wheels . . . a vehicle! He grabbed the torch firmly, tugging it from his pocket. Ran the watery beam over the room. Found a door. A machine-shop, a garage – *another* garage? He moved quickly towards the door, turned the handle, opened it. Flung the beam of the torch like a challenge into the darkness. Dared not breathe. Dusty, paraffin-smelling silence.

Oil-drums, tool trolley – his throat was tight, he could not swallow – a metal blade? Wires gleamed like spider's threads. The moonlight from small windows in the eaves was faint, he had to wait until his night-vision adjusted to it. Meanwhile, he flicked the beam from spot to spot. Another knifelike blade, hanging in darkness. Wires, the dull flank of some machine . . .

Propeller blades. The fuselage of an aircraft. It was, it was – Christ-in-Heaven, it was almost *that* aircraft! He saw vividly the dust rising in a cloud from the road, saw his younger self looking up from his book, rising in astonishment from the slouch he had adopted outside the gas station's small office . . . *that* aircraft! An old biplane, prop-driven, just like the crop-duster which had been the first, the very first he had flown . . .

His mouth was dry with excitement, even as in the same moment his eyes were wet with disappointment. He had identified the pieces of the airplane's jigsaw, and seen its engine lying beside the fuselage on the concrete floor, the biplane's panels and flaps littered around it like the debris of a wreck. It was an airplane, but he could not use it.

He dropped weakly to his knees, his head bowed. His growl of refusal became more like sobbing. It wouldn't fly, he could never make it fly.

SIXTEEN

consider the phoenix

The Botanical Gardens lay blankly white with snow, the panes of glass in its iron-framed hothouses were steamed and dreary like the windows of passing buses. The glass through which he looked was also misting, along the whole length of the gallery. The lake lay beyond the gardens, and beyond that the last of the daylight caught the tips of the Mont Blanc range. The snow-flanked mountains marched into the distance, into other countries. Defence Minister Zaitsev considered them, rubbing his chin with his left hand, cupping his elbow with his right. It was an almost philosophical pose, he realized, but appropriate to the television solemnities taking place in the gallery of Geneva's Palais des Nations.

Then he turned his back on the view. He had been outside the Soviet Union many times, but to the West only perhaps on three or four occasions. He always seemed to look at such places through thick glass.

He gave his attention to the Soviet Foreign Minister, Vladimir Shiskin, who stood beside him. He had not been as successful as Zaitsev in appearing engrossed by the view. His square, sallow features – Zaitsev had to lower his eyes to the man's face, Shiskin was a short man – were alert like those of a cornered animal. While he appeared to stare across Lake Geneva, Zaitsev's thoughts had not, for a moment, left the subject that had raised itself between them. Shiskin, of course, had had to be briefed. As the most prominent pro-army member of the Politburo, apart from himself, it had been necessary to tell him – unfortunately necessary – of the compressed launch schedule for the laser

470

weapon. It would be Shiskin who would prepare, then mollify, Nikitin.

'You're satisfied, then?' Shiskin repeated. 'This is not a move of desperation?'

'No, it is not a desperate move.' Zaitsev smiled sardonically. 'Is that *your* question, Vladimir Yurievich, or does it originate with another of our little group? Were you told to ask it?'

'It is – a general feeling, my friend. A general feeling.' Shiskin seemed to acquire stature from his fiction of consensus. Zaitsev glanced at the television monitor to his left. Farther along the gallery, Nikitin and the American President were reassuring the world; basking in their separate lies. Behind them, the town's miniature image retreated into the evening darkness. The finger-tip mountains were purpled, indistinct. Zaitsev glanced through the windows again, then back to the screen. Somehow, the shrunken image of Geneva and its landscapes satisfied him more.

'Very well,' he said. 'And are you sure of our party?' He watched Shiskin's eyes. They were doubtful – as was the group they reflected. Afraid, naturally. But not deserters, not yet.

'Confident.'

'Then assure them Rodin knows exactly what he is doing – and that what he is doing has the full approval of *Stavka*.'

Rodin was – what? Panicking? Possibly . . . but that was an easy thing to do, at the eleventh hour. On the brink of *Lightning*. And – destroying the American shuttle as soon as possible would bind their group on the Politburo more closely to *Stavka* and the army. Nevertheless, Zaitsev wished he had spoken personally to Rodin . . . what exactly was happening at Baikonur? *Was* anything amiss?

He rubbed his chin once more, his contemplative gaze directed at the television monitor, from which the voices of Nikitin – speaking in English in honour of the occasion – and Calvin issued like those of distant children, crouched in separate corners of the room, speaking to each other through tin cans connected by string.

'Consider the Phoenix,' he murmured.

'What –?'

'The Phoenix. The army mustn't be allowed to burn to ashes just in order to be reborn . . . must it, Vladimir Yurievich?'

'I don't see –'

'Don't you? We are here, you and I and the others, precisely because the old men were removed. Policies have changed. Nikitin dreamed of a twenty-first century army, high technology to the forefront . . . before he decided to give the people toys to play with! He's reneging on solemn promises made to the army – for the sake of gadgets in the shops! Computer games instead of thinking missiles!' Zaitsev smiled at his own grandiloquence. 'He wants the Phoenix to burn itself to death and *not* rise from its own ashes. We have to prevent that. If we do not, history will judge us.' His tone was calculated, but he found himself impressed by his sentiments. Perhaps it was the proximity of the monitor and the events it foretold, perhaps the distant mountains, perhaps the American entourage or even all the marble from all over the world that decorated this place . . . anyway, Shiskin was nodding docilely, attempting stature once more.

'I agree, my friend. We *all* agree.' Shiskin sighed.

'Good, good . . .' Calvin was speaking from the monitor. Zaitsev looked along the gallery. In reality, it was too confined for the televised press conference, but the backdrop of the city, lake and mountains was considered too delicious to be omitted. The world's press representatives were crushed together on a steeply-raked dais and seated on narrow chairs; like an audience at an intimate little theatre club. The larger settings of the Salle des Pas Perdus and the great Assembly Room were reserved for the climax of the drama the following day. Farce? No, Zaitsev could not quite call it that. The Treaty was still dangerous . . . not quite a farce. All the elements of one, but no one in the theatre was laughing yet. He nodded slowly to himself, and realized he was nodding in time to Calvin's portentous phrases as if they were soft, commanding taps upon a military drum.

'Good, good,' he repeated, as if approving Calvin's sentiments. Then he chuckled, a sudden and unnerving noise. 'We won't fail,' he announced. The certainty of the words seemed, even to

472

him, clouded with fervour. 'We can't afford to,' he added. 'And failure is impossible.' Yes, he had achieved the right confidence of tone. He slapped his broad hand onto Shiskin's shoulder. 'Cheer up, Vladimir Yurievich, cheer up! We're almost at the winning post!'

He glanced from the screen beside them to the misting glass of the huge window. Garish lights from the city, encroaching darkness masking the lake. The mountains glimmering like weary ghosts of themselves. He shivered. He found Geneva an alien place, as if he had no business there, no right to be there.

Zaitsev removed his hand from Shiskin's shoulder, sensing that its pressure was no longer reassuring; maybe even threatening.

The press gallery broke into applause. The conference was at an end. The purpled, garishly lit darkness outside the windows seemed to rush headlong against the glass.

Foggily, he saw that it was ten o'clock. He did not understand why the hands of the old-fashioned clock on the wall should impinge quite so vividly, but they did. For a moment they obtruded more than the pain of the blows, more than the fear of Serov's unbridled rage.

Priabin fell heavily again. Serov's boot struck him in the side, sinking into his ribs. The pain slowly, irresistibly penetrated his dulled, disorientated awareness. No one else touched him. Just Serov. No one asked him questions, not even Serov. There was just the beating. *I owe you pain*, he'd announced with the voice and manner of a bank clerk; except that his eyes were fierce and greedy. At first, his people had held Priabin, but with the second flurry of blows – he could only use his right hand – and the second bout of kicks while he lay huddled foetally on the floor, Serov's men served only to drag him each time to his feet then let him go so that Serov could bull against and into him.

No questions, nothing but the beating . . . he was quite vividly aware he was becoming drunk with pain. He saw Gant drop out of sight from the MiL's main cabin, over and over again like an unending loop of film. Mostly, however, he saw Anna's dead face, Rodin's limbs splayed on his bed, Katya's form disguised by the heap of coats he had thrown over her. Gradually, these recurring images explained the beating. He had deserved it –

– and however horrible, he allowed no part of him to oppose or struggle. It was unimportant that it was Serov administering the blows.

Kick in the head, his hands had not covered it quickly enough –

– a red mist, his agonized coughing and groaning much too loud in his ears, inside his head, huge noises . . . his body could no longer tense in expectation, he felt his ribs grinding together. Gouts of pain bloomed, died, spread again, were replaced by others; an artillery bombardment. His hands moved in a slow, lost way down to his groin, clutching at that more fiery area of pain. Red mist . . .

. . . slowly, frighteningly slowly, clearing to a wet grey fog, and the noises in his ears becoming those in the room rather than in his body . . .

. . . tried to look for the clock but could not locate it. Red second hand strutting, couldn't find it – he heard himself groaning, but almost as close to him he could hear heavy, laboured breathing . . . boots – he flinched.

The fog cleared enough for him to see through a gauzy spider's web just in front of his eyes. He feared for his sight. Boots, Serov's boots, bloodstained – blood on the bent trouser knee, Serov's hands clasped together, already showing the blue of bruising, caused by uniform buttons, by Priabin's teeth, which ached and seemed loose . . . like his whole head as he moved it fractionally to look up into Serov's face. Serov, leaned forward, staring intently at him, his mouth wet and hanging open as he dragged in air . . . hands. Not clasped – the spider's web clearing a little more, thank God! – but the bruised one holding the other gently, almost kindly . . . that one was white, unmarked. Priabin made a precise inventory of Serov's hands. It seemed like a test he must pass. Short fingernails, coloured not with dirt but blood . . . the difference between the two hands?

474

Serov must have, must have, must have . . . broken his arm or wrist or something when he jumped . . . yes, *yes*! The memory from a few minutes before struck him with the force of some epochal discovery of science or philosophy, thrilling him. He remembered seeing Serov's left arm in a sling when they brought him into this room!

'Colonel, sir?' someone murmured. He hardly caught the words. The pain seemed to have been increased like the volume of a radio just at the moment he fully remembered about Serov's arm and his vision finally cleared. His body shrieked with pain. He grunted, dribbling blood. It tasted of salt. He moved his thick tongue around his teeth . . . loose? He prodded each tooth with his tongue, escaping the pain which cried and rushed through the rest of him, by narrowing his awareness. Left side, upper, lower . . . right side, lower, upper . . . front, the vanity teeth, one by one. Priabin became absorbed in the examination of his teeth.

Until dragged to his feet. Every part of him protested against the movement. They held him in front of Serov, and his body winced and hunched into itself at the suggestion of further pain.

'Sit him on a chair!' Serov's voice seemed to roar. His bruised hand waved towards Priabin, who tried to duck. Serov laughed.

Priabin felt his body dumped onto a chair, the chair prevented from tipping backwards by someone's hand. The angles and edges of the chair created fresh areas of suffering. His consciousness slowly returned to his slumped body. He looked up. Serov, clearly in focus, was watching him, his bruised hand cradling his other elbow gently.

The clock. The second hand. Ten-ten . . . where was he?

He looked slowly, cautiously around him. Three GRU uniforms, anonymously filled . . . no, one of the faces belonged to the lieutenant who had brought him back. And Serov. Screens, too. A computer console and a large-scale map projection. A glass wall to the room, tinted and almost opaque. The dull glow of numerous lights coming through it. Rows of what might have been spectators dimly to be perceived. Mission control —?

'Where's he gone, Priabin?' he heard Serov ask, and was irritated by the intrusion. His body seemed to be gradually swallowing his bruises and the rushes of pain in a general ache. He held his ribs. Pain, but no tearing sensation when he breathed. Not broken, then.

'Who?' he replied automatically. His voice was thick. He gingerly took out a handkerchief and spat into it. Like consumption; bright blood in the saliva. 'Who?' he repeated.

'You know who.' Serov's voice seemed tired, as if the real purpose of their encounter was already accomplished. 'The American. Where is he?'

Priabin carefully shook his head. Pain lurched like a solid mass from temple to temple.

'No idea.'

'Why didn't *you* go, too?'

'No idea.' Priabin dabbed his swollen lips with the handkerchief and then inspected the daubs of blood. Wiped his bruised, numb chin. 'Bloody stupid, wasn't it?'

Serov sat forward on his chair, growling like an animal.

'What's the matter with you Priabin? Where *are* you, for Christ's sake?'

Priabin shrugged, wincing against the pain the tiny gesture evoked. 'Nowhere,' he murmured. Almost anaesthetized. Strange – his whole body seemed to be going warmly numb, as if he were falling luxuriously asleep in a soft bed. 'Nowhere . . .'

'Move him over to the console!' Serov snapped, rising from his chair. It tipped over onto its side. 'Let him look at the map. It might jog his memory! Come on, Priabin – do some of our work for us . . . tell us where you think he is. While you still can!'

As Priabin was lifted and shunted across the room still seated, he saw on one of the screens a glowing image of the launch pad. The erector cage starkly lit, the flank of the giant G-type booster stages splashed white and coldly blue. It didn't matter where Gant was, after all – it didn't matter a jot . . .

The torch beam sufficed for his narrowed consciousness. He made no search for the mains switch, no move to use the shrouded inspection lamps whose cables curled like dead black snakes across the littered, dusty concrete floor of the hangar. Touching upon, sliding across, illuminating only parts and sections of angles, surfaces, planes, the torchlight was enough. He was afraid of greater light, not because the windows were open to the sky and his presence would be betrayed, but because he feared to see the whole expanse of the place at once. Some kind of hope proffered itself always just out of range of the torch's beam.

Gant moved slowly, cautiously around the airframe. His inspection had taken him perhaps fifteen minutes, a period of deliberate delay. The torch had picked out the little peaks of hopelessness as it settled on the skeletal airframe, the dismembered engine, the discarded flaps. Yet he had remained with the Polish-built Antonov biplane, fearing to move farther back into the darkness, back towards –

– metal blades, leading edges of wings, struts, flaps, the flank of a second fuselage. He was deeply afraid of inspecting the second biplane. It might prove even more skeletal and useless than this first one. So he waited for the tide of defeat to ebb. He knew it would. It was just a matter of time. His father snickered cruelly at the back of his mind, and Charley's voices rustled in the darkness like the scurrying of rats. As long as he encountered no new and greater blow, his sense of survival would re-emerge.

He flicked the torch's beam at his watch. Ten-thirty. Gant poised himself, breathing quickly and deeply to calm himself. Flicked the beam of the torch out in front of him, washing it weakly over the propeller blades, then engine cowling, *engine cowling* – the words reverberated like the echoes of thunder among mountains. He saw, with a great sigh of relief, the oily gleam of exposed valve gear . . . fuselage, tailplane almost out of reach of the beam . . . then the concrete floor, sweeping the torch back and forth, back and forth looking frantically for signs of dismantling, disembowelling.

Clear, *clear*!

Moonlight.

The darkness had held for almost half an hour, and he had been grateful for that. Now that the clouds had released the moon once more and faint, sheening light grew in a row of pale squares along one side of the building, he was as startled as if the main light-switch had been thrown. The second Antonov An-2 was ghostly in the moonlight, unreal. He moved towards it with a reluctant lurch.

Stopped. Turned back, searching along the fuselage of the first airframe. Pulled the shrouded inspection lamp and its trailing lead with him, heading back towards the second Antonov. The noise of the shroud as he slid it across the lamp tinkled in the chill, dead air. He switched off his torch, its beam beginning to fail now, and turned on the lamp. Its diffused glow glided along the Antonov's side.

Engine. Fourteen hundred horsepower, turbo-prop. Entire, intact. He moved along the fuselage. Ducked down, thrusting the lamp in front of him, then stared into the main cabin. It was the agricultural variant, just like the other biplane. Two crop-dusting airplanes wintering in this hangar, undergoing their major servicing before the spring. The metal of the chemical tank gleamed in the darkness of the cabin. He moved on.

The open inspection panel and the gap of darkness behind it made him shiver, as if newly aware of the cold. It had been too good to be true, too good . . . the battery was missing. His fist banged the tail of the Antonov, hard. A hollow, booming noise, as if the whole airframe was empty.

'Shit . . .' he breathed. 'Shit, shit . . .' Over and over; its ordinariness recovered him, as if the expletive could only be applied to what was remediable. Find the battery, it has to be here, refit the battery after you find it . . . but that was sufficiently far into the future to open the perspective of his awareness, and he clamped down on the idea. His father's snickering ceased in his head; it *was* the scurry of a rat somewhere in the hangar.

Tour of inspection. He turned, gathering and coiling the lamp's lead as he followed it back to the first airframe. His step was careful but quick. He sensed himself moving across experiences rather than within them.

He passed the engineless biplane and moved towards the door

through which he had first entered from the lean-to. He passed the diffused light over what was evidently a workbench. Spider's web. A white powder that was not dust covered everything except the surface of the bench. DDT? Residue of some dry chemical they'd been using to dust . . . . A copper tank rested on trestles, its filler lid opened. He passed it, paying out the coiled lead. He was hungry. He felt in the parka's pockets until he found the bar of chocolate from the emergency rations. Unwrapped it with clumsy fingers, broke off a large piece, and filled his mouth as completely as a child might have done. He chewed awkwardly. The sweetness assailed his teeth, as he reached the door to the lean-to.

He realized it formed a suite of offices; if they could be called offices. He checked the first one, the off-duty room. Dirty cups. He moved to the table, rubbing with a gloved finger at the rings left by coffee-mugs, dabbing at the grains of spilt sugar. He picked up the sugar bag with a snatching movement, shining the lamp into its crumpled, open neck, and softly squeezed the base of the bag. The sugar moved and altered like a tiny landslide. It hadn't been here for weeks, not even days. The coffee-stains erased easily. He heard his own harsh breathing. They were servicing the two Antonovs now, each day, each daylight.

His gaze swung along the line of moonlit windows, then down to the face of his watch. Ten-forty. Daylight would be —? Seven-thirty, but they might not come until . . . the future intruded and he angrily shut it out. Where did they sleep? Not here, they would have heard him by now, there would be heaters working . . . at the collective? The lamp revealed the ancient stove in the corner and a pile of chopped logs near it. Easy chairs, stuffing and springs gaping, grease drums, a calendar on one wall. He turned and left the room, obeying a new urgency that was not panic, rather familiarity. This was the kind of place he knew.

The next room was perhaps three times the size of the off-duty room. An opened crate contained a new nine-cylinder engine — why hadn't they installed it already? A lathe, crated propellers, an air compressor.

The third room was locked. A faded, stencilled notice claimed

479

it to be the Radio Room. He did not bother to force the lock. The fourth room was unlocked. The door opened with a creak. Something scuttled away in the moonlit shadows. Shelves in the lamplight; manuals, sheaves of documents, ring-binders, box folders. A battered desk, an IN-tray visible, even its companion, the OUT-tray. He flicked the light across the papers they contained. There were other questions wearing like blown sand at his apparent calm. It wasn't just the battery, it was whether the second Antonov was airworthy, whether it would take him – stop it!

The lamp opened his perspective rather than kept it closed and narrow. The papers – their headings, their insignia and crests, their information, threatened his present stability. He did not want to remain in what he realized was the chief engineer's office, but the search for the Antonov's missing battery was futile unless these documents answered the questions which he could no longer avoid. He passed the lamp over a row of clipboards hanging from a series of nails and screws. One of the more official-looking letters in the OUT-tray had authorized an air test and was dated six days previously. No, no . . . the third clipboard revealed two freshly made out cards, one labelled Compass Correction, the other Airspeed Correction. They were both twice initialled and dated two days earlier. The box file on the desk revealed a sheaf of papers and their unseparated carbons. The sheets itemized every aspect of the Antonov, its faults and their repair. It had to be the second Antonov, let it be the second –

His hand flicked feverishly through the papers on the desk. He was a burglar become a vandal, no longer caring to preserve any sense that he had not been there. Yes –? No, no, no, no – *yes!* Reference numbers tallying – he found the reference number of the Antonov without its engine – the repairs and the air test both referred to the other airframe, the one that was intact.

He slammed the box file shut and tucked it beneath his arm as he left the office. The place was once more familiar, even when the moonlight disappeared and the lamp was the place's only light. He crossed the hangar with confidence. He felt the dust of the DDT or whatever it was on his fingertips, noticed it on the toes of his boots in the swinging light of the lamp.

As he reached the second Antonov, the moonlight returned. He hurried now, as if the pale window squares revealed some inkling of daylight. Ten forty-five. There were small fabric flags attached to various components, each one accompanied by a card which was rubber-stamped and detailed the repair effected. Except for the battery compartment. Only the flag bearing the Cyrillic legend, ATTENTION. Kneeling, he flicked through the sheaf of forms and reports in the box file. Found –

BATTERY TIME EXPIRED AND U/S. It was dated the previous day . . . ? He flicked the lamp's glow towards the undercarriage. New tyres, but they bore evidence of at least one take-off and landing . . . the air test must have been done – then they'd used the battery from the other Antonov, the one that needed a new engine!

Where was it, then? He saw his quickened breathing as puffs of distress in the lamplight. *Where was it?* The lamp remained on the undercarriage. Mud, a few blades of grass . . . where was the battery? He hugged the box file like a life-jacket. It *had* been air-tested, then the battery had been removed, why? Was it faulty . . . ? Christ, don't let it be faulty! He stood up slowly, weighing his strength as much as his mood. Then he moved to the far side of the hangar, paying out the coiled lead of the lamp once more. He stepped over the bonding wire that earthed the airframe, feeding the lamp underneath it, then continued. He moved along the far wall until he found a door labelled Battery Room. He swallowed noisily, even though his mouth seemed dry.

The door was unlocked. He played the lamplight over the bench, over the charger, which hummed and seemed to stare at him with a single red eye. He moved closer, afraid to study the dials along the charger's top. There were two batteries, both connected. One of them was brand-new, the other was used, but it wasn't covered with the fine white powder that coated everything that had been left lying in the hangar for any length of time. He touched it, inspected his finger, to make sure.

481

Looked.

The new battery had only just been put on charge. The quivering needle on the dial was still way up. The second, the second – the needle was a little over half-way to its stop. The second battery was half-charged.

Not *enough*! It would be hours, whole *hours* yet, before the battery was able to start the Antonov. Three, four hours perhaps, too long, far too long . . .

He saw that the lamplight seemed to be trembling, as if on the point of collapse; quivering like ice about to crack open. He could not stop his hand shaking.

Telescope. Rodin's features, his questions and even the concerns that dimly lay behind them, all seemed as if viewed from the wrong end of a telescope; made tiny and out of focus and unimportant. *Where is the American? What information does he possess? What does he intend to do, where is he hiding now? Where is he heading?* The questions were all so predictable. *What have you told him of* Lightning – *what does he* know? As if it mattered . . .

As he looked at Rodin's face, Priabin felt his own bruised features, his swollen lips, the dried blood, the puffy dough his skin had become. The clock with its strutting red second hand showed eleven-fifty. It was almost two hours since Serov had beaten him. It was the tiredness, the detachment that surprised Priabin. He could not give a toss for any of it any more. Not even for this old man's hesitant, uncomfortable probing with regard to the death of his son. *What – was his . . . mood when you spoke to him? You must be responsible – you frightened him . . . What did he tell you, how did he seem to you . . . ?* Not one atom of it mattered to Priabin.

He looked down at the loosely-cupped hands resting in his lap. There were things he could grasp, hold on to, if he could make the effort to reach out to them, important things. Serov's interrogation whirled in his head like sparks from a windblown fire. There had been no more violence, only questions and a mounting impatience. Eventually, while he sat on in front of the computerized, shifting map, without answers, Rodin had arrived.

What did you learn? he'd asked when he saw Priabin's face. *This wasn't interrogation, this was gratuitous*, Serov had answered mockingly. *Comrade General . . . the American would not have told him . . .*

. . . get out, Serov, leave him with me, get your people out of here – get out!

The questions had dripped slowly, hesitantly onto Priabin's mind which, like a sloping roof bearing rainwater, could not hold them. They ran away somewhere, out of his consciousness. After some time had passed, he realized most of them related to Valery Rodin.

The screens in the room reflected Rodin's state of mind quite clearly. The launch pad, the slow, ponderous approach of the *Raketoplan* on its transporter, the waiting erector cage, the glare of lights. Now, the erector cage was around the shuttle craft, they were about to use the express hoist to raise the spacecraft on top of the booster stages. Rodin was preoccupied, obsessively so, his son's death forgotten now.

Priabin heard Rodin's breathing, magnified by the silence in the room. He sensed the man's sheen of success; yet there was some obscure sense of unrest, even unease. He shook his head and groaned at the lurching pain. Rodin looked round quickly, his features registering distaste as he saw Priabin's damaged face. Self-consciously, Priabin touched at his jaw, his swollen, awkward lips, before he spoke.

'All going according to plan, then?' he sneered. The words were indistinct, pathetic.

Rodin's eyes gleamed. He cupped his sharp chin in one hand. The other waved dismissively at the room, at the screens; at Priabin. Yet there still seemed that unease.

'Quite so, Colonel – quite so,' his voice remarked coolly. Perhaps Priabin was mistaken. This was the hour of the man's success . . . yet –? His questions regarding his son had been asked as if at the behest of someone else, like a favour. Valery's mother? Was there a mother?

483

Priabin did not wish the questions to intrude. He wanted only to be detached, indifferent. It was all over anyway, young Rodin, Katya, Anna — even Gant, wherever he was — all over. So, stop being a policeman, he told himself. The questions insisted.

'You're mad,' he goaded. His aching face reminded him of physical punishment as Rodin's eyes glared. But he continued: 'It will all come out, comrade General, even in *our* deaf-and-dumb society, it'll come out. Fifty years' worth of priceless propaganda you'll have handed the Yankees on a plate, General!' His attempt at laughter became a racking cough which doubled him over on his chair. When he looked up again through wet eyes, he saw the disdain on Rodin's face.

'Your body has the strength of your opinions,' the general observed quietly again turning to the television screen which absorbed his attention.

In a glare of arc-lights, the vast trelliswork of the erector cage was lifting the shuttle craft as delicately as a toy from the flatcars on which it had rested. It was being tilted through ninety degrees so that it would point skyward before the cranes raised it on top of the boosters. Somehow, to Priabin, it was strangely primitive; a poor, out-of-date copy of the high-technology of the American shuttle and its vast external fuel tank and the two solid rocket boosters; gleaming and sleek and filled with power on a sunny Florida morning. He'd seen countless launches of the American shuttle. The *Raketoplan*, smaller and riding on a huge missile, seemed like some vulgar, dubious imitation. Nevertheless, he watched, as fascinated as Rodin himself appeared to be. The shuttle swung through forty degrees like the elevation of some enormous gun from an old war.

New war . . .

Priabin swallowed drily.

'He killed your son,' he murmured. Rodin appeared half-disturbed from his concentration, then he whirled to face Priabin, his features ashen. Rodin's hatred made Priabin blanch, but he swallowed once more, then added: 'Serov killed your son, or had him killed. You know, though, don't you? At least you —'

'Be *silent*!' Rodin stormed, his cheeks white, his lips faintly blue. He made as if to move towards Priabin, but then forced himself to remain still. Then he shouted: 'You do not understand, Colonel, you simply do not *begin* to understand!'

'But you know, or suspect?' he insisted.

'And why should you care, Colonel?' The shuttle craft's nose pointed at perhaps sixty degrees into the glare of the lights and the night beyond them. 'To save your own miserable life? To place me like a barrier between yourself and Serov?' He snorted with contempt. 'Serov intends to have you shot.'

'With respect, that's obvious, General.'

'And you would like to take the mad dog down with you?' Then Rodin added in a quieter voice: 'The woman was your mistress, I suppose?'

Priabin shook his head, ignoring the surge of heavy pain between his temples. 'No. I just liked her,' he said tiredly.

'Then – what do you hope to gain by your accusations against Serov?'

The shuttle's nose was travelling through seventy degrees to the horizontal, locked in its cage. Priabin sensed the vast hydraulic forces, the sheer size and mass and effort of the silent, diminished scene. The express hoist would move the *Raketoplan* up the side of the launch gantry like an outside lift rising past the floors of some ultra-modern hotel. Then the craft would be settled on the booster stages. His stomach felt hollow as he realized that they would launch in perhaps as little as four hours . . . it was twelve. Midnight. He felt the need to make his words count, have effect, though he had little sense of objective. Did he just want to needle Rodin?

'I don't give a shit about Serov,' he said, shrugging with studied casualness.

'Then what? Assuming I believe yo ndifference to Serov.'

'Just the truth.' Again, Rodin snorted in derision. His attention returned to the screen.

Surprised at himself, Priabin wondered why and how he had become re-involved. Why did he want Gant to escape, make it to somewhere? Where? A KGB office? Ludicrous. It didn't matter, the future was too vague to consider, his mind too weary. But, if

Rodin acted against Serov, then the hunt for Gant would lose its edge, *might* lose its edge, he corrected himself. Serov was the slave-driver – if someone else took command, it might just leave a door ajar through which Gant could slip.

He doubted it all. Its slender contact with reality, with *that* happening inexorably on the screen, mocked him. Yet he persisted simply because he was no longer totally absorbed with guilt and self-pity. He did not wish it to leave him, he still desired the embrace of guilt. He still wanted to go on paying, even after the beating, but guilt had lost its strength. Katya, Valery Rodin, Viktor, Anna – all of them were slipping back into the dark. The immediate insisted its presence.

'Just the truth,' he repeated, afraid he had lost Rodin, who was staring at the screen. The shuttle craft did not appear to be tilting any further skywards. A delay?

'What?' Rodin murmured absently; irritated.

'He had your son killed!' Priabin shouted. 'What are you going to do about it?'

'What did you –?' Rodin turned, his features enraged.

'He killed your son like he killed your son's friend, the actor! Do you want me to spell it out? K-i-l-l-e-d, *killed!* He's a mad dog, you said it. Rabid. Your son let slip your precious secret. Your son was going to Moscow, wasn't he?'

'Yes.'

'Never mind! I was going with him. He'd agreed to talk! Serov knew that, or suspected it, and got rid of him. Like tipping rubbish down a disposal chute. Just got rid of him and made it look like suicide! Now will you do something about it?'

Rodin was still, but his body seemed to sway minutely.

Adopt revenge as the motive, Priabin told himself coldly. Just get rid of Serov, you can't control anything more than that. Get rid of Serov.

The door opened. Serov entered, his features impassive. Rodin turned towards him, with the clockwork movement of an automaton. Had Serov heard? The man's face betrayed nothing but urgency, his own security concerns.

'Comrade General,' he urged deferentially, 'we must have

486

these operating consoles, the computer map. The search is being hampered while we are excluded from this room, comrade General.'

The silence thudded in Priabin's ears. Rodin stared at Serov without moving. Then he turned his face towards Priabin. His eyes were bleak grey pebbles, his lips compressed into a straight, expressionless line. Priabin saw the turmoil for an instant, reflected in a tic at the corner of Rodin's mouth. Then it seemed his will was able to still that involuntary reaction, because it ceased almost as soon as it appeared.

Eventually, he looked at Serov and said: 'Very well. Find him — find that American!'

'We will, General, we will.'

'Be certain you do, Serov.' Rodin turned suddenly to Priabin, and he snapped: 'Colonel Priabin, come with me now!'

'But, General —'

'Be silent, Serov. The Colonel is now *my* prisoner.'

He waved the shrouded lamp over his wrist. Midnight. Then, once more, he dipped the lamp into the blackness of the chemical tank in the Antonov's cabin. Dry, clean, no residual scent of the crop-dusting chemicals they had used last season. He nodded vigorously. It would work, just so long as he could fuel up the airplane. It *would* work, he reiterated to convince himself. The chemical tank had about a three hundred gallon capacity; greater than the Antonov's upper-wing fuel tanks. He assessed the aircraft's range at perhaps as much as five hundred miles. With the chemical tank filled with aviation fuel, he would more than double that range.

Eleven hundred miles. Pakistan or Turkey. Across the border. His chest was tight with excitement as he once more recited the figures. His body felt warmed by self-satisfaction.

The wing tanks were full. All he required was to find the fuel store. It must be outside the hangar. He hadn't seen it on his approach. It had to be behind the hangar, out in the dark where the dirt runway undoubtedly was. His imagination reached out, and faltered. He couldn't get the airplane out of the hangar unless he started up the engine. That noise might bring –

– and he wouldn't have time to fuel up the chemical tank if he aroused interest.

He stood up in a crouch and climbed out of the cabin, the lead for the lamp dropping noisily onto the concrete as he jumped down. He couldn't check the flaps because they operated electrically. He'd checked everything that worked by cable, mechanically – the rudder, the ailerons, the flying controls. Checked the oil levels, the maps in the cockpit – sat in the pilot's seat, sensing the separate, unfamiliar life of the Antonov; sensing, too, its resemblance to that first crop-duster. Familiarity had been a small victory. He had jettisoned as much from the cabin as he could – most of the cabin lining, stowed equipment, the noise-reducing plywood of the fuselage walls. He had checked each of the repair cards. The Antonov would fly, but only for five hundred miles until he found extra fuel. Half the way home –

. . . *like repairing a bicycle, kid* . . .

The memory had made him grin involuntarily. He'd said that, twenty-five years ago as he let Gant help him service the crop-duster, after their first flight together. Gant had checked the pressure in the Antonov's tyres and remembered the words. *Like repairing your bicycle, kid* . . .

He switched off the lamp, and crossed the now-familiar hangar in pale moonlight. He opened the judas-door and stepped through it. He shivered in the icy cold, came more awake. He hunched into the folds of the parka, its hood dragged over his head, and rounded the side of the hangar. The wind howled in pursuit. He ran.

The battery needed perhaps two, three more hours to be fully charged. He could not cut it finer, dare not. If he drained the battery trying to start the engine, he was lost. Fuel was the necessity.

Wire, a small compound, tarpaulin. He sucked in air greedily, his teeth set in what might have been a grin. He rattled the lock. He needed something to cut the chain or snap the lock – have to go back. Gant bent down and studied the anonymous, heaped shape that was the outline of the tarpaulin. It was loosely fixed, great gusts of wind rippling it like the back of an aggressive animal. Flaps of it flew and cracked. He waited, the tension coming back into his frame.

TURBINE FUEL . . . He held his breath and waited for the wind to reveal the drum once more, reveal the stencilled Cyrillic lettering stamped on it. Eventually, TURBINE FUEL appeared. By the size of the tarpaulin, there had to be in the region of thirty drums beneath its cover. He rose and looked at the wire fence. Pointless to climb, he had to open the gates. Smash the lock. The thought of the small violence satisfied him.

He had found the fuel he needed. If he employed the pump on the chemical tank to feed the fuel via a hose to the wing tanks, the whole jury-rig would work; it *would* work. He turned away from the rattling tarpaulin towards the hangar. Twelve-ten. By four, then, with luck . . .

He listened intently, saliva filling his mouth. He wasn't mistaken. He knew the wind was carrying the noise of an approaching engine. He cocked his head to one side. Small vehicle by the noise. Coming closer. He ran scuttling towards the side of the hangar. As the moon slid behind a great billow of cloud, he saw headlights bouncing crazily as the vehicle followed the undulating dirt track from the collective. Light splashed on the firs, on the hangar. Gant crouched in the shadows.

The engine noise died. He heard the brake cranking on. Heard voices, two of them, even one man's luxurious yawn, the other's comment on the chill of the night. One of the men rattled the doors of the hangar, the other's voice disappeared into a muffled distance – Christ, if he was going to walk right around the hangar! The rifle was in the hangar – he grabbed at his pockets frantically. Found the Makarov pistol he'd snatched up in the MiL's cabin, eased a round into the chamber, holding his breath at the magnified noise of the action. Christ –

'. . . aircraft in here?' he heard.

'So those lazy sods said. Why the hell they couldn't have told us that in the first place!'

'Got the keys?' The walking man had returned to his companion. The barrel of the Makarov was icy against Gant's cheek. He pressed further into the shadows, his gaze intent upon the corner of the hangar.

'Let's have a look-see, then.'

The small, metallic noises of unlocking the padlock on the main doors, the creak of wood, the grunt of a man straining against the wind with the great sailplane of one of the doors.

'Fucking little door was open all the time!' one of them exclaimed.

He heard the large door slam back into place, shuddering as it did so, banging again and again in the wind. He strained to listen, ear against the wall, but only muffled exclamations reached him from inside the hangar. If they found, if they guessed –

Light sprang from the window above his head, making him flinch. Wildly, he looked around. An empty oil drum lying on its side in the straggling grass. He stepped out of the shadows, pocketing the gun. Dragged the drum, which whispered hollowly as he touched it, directly under the window. Climbed onto it, taking the gun once more from his pocket, slipping off the safety catch. He looked down into the hangar.

And flinched back instantly as one of the uniformed men turned in his direction. Waited, no breathing, then raised his head cautiously. They were looking at the Antonov. One of them was pointing at the litter of material he had removed from the cabin. Tossing his head in amused puzzlement, tapping one finger to his forehead. Two GRU uniforms, perhaps even the two he had failed to kill earlier on the embankment. Returning in the long swing of their patrol to the collective, learning this time of the hangar, its two aircraft ... reassured they wouldn't fly?

He watched one of the two, a corporal, move towards the door, then through it. The remaining soldier had lit a cigarette, taken a flask from the pocket of his parka. He swigged violently, wiped his chin, licked the back of his hand. Gant stepped down from the oil drum, crept cautiously along the side of the hangar. Returning moonlight searched him out. The wind slapped his parka's

490

skirts against the building's wall, and he grabbed the garment closer around him. Paused at the corner.

Listened.

'. . . say neither of them's capable of flying . . . bits missing, sir. I don't know what bits, sir! Sorry, sir . . .' The man's words were interrupted or accompanied by a tinny squeak from the UAZ's radio. The corporal was standing by the vehicle, leaning against the door, microphone in his hand, the other hand scratching his cheek. 'That's what he said, sir, the collective's engineer. Neither of them can fly . . . what, sir? OK until further orders, yes, sir. Over and out.' He threw the microphone into the cab of the UAZ. Gant darted back into the shadows of the hangar. His whole chest and stomach seemed empty as he heard the corporal call out: 'Ivan, you lazy sod! Officer says we're to stay here until further orders! Have a break, he says, but stay sharp! Suits me.'

Until further orders.

He was trapped, separated from the Antonov, unless he killed both of them. And if he did that, he'd raise the alarm for certain. As soon as they failed to call in – *every hour, half-hour, every fifteen minutes?* – the gunships would come looking for him, certain of his whereabouts. He couldn't kill them. He couldn't do anything.

'We are at T minus three hours, final countdown continues.'

Wild cheering, as if the words had released tensions in a great wave that rushed through mission control. Priabin felt battered by its strength. On screen after screen, in front of him and to each side, the shuttle craft stood on top of its massive booster stages. The last of the liquid oxygen fumed away from the flanks of the vast machine, the skeletal gantry threw its shadows down the chequerboard pattern on the missile's side. The cheering went on, deafening and exaggerated. Even the guard at his side had a wide grin on his face, as he puffed at his cigarette. Priabin ignored the cigarette the guard had given him. On the huge fibre-optic map twenty feet away the undulating course of the American shuttle *Atlantis* across the planet looked like the measurement of a regular sine wave.

491

Rodin's voice was amplified and mechanical over the P/A, but still betrayed the man's excitement as it reached every part of the room.

'Gentlemen, we are on schedule,' he announced. A renewed ripple of applause as he stated the self-evident, luxuriating in it. Priabin could see the general, behind glass like a zoo exhibit, looking out at his kingdom. 'We shall be commencing the transfer of the liquid hydrogen to the booster stages in approximately two minutes' time. The *Raketoplan*'s crew will be boarding the craft within the next five minutes. Thank you, gentlemen – keep up the good work!' More applause, sounding now like a frantic desire to maintain an already overheated emotional atmosphere. Dying away reluctantly.

On one screen, the vehicle carrying the three members of the shuttle's crew drew up at the base of the launch gantry. Priabin watched as the men, already suited and helmeted, and carrying their life-support packs like white suitcases, lumbered towards the lift to take them the hundred or more metres to the shuttle. From the television monitor, there was faint cheering from the ground personnel. Priabin looked at his guard, then drew heavily at his cigarette. His face and body's aches had subsided into a general discomfort. Rodin had even had a nurse to dab his cuts and bruises, inspect the darkened flesh over ribs and buttocks – and pronounce upon the degree of injury Serov had inflicted. One damaged rib, otherwise no more than heavy bruising and abrasions. There was sticking plaster on his forehead, but the stinging of the antiseptics and the adrenalin solution to stem the blood flowing from his cleaned cuts had faded.

Rodin had talked to him; wary of him, massively resentful at some moments, indifferent at others. But though he had Priabin guarded, he did not have him removed to a cell. Nor handed back to Serov. As if he wanted Priabin to see him succeed, witness every moment of *Lightning*. And yet it seemed that Rodin himself was plagued by something other than the launch. His son, Priabin, suspected. He did not wish to hear about him, he was able for long moments to ignore his son's death, but the thought seemed to keep returning to him.

Priabin turned to look across the room towards Serov's windows. The security monitoring unit of mission control was raised above the main floor. A row of tinted windows. He could see nothing more than occasional shadows passing to and fro behind the glass. He had not prevented Serov from continuing the search for Gant. Rodin had ignored – or suppressed – what he had said concerning the GRU colonel's murder of his son. Perhaps the idea cast doubt on too many of Rodin's unthinking beliefs?

He turned back. Rodin had left his glass booth and was walking towards him and his guard – who snapped to attention. Priabin was immediately attentive. Rodin's walk was stiff, parade-like, as if he was too aware that others were watching him. Yet he barely acknowledged the smiles and salutes that hemmed him in like a corridor. He marched directly towards Priabin, halting in front of him.

He paused only to wave the guard aside. 'Come,' he ordered. There appeared little strength in his voice. Priabin walked at his side.

They mounted the steps between the amphitheatrical ranks of consoles and their operators. Instructions, repeated acknowledgements, orders, measurements, hummed around them. It was difficult to catch what Rodin was saying in a quiet, unfamiliar voice. Priabin strained to hear.

'. . . a priority message – came two hours ago . . . didn't regard it as important, only just read it – wife . . .' The telemetry, the countdown, the shuttle's status, the voice of the mission commander as he boarded the craft, rising and falling like waves. Priabin could not believe what he heard; more, could not believe the voice in which the information was relayed to him. The launch became unimportant. '. . . hospital, suffering from an overdose . . . my wife?' The tone of querulous enquiry was hard to accept as real. '. . . took sleeping tablets – rushed her to hospital . . . critical, they say . . .'

Priabin halted beside Rodin at the top of the steps. Cigarette-smoke hung heavily there, despite the air-conditioning. The noises of the room were murmurous, oppressive, as was its temperature. Incredible. Rodin seemed out of his depth. Stunned and incapable. Priabin glanced quickly towards the tinted windows of the security room. Now, *now* he could finish Serov, with Rodin in his present state of numbed shock. *Now –!*

Something startled him into wakefulness. Drugged as he seemed, he knew immediately he must make no noise. He rubbed his face roughly, cleared his eyes into focus. Pale light from the low moon illuminated the doors of the hangar and the UAZ still parked in front of them. And the opening of the small door and the form of one of the GRU men coming through it; eating and stretching luxuriously.

The bleep of the radio's signal had summoned the man and woken Gant. A tinny voice succeeded the signal, which had itself sounded impatient. The voice was sharp and near on the icy air. The wind appeared to have dropped, as clouds galleoned slowly across the stars.

He listened. The tractor's rusty red body and huge rear wheels masked him even more effectively than the shadows of the pines beneath which he sat, wrapped in the fold of the parka, hood over his head and face. He had eaten the chocolate and biscuits from the emergency rations, kept the stale taste of inactivity and impending defeat from his mouth with the water bottle. Ordinary, ludicrous things. He had done them because there was nothing else; he could not kill them and give the alarm, he could not reach the Antonov, he could not fit the battery, he could not fill the chemical tank with fuel, he could not tow it to the fuel dump by using the tractor . . . which others had used, its towbar indicated. The pieces of the puzzle lay about him and he knew its solution; but was powerless to act.

As he listened, he looked at his watch. Just before two in the morning. The guards called in or were called every thirty minutes. Routine. No one seemed to want to move them on. He had taken up his position beside the tractor because from it he could watch both the road to the collective, the sky to the north from which direction the gunships would come, and the hangar and the UAZ. It was like climbing voluntarily into a hospital bed in an intensive care ward, so trapped did he feel, so bereft of a future. Only the battery was charging; that was the only progression.

The guard was almost forty yards away, yet he caught nearly every word spoken.

'. . . as the grave, sir. Sure. Oh, yes – we've patrolled regularly.' They hadn't left the comparative warmth of the hangar except to call in or to answer a call. Once, one of them had come through the small door, urinated briefly against the hangar wall, presumably because he couldn't locate the toilet inside, and hurried back in out of the cold. They had kept the lights switched off, as he had heard them ordered to do. Torchlight had flickered in there from time to time. 'Matter of fact, that's why I was a bit late, sir . . . just finished my patrol . . . nothing doing, sir – picked the wrong . . . yes, sir, of course, sir!' Gant felt himself drawn into the one-sided conversation, as into warm sleep. He rubbed his arms, waking himself. 'Me, sir? Back on patrol, leave the private here, sir – yes, sir!' The corporal actually stood to attention for a moment before he flung the microphone back into the vehicle with a muttered curse. He opened the judas-door and bellowed: 'You jammy bastard, get out here! Come on, move it!'

'Corp –' Gant heard from inside.

'Don't corp me, you lucky sod! I'm to go back on routine patrol, son, while you take time out here smoking fags and guzzling vodka!'

'Sorry, corp –'

'You will be, son – you will be,' the corporal murmured, leaning over the other soldier. 'Right, I'll be back in an hour, maybe more. I'll leave the walkie-talkie with you – make sure you keep in touch. And make sure you do the patrols, my son – understand?'

'Yes, corp.'

'Jammy bastard!'

Gant watched as the corporal climbed into the UAZ and started the engine. It roared in the silence, then the vehicle moved off quickly, churning up dust, squealing along the track towards the collective, its headlights bucking and bouncing like a runaway horse. Its engine noise faded. The private raised two fingers vigorously, twice, then turned back to the judas-door. He paused, then ducked his head and re-entered the hangar, closing the door behind him.

Gant's hands jumped and twitched with tension-becoming-excitement. He climbed awkwardly to his feet, stamping them at once to rid his legs of cramp and cold. He wasn't tired now. He had no further time to waste. Two o'clock. His hand banged the tractor's huge rear tyre like the shoulder of an old friend.

Crouching, he moved swiftly across the forty yards of open ground to the side of the hangar, the Makarov ready in his right hand in case –

The judas-door did not open. He paused, breathing deeply, then hurried once more, around the building's circumference, towards the lean-to, approaching it from the rear of the hangar. His boots brushed through straggling, icy grass. He found the loose panel of corrugated sheeting, knelt, then wriggled into the hangar. Moonlight gave him enough light to see by. He moved carefully past empty drums, cans, boxes, the fat tyres – flicking on the torch only to locate the handle of the door. Touched it, breathed softly, remembered whether or not the door had squeaked when he had first opened it – *no* – opened the door. The pale darkness of the hangar rustled. Smell of paraffin, dust, oil, sausage. He waited in the crack he had opened, sensing rather than seeing the details of the hangar. Moonlight on the nearer Antonov.

Where? Where was the guard? Impatience surged through him. Close. The hairs rose on the back of his neck. Something scuffled, a bootheel rather than a rat. Close.

He slipped through the gap in the dor. Paused, head turning slowly from left to right, right to left . . . Breathing? Could he hear that much, that clearly? His shoulder quivered as if anticipating a hand falling heavily on it. He saw the door to the off-duty room was open. A poor light filtered from it like a leak of yellowish water. Rustling . . . ? The turning of pages. A grunt of what might have been satisfaction. The shuffling of feet. There was no time, no space for the complications of hitting the guard, tying him, being aware of him through the hour or so that still lay ahead. He had to kill him.

Gant studied the floor between himself and the open door. The light – of a torch? – seemed a little stronger, yet hardly spilled beyond the dark rectangle of the door. The man could be sitting on one of the battered easy chairs, or standing at the table. He would have no more than moments in which to locate, aim, kill. It was six steps to the open door.

Noise of gurgling, like a distant tap. The man was drinking something. There was nothing between himself and the door. He moved on tiptoe, pausing between each step. Sigh or grunt, magnified. Rustling of pages, a muttered oath regarding the light, the scraping of chair legs – table, then . . .

He was in the doorway, the Makarov level with his hip. A pool of torchlight, some glossy pages open on the stained table; the bulk of the soldier already half-risen. He did not distract himself with a glance at the man's face, but simply fired twice.

The body began falling in slow-motion, but the sense of having killed snapped Gant's time-sense back to normality. The body slid towards the table, moving it in a painful scrape on the floor, then toppled backwards, half over one of the ragged chairs. To lie motionless.

Gant waited, the noise of the two shots separating then blurring as they echoed in his ears. Over. He felt nothing. The man had been no more than a voice, then a dark form. His face was hanging over the chair's arm, out of sight and Gant had never seen his features. He moved forward into the room, his hand touching the magazine – a naked girl – then the torchlight located the walkie-talkie. A moment of fear because he was alone with the machine and felt its contact with the UAZ, with Baikonur.

He left the room quickly, shutting the door behind him, and crossed the hangar to the Battery Room. Flicked the beam of the torch, fading noticeably, at the dials. Almost, almost –

certainly charged enough by the time he . . thoughts tumbled. He regimented them like a hand of cards.

Engineer's office. He crossed the concrete floor, collecting the lamp and its coiled lead on his way. Quickly, quickly . . . his hand dabbed along a wooden board littered with keys hanging from hooks. TRACTOR, one was labelled. He snatched off the keys, then the ignition keys for the Antonov. Then returned to the store-room, wiping the glaze of the lamp around its dusty, littered space until he found a crowbar. Keys, means of opening the fuel compound . . . two down.

Waved the lamp again, crouched on his haunches, scuttled like a crab in that position, poking the light into dark corners. Webs, the hardly-noticed scurry of a rat he never saw, dirt on his fingertips, spilt paint long dried – a length of rubber hose. Triumphantly, he tugged it out from behind stacked, empty boxes and drums which had once held the chemicals used in crop-dusting. Hardly pausing, he returned to the hangar, climbing into the second Antonov as if returning to a familiar location. As he squeezed into the cockpit, he felt his frame too big for the interior of the aircraft; as if it could hardly contain his energy. In the light of the lamp, he inspected the panel which operated the pump for the chemical tank. Stuck-on labels. POWER On-Off; PUMP On-Off. Just the two switches and a lamp to register they were operating. Primitive. Familiar. He returned to the cabin, bending to inspect the spray outlet. No spray bars had been fitted to the underside of the fuselage. The outlet pipe ran into the floor of the plane.

He jumped down. And it ran through it. Yes, he could fit the hose easily, when he needed to refuel from the chemical tank to the wing tanks. He could fill the tank from the input on its top surface, using the hose still in his hand. He threw it into the interior of the Antonov.

Wobble pump. Or whatever they used to fill the tank with its chemicals – where?

Two-fifteen. No pump. He began patrolling the walls of the hangar for a second time, flashing and slipping the light carefully over every surface, every shadowy gap. No pump. Two twenty-five. He was aware of the walkie-talkie in his pocket, its link with the UAZ and with Baikonur – with Serov – aware too, of the videotape, the cassette from the camera Priabin had used . . . aware most of all of time. He had glanced at each minute that passed on the face of his watch.

He stood in the middle of the hangar, having completed his second unsuccessful patrol. *Do something else*. Two-thirty. He had done nothing, nothing so far – just a length of hose and the death of a man – do something else. Shuffle the cards, *do something else!*

He crossed to the doors. He still could not nerve himself to switch on the hangar's main lights. He left the lamp, at the limit of its lead – caught on something? He could not delay to check. Reached the doors. Still unlocked, left that way by the corporal, found the handle, began to wind at it, listening to the magnified creaking of the two doors as they slid apart on their protesting metal rails. Moonlight crept forward like an inquisitive, wary animal. He opened them to their full extent.

He stood looking out at the shadowy form of the tractor parked beneath the firs. The refuelling pump could be at the dump, locked in with the tarpaulin-covered drums. It didn't matter. Now, he had to move the aircraft.

He ran across the moonlit space. Little or no wind. His cheeks were numbed by his speed through the icy air. He climbed into the tractor's cab, dabbling his fingers like those of a blind man for the ignition. Held his breath, switched on. The engine coughed, died. A second time, then a third. The noise of the engine turning over but refusing to fire was a violent, alarming sound in the silence. He could not help glancing repeatedly over his shoulder, in the direction of the collective's huddled buildings almost a mile away.

The engine caught, still reluctant, then roared as he over-accelerated. He slipped off the brake, heard the engine settle, then dragged the wheel over, turning the tractor out of the shadow of the trees towards the hangar. His head turned rapidly from side to side. Nothing.

He drove the tractor into the darkness inside the hangar. The two aircraft assumed identity slowly as his vision adjusted to the lack of light. He tugged on the tractor's brake and jumped down. The silence after he switched off its engine was solid, pressing on his eardrums like a shockwave. He inspected the towbar with his torch. Yes, it had been used to tow the Antonovs in and out of the hangar.

Snatching up the lamp once more, he inspected the second Antonov's undercarriage. Two towing lugs. Good.

He climbed back into the tractor cab and started the engine – first time, he breathed out hugely. Very slowly, carefully, he turned the tractor – familiar again, like the airplane; a machine that belonged to *his* past. Then he backed it up to the Antonov's nose, juggling with the reluctant steering wheel until he heard the towbar clunk against the undercarriage strut. Stopped. Jumped out, checked the towbar's alignment with the towing lugs.

Two thirty-eight. He felt relief rob him of all strength for a moment and make his head spin with dizziness, then he raised the towbar and dropped it over the towing lugs, locking the two machines into a single unit.

Immediately he looked up at the gap of moonlight through the wide-open doors. Looked then at the wingspan of the Antonov, the four dull leading edges of the wings. He remembered the doors of the KGB hangar closing against the MiL's desperate race towards the air.

He stood for a moment, trying to retain the sense of his tasks as a hand of cards. Hose, rifle, keys, fuel outside – pump? – tractor . . . two-forty. Battery . . . he would have to manhandle the large battery onto the tractor and transport it to the Antonov after he had fuelled up the tank in the cabin. It was charged, or almost charged – it would start the airplane, if he could get it into the tail section and wired up. He felt unequal to it. It came down to whether he could lift the battery onto the tractor, then once more into the airplane. Just that; brute strength.

And the adrenalin of panic . . . leave it for the moment – *leave* it! He climbed with great effort into the cab of the tractor, wiping the smear of his exertions and fears from the inside of the windscreen with his gloved hand, then with the sleeve of the parka. Turned to look back at the Antonov –

– jumped down and unclipped the bonding wire from the undercarriage, throwing its crocodile clip and length of wire away from him like a reckless gesture of success.

He paused, then started the tractor once more, creeping the lumbering vehicle slowly towards the open doors. The image of the KGB hangar's similarly open doors kept flashing like a strobe light on the retinae of his eyes, making his body jump and tremble with anticipated disaster . . . just the tip of one wing, just the merest collision, just, just . . . the doors of that other hangar kept grinding closer together.

He gripped the wheel fiercely, yet his touch on its movements was delicate as he held the tractor to the adjudged centre of the gap. Five yards, four . . . the tractor passed through the doors, they were alongside then behind him. Already, the propeller blades were glinting with moonlight in the tractor's side-mirror.

He glanced back quickly, then relied upon the mirror to his right, watching the Antonov's starboard wings, watching the longer upper wing of the biplane, watching, watching . . . he wasn't breathing, his head was light with concentration . . . watching . . .

Through.

He grunted aloud. The Antonov rolled gently out into the open. At once, he turned the tractor's wheels, heading the aircraft through a wide semi-circle towards the fuel dump at the back of the hangar.

Sweat bathed his forehead, freezing to an ache almost at once. The noise of the tractor dinned at his eardrums.

Two forty-five.

The moon was old, low, sliding towards morning near the horizon. Daylight, a thousand miles . . .

'Gentlemen, *another* countdown adjustment – it is now T minus fifty minutes and counting.'

Cheering, diffuse and roaring like a distant sea from beyond the tinted glass.

'Turn that bloody thing *off!*' Serov barked. 'For *Christ*'s sake — you're like a bunch of fucking *kids!*' Someone moved to switch off the only television screen relaying the scene in mission control, then to the P/A speaker on one wall. Serov drew angrily on his cigarette. The ashtray on the table was filled with crushed and twisted butts. A dozen or more cardboard filters. 'Let Grandpa Rodin get on with his game — *you*'ve got *your* work cut out right here!'

The security room was hazy with smoke, stale-smelling and crowded, though there were no more than half-a-dozen in the search coordination team. The cheering died away beyond the tinted glass. They were all tired, all frustrated, all edgy, none more so than he. Childish rage brought no rewards, but seemed necessary. He waved a hand.

'All right, all right — back to work, back to work!' Like a hen fussing. It wasn't their fault — but it would be *his* fault if they didn't locate and bring in the American pilot. He looked at his watch.

Three-ten. Dear Christ, three in the morning! Gant had been out of his hands since before four — almost twelve hours.

Had Priabin still been his prisoner — well, who could have said, he admitted with a grin, whether he would still have been alive? . . . though why Rodin kept him hanging around him like a court buffoon, God alone knew the answer.

Was there any danger there? He'd asked himself that question fifty, a hundred times, mostly with confident indifference. But he realized Rodin could no longer believe Priabin had driven his son to suicide. Had he still done so, he wouldn't have been able to bear the sight of him, would have had him locked up, even shot.

Serov patted his pocket. The tapes from Mikhail. Should he give them to Rodin, or not? They'd convince, almost by themselves, that the pressure of Priabin's interrogation had snapped Valery Rodin's reason, driven him to a desperate act of suicide . . . wouldn't they? Perhaps they should be used?

He wandered to the line of tinted windows. Almost at once, he

502

located Rodin surrounded by his staff, in front of the huge telemetry map which showed the snaking orbit of the American shuttle. Pointing, waving his arms – completely mad. Serov felt detached from the whole vast room down there. Where was Priabin? Had Rodin got rid of him at last?

No, there he was, still guarded. Playing – dear Jesus, playing *cards* with his guard and two white-coated technicians, away in one corner. *Cards!* The scene was surreal. What was he doing? Why was he still there?

He would not admit that Priabin worried or unnerved him.

He turned from the windows and the thought abruptly. The radio reports, the replies of his team, filled the stale air of the room with their own enervating urgency. Priabin's image nagged at his thoughts for a moment or two, then Gant replaced him. He had to have the American. That would be the basis of any stand-off, would be the yardstick. Even the lifeline, he admitted with great reluctance.

And yet all these reports and acknowledgements are empty, *negative* –!

The team had their backs to him like chastened pupils. Bent over radios, VDUs, maps. The large screen standing vertically on its trolley in one corner was no more technological or revelatory than an empty blackboard in a classroom. Its colours and markings faded, flowed like dyes running in woollen garments, the kind of cheap rubbish they sold in many stores . . . the colours re-formed in a new pattern. The map was computer controlled, constantly updated from its accompanying console. Fifty different images of nothing had been its contribution thus far!

He strode over to it, confronting it, a new cigarette between his lips on which he drew loudly, repeatedly. Baikonur's south-western quadrant occupied the fibre-optic screen. Marks and dots and squiggles crawled and moved on its surface like thunderflies on a pale wall. He studied the map, replacing its images with as many of the locations as he could recall. The river, bending away towards the bottom of the map, the old town straggling out into the desert and the country reclaimed and cultivated through irrigation. The bottom half of the projection was a grid-pattern like the aerial view of some American or new Siberian city. Collectives, clumps of trees, the tracks and roads that wound through the canal and dyke system, individual cottages and huts; barns, stores, sheds, hen-coops, garages. Every building was represented. And yet he wanted to lash out at the map with his good hand – the fist that had so damaged Priabin's pretty face – and reduce the map to a jigsaw of coloured shards on the floor.

Every man at his disposal, army, GRU and even police – he had excluded Priabin's KGB and confined some of them *pending further enquiries*, as he had instructed sardonically – every mobile or air unit was represented on the map. A separate colour or shade of a colour indicated the areas they had searched. Like a dye introduced to the body and shown up by X-ray; areas clear of disease. These blotches merged at many points. Soon, the whole map would be a single smear of colour declaring that the American had escaped.

He refused to believe it. The unit designations wobbled and disappeared, then reappeared as positional reports were updated. The map did everything, it was supremely sophisticated, advanced. And utterly useless!

'What else can we *do*?' he exploded. He saw their shoulders twitch, heads snap up. One or two of them turned at once to look at him; others were more cautious. Yet it was not anger so much as frustration he expressed. 'Tell me – boys, tell me. What the hell are we *missing*?'

They had all turned now, except the map operator, feeding in yet another stream of positional information. Clear here, clear, nothing, nothing . . . and yet *he's in there somewhere!*

'Well?' he asked again, attempting bluffness. 'What are we missing?'

'Sir – nothing . . .' It was the lieutenant who had brought him the news about the MiL – and brought him Priabin.

'Nothing?' he replied acidly, barely controlling another outburst of temper. 'Nothing?'

'Sir, we've never done *anything* as thoroughly as this!' He had accepted the role of spokesman, reluctantly, of course. 'We've covered everything. He hasn't got a vehicle — we've traced everything on wheels out there. He can't have got back into Leninsk or Tyuratam on foot . . .' The lieutenant's face was screwed up like that of a child seeking an answer; a genuine attempt to help the teacher. But his shoulders shrugged at the same time.

'All right. I'm not criticizing —' Serov began. Then he bellowed: 'Shit — for *Christ*'s sake —! All this equipment, all the routines, the systems — how much are they worth now? Two fucking kopecks is about the mark, wouldn't you say?' He turned his back on them and strode across the room towards the tinted windows. Saw Priabin immediately. Still playing cards. *The man was laughing at him!*

He turned back to the men in the room, his face enraged. Gant was on foot, he had to be, or holed up somewhere. On the collectives, they were turning out their bedrooms, their cup-boards, their privies for any sign of him. Everything had been or was being searched. It was ridiculous, unbelievable that they could find no trace of him!

'Ask them,' he said hoarsely, waving a hand in front of him. It was an admission of bafflement, of weakness, but he had to make it. Then he'd settle Priabin's hash. But, first; 'Ask them — every officer out there . . . I want *ideas!* Call every one of them in turn and ask for their ideas.'

'Sir, that could take —'

'I don't care how long it takes!' Serov stormed. 'They're the people on the spot. Ask them. Well, get on with it — get started!'

He was hot, sweating profusely with his efforts at the wobble pump. He paused only to wipe his sleeve across his brow or to glance at the watch on his wrist. Nothing else interested him; he was unconcerned with the cold, empty landscape around him. He was oblivious to the walkie-talkie thrust into his breast pocket. He had almost filled the chemical tank in the Antonov's cabin with kerosene. It was three-thirty in the morning.

He worked furiously at the pump, bobbing over it like some

505

frantic lifeguard over the body of a rescued swimmer, attempting to empty him of water. Watch, brow, pump – his horizons. In his haste, he had knocked over a drum of petrol. Its sweet smell made his head spin. The odour was all around him like an invisible cloud.

Three thirty-two. He checked the gauge. He had transferred two hundred and ninety gallons to the chemical tank. Empty drums lay on their sides around him like litter. Spilled kerosene and petrol stained the ground. The loosened tarpaulin crackled and snapped behind him in the occasional gusts of wind. Helicopters had passed in the distance, always to the north. No vehicles had come down the track towards the hangar or the fuel compound.

He cradled his back in his hands for a long time, while his breathing returned to normal. Eventually, he crossed to the tractor. His strength seemed to ebb at the thought of the battery and its weight. *You can lift it, you can . . .* He glanced at the Antonov. Close now, close.

He touched the ignition key of the tractor. Noise blurted from the walkie-talkie against his breast, stunning him. He whirled round in his seat as if someone was behind him. The noise slowly resolved into a human voice. Into a demand for an acknowledgement from the dead GRU private.

He dared not answer.

His eyes frantically studied the night sky, examining individual stars, expecting them to shift, move, resolve themselves into navigation lights. They did not.

'Acknowledge –'

They knew the man's name, his rank, his number. They wanted to speak to him, question him.

He dared not reply.

But if he didn't, they'd come –

fires in the night

He dared not acknowledge.

Gant turned the ignition key and the tractor's engine roared. The noise clamoured, drowning the small, insistent voice from the walkie-talkie. He put the tractor into gear, turning the wheel with a strength that surprised him; comforted him, too. The battery's bulk seemed to have increased. It dominated his thoughts. He accelerated along the side of the hangar, his eyes constantly checking the sky above and around him. Only stars, only the fading moonlight –

The voice was apparent again. While it repeated its summons over and over, it lost its threat. He turned into the hangar. The huge rear tyres crushed something that cracked audibly, the wingtip of the stripped Antonov brushed against the top of the cab. He felt a tug at the tractor, heard a tearing noise. The door of the Battery Room was visible ahead of him as he turned on the tractor's headlights. Splashing light no longer mattered. He halted the tractor and stepped down.

As he entered the confined space of the room and the engine noise diminished, he realized that there was no sound from the walkie-talkie. He held it to his ear for a moment – no, nothing. He almost wanted to shake it like some clockwork toy that refused to work, but thrust it back into his breast pocket. He looked at his watch. Three thirty-eight. It had begun; suspicion, realization, counter-activity.

Breathing deeply, he checked the dials on the charger. The battery was almost fully charged. He unclipped the leads, tested the bulk of the battery, felt for the carrying handle . . . it hardly slid more than a few inches as he heaved at it. He groaned aloud.

Stood back. The bench on which the battery rested was a few feet from the floor. He would damage the battery for certain if he dropped it –

– come on, *come on*, he raged at himself. *Try!*

He turned to the tractor, headlight-eyes staring at him, making him blink and squint. Come *on!*

He moved behind the bench, pushing at the battery. It slid reluctantly to the edge, almost teetering there, in danger of falling. He checked, then moved alongside the battery. He was sweating feverishly. He gripped the carrying handle in both hands, and tugged. The battery slid off the bench onto the floor with a hideous concussive noise. He flashed the torch but could find no damage. Back bent, he dragged the battery by its handle out of the Battery Room, across the dusty concrete to the tractor. His breathing was like a punctuated groaning.

This was the last thing, the last task. He gripped his arms around the battery, heaving and straining at it. He staggered with the weight, lurching against the side of the tractor, thrusting the battery like a ram against the cab, against, in, *into* the cab . . . gasped for breath, back aching, arms numb. He looked at the battery resting innocently on the floor of the cab, near the pedals.

Almost at once, a sense of his peril returned, and all but doubled Gant up with stomach cramps. He forced himself up into the cab. Accelerated slowly, the cramps passing. He drove out of the hangar, almost afraid to look up. Then making himself quarter the sky. Stars, moon, darkness. Nothing moved. Nothing on the track, either. He rounded the hangar, heading towards the clearly visible aircraft. Drew up next to it.

Three forty-three.

He slid the tractor inch by inch alongside the open battery compartment in the Antonov's tail. His hands were light on the wheel, his foot gentle on the pedal. He watched over his shoulder. Closer, closer. He could not attend to the night sky now, his horizon had become the edge of the cab, the distance to the open flap.

Yes!

He switched off the engine and jumped down. Silence

gradually seeped into his hearing. Silence, still. Only minutes now.

He would have to heft it into the compartment before rigging it. Stow and rig – how long? *It won't matter shit if you don't get it into the compartment!* He positioned himself, feet slightly apart, arms at each side of the battery, then he bent and strained, as if about to hurl the battery into the open flap. Paused, tried to raise his body, move his arms as they cracked with the strain. Lifted the battery, staggered in a turn, expelling his breath in a huge shout –

The battery banged into the compartment – he lurched forward with the effort and with the frantic desire to stop it falling backwards towards him. If it did, then he would never be able to hold it, would fall with it –

His imagination was feverish with anticipation, so that his hands felt as if the battery was beginning to topple. He thrust at it frantically, struggling it further into the compartment, finally feeling it tilt into the shallow tray in which it was normally secured. Heaved at it again without any sensation in his hands that its bulk had been squared as he intended – then he dimly felt it drop firmly into the tray and remain still. He kept his hands on the battery to calm them as sweat broke out all over his body, as if produced not by his effort but by the trembling weakness afterwards. *Christ –!*

He wiped his mouth with the back of one quivering hand. Three forty-five.

Where were they now? Suspicion or realization? Even counter-activity? Somewhere between realization and action, he decided. Close –

T minus fourteen minutes.

The countdown clock in the security room had been re-adjusted once more as Rodin shaved further minutes from the launch procedures. Serov glanced up at it. It seemed to bear little relationship to the activities of the room and its occupants; as if the tinted windows comprising the wall between himself and the rest of mission control had become completely opaque. The scenes on the television screens were unaccompanied by noise or words. Launch pad, the strange steam of vaporizing fuel, the garish lights, the images from the flight deck of the shuttle craft; all somehow less real than the fibre-optic map and the radio connection with one corporal driver.

'Why not?' he repeated. 'Why can't you raise him?' He addressed the words to the ceiling. If the man failed to pick up his words, they would be repeated by the radio operator. He wished to remain detached.

But why did the countdown clock intrude at the very edge of his peripheral vision? It had nothing to do with the American. He could not ignore it. Thirteen minutes thirty. It was three-forty in the morning, his eyes were gritty with tiredness, his body stale and beginning to acquire an odour within its uniform. Yet his brain refused to be weary; it leapt and jumped with electricity.

He turned his back completely on the countdown clock.

'Well?' he demanded.

'. . . no idea, comrade Colonel,' he caught by way of reply.

'And there were *two* aircraft in that hangar?'

'Yes, comrade –'

He interrupted: '*You* were certain they were unusable?'

'The chief engineer explained –'

'What did he say – *exactly*?' Three forty-one. Time seemed to be accelerating. His mind obeyed the diminishing time, but not with anxiety or fear but with a sense of keeping pace, even overtaking. His body itched for action. '*Exactly!*'

All the checks, all the calls they had made, and only one failure to respond . . . this one, a GRU private guarding two aircraft.

'One of them was stripped right down – we could see that for ourselves.'

'And the *second* one?' His tone was at one level of intensity, the volume of his words raised but constant; as if addressing a large crowd.

'. . . battery on charge ready to . . .' he caught, but his mind had plucked up his attention. He was ahead of the explanation, outrunning the passing moments.

'Then it is *only* the *battery*!' he bellowed at the ceiling, his head

510

spinning, the windows now completely black and opaque. 'If the battery were replaced in the aircraft it could *fly!*'

'Comrade Colonel, I don't –'

'Idiot!' he yelled. There was a triumph in his voice, large and unarticulated. But, even as he shouted the single word, he felt that failure had gripped his throat, constricting it. He could already, he could – dear *God*, the American had an *aircraft!* The windows no longer seemed opaque. The whole of mission control's huge extent rushed against the glass, clearly visible. He could at once pick out Rodin on the far side of the room, behind a glass panel similar to the one which divided him from the main room. Opponent. 'Idiot!' he choked. 'And now we can't raise your companion – do you think by any remote chance he might be *dead*?' He waved his hand. 'Cut that clown off! Get me the collective's chief engineer – whoever *knows* about that plane! Hurry!'

He paused on some mental outcrop. He glanced at the upright map, its violent colours shifting and blending and then standing out starkly like lights at evening. What should he –? What decision? A wrong move and –

What, what, *what*?

He dimly felt his nails digging into his palm. He was aware of mission control, aware of the countdown clock, which now seemed to have raced ahead of him. *What should he do?*

Voice of the radio operator calling the collective. No one would be attending to the radio at this time in the morning! Mistake –

'Cancel that call!' he yelled, surprising them and himself. Their faces turned to him, expectant, even demanding.

American . . . aircraft that needed only a battery . . . three forty-three in the morning . . . the temperature of the room, his mind a vast darkness lit with fires . . . his collar tight, faces looking in his direction, looking *for* direction.

Noise from the radio, another radio, a gunship calling in – map, colours flowing, then solid for a moment, white like a star. Gunship –

'Order – *order*,' he repeated more clearly, growling his throat free, 'that gunship to pick me up – *now!* Order the *nearest* gunship to pick me up – order the others to rendezvous at, at the collective's hangar. Quickly, quickly, *man!'* He sounded breathless, young and somehow absurd. But they obeyed. 'Ask how long rendezvous will take, how long it will take to pick me up here.' His hands waved like those of a conductor, drawing sense from the chaos in his own head. '. . . at the collective, wait until I get there – *hurry!'*

He grabbed up his greatcoat and cap, even his gloves, from the chair against the windows where he had left them a long time before. Saw Priabin, who was at that moment looking up at him. From his hand of cards –

Serov almost raised his hand, almost clenched his fist at the KGB colonel, to threaten, to crush all in a single gesture. But did not . . . Priabin. His time was close. The American first.

'Hurry!'

Three forty-four. Ten minutes to launch time.

Ten minutes to launch time. Dimly, Priabin could make out Serov's bulk, his saturnine features beyond the tinted glass. Three forty-four on half the clocks in the room, ten minutes to launch on the other half. And the countdown ringing mechanically through the whole vast area. Cards in his hand – ridiculous, crazy. Serov's image more real at the glass for a moment than anything else. Then the man disappeared. Something of the urgency with which his shadow vanished communicated itself to Priabin, and his voice faltered in his bid. Bridge. Himself, surprisingly the guard – patronizing thought – and two computer technicians whose tasks were completed. At a loose end, like many others; catered for by a rest area in one corner of the huge room, marked off only by a ring of chairs. Cards, tobacco – no drink, naturally – the atmosphere of some company's staff club. Ludicrous.

Serov's sudden urgency worried Priabin.

'What was that, Colonel?' the guard asked almost affably. His tone suggesting Priabin wasn't a prisoner. 'What did you bid?'

'Two clubs,' he replied automatically. Serov's purpose – himself or Gant? It had to be one or the other. Immediately, his

512

bruises ached again, his face a mask of dull pain. 'Two clubs,' he repeated like a spell.

'No bid,' one of the technicians murmured, tapping ash from his cigarette, after pausing for a moment to regard the magnified voice of the countdown.

'Nine minutes thirty and counting.'

The room murmured, called, moved around them like a tropical forest, its noises and activities lush and dense. Unreal. If he turned his head even slightly he could see, through the glass panels of the command booth, Rodin and his senior staff grouped like visiting dignitaries. Priabin felt anaesthetized. The room worked on him like a strange new drug, inducing a pleased, satisfied tiredness. The guilt had left him – even the heap of coats under which he had buried Katya was no longer clear in his imagination. Anna and Valery Rodin had retreated to an even greater distance. There was only the room and the lunacy of playing bridge with his captors while the countdown rushed towards launch time.

'T minus nine minutes and counting.'

Serov emerged from the door below the tinted glass windows of the security room. Hurrying, urgent, almost possessed. And yet he spared a glance for Priabin. And a quick, greedy smile. Priabin's head cleared. It could only be Gant.

Serov strode towards one of the control room's doors, pursued by two of his team. Greatcoat over his arm, cap in hand, hurrying as if late for an appointment. Priabin turned to where Rodin stood amid his staff officers. He hadn't noticed Serov's departure.

Serov had found Gant, at least knew where he could lay hands on him. And seemed assured of doing so. The grin of success. Priabin was shaken out of his lassitude. Rodin – Rodin had simply walked away from him at the top of the steps, after his confidences regarding his wife. Simply walked away and had addressed no word to him since then. Obsessed with the count-down, the launch.

And now Serov, too, was preoccupied. Rodin would launch and Serov would capture Gant. *Lightning* would happen.

Gant released the brake. It seemed a massive effort. The Antonov struggled forward, unleashed and awkward, then bumped and rolled across the sand and straggling grass towards the flattened, undulating runway. The wind was light, less than five knots, and blowing at an angle across the runway. No problem.

He increased the engine power. The Antonov bucked over the uneven ground. Its power was feeble, yet it was enough for him. The din of the engine banged like hammers in the cockpit and echoed down the narrowing fuselage behind him. The large-scale local maps lay open on the co-pilot's seat, an adjustable light dimly glowing on their contours. Beneath them, a school atlas. He had found it thrust into a door-pocket, and could not imagine why it was there or what it had ever been used for. On a cramped, ridiculous scale, desert stretched away for hundreds of miles in every direction. Gant did not concern himself with it.

He bent forward, craning his head in order to quarter the dark sky. Stars still in their vast orbits, no firefly movements among them. Luck was holding, had to hold –

He watched the needle on the torque meter as the wheels of the undercarriage jolted the aircraft onto the edge of the runway. Tyuratam and Baikonur were like a false dawn along the starboard horizon. He turned the aircraft, paddling the rudders, his two hands gripping the old-fashioned, primitive column. Old-fashioned but familiar.

He sensed the fat tyres sitting on the runway, sensed the engine revs reach his requirement, sensed the slipstream buffet the rudder; sensed the flaps, all and every detail of the old Antonov. He was ready. Airborne, he would quickly become lost in the vastness surrounding the Baikonur complex . . . his luck was holding . . . he increased the power to the engines, sensed the light breeze, watched the starlit sky and its few weary, lumbering clouds, released the brakes, wanted to cry out as the airplane skipped forward on its tyres.

He switched on the radio. Before, he had to remain silent and unknowing so that he might effect his escape, but now it did not matter, he needed to hear where they were.

– moving lights, even before he began tuning the radio. They had come. He saw the billow of the nearing navigation lights as the gunship dropped out of the darkness towards him. *Ahead of him*.

The radio blurted. He had gone on tuning it automatically, with dull and cold fingers. Challenge. Bellowing in the noisy cockpit.

He felt the confidence of only seconds before retreat like a shockwave through his body; chest, stomach, legs —

— then the shockwave of the gunship's downdraught was the one sensation that was real as the Antonov shivered throughout its length. The two-handed column quivered in his hands. He sensed then saw the gunship's shadow settle over him like a cloak, darkening the stars. The radio yelled orders at him. The situation had been snatched from him just as the whirlwind around him threatened to snatch away the control column. The Antonov wobbled, swerved, as fragile as a child's bicycle out of control.

Serov's voice.

'You will stop the aircraft, Major Gant. You will come to a complete halt.'

Stars winking to the west, ahead. The runway rose gently to a close and false horizon; like a springboard that could fling him into the air. Dust whirled around the cockpit, stiff uprooted blades of grass rattled on the perspex, tiny stones and grit showered and bounced like hail. His vision was rapidly becoming obscured. Air intake. Dust clogging it, stones damaging it, wrecking the engine, the propeller. The gunship sat above him like a squat black beetle with a grey underbelly. He watched it, keeping the Antonov's heading along the runway but cutting its speed to a crawl. It was no longer an airplane, only a toy.

The gunship moved slightly further ahead of him and lowered as if on a thread. It was blocking his path. The undercarriage was down. The wheels alone could do enough damage . . . Serov would undoubtedly crash the machine into him if that was the only way to prevent his taking off. And in the downdraught, he could not rely on the Antonov's stability and lift. He could *not* take off.

'You will stop the aircraft and switch off the engine! You will leave the aircraft —'

Gant could see his face and form at the main cabin door. Microphone and loudhailer. Imperatives.

The engine coughed with an almost human noise on the surrounding dust. The Antonov was barely moving forward. Serov wanted him alive, wanted that triumph.

He could see the hangar, the low moon stained brown by the dust, the feeble stars, the fading runway ahead of him, the fuel store.

The cockpit shrank around him, its elements encroaching. Other voices answered and bayed with Serov's over the open channel. Call-signs, acknowledgements, eagerness and confidence. They had crept up on him in the darkness. The cockpit impinged, each element like a sharp needle. The maps, the ridiculous school atlas opened to a vast area of the Soviet Union, each instrument — radio, gyro compass, altimeter — *useless!* Temperature, fuel, revs . . . fire extinguisher, flare pistol, *Mayday, Mayday* . . .

'You will halt the aircraft and leave it with your hands in the air!'

Call-signs, acknowledgements, eager anticipation in every voice. All coming at maximum speed, location confirmed. Icy panic. He had two minutes before the next gunship, less than that before the first ground patrol in a UAZ or a truck arrived. General alert — all units to converge. Imperatives.

Two minutes — one gunship was sufficient, blocking his vision as its grey belly loomed out of the dust cloud. Stones rattled on the perspex, the engine coughed.

'— leave the aircraft!'

Mayday —

The gunship was no more than fifteen feet off the ground, ready to anticipate and counter any move he made. Hanging in the night, blocking the runaway. Fifteen feet up, no more . . .

The idea came slowly, as if he were squeezing juice from an old, dry lemon. *Mayday* —

Hangar, fuel store, the litter of empty drums, the, the – *full drums* – Mayday, *Mayday!*

He manoeuvred the aircraft slowly, innocently, off the runway. The gunship slid alongside and slightly ahead, wary, but confident and alert. Serov was poised in the cabin doorway, braced against the frame, microphone in one hand, the other, holding the loudhailer, waving imperiously.

The MiL's pilot was assured, expert. Serov assumed that surrender lay in getting the Antonov off the runway. Gant felt the biplane bounce and roll, then he slid back the cockpit window. Dust swirled in. Ground speed less than ten miles an hour; crawling to a halt. Serov was waving him on now, the loudhailer gesturing him towards the hangar.

'You will now halt the aircraft.'

Call-signs, acknowledgements, airspeeds, distances. Just above a minute and a half. It had to be now.

Mayday.

He reached carefully for the emergency flare pistol, and cocked it. Headlights in the distance bounced through dark trees. The gunship hovered close to the fuel store, fifteen feet above . . . a second more, two seconds, above, above – *now!*

He fired the flare pistol into the dense mass of fuel drums. Vapour from the fuel he had spilt and from half-used drums, glowed like a frosty haze before it ignited. The tarpaulin flared like old straw. Then a moment in which the whole fuel store glowed. Before –

Orange flame. He choked on the smoke and the dust in the cockpit. His eyes watered. A huge roar of orange. Serov was clearly visible for a moment, burning. Then he fell into the bonfire Gant had created. The gunship lurched, then toppled, slowly at first, flame inside the cockpit as well as surrounding it.

Gant watched in his mirror as he turned the Antonov away, opening the throttles to hurry the machine away from the fire. The MiL sagged onto the bonfire like a weary bird onto a nest. Phoenix. Serov *wouldn't* rise from the ashes.

He saw then only a rectangle of orange light stippled with flashes of greater heat. There was no detail in the mirror. The wheels of the Antonov bounced onto the runway. He turned the aircraft to head west, and the first rise of the undulating runway rushed towards him. The gouting flames to port of him were no more than the burning of stubble. Orange, white plumes, rolling smoke, the gunship dissolving, breaking open. Nothing left alive.

He looked at his groundspeed. Forty-five. The rise was like a mouth opening to swallow him. Fifty miles an hour. The wing-tips glowed with reflected orange light, the whirling propeller was made visible by the glare, so that it became a mirror. The interior of the cockpit and his hands on the column were daubed by splashes of the same livid colour. A false dawn. He lifted the Antonov into the air; his body seemed to return, but it felt light, buoyant. The aircraft climbed fragilely but steadily. Sixty, seventy mph, a hundred . . . time was opening and spreading now like a great ripple, becoming safer with each second that passed. A couple of hundred feet up.

Gant levelled the aircraft below radar height. Invisible. In a moment, he would bank to the south-west, after everyone on the ground who might have seen him could swear he headed directly west. Pale desert stretched away on every side. The feeble dark clumps of firs were like the remnants of a buried fortress wall. There was nothing out there, nobody. Double back, he thought, show them where you are just once more – or fly south-east . . . ?

The fire below remained in his mirror as it dulled on the wingtips and inside the cockpit.

A pillar of fire ascended to starboard, to the north. It was as if some gigantic mirror caught the light from the bonfire of the gunship. The column of flame rose hundreds of feet into the night and went on climbing. Its cloudy base spread, roiled and then faded. The pillar of smoke and flame continued to rise. He knew what it was.

It surged thousands of feet, whole miles, into the sky. He knew.

Lift-off. Launch commit. Lift-off.

He was alive, but he had already lost. They'd launched the

shuttle, and the laser weapon was aboard. *Lightning*. They'd begun it.

A fireworks display. But the analogy diminished the event. The huge map with its winking lights representing radar stations and the wiggling course of the American shuttle seemed shrunken. Instead, Priabin's gaze and that of everyone in the control room had become fixed on the large-screen projection against a distant wall. The column of smoke, lit from within, the falling aside of the skeletal structure of the launch gantry, the boiling fumes, the huge, enveloping, frightening roar of fire were all somehow slowed, so that he could sense the great forces, the huge weight to be thrown into the sky. The needle of the vast missile, the fragile toy of the *Raketoplan* perched on top of it as if impaled by the great steel spear. He found it hard to breathe, and then only shallowly. The whole room seemed not to be breathing.

There was only the magnified voice of the countdown. *Booster ignition . . . we have a launch commit . . . shuttle craft* Kutuzov *has cleared the tower . . .*

. . . cheering beginning like the slow opening of one great mouth. The sound elongated like the slow-moving film he could see on the screen. His chest felt tight.

. . . principal stage engines look good . . . T plus four seconds . . .

A jolt to the image on the screen as the rocket motors of the principal stage of the booster passed out of shot, to be replaced by the image from a more distant camera. The pillar of cloud was glowing from the fire within it as it rose above the launch pad, climbing into the night; extinguishing darkness. Little else could be seen. The cameras peered into the dark, but the weathercock-like shuttle riding on the hundred-metre-high needle was invisible. The cameras swung upwards, as if raised by the cheering and self-congratulatory voices in mission control. *Atlantis'* orbit writhed like a long white worm on the principal map, which winked now with new lights; telemetry stations tracking the launch.

The noise of success went on and on. *T plus fifty seconds*. Mach 1.

One minute and twenty seconds to first stage separation . . . Kutuzov, *you're still looking good* . . . Strange that the very jargon of the launch was so American, so much an imitation of what happened in Florida and Texas. Kedrov, he thought, Kedrov with his foolish dreams of America would have been wounded by the ironies of mission control's single voice.

Thinking of Kedrov and realizing that the man was probably dead already, Priabin glanced up at the row of tinted windows behind which lay the security room. And what Serov had left behind of his team.

Gesticulating hands and arms. Signals of anger, surprise. A uniformed officer was standing close to the windows and Priabin could see him quite clearly. The noises of mission control were becoming more routine, less excited, as if they, too, were intrigued by the scene in the security room. Two men facing each other now, shouting silently; like a domestic quarrel behind glass.

. . . *altitude fifteen miles and looking good*, Kutuzov. On the big projection screen, the pillar of cloud was thin and without the power to impress, the orange flame at its tip hardly visible. *T plus two minutes, first stage separation* . . . *Control, this is* Kutuzov — *ready for first stage separation* . . . *first stage burnout, we have first stage burnout*. Priabin glanced again at the tinted windows. They were still arguing, hands being rubbed almost desperately through untidy hair. The projection screen showed the tiny flick of light and smoke as the giant first stage of the booster fell away and the second stage motors ignited. *Ignition of second stage successful* . . . *Roger*, Kutuzov, *we can see that. You are negative return*, Kutuzov . . . *Roger, mission control, we are negative return* . . .

They could no longer return to Baikonur, they were too high and too far into the flight. Priabin turned away from the screen and ignored the voices because there was no possibility of doing anything . . . but, that — argument? Why were they shocked and panicking up there in the security room? Gant —?

They moved away from the windows. The officer had been staring in Rodin's direction for some seconds before turning away. What was it?

He turned to his guard, lounging in his chair, idly watching the projection screen and the fibre-optic map. Winking telemetry, the worm of the American shuttle's plotted orbit, the new red stripe that revealed the course of the *Kutuzov*.

'I want to go up to the security room,' he announced.

The guard shrugged, and seemed to study Priabin's bruised and swollen features. 'OK,' he said. 'I'll have to come, Colonel.' Priabin nodded and turned towards the tinted windows. What was it? They were frightened. He could tell that almost as easily as if he had been in the room. A peculiar sensation plucked at his chest as he climbed the concrete steps. The corridor was chill and unfinished. It had been little more than a grey blur when he followed Rodin along it, having been rescued from Serov's malevolence. Had something happened to –? Pray God it has, he replied to his own silent question. The guard's boots pursued with leisurely clicks and echoes. He opened the door of the security room.

A high voice strained and shouting from the radio. A still-panicked reception of the words. '. . . still burning. No, there's *no* bloody hope of anyone being alive in that lot! Burned to a crisp, the whole bloody crew! What would you expect, you *prick*?'

'Calm down!' the lieutenant cried back at the microphone which abused him. Sweat was a grey sheen on his pale forehead, his narrow, dark features were lopsided with indecision and imagined pain; someone else's agony. What had –?

'What the hell's going on?' he asked the nearest member of Serov's team, a corporal with radio operator's flashes on his sleeve. He shook him excitedly. 'What is it?'

The corporal ran thick fingers over cropped fair hair. His eyes were blank with shock. '. . . American bastard got the Colonel,' was the one thing Priabin heard with clarity.

A fierce, even shameful delight spread through him. He grasped the fact, the implications immediately. And was glad. Serov was dead. Gant had killed Serov?

'How? How, man, how?' He was shaking the corporal by the upper arms. The lieutenant's eyes were narrow with suspicion.

From a wall-speaker, the voice of mission control continued; seemingly incongruous now.

... *second stage separation complete – looking good*, Kutuzov. *Altitude, eighty miles, speed eighteen thousand kilometres per hour* ...

The distances and speeds were hard to grasp, the dialogue flip and stagey – Serov was *dead*! He felt his body shiver with relief.

The lieutenant snapped: 'Your American friend blew up a fuel dump – incinerated the Colonel's helicopter! *That*'s how!' There was awe, and shock, but the respect implied by the use of Serov's rank seemed imposed only by death.

'And Gant – the American?' Priabin returned.

'Gone – taken off. Certainly not destroyed.'

The lieutenant's hand waved towards the room's fibre-optic map and the console operator beside it who was feeding in the search coordinates. He alone seemed unaffected by the incineration of the gunship.

On the map, the elements of the search buzzed like frantic fireflies, small lights maddened by an insecticide. Gunships, other aerial units, ground units. Small lights, but giant, awkward, lumbering attempts to form a net. Gant, he knew, was already gone. The rat in the corner did not panic – it bit the weakest ankle and then fled as it was hunted with increasing desperation. That was Gant. His survival was his only priority.

They'd lost him, anyway. That was already obvious. So Priabin began to consider the video cassettes that Gant had with him and Gant's eventual destination. Turkey or Pakistan. With an aircraft, Gant would attempt to make a complete escape. All one thousand miles of it.

The lieutenant was in contact with Rodin. For an instant, Priabin began to reach out a restraining hand. The lieutenant's eyes were instantly alarmed, and he barked at the guard lounging near the door:

'This man is your prisoner – guard him!' He glared at Priabin. Shock had been replaced by activity, and by a common identity of service with Serov. Priabin was KGB, Priabin had been with the American. The corporal slouched beside Priabin, his rifle barrel nudging at his arm as if to mock rather than arrest.

'Sir,' the guard murmured with undisguised insolence.

Priabin heard Rodin's voice. The lieutenant's face was satisfyingly pale. It had taken him whole minutes to interrupt Rodin's unalloyed triumph. Eventually, he lowered the telephone and muttered: 'He's coming up.'

. . . third stage separation . . .

Roger, Kutuzov *– still looking good . . .*

The reduced image of the main control room's map showed the red path of the launch moving across the world; on course, undeviating. The shock of Serov's death retreated from Priabin, and he became aware that it was too late, that Gant had too far to go – even if he made it.

Kutuzov, *this is Baikonur control. Go for OMS-one burn . . .*

Roger, Baikonur. Going for OMS-one . . .

The shuttle craft was on the point of employing its own engines, not those of the G-type booster. In another forty minutes or less it would be established in orbit and preparing to launch the laser weapon from its cargo bay. Gant was a thousand miles and hours too late . . .

Rodin flung open the door. There were others behind him, perhaps four or five staff officers of senior rank, but they were like extras accompanying a star performer. His face was pinched with rage, his eyes pale and gleaming. He hardly noticed Priabin as he crossed to the lieutenant.

'What is this? What has *happened*?'

'Comrade General, sir, the American –'

'You told me *that*!' he shouted back. 'Where is the American now?'

The lieutenant shook his head falteringly. 'He's – he's disappeared, comrade –'

Rodin turned to the staff officers who now crowded the room, making it hot and annexed. 'I *knew* this would happen – didn't I warn you, didn't I warn *him*?' There were no dissenters. Nor was there anything of Priabin's own strange satisfaction in Rodin's reaction. It was purely a military and security matter. For the moment, his son had never existed or come into contact with Serov. Priabin glanced at the wall clock. Almost ten minutes into the launch. Perhaps six minutes since the moment he had first noticed the panic behind the tinted glass. Rodin clenched his fists in impotent fury.

'We're in the middle of nowhere,' Priabin said. Rodin's head jerked up, as if he had received a blow. Only slowly did he recognize the speaker, and even more slowly did suspicion and dislike clear from his features.

'And he knows it,' Rodin replied finally, as he slapped one clenched hand into its companion palm. The looks were puzzled, as if Rodin and himself were two people employing a secret language. 'And he damn' well *knows* it!' Rodin repeated, and the breathy words might have contained admiration. Then he snapped at the map's operator: 'Enlarge the map area – full extent! No, again – again! Smallest scale!'

The operator typed frantically at his keyboard. The map, like a rectangle of stained glass upright on a trestle, changed in a series of eye-hurting jolts. Each time, the area covered by the map enlarged. It was the effect of a camera rushing away from a place, a jerky, interrupted view such as the cosmonauts aboard the shuttle might have had, if they ever looked down and back. Finally, when the operator looked up, the blue smear of the Caspian's eastern coastline soiled the left-hand edge of the map, yellow desert filled the bottom half, the Aral Sea was little more than a large puddle, and mountains began to rise in the south-eastern corner. Millions of square miles – hundreds of thousands, at the least.

Rodin studied the map then turned on Priabin.

'You think he's won?' he said. It was hardly a question.

'No,' Priabin admitted. 'I think he's lost . . .'

As if to confirm some pessimistic hospital diagnosis, the voice of the shuttle commander was suddenly loud in the room.

'Baikonur Control, this is *Kutuzov*. We have OMS cut-off.' The voice warmed Rodin's chill features.

'I think you're right,' he said, and turned back to the map.

'He could still be anywhere in that nowhere,' he added in a murmur.

'Flying low and on an erratic course,' Priabin replied. Again, they seemed the only two insomniacs in a room of sleepers; the only two who understood each other and the situation. 'There's no one out there to see or hear him . . . hardly a soul, anyway. He's gone.' He sensed the pleasure in his voice, but did not regret it. And Serov *was* dead.

'You think so?' Rodin asked.

The general had turned to him now, not as to some trusted adviser but rather to an opponent who had somehow earned his respect. And who would be beaten and eliminated, Priabin realized. There was a cold and malevolent glitter in the old man's eyes. Valery and Serov were both dead. His son was off his conscience.

Priabin, nevertheless, nodded in a studiedly casual way.

'I think so,' he repeated, moving closer to Rodin. He pointed at the map. 'It will be dark for another three hours and more. He's amid ground-clutter as far as radar's concerned, this whole area is uninhabited for the most part – he's the best pilot they have. *We* know that only too well! He's gone, General. He's gone, all right.'

Rodin paused, then his fingers clicked and he snapped out: 'Fuel! He exploded the fuel store, you said. How much fuel did he take on board – any? Well, do you *know*?'

Voices leaking from the radio, as depressing as continuous rain against summer windows. *Not here, gone to earth, no trace, not here, gone . . .*

Their content never varied. Gant had, to all intents and purposes, disappeared. Almost, Priabin thought with an irony which he savoured, as if the aircraft he flew was invisible.

'Sir – I have an answer!' the lieutenant announced breathlessly.

'Well?'

'Most of the store was destroyed . . . some empty drums were away from the fire – the aircraft would have been fuelled up, anyway, comrade General, sir – so what –?'

'What has he done? I don't know, Lieutenant – but I am willing to stake that he has more than enough fuel for his journey. Wouldn't you, Priabin?'

'You're convinced, then, too?' Priabin agreed.

Rodin nodded. 'Oh, yes, this American is trying to make it all the way home.'

'Which means,' Priabin realized, blurting out the words as if they were a cry of pleasure, 'you have to stop, cancel *Lightning* until you catch him!'

'I shall cancel nothing.'

'Unless you catch him it doesn't matter if it takes him a *month* to get home! He has the *proof!*'

'Then he must be found!'

'You have to stop it.'

'No!' Rodin thundered. 'The American has to be *found!*'

'You won't be able to do that, General.'

Rodin studied Priabin with a malevolence that distorted his features. He rubbed his chin feverishly. His eyes gleamed.

'You think not? That's some old agricultural variant of an Antonov he's flying – a crop-spraying aircraft. Wherever he is headed, south or west – and however deviously – he can't travel fast enough. He's racing daylight and he can't win!' He turned his back to study the enlarged area shown on the map. His left hand waved vaguely yet repeatedly, as if he were conjuring something from the computer image. In the centre of the display, the maddened insects of the search continued to buzz and jerk and twist in their separate courses. Rodin continued speaking, addressing no one other than Priabin. 'I calculate he will have to run for a full hour in daylight, whichever route he takes.' He turned back to Priabin. 'Which means we shall set a trap for our friend. Using every aircraft and helicopter we can lay our hands on. West and south – slam the doors in his face. Mm?' His confidence had become amused. 'Well, Colonel?'

After a long silence, Priabin said: 'I see. You'll be waiting for him. However –'

'However nothing! We'll find him – and kill him. Meanwhile, there's work to do.' He glanced at the men in the room as if for the first time. 'Lieutenant – you will continue the search within the Baikonur perimeter. His aircraft may have been damaged in the – explosion.' There was only the merest hesitation in his voice. 'Responsibility for coordinating the larger search will pass to me.'

'Sir!' the lieutenant snapped out.

Rodin turned to his staff officers, who became animated, full of small, impatient movements.

'Gentlemen – we have a laser weapon to place in orbit – shall we go?' Heartiness answered by smiles and the bright eyes of younger men than they were. Rodin was blithe. He had no doubt that Gant would be caught, Priabin thought, no doubt at all.

I'm in no doubt, either, he was forced to confess. Gant would be running for Turkey, he wouldn't risk Afghanistan again, the way he had come in. He was going west. Where the forces that could be mounted against him were massive, the entire Caucasus and Transcaucasus military districts. They were front-line, not like Central Asian district. Aircraft, missiles, helicopters. And Gant would be running the gauntlet to the border for a whole hour of daylight. The desperation of their need to destroy him would ensure their success. By the time it was daylight, Rodin would have destroyed the American shuttle. From the moment that happened, the whole country couldn't afford Gant's survival.

Rodin waved his hand; dismissing everything with the gesture except *Lightning* and Gant.

'You will accompany us, Colonel,' he snapped, leaving the room.

The hidden striplight over the bathroom mirror gave his features an unhealthy, exaggerated pallor. He inspected his face minutely, reminding himself to use the eye-drops to clear the red streaks from his eye-white. He tossed his head without amusement. Nikitin and his entourage were waiting until they saw the whites of his eyes. They were in no hurry to open fire. He rubbed his chin. Get rid of the stubble, the shadow, too. If he slept – take

527

the pills – the dark stains beneath his eyes might fade enough. If not, then make-up would do it.

At the banquet given by the President of the Swiss Republic for the visiting dignitaries, he had waltzed with his host's plump wife, her white, smooth arm resting lightly on his shoulder, heavily manacled with diamonds. Their glancing lights had become almost hypnotic. While they danced, he automatically moving and responding to the woman's platitudes, he had re-called the Inauguration Ball and the first dance with Danielle as First Lady. The roars of applause and inebriated and triumphant voices had drowned the quieter whispers and imperatives of the lobbyists and place-seekers and time-servers. Later, Joni Mitchell had sung; people had talked of another Camelot. Ridiculous, but possible to believe then, that first night.

Invitation to the dance; of folly. He had tripped as lightly as Dorothy down a yellow brick road of his own devising. It was in reality a Soviet illusion, dazzling him like the diamonds on the wrist of the Swiss President's wife. The prize had been peace and a place in history. He had made a greedy snatch at both of them; and lost both.

He shook his head. No, you haven't lost your place in history, he instructed himself. Just switched roles, hero-into-villain. You'll be remembered, boy, and how . . .

The sun had come up, clear and cold, that morning after the Inauguration Ball. On the White House lawn, heavy, clean snow. The Washington Monument like an inverted icicle, the Lincoln Memorial, distant, clean and massive against the pale sky. He'd breathed deeply, and he could hear, as if in his blood, Martin Luther King's speech from the steps of the Memorial and the vast murmur of the crowds. Portentously, he had mur-mured, clutching his arms across his chest because of the cold, *I have a dream, too . . .*

. . . not any more you don't, he told the now-haggard image in the mirror which was tiredly cleaning its teeth. Not any more.

The satellites and the shuttles were obsolete. As from tonight, with the launch of the Soviet *Raketoplan*. The US was ten years behind, however much money Congress and the administration approved once the truth came out. From tonight, while he had waltzed with a platitudinous, plump Swiss wife with too many diamonds on her throat and wrist, they could do anything they wanted – shoot down satellites, shoot down *Atlantis* or any of the shuttles, anything they wanted. He couldn't call their bluff. He had no proof, there *was* no proof!

Dick Gunther had whispered in his ear, during the fish course, that the Soviets had confirmed the launch from Baikonur. *An historic occasion . . . a glimpse of the future* – was there an irony in that statement? Nikitin had joked about the rendezvous in orbit with *Atlantis*. Exchanging comic books and chocolate bars, was that what he had said? Yes, adding *while we make the real exchange here, my friend*.

He spat toothpaste and saliva into the wash basin, swilled out his mouth. Strangely, there was still that stale taste.

The scent of the turbine fuel was heady and sweet on the chilly, dark desert air. The smell hung about the Antonov because the late night was windless and empty. The faint hissing of the fuel in the hose and the whirring of the pump could not be heard above the Antonov's feathering engine. The wing quivered beneath his feet. He had to keep the engine idling to operate the pump driving the fuel from the chemical tank into the tanks in the wings. He had squatted on his haunches on the wing, the light of the torch dimly illuminating the pages of the school atlas open on his knees. The yellow-brown of desert stretched around the position of his index finger. He was two and a half hours from Baikonur and four hundred miles to the south-west of the complex – *there*, still more than a hundred miles east of the Caspian Sea. He fixed the point in his mind where he would cross the coast, then traced his route towards the oil wells marked south-east of Baku. Their flares in what remained of the night would give him a visual fix as he passed to the south of them, just above the water.

He closed the atlas with a snap, listening to the noise of the engine. Everything was familiar, gave confidence. The noises of an airplane, the empty night. He stood up and stretched.

Stretched away tiredness and cramp. The five hundred and more miles ahead of him, the four hours' flying, distanced him from past and future. They would not find him, not while it remained dark and the land was empty; and he had no need, not yet, to consider the dawn and the trap waiting to be sprung at first light. It was easy to understand what Rodin would decide, and easy, for the moment, to ignore it. It was like a time-out called by both teams. He'd seen the distant navigation lights of aircraft against the stars. Heard voices on the radio, picked up glimpses of them on radar. But it had all been unreal, not dangerous.

He looked up at the night. The moon had gone. Five in the morning, local time. His westward flight extended the night, as if he carried darkness with him like a cloak, which would disappear a hundred miles short, almost an hour before he reached the Turkish border. As soon as they saw him – and he knew they would – he would scream *Mayday* on the broadest waveband; scream the whole story.

Gant shook his head.

He had begun to believe in his survival. He did not want to envisage daylight. He rubbed his eyes. Navigating by compass and the stars – and the school atlas – tired him, the noise of the Antonov was a constant assault, but those things did not matter. They were elements of surviving, and familiar. He could cope. Distance from Baikonur was like a constant, measured flow of adrenalin.

In every direction, emptiness undulatingly stretched away from him. The uninhabited northern part of the Kara Kum desert. Somewhere, a rock split, the noise like gunfire, startling him. The shock had no reverberation. He was calm. The whole ball game now, that was what he wanted. The videotape cassette delivered; the means of winning. It meant he had to survive, cross the frontier. It was him now, against everyone and everything, and the idea did not unnerve him. Not yet.

The wing tanks should be almost full by now.

'One half-orbit distance achieved, *Kutuzov*.'

'Roger, control. Forty-five minutes since satellite release. Countdown to PAM ignition at — fifteen seconds and mark. Over.'

'Roger, *Kutuzov*. Fifteen seconds and counting.'

Rodin was smiling. It was as if there were two smiles on his lips at the same moment. The small one at the fiction of referring to the laser weapon as a satellite — in the event of transmission interception and decoding — and the larger satisfaction of the countdown, like that of a cat with cream on its whiskers. Ten seconds were all that remained until the payload assist module's — PAM's — small solid-propellant motors automatically fired to lift the laser battle station towards its thousand-mile-high orbit over the Pole.

Kutuzov was in a two hundred-mile-high orbit, circling the earth every ninety minutes. Its cargo doors had opened an hour and a half before, the shuttle had manoeuvred into position, the laser weapon on its motors had been set spinning in the hold, then unlocked to drift away from the shuttle. Now, half an orbit later, its motors were about to fire. Five seconds.

Priabin stood at the back of the narrow command room like a newspaper reporter allowed to observe events without playing any part in them.

Everything had gone smoothly, there had been no hitches. Rodin was winning his race with Gant and with his own country. To watch him was like being told that one's calm, elderly neighbour was a dangerous madman, then becoming alert for signs of disorder, irrationality, even violence. But there was nothing. The general was blithe, tense at moments, jocular, expansive, silent in turn. There were no signs of madness, simply the sense that this room and the vast control room below its windows were his entire world. Institution. They were all mad here. And unstoppable. He knew that with only too great a certainty. He was there because it amused Rodin to have him witness his own helplessness. *Watching history unfold, mm, Priabin?* he had snapped at him at one moment — when the cargo doors of the shuttle opened and the camera displayed the action

531

on a dozen screens at once. *A rare privilege*, he had added, *for a mere policeman*. Laughter in the crowded, orderly room.

They had no thought of consequences, only of authority. The demonstration of their power. Outside this institution of theirs, with its intoxicating illusion of omnipotence, there existed only the Politburo. No other world, no populations, no enemy country, no other superpower. They were engaged in a struggle with their political masters – soon their servants? Priabin nodded in gloomy confirmation. If they didn't cause a war, they'd win what they wanted. The institution would control *everything*.

The madhouse. The efficient, normal-seeming, clubby madhouse.

Ignition of the PAM's motors. Priabin winced and waited for the voice of the shuttle's commander to confirm motor ignition. He could clearly envisage the laser weapon flashing up into the darker darkness, away from the earth. Rodin was as remote as *Kutuzov* and the now-moving *Lightning* weapon.

PAM-T plus ten seconds.

'Baikonur, this is *Kutuzov*.'

'Go ahead, *Kutuzov*.'

The voices were uttering feed-lines to arouse the pleasure of this room's inhabitants. He glanced at a screen beside him.

Before the shuttle commander could reply, he heard someone say in a surprised, even pained voice: 'Comrade General, we're not getting a confirm signal from the PAM –'

Then the *Kutuzov* voice: 'Baikonur, PAM ignition nonfunctional. Repeat, we do not have PAM burn.'

Rodin's cry broke in the room, startling men who, a moment earlier, had been somnolent with anticipated pleasure.

'What has happened? *Answer me*! What's wrong, *Kutuzov* – what has gone wrong?' It shook Priabin to attention. On the screen beside him, the fibre-optic map showed the twin wiggles, red and white, of the two shuttles' orbits, separated by half the world. On a second screen, the open cargo doors of the *Kutuzov* and the empty cargo bay.

No ignition, then –

No ignition!

'Baikonur, this is *Kutuzov*. We're showing a non-ignition on the PAM's motors –'

'Back-up!' Rodin cried.

'Back-up systems show non-ignition, sir.'

'Manual emergency trigger!'

'No response from the PAM motors, sir.'

There was a tight, stifling silence in the room, the only chatter from machines, the humming and clicking of electrics.

'Sir, telemetry reports tracking the – satellite . . .' The officer remembered the fiction. 'It hasn't left orbit, sir. It's not moving.'

Priabin glanced towards a clock on the wall. Six forty-five. Recognition of time made him think of Gant. Two and a half hours or more since he had taken off, incinerating Serov and a gunship crew to enable him to do so. Perhaps he was halfway, or less, to Turkey. Time, time . . . delay.

'Not moving?' It was a challenge rather than a question.

'Telemetry confirms the weapon is stationary in its original orbit.'

'Where it cannot be targeted and fired!' Rodin stormed.

Time . . .

Had the solid-fuel motors on the weapon fired, there would have been a maximum of two hours before the battle station reached its final altitude and been ready to fire at the American shuttle. Time . . . how much time *now*? A systems failure in the ignition of the PAM had elongated time like elastic, stretching it in . . .

Gant's favour?

No, Gant would be stopped at the border. Daylight would be the brick wall with which he would collide and die.

Priabin found himself staring across the room at Rodin, who was glaring in his direction; as if he were the jinx who had caused this ill-luck. But the time was unusable. He was Rodin's prisoner, he reminded himself, now aware of the lounging guard – a new one, the other having been relieved an hour ago.

Rodin was huddled with his senior officers. Voices debated, urged and rejected. Radio channels crackled, the voices of mission control and the shuttle waited. Priabin edged towards the windows. Looking down, he saw the huge map; colours flared, lights winked and moved. The combined forces of two military districts were being mobilized, marshalled into the shape of a trap. A team handpicked by Rodin controlled, by proxy, hundreds of aircraft and helicopters, thousands of men. He turned away from the depressing vision it formed. He realized that all the delay to the firing of the laser weapon would do, would be to prevent Rodin from destroying the *Atlantis before* Gant died. Nothing had changed.

And Rodin seemed to realize it, too. His face was still angry, and filled with cold authority. But his eyes and mouth were calm. His hands unclenched. A temporary setback; revert to original time-table. Gant, *then* the shuttle.

'*Kutuzov*, this is Rodin,' Priabin heard him say. 'I want a link-up with the – *satellite* during your present orbit of the earth, and an EVA to inspect and repair the systems failure. Acknowledge.'

A man floating in space, repairing the malfunctioning motors. A matter of hours, no more. Rodin's features gleamed with satisfaction when the shuttle commander acknowledged. He put down the microphone and slapped his hands together loudly, like a noise to frighten children engaged in a party game in the dark.

'Gentlemen, we have work to do!' he cried. 'As tight a schedule as possible – and no more delays!' He glanced again in Priabin's direction, then beckoned him. 'Come, Colonel, you can give us your expert opinion on the preparations we're making for Major Gant!'

EIGHTEEN

acts of desperation

A Sukhoi fighter, too eager, flashed across the nose of the Antonov, the sun glistening on its silver fuselage. Then it was gone. Gant craned to follow its path, and saw it winking like a signal-lamp as it banked then began to climb out of the sand-brown of the country below into the pale morning sky.

And others . . .

Full daylight. Eight o'clock, and they had found him. The radio could not be retuned to their Tac-channels and the radar was too rudimentary to show more than a smudged impression of the hostile landscape ahead. After crossing the Caspian and the flat marshes and plain to the west of it, he had sneaked through the mountains like a thief, for hours it seemed. Sliding around and over and through, hugging the contours of the country as the night faded into grey-then-blue. Temperature mounting, the past hours becoming no more than a mocking illusion of safety and cleverness, tension holding him like a straitjacket. Now, morning and the aircraft.

He flung the lumbering, though small, Antonov severely to port, shocked at the leap of a mountain into the centre of the cockpit windscreen. He wrenched on the steering handles of the column, throwing the crop-sprayer away from the mountain's snow-streaked flank. At once, he was straining to relocate the Sukhoi, the *Fencer* variable-geometry fighter. He had glimpsed the pilot's helmet and the aircraft's eagerness. He ignored the other occupant of the cockpit, the weapons officer. It was the pilot's skill that would kill him.

As the fighter flipped into a looping turn and came back towards him, he saw the flare of a missile igniting. He pulled up the Antonov's nose as if reining in a wild horse. Sky swung crazily across the windscreen, the tail of the aircraft seemed as if tearing free of thick mud – then the thin, steamlike trail from the missile passed away beneath him. The peaks of the mountains around him gleamed with sunlight. The Sukhoi rushed below him and flicked belly-outwards around an outcrop of brown, snow-marked rock. And was a mile away before it began to turn.

The primitive radar, which only scanned forward, showed him no signs of other aircraft. But he knew that they were only minutes away at best. Aircraft and gunships. Slower and more manoeuvrable than the Sukhoi.

The border was less than fifty, less than *forty* miles away now. He had come nearly nine hundred miles in darkness and safety at zero feet and with mounting excitement. And now it was over. He dipped into the uneasy safety of the mountains once more.

The Sukhoi turned lazily and looked for him again. A silver signal at the far end of a tunnel-like valley, rushing closer. Enlarging in his mirror. Hopeless –

The retinal image of the detonating missile was like a distant omen. The *Fencer* grew like a rushing silver fish in his mirror, attacking along the valley. It was time, the moment for Mayday – and even as he thought it, it was already too late. Cannon fire from the fighter flashed alongside and past the cockpit, shook and flung dust and snow from the nearest hill-flank. Then the Antonov rocked in the shockwave of the *Fencer*'s passage. Two tinted facemasks were turned in his direction – it was as if he could see boyish grins behind them – and then the aircraft lifted sharply up and away to begin its turn. The Antonov, as if in surrender, entered a gap of clear air above mountain pasture, the hill-slopes falling sharply away on every side. Snow-covered grassland, dotted huts, a thin trail of smoke climbing into the morning air. The detail emphasized the lumbering, frail slowness of the crop-sprayer. Gant swallowed and wiped the perspiration from the edge of the old leather flying helmet. The *Fencer* began falling like a meteorite towards him.

Weapon load – he'd glimpsed the underwing pylons on the

starboard side which included medium-range air-to-air missiles and the AA-8 snapshoot missiles designed especially for dogfights. And a multi-barrel gun beneath the belly. As the *Fencer* had turned, he had seen the port wing and the bulk of two 57mm rocket launchers.

It swooped down behind him. The radar screen began filling with shapes. Six, seven —

Mayday.

The *Fencer* loomed —

Underwing flame. He had to climb, to broadcast his Mayday cry, his code-ident, *Winter* —

The Antonov rocked, bucked, tried to free itself of his grip on the column. His wrists bulged with muscle and vein. Smoke, he smelt smoke . . . but the Antonov turned as he wished as the *Fencer* flashed over him with a cold shadow.

Gant knew the *Fencer*'s armaments, the speed, climb-rate, turning circle, time-to-return to an attack . . . and the old Antonov was a weaponless biplane, a survivor from an age before modern dogfights.

The Sukhoi was now swinging down behind him in the mirror, where smoke was streaming from the aft section of his 'plane. Gant felt chilled as he identified the location of the fire, and the rudder and the column felt weak and distant under his hands and feet.

The fighter sped past and above and swung into a scissors manoeuvre. The pilot's reinforcements would be closing. Gant was supposed to follow — he was already heaving the column into a break which would confirm he was obeying the pattern of the manoeuvre —

— smoke. Controls OK, but limited life.

It was like a crazy, clever movie, past versus present or future. The *Fencer*'s patience was wearing thin as he curved back to complete the second figure of the scissors manoeuvre. He over-shot because it was much slower than in training, but the boy in the Sukhoi had already begun to adjust.

As the smoke crept in, Gant knew his cockpit time was running out . . . the main cabin would be filled with smoke now, the airplane was becoming leaden and dull and the mountain-sides ahead of him offered a shelter he could not reach. Smoke trailed out from the tailplane like a signal, answered by thin trails of smoke from hut chimneys on the ground. The thirty-seven miles to the border were impossible.

The *Fencer* came down like a sabre.

There is a stalemate in the scissors . . .

. . . so said the manual. The boy in the Sukhoi understood the manoeuvre. His forward airspeed had become reduced, he was crawling through the air. *The winner will be the fighter with the slowest forward velocity . . .*

The Antonov was the slower in any race but it was unarmed — — and hit.

Clean air.

Ground.

Instruments . . .

He would have to climb, and pulled back the column without expectation. The nose of the old biplane nuzzled into the sky. Only the Mayday signal was left to Gant, however much he resented the fact. The radio signal had to reach across the Turkish border like the scattering from a hand sowing grain. There was only that — and survival.

But not in the air. The fire, he knew, would be creeping along the fuselage from the tail section towards the main cabin. None of the controls seemed to have been damaged, the biplane could still be manoeuvred, and the Sukhoi, even with its wings and airbrakes fully extended was still not able to make the requisitely tough turns to break the stalemate of the scissors . . .

The *Fencer* was not an opponent, merely a factor. When the others arrived, they would build an aerial box from which he could not escape. It could be no more than a minute now before that process began . . . *climb!*

Mayday.

As the biplane's sluggish nose lifted, the Sukhoi flashed around and beneath, surprised by his disobedience. Then he climbed. The sun behind them reddened the star the fighter made as it rose. The boy-pilot would come head-on now, firing everything, because on his screens the others were rushing in like sharks. *He* wanted the kill.

Villages, huts, settlements below . . . a long, wide valley, lush beneath snow. From the school atlas on the co-pilot's seat, this was the target for the signal. Smoke billowed, hardly dispersing in the airflow. The snapshoot missile had ignited without damaging. The 'plane was being eaten by the fire, but everything still worked.

Here he had to.

Sukhoi, finally swinging up and around to kill.

Altitude just, just *enough*!

Mayday. Heat in the cockpit, smoke everywhere, billowing and acrid.

'Mayday, Mayday – this is *Winter Hawk*. I repeat, this is *Winter Hawk* . . .' Behind his tinted facemask, the young pilot of the *Fencer* would let his smile grow at the panic of the distress call and the unfamiliar codename. 'This is *Winter Hawk* . . .' In control rooms, cockpits, radio posts, they'd hear it and be satisfied. The American pilot hadn't made it, he'd lost . . . he was crying for help. He gave his position, over and over, he repeated the codename, the Mayday, then his position again. And, because the hunt knew what he had, he ended: '*Winter Hawk* successful, repeat successful. Mission accomplished.' When he had repeated the final sentence of his message, he flicked off the radio and coughed in the acrid atmosphere. The radio had become irrelevant. The cockpit was hot, stifling.

. . . and now the burning . . .

Vietnam. Pulling at the hood of the ejector seat, the cockpit perspex banging away from above him, the seat exploding out of the Phantom, rotating like a ball so that he saw sky, jungle, sky, the Phantom pursuing its course, streaming dark, oily smoke. Sky, jungle – the seat drifting away from him, then the neck-wrench and physical blow of the chute opening above him . . . then the airplane exploding into bright fragments wrapped in billowing orange. Then dropping towards –

Here he had no ejector seat, only the parachutes stowed in the burning main cabin. He heard the Antonov's automatic fire alarm for the first time, as if it had only begun that moment. He switched to autopilot, and sensed the cockpit alienate him; finish with his services. He unbuckled his seat belt and stood up, dragging off the tight old leather flying helmet, throwing it aside. Bending low he gripped the hot door handle and opened the cabin door. Smoke was opaque, choking. He clutched his handkerchief over his nose and mouth. His last glimpse through the cockpit windscreen had shown him new stars winking as they approached and the mountains beginning to loom ahead of the course he had set.

He fumbled in the cabin like a blinded animal. Caught up the kitbag which contained the cassettes of film and videotape. Rifle next, snatched from its mount on the fuselage. Orange fire glowing at the end of the cabin. Smoke everywhere. Now, the burning of systems, ailerons, struts, linkages, control mechanisms. At any moment, the Antonov would be unable to respond to the autopilot and begin to fall out of the morning.

Glasses, rifle, spare ammunition clips, cassettes . . . chute, *chute* – his mind raced towards becoming out of control. Emergency pack, compass . . . the linkages were buckling, beginning to distort. He felt the Antonov lurch tiredly, then resume its illusion of calm passage.

He heaved the chute from its locker and awkwardly, hunched and coughing, wrestled his arms into the harness. Then touched the ripcord. He eased around the chemical tank and reached the door –

– flung it open. Smoke was torn and hurled around him. The wind cried. The fire leapt nearer. The biplane lurched again, then seemed to decline into a lazy, certain fall, banking over the valley towards the nearest hillside. Brown and snow-streaked. The slipstream tore at Gant's clothing, flapping the parka like stiff folds of tarpaulin. He gripped the edges of the door-frame with white hands. Looked down, then quartered the sky as the Antonov's dying fall moved his vision like a lazy camera.

The Sukhoi *Fencer* was coming head-on now, and he could hear the boom of its engines echoing off the hills. The boy would hang a curtain of shells and rockets just ahead of the biplane, into

540

which the old Antonov would lumber like a weary tiger into a pit. As he squinted into the slipstream, his eyes watering, Gant saw the Sukhoi growing in size, until the ripple of little ignitions beneath its wings indicated the hanging of the curtain. The *Fencer* was nose-up, then it pulled steeply away and banked, slipping behind a creased mountain flank. Two new silver fuselages winked in the sun.

Gant poised himself. The Antonov's fall was almost graceful, delicate. He glanced at the tailplane, then at the fire behind him. He thrust out from the cabin door into the slipstream, feeling it leap on him, buffet and move his body even as he fell away from the Antonov. Altitude, five hundred and fifty feet, no more. It was low to jump . . . just all right? The mountain loomed – all round him, it seemed – and the biplane curved eerily towards it. He swivelled his gaze but could not see the *Fencer*.

Impact. Not with the mountainside but with the curtain of shells and rockets. The Antonov disintegrated. Skeletal remains were illuminated like black matchsticks within the ball of orange fire . . . which became smoke. Debris drifted down –

– like himself.

Ripcord.

Jerk as if someone were wrestling with him and trying to break his back. He looked up. The chute opened slowly, like a demonstration.

Where was the *Fencer*, how near the closest of the others, how long to fall . . .?

The snow filled the valley, now wide enough to be a plain. The wind drifted him towards the huge mountain. His hands tugged, altering his course minutely. Perhaps two hundred feet up now, no more . . . where was the *Fencer*? How close was the nearest gunship?

The *Fencer* pilot had not seen him jump. Perhaps the others were too far off to reach him. One-fifty feet. He felt himself hanging in the wind like a target in a fairground booth.

The lower slopes of the mountain gave him his best chance. The pall of smoke from the biplane hung above him, as the debris raced him towards the snow. He was too close to the mountainside to reach the flat terrain covered with soft snow. The wind drifted him and he fought against it, tacking like a sailor with a hundred tiny adjustments to avoid being thrown against the rock face. He was unaware of his own breathing, his mind was at a great distance. Hands only, his weight, the force of the wind, the brown, snow-streaked rocks, the trees below.

And the sky, the silver fuselages taking on distinct shape and proximity. And the first gunship no bigger than a beetle as yet. *Mayday*. There had been no other way. He could not have survived in the sky.

He jerked on the chute's cords, feeling his body swing away from hard rock, then he seemed to plummet into a narrow crevasse. Feet struck, cold and shock registering together. He rolled, covered at once in snow, his nostrils and mouth filled with it, choking him. It buried him, cutting out all light and air. He could just make out the noise of firing and registered the thud of cannon fire or rocket attack through the rock beneath and around him. Darkness. Suffocation –

Time passed somnolently on the giant screen portraying the repairs to the laser weapon's payload assist module. The sensation of such lumbering slowness scratched at Priabin's nerves. It was as if time itself imprisoned him, not the bored and chewing guard who lounged opposite him. He wanted to scream away the tension that gripped his chest and made it difficult to breathe. Ten o'clock in the morning, local time. Already half an hour of daylight on the Turkish border. The idea brought a fresh choking sensation. There was nothing *he* could do, however much he wanted to.

The repair work had been in progress for more than three hours. On the screen, the bloated form of one of the cosmonauts hung in the blackness alongside the laser weapon. The faulty payload assist module had been detached and returned to the *Raketoplan*'s cargo bay in order to effect the necessary repairs. Now, as he watched, a second cosmonaut – only the shuttle's pilot had remained aboard *Kutuzov* – hovered into view, propelling slowly ahead of him the module's bulk. It was one-third of the battle station's size and circular, except where its single rocket motor narrowed into a funnel. The cosmonauts, even wearing their backpacks, seemed dwarfed by the two machines they now had to reunite. It was perhaps a matter of less than two hours . . . then a further two hours, and —

Rodin — where was Rodin? He looked up towards the windows of the command room. Figures behind glass. Yes, there he was, arms moving in emphasis, the mad conductor of this mad orchestral score. Unable to settle or remain still. Moving between *Lightning* and Gant. Shaped by the progress of the repairs — which had gone well — and the hunt for the invisible Gant.

On the screen, the payload assist module was nudged towards the laser weapon, approaching it with the caution of a servant bearing bad news. The two cosmonauts, using their backpacks and yet still moving with almost stonelike slowness, closed on one another, handling the inertia of the PAM, slowing it, directing its bulk beneath the waiting battle station. Time was elephantine, but its hurry made him want to shriek. This was *all* the time there was. Four hours — and when they had passed, the world would have changed.

He rubbed his hand through his hair. Then drank cold coffee. The guard, on the other side of the foldaway table on which breakfast had been served — with a sense of mockery clearly emanating from Rodin, who must have organized the meal — belched softly, then picked his back teeth with a spent matchstick. Priabin had eaten as if on holiday — or like the proverbial condemned man, he corrected himself.

On the giant screen, the two cosmonauts danced with heavy, slow movements around the PAM, manoeuvring it into position. Their dialogue and the replies and instructions of mission control were no more than a background noise, like muzak.

The hours of Gant's continuing escape had been like a mounting fever, maddening Rodin. His figure had vanished from the windows of the command section. Priabin, itching with a renewed assault of tension, watched the door below the line of windows. As if waiting for an actor to enter, stage right. Hearing a babble of sound that could not submerge itself into the dialogue with *Kutuzov*, he turned his head.

At the map table, someone was looking up towards the door into the main room, other officers were bending closer to the table. The excitement was unignorable. They'd found him, he'd been sighted . . .

Rodin strode across the room towards the table. Priabin stood up. The guard seemed indifferent to his movement. Rodin's voice was peremptory with enquiry, but bearing an undercurrent of congratulation in it, too. His staff officers crowded around, peering, gesticulating. There was no doubt about it. The dialogue with the shuttle and the images on the giant screen were peripheral, almost subliminal. The centre of the room was the map table.

Priabin felt physically sick with utter weariness. He tasted the fat in which his breakfast had been cooked; the coffee seemed lodged at the back of his throat. He tasted too many cigarettes. He understood why he had watched the passage of slow time only on the screen and not looked at any of the numerous clocks in mission control. Subconsciously, he had known the exact moment dawn had broken over the border and seeped through the Caucasus mountains. And every minute since then had wound him like a watchspring, tighter and tighter. His hand gripped the edge of the rickety table. He felt dizzy. Words leaked like the chants of a distant but approaching mob.

'. . . hit . . . confirmed hit, on fire . . .'

'Head-on . . . can't get away.' Voices from headphones, tinny and stridently unreal, from remote microphones, repeated and emphasized by the group around the table. Hands tracing shapes and courses, heads bent to peer at the culmination. '. . . is it, sir!'

'. . . *there*.'

'. . . contact lost. Gunship has visual . . .'

'What of −?'

'Here, just here!'

'. . . destroyed . . .'

Priabin was less than halfway across the room to the table. Peripherally, he saw the two cosmonauts like great white grubs on the screen. The battle station and its PAM seemed one single object now. And that was it, all of it. Then he heard:

'Fireball – *completely* destroyed!'

Cheering, congratulation – nausea returning, on which he gagged. Looking up after a moment, he saw Rodin staring in his direction. The general's smile was one of cold, certain satisfaction. His right hand, slightly extended, was closed in a firm grip.

'. . . chute opening – there's a parachute opening, comrade General!'

Rodin seemed to falter, as if ill or dizzy.

Priabin felt his limbs unfreeze. He hurried to the table. A staff officer moved as if to interpose his body between the general and some attack. Rodin glared into Priabin's eyes like a hard, explosive light.

'What –' Priabin began.

'. . . *devil's* luck!' he heard Rodin exclaim in a pinched, cheated voice before the old man turned to the map table. His knuckles whitened on the table edge.

'. . . gunship may get there,' someone said breathlessly. The atmosphere around the table was choking and airless. 'Two more aircraft closing quickly.' The tone was that of someone repeating an unviable alternative to a set of facts. 'Down – he's down!'

'Kill him,' Rodin managed to say. '*Kill him!*'

'The gunship's going in – tricky, they've spotted him, the chute's dropping over him, marking the spot. Rocket and cannon, sir – they're using everything . . .'

Rodin lurched rather than walked away from the table. His hand waved the others away from him. The subliminal noises of the dialogue with the shuttle impinged on Priabin's hearing. It was as if he had lowered the volume of voices around the map, not wishing to hear.

'. . . can't see anything now . . .'

'He can't survive that, surely?'

'Let the gunship take care of it . . . how many more in the immediate area – what? Let them wait until the snow's cleared –'

Someone had taken command for the moment. Priabin heard

no more, squeezing the voices from his head like water from a sponge. Rodin was beside him, his eyes filled with apprehensions and blame.

'You —' he said.

Rodin seemed to have aged. When a lieutenant appeared beside him and saluted, it was some moments before his presence seemed to register.

'What —'

'Sir, *Stavka*, sir . . .' He held out a message form, hastily scribbled upon. 'Coded signal. They're awaiting —' Rodin waved the man away, snatching at the flimsy sheet and tearing it. The lieutenant subsided to attention some yards away. The noise at the map table had subsided, too, into a concentrated murmur. Time had dragged free of the elephantine images on the screen and raced now. Moments only before Gant was obliterated like the old aircraft in which he had escaped —

— not quite escaped.

Rodin waved the message form beneath Priabin's nose.

'Decision postponed,' he said. 'Decision *postponed*! That's *Stavka*'s position . . .' He turned, glanced at the table, and then faced Priabin once more. 'One man, and they're afraid of him. I shall acknowledge . . .' He smiled, very faintly and with evident cunning. 'I shall inform *Stavka* that no proof exists, that the American has no proof.'

'You can't —'

'I will. At once.'

Priabin's frame quivered. He felt an ague of fear. It was as he had suspected. Rodin was beyond logic. As if in explanation, Rodin added:

'My wife died an hour ago . . . she never recovered consciousness.'

It was like a bulletin rather than an expression of loss. The indifferent voice of printed lines in a column of newspaper deaths. All restraint had gone. His face displayed no signs of grief, and little shock. The man had been hollowed out like a rotten tooth. There was nothing left inside him. Only the uniform and what he believed was his duty were left.

Mad. Dangerously, frighteningly mad. To himself, Rodin was sane and certain.

Priabin whirled around to the table behind them.

'The gunship's spotted him!' someone called out. 'Where's the closest back-up aircraft?'

'It's twenty miles to the border – fifteen at least!'

'Not in a million years – no chance . . .'

Priabin turned away. Rodin was smiling, almost sympathetically. Yes, his emptiness was justified. They'd kill Gant, recover the cassettes, and no one would ever know. No one. Gant was a dead man . . .

'OK, Dick – what can we *do*?'

Shock, hope, deep anxiety all fought against the clinging of the valium he had taken in order to assure himself of sleep. He struggled to a more erect position against the padded headboard of the bed. Gunther was still leaning over him like a doctor.

'What can we do?' he repeated, looking at his hands. They quivered to the register of a distant earthquake. The signal from Gant had shocked with its sudden glimpse of the impossible, and he felt he had not caught his breath since then.

Gunther's briefing continued to assail him, like the effect of successive waves against an old, crumbling sea wall. He wanted to give in to hope, and was terrified of its illusory beauty. Gant, *alive* –

'We *can't* go in, Mr President,' Gunther offered, as if replying to some wild suggestion already voiced. 'That's not possible. Their activity in the air, and now on the ground, is – well, sir, it's frantic.'

'Then they'll –?'

Danielle had slipped out of bed as soon as Gunther's knock had woken her. Calvin smelt coffee, heard the plopping of the percolator. She moved against subdued lighting like an illusion. Part of the illusion of hope that surged in his head like drink. He rubbed the putty-like contours of his face with both hands.

'Sir, I don't *know*! We don't know whether he has *Cactus Plant* with him, we only know that he transmitted the Mayday signal, he used his code-ident, and he said *mission accomplished* . . . their response confirms he has something, some proof, but we can't even begin to guess what it is. His aircraft was shot down, whatever it was – but he has to be alive.'

'You're certain?'

'They're not looking for a body – not with those forces. Sure, they're putting out a smokescreen – searching for a crashed transport airplane is the story – but they're using *speznatz* codes and channels and paratroops – just to look for bodies?' Gunther raised his hands. 'There are *Desantnyye Voyska* units in the area – they've just been parachuted in and there are more on the way. Sir, he's alive and in big trouble. He *must* have the proof we need!'

'And they're terrified he's going to get it out – to us,' Calvin murmured. Then he looked up into Gunther's shadowed face. 'But how in hell can we?' He raised his hands in a gesture of defeat and surrender, but slapped them impatiently back onto the bedclothes. '*Hell*, what can we *do*?'

'John,' he heard Danielle say, her voice strangely pained. He looked up. Her dark hair clouded around her small face. 'He's alive. It doesn't matter . . .' Her voice trailed away into the empty shadows of the room. He nodded, as if she had been his spokesperson and voiced exactly what he had intended to say.

Gunther stepped back as Calvin swung his legs out of bed, stood up, and put on his dressing-gown. One of his jokes. Donald Duck across the shoulders of the towelling material. And a NASA shuttle badge sewn on the breast pocket. But, as if he had donned a uniform, his movements became at once crisper, more alert. He rubbed his hair to tidiness.

'You'll come down –?' Gunther began.

'Yes. At once.' He thrust his feet into his slippers, and held Danielle's wrists briefly as she handed him coffee. The Presidential seal minutely painted on the white china. He nodded reassuringly at his wife. Her face seemed a mirror of his own. Hope fading, the anxiety mounting. 'Yes, I'll come down to the code room. What monitoring do they have down there?'

'Full links with the Pentagon, the NSA, Langley.'

'Good. What have we —?'

'There's a KH-11 satellite over the Caucasus. Full daylight and little cloud cover. Good transmission situation. Washington can see quite a lot of the activity. Gunships, fighters, troop transports — and now troops on the ground in numbers.'

'Terrain?'

'Mountainous, all the way to the border. Difficult for him.'

'And for *them*!'

He passed the empty cup back to Danielle. Thrust his hands into his pockets.

'How far inside is he?'

'Between ten and fifteen miles, their best estimate.'

'That little?'

'That little. Maybe that's as bad as a hundred, even a thousand. They have crack troops swarming all over the place.'

'Dick, don't *say* that! The man got out of Baikonur in an *airplane* . . . now, how the hell did he do that? He could —'

But Gunther was shaking his head.

'They can't afford to let him.'

'He has to stay alive! He has to make it . . . Dear-Christ-in-Heaven, we can't lift a finger to help the guy!'

'Not unless you want to start the next war.'

Calvin nodded absently. 'I realize that, Dick,' he murmured. 'At least —' He looked up, grinning suddenly before his face resumed its solemn expression. '— part of me does. OK, we can't go after Gant. But we can have people on the border, *right* on the border, and we can be watching from the air. What do we have up?'

'AWACS is watching the whole thing.'

'Good. Then I have to talk to the Turkish President right away.'

'We anticipated that, Mr President.'

'Right, then let's be clear what we're talking about here. We have to enlist the aid of one of our NATO allies . . . wait! Would *they* cross into . . . ?'

Gunther looked gloomy. 'They want him awful bad,' was all he said.

Calvin rubbed his hair.

'Then I have to prepare one of our allies for a possible Soviet troop incursion into their territory . . . if Gant makes it that far. God knows what I tell the Turkish President!' He was pacing the room urgently, as if attempting to walk off the last lingerings of the valium; or of fear. 'Ten miles – maybe as little as that?' Gunther nodded. 'Dear *God*, we can only sit and wait this thing out! I feel like an actor waiting to come on – but no one's supplying my cue.' He turned slowly, looking at the room as if it were some kind of command centre reflecting the powers of his office. And shook his head. 'All we can do is make sure we're there to meet him, if he gets out. And he has the proof we *need*!' The tone was singular, not plural. He felt a thrill of enraged frustration that deepened almost at once into fear. He was racked by hope and terror. The proof *I* need, the *proof*, he heard again and again in his head. The proof I need.

'Mr President –?' Gunther began.

'Yes, yes, I'm coming. Give me just a moment to dress.'

Treeline.

The treeline was what had saved him, he admitted once more. Temporarily saved him; just as it temporarily concealed him.

His back was against a rock, he was sitting hunched on pine needles. The snow was patchy beneath the trees, much of the forest floor tinder dry. He held the small glasses he had taken from the Antonov to his eyes, and watched them moving below, around, opposite. All of them . . .

. . . all of them *speznatz*, experts.

The morning was icy cold and clean. Sound was restricted to the occasional crackle of a distant radio or transceiver carried on the sharp air, and the throb of troop helicopters and gunships winding through the mountains or floating above the wide plain of Ararat. Beyond the troops and the machines hanging in the air and the occasional fattening stripe of a vapour trail, he could see Turkey in the distance, where the landscape seemed cardboard and flat through the glasses. The twin peaks that dominated the plain to the West were those of Mount Ararat, in Armenia — *Turkish* Armenia. Gant knew that from the pages of the school atlas. And knew little more than that.

Far below, the main road parallelled the border. To the north-east, a haze of industry hung where the town of Yerevan must be. Snow, brown flanks, foothills, the wide plain, and the river Araxes, followed in swift, blurred succession as he swung the glasses down. He was in the niche of border between three countries.

Speznatz . . .

He involuntarily looked at his watch. The sleeve of the parka crackled with dried, half-frozen snow-melt as he tugged it back from his wrist. Nine-fifteen. Just over an hour since he had baled out. And they had attempted to obliterate him with rocket fire from the first of the gunships to reach him. Had he been able to control the chute as well as he would have chosen . . . he would have struck the snow of the plain dead. In pieces; burning rags of clothing and flesh hanging loosely from the cords of the chute. He shivered, and was chilled through.

The shallow crevasse had saved his life. Trees had beckoned below and he'd struggled feverishly down the precipitous slope, coughing and spitting out melted snow, banging against rocks, tripping often. Then he'd reached the first stunted trees, rolling over and over beneath them until a slim bole winded him and fetched him up half-lying, half-sitting, breath heaving. It had taken them three-quarters of an hour to land the *speznatz* troops or parachute them in. In that time, he had worked his way further down the mountain, beneath the thickening, stronger trees. To wait — and recover. Now, he must move again.

He raised the glasses. A slow vapour trail streaked the sky to the west, across the border in Turkey. As if it was some kind of signal that they had received his Mayday call.

A gunship slid up the side of the mountain, dragging its shadow like a cloak across the snow. Irrelevant. They couldn't find him, not beneath the tree cover. The *speznatz* could —

— and would.

They worked, like most special forces, in four-man units. Or, as now, in multiples of four. And in touch with each other. They could napalm the mountainside from gunships or MiGs, but he knew they wouldn't. They had to be sure, certain sure, he had died. They wanted the cassettes that were the evidence, and they wanted the body. Perhaps most of all, that. They wanted the body, to be certain.

It was time to move. To survive. The nearest troops that he could see were perhaps four or five hundred yards away, below and to his left, trudging up a snow-hidden track, backs bent, guns clearly visible. A four-man unit.

Far below and across the plain, a train appeared as if sliding wormlike out of the undulating earth, smoke billowing up into the air. Railway, road, river; border. Open country. Gant rose onto one knee.

They were toiling alertly up the slope where the trees opened out to reveal a winding track. Rifles slung across their chests — new AK-74s, not like the old Kalashnikov he held in his hands — packs, camouflage overalls ... other weapons, a Dragunov sniper's rifle carried by the sergeant, and slung at one trooper's side, an RPG-7 rocket launcher. If they found only the remaining bits of him, it would be enough.

Four hundred yards.

Everything had become simple, even stark. They wanted him dead, and the proof recovered. He was the only fly in their ointment. He wanted to survive. Even the proof and their concern over it were unimportant. There was only their need to kill him and his desire for survival. Which made the sighting through the foresight's cylinder and the open, U-shaped notch of the rearsight easy, almost like squinting into a small telescope. And made the metal of the unfolded stock as comfortable as that of a favourite hunting rifle. Single shot.

Once, twice, three times.

Surprise, although half-expected, although their nerves were alert. Heads up for an instant before the inertia of training and experience threw their bodies aside from the track towards rocks or tree-boles. Enough surprise for one of the camouflaged bodies to fall awkwardly and roll over, and for a second to have to lunge limpingly towards cover. The fourth, fifth and sixth rounds missed. He quite clearly saw snow plucked up by each of the bullets.

Then he moved, farther back into the trees and to his right, body bent and weaving below and around stinging branches. Ten seconds, eleven, twelve –

– they were good. Behind him, trees shuddered and split and became engulfed in fire as the projectile from the RPG-7 struck and detonated with a roar. He felt the shockwave slap at his back. One dead, a second out of the hunt, the hornets' nest stirred with the long stick of violence. He rushed on, thin branches whipping at him, the rifle swinging rhythmically back and forth across his chest – the pack containing the film and video cassettes banging softly, familiarly on his lower back. He was running north.

Above the noise of his breathing, he heard one of the gunships drive in towards the trees behind him. Noise, then light flashing on the snow lying on the branches over his head. Fierce orange light like a winter sunrise. They'd used the RPG-7's hit as a marker and demolished the immediate area around it. He stopped, and had to lean against a tree to control the shaking of his body. He turned, reluctantly.

A fire seared and glowed like the mouth of a furnace perhaps three or four hundred yards away. He felt the shockwave ebbing through the forest and through his body. His heart continued to pound. The glow began to subside but, higher up, the branches were alight. Resinous, smoky scent, licking flame. A marker, a signal – *here he is, come and get him.*

Beneath the trees he was safe – no, just safer. He concentrated, remembering the scene through the glasses like a map now glanced at. He had to go down, eventually . . . They'd know that. And they *had* maps. They'd know the tracks, all the routes down; the possible, the dangerous, the impossible. The light was dying on the glinting snow above his head. The gunship's rotors beat farther off now, a painter standing back from a completed canvas. The *speznatz* troops would be moving again, up towards the outcrop he had occupied and where the fire still burned.

He turned away, his breathing under control, his heart

quieter. The adrenalin surged. Ducking low, he once more began running, his feet crackling like flames across dead pine needles.

Priabin hit the guard clumsily. His arms flailed again and again once the first blow had been struck because the guard still had hold of the rifle – it could not be tugged from his grasp – and the barrel kept straining towards Priabin's stomach. The guard's body banged against the metal of the double doors behind him. His face registered pain, but had moved out of shock into malevolence, fear for his life.

Again, again – face, chest, arms, most of the blows doing little damage. His knuckles numbly hurting, blood on them.

The guard slumped down the doors into an awkward sitting position, loosening his grip on the rifle and moaning softly just once. After that, the only sound was Priabin's harsh breathing, snatched between the sucking of his bruised and skinned knuckles. He was bent almost double with the effort he had undergone.

He glanced to either end of the alleyway between the main assembly building and a low shed with a corrugated roof and breeze-block still plain beneath stained whitewash. If there was anyone, if they had heard the banging against the door –?

. . . *just caught short – have to go here, OK?* The guard had followed him, amused . . . He had had to force a conversation with the man, through nerves and the mounting fear of the proximity of the guard and his rifle . . . *where did you say they were keeping that poor bastard? Kedrov the spy, yes that's him* . . . He had foolishly repeated every word the guard had uttered, as if to memorize a complicated sequence of instructions. A thin stream of urine. The biting cold of the midday air because he wasn't wearing a greatcoat or cap or gloves. He finished urinating. Knew he could simply go back inside and wait for the inevitable – the unavoidable. He had turned to the guard, zipping his flies, smiling awkwardly. Rifle, guard nodding, his bulk larger than Priabin's.

The EVA was over, the crew was back aboard *Kutuzov*. The shuttle had used its small clusters of rockets to move away from the laser weapon. Firing of the rocket of the PAM was thirty minutes away. The countdown was at two hours —

— he had lashed out at the guard's chin and missed, grazing the reacting man's ear. Moved, hit again and again, wrestled with the gun . . .

Two hours. At the end of that time the laser battle station would have achieved its thousand-mile-high orbit above the pole and would have been aligned on its target, *Atlantis*. Rodin would commence the firing sequence and the American shuttle would be vaporized. It would disappear. And, and . . . unthinkable.

He had not intended action. He was deeply frightened now that he had done so. The guard seemed to be snoring in his unconsciousness, his face chilly with cold, his hands slackly on the rifle. Priabin snatched at it, unhooking its strap from around the man's neck. The guard's head flopped horridly, as if he were dead. Priabin flinched away from him. He had not intended — but the tension had mounted in him because of his inactivity.

The scheme was patchy. It involved Kedrov . . . it involved stopping the firing of the weapon. He could do nothing else, stop nothing *except* the firing sequence. Kedrov *had* to know how it could be done. If he did not, then —

Priabin looked down at the guard. Irrevocable. He was committed now. He shivered with reaction, gripping the rifle tightly, squeezing its warmed metal. Glanced to either end of the alley in a panicky, sweaty haste. His body felt hot now. He had to rid himself of the guard, put him, tie him — where?

He rolled the guard away from the double doors with his foot. It seemed a huge effort. He needed a vehicle to get to GRU headquarters, he needed a means of entering that place, he needed, he needed —

— to get the guard out of sight, don't think ahead, just do this, do this . . . come on, come on, *break* —! He twisted the folding stock of the AKMS in the chain and padlock. Sweat sheened his forehead, his muscles had no strength, the flimsy chain seemed insuperable . . . and parted slowly, with a slight creak like the opening of a window.

He pushed the doors open. Darkness. The light seemed to spill in slowly. It illuminated boxes, shelves, tins – of paint. He wanted to laugh. A paint store. And the doors had been seriously in need of painting.

He dragged the guard into the darkness, found the man's handkerchief and gagged him with it, tying his own around the man's mouth to keep the wad in place. The rifle was banging on his back as he worked, and seemed omnipresent. But he could not use it, not on an unconscious man. Mistake, mistake –

– everything you've done so far is a mistake, he told himself. You can't do it, anyway, so shut up about it . . .

The man's belt and webbing. Hands and feet together behind him, a reversed foetal position. He tightened the straps viciously, perhaps because he couldn't kill him.

He stood in the air for a moment, breathing labouredly. Hands on his hips. Then he picked up the chain and rethreaded it through the door-handles. Hid the broken link as well as he could, left the lock dangling as if still effective. Glanced along the alleyway once more. Still no one. He looked a last time at the door. The chain appeared sound. He began running along the alleyway, his memory of this place playing in his mind like a very old film; stained, patchy, flickering. But *there* –

He forced himself to remember. Main assembly building, attendant stores, workshops, other facilities . . . car parks. Car parks. Military and civilian. He needed something like a UAZ jeep, something that would not be suspicious, not out of place, still free to move around the high security area. Car park –

– left now, then right. He moved incautiously, like a rat seeking reward through its familiar maze, down the alleyways between the crowding complex of buildings. He saw no one.

Until he reached the open space of the car park. Civilian and military vehicles parked within regimented white lines. The car park was almost full. Two men were lounging against a wall, smoking, white lab coats beneath their open topcoats. Fur hats. They were fifty yards away, and uninterested. All they could see was a uniform; a capless officer with a rifle. Baikonur was full of officers. A military driver stepped out of a UAZ, other men were leaning out of a canvas-hooded truck. As his breathing calmed, he began to see how many people there were. He began to stroll. He was not out of place here . . . you are not, you are not out of place, *you are not*.

The truck drove off, smoke pluming from the exhaust. The driver of the UAZ was carrying a metal box, sealed and locked. Priabin passed him with only a single line of parked cars between them. The guard hardly glanced in his direction after saluting casually. He had not even noticed the KGB flashes.

He reached the UAZ and turned. The soldier with the metal box entered the building where the two technicians were lounging against the wall. Priabin glanced into the vehicle. The key was in the ignition. A lucky rabbit's foot dangled from it. Dear *God* —

He watched the technicians, but could not wait. They wouldn't know, would they —? They wouldn't know which vehicle it was.

He climbed in, placing the rifle on the passenger seat. His hands gripped the wheel. They had begun shaking. He looked up at the pale midday sky. Cloudless above a cold desert. It was as if the keys had been left here, as if the guard had been unawares — on purpose. Rope with which to hang himself; a trap. Luck, he kept telling himself, *luck* . . . they're not watching you . . . luck.

He turned the key. The engine caught, and he revved it as if shouting defiantly at someone. He turned the wheel and headed for the road, bumped over the low kerb, then was heading south towards Tyuratam.

Fifteen minutes, ten perhaps.

He had watched the firing of the shuttle's small auxiliary manoeuvring rockets, the sliding away of the laser weapon — or so it seemed from the camera's view aboard *Kutuzov* — until it was a pinprick less bright than some of the stars. He had listened to the voices from the shuttle, the voice of mission control. He had listened to the revised countdown, he had listened to Rodin's public-address voice as he bestowed congratulation to every part of the vast room. He had looked, he had listened –

– until the lid had blown off his rage and frustration and guilt at doing nothing. He had to do something, he had to try to stop Rodin – who was capable of anything. There was no one else to stop him . . . Gant was as good as dead . . . *He* had to do something –

– and the trigger was knowing that Gant was still alive . . . *he's running into a box . . . we have him all but pinpointed . . . only the two casualties so far . . . ten minutes and he's ours –*

Priabin glanced wildly at his watch. Since he'd heard that report from the Armenian border with Turkey, fifteen minutes had passed. He knew Gant was alive and was just as certain he would soon be dead – odds of as much as fifty to one, all his opponents *speznatz* troops, no way out – and *he* had to do something . . . as if it was his *turn* to act.

Buildings encroaching, the darkness of the huge war memorial ahead of him. The cobbles of the square shaking the UAZ's suspension. GRU headquarters. He turned down the ramp into the underground garage from which he and Gant – and *Katya* – had escaped the previous day . . . evening . . . it had all happened in that little time. Now, he was walking back in – driving! *Here I am!*

How the hell could he avoid being recognized? It was *crazy*!

Slowly, carefully, he parked the UAZ. Petrol was nauseous, the damp chill of the place reached into him at once. He glanced at the rifle on the passenger seat. Folding stock, length of weapon when the stock was folded almost twenty-seven inches. Just over two feet. *He hadn't a greatcoat under which to conceal it!*

A greatcoat walked towards him, unsuspecting, merely observing routine. Corporal's stripes, a man smaller than Priabin. A GRU greatcoat. The corporal slapped his gloved hands together for warmth. Again, a fleeting sense of a trap . . . enough rope, as if they *wanted* him there. Then the duty-corporal was at his side, hands coming together slower than before, as if to catch a moth, because he had seen the rifle on the seat in the moment before Priabin raised the barrel towards him. Priabin altered the aim so that the barrel pointed into the corporal's face. Shock, and recognition of the KGB uniform, perhaps even of the colonel inside it. He might have been one of them in the garage yesterday, when they had Serov as a shield, he and the American. The man's face printed out recognition and memory like a computer screen.

'Yes,' Priabin said, nodding. 'Take off your coat . . . no, wait. Step back!' He removed the ignition key and got out of the vehicle. 'Keep your hands down!' He motioned with the gun. 'Let's go back into your warm little booth, shall we, corporal?'

Sullenly, the soldier turned away and began walking. Footsteps echoed. Priabin's overlapped in the damp silence. He watched the lift doors as they passed them, then watched the floor indicator. No one.

Greatcoat.

The soldier opened the door of his glass-sided sentry-booth, and hesitated, as if waiting –

– to be struck. Priabin hit him across the back of the head with the AKMS. Coffee spilled from a mug against which the corporal lurched. Papers and a clipboard came off his desk-shelf and fell about him. The whole booth seemed to list with the weight of his collapse.

Which was below the level of the glass, out of sight. Priabin kicked the man's legs away from the door, then bent to tug and heave at the body – should have got him to remove, doesn't matter, get on with it – until he had pulled the corporal out of his greatcoat.

The sleeves were too short. He pulled off the man's gloves, then scrabbled in a corner for the fur hat with its small red star. Stood up and buttoned the coat. It wasn't too tight, just short in the sleeves and the length. He looked down. Distinguishing stripe on his trousers, just visible. He had to risk it. He tugged on the gloves and slung the rifle over his shoulder. Adjusted the fur hat. Studied the guard. Quick, if you're still in there by the time he recovers you'll be too late anyway.

He grabbed up the keys and locked the glass booth. It rocked as he tested the door with a furious jerk. Glancing back from the lift, it was unsuspicious; unless anyone officiously wanted to know the sentry's whereabouts.

The doors grumbled open. The lift was empty. What was it the guard had said? Kedrov was in one of the *hospital* rooms. To him, it had been a joke, like a salacious insult. Second floor, towards the rear of the building. He pressed for the second floor. The doors closed. The image of the trap again. He heard his own breathing magnified. Stamped with nerves, his arms clutching across his chest and stomach as if he were being assaulted. There was getting out again, taking Kedrov even, then what to do? He hadn't any idea, not really, if he was brutally honest, he would not be able to stop it, he wasn't technical, not in the least.

The doors sighed open at the second floor.

NINETEEN

high frontiers

The trees were opening out. If they caught him on exposed rock, the gunships would no longer be frustrated by the tree-cover and would drive in. It would be over in moments. One of them was close over his head, hanging noisily, its din alone an effective aid to terror. They were drawing the trap close like the neck of a bag. Tight.

He'd tried, with increasing desperation, to maintain his altitude above the foothills and the plain. They wanted to drive him either down to the open ground, or up beyond the treeline. And yet, even though he'd succeeded, the *speznatz* troops behind and around him appeared content. He was still ten miles or more from the border, however much distance he'd travelled. He was still inside their country, moving only parallel to the border, north-east towards the haze that hung above Yerevan.

They didn't mind. He had remained in the trees, high and concealed, but they were sure of him. They couldn't pinpoint him, but they'd have thermal imagers by now. He was warmer than the cold sap of trees. They'd have caught glimpses of him. The transport MiLs had done too accurate a job of landing reinforcements for them not to be aware at least of his general direction and position.

The slopes were steepening now, there were few tracks. The snow was thicker as the trees thinned. They had driven him higher and the country was changing, too. Ravines and narrow canyons, black knife-edges of rock, frozen streams and waterfalls. Trees clung precariously to the landscape; as he did.

His back pressed to rock, he moved in a cloud of his own breath along a narrow ledge screened by a few thin trees from the pale sky. The camouflage of a gunship slid past less than a hundred feet away. Gant felt the downdraught tugging at his parka, tugging at his balance. The machine moved on, blind to his presence, simply waiting. He paused. Sweat dampened his forehead and his armpits were chilly with it. Slowly, he moved on.

They were ahead of him. He'd seen some of the transports, sensed others. Troops had been lowered from ropes or landed in small clearings above and below, and ahead of him. Behind him, others had followed his trail of snapped twigs and branches, trodden litter on the forest floor, disturbed snow on the firboles. Signs of his passage cried out for their attention.

He reached the end of the ledge. The crack of the ravine glinted with ice and a frozen stream at its bottom. He looked up, then around. Nothing. The noise of the MiLs had receded. Eye of the storm. Silence. He waited, but distinguished no noises that indicated stealth or the springing of the trap. The ravine dizzied him as he looked down into it. He would have to jump the ravine now that the ledge had petered out. Push himself outwards away from the rock at his back, as if to fly . . . hands grabbing the opposite side of the ravine, holding on –

Gant swallowed. A radio crackled momentarily until stilled by a harsh whisper. His body shook with reaction. The trees concealed them now. The morning air magnified, made sounds louder and closer, but *how close*? He strained to hear other noises, boot on rock, the rustle of pine-litter, the click of a round of ammunition levered into the chamber. He heard nothing, except the now-background throbbing of gunship rotors. The rock arched above him like a shell. The ravine was below him. The trees were thin – too thin – above and to his left, the way he had come. They would see him easily.

He rubbed one hand over his face, which seemed unformed, loosely put-together. His mouth was wet with saliva. He listened once more, looking down into the ravine and fighting the dizziness. The mouse-scrape of boots through the pine needles rotting on the ground. Eventually, he heard at least one man moving. Then a second, perhaps a minute later, and realized the neck of the bag, the trap itself . . . was there, precisely *there*.

They'd designed it that way. His sense of his immediate surroundings had enlarged, he'd noticed the way the slope fell sheer away beyond the ravine and an outcrop of bare rock. He could glimpse the plain far below through the last of the poor trees. If he reached the outcrop by jumping across the ravine, he could not go down . . . nor continue north because the ground rose steeply and there were no trees. Below him, only the ravine, where he would lie until they abseiled or climbed down to reach the cassettes in the kitbag slung across his body.

He pressed back against the rock. They wanted to drive him upwards, onto bare rock, to flounder through the snow until they surrounded him.

He stared down again. The tiny frozen stream glinted like a snail-track down there. The ravine was perhaps fifty feet deep . . . no, it fell away down a slope that twisted out of sight. In summer the stream would rush down it towards the foothills and the plain. Crazily, he wondered whether he could follow the course of the stream, out of sight of the hunt. Could he even get down there? If he fell, he would break bones. Be finished. He listened above and stared below, estimating the width of the ravine, its roughnesses, the steepness of the frozen stream's descent. He shivered. It was dark in the ravine, as narrow as a straitjacket.

He heard more small noises above him. They were closing in on the ledge, knowing he was not to the south or the north, knowing he could go no other way. The gunships seemed to have been called off.

He lowered himself slowly, carefully, until he sat on the ledge, his feet dangling into the ravine. He breathed deeply twice, three times, then gingerly turned his body so that he was hanging, weight on his forearms and wrists, into the crack in the rock. He glanced to right and left. Empty. They hadn't linked up yet and weren't using the radios, to avoid giving their positions away. When they met, they'd cast about urgently to locate him.

He, too, was making noises now, the scrabbling of his boots for toe-holds. His toes were numb with damp cold and moved inside the KGB uniform boots sullenly, reluctant to assist him. His eyes came level with the ledge, then he lowered himself further into the ravine. Bile was sour at the back of his throat as fear surged. Finger-holds, boots scraping, his arms aching because he had to move so slowly in order not to give himself away with noise. Finger-holds, toe-holds. He eased his body into a half-crouch, seeking new finger-holds. The rock was smooth, but cracked and pitted like scored metal. And icy cold. Down –

Caterpillar. Straightening, then arching, then straightening. Each tiny sound was a failure and an alarm. He descended the side of the ravine as it narrowed and darkened. Was it wide enough? His body seemed to ask the question with a flood of panicky heat.

Twenty feet down, thirty perhaps now. Caterpillar. His arms and legs were aching, his fingers stiff and clawlike. Icy cold. The rifle, slipping round on its strap from his back, rattled against the rock. He paused. Looked up.

They'd linked up from north and south. He heard the crackling of a radio and the urgency of muffled words. They were very close, and alarmed that he had disappeared. Caterpillar. His back protested, his legs were quivering with weakness and effort, his arms were shrill with pain. Forty feet . . .

The ravine echoed his breathing, every tiny noise of his descent. It was a funnel for sound. They'd hear, any moment they'd hear.

His grip slackened, he scrabbled for it, felt his boots distantly attempt purchase, then his body, suddenly seeming much heavier, slid the last feet. He buckled into a foetal position, onto the surface of the frozen stream, hands scraped raw, his cheek bruised and bleeding. Inertia moved him downwards almost at once as he rolled onto his back. Like a fairground helter-skelter chute, the stream moved him.

The face above him looked down, fifty feet away. Gant slid helplessly, as the shout of alarm reached him and a second face appeared. At once, the noise of a rifle and the cry of bullets from the surface of the rock. With a huge effort, he rolled into the shadow of a small outcrop. And sat hunched until someone ordered the firing to stop.

Silence again, then.

Ropes.

Unslung from packs, dropped like writhing snakes into the ravine, curled on the ice perhaps fifty yards away. The noise of boots on the ledge, then seeking for purchase on the wall of the ravine. A lamp flickering over the coiled ropes, over the ice so that it glimmered, and over the outcrop beneath which he huddled. The bulk of the first man to descend. He could shoot the climber – and be shot himself. He immediately abandoned the idea. And stretched his limbs carefully, checking their mobility, their lack of pain. His hands were beginning to warm, held beneath his armpits. His feet were still cold and numb.

He had to move, now. Out of sight as the stream bent in its channel. The ice was like glass, without purchase. He climbed to his feet, his back using the rock behind him to keep his body upright. His feet careful of the ice, testing its smoothness, his eyes studying the downward course of the stream, the angle of descent.

The sense of his mistake, his fatal error, assailed him, while his body went on making its independent attempt to survive. He had walked into an even more certain trap than the one they had set. The climber was half-way down the ravine's side, abseiling like a careful spider, face turned repeatedly in his direction, rifle across his chest ready to respond to any action of his.

He looked up at the other faces, then at the protecting outcrop and at the lamp swinging back and forth along the dark channel. And then fired –

– and ran, stumbling and bent double, scraping his side along the rock, his feet constantly slipping, the gunfire hideously loud behind him and cutting across the cry of surprised pain from the fallen climber . . . who lay still, he saw as he half-turned from a collision with the ravine wall. He reached the curve of the stream and tumbled onto the ice, skittering down its slope like a flung stone. Slowing gently.

He rose onto all fours, panting like a wearied dog. He had killed another of them. They'd want him. They could move quickly

565

above him, once away from the ledge, along the outcrop. He estimated it was now seventy feet to the lip of the ravine. He was a more difficult target, they'd be reluctant to descend from any other place than the ledge, now out of his sight. For the moment, they'd hesitate.

He heard his name called, booming through some kind of loudhailer. Above the noise of returned rotors. Magnified and wailing down the ravine like a wind.

Using the Kalashnikov as a crutch, he got to his feet. There would be two more on the ice by now, abseiling down from the ledge. He moved with infinite caution, one foot shuffled in front of the other, sliding step by step down the slope, using the ravine wall as a brake on his progress, dragging his shoulder against the rock. Looking back every second or third step, waiting for them to appear; counting his breaths, his heartbeats, passing seconds, distance – anything to prevent the paralysis induced by desperation from overtaking his legs and feet. He could hear radios, rotors, the clatter of equipment.

Single shots. Whining off the rock. Chips of it struck his face and hands. He returned their fire even though he could not see them. A lamp flicked its beam out towards him. He fired again. They returned fire more heavily. Still single shots. His name boomed through the loudhailer, sapping his will.

Darkness. The belly of a gunship hung over the ravine like the stomach of a huge, bloated spider. A face peering down from the main cabin. A scattering of seed, even as he fired upwards and the face and hand were withdrawn. Seed falling stonily, rattling into the ravine. He stumbled as he ran, hearing single shots behind him, hearing the hideous, magnified rattling of the grenades. He fell, rolled and skidded, bullets passing over his head, slid on, head tucked into his arms, body foetal, feet in the air because he did not want any braking effect from his boots, rifle tucked into his belly, kitbag containing the cassettes following him down the headlong slope of frozen water. Explosions, cracks rushing after him jaggedly – he could see them as the flame of the grenades faded on his retinae. He was still being carried forward and downwards by inertia and the slope, but the cracks raced more swiftly, seeming to overtake him . . . until they petered out.

Banging against an outcrop, aching in a new place, he looked up. The MiL's belly was fat and dark above him again, and the face was looking down cautiously. He raised the old AK-47 and fired a short burst. The face became surprised, then marked, then unassembled as the rounds destroyed it. The body fell away from the helicopter to hang grotesquely by its safety harness, just on the lip of the ravine.

Moments. He had bought a few precious moments.

He could not accept the information of his eyes. A blank, black wall of rock fifty or sixty feet from him. Even with the hollow circles of fuzzy light still in the centre of his vision he was certain, though he could not accept it. It had to be an illusion, not a dead-end.

He forced himself to listen. The gunship had moved away with a roaring noise. His ears seemed deafened. The body was gone. The cracks in the ice had not reached within twenty yards of him. His two pursuers were being more cautious now.

The glimmer of the frozen stream simply became black rock. It turned to neither side. It just ended.

He crawled towards it, the hollow rings of light on his retinae vanishing. To confirm the dead-end. There was no possibility of self-deception now. It was there, black and a hundred feet high, a solid wall of rock.

He groaned as he paddled down the slope on his stomach. Dead-end.

His head turned to look up. The MiL had not returned, the pursuers were still out of sight. They had all the time they needed. The surface of the ice seemed to cloud like a mirror with his exertions, his hands were numb. In the strange quiet he could hear his own efforts — heart, lungs, boots scrabbling, hands sliding, weapon scratching at the frozen stream like an ineffectual icepick. All Gant became aware of was himself. His head was empty. There was no Vietnam, no father, no past – nothing . . .

The frozen stream disappeared, dropping like old lava into a hole it had carved in the rocks during slow millennia. Flung out from the lip of the hole, it was like a silver, jutting beard. Gant stared unrealizing over the lip of what might have been a dark cauldron where nothing boiled. Heart, lungs, the other noises stilled. The whack of rotors seeping back in. And, before that noise loudened, he heard a radio's crackling and orders snapping muzzily down the funnel of the ravine. He was outside himself once more.

A dark hole in the floor of the ravine. The river dodging beneath some too-hard outcrop, the cliff-face he had thought was a dead-end. Dropping into — what?

Flash of a lamp like a splash of water somewhere on the ravine wall behind him. Radios, the urgency of the hunt overriding stealth. The rotors banging down like a yell into the cleft, echoing deeper into the ground through the hole into which he stared.

Gap.

Rough, contoured, ragged rock. Hand-holes, foot-holds. He glanced behind him as he turned around, then backed with the utmost, panicky care into the hole. Just as he had done into the ravine itself. Toes, hands, rifle rattling against the frozen water, the noise of dripping echoing in the blackness below him . . . around him as his head came below the lip of the hole and he moved sideways where his feet sensed then discovered a narrow ledge. He scrabbled his left hand in the kitbag, clutching the torch after touching the cassettes of videotape and film. He flicked on the torch and looked down into undefined, uncertain depth. Icicles — stalactites — but nothing growing up from the floor of what the light suggested was a cave, even a cavern. He could not see the floor, but wiped the torch's beam over the immediate rocks, and their contours were stark and easy to traverse. Having put the torch back into the bag, he slowly began to move to his right.

A sense of burial alive and of safety, conflicting and battling in his chest. He hung there for long moments, wrestling with and overcoming the claustrophobia. Eventually, he felt his heartbeat becoming calmer.

His hands became more confident. His feet shuffled and tested, as he moved away from the hole in what was now the roof of the cavern, moved away, too, from the glimmering sheet of silver that trailed away into the blackness.

He caught the sounds of hammering, less real than the dripping of the water around and below him. Hammering –?

A lamp flashed down the frozen length of the stream, and something hissed as it fell in the darkness away to his left. The lamp had dazzled him. Then he heard the noises of a body lowering itself into the cavern. He had heard a piton being hammered in, a rope uncoiled and dropped.

His hands seemed frozen to the rock, his feet rooted. His own breathing became audible once more.

The guard, who had been sleeping on a chair opposite Kedrov's bed when Priabin had entered the room, stared at them, his eyes, above the torn sheet used to gag him, filled with sullen dislike. His hands were tied behind his back, then to his feet. Kedrov seemed unable to ignore the man, or to accept Priabin's desperation as genuine.

Twelve twenty-six. He had been in that room for eight minutes. There was a corporal in the garage who might recover at any moment, a doctor might walk in, Kedrov's guard was tied up . . . the dialogue continued in his head, snapping back and forth across the widening chasm of his nerves. But he couldn't force Kedrov to leave, the man had only to open his mouth to alarm the whole of GRU headquarters. He had walked into the tiger's cage to rescue – a piece of meat that did not have the consciousness to want to be saved.

Leave him, then –

Kedrov's eyes were dull, wide-pupilled, slow to focus. The drug-interrogation had left him spent; just about back together rather than Humpty-Dumpty, but without will or resolve. And he seemed to know nothing!

'Look, come with me now, trust me,' Priabin pleaded once more.

Kedrov looked dazed by the remark, as if by tragic domestic news. Priabin guessed there was less than two hours before final target acquisition by the laser battle station on the helpless American shuttle – *and this, this dummy won't move, won't wake up* –! 'Trust me,' he repeated, but his harsh tone alarmed Kedrov, who flinched into the corner of the room. He was standing like some mental defective, cowering even though he was standing upright, hands flat against the walls.

'No . . .' Kedrov sighed plaintively. He was in some sort of suspension here, a place out of time. He felt safe. Even the armed guard had become familiar. Priabin had roughly rearranged his tiny world and frightened him with its new, uglier image.

'For Jesus Christ's sake, man, I'm here to save your *life!*' Priabin hissed, his voice dropping violently in volume after the first two words as he remembered the corridor outside, the danger of the building around this room. His hands went forward in a plea. 'Look, you have to come, you have to help me . . . you have to save your own life, don't you?' He shifted on the chair, his impatience heating his body, his back aware of the door behind him against which the chair and his weight were placed.

Kedrov seemed puzzled, as at some advanced mathematical concept. How much damage had Serov's drugs done to him? Would he be of any help, anyway? Jesus . . . twelve twenty-seven.

The guard's removed uniform, even his boots, lay on the bed like a spread corpse. It would be easy for them to get out if only Kedrov would put on the uniform . . . *put it on, you stupid bugger, for God's sake!*

He couldn't explain his plan to Kedrov, not in front of the guard, who would eventually be found . . . *knock him out, place the unconscious form under the bedclothes, it might be hours before* . . . but Kedrov remained intractable.

He stood up, wary of leaving the door . . . jammed the chair beneath the door handle. Kedrov stood in his corner, for all the world as if he had wet his trousers, his face helpless, bruised by the mystery and danger brought into the room by Priabin. Priabin moved towards him, hands held out in front of him, palms outward.

'Listen,' he said confidingly. 'Listen. Serov's dead, you know that, but that isn't the end of it, Filip – yes, I was after you, too, I admit that . . . but you know about *Lightning* . . .' Kedrov shook his head violently. 'Yes, you do – I have to do something about that, and you have to help me. You have to help me, Filip. Only *you* can.'

He was standing only a yard from the man now. Thin pale hair awry, his face wizened and aged by the past few days, body pressed into the corner of the room. Priabin took him by the shoulders. Kedrov flinched.

He leaned his head towards Kedrov, and whispered. 'There has to be a transmitter, doesn't there?' he asked, sensing a great reluctance in himself. Kedrov seemed puzzled only by the fact that he was whispering. He could not risk the guard hearing, but he had to *know!* 'A secret transmitter to put *Lightning* into operation . . . the general can't just press a button in front of everyone in mission control now, can he?' All the while, he was gently shaking Kedrov's shoulders, as if waking – Anna, he thought for a moment, then concentrated on the familiar, gentle tone of voice he felt required to use. 'Some of them know, but not all. It's a secret, after all, so he can't press the button in full view of everyone, can he? People like you who aren't army . . . see what I mean?' Did it sound feasible now, put into words? Or did it sound ludicrous? Perhaps they all *did* know. No, his guard didn't seem to, the technicians with whom he had played bridge had always referred to *Linchpin*, and to the objective as being the placing of the weapon in orbit . . . oh, yes, they were going to test the weapon, some time, on a dead satellite, maybe . . . they hadn't known anything more than that. It would be senior telemetry people, senior staff officers, the crew of the shuttle, Serov and his second-in-command.

'See what I mean?' he persisted. Twelve twenty-nine. Shake his shoulders, gently, *come on, Sleeping Beauty, wake up*. Priabin felt sweat gather around his throat, beneath his arms. 'They would have to have a secret transmitter, even a small control room, in order to align the weapon, acquire the target, and fire the laser beam . . . don't you see, Filip?' *Come on, come on, you fucking cretin, understand – say yes, oh, Christ, please say yes!* 'See?' he managed to murmur sweetly, stepping back.

Kedrov nodded. His face had been screwed up in concentration. Suddenly, his brow unfurrowed, he looked younger. And he nodded eagerly like an idiot understanding a simple instruction. Thank *God*! Then he seemed to see Priabin's uniform and become frightened again. Priabin forced himself to smile, and leaned forward, taking his shoulders again, feeling their flinch then relaxation.

'They'd have to be able to tap into the central control system, use its information for aligning and testing the weapon, and then fire it secretly . . . or they've got a duplicate of the entire weapon control system, down to tracking radars . . . ?' He could not keep the doubt from his voice. He wasn't telling, after all, he was asking. Kedrov ought to know if he was on the right track. 'Wouldn't they?'

Again, Kedrov nodded slowly, his face brightening. *Christ, am I right or not?*

'Look, Filip, help me with this and I'll help you get to the West. God help me, I'll get you to the West. Understand?' He was shaking the man too vigorously now, but could not prevent himself. The room stifled him. It was going down the drain, he was running out of time, and he had no idea what to look for, where to look, or whether his idea was even feasible . . . come on, for Christ's sake, *come on* –! 'Help me?' he pleaded, no longer whispering. 'Help me!'

Hot, tense silence, as if the room was in the tropics, a storm gathering beyond the blinds. He released Kedrov's shoulders. The silence went on, pressing around Priabin's temples. The guard's presence was vivid.

Eventually, Kedrov spoke. Normally, it seemed.

'To the West? To America? All the way to *America*?' Priabin nodded, stifling the noise and expression of his relief. Trying not to shiver with gratitude. 'How will you do it?' The cunning of a simpleton. Kedrov was detached, half-awake. Like hashish effects.

'Of course I'll do it! If we can do this, I can use my authority to get us out by car, train, even aeroplane, if you want . . . you'll be coming to Moscow with me. From there, it will be easy. Don't you see how grateful the Americans will be? They'll make you a millionaire!' He slapped Kedrov's upper arms in a pretence of delight. *Come on, come on* . . . twelve thirty-two. Fourteen minutes in the room – and they hadn't come with lunch for Kedrov and the guard, they could be here at any moment – Calm *down*! Oh, Christ, Kedrov, you fell for the line about America once, *do it again!*

'A millionaire . . . ?'

'If you save their shuttle, yes!'

'And you could . . . ?'

'I can!'

Strained silence. Priabin listened behind him, to the corridor beyond the door. Nothing . . . come on –

'All right, all right, Colonel – I'll come!' He had looked at the guard just before he spoke. It must have been the contemptuous hatred in his eyes. Kedrov had shuddered. The guard had pulled down the last remnants of the illusory world of this safe room. 'Yes, yes!' he continued. 'We must hurry.'

'Put on his uniform – quickly, Filip,' Priabin said, moving at once to the door, the rifle now in his hands, snatched up from the top of a low table. 'Put on the uniform and let's get out of here!'

He had been working towards the increasing, diffused light for whole minutes. They were behind him; radios crackled like small, repetitive explosions in the cave system. He had found the stream again, lying like a spread, ghostly cloth along the floor of another cave, and had followed it towards the dim glow some-where ahead.

Then the stream had vanished into the rock, dropping out of sight. He had felt abandoned. Had had to force himself to continue, climbing down through a narrow crack, flashing the torch by shining its thin beam through the material of one of his woollen gloves to mask its reflections from the icy walls. He had become accustomed to the darkness and the echoing emptiness of the caves. The light was stronger in this lower cave, but there was still no sign of the stream. It had to issue somewhere – had to, it was his way out . . . panic jumped like a thermometer plunged into boiling water.

He moved slowly towards the light. It had been coming up through the crack, through other crevices in the rock. Its source was in this cave. He listened through the blood drumming in his ears. Ropes hissed as they uncoiled, radios crackled; all noise was magnified. He looked behind him, but the darkness was still intact back there. He kept to the wall of the cave, stepping with infinite stealth and care, to avoid being outlined by the light, which now seemed to be slipping towards him from beyond a bend. His breath was visible now, as well as being audible to him.

A shadowy curtain. Just twenty or thirty yards from him – what . . . ? The light was diffuse, almost greenish. Puzzling. As he reached it, he removed his glove and touched the wall of dull, solid light. Ice!

It was the stream issuing from above him, masking this opening, pouring frozenly past the gap. He exhaled in noisy relief. A frozen waterfall.

Bullets plucked and stung at the ice near him. He jerked his hand back and turned. The flashes from invisible muzzles were forty or fifty yards behind him. He crouched back against the rock, his head turned back towards the ice –

– where a shadow dangled and shifted beyond the waterfall, and something banged against the ice as if knocking at a door. He switched the Kalashnikov to automatic. Light was leaking more strongly around the edges of the waterfall as if it was no more than a curtain hurriedly drawn across this gap to the outside world. He aimed, then squeezed the trigger, flinching against the thought of ricochets.

The waterfall starred and crazed like a windscreen in a high-speed accident. The steel-cored bullets penetrated the ice just where the shadow dangled. At once, it became a different outline, somehow heavier and inanimate. Fire increased behind him in response to his own shooting, bullets winging away or lodging in the crazed waterfall. He edged onto the ledge at the side of the ice, its scarred green surface only inches from his face. Pressing his back against comforting rock, he inched along the ledge, into –

– sunlight hurting his eyes, almost blinding him. Into a plucking wind, rattling the parka and seeking to dislodge him. The shadow he had seen through the waterfall was as diffuse as before, as he tried to focus his wet eyes. The shadow took on substance. Hanging from a nylon rope. Foot and hand holds kept the body upright, almost alert. The camouflage jacket was torn by bullets, and was wet with melting ice-chips and blood.

There was more firing behind him. He looked up. The rope came down from a cliff-top perhaps fifty feet above him. It might only be a ledge or outcrop, or the slope of the mountainside. He had been descending steadily. The mountain may have sloped like a roof, following that descent. The rope trailed away down into a canyon. A river rushed past the point where the frozen stream ended. There was a single railway line, and a railway tunnel. Between the track and the river, was a broad, four-lane highway. The canyon wound downwards towards the plain of Ararat, towards, towards –

A railway junction. The one he had seen through the glasses. The river below met the Araxes there. It was the road junction too. A military highway, for certain, wide enough for tank transporters and the heaviest army vehicles. It *was* the border. Perhaps two or three miles away. Say two . . .

Safety. He glanced up. Where was the rest of this *speznatz* trooper's unit? What of those behind him? There must be at least three of them still alive – hurrying now towards the waterfall and the cave mouth, knowing he had made an exit which they could still prevent from becoming an escape.

It was automatic, almost. A reflex. He used the folding stock of the Kalashnikov like a hook, catching the rope that dangled freely beneath the body. Pulling it towards him. Touching it with his gloved fingers. The sunlight seemed paler now, his eyes could cope. He gripped the rope. Glanced down, then at the waterfall's close edge. Then tugged on the rope. The body twitched but the rope was firm. He held it in both hands, after slinging the rifle across his back, and jumped.

His feet came back with a hollow boom against the crazed waterfall like a signal to those inside. *He* was now the shadow, the easy target.

He abseiled. Hands burning, legs ricocheting like falling sticks off the rocks, off the frozen water, off ledges and outcrops. He bounced, dreading the weakness of his ankles, the proximity of the rock, anticipating injury, and the quick, certain fall that would follow. He paused, straining to recover his breath, his hands waking to a shriek of pain and heat. He looked down. Forty feet below him, the end of the rope twisted and wriggled like an injured snake.

He dropped down further, gathering momentum once more. The gleam of polished track, the rock enlarging and blurring close to his face, the thud and ache of his feet and legs – the end of the rope. He slithered to a sitting position at the bottom of the rope. It was another hundred feet to the railway line and the highway, but it did not matter, the slope was shallower now.

It was only a moment before ropes whistled and rattled down beside him. The noise of distant rotors picked up, quickening and nearing. He glanced at the sky above the canyon. A dot, beating-up the twists of the river towards him. Frantically, he weaved through the jagged outcrops, jumping, sliding, dodging. Shots had to be ignored until he was hit . . . he wasn't hit, not hit, not yet, not hit . . .

He slithered the last yards, now perhaps a hundred feet away from the fall of the stream. The railway track and the road ran due south, down towards the enlarging gunship driving up the canyon. Its noise had begun to echo from the cliffs. He reached the railway. Bullets struck near him. The tunnel was a hundred, two hundred yards away –

– one fifty, he decided, already running. He adjusted his step to the gaps between the sleepers, more and more assuredly landing on those that fell below each stride. Concentrating his attention on his leading leg, counting, marking off, selecting the next sleeper. The river was below and to his right; he heard the gunship's noise. He dismissed the shots, those he heard . . . not hit, not yet, not hit . . .

The tunnel, wobbling in his vision as he glanced up, was closer. The gunship barely recognizable through his fear and effort, was much closer, moving at a terrifying speed that made his legs seem leaden, his body exhausted. He was slowing down, almost still, out of energy . . . the gunship came on, the tunnel hardly neared, the sleepers were blurred, grey concrete lines drawn like trip-wires across his path. He felt lightheaded, off-balance; the tunnel was receding now, indefinite, illusory.

The gunship swung away to his right but he could not follow it, he had to concentrate on the blurred sleepers. The rotor noise and engine note changed. It was transforming itself into a stable firing platform.

The mouth of the railway tunnel, carved through the rock of the canyon, was illuminated in a glare. Rocket fire. Rock groaned and split in the midst of the noise of the explosion. Dust surrounded him as the shockwave knocked him off his feet, against the side of the tunnel.

'Then you don't know!' It was a childish wail of disappointment from Priabin. He banged his fist against the thin wall and the noise seemed to echo in the empty place. Kedrov flinched and backed slightly across the room. There was a bare wooden table between them. 'You don't *know!*'

Priabin's fist banged against the wall once more. The greasy, faded wallpaper showed two smeared marks. The kitchen still smelt of stale cooking, though the place had been empty for days. He could sense the fear that remained. He had had to kick the padlocked door open. The UAZ was parked in the cobbled lane behind the yard. Priabin had been unable to think of anywhere else to go to earth except the kitchen behind Orlov's shop.

Sugar was crystally smeared on the table; rings from cups and bottles. His breath clouded in the cold. Kedrov's white, apprehensive face enraged Priabin. He looked at his watch. One-eighteen. At most, he had no more than fifty minutes.

'Where?' he pleaded with Kedrov. 'Just give me *some* idea where to look!' Kedrov's pasty skin seemed anxious to please, his mouth and eyes mobile with the search for some answer. But he could only shrug, then grin wanly. 'Oh, for God's sake, sit down!' he bellowed at the technician, who then shuffled a chair from the table and perched himself upon it like some prim, maidenly visitor uncertain of the moral uprightness of the household.

Priabin sat down heavily opposite Kedrov. His head whirled with futility, with a sense of irrevocable steps taken to no purpose. He seemed to have used up whatever energy he normally possessed. He placed his hands on the table, as if clasping some invisible cup or mug. He looked tiredly at Kedrov.

'Listen, Filip – we have to think. There has to be something . . .' Kedrov screwed up his features helpfully, but said nothing. Priabin sighed. One forefinger began shunting the hard, sticky grains of spilt sugar across the table, as if he were moving chesspieces. A lethargy of defeat held him in his chair. He struggled to continue what he knew he must say. 'It has to be secret, doesn't it?' Kedrov nodded, his head wagging with as much significance as a puppy's tail. He was abstracted in dreams of America and wealth, which worked on him like the after-effects of the drugs they had administered. 'They would have to hide their secret control centre, wouldn't they – however big or small, whatever it contained?' Again, Kedrov nodded. His eyes, however, seemed clearer, as if he had more fully awoken.

'Yes, they would.'

Priabin continued: 'Then let's think along those lines once more, mm?' His voice was filled with a false bonhomie. 'They have to have a transmitter, and it has to be one they don't have to account for – doesn't it? I mean, Rodin can't just use the main control room if he intends *firing* the weapon, can he?'

'No.'

'Then, there you are! An underground site, separate – well away from the control complex . . . and the transmitter would have to be hidden, too. So, that's underground until the moment it's needed – wouldn't it be?' Kedrov's hand was tapping the

578

table, his interest aroused just as Priabin felt the energy of his questions drain away, and his leaden body drag at his thoughts. He was angry, too – angry with Gant. Why had the bastard had to die? 'So – *where is it?*' he growled. He had asked these questions, all of them, so many times.

'They . . .' Kedrov began, but seemed abashed by Priabin's sullen glare.

'Go on!'

'They'd need . . . well, Colonel, I think they'd need something like a missile silo . . .' Again, his voice faltered. Priabin's waving hands encouraged him. 'That would be the easiest way to get the transmitter up and down when they needed it. It would come up out of the silo just at the right moment, then disappear as soon as they'd – finished . . . ?' He shrugged again, a gesture which irritated Priabin unreasonably.

He applauded ironically, his face sneering.

'Christ, you're a bloody *genius*, Filip – you really are! Do you know how many silos there are around here? Do you? Hundreds – probably *thousands!*' His despairing hands slapped down hard on the table. 'Christ –!'

'It's all I can think of,' Kedrov muttered placatingly after a while. Priabin glanced at his watch. One-thirty. They'd already been in Orlov's kitchen for half an hour. He pushed at stubborn grains of sugar that had adhered to the table. His face was distorted with concentration on the task. They'd discussed, argued, refined, dismissed, reiterated . . . all for nothing. Of course it had to be a silo – but there really *were* hundreds of the bloody things! The discussion had gone round and round. 'It would have to be one of the abandoned sites, wouldn't it – like the one I hid in?'

'What?' Priabin snapped, as he arranged the grains of sugar into a neat little heap. He did not look up.

They'd be looking for them by now. The corporal, whose body was still slumped on the floor of his booth when they came out of the lift, would have recovered by now and raised the alarm. The bedclothes would have been pulled back on Kedrov's bed to reveal the guard. It was less than forty minutes before target

579

acquisition was completed and the weapon fired. The American shuttle would disintegrate. An act of war would have been committed . . . the whole bloody Treaty and everything else would be down the toilet and people like Rodin would be in charge, finally and for good. He realized he was shaking his head. It didn't bear thinking about – the army, the fucking army in charge of everything! Dear God –

'It would have to be an abandoned site, and probably a remote one . . . out near the edge of the security area . . . they would have to have had work done, a lot of work, and they wouldn't have wanted anyone to see what they were up to.' Kedrov's voice had an air of discovery about it, an excitement. Priabin looked up at him, glowering, and Kedrov faltered. 'Wouldn't it?' he asked plaintively.

Priabin sighed. He noticed that his left foot was tapping restlessly. The lethargy seemed to have evaporated, leaving him tired, but fidgety and unsettled. He studied the technician's too-young, half-matured features. No sign of the after-effects of the drugs now.

'Go on,' he said heavily. 'I'm listening.'

Kedrov waved his hands over the table like a magician, to emphasize the quickening babble of his words.

'There are lots of abandoned sites, I agree, but there would be signs of recent work . . . silo repairs, heavy vehicles, fresh tunnelling, that sort of thing.' He reminded Priabin of a faulty sodium streetlamp, flickering, glowing red, but never quite blooming into full light. Priabin willed him to be precise. 'They'd need all kinds of people to help – scientists, technicians, computer people . . . a whole team to set it up.'

'A bloody pity you weren't one of them!' Priabin snapped at Kedrov, making him shy backwards in his chair. 'Think, man – think!' Anger fuelled his curiosity. His fist banged the table in repeated soft blows of emphasis. 'Didn't you hear *anything*? Wasn't there gossip, rumour, while they were building whatever they built? Listen, Kedrov – you're talking about a million dollars here! *Your* million dollars. The Americans would be fucking *overjoyed* to give you that kind of money if you save their precious shuttle! A home overlooking Central Park, a big car, a pile of money – now bloody *work* for it!'

'There's so much secrecy in this country – especially in this place –'

'Don't give me politics!'

'You're the policeman! Why can't you answer the question for yourself?' Kedrov's face had reddened, become more animated. He resented Priabin's bullying. 'The stuff they would need – where did they get it? How did they cover up what they – *diverted*?'

'All right – all right,' Priabin said. '*Who* worked on it?'

'I don't –'

'Yes you do.' He brushed his hands across the table, as if to remove the evidence of wasted time, the grains of sugar. Patterns vanished. 'People going on – on unexpected leave, or being transferred all of a sudden, without warning . . .' He looked up from the table. 'There must have been some strange comings and goings?'

Kedrov screwed his features into concentration. Priabin tried to think. Diversion of resources . . . ? The army couldn't simply requisition what it wanted, not for *Lightning*. It would have to – appropriate what it required. Rodin would have to falsify the dockets, sign bogus requisitions, even pinch the stuff from storeroom shelves.

'What – sort of thing do you mean?' Kedrov asked eventually, his face blank of inspiration. Priabin felt anger rise unreasonably into his throat.

'There must have been people you knew who worked on the project!' he shouted, angry in a new and momentary sense because Kedrov flinched away from him like a frightened child. He shouted more loudly, desperately: 'For Christ's sake, you stupid bugger! People working on *Linchpin* had to be working on *Lightning* at the same time! There aren't enough clever sods in the whole bloody country to have two different teams at work – especially not in the army! So – think of someone you know who went missing, or went on a long and unexpected leave – holiday that wasn't due, a sudden illness you knew nothing about . . .

caught the pox when he was a queer or AIDS when he lived like a monk – think, you silly little sod, we're running out of time!'

He stood up, exasperation and a premonition of utter failure making his body intolerably hot and uncontrollable. He walked away from Kedrov, not wishing to see the child's pretence to helpfulness on the tortured face. He ought to be sucking a pencil, just to add the final touch! Kedrov's silence seemed to extend into minutes, to press like a heavy weight of cloth around Priabin's head until the pressure of the situation threatened a further explosion of temper, of utter rage.

He heard Kedrov saying: 'I suppose there's old Grisha Budin . . . he wasn't really an alcoholic – it never interfered with his work. Just a piss-artist like the rest of us –'

Priabin wanted to squeeze the throat that was uttering such incredible rubbish –! Instead, he turned with a mannequin's slowness and poise, and said almost sweetly: 'What did you say?'

Kedrov looked hopefully up at him, glad as a dog that he seemed no longer angry.

'Grisha Budin – computer programmer . . . my friend.'

'What about him?' The effort to control his anger seemed impossible to maintain. His bland, blank, *stupid* face –!

'So?' he said.

'I was just saying . . . he was transferred to secret duties for a whole two months before they sent him away.'

'In Baikonur?'

'They said not – he said yes, when he came back. Nudge and wink, that was all . . . he didn't really say anything except that he'd been working right next door. That's the way he put it – *right next door.*'

'Does it help us? When was it?'

'Three months ago. I can recall other people now, people I didn't know – going on holiday, just like you said, or being transferred without warning. Computer people, telemetry experts, that sort of person.'

Priabin slapped the table with his open palm.

'There *was* fiddling,' he admitted, nodding his head. 'I remember now. Viktor and Katya –' He paused for a moment, then continued in a hoarser voice which he kept having to clear. '– were in charge of the investigation. Central Electronic Stores was the major target. Stuff disappearing at an alarming rate over a period of six or eight months . . . the bloody army weren't very helpful, even though they were blaming civilians. We found some of the pilfered stuff for sale on the black market, but there was bigger stuff that vanished without trace. We weren't getting anywhere, so I ordered it dropped.' He rubbed his face with his hands. 'It's all circumstantial and too vague,' he sighed. 'It could mean something or nothing . . . and it still goes nowhere near telling us *where*.'

Priabin reached into the greatcoat and drew out the large-scale map of Baikonur he had removed from the UAZ. It cracked and rustled as he unfolded it. His finger dabbed at the map. 'There, there, even *there*. There are abandoned silos everywhere!'

Kedrov turned the map so that he could study it more easily. 'One of them is too distant – we couldn't get there . . . two others are too exposed, too close to new roads. That one's the most isolated in terms of what else is in the vicinity.' His finger tapped at the map. 'They were abandoned in the early '60s. A small group of silos, I think.'

'Come on, then!' Priabin snapped, getting suddenly to his feet, tucking the map untidily under his arm like a newspaper. 'We've got thirty minutes!'

tunnels

He was propped against the wall of the tunnel like an abandoned doll, legs splayed and numb, head drumming with the blow of the shockwave. The downdraught whirled up dust and brick rubble which stung his face and filled his nose and eyes. Nausea welled in his throat. He clutched the rifle tightly in his hands.

Then the ugly nose of the gunship drifted into view, dropping like a spider into the arching gap of daylight that was just clearing of dust. Gun, rockets, missiles slung beneath its stubby wings.

It can't see you, it can't, can't . . .

He struggled to convince himself, his body running the tape-loop over and over, prompting an effort at survival. He struggled to his feet, his weight resting heavily against the icy, wet stonework. The nose of the MiL intruded like that of a hungry cat into a mousehole. Snuffling and eager, violence assured.

The walls of the tunnel were splashed with bright, crude light. Rails gleamed. Gant cringed back farther into the shadows of a narrow archway which was too cramped to conceal him more than momentarily; but for now the light washed just in front of him.

If only his legs would regain some kind of mobility, if only his head would clear, if only the noise would stop dinning off the walls. He kept his gaze away from the dust-hazed light.

The MiL rumbled a few feet closer, as close as it dared. *There's only a single track*, he heard some distant part of his mind confirm, *the rotor span is sixty feet, it can't come in after you*. It would wait, just so long as he didn't move, until troops had abseiled down from the waterfall or came up in trucks along the military highway. Or until it dropped its own troops, if it had any aboard. It was only a moment's pause.

Its ugly snout continued to swivel and sniff at the tunnel's mouth. Dust and debris seemed as if lifted and flung by a hurricane. The light of the lamp was foggy. Water splashed on his face and hands in large, uprooted droplets. The force of the downdraught thrust at him like a hand.

He was perhaps fifteen yards from the entrance. He glanced to his left, down the length of the tunnel. He was two miles from the border. He could see no blob or even prick of light – the tunnel must curve in its passage under the mountains as it followed the course of the river. He must run.

The MiL's cabin door was open. The wheels of the helicopter were no more than feet above the rails. Shapes dropped quickly. Gant felt the gravel under his feet shivering as at the first tremors of an earthquake. Three of them, and more coming behind, down the cliffs or up the road. Then, above the din, a voice bellowed distortedly through a loudhailer.

'You can't escape, Major – we know what you have! There's no way you can get out of here!'

The first of the men had entered the tunnel, and was clearly silhouetted. He restrained the curl of his finger on the rifle's trigger. He fumbled instead for the kitbag, tugging open its drawn-tight neck, and drew something out. It was the right shape, what he wanted . . . the first soldier moved cautiously closer, the MiL's nose snuffled with what seemed an increased appetite. Torches flicked on, weak fireworks beside the glare of the lamp.

Lamp, infra-red, low-light TV –

He raised the flare pistol from the kitbag and fired, turning his head away, clenching his eyelids shut. The cartridge struck the opposite wall of the tunnel, exploding against the brickwork, hissing like a cauldron before it glared brighter than the lamp. Smoke made him cough, the light was white beyond his eyelids, even though he had crooked his arm across his eyes. The noise of the rotors was distanced by the adrenalin that surged through his body.

Run, run –

He stumbled, still not daring to open his eyes, his left hand guiding him by scraping along the tunnel, so that the rope burns began to pain him once more. Fear for his ankles, his footing, grew in his mind as he stumbled on. The glare was still evident, even through his eyelids. The loudhailer bellowed. He felt light-headed. He was becoming careless of his footing. He opened his eyes into slits. Light, still lurid on the wall, hurt the backs of his eyes.

Wild shooting behind him. He heard no ricochets. He paused. Watched his shadow dying on the rock. Far ahead of him, he could see a tiny speck of daylight. The tunnel was clear and the exit was at least half a mile away. The light from the flare was dying now. Within seconds, their retinae and infra-red would recover. He breathed in deeply and thrust the flare pistol back into the kitbag. The MiL was out of sight around the bend of the tunnel. His heart was large and painful in his chest as he ran on. He could hear his own footsteps echoing off the walls, as if pursuing him. The noise of the rotors had almost gone now . . .

The patch of daylight, recognizable now as the mouth of the tunnel, darkened. Was filled by something. Cutting off his escape.

'Yes, comrade General, all systems are functioning properly.'

'When can we cut the links with central control?'

'In ten minutes, comrade General, target acquisition will be completed and we'll be locked on here.'

'Ten minutes . . . and how long before –?'

'Two minutes after the platform is raised to the surface, the transmitter will be aligned and locked-on.'

'Twelve minutes. Good. You have my order to proceed with *Lightning* – to its conclusion.'

'Very good, comrade General Rodin. Countdown at – eleven minutes, fifty seconds – mark and counting.'

'In the tunnel? How can they be sure —?'

'Mr President, we're monitoring their radio traffic. It's being screamed all over their Tac-channel.'

'How many troops do they have on the ground — close to him?'

'Maybe as many as a dozen *spetsnaz* units in the immediate area — a lot more in reserve . . . a dozen or so gunships and there are whole convoys of troop-trucks on the main highway —'

'Then he has to have something *decisive*.'

'That's our thinking, Mr President.'

'Then we have to get him out.'

'I don't think we can —'

'Listen to me — the Turkish government has pushed army units right up to the border . . . they have air cover, all we asked for. The price we're having to pay doesn't matter. The Turks have been *cooperative*. Now, we have to do *more* than they're doing!'

'Mr President, we can't afford an incident, not now, not *today*.'

'Dick, all of you — we can't afford *not* to have an incident!'

'What do you want, Mr President?'

'Small, fast, light helicopters — how many do we have in the area, General — *us*, not the Turks?'

'I'd have to check that, Mr —'

'Then do it!'

'Mr President — John, have you thought of . . . ?'

'Consequences, Dick? Yes, I've thought of very little else. I can assure you on that. But, understand me, Dick — Gant is alone . . . we thought we'd lost him when he went underground. He's still alive and their efforts to make sure he doesn't stay that way means he has something that could help us get out from under. I can't afford to lose that!'

'He's in the tunnel. They'll go in after him even if they haven't already done so. Sir, what can helicopters do for him?'

'I don't *know!* Christ Almighty, Dick, I'm supposed to be the President of the United States! That ought to count for something . . . it obliges me to *try!*'

'They'll shoot anything down that's carrying the stars and stripes . . . maybe anything with a red cross on it for all I know!

587

They're down to the wire on this, just as we are, sir. John, think about it, please.'

'The guy's a mile and a half from the border, Dick! What's to think about?'

'The next war?'

'Starting from *this*? If we don't have what Gant has, then we'll *lose* the next war!'

'What chance do they have of finding him?'

'How the hell would I know, Dick?'

'You'll be killing anyone you send into that – that hornets' nest over there.'

'Dick, I *know* that! I don't need reminding.'

'What about the Turks?'

'Who's to know? They'll back up anyone coming back across. While they're protesting about what we're doing, Gant will either be back here . . . or he won't.'

'Mr President, sir –'

'What is it, General?'

'We have two small Hughes Defender helicopters, observing along that stretch of the border. They could be in the area of that tunnel in – two minutes, maximum. So I'm guaranteed. From the time you give a direct order for them to cross, Mr President.'

'John –!'

'Thank you. Look, Dick, the Turks are already screaming at the Soviets here in Geneva and in Moscow about the *provocative troop movements* on the Armenian border – if the Defenders can find him, it might work.'

'John, think about this, please!'

'The time for thinking is over. General – give them the order to go in – give them anything they need, but get them in!'

Tyuratam was little more than a smudge to the south-east. Priabin looked back along the narrow, potholed road. It was empty, like the clean and dangerous sky. He slung the rifle across his back, shifting it to comfort, then wrenched the toolbox out of the UAZ with an angry yet purposeless strength. It had taken them twenty minutes to get here, to this God-forsaken place. What would he need? What would he *do*?

'Come on,' he growled, and began climbing the long, gentle slope in front of them.

The wind strengthened, soughing across empty country. There had been the frozen, rutted tracks of heavy lorries after they had turned off the highway. Did they mean anything? Kedrov scuttled beside him like a dog being taken for a walk, grating on Priabin's raw nerves. There was no hint of optimism in his hurried stride.

They reached the crest of the slope. The sticks and trellises of the main telemetry complex were only slightly closer than the haze of the old town. He glanced around him wildly. The country was not utterly flat, but undulated gently, pockmarked with dips and hillocks. It looked like some piece of ground that had been heavily shelled. No-man's-land.

'New wire,' Kedrov murmured, his hand touching the bright barbed wire at which they had halted. A warning notice, two more farther off. *Death to all intruders*, or something of the kind. They put notices like that outside every officers' pisshouse! There were no guards, no dogs, nothing!

'Christ!' he cried out. 'Look at it! There's nothing here except the old silos!'

'New wire,' Kedrov persisted.

'That's what we came out here to find?'

'No. Signs of recent work!' Kedrov snapped back at his cynicism.

Priabin scanned the landscape in front of him. Heavy tyres, rubble heaped and scattered, but nothing, nothing *real*. He bent down and scrabbled in the toolbox. Found the heavy-duty pliers, checked their edges.

'Watch out!' he ordered. 'I'm not climbing through this lot. Let's see if these will cut —' He grunted with effort, struggling and twisting the wire, attempting to cut through it. Even in the icy wind, sweat prickled on his forehead and was damp inside his shirt. The wire would not cut. Furiously, he kicked at one of the wooden posts holding the wire taut. Then kicked again and again. It struggled out of the grip of the frozen earth and leaned drunkenly, dragging the four strands of wire towards the ground.

He stepped across the sagging wire.

'Come on – and bring the toolbox!' Which is no bloody use whatsoever, he told himself.

The earth and the icy puddles cracked and ripped as they hurried across the empty landscape.

'What should we look for?' he demanded.

'Signs of repair – lack of rust . . .' Kedrov's voice faded into uncertainty.

More ruts from heavy tyres, even the tracks of a bulldozer. A hundred yards and more from the new wire they reached a silo shaft's steel doors, which were pitted and rusting. Priabin stood on them, stamping a din from the metal, as he gazed around him. He could distinguish as many as forty – well, thirty – of these silo entrances scattered over the ground and looking like giant anti-personnel mines. They rose only a few feet above the surface, while the shafts beneath them descended hundreds of feet into the earth.

'Don't waste time – split up, check as many as you can! Oh, Christ, all right, I'll take the toolbox!' He bared his teeth. 'Get moving!'

There was a moment of pathetic doubt on Kedrov's face, and the after-drug vacancy returned, then he turned to scan the landscape, picking out the closest silos.

'I'll shout,' he offered, 'and wave, if I find anything.' It was as if he had patted Priabin's forearm to comfort him. He seemed to draw on some reserve of optimism, and smiled encouragingly.

Priabin's arm ached with the weight of the toolbox, and even the rifle seemed heavy across his shoulders. He scuttled towards another shaft, turning only once to see Kedrov blown like a brown rag across the landscape. The second and third sets of silo doors were dirt-encrusted, with stiff blades of grass appearing to spring from the metal. He hurried on.

Four now, all of them unused for years. Six, and still nothing but pitted doors and the mouths of air ducts with rusty wire grilles across them, but tyre-tracks and caterpillar-track indentations going everywhere and nowhere. He transferred the toolbox once more from his left hand to his right. He seemed to be staggering along now, buffeted by the icy wind. If he so much as thought for a moment about his task, it would be like colliding with a solid wall.

The wind shouted, faintly.

Groggily, he looked up. A brown scarecrow was waving its outstretched arms . . .

Kedrov. Waving and shouting like a drowning swimmer.

He ran towards Kedrov, who seemed to be dancing with excitement. Pieces of abandoned metal glinted in the sun. Not rusty, then . . . even half-bricks, oil-stains, too, scraps of electrical cable.

'What —?' he gasped at Kedrov, dropping the toolbox, bent double to catch his breath. 'What is it?'

'These doors have been replaced — look!'

The metal doors of the shaft, tight shut, gleamed like a polished mirror. Rodin was down there somewhere, he knew it!

'Thank God,' he breathed. 'How do we get down there? What do we do?'

'The closest air shaft's over there, about sixty yards away. We climb down the tunnel, find the doors to the silo shaft . . .'

'And —?'

'Get into the shaft through the servicing doors. Stop the thing coming up . . . cut the *wires!*' It was the exasperation of a technician towards the technically illiterate. Kedrov seemed to have found his daydream of America once more. Priabin nodded.

'You'll have to help.'

'I can't go down there.'

'I don't care if you didn't like it last time, you're coming with me!'

Priabin knelt down, and pressed his cheek to the icy metal of the closed doors. He heard, faint but distinct, the humming of machinery or electrics. And a rumbling noise, as if a train were

591

passing through the earth a long way down. It *was* down there! He got to his feet.

'Good, down the air shaft, then. Come on.'

They ran to the air shaft's rusty grille. The jack-handle from the toolbox levered the mesh away from the mouth of the narrow shaft. A flight of rungs set in the concrete disappeared into the darkness . . . no, there was a faint glow of light from the bottom. He turned and began to climb backwards into the shaft, his feet feeling for the nearest rungs. He gestured at Kedrov to hand him the toolbox.

'Come on!' he yelled. His voice echoed betrayingly down the shaft.

Kedrov was not looking at him. His head was turned towards the silo. Then his face snapped back, mouth open, eyes wide.

'The doors are opening –!'

'What?'

'The doors – they're opening – it must be coming up!'

Priabin scrambled out of the shaft like a demented old man. He even crawled a few paces before getting to his feet, eyes staring wildly towards the silo. A hole in the ground now, no gleam of metal. He wanted to scream away the adrenalin coursing through his veins. He was too late, he could do nothing. *Rodin* had won –! The thought obsessed him. There was no room for any speck of rationality in his head.

Rodin . . .

He was down there, hundreds of feet below him, just *there!* He banged the jack handle on the frozen ground, feeling the shock pass through his wrist and arm and reach his shoulder. Rodin was down there, laughing while he started the next fucking war –!

'Look!' Kedrov was shaking his arm, and pointing. Priabin whirled on him, the jack handle raised. 'Look!'

It was coming out of the silo like some nightmarish plant, its growing cycle speeded up by a time-lapse camera. Dish aerial, transmitters, the platform on the metal stalk of an old missile hoist. Twenty feet into the air. It grew further and began to move. The dish aerial seemed to turn in their direction like a single, silver eye, then tilted towards the pale afternoon.

'Christ, oh, *Christ*,' he heard himself muttering.

Kedrov was separate from his desperation. Detached and blown like a brown leaf across the sixty yards to the silo.

'Wait – *wait!*' he bellowed.

And was running, stumbling like an exhausted athlete. The jack handle like a heavy baton in his hand. Ahead of him, he could see the skirts of Kedrov's stolen greatcoat flying in the wind, his arms waving as if he were swimming against the air's current. The plant had grown taller, thicker-stemmed. Its silver eye winked in the sun, watching the sky, swivelling. The spars and sticks of the other aerials and transmitters seemed to move, too.

He was out of breath, dragging in lungfuls of air as if at some great altitude. His chest was tight and aching.

Kedrov was standing at the base of the platform, looking up. Smooth, sheer metal for thirty feet, impossible to climb. Hopeless . . . metal gleamed and shone, mocking him. The platform hummed with electricity and purpose. The winking eye of the dish aerial halted in its movements. Stared directly at some invisible target.

'It's locked on!' Kedrov shouted in his ear. 'Locked on!'

The cables, bunched into a rope, travelled back into the silo shaft, down hundreds of feet to Rodin's finger on the button. The signal was about to be transmitted.

He swung the jack handle at the cables, disturbing them and leaving no mark on the heavy nylon sheathing that protected the wiring. He felt his left hand forced open. He released his grip on whatever he had held. Kedrov knelt by the bunched cables, straining with the heavy pliers. Groaning as he did so, veins standing out on his forehead, sweat sheening it. The wind sang through the transmitters and aerials in an unearthly, crowing way.

Priabin knelt down, too, and took the cables in both hands. Heaved at them.

Kedrov wrenched rather than cut. His hands were white with

593

effort. It was no use – if it was, Kedrov would electrocute himself as soon as the metal touched the wires inside.

He heaved again at the reluctant cables. What did he think he was doing anyway? He gazed upwards and then wildly around him.

Frenziedly, he wrenched the Kalashnikov from his shoulders and pointed it at the cables, as if about to fire into them . . . his head whirled crazily, there was no rationality. The weapon was useless to him. He raised it as if to throw it aside. He'd never even learned to fire it accurately, years ago during basic training. Cleaning, loading, aiming – even bayonet practice . . . the thing was useless, *useless!*

Then he remembered. Yes! He knelt down, his hands fumbling to detach the bayonet in its scabbard from above the magazine. 'Get away!' he yelled at Kedrov, whose shadow interfered with the light. He struggled with the bayonet, then threw the gun away from him, and held up the tool he had constructed.

. . . *with the bayonet and the insulated scabbard, an effective wire cutter is made* . . .

The instructor. They'd laughed in the junior officers' mess afterwards – *who wants a wire cutter, we're not trying to escape, are we?*

He attacked the sheathing of the cables, hacking, sawing, shearing at it. Strips of nylon, cord within, bare copper gleaming – one, two, three, four. He worked like a madman, mutilating the cables. His hands were torn and bloody from frayed wiring and the sharpness of the nylon . . .

. . . eventually, he finished.

The interlocked bayonet-and-scabbard tool rattled and clunked as it slid down the silo shaft. Priabin lay on his back, chest heaving, staring at the sky. Kedrov was no more than a shadow in his peripheral vision. His body was a single, feverish ache. Nothing mattered now, nothing –

– Rodin, Rodin . . .

He let the name fade in his mind, like a figure retreating down a long, empty corridor.

The sky was clean.

Except for Kedrov's shadow.

'I — don't know if we were in time,' Kedrov said, his voice hardly audible above the noise of the wind through the aerials. 'They may have transmitted the firing command — we wouldn't know . . .'

When the words had taken effect on Priabin's consciousness, he groaned, rolling onto his side as if to hide under non-existent bedclothes.

Rodin, *Rodin* —!

Train.

Almost at once, he could smell the smoke. The tunnel thrust the locomotive's bellow of steam and damp smoke along its length towards him. The rail beneath his left boot quivered, then thudded rhythmically. His heart thudded like the rail, but with relief; almost threatening to overwhelm him. He could only lean back against the wet brickwork and watch. The locomotive and its burden roared down the tunnel towards him.

The parka became sodden almost at once from the running water washing down the wall. The smoke made his eyes water, his throat constrict. And yet he knew he had to move, however terrifying this huge rush of metal. The train blocked the entrance to the tunnel, preventing any gunship from making its descent to cut off his escape.

There was a halo of light dimly marking the train's outline, a tiny gap of air between its bulk and the walls. Sparks, the billowing of wet smoke and steam, the glow of the boiler's fire. He turned his cheek to the rough brickwork, and wetness soaked into his taut skin. Already, the realization seeped, they would be working their way along the same wall, thinking they, too, could use the train's passage. He had to move *now*.

He began to slide-run along the curve of the wall. His shoulder scraped against the bricks and the jutting rock, his feet unbalanced and his whole body leant like a drunk into the wall, away from the track. The train enlarged, yelling and threatening.

Seeming too big for the tunnel. The dim halo of light had disappeared. He checked in mid-stride.

The breath he snatched at was foul with smoke, making him cough. His ears were filled with the din of the locomotive. Sparks jumped and spat like fireworks only a hundred yards away as the train rushed towards him.

Somehow, he made himself run on, towards the thing that filled the darkness with noise and fire. The beam of its lamp polishing the track but eluding him. His shoulder pressed against the wall. The pressure and inertia of the train quivered in the brick, the gravel under his feet seemed like quicksand.

And then it was passing him, and moving with a totally unexpected slowness, labouring up the canyon's long incline. One man in the locomotive's cab was bent to the raging fire, the other stood as still as a statue commemorating a long-ago war. Then the first of the goods wagons was level with him, and some animal or other lowed like a fog-warning. Other beasts joined its cry. Cattle-trucks. Helpless animals, in transit to an abattoir.

His cheek was still warm from the blaze of the fire. He had to pause to beat at sparks that had flown onto his legs from the flanged wheels of the trucks. Then moved on in his unbalanced fashion, down the length of the long, slow train which creaked and thudded and clanked; and lowed.

Smoke roiled about him so that he could hardly breathe. He was terrified by the sight of cattle snouts jutting through slats into the tunnel's madness. He heard hooves banging against the floors and sides of trucks as they lurched past.

The train was incredibly long. Its noise seemed as if it would never stop. He felt he would never rid himself of the lowing of the cattle. He had to be in the open before the end of the train entered the tunnel. The trucks moved by so slowly. He couldn't be running that slowly. Then he saw the light increasing.

The second locomotive, at the rear of the train, pushing it up the long incline towards Yerevan's abattoirs, was at the maw of the tunnel and was then swallowed. The driver's face, looking down at him, was white and shocked, and the glow of the fire was dimmed by the early afternoon light. The track ahead of him was clear.

He saw the bridge, and heard the throb of rotors, and the scream overhead of the first MiG or Sukhoi fighter. He felt shrunken, a tiny figure on a narrow thread of track that ran from tunnel to bridge. He stared wildly around and above him, looking for the gunship, waiting for its attack; hearing, despite the noise of its approach, the sound of lorries moving on the highway below him. He felt pinioned by noise. Then he saw the gunship beating down towards him, rotors tilted, snub nose head-on to him. He would never – even if he could move – make the bridge before it opened fire. The passage of the train still rumbled in the ground beneath his feet. He raised the Kalashnikov in a futile gesture as the helicopter enlarged, its black tinted glass and snub nose sweeping over his head, the down-draught plucking at him as if to cuff him aside.

There was black glass everywhere as it turned to face him, swinging violently into the hover, so that he could see the gun and the missile pod. It hung in the air, its skis only feet above the railway track – between him and the bridge. Olive-drab paint.

He knew quite certainly that he would die there, framed in the tunnel entrance. They could be no more than thirty yards or so away now. He was trapped between the *spetsnaz* troops behind him and the gunship which stared at him with its huge, black glass eyes. Gant shivered. The rifle pointed foolishly, like a child's stick. He seemed to have stopped breathing. The only sound he could hear was the noise of the small, light gunship.

Familiar . . . ?

Military. Olive-drab. Insect eyes.

Familiar –?

The helicopter stared at him, no more than twenty yards away. The helicopter . . . the, the – Hughes Defender stared at him, and at that same unnerving moment that he identified the aircraft he saw an arm waving him forward from the port insect-eye – the eye was a door which had swung open. The helicopter was American!

Relief . . . disbelief. The conflicting feelings seemed to shake

597

him like a storm. It had to be an illusion, it couldn't be a Hughes, a Hughes couldn't be here –

– even as he began running towards it, obeying the still-waving arm.

The Defender lifted slightly, delicately adjusting itself in the air, then settled onto its skis. Then all he saw was the arm, waving once more. But he had glimpsed the white star on the helicopter's flank and the legend, US ARMY. The pilot had shown them to him like a guarantee. Ten yards away, five. The gesticulating arm came closer, closer, *closer* . . .

He staggered against the fuselage. Bullets clanged against the metal. He looked down with what might have been surprise. His left thigh was burning with pain and stained with something dark and wet, which spread even as he watched it. His whole frame began to quiver. Fuzzily, he could see two soldiers at the tunnel entrance, one of them kneeling, taking better aim, the other standing as stiffly as a member of a firing-squad.

He groaned with pain. Something pulled at his shoulder, then a hand grabbed his arm, wrenching him off his feet. The rotors idled noisily above his head, the two soldiers were still and patient and certain, his leg shrieked as he was dragged into the cockpit of the helicopter and it twisted under him. The whole of his thigh seemed black with blood as he looked drunkenly down, slumped in the co-pilot's seat. His face leant against the pilot's uniform. The flying overalls bore the name PRUITT. Then he was pushed away from Pruitt, to loll in his seat as the rotors picked up speed and volume. Bullets careened off the metal of the fuselage.

'Fasten your seatbelt, Major!' Pruitt snapped, his hand pointing forcibly at Gant's lap. Instinctively, Gant moved to obey, and his leg cried out again. 'You all right?'

The Hughes was twenty feet or so up in the air, hardly moving. Gant groaned, then shouted:

'For Christ's sake – go!'

He tightened the seatbelt automatically, then fumbled with his belt. The small helicopter flicked into the air like a spun coin, dizzyingly, making his leg protest with a flash of red behind his quickly-clenched eyelids. He felt sick. He forced himself to open his eyes, as if in response to the noise of bullets against the Defender's fuselage. Pale flickers of flame down on the track. A bullet flew off the cockpit's perspex, scarring it. The Hughes yawed wildly before Pruitt corrected its course. Gant felt the aircraft drop like a loosened boulder, down the canyon wall.

With a feebly waving hand, he pointed urgently towards –

– the military highway and its road tunnel to the frontier. Broad tunnel. Even as he saw the first of the MiL gunships, its stubby wings overloaded with rockets and missiles, dive in pursuit of them. There was a second one, farther off. Gant tightened his belt into a tourniquet around the top of his thigh, grinding his teeth against the increased pain. Each manoeuvre of the Hughes seemed to wrench at the damaged sinews and muscles and act like a pump on the blood he was trying to staunch.

Pruitt drove the Defender downwards – rotor span twenty-seven feet, only *twenty-seven*, Gant told himself, the words taking the pattern of his grinding teeth and accompanying their noise inside his head. He slumped back in the co-pilot's seat. Pruitt levelled the helicopter before the mouth of the road tunnel, abruptly, so that Gant yelled aloud. Then the tunnel swallowed the tiny aircraft.

'Hell –!' he heard Pruitt distantly exclaim, his head filled with pain as if it were noise, the lights set in the tunnel's roof seeming to hurt his eyes, as if they, too, were connected with his wound. He had clamped his hand over his thigh. His finger and thumb had felt the entry and exit wounds of the bullet's passage. He was bleeding more slowly.

The tunnel was wide enough to take a MiL-24, not just the smaller Hughes, but they'd have to be more careful. The second gunship could hop to the other end of the tunnel, but the Hughes was armed with missiles and a Chain Gun and they'd have to be careful, too . . .

He was hardly conscious, because now the tunnel lights seemed hypnotic, extending into a blur . . . The pain in his thigh, steadily mounted through his whole frame and seemed to throb in rhythm with the passage of the lights. Pruitt's wild elation was no more than a distant sighing.

The tunnel ended like a bright mouth opening.

The Plain of Ararat. Daylight and gunships. They were as unreal, as unimportant to Gant as smears on the perspex. He vaguely glimpsed a border crossing, poles and booths and vehicles straggling across the highway. Then it was gone. He could not be certain he had seen it, was increasingly unaware of the dimensions of the cockpit around him, the presence of the pilot. Then Pruitt jerked the helicopter up and away.

Something exploded astern of them against the canyon wall. Gant did not turn his head to look back. He felt an increase in the Defender's speed, and sensed the ground further away below. The plain spread out ahead of them, as grey-white and unfeatured as an unrolled bale of cloth. His head felt heavy, and yet without substance.

Turkey. He knew that . . .

More gunships.

Hughes helicopters, and a Bell Hueycobra. Their shapes familiar, comforting. Jets higher and farther away. Turkey. The border was already invisible behind the last slopes of the foothills as the Defender skimmed the snowbound plain. The whiteness, he could see now, was smeared by the passage of a steam train and trellised by cleared roads and highways. The twin peaks of Mount Ararat gleamed in the distance.

A second Hughes Defender slid up close to port. Its pilot raised a thumb. An unarmed Turkish air force Jetranger rose like a cork to the surface of water and took up station behind them. It was a target for any missile that might be launched across the border. The Hueycobra bobbed to starboard as they closed ranks around Pruitt, around Gant. He was protected, safe. His leg burned with a fresh agony. There was something he had to do besides sleep, besides surrender to the pain – something . . .

His hands groped towards the instrument panel. Pruitt, understanding his feeble efforts, thrust the co-pilot's headset into his hands and opened the Tac-channel. As if lifting a great weight, Gant slowly slid the headset on. Voices blurted in his ears, showering the ether with congratulation. Strangely, they seemed to evoke the sensation of some long staircase he must climb, urgently. He groaned at the idea of further effort.

'Come on, Major –!' he heard Pruitt urge, but the pilot's voice was very faint.

The pain threatened afresh. He began talking quickly, afraid it might finally overwhelm him. They had to be told; they had to know. The cockpit was as vague and unfeatured as the pale sky and the carpet of snow. The instruments were blurred, his sense of Pruitt beside him diminished.

'. . . *Winter Hawk*,' he felt himself repeating, over and over. His own exclamations of pain were more real. He heard himself grinding his teeth as a noise inside his head, as if bones were being moved in his skull. '. . . I have the proof, yes . . . definite proof . . .' It did not matter who was listening, how far up that staircase in his mind he had climbed in less than a minute. Some general, a CIA deputy director – who cared? He remembered something else, then, with a huge, sickening effort, and said: 'They have the weapon, it's – already in orbit . . . intend to use it, against the shuttle – *Atlantis* . . .' It was so difficult to remember the shuttle's name. A cleared road lay below him, Pruitt was following its grey line through the snow. Someone asked him a question – one of the voices that babbled at him and kept him from sleep, allowing the pain to enlarge. He merely repeated: '. . . the target is the shuttle, yes – I saw the launch, the weapon is in orbit at this – moment . . .' Then, finally: 'Man, I don't give *shit* what you do, just *do* it!'

Fuzzily, as he leaned forward to cut off the channel, he saw a helicopter bearing a gigantic red cross drift like a dirigible across their course. He sighed, and surrendered to the pain and to his weariness. His head burned as intensely as his leg. It's all right now, he assured his wound. All right. He'd survived. His message and what they did about it did not matter any more. He'd survived . . .

POSTLUDE

'Negotiations and love songs,
Are often mistaken for one and the same.'

PAUL SIMON: *Train in the distance*

'. . . it is therefore in a gesture of the most profound respect for the importance of today, and out of the new friendship that exists between our two countries and across the whole of our planet – that the government of the Union of Soviet Socialist Republics wishes to include a new clause in our solemn Treaty.

'We propose, out of our sincere desire for peace in the world, to include all space weapons systems, whether real, experimental or merely theoretical, within the terms of our agreement. All space weapons and all research into such weapons will now become subject to the terms of the Nuclear Arms Reduction Treaty . . .'

John Calvin applauded, together with every member of every delegation assembled for the signing session in the Assembly Room of the Palais des Nations.

Projected on a huge screen at one end of the hall, the US shuttle *Atlantis* hung above the beauty of the blue-white-green earth. Beside it, the Soviet shuttle, *Kutuzov* floated innocently against the planet. He glanced from the screen towards Dick Gunther. Gunther shook his hand in a slight, quivering gesture.

Close, too damn' close, the gesture stated.

Calvin nodded and then looked down at the Treaty, waiting to bear his signature. And only then, staring at the paragraphs and clauses that were somehow out of focus for a moment, did he smile genuinely and with vast relief.

ABOUT THE AUTHOR

Craig Thomas was born in Cardiff in 1942, and educated at Cardiff High School and University College, Cardiff, where he was awarded his MA in 1967. His first novel, *Rat Trap*, and his first bestseller, *Firefox*, were both published while he was still a schoolmaster. The success of *Firefox* on both sides of the Atlantic enabled him to become a professional novelist. Since 1977, he has published eight other novels (two under the pseudonym *David Grant*), many of which have become bestsellers. A film of *Firefox*, starring Clint Eastwood, appeared in 1981. His sales now exceed nine million copies worldwide.

Craig Thomas' other novels include *Wolfsbane*, *Snow Falcon*, *Emerald Decision* and *Moscow 5000* (as *David Grant*), *Sea Leopard*, *Jade Tiger*, *Firefox Down* and *Bear's Tears*.

Craig Thomas is married and lives with his wife and an aging tortoiseshell cat near Lichfield in Staffordshire. His pastimes include gardening, watching cricket, listening to music and reading.